Chain of Thorns

Also by Cassandra Clare

THE MORTAL INSTRUMENTS

City of Bones

City of Ashes

City of Glass

City of Fallen Angels

City of Lost Souls

City of Heavenly Fire

THE INFERNAL DEVICES

Clockwork Angel

Clockwork Prince

Clockwork Princess

THE DARK ARTIFICES

Lady Midnight

Lord of Shadows

Queen of Air and Darkness

THE LAST HOURS

Chain of Gold

Chain of Iron

Chain of Thorns

THE ELDEST CURSES

With Wesley Chu

The Red Scrolls of Magic

The Lost Book of the White

The Shadowhunter's Codex

With Joshua Lewis

The Bane Chronicles

With Sarah Rees Brennan
and Maureen Johnson

Tales from the Shadowhunter Academy

With Sarah Rees Brennan, Maureen Johnson,
and Robin Wasserman

Ghosts of the Shadow Market

With Sarah Rees Brennan, Maureen Johnson,
Kelly Link, and Robin Wasserman

THE LAST HOURS

BOOK THREE

Chain of Thorns

CASSANDRA CLARE

WALKER
BOOKS

First published in Great Britain 2023 by Walker Books Ltd
87 Vauxhall Walk, London SE11 5HJ

2 4 6 8 10 9 7 5 3 1

This book has been typeset in Dolly and Pterra

Printed and bound by CPI Group (UK) Ltd, Croydon CR0 4YY

British Library Cataloguing in Publication Data:
a catalogue record for this book is
available from the British Library

ISBN 978-1-4063-5811-7
ISBN 978-1-5295-1633-3 (Australian HB)
ISBN 978-1-5295-1067-6 (Export/Airside PB)
ISBN 978-1-5295-1636-4 (Illumicrate)
ISBN 978-1-5295-1635-7 (FairyLoot)

www.walker.co.uk

FSC
www.fsc.org
MIX
Paper | Supporting responsible forestry
FSC® C171272

For Emily and Jed.
I'm glad you finally got married.

We must learn to suffer what we cannot evade; our life, like the harmony of the world, is composed of contrary things—of diverse tones, sweet and harsh, sharp and flat, sprightly and solemn: the musician who should only affect some of these, what would he be able to do? he must know how to make use of them all, and to mix them; and so we should mingle the goods and evils which are consubstantial with our life; our being cannot subsist without this mixture, and the one part is no less necessary to it than the other.

—Michel de Montaigne, *Essays*

Prologue

Later James could only remember the sound of the wind. A metallic scream, like a knife drawn across a shard of glass, and far below that the sound of howling, desperate and hungry.

He was walking upon a long and trackless road: it seemed no one had come before him, for there were no marks on the ground. The sky above was equally blank. James could not have said if it was night or day, winter or summer. Only the bare brown land stretching before him, and the pavement-colored sky above.

That was when he heard it. The wind, kicking up, scattering dead leaves and loose gravel around his ankles. Growing in intensity, the sound of it nearly covered the oncoming tread of marching feet.

James whirled and looked behind him. Dust devils spun in the air where the wind had caught them. Sand stung his eyes as he stared. Hurtling through the sandstorm blur were a dozen—no, a hundred, more than a hundred—dark figures. They were not human, he knew that much; though they did not quite fly, they seemed to be part of the rushing wind, shadows furling around them like wings.

The wind howled in his ears as they shot past overhead, an interlocking clutch of shadowy creatures, bringing with them not just a physical chill but a sense of cold menace. Under and through the sound of their passage, like thread weaving through a loom, came a whispered voice.

"They wake," Belial said. "Do you hear that, grandson? They wake."

James jerked upright, gasping. He couldn't breathe. He clawed his way up, out of the sand and shadows, to find himself in an unfamiliar room. He closed his eyes, opened them again. Not unfamiliar: he knew where he was now. The coaching inn room he shared with his father. Will was asleep in the other bed; Magnus was somewhere down the hall.

He slid out of the bed, wincing as his bare feet made contact with the cold floor. He crossed the room silently to the window, gazing out at the moonlit, snowy fields that covered the ground as far as the eye could see.

Dreams. They terrified him: Belial had come to him through dreams as long as he could remember. He had seen the bleak kingdoms of the demons in his dreams, had seen Belial kill in his dreams. He did not know, even now, when a dream was just that, a dream, and when it was some terrible truth.

The black-and-white world outside reflected back only the desolation of winter. They were somewhere near the frozen River Tamar; they'd stopped last night when the snow had gotten too thick to ride through. It had not been a pretty, flurrying shower either, or even a chaotic, blowing squall. This snow had direction and purpose, beating down at a sharp angle against the bare slate-brown ground, like an unending volley of arrows.

Despite having done nothing but sit in a carriage all day, James had felt exhausted. He'd barely managed to force down some hot soup before making his way upstairs to collapse into bed. Magnus and Will had remained in the saloon, in armchairs near the fire, talking in low voices. James guessed that they were discussing him. Let them. He didn't care.

It was the third night since they'd left London, on a mission to find James's sister, Lucie, who had gone off with the warlock Malcolm Fade and the preserved corpse of Jesse Blackthorn, for a purpose dark and frightening enough that none of them wished to speak the word they all dreaded.

Necromancy.

The important thing, Magnus stressed, was to get to Lucie as soon as possible. Which was not as easy as it sounded. Magnus knew that Malcolm had a house in Cornwall, but not exactly where, and

Malcolm had blocked any attempt at Tracking the fugitives. They'd had to fall back on a more old-fashioned approach: they stopped often at various Downworld watering holes along the route. Magnus would chat with the locals while James and Will were relegated to waiting in the carriage, keeping their Shadowhunter selves well hidden.

"None of them will tell me anything if they think I'm traveling with Nephilim," Magnus had said. "Your time will come when we arrive at Malcolm's and must deal with him and Lucie."

This evening he'd told James and Will that he thought he might have found the house, that they could easily make it there with a few hours' journey the next morning. If it was not the right place, they'd journey on.

James was desperate to find Lucie. Not just because he was worried about her, although he was. But because of everything else happening in his life. Everything that he had put aside, told himself not to think about, until he found his sister and knew she was safe.

"James?" The sleepy voice cut into his thoughts. James turned away from the window to see his father sitting up in bed. "Jamie *bach*, what's the trouble?"

James gazed at his father. Will looked tired, his mane of black hair disarrayed. People often told James that he was like Will, which he knew was a compliment. All his life, his father had seemed the strongest man he knew, the most principled, the most fierce with his love. Will did not question himself. No, James was nothing like Will Herondale.

Resting his back against the cold window, he said, "Just a bad dream."

"Mmm." Will looked thoughtful. "You had one of those last night too. And the night before. Is there something you'd like to talk about, Jamie?"

For a moment, James imagined unburdening himself to his father. Belial, Grace, the bracelet, Cordelia, Lilith. All of it.

But the picture in his mind did not hold. He could not imagine his father's reaction. He could not imagine speaking the words. He had held it all inside so long, he did not know how to do anything but hold on further, tighter, protecting himself the only way he knew how.

"I'm just worried about Lucie," James said. "About what she might have gotten herself into."

Will's expression changed—James thought he saw a flicker of disappointment cross his father's face, though it was hard to tell in the half dark. "Then go back to bed," he said. "We're likely to find her tomorrow, Magnus says, and it would be better to be rested. She might not be pleased to see us."

1
Twilight Days

My Paris is a land where twilight days
Merge into violent nights of black and gold;
Where, it may be, the flower of dawn is cold:
Ah, but the gold nights, and the scented ways!
—Arthur Symons, "Paris"

The gold floor tiles gleamed under the lights of the magnificent chandelier, which scattered droplets of light like snowflakes shaken from a tree branch. The music was low and sweet, rising as James stepped out from the crowd of dancers and held out his hand to Cordelia.

"Dance with me," he said. He was beautiful in his black frock coat, the darkness of the cloth accentuating the gold of his eyes, the sharpness of his cheekbones. Black hair tumbled over his forehead. "You look beautiful, Daisy."

Cordelia took his hand. She turned her head as he drew her out onto the floor, catching a glimpse of the two of them in the mirror at the far end of the ballroom, James in black and she beside him, in a daring dress of ruby-red velvet. James was looking down at her—no—he was gazing across the room, where a pale girl in an ivory dress, her hair the color of creamy-white rose petals, was looking back at him.

Grace.

"Cordelia!" Matthew's voice made her eyes snap open. Cordelia, feeling dizzy, put a hand against the wall of the changing room for a moment to brace herself. The daydream—daymare? It hadn't turned out to be that pleasant—had been awfully vivid. "Madame Beausoleil wants to know if you require any aid. Of course," he added, his voice full of mischief, "I would render the help myself, but that would be scandalous."

Cordelia smiled. Men did not usually accompany even wives or sisters into a dressmaker's shop. When they had arrived for their first visit, two days ago, Matthew had deployed the Smile and charmed Madame Beausoleil into allowing him to remain in the store with Cordelia. "She does not speak French," he had lied, "and will require my assistance."

But letting him into the shop was one thing. Letting him into the trying-on closet, where Cordelia had just finished donning an intimidatingly stylish red velvet dress, would indeed be *un affront et un scandale!*—especially in an establishment as exclusive as Madame Beausoleil's.

Cordelia called back that she was all right, but a moment later there was a knock on the door and one of the *modistes* appeared, wielding a buttonhook. She attacked the closures at the back of Cordelia's dress without requiring any instruction—clearly she had done this before—and pushed and pulled at Cordelia as if she was a stuffed mannequin. A moment later—her dress fastened, her bust lifted, and her skirts adjusted—Cordelia was decanted into the main room of the dressmaker's salon.

It was a confection of a place, all pale blue and gold like a mundane Easter egg. On their first visit Cordelia had been both startled and oddly charmed to see how they displayed their wares: models—tall, slender, and chemically blond—promenaded up and down the room, wearing numbered black ribbons around their throats to show that they were displaying a particular style. Behind a lace-curtained door was a wealth of fabrics one could choose from: silks and velvets, satin and organza. Cordelia, upon being presented with the trove, had silently thanked Anna for instructing her on fashion: she had waved away the lace and pastels and moved quickly to select what she knew would suit her. In only a couple of days the dressmakers had whipped up what she had ordered, and now she'd returned to try on the final products.

And if Matthew's face was anything to go by, she had chosen well. He had settled himself into a black-and-white-striped gilt chair, a book—the scandalously daring *Claudine à Paris*—open on his knee. As Cordelia left the cupboard and came to check the fit in the triple mirror, he looked up, and his green eyes darkened.

"You look beautiful."

For a moment, she almost closed her eyes. *You look beautiful, Daisy.* But she would not think about James. Not now. Not when Matthew was being so kind, and loaning her the money to purchase these clothes (she had fled London with only one dress and was desperate for something clean to wear). They had both made promises, after all—Matthew, that he would not drink to excess while they were in Paris; Cordelia, that she would not punish herself with dark thoughts of her failures: thoughts of Lucie, of her father, of her marriage. And since they'd arrived, Matthew had not so much as touched a wineglass or a bottle.

Pushing aside her melancholy, she smiled at Matthew and turned her attention to the mirror. She looked almost a stranger to herself. The dress had been made to measure, and the neckline dipped daringly low, while the skirt clung about her hips before flaring out, like the stem and petals of a lily. The sleeves were short and ruched, baring her arms. Her Marks stood out stark and black against her light brown skin, though her glamours would prevent any mundane eyes from noting them.

Madame Beausoleil, who kept her salon on the Rue de la Paix, where the most famous dressmakers in the world the House of Worth, Jeanne Paquin—were situated, was, according to Matthew, well acquainted with the Shadow World. "Hypatia Vex won't shop anywhere else," he'd told Cordelia over breakfast. Madame's own past was shrouded in deep mystery, which Cordelia found to be very French of her.

There was very little under the dress—it was apparently the mode in France for dresses to skim the shape of the body. Here, slim stays were worked into the fabric of the bodice. The dress gathered at the bust with a rosette of silk flowers; the skirt flared out at the bottom in a ruffle of gold lace. The back dipped low, showing the curve of her spine. It was a work of art, the dress, which she told Madame (in English, Matthew translating) when she bustled over, pincushion in hand, to see the results of her work.

Madame chuckled. "My job is very easy," she said. "I only must enhance the great beauty already possessed by your wife."

"Oh, she's not my wife," Matthew said, green eyes sparkling. Matthew loved nothing more than the appearance of scandal. Cordelia made a face at him.

To her credit—or perhaps it was just that they were in France—Madame did not even blink. *"Alors,"* she said. "It is rare I get to dress such a natural and unusual beauty. Here, the fashion is all for blondes, blondes, but blondes cannot wear such a color. It is blood and fire, too intense for pallid skin and hair. They are suited by lace and pastel, but Miss . . . ?"

"Miss Carstairs," Cordelia said.

"Miss Carstairs has chosen perfectly for her coloring. When you step into a room, *mademoiselle*, you will appear as the flame of a candle, drawing eyes to you like moths."

Miss Carstairs. Cordelia had not been Mrs. Cordelia Herondale very long. She knew she should not be attached to the name. It hurt to lose it, but that was self-pity, she told herself firmly. She was a Carstairs, a Jahanshah. The blood of Rostam ran in her veins. She would dress in fire if she liked.

"Such a dress deserves adornment," said Madame thoughtfully. "A necklace of ruby and gold. This is a pretty bauble, but much too tiny." She flicked at the small gold pendant around Cordelia's neck. A tiny globe on a strand of gold chain.

It had been a gift from James. Cordelia knew she should take it off, but she was not ready yet. Somehow it seemed a gesture more final than the slashing through of her marriage rune.

"I would buy her rubies willingly, if she let me," said Matthew. "Alas, she refuses."

Madame looked puzzled. If Cordelia was Matthew's mistress, as she'd clearly concluded, what was she doing turning down necklaces? She patted Cordelia on the shoulder, pitying her terrible business sense. "There are some wonderful jewelers on the Rue de la Paix," she said. "Perhaps if you glance in their windows, you will change your mind."

"Perhaps," said Cordelia, fighting the urge to stick her tongue out at Matthew. "At the moment, I must concentrate upon clothing. As my friend explained, my valise was lost on the journey. Would you be able to deliver these outfits to Le Meurice by this evening?"

"Of course, of course." Madame nodded and retreated to the counter at the opposite end of the room, where she began doing figures with a pencil on a bill of sale.

"Now she thinks I'm your mistress," Cordelia said to Matthew, hands on her hips.

He shrugged. "This is Paris. Mistresses are more common than croissants or needlessly tiny cups of coffee."

Cordelia humphed and disappeared back into the changing room. She tried not to think about the cost of the outfits she'd ordered—the red velvet for cold evenings, and four more: a black-and-white-striped walking dress with a matching jacket, an emerald satin trimmed in eau de Nil, a daring black satin evening gown, and a coffee silk with gold-ribbon trim. Anna would be pleased, but it would take all Cordelia's savings to pay Matthew back. He had offered to take on the cost, arguing that it would be no issue for him—it seemed his grandparents on his father's side had left a great deal of money to Henry—but Cordelia couldn't allow herself to accept it. She'd taken enough from Matthew already.

Having put her old dress back on, Cordelia rejoined Matthew in the salon. He'd already paid, and Madame had confirmed delivery of the dresses by that evening. One of the models winked at Matthew as he escorted Cordelia out of the shop and into the crowded Paris streets.

It was a clear, blue-sky day—it had not snowed in Paris this winter, though it had in London, and the streets were chilly but bright. Cordelia happily agreed to make the walk back to the hotel with Matthew rather than flag down a *fiacre* (the Parisian equivalent of a hansom cab). Matthew, his book tucked into the pocket of his overcoat, was still on the subject of her red dress.

"You will simply shine at the cabarets." Matthew clearly felt that he had scored a victory. "No one will be looking at the performers. Well, to be fair, the performers will be painted bright red and wearing false devil horns, so they might still attract some notice."

He smiled at her—the Smile, the one that turned the sternest curmudgeons to butter and made strong men and women weep. Cordelia herself was not immune. She grinned back.

"You see?" said Matthew, waving an arm expansively at the view before them—the wide Parisian boulevard, the colorful awnings of shops, the cafés where women in splendid hats and men in extraordinarily striped trousers warmed themselves with cups of thick hot chocolate. "I promised you would have a good time."

Had she been having a good time? Cordelia wondered. Perhaps she had. So far, she'd been mostly able to keep her mind off the ways she'd horrifically failed everyone she cared about. And that, after all, was the very purpose of the journey. Once you had lost everything, she reasoned, there was no reason not to embrace whatever small happinesses you could. Wasn't that, after all, Matthew's philosophy? Wasn't that why she had come here with him?

A woman seated at a nearby café, wearing a hat laden with ostrich plumes and silk roses, glanced from Matthew to Cordelia and smiled—approving, Cordelia assumed, of young love. Months ago, Cordelia would have blushed; now she simply smiled. What did it matter if people thought the wrong things about her? Any girl would be happy to have Matthew as a suitor, so let passersby imagine whatever they wanted. That was how Matthew managed things, after all—not caring at all what others thought, simply being himself, and it was astonishing how it allowed him to move easily through the world.

Without him, she doubted she could have managed the journey to Paris in the state she'd been in. He'd gotten them—sleep-deprived, yawning—from the train station to Le Meurice, where he'd been all smiles, sunny and joking with the bellman. One would have thought he'd rested in a featherbed that night.

They'd slept into the afternoon, that first night (in the two separate bedrooms of Matthew's suite, which shared a common living room), and she'd dreamt that she'd poured out all her sins to the Meurice desk clerk. *You see, my mother is about to have a baby, and I might not be there when she does because I am too busy gallivanting with my husband's best friend. I used to carry the mythical sword Cortana—perhaps you know of it from* La Chanson de Roland*? Yes, well, I turned out to be unworthy of wielding it and gave it to my brother, which also, by the way, puts him in potentially mortal peril from not one but two very powerful demons. I was supposed to become my closest friend's* parabatai*, but now that can never* *happen. And I allowed myself to think that the man I love might have loved me, and not Grace Blackthorn, though he was always direct and honest about his love for her.*

When she'd finished, she looked up and saw that the clerk had Lilith's face, his eyes each a tangle of writhing black snakes.

You've done well by me, at least, dearie, Lilith said, and Cordelia had woken up with a scream that echoed in her head for minutes after.

When she woke again later to the sound of a maid throwing the curtains back, she had gazed out in wonder on the bright day, the roofs of Paris marching away to the horizon like obedient soldiers. In the distance, the Eiffel Tower, rising defiant against a storm-blue sky. And in the next room, Matthew, waiting for her to join him in an adventure.

For the next two days, they had eaten together—once at the gorgeous Le Train Bleu inside the Gare de Lyon, which had amazed Cordelia: so pretty, like dining inside a cut sapphire!—and walked together in the parks, and shopped together: shirts and suits for Matthew at Charvet, where Baudelaire and Verlaine had bought their clothes, and dresses and shoes and a coat for Cordelia. She had stopped short of allowing Matthew to buy her hats. Surely, she told him, there must be some limits. He suggested that the limit should be umbrellas, which were essential to a proper outfit and doubled as a useful weapon. She'd giggled, and wondered then at how nice it was to laugh.

Perhaps most surprising, Matthew had more than kept to his promise: he consumed not a drop of alcohol. He even withstood the disapproving frowns of waiters when he declined wine at their meals. Based on her experience of her father's drinking, Cordelia had expected him to be sick with the lack of it, but to the contrary, he had been clear-eyed and energetic, dragging her all over central Paris to the sites, the museums, the monuments, the gardens. It all felt very mature and worldly, which was surely the point.

Now she looked at Matthew and thought, *He looks happy.* Honestly, plainly happy. And if this trip to Paris might not be her salvation, she could at least make sure it was his.

He took her arm to guide her past a broken bit of pavement. Cordelia thought of the woman at the café, how she had smiled at them, thinking them a couple in love. If only she knew that Matthew hadn't so much as tried to kiss Cordelia once. He had been the model of a restrained gentleman. Once or twice, as they bid each other good night in the hotel suite, she had thought she caught a look in his eyes, but perhaps she was imagining it? She wasn't entirely sure what she had expected, nor was she sure how she felt about—well, anything.

"I am having a good time," she said now, and meant it. She knew she was happier here than she would have been in London, where she would have retreated to her family home in Cornwall Gardens. Alastair would have tried to be kind, and her mother would have been shocked and grieving, and the weight of trying to bear up under it all would have made her want to die.

This was better. She'd sent a quick note home to her family from the hotel's telegraph service, letting them know she was shopping for her spring wardrobe in Paris, chaperoned by Matthew. She suspected they would find this odd, but at least, one hoped, not alarming.

"I'm just curious," she added as they approached the hotel, with its massive facade, all wrought-iron balconies and lights shining from its windows, casting their glow over the wintry streets. "You mentioned that I would shine at a cabaret? What cabaret, and when are we going?"

"As a matter of fact, tonight," Matthew said, opening the hotel door for her. "We will be journeying to the heart of Hell together. Are you worried?"

"Not at all. I am only glad I chose a red dress. It will be thematic."

Matthew laughed, but Cordelia couldn't help but wonder: journeying into the heart of Hell together? What on earth did he mean?

They did not find Lucie the next day.

The snow had not stuck, and the roads at least were clear. Balios and Xanthos trudged along between bare walls of hedges, their breath puffing white in the air. They came to Lostwithiel, a small village inland, in the middle of the day, and Magnus headed into a public house called the Wolf's Bane to make inquiries. He came out shaking his head, and though they made their way regardless to the address he'd been given earlier, it turned out to be an abandoned farmhouse, the old roof falling in on itself.

"There is another possibility," Magnus said, clambering back into the carriage. Flakes of fine snow, which had likely flurried off the remains of the roof, were caught in his black eyebrows. "Sometime last century, a mysterious gentleman from London purchased an old ruined chapel on Peak Rock, in a fishing village called Polperro. He restored the place but rarely leaves it. Local Downworld gossip is he's a warlock—apparently purple flames sometimes leak from the chimney at night."

"I thought a warlock was supposed to live *here*," Will said, indicating the burned-out farmhouse.

"Not all rumors are true, Herondale, but they all must be investigated," said Magnus serenely. "We ought to be able to get to Polperro in a few hours, anyway."

James sighed inwardly. More hours, more waiting. More worrying—about Lucie, about Matthew and Daisy. About his dream.

They wake.

"I shall amuse you with a tale, then," said Will. "The tale of my hellride with Balios from London to Cadair Idris, in Wales. Your mother, James, was missing—kidnapped by the miscreant Mortmain. I leaped into Balios's saddle. 'If ever you loved me, Balios,' I cried, 'let your feet now be swift, and carry me to my dear Tessa before harm befalls her.' It was a stormy night, though the storm that raged inside my breast was fiercer still—"

"I can't believe you haven't heard this story before, James," said Magnus mildly. The two of them were sharing one side of the carriage, as it had become quickly apparent on the first day of their journey that Will needed the entire other side for dramatic gesturing.

It was very strange to have heard tales of Magnus all James's life, and now to be traveling in close quarters with him. What he'd learned in their days of travel was that despite his elaborate costumes and theatrical airs, which had alarmed several innkeepers, Magnus was surprisingly calm and practical.

"I haven't," said James. "Not since last Thursday."

He did not say that it was actually rather comforting to hear it again. It was a tale that had been told often to himself and Lucie, who had adored it when she was young—Will, following his heart, dashing to the rescue of their mother, who he did not yet know loved him, too.

James leaned his head against the carriage window. The scenery had turned dramatic—cliffs fell away to their left, and below was the uproar of pounding surf, waves of gunmetal ocean smashing against the rocks that reached knobbled fingers far out into the gray-blue sea. In the distance, he saw a church atop a promontory, silhouetted against the sky, its gray steeple seeming somehow terribly lonely, terribly far from everything.

His father's voice was singsong in his ears, the words of the story as familiar as a lullaby. James could not help but think of Cordelia, reading to him from Ganjavi. Her favorite poem, about the doomed lovers Layla and Majnun. Her voice, soft as velvet. *And when her cheek the moon revealed, a thousand hearts were won: no pride, no shield, could check her power. Layla, she was called.*

Cordelia smiled at him over the table in the study. The chess game had been set out, and she held an ivory knight in her graceful hand. The light from the fire illuminated her hair, a halo of flame and gold. "Chess is a Persian game," she told him. "*Bia ba man bazi kon.* Play with me, James."

"*Kheili khoshgeli,*" he said. He found the words easily: they were the first thing he'd taught himself to say in Persian, though he had never said them to his wife before. *You are so beautiful.*

She blushed. Her lips trembled, red and full. Her eyes were so dark, they shimmered—they were black snakes, moving and darting, snapping at him with their teeth—

"James! Wake up!" Magnus's hand was on his shoulder, shaking him. James came awake, retching dryly, his fist jammed into his stomach. He was in the carriage, though the sky outside had darkened. How much time had passed? He had been dreaming again. This time Cordelia had been dragged into his nightmares. He sank back against the cushioned seat, feeling sick to his stomach.

He glanced at his father. Will was looking at him with a rare stern expression, his eyes very blue. He said, "James, you must tell us what is wrong."

"Nothing." There was a bitter taste in James's mouth. "I fell asleep—another dream—I told you, I'm worried about Lucie."

"You were calling for Cordelia," Will said. "I have never heard anyone sound as if they were in such pain. Jamie, you must talk to us."

Magnus glanced between James and Will. His hand was on James's shoulder, heavy with its weight of rings. He said, "You cried out another name too. And a word. One that makes me quite nervous."

No, James thought. *No*. Out the window, the sun was setting, and the rolling farms tucked between the hills glowed dark red. "I'm sure it was nonsense."

Magnus said, "You cried out the name Lilith." He regarded James levelly. "There is much chatter in Downworld about the recent happenings in London. The story as I have been told it has never quite sat well with me. There are rumors, too, of the Mother of Demons. James, you don't need to tell us what you know. But we will put it together, regardless." He glanced at Will. "Well, I shall; I can't promise anything for your father. He's always been slow."

"But I have never worn a Russian hat with fur earflaps," said Will, "unlike some individuals currently present."

"Mistakes have been made on all sides," said Magnus. "James?"

"I do not own an earflap hat," James said.

The two men glared at him.

"I can't say it all now," James said, and felt his heartbeat skip: for the first time he had admitted there was something to say. "Not if we're going to find Lucie—"

Magnus shook his head. "It's already dark, and starting to rain, and the way up Chapel Cliff to Peak Rock is said to be a precarious one. Safer to stop tonight and go tomorrow morning."

Will nodded; it was clear he and Magnus had discussed their plans while James was asleep.

"Very well," Magnus said. "We will stop at the next decent inn. I'll book us a saloon room where we can talk privately. And James—whatever it is, we can sort it out."

James doubted that very much, but it seemed pointless to say so. He watched the sun vanish through the window instead, reaching his hand into his pocket as he did so. Cordelia's gloves, the pair he had taken from their house, were still there, the kidskin soft as flower petals. He closed his hand around one.

* * *

In a small white room near the ocean, Lucie Herondale was drifting in and out of sleep.

When she'd first awakened, here in the strange bed that smelled like old straw, she'd heard a voice—Jesse's voice—and she had tried to call out, to let him know she was conscious. But before she could, exhaustion had swept over her like a cold gray wave. An exhaustion she had never felt before, or even imagined, deep as a knife wound. Her fingertip grip on alertness had slipped, tumbling her into the darkness of her own mind, where time swayed and lurched like a ship in a storm, and she could hardly tell whether she was awake or asleep.

In the moments of lucidity, she had pieced together only a few details. The room was small, painted the color of an eggshell; there was a single window through which she could see the ocean as its waves rolled in and out, a dark gunmetal gray tipped with white. She could hear the ocean too, she thought, but its distant roar often came mixed with much less pleasant noises, and she could not tell what of her perception was real.

There were two people who came into the room from time to time to check on her. One was Jesse. The other was Malcolm, a more diffident presence; she knew somehow that they were in his house, the one in Cornwall, with the Cornish sea pounding the rocks outside.

She hadn't yet been able to speak to either of them; when she tried, it was as though her mind could form the words, but her body would not respond to its commands. She could not even twitch a finger to call attention to the fact that she was awake, and all her efforts only sent her back into the darkness.

The darkness was not only the interior of her mind. She had thought it was, at first—the familiar darkness that came before sleep brought the vivid colors of dreams. But this darkness was a *place*.

And in that place, she was not alone. Though it seemed an emptiness through which she drifted without purpose, she could sense the presence of others, not alive but not dead: bodiless, their souls whirling through the void but never meeting her or one another. They were unhappy, these souls. They did not understand what was happening to them. They kept up a constant wailing, a wordless cry of pain and sorrow that burrowed under her flesh.

She felt something brush against her cheek. It brought her back to her body. She was in the white bedroom again. The touch on her cheek was Jesse's hand; she knew it without being able to open her eyes, or move to respond.

"She's crying," he said.

His *voice*. There was a depth to it, a texture it had not possessed when he had been a ghost.

"She might be having a nightmare." Malcolm's voice. "Jesse, she's fine. She used up a great deal of her energy bringing you back. She needs to rest."

"But don't you see—it's *because* she brought me back." Jesse's voice caught. "If she doesn't heal . . . I could never forgive myself."

"This gift of hers. This ability to reach through the veil that separates the living and the dead. She has had it all her life. It is not your fault; if it is anyone's, it is Belial's." Malcolm sighed. "We know so little about the shadow realms beyond the end of everything. And she went quite far into them, to pull you back out. It is taking her some time to return."

"But what if she's trapped somewhere awful?" The light touch came again, Jesse's hand cupping her face. Lucie wanted to turn her cheek into his palm so badly it hurt. "What if she needs me to pull her out, somehow?"

When Malcolm spoke again, his voice was more gentle. "It's been two days. If by tomorrow she is not awake, I may attempt to reach her with magic. I will look into it, *if*, in the meantime, you stop standing over her, fretting. If you really want to make yourself useful, you can go into the village and bring back some things we need . . ."

His voice wavered, fading into silence. Lucie was in the dark place again. She could hear Jesse, his voice a far-off whisper, barely audible. *"Lucie, if you can hear me—I'm here. I'm taking care of you."*

I am here, she tried to say. *I can hear you.* But like the time before and the time before that, the words were swallowed up in shadow, and she fell back into the void.

* * *

"Who's a pretty bird?" Ariadne Bridgestock said.

Winston the parrot narrowed his eyes at her. He offered no opinion on who might or might not be a pretty bird. His focus, she was sure, was on the handful of Brazil nuts in her hand.

"I thought we could have a chat," she told him, tempting him with a nut. "Parrots are meant to talk. Why don't you ask me how my day has been so far?"

Winston glowered. He had been a gift from her parents, long ago, when she had first arrived in London and was longing for something colorful to offset what she found to be the dreary grayness of the city. Winston had a green body, a plum-colored head, and a scoundrel's disposition.

His glare made it clear that there would be no conversation until she provided a Brazil nut. *Outmaneuvered by a parrot*, Ariadne thought, and handed him a treat through the bars. Matthew Fairchild had a gorgeous golden dog as a pet, and here she was, stuck with the moody Lord Byron of fowl.

Winston swallowed the nut and extended a claw, wrapping it around one of the bars of his cage. "Pretty bird," he chortled. "Pretty bird."

Good enough, Ariadne thought. "My day's been rotten, thanks for asking," she said, feeding Winston another nut through the bars. "The house is so empty and lonely. Mother just rattles about, looking woebegone and worrying about Father. He's been gone for five whole days now. And—I never thought I'd miss *Grace*, but at least she'd be company."

She didn't mention Anna. Some things were none of Winston's business.

"Grace," he croaked. He tapped at the bars of his cage in a meaningful manner. "Silent City."

"Indeed," Ariadne murmured. Her father and Grace had left on the same night, and their departures must have been connected, although Ariadne wasn't sure exactly how. Her father had rushed off to the Adamant Citadel, intending to question Tatiana Blackthorn. The next morning Ariadne and her mother had discovered that Grace was gone too, having packed her meager things and left in the dead of night. Only at lunch did a runner bring a note from Charlotte, letting them know that Grace was in the custody of the Silent Brothers, speaking with them about her mother's crimes.

Ariadne's mother had swooned with agitation over this. "Oh, to have unknowingly sheltered a criminal under our roof!" To this Ariadne had rolled her eyes and pointed out that Grace had gone of her own volition, not been dragged out by the Silent Brothers, and that it was Tatiana Blackthorn who was the criminal. Tatiana had already caused a great deal of trouble and pain, and if Grace wished to give the Silent Brothers more information about her illegal activities, well, that was just good citizenship.

She knew it was ridiculous to miss Grace. They had rarely spoken. But the feeling of loneliness was so intense, Ariadne thought, that just having someone *there* would surely alleviate it. There were people she actively wished to talk to, of course, but she was doing her best not to think about those people. They were not her friends, not really. They were Anna's, and Anna—

Her reverie was interrupted by the harsh jingle of the doorbell. Winston, she saw, had fallen asleep, hanging upside down. Hastily she dumped the remainder of the nuts into his food dish and hurried from the conservatory toward the front of the house, hoping for news.

But her mother had gotten to the door first. Ariadne paused at the top of the stairs when she heard her voice. "Consul Fairchild, hello. And Mr. Lightwood. How kind of you to call." She paused. "Do you perhaps come with news of Maurice?"

Ariadne could hear the fear in Flora Bridgestock's voice, and it rooted her to the floor. At least she was around the bend of the stairwell, out of sight of the door. If Charlotte Fairchild had brought news—bad news—she would be more willing to tell her mother without Ariadne there.

She waited, gripping the newel post on the landing, until she heard Gideon Lightwood's gentle voice. "No, Flora. We've heard nothing since he left for Iceland. We were rather hoping that—well, that *you* had."

"No," her mother said. She sounded remote, distant; Ariadne knew she was struggling not to show her fear. "I assumed that if he was in touch with anybody, he would be in touch with the office of the Consul."

There was an awkward silence. Ariadne, feeling dizzy, suspected Gideon and Charlotte were wishing they'd never come.

"You've heard nothing from the Citadel?" her mother said at last. "From the Iron Sisters?"

"No," admitted the Consul. "But they are a reticent bunch even under the best of circumstances. Tatiana is likely a difficult subject to question; it's possible they simply feel that there is no news yet."

"But you've sent them messages," said Flora. "And they haven't responded. Perhaps—the Reykjavík Institute?" Ariadne thought she heard a note of her mother's fear slip past the battlements of her politeness. "I know we cannot Track him, as it would be over water, but they could. I could give you something of his to send them. A handkerchief, or—"

"Flora." The Consul spoke in her kindest voice; Ariadne guessed she was, by now, gently holding her mother's hand. "This is a mission of the utmost secrecy; Maurice would be the first to demand we not alarm the Clave at large. We will send another message to the Citadel, and if we hear nothing back, we will launch an investigation of our own. I promise you."

Ariadne's mother murmured assent, but Ariadne was troubled. The Consul and her closest advisor didn't visit in person because they were merely eager for news. Something had them worried; something they had not mentioned to Flora.

Charlotte and Gideon took their leave among further reassurances. When Ariadne heard the door latch shut, she came down the stairs. Her mother, who had been standing motionless in the entryway, started when she saw her. Ariadne did her best to give the impression that she had only just arrived.

"I heard voices," she said. "Was that the Consul who just left?"

Her mother nodded vaguely, lost in thought. "And Gideon Lightwood. They wanted to know if we'd had a message from your father. And here I hoped they had come to say *they'd* heard from him."

"It's all right, Mama." Ariadne took her mother's hands in her own. "You know how Father is. He's going to be careful and take his time, and learn all he can."

"Oh, I know. But—it was his idea to send Tatiana to the Adamant

Citadel in the first place. If something's gone wrong—"

"It was an act of mercy," Ariadne said firmly. "Not locking her up in the Silent City, where she would no doubt have gone madder than she already was."

"But we did not know then what we know now," her mother said. "If Tatiana Blackthorn had something to do with Leviathan attacking the Institute . . . that is not the act of a madwoman deserving pity. It is war on the Nephilim. It is the act of a dangerous adversary, in league with the greatest of evils."

"She was in the Adamant Citadel when Leviathan attacked," Ariadne pointed out. "How could she be responsible without the Iron Sisters knowing? Don't fret, Mama," she added. "It will all be well."

Her mother sighed. "Ari," she said, "you've grown up to be such a lovely girl. I will miss you so, when some fine man chooses you, and you go off to be married."

Ariadne made a noncommittal noise.

"Oh, I know, it was a terrible experience with that Charles," her mother said. "You'll find a better man in time."

She took a breath and set her shoulders, and not for the first time, Ariadne was reminded that her mother was a Shadowhunter like any other, and confronting hardships was part of her job. "By the Angel," she said, in a new, brisk tone, "life goes on, and we cannot stand in the foyer and fret all day. I have much to attend to . . . the Inquisitor's wife must hold down the household while the master is away, and all that . . ."

Ariadne murmured her assent and kissed her mother on the cheek before going back up the stairs. Halfway down the corridor, she passed the door to her father's study, which stood ajar. She pushed the door open slightly and peered inside.

The study had been left in an alarming shambles. If Ariadne had hoped that looking inside Maurice Bridgestock's study would make her feel closer to her father, she was disappointed—it made her feel more worried instead. Her father was fastidious and organized, and proud of it. He did not tolerate mess. She knew he had left in haste, but the state of the room brought home how panicked he must have been.

Almost without thinking, she found herself straightening up:

pushing the chair back under the desk, freeing the curtains where they'd become folded over a lampshade, taking the teacups out into the hallway where the housekeeper would find them. Ashes lay cold in front of the grate; she picked up the small brass broom to whisk them back into the fireplace—

And paused.

Something white gleamed among the ashes in the fireplace grate. She could recognize her father's neat copperplate handwriting on a stack of charred paper. She leaned closer—whatever kind of notes had her father felt he needed to destroy before he left London?

She took the papers out of the fireplace, flicked the ash from them, and began to read. As she did, she felt a piercing dryness in her throat, as if she were near choking.

Scribbled across the top of the first page were the words *Herondale/ Lightwood.*

It was an obvious transgression to read further, but the name Lightwood burned its letters into her eyes; she could not turn aside from it. If there was some sort of trouble facing Anna's family, how could she refuse to know it?

The pages were labeled with years: 1896, 1892, 1900. She flipped through the sheets and felt a cold finger creep up the back of her neck.

In her father's hand were not accounts of money spent or earned, but descriptions of events. Events involving Herondales and Lightwoods.

No, not events. Mistakes. Errors. Sins. It was a record of any doing of the Herondales and Lightwoods that had caused what her father considered problems; anything that could be characterized as irresponsible or ill-considered was noted here.

> 12/3/01: *G2.L absent from Council meeting without explanation. CF angry.*
>
> 6/9/98: *WW in Waterloo say WH/TH refused meeting, causing them to disrupt Market.*
>
> 8/1/95: *Head of Oslo Institute refuses to meet with TH, citing her Heritage.*

Ariadne felt sick. Most of the deeds noted seemed petty, small, or hearsay; the report that the head of the Oslo Institute would not meet with Tessa Herondale, one of the kindest ladies Ariadne had ever known, was revolting. The head of the Oslo Institute should have been reprimanded; instead, the event was recorded here as if it had been the Herondales' fault.

What was this? What was her father thinking?

At the bottom of the stack was something else. A sheet of creamy-white stationery. Not notes, but a letter. Ariadne lifted the missive away from the rest of the stack, her eyes scanning the lines in disbelief.

"Ariadne?"

Quickly, Ariadne shoved the letter into the bodice of her dress, before rising to face her mother. Standing in the doorway, Flora was frowning, her eyes narrowed. When she spoke, it was with none of the warmth she'd had in their conversation downstairs. "Ariadne—what are you doing?"

2
Grey Sea

Grey rocks, and greyer sea,
And surf along the shore—
And in my heart a name
My lips shall speak no more.
—Charles G. D. Roberts, "Grey Rocks, and Greyer Sea"

When Lucie woke up at last, it was to the sound of waves and a bright, wintry sunlight as sharp as the sheer edge of glass. She sat upright so quickly her head spun. She was determined *not* to go back to sleep again, *not* to fall unconscious, *not* to return to that dark, empty place full of voices and noise.

She threw off the striped afghan she'd been sleeping under and swung her legs out of bed. Her first try at standing was unsuccessful; her legs buckled, and she tumbled back onto the bed. The second time she used one of the bedposts to pull herself upright. This worked slightly better, and for a few moments she swayed back and forth like an old sea captain unused to land.

Other than the bed, a simple wrought-iron frame painted eggshell white to match the walls, there was little furniture in her small room. There was a fireplace in whose grate embers crackled and smoldered with a faint purple tinge, and a vanity table of unfinished wood, carved all over with mermaids and sea serpents. Her own traveling trunk sat reassuringly at the foot of the bed.

Eventually, her legs fizzing with pins and needles, she made her way to the window, set into an alcove in the wall, and looked outside. The view was a symphony of white and deep green, black and palest blue. Malcolm's house seemed to be perched halfway up a rocky cliff, above a pretty little fishing village. Below the house was a narrow inlet where the ocean sloshed into the harbor and small fishing boats rocked gently in the tide. The sky was a clear porcelain blue, though it had obviously snowed recently, judging from the sugary dusting of white on the village's pitched roofs. Coal smoke from chimneys sent black threads up into the sky, and waves crashed against the cliff below, foaming white and pine green.

It was lovely—stark and lovely, and the expanse of the sea gave Lucie an odd, hollow feeling inside. London seemed a million miles away, as did the people in it: Cordelia and James, her mother and father. What must they be thinking now? Where in Cornwall did they imagine she was? Probably not here, gazing at an ocean that stretched all the way to the coast of France.

To distract herself, she wiggled her toes experimentally. At least the pins and needles were gone. The rough wood planks of the floor had been worn down over years so they felt as smooth against her bare feet as if they had been newly polished. She slid across them to the vanity table, where washbasin and cloth awaited her. She nearly groaned when she caught sight of herself in the mirror. Her hair was matted and flyaway, her traveling dress crushed and wrinkled, and one of the buttons on a pillow had left a penny-sized dent in her cheek.

She'd have to beg Malcolm for a bath later, she thought. He was a warlock; surely he could produce hot water. For the moment, she did her best with the washbasin and a cake of Pears soap before she peeled off her wreck of a dress, tossed it into a corner, and flung open her trunk. She sat staring for a moment at the contents—had she really packed a *bathing costume*? The thought of swimming in the ice-green waters of the Polperro harbor was terrifying. After moving aside her axe and gear jacket, she selected a dark blue wool dress with embroidery around the cuffs, and set to work making herself look presentable with hairpins. She had a moment of panic when she realized her gold locket was not around her neck, but a minute's hasty searching turned it up on the nightstand beside her bed.

Jesse put it there, she thought. She could not have said how she knew that, but she was sure of it.

She was suddenly desperate to see him. Kicking her feet into low boots, she slipped out of the room into the corridor.

Malcolm's house was significantly larger than she had thought; her bedroom turned out to be one of six on this level, and the stairs at its end—carved in the same manner as the vanity table—led to a high-ceilinged open parlor suitable for a manor. There was obviously no room for both the high ceiling and the bedrooms above, a disorienting effect; Malcolm must have enspelled the house to be as large as he liked on the inside.

There was no indication of anyone else being home, but there was a steady rhythmic thump coming from somewhere outside. After a moment of searching, Lucie located the front door and stepped outside.

The bright sunlight had been deceptive. It was *cold.* The wind sheared across the rocky cliffs like a knife's edge, cutting through the wool of her dress. She wrapped her arms around herself with a shiver and turned in a quick circle, taking everything in. She had been right about the house—from outside, it seemed very small indeed, a cottage that could have fit three rooms or so. Its windows appeared boarded up, though she knew they weren't, and its whitewash was peeling, roughed away by the salt air.

The frostbitten seagrass crunched under her shoes as she followed the *thump, thump* sound around the side of the house. And stopped in her tracks.

It was Jesse. He stood with an axe in his hands, next to a pile of firewood he'd been splitting. Lucie's hands shook, and not just with the cold. He was *alive.* The force of it had never hit her so hard before. She had never seen him like this—never seen the wind lift his black hair, or seen the flush of exertion on his cheeks. Never seen his breath puff out in white clouds as he exhaled. Never seen him breathe at all; he had always been in the world but not part of it, untouched by heat or cold or atmosphere, and here he was breathing and *living,* his shadow stretching out behind him across the rocky ground.

She could not stand it a moment longer. She ran to him. He had time only to look up in surprise and drop the axe before she had thrown her arms around his neck.

He caught her against him, gripping her tight, fingers digging into the soft fabric of her dress. He nuzzled his face down into her hair, breathing her name, "Lucie, *Lucie*," and his body was warm against hers. For the first time she experienced the scent of him: wool, sweat, skin, woodsmoke, the air just before a storm. For the first time, she felt his heart beating against hers.

At last they drew apart. He kept his arms around her, smiling down into her face. There was a little hesitance in his expression, as if he were unsure what she thought of this new, real, and living Jesse. Silly boy, she thought; he ought to be able to read it all in her face. But maybe it was better if he couldn't?

"Awake at last," he said. His voice was—well, it was his voice, she knew his voice. But it was so much more physical, more present, than she'd heard it before. And she could feel the vibration in his chest as he spoke. She wondered if she would ever get used to all these new details.

"How long was I asleep?"

"A few days. Nothing much has happened; mostly we've just been waiting for you to wake up." He frowned. "Malcolm said you would be all right eventually, and I thought—" He flinched and held up his right hand. She winced to see the torn red skin. But Jesse seemed delighted. "Blisters," he said happily. "I've got *blisters*."

"Rotten luck," Lucie said sympathetically.

"Not at all. Do you know how long it's been since I had a blister? A scraped knee? A missing tooth?"

"I hope you don't knock out all your teeth in your new delight at being alive," said Lucie. "I don't think I could lo—like you as well as I do if you were toothless."

Oh, dear. She had almost said *love*. At least Jesse seemed too enchanted with his new injuries to have noticed.

"How shallow," Jesse said, winding a strand of her hair around his finger. "I should like *you* just as well if you were bald and shriveled like a desiccated acorn."

Lucie experienced a terrible desire to giggle. She forced herself to scowl ferociously instead. "Honestly, what on earth have you been doing out here chopping wood, anyway? Can't Malcolm magic up some wood if it's needed? Where *is* Malcolm, by the by?"

"Went down into the village," Jesse said. "Ostensibly to buy supplies. I think he likes the walking; otherwise he'd probably just magic up food, like you said. Most days he's gone all afternoon."

"Most days?" Lucie said. "You said a few days—how long has it been?"

"This is the fifth day we've been here. Malcolm used his magic to determine that you were safe and only needed natural rest. A great deal of it."

"Oh." Lucie stepped back, alarmed. "My family will be coming after us, surely—they'll want to know everything—they'll be furious with me—and Malcolm—we must make a plan—"

Jesse frowned again. "They won't have an easy time finding us. The house has been very heavily warded against Tracking and, I suppose, most everything else."

Lucie was about to explain that she knew her parents, and they were not going to let something like impenetrable wards stop them from ferreting out where she was, but before she could, Malcolm came around the corner, walking stick in hand, his boots crunching on the frozen ground. He was wearing the white traveling coat he'd had on when she last saw him, in the Institute Sanctuary. He had been angry then; frightened, she thought, of what she'd done. Now he only looked tired, and more disheveled than she'd expected.

"I told you she'd be fine," he said to Jesse. He glanced at the firewood. "Excellent work," he added. "You'll be feeling stronger every day if you keep that up."

So the task of splitting firewood was more about Jesse's health than anything else. It made sense. Preserved or not, his body had surely been weakened by seven years of being dead. Of course, Belial had possessed Jesse, used his body as a puppet, driving him to walk miles all over London, to—

But she didn't want to think about that. That had been in the past, when Jesse did not really inhabit his body. All that was changed now.

Jesse examined the pile of unsplit logs behind him. "Another half hour at most, I think, and I'll be done."

Malcolm nodded and turned to Lucie. There was an odd blankness to the way he looked at her, Lucie thought, and felt a stir of unease. "Miss Herondale," he said. "May I speak to you in the house?"

"Now, I've prepared *this* sheet with a solution of hartshorn," Christopher was saying, "and when the flame is applied via a standard combustion rune—Thomas, are you paying attention?"

"All ears," said Thomas. "Absolutely countless ears."

They were downstairs at the Fairchilds' house, in Henry's laboratory. Christopher had asked Thomas to help him with a new project, and Thomas had leaped at the opportunity for something to distract him.

Christopher pushed his spectacles up his nose. "I see that you're not sure the application of fire will be necessary," he said. "But I keep a close eye on the mundanes' developments in the area of science, you know. They have recently been working on ways of sending messages from one person to another, at a great distance, first through lengths of metal wire, and more recently through the air itself."

"What's that got to do with you setting fire to things?" said Thomas—in his opinion, very politely.

"Well, to put it plainly, mundanes have used heat to create most of their technology—electricity, the telegraph—and we Shadowhunters can't fall behind the mundanes in what we can do, Thomas. It will hardly do if their devices give them powers we can't match. In this case, they can send messages at a distance, and well—we can't. But if I can use runes—see, I singe the edge of the parchment here with a flame, and fold it over, and Mark it with a Communication rune *here*, and an Accuracy rune *here* and *here* . . ."

From upstairs, the doorbell chimed. Christopher ignored it, and for a moment Thomas wondered if he should answer it himself. But at a second and third chime, Christopher sighed, put down his stele, and headed for the stairs.

Overhead, Thomas heard the front door open. It wasn't his intention to eavesdrop, but when Christopher's voice drifted down to him, saying, "Oh, hullo, Alastair, you must be here to see Charles. I think he's upstairs in his study," he felt his stomach swoop inside him like a bird diving for a fish. (Then he wished he'd come up with a better mental analogy, but one either had a poetic turn of mind, like James, or one didn't.)

Alastair's reply was too low for him to hear. Christopher coughed and said, "Oh, just down in the lab, you know. I've got quite the new exciting project—"

Alastair interrupted him to say something. Thomas wondered if Christopher would mention that Thomas was there. But he did not; he only said, "Matthew's still in Paris, as far as we know. Yes, I'm sure Charles wouldn't mind a visit . . ."

The bird in Thomas's stomach flopped over dead. He leaned his elbows on Christopher's worktable, trying to breathe through it all. He knew he shouldn't be surprised. Alastair had made it clear, the last time they saw each other, that there could be nothing between them. And the main reason for that was the hostility between Alastair and Thomas's friends, the Merry Thieves—who disliked Alastair for very good reason.

Thomas had woken up the next morning with a clear thought in his mind: *It's time—it's past time—for me to tell my friends about my feelings for Alastair. Perhaps Alastair is right and it is impossible—but it will definitely remain impossible if I never try.*

He had meant to do it. He had gotten out of bed absolutely determined to do it.

But then he learned that Matthew and James had both left London in the night, and so his plan had to be delayed. And in fact, not just Matthew and James were gone. Cordelia and Matthew, it seemed, had gone to Paris, while James had gone off with Will to look for Lucie, who had, it seemed, taken it into her head to visit Malcolm Fade at his cottage in Cornwall. Christopher seemed to accept this tale without question; Thomas did not, and he knew Anna didn't either, but Anna had been firm in her refusal to discuss it. *One gossips about one's acquaintance, not one's friends,* was all she would say. Anna herself looked pale and tired, though perhaps she'd gone back to having a different girl in her room every night. Thomas rather missed Ariadne and he suspected Anna did too, but the one time he'd brought her up, Anna had almost slung a teacup at his head.

Thomas *had* considered these last few days telling Christopher of his feelings, but while Christopher would be kind about it, he would feel awkward about knowing something James and Matthew didn't, and it was James and Matthew who truly disliked—hated, even—Alastair in the first place.

And then there was the issue of Charles. Charles had been Alastair's first great love, though it had ended badly. He had been wounded in an encounter with Belial, and though he was convalescing, Alastair seemed to feel he owed him support and looking after. While Thomas could understand this from a purely moral standpoint, he was tormented by the thought of Alastair mopping Charles's feverish brow and feeding him grapes. It was all too easy to imagine Charles laying a hand on Alastair's cheek and murmuring his gratitude while staring deeply into Alastair's gorgeous dark eyes with their long, thick lashes—

Christopher returned from upstairs, nearly causing Thomas to leap out of his chair. Christopher, thankfully, seemed blissfully unaware of Thomas's inner turmoil, and immediately went back to the workbench. "All right," he said, turning toward Thomas with a stele in hand, "let's try again, shall we?"

"Sending a message?" Thomas asked. He and Christopher had "sent off" dozens of messages by now, and while some of them had disappeared into thin air or raced up the chimney, none had ever gotten to their intended destination.

"Indeed," Kit said, handing over a piece of paper and a pencil. "I just need you to write a message, while I test this reagent. It can be any sort of nonsense you like."

Thomas sat down at the workbench and stared at the blank page. After a long moment, he wrote:

> *Dear Alastair, why are you so stupid and so frustrating, and why do I think about you all the time? Why do I have to think about you when I get up and when I go to sleep and when I brush my teeth and right now? Why did you kiss me in the Sanctuary if you didn't want to be with me? Is it that you don't want to tell anyone? It's very annoying. —Thomas*

"All right, then?" Christopher said. Thomas started and quickly folded the page into quarters, so its contents were hidden. He handed it over to Christopher with only a slight pang. He wished he could have shown the words to someone, but he knew it was impossible. It had felt good to write it all down, anyway, he thought, as Christopher lit a match and touched it to the edge of the page. Even if the message was, rather like Thomas's relationship with Alastair, going nowhere in the end.

Considering the horror stories her mother had told her, Grace Blackthorn had expected the Silent City to be a sort of dungeon, where she would be chained to a wall and possibly tortured. Even before she reached the City entrance in Highgate, she had begun to think of what it would be like to be tried by the Mortal Sword. To stand on the Speaking Stars and feel the Silent Brothers' judgment. How it would feel to be compelled—after so very many years of lying—to tell the truth. Would it be a relief? Or would it be a terrible agony?

She supposed it did not matter. She deserved the agony.

But she had not been clapped in irons, or anything of the sort. Two Silent Brothers had escorted her from James's house in Curzon Street to the Silent City. The moment she had arrived (and it was indeed a dark, forbidding, shadowy sort of place), Brother Zachariah—who she knew to be Cordelia's cousin, once James Carstairs—had come forward as if to take charge of her.

You must be exhausted. His voice in her mind was quiet, even kind. *Let me show you to your chamber. Tomorrow will be early enough to discuss what has happened.*

She had been stunned. Brother Zachariah was a figure that her mother had referred to, more than once, as a demonstration of the Herondales' corrosive influence over the Nephilim. "His eyes aren't even sewn shut," she'd snap, not even looking at Grace. "Only special treatment for the ones that the Lightwoods and the Herondales favor. It's obscene."

But Brother Zachariah spoke to her with a gentle kindness. He had led her through the cold, stone-walled City to a small cell, which she had been imagining as a sort of torture chamber, where she would sleep on cold stone, perhaps bound with chains. In fact, while it wasn't luxurious by any means—a windowless stone chamber with little privacy, as the large door was made up of narrowly spaced *adamas* bars—compared to Blackthorn Manor, it was downright homey, containing a fairly comfortable bed of wrought iron, a battered oak desk, a wooden shelf lined with books (none of any interest to her, but it was something). Witchlight stones had even been placed haphazardly around, as if an afterthought, and she recalled that the Silent Brothers did not need light to see.

The most uncanny element of the place was that it was impossible to tell when it was day or night. Zachariah had brought her a mantel clock, which helped, but she wasn't fully confident that she was keeping track of which twelve o'clock was noon and which midnight. Not that it mattered, she supposed. Time stretched out here, and compressed like a spring, while she waited between the moments that the Silent Brothers wanted to speak with her.

When they did want to speak to her, it was bad. She could not pretend otherwise. Not that they harmed her, or tormented her, or even used the Mortal Sword upon her; they only questioned her, calmly but relentlessly. And still, it was not the questioning that was bad either. It was telling the truth.

Grace had begun to realize that she only really knew two ways to communicate with others. One was to wear a mask, and to lie and perform from behind that mask, as she had performed obedience to her mother, and love to James. The other was to be honest, which she had only ever really done with Jesse. Even then she had hidden from him the things she was ashamed of doing. Not hiding, she was finding, was a painful thing.

It hurt to stand before the Brothers and admit to all she had done. *Yes, I forced James Herondale to believe himself in love with me. Yes, I used my demon-given power to ensnare Charles Fairchild. Yes, I plotted with my mother the destruction of the Herondales and Carstairs, the Lightwoods and Fairchilds. I believed her when she said they were our enemies.*

The sessions exhausted her. At night, alone in her cell, she saw James's face the last time he had looked at her, heard the loathing in his voice. *I would throw you onto the street, but this power of yours is no better than a loaded gun in the hands of a selfish child. You cannot be allowed to continue to use it.*

If the Silent Brothers intended to take her power—and they were welcome to it—they had shown no signs of it yet. She sensed they were studying her, studying her ability, in ways she herself did not understand.

All she had to comfort herself was the thought of Jesse. Jesse, who Lucie must surely have raised, with Malcolm's help. They would all be in Cornwall by now. Would Jesse be all right? Would returning from the shadowy lands he had inhabited so long be a terrible shock for him? She wished she were there, to hold his hand through it, as he had helped her through so many terrible things.

She knew, of course, that it was entirely possible that they had failed to raise Jesse. Necromancy was near impossible. But his death had been so unfair, a terrible crime based on a poisonous lie. Surely if anyone deserved a second chance, Jesse did.

And he loved Grace as his sister, loved and cared for her in a way that nobody else did, and perhaps, she thought, nobody else ever would. Maybe the Nephilim would put her to death because of her power. Maybe she would rot in the Silent City forever. But if not, a living Jesse was the only way she could imagine any kind of future life for herself at all.

There was Christopher Lightwood, of course. Not that he loved her; he barely knew her. But he had seemed legitimately interested in her, in her thoughts, her opinions, her feelings. If things had been different, he could have been her friend. She had never had a friend. Only James, who surely hated her now that he knew what she had done to him, and Lucie, who would soon hate her as well, for the same reason. And really, she was just fooling herself if she thought Christopher would feel any differently. He was James's friend, and loved him. He would be loyal, and despise her . . . she could not blame him . . . .

There was a sound, the telltale scrape of the room's barred door opening. She sat up hastily on her narrow mattress, smoothing down her hair. Not that the Silent Brothers cared how she looked, but it was force of habit.

A shadowy figure regarded her from the doorway. *Grace,* Zachariah said. *I fear the last round of questioning was too much.*

It had been bad; Grace had nearly fainted when describing the night her mother had taken her to the dark forest, the sound of Belial's voice in the shadows. But Grace did not like the idea of anyone being able to sense what she felt. She said, "Will it be much longer? Before my sentence is pronounced?"

You wish for punishment that badly?

"No," Grace said. "I only wish the questioning to stop. But I am ready to accept my punishment. I deserve it."

Yes, you have done wrong. But how old were you when your mother brought you to Brocelind Forest to receive your power? Eleven? Twelve?

"It doesn't matter."

It does, said Zachariah. *I believe that the Clave failed you. You are a Shadowhunter, Grace, born to a Shadowhunter family, and abandoned to terrible circumstances. It is unfair to you that the Clave left you there for so long, without intervention or even investigation.*

Grace could not bear his pity; it felt like tiny needle marks against her skin. "You should not be kind to me, or try to understand," she snapped. "I used demonic power to enchant James and make him believe he was in love with me. I caused him terrible pain."

Zachariah regarded her without speaking, his face eerily still.

Grace wanted to hit him. "Don't you think I deserve punishment? Mustn't there be a reckoning? A balancing of things? An eye for an eye?"

That is your mother's thinking about the world. Not mine.

"But the other Silent Brothers. The Enclave. Everyone in London—they will want to see me punished."

They do not know, said Brother Zachariah. For the first time, Grace saw a sort of hesitation in him. *What you have done at your mother's behest remains known only to us, and to James.*

"But—why?" It made no sense; surely James would tell his friends, and soon enough everyone would know. "Why would you protect me?"

We seek to question your mother; the job of that will be easier if she believes you are still on her side, your powers still unknown to us.

Grace sat back on the bed. "You want answers from my mother because you believe I am the puppet, and she the puppet master, the puller of strings. But the true puppet master is Belial. She is obedient to him. When she acts, it is at his behest. He is the one to fear."

There was a long silence. Then, a gentle voice inside her head. *Are you afraid, Grace?*

"Not for myself," she said. "I have already lost everything I had to lose. But for others, yes. I am very afraid indeed."

Lucie followed Malcolm into the house and waited while the warlock divested himself of his traveling coat and walking stick in the entryway. He led her into the parlor she'd passed through earlier, with its high ceiling, and with a snap of his fingers set a roaring fire in the grate. It occurred to Lucie that not only could Malcolm acquire firewood without Jesse needing to chop it for him, he could probably keep fires going with no wood whatsoever.

Not that she minded watching Jesse chop wood. And he seemed to be enjoying it, so it was beneficial for the both of them.

Malcolm gestured her toward an overstuffed settee into which Lucie thought she might sink so far she would be unable to get up again. She perched on its arm. The room was quite cozy, actually: not at all what she would have associated with Malcolm Fade. Satinwood furniture, worn to a soft patina, upholstered with tapestry and velvet fabric—no effort had been made to match the pieces, though they all looked comfortable. A rug embroidered with pineapples covered the floor, and various portraits of people Lucie did not recognize hung upon the walls.

Malcolm remained standing, and Lucie assumed he would now lecture her about Jesse, or interrogate her regarding what she had done to him. Instead he said, "You might have noticed that although I have *not* been unconscious for several days after an act of unpracticed sorcery, I am looking somewhat the worse for wear."

"I hadn't noticed," Lucie said, though she had. "You look, er, quite polished and put-together."

Malcolm waved this off. "I am not fishing for compliments. I mean to explain that these last days, while you have been sleeping off the effects of the magic you performed, I have been taking the opportunity of being back in Cornwall to continue my investigations into Annabel Blackthorn."

Lucie felt a nervous fizzle in her stomach. Annabel Blackthorn. The woman Malcolm had loved, a hundred years ago, and who Malcolm had long believed had left him to join the Iron Sisters. In truth, her family had murdered her rather than allow her to marry a warlock. Lucie flinched, remembering the look on Malcolm's face when Grace had told him the truth of Annabel's fate.

Warlocks did not age, yet Malcolm seemed somehow older than he had a short time ago. The lines of strain about his mouth and eyes were pronounced. "I know that we agreed you would call up her spirit," he said. "That you would allow me to speak to her again."

It seemed odd to Lucie that warlocks could not, themselves, call up those dead who no longer haunted the world, but had passed into a place of peace. That the terrible power in her blood allowed her to do something even Magnus Bane, or Malcolm Fade, could not. But there it was—she had given Malcolm her word, though the hungry look in his eyes made her shiver a little.

"I did not know what would happen when you raised Jesse," Malcolm said. "For him to have come back as he has—with breath and life, perfectly healthy, perfectly cognizant—is more miracle than magic." He took a ragged breath. "Annabel's death was no less unjust, no less monstrous, than what happened to Jesse. She deserves to live again no less than he. Of that I am certain."

Lucie did not bring up the detail that Jesse's body had been preserved by Belial in a strange half-living state, and Annabel's surely hadn't. Instead she said anxiously, "I gave you my word, Malcolm, that I would call up her spirit. Let you commune with her ghost. But no more than that. She cannot be . . . brought back. You know that."

Malcolm seemed barely to hear this. He threw himself down into a nearby chair. "If indeed miracles are possible," he said, "though I have never believed in them—I know of demons and angels, but have put my faith in science and magic only—"

He broke off, though it was too late for Lucie's unease. It was vibrating at a high tempo now, like a plucked string. "Not every spirit wishes to return," she whispered. "Some of the dead are at peace."

"Annabel will not be at peace," said Malcolm. His purple eyes looked like bruises in his pale face. "Not without me."

"Mr. Fade—" Lucie's voice shook.

For the first time, Malcolm seemed to notice her anxiety. He sat up straight, forcing a smile. "Lucie. I understand that you barely survived raising Jesse, and that you are significantly weakened. It will hardly do any of us any good if calling up Annabel sends you back into unconsciousness. We must wait for you to be stronger." He gazed at the fire as though he could read something in the dance of its flames. "I have waited a hundred years. Time is not the same for me as it is for a mortal, especially one as young as you are. I will wait another hundred years, if I must."

"Well," said Lucie, trying to keep her voice light, "I hardly think I will need *that* long."

"I will wait," Malcolm said again, speaking perhaps more to himself than to her. "I will wait as long as it takes."

3
The Slow Dark Hours

But is there for the night a resting-place?
A roof for when the slow dark hours begin.
May not the darkness hide it from my face?
You cannot miss that inn.
—Christina Rossetti, "Up-Hill"

James estimated that he'd been talking for about a month.

Magnus, who seemed able to detect comfortable coaching inns from a distance, had found them one on the road to Polperro. Once Balios and Xanthos had been safely stabled, Will had booked the three of them a private dining room on the inn's ground floor, where they could eat and talk in private.

Not that James had eaten much. The room was nice enough—old-fashioned, with dark wallpaper and worn rugs, a wide oak table in the center—and the food seemed decent. But once he'd started talking about the events of the past few weeks, he'd found it hard to stop; after all the secrets and lies, the truth poured out of him like water from a jug. Even then, he'd had to remain careful to keep the secrets that weren't his to tell: he said nothing of the pledge Cordelia had accidentally made to Lilith, only spoke of Lilith impersonating Magnus to trick them.

"I know I ought to beg your forgiveness," James said, when his voice had run dry. "I should have told you all of this, but—"

"But you were not the only one affected," said Will. He looked tense, the lines beside his eyes unusually prominent. "And so you kept your mouth shut to protect your friends and your family. I am not entirely an idiot, James. I do understand how these things work."

Magnus uncapped a decanter of port and poured a thimbleful into Will's and James's glasses. "I am worried. Belial should not have been able to return to our world after the blow Cordelia dealt him with Cortana. But he *did* return, through a plan he must have put in place years ago, back when Jesse Blackthorn was only a baby—"

Will was looking furious. "*This* is why we should never have tolerated Tatiana Blackthorn's bizarre behavior with her children. What could it harm, not to let the Silent Brothers do Jesse's protection spells? What harm indeed. Thank the Angel that Maurice went up to retrieve her from the Adamant Citadel. The Silent Brothers are going to need to get the whole story out of her."

"Why didn't you tell the Enclave," Magnus said to James, not unkindly, "if you knew Belial was responsible?"

"He didn't tell the Enclave," Will said, "because if the Enclave found out that Belial is his grandfather, is Tessa's father . . . well, the consequences could be quite dire, for our family. For Tessa. I knew also, and I also said nothing, for the same reason. James cannot be blamed for that."

"Does anyone else know?" said Magnus.

"Only my closest friends," James said. "Cordelia, of course, and Matthew . . . and Thomas and Christopher. And Anna. They will keep the secret. I trust them with my life," he added, perhaps a little defensively.

Will exchanged a look with Magnus that James couldn't read. Slowly Will said, "I am glad that you at least had your friends to confide in. I wish you had told me as well, James." He looked sad for a moment. "It breaks my heart to think of you being tormented by these dreams of Belial, and keeping them a secret besides." He picked up his glass, as if he'd just noticed it was there, and took a sip. "I've seen death myself," he said quietly. "I know how terrible it is to witness it."

His father's eyes flicked away from them for a moment, and James wondered what he meant—and then, with a start, remembered that long ago, Will had held Jessamine while she died in his arms. He was so used to her ghostly presence in the Institute that it was easy to forget the trauma her death must have brought to them all. His father made it easy to forget; his usual sanguine demeanor did a good job of hiding all that he had been through.

Magnus cleared his throat, and James looked over to see his luminous cat's eyes peering at him thoughtfully. Will caught this and sat up in his chair, returning from his reverie. "What are you thinking of, Magnus?"

"Only that Belial was willing to wait a long time for his plan regarding Jesse to come to fruition," said Magnus. "I wonder what other plans he might have made in the meantime. Plans of which we have no knowledge." His eyes glittered at James. "I must ask. What were you dreaming of, in the carriage? When you woke up screaming?"

There was a guilty knot in James's chest. He was still keeping a secret, after all—Cordelia's secret. "I dreamed of a gathering of shadows," he said. "I stood in a fire-blasted place and saw monstrous creatures rushing through the air."

"Were they demons?" said Magnus.

"I don't know," said James. "Their forms were shadowy and diffuse, and the light was dark. . . . It was as though I could not fully focus my eyes on them. But they are part of some plan of Belial's. He spoke to me."

"What did he say?" said Magnus quietly.

"'They wake,'" said James.

Will exhaled loudly through his nose. "Well, *that* isn't very helpful of him. What wakes?"

"Something that was sleeping?" suggested Magnus. "In the past, it seemed that Belial wanted you to see his actions clearly. Now he wants you in the dark."

"He wants me to be afraid," James said. "That's what he wants."

"Well, don't be," said Will decidedly. "As soon as we find Lucie, we will return to London. Now that you've told us the situation, we can muster every resource at our command to deal with this thing."

James tried to look as if the thought heartened him. He knew his father had faith, a kind he did not, that even the most intractable problem could be overcome; still James could not imagine a life in which he was not tied to Belial. The connection would exist as long as Belial lived, and as James had been reminded many times, a Prince of Hell could not die.

"Are you not going to drink your port?" said Magnus. "It might steady your nerves a bit, help you rest."

James shook his head. He felt sick, looking at the alcohol, and he knew it was not only his nerves. It was Matthew. Memories had been coming back to him, ever since he had rid himself of the bracelet—memories not just of events, but of his own thoughts and feelings, things he had forgotten, things pushed to the back of his mind. His feelings for Cordelia . . . his desire to remove the bracelet itself . . . but also his worries about Matthew's drinking. It was as if the bracelet's influence had insisted that there was nothing wrong with Matthew, that he need not concern himself with anything except that which the bracelet wanted him to concern himself. It had grown clearer and clearer to him that something was terribly wrong with Matthew, and that it was getting worse, but the bracelet had ensured that he couldn't hold on to the thought, couldn't focus on it. He recalled the London Shadow Market, a snowy alley, his snapping at Matthew, *Tell me there is someone you love more than that bottle in your hand.*

He had known, but he had done nothing. He had allowed the bracelet to guide his attention elsewhere. He had failed his best friend. He had failed his *parabatai*.

"Well, you need sleep," Magnus said. "Dreamless sleep, if possible. I was hoping to use the more mundane methods of getting there, but . . ."

James swallowed. "I don't think I can drink it."

"Then I'll give you something else," Magnus said decisively. "Water, with something more magical than mere fortified wine. How about you, Will?"

"Certainly," said Will, and James thought he still sounded lost in thought. "Bring on the potions."

That night James slept like the dead, and if his father rose in the middle of the night to check on him as if he were a small boy, if Will sat beside him on his bed and sang to him in rusty Welsh, James did not remember it when he woke up.

* * *

"As you can see," Matthew said, throwing out his arm to embrace the whole of the Boulevard de Clichy. He was wearing a fur greatcoat with multiple capes, which made the gesture all the more dramatic. "Here is Hell."

"You," Cordelia said, "are a very wicked person, Matthew Fairchild. Very wicked." She couldn't help but smile, though, half at Matthew's expectant expression and half at what he'd brought her to Montmartre to see.

Montmartre was one of the most scandalous neighborhoods in a scandalous city. The notorious Moulin Rouge was here, with its famous red windmill and half-naked dancers. She had expected them to wind up there, but Matthew, of course, had to be different. Instead he had brought them to the Cabaret de l'Enfer—quite literally, the Cabaret of Hell—a place whose front entrance had been carved to look like a demonic face, with black bulging eyes and a row of fanged teeth at the top of its open mouth, which served as the door.

"We needn't go in if you don't want to," Matthew said, more seriously than usual. He set a gloved finger under Cordelia's chin, raising her face to meet his gaze. She looked at him in some surprise. He was bareheaded, and his eyes were a very dark green in the light spilling from L'Enfer. "I thought it might amuse you, as the Hell Ruelle did. And this place makes the Ruelle look like a child's playroom."

She hesitated. She was aware of the warmth of his body, close to hers, and the scent of him: wool and cologne. As she hung back, a richly dressed couple emerged from a *fiacre* and headed inside L'Enfer, both giggling.

Wealthy Parisians, Cordelia thought, slumming it in a neighborhood famous for its poor artists, starving in their garret flats. Light from the gas torches on either side of the doors fell upon their faces as they entered the club, and Cordelia saw that the woman was deadly pale, with dark red lips.

Vampire. Of course Downworlders would be drawn to a place with a theme like this one. Cordelia understood what Matthew was doing: trying to give her the excitement of the Hell Ruelle, in a new place, without the weight of memories. And why not? What was she afraid of, when there was nothing left for her to lose?

Cordelia squared her shoulders. "Let's go in."

Inside, a staircase led sharply downward into a cavernous den lit by torches behind sconces of red glass, which gave the view a tinge of scarlet. The plaster walls were carved in the shapes of screaming faces, each one different, each one a mask of dread or agony or terror. Gilt ribbons hung from the ceiling, each bearing a line from Dante's *Inferno:* from MIDWAY UPON THE JOURNEY OF LIFE, I FOUND MYSELF WITHIN A FOREST DARK to THERE IS NO GREATER SORROW THAN TO RECALL IN MISERY THE TIME WHEN WE WERE HAPPY.

The floor had been painted in swirls of red and gold—meant, Cordelia expected, to evoke the eternal fires of the damned. They were at the back of a single large room, high-ceilinged, which sloped downhill gently toward the stage at the far end; in between were innumerable café tables lit by softly glowing lights and mostly filled with Downworlders, though there were a few mundanes, elaborately costumed, glasses of green absinthe at their elbows. No doubt they thought the Downworlders to be other mundanes, in amusing costumes.

The show had clearly not yet begun, and the crowded tables were abuzz with conversation. There was a brief interruption as a variety of heads turned to look at Matthew and Cordelia, leading Cordelia to wonder how often Shadowhunters came here, and whether they were fully welcome.

Then, from the far corner, a chorus of high-pitched voices cried, "Monsieur Fairchild!" In the strange, variegated light of the flames, Cordelia could see that it was a table packed with what she thought were perhaps brownies? Or pixies? In any case, they sported wings of various rainbow colors; each was no more than a foot tall, and there were about twenty of them. They clearly all knew Matthew, and more strikingly, they all seemed very pleased to see him. In the middle of their table (built for customers of human size) was a large punch bowl half-full of a glittering beverage, which a few of them were using as a swimming pool.

"Old friends?" Cordelia said, with some amusement.

"Anna and I once helped them out of a jam," Matthew said. He waved cheerfully at the faeries. "It's quite a tale, involving a duel, racing carriages, and a handsome prince of Faerieland. At least, he said he was a prince," Matthew added. "I always get the feeling that everyone in Faerie is a prince or princess, rather like everyone in Lucie's books is a secret duke or duchess."

"Well, don't keep your handsome prince to yourself." Cordelia poked him in the shoulder. "I think I'd like to hear this tale."

Matthew laughed. "All right, all right. In a moment. I must talk with the proprietor."

He ducked away for a moment to speak to a faun whose antlers seemed far too large to allow him to pass through the building's front door. There was a great deal of friendly nodding before Matthew returned and offered Cordelia his hand. She allowed herself to be led to a table close to the stage. When they sat, she saw that the glowing lights were not candles, as she'd assumed, but luminous faeries even smaller than the ones who had greeted Matthew.

Will-o'-the-wisps, perhaps? The one at their table was sitting in a glass bowl, legs crossed, wearing a small brown suit. He glowered at them as they sat.

Matthew tapped on the glass. "Not the most exciting job, is it?" he said sympathetically.

The faerie in the glass shrugged and revealed the tiny book he was holding. A small pair of spectacles sat on his nose. "One must make a living," he said in a distinctly German accent, and went back to reading.

Matthew ordered coffee for both of them, drawing (and ignoring) a stern, disapproving look from the waiter. Cabarets likely made most of their profit from selling drinks, but Cordelia didn't care; she was proud of Matthew's efforts to be sober.

Matthew leaned back in his chair. "So," he said. "Last year Anna and I were at the Abbaye de Thélème, a nightclub with a monastic theme, with cancan dancers dressed as priests and nuns. Very shocking for mundanes, I gather, rather as if I opened a cabaret where Iron Sisters and Silent Brothers posed nude."

Cordelia laughed, earning a glare from the table faerie. Matthew went on, weaving with words and hands an amusing tale in which a faerie prince pursued by demonic assassins hid beneath his and Anna's table. "Swiftly," he said, "we armed ourselves. We had not been allowed to bring weapons inside—house rules—so we had to improvise. Anna slew a demon with a bread knife. I crushed a skull with a cured *jambon*. Anna hurled a wheel of cheese like a discus. Another evildoer was dispatched with a freshly pulled shot of steaming espresso."

Cordelia had folded her arms across her chest. "Let me guess. The faerie prince had enraged the Downworlders of France by ordering a steak well done."

Matthew ignored this. "A demon was set upon by a number of small, noisy dogs whose owner had brought them inexplicably to the cabaret—"

"None of this is true."

Matthew laughed. "As with all the best stories, *some* of it is true."

"*Das ist Blödsinn,*" muttered the lamp faerie. "Seems a load of nonsense to me."

Matthew picked up the lamp and moved it to another table. By the time he returned, the waiter had served them coffee in tiny pewter cups. As Matthew slid back into his seat, he said, in a low voice, "Have you a stele with you? Or any weapons?"

Cordelia tensed. "What's happened?"

"Nothing," Matthew said, playing with the handle of his coffee cup. "I realized I have just finished telling you a tale of improvised weapons, but you . . ."

"Cannot wield a weapon at all, lest I do it in *her* name." Cordelia tried and failed to keep the bitterness from her voice; she did not want to speak the name of Lilith aloud, nor did she wish to give Lilith, even indirectly, the satisfaction of her fury. "But I do miss Cortana. Is that odd, to miss a sword?"

"Not if the sword has a great deal of personality—which Cortana does."

She smiled, grateful at his understanding. She did not think he would like that she had given the sword to Alastair for safekeeping. Her brother and Matthew continued to dislike each other. So she had kept it to herself; besides, she had no idea where Alastair had hidden it. Before she could say anything else, the lights began to go down above them, and to come up on the empty stage.

Conversation died down, and a silence hung in the air, suddenly eerie. Into that silence came the tapping of shoes, and after a few moments a woman emerged onto the stage. *Warlock*, Cordelia guessed; she had that indefinable aura about her, of controlled power. Her hair was iron gray, knobbed into a chignon at the back of her head, though her face was youthful enough. She wore a deep blue velvet robe, embroidered all over with the symbols of the planets and stars.

A blue silk blindfold was tied around her eyes, but it didn't appear to prevent her from knowing when she had reached the middle of the stage. She reached her arms out toward the audience and opened her hands, and Cordelia gasped. In the middle of each palm was a long-lashed human eye, bright green and sharply knowing.

"Quite a warlock mark, don't you think?" Matthew whispered.

"Is she going to tell fortunes?" Cordelia wondered.

"Madame Dorothea is a medium," said Matthew. "She claims she can speak to the dead—which all spiritualists claim, but she *is* a warlock. It's possible there's something to it."

"Bon soir, mes amis," said the warlock. Her voice was deep, strong as coffee. For such a small woman, her voice carried loudly to the back of the room. "I am Madame Dorothea, but think of me as Charon, child of Night, who plies his ferryboat over the river that divides the living and the dead. Like him, I am equally at home with life and death. The power I have through these"—and she held up her hands—"my second set of eyes, allows me to glimpse the worlds between, the worlds beyond."

She moved to the edge of the stage. The eyes set into her palms blinked, turning back and forth within their sockets, examining the audience.

"There is someone here," Madame Dorothea said. "Someone who has lost a brother. A beloved sibling who cries out now to be heard . . . by his brother, Jean-Pierre." She raised her voice. "Jean-Pierre, are you here?"

There was an anticipatory silence, and slowly a middle-aged

werewolf rose to his feet at one of the back tables. "Yes? I am Jean-Pierre Arland." His voice was quiet in the emptiness.

"And you have lost a brother?" Madame Dorothea cried.

"He died two years ago."

"I bring you a message from him," Madame Dorothea said. "From Claude. That was his name, correct?"

The whole room was silent. Cordelia found that her own palms were damp with tension. Was Dorothea *really* communing with the dead? Lucie did it—it was possible—Cordelia had seen her do it, so she didn't know why she felt so anxious.

"Yes," said Arland warily. He *wanted* to believe, Cordelia thought, but he was not sure. "What—what does he say?"

Madame Dorothea closed her hands. When she opened them again, the green eyes were blinking rapidly. She spoke, her voice low and gruff: "Jean-Pierre. You must give them back."

The werewolf looked baffled. "What?"

"The chickens!" Madame Dorothea said. "You must give them back!"

"I . . . I will," Jean-Pierre said, sounding stunned. "I will, Claude—"

"You must give them *all* back!" Madame Dorothea cried. Jean-Pierre looked around him in a panic, and then bolted for the door.

"Maybe he ate them," Matthew whispered. Cordelia wanted to smile, but the odd feeling of anxiety was still there. She watched as Dorothea gathered herself, glaring at the audience through her open palms.

"I thought we would get to ask questions!" someone cried from a corner of the room.

"The messages come first!" Madame Dorothea barked in her original voice. "The dead sense a doorway. They rush to deliver their words. They must be allowed to speak." The eyes in her palms closed, then opened again. "There is someone here," she said. "Someone who has lost her father." The green eyes swiveled and came to rest on Cordelia. *"Une chasseuse des ombres."*

A Shadowhunter.

Cordelia went cold as whispers flew through the room: most had not known Shadowhunters were in their midst. She looked quickly at Matthew—had he known about this?—but he seemed just as surprised as Cordelia was. He slid a hand toward hers on the table, their fingertips brushing. "We can leave—"

"No," Cordelia whispered. "No—I want to stay."

She looked up to find Madame Dorothea gazing fixedly at her. The lights at the edge of the stage cast her shadow back against the wall, massive and black. As she raised her arms, the sleeves of her robe appeared as dark wings.

"Cordelia. Your father is here," Madame Dorothea said simply, and her voice was oddly quiet now, as though she were speaking so only Cordelia could hear. "Will you listen?"

Cordelia gripped the edge of the table. She nodded, aware of the gaze of the whole cabaret. Aware that she was exposing herself, her grief. Unable to stop, regardless.

When Madame Dorothea spoke again, her voice was deeper. Not gruff, but modulated, and in English, without the trace of a French accent. "Layla," he said, and Cordelia tensed all over. It was him. It could be no one else; who else would be aware of the family nickname? "I am so sorry, Layla."

"Father," she whispered. She glanced quickly at Matthew; he looked stricken.

"There is much I would tell you," said Elias. "But I must warn you first. They will not wait. And the sharpest weapon lies close at hand."

There was a murmur in the club, those who could speak English translating for those who could not.

"I don't understand," Cordelia said, with some difficulty. "Who will not wait?"

"In time there will be sorrow," Elias went on. "But not regret. There will be quiet. But not peace."

"Father—"

"They wake," Elias said. "If I can tell you nothing else, let me tell you this. They are waking. It cannot be stopped."

"But I don't understand," Cordelia protested again. The green eyes in Dorothea's palms stared at her, blank as paper, without compassion or sympathy. "Who is waking?"

"Not we," Elias said. "We who are already dead. We are the lucky ones."

And Madame Dorothea collapsed to the ground.

4

Blessed Ghost

I moved, and could not feel my limbs:
I was so light—almost
I thought that I had died in sleep,
And was a blessed ghost.
—Samuel Taylor Coleridge,
"The Rime of the Ancient Mariner"

Malcolm could barely remain at the table for the few minutes it took to eat dinner. In fact, he had seemed impatient when, hours after the sun had set, Lucie had pointed out that they needed to eat. She suspected it had been a long time since Malcolm had had a houseguest. And probably, he rarely bothered to sit and eat a full meal at his dining table. Probably he just magicked himself up some food whenever he got hungry, wherever he was.

Though he had grumped about it, he eventually produced plates for them of what he explained was simple but traditional Cornish fishing village fare: pilchards—a sort of tiny fish—grilled over a wood fire; great hunks of bread with a crust you could break teeth on; a creamy round cheese; and a jug of cider. Lucie had torn into the food, feeling as though she hadn't eaten in days—which, she realized, she hadn't.

Jesse had eyed the pilchards warily, and the pilchards had glassily eyed him back, but eventually he had made his peace with the situation and eaten a few. Lucie was so caught up in watching Jesse eat that she nearly forgot how hungry she was. Though he must have eaten during the time she'd been sleeping, it was clearly still a revelation to him. With each bite he closed his eyes; he even licked spilled cider from his finger with a look that made Lucie's insides feel muddled.

Halfway through the meal, it occurred to Lucie to ask Malcolm where exactly he had gotten the food, and she and Jesse exchanged looks of dismay when he admitted he had nicked it from a local family who had been about to sit down to dinner. "They'll blame the piskies," he said, which were apparently a type of mischievous local faerie.

After a moment of guilt, Lucie had considered that it wasn't feasible at this point to return the table scraps, and tried to put it out of her mind.

The moment their plates were empty, Malcolm leaped up and departed again, leaning back into the dining room only to tell them that they should feel free to put the kettle on, if they wished, and then leaving so quickly that the front door rattled on its hinges as he slammed it closed behind him.

"Where does he go, I wonder?" Jesse said. He delicately bit the edge of a treacle tart. "He's off most of the time, you know. Even while you were unconscious."

"I don't know where he goes exactly," Lucie said. "But I know he's trying to find out more about what happened to Annabel Blackthorn."

"Oh, his great lost love?" Jesse said, and when Lucie looked surprised, he smiled. "Malcolm told me a bit. That they loved one another when they were children, and her family disapproved, and he lost her tragically, and now he doesn't even know where her body is buried."

Lucie nodded. "He always thought she had become an Iron Sister, but it turned out that never happened. That's just what her family told him, to stop him looking for her."

"He didn't tell me that part. He did tell me that I shouldn't worry, because the Blackthorns who lied to him were only very distant relations of mine."

"Oh, dear. What did you say?"

He gave her a wry look. "That if I were to be responsible for the poor behavior of my relatives, I had bigger problems closer to home."

The reminder of Tatiana made Lucie shiver. Jesse looked immediately concerned. "Shall we go into the drawing room? There's a fire on."

This seemed a fine idea to Lucie. She had brought her notebook and pens down from the trunk in her bedroom and had thought she might try to write a bit after dinner.

They went into the room, and Jesse busied himself finding Lucie a shawl to wrap herself in, before going over to the fireplace and kneeling down to prod at the glowing embers with a poker. Lucie, for once feeling no desire to pick up a pen, curled up on the settee and watched him. She wondered if she would ever stop marveling at the *realness* of this new Jesse. His skin was flushed from the heat of the fire; he had pushed his sleeves up to his elbows, and the muscles in his forearms flexed as he moved.

He rose and turned toward her. Lucie breathed in sharply. His face was beautiful—she had known that, of course she had, it was the same face as always—but before it had been washed out, faded, distant. Now he seemed to glow with a pale fire. There was texture and depth to him that had not been there before, the sense of something real, something that could be touched. There were the faintest of shadows below his eyes, too—had he not been sleeping? Sleeping must be so strange to him; it had been so long since he'd done it.

"Jesse," she said softly. "Is something wrong?"

The corner of his mouth curled a little. "You know me so well."

"Not that well," she said. "I know you seem bothered, but not why."

He hesitated a moment, then said—in a reckless sort of way, as if he were throwing himself headlong into an unknown darkness, "It's my Marks."

"Your—Marks?"

He held out his bared forearms to her. She stood up, throwing off the shawl; she was quite warm enough. She came closer to him; she had not really noted the Marks before, since nearly everyone she knew bore them. On the back of Jesse's right hand was the old scar of a failed Voyance rune, and inside his left elbow, a rune of Angelic Power. There were four more, she knew: Strength, on his chest; Swiftness and Precision, on his left shoulder; a new Voyance rune, on the back of his left hand.

"These are not mine," he said, looking at the Voyance and *enkeli* runes. "They belong to dead people—people Belial murdered, using my hands to do it. I always wanted runes, since I was a child, but now I feel as if I am wearing the marks of their death on my body."

"Jesse. It's not your fault. None of it was your fault." She took his face between her hands, forced him to look directly at her. "Listen to me. I can only imagine how awful it must feel. But you had no control over any of it. And—and when we get back to London, I'm sure the runes can be removed, and you could have new runes put on, ones that would be *yours*, that you chose." She tilted her head back. Their faces were inches apart. "I know what it is like, to be gifted by Belial with something you did not ask for, did not want."

"Lucie—that's different—"

"It's not," she whispered. "You and I, we are alike in that way. And I only hope—that I can always be as brave as you have been, bear up as well as you have—"

He kissed her. She gave a little gasp against his mouth, and her hands slipped down to his shoulders, clutching at him. They had kissed before, at the Shadow Market. But this was something else entirely. It was like the difference between having someone describe a color to you and finally seeing it yourself.

His hands slid into her hair, tangling in the thick strands; she could *feel* his body change as he held her, feel the tightening in his muscles, the heat blooming between them. She opened her mouth to him, feeling wild, almost shocked at her own lack of restraint. He tasted of cider and honey—his hands moved downward, cupping the wings of her shoulder blades, following the arch of her back. She could feel the racing beat of his heart as he rocked her against him, hear the deep groan low in his throat. He was shaking, whispering against her mouth that she felt perfectly perfect, perfectly alive, saying her name: *"Lucie, Lucie."*

She felt dizzy, as though she were falling. Falling through darkness. Like the visions, or dreams, she'd had in her half-consciousness in bed. It felt like it did when she had raised him, like she was losing herself, like she was losing anything that connected her to the real world at all.

"Oh—" She drew away, disoriented and blinking. She met his blazing green eyes, saw the desire darkening his gaze. *"Bother,"* she said.

Flushed, and very disheveled, he said, "Are you all right?"

"I was just dizzy for a moment—probably still a bit wobbly and tired," she said disconsolately. "Which is dreadful, because I was enjoying the kissing a great deal."

Jesse inhaled sharply. He looked dazed, as if he'd just been shaken awake. "Don't say things like that. It makes me want to kiss you again. And I probably shouldn't, if you're—wobbly."

"Maybe if you just kissed my neck," she suggested, looking up at him through her lashes.

"*Lucie.*" He took a shuddering breath, kissed her cheek, and stepped back. "I promise you," he said, "I would have a difficult time stopping there. Which means I am going to now pick up a poker and respectably tend to the fire."

"And if I try to kiss you again, you'll hit me with the poker?" She smiled.

"Not at all. I will do the gentlemanly thing, and hit *myself* with the poker, and you can explain the resultant carnage to Malcolm when he returns."

"I don't think Malcolm is going to want to stay here that much longer." Lucie sighed, watching the sparks leap up in the grate, dancing motes of gold and red. "He will have to return to London at some point. He *is* the High Warlock."

"Lucie," Jesse said softly. He turned to watch the fire for a moment. Its light danced in his eyes. "What is *our* plan for the future? We will have to go back to the world."

Lucie thought about it. "I suppose if Malcolm throws us out, we can go on the road and be highwaymen. We will only rob the cruel and unjust, of course."

Jesse smiled reluctantly. "Unfortunately, I hear there has been a tragic reduction in the ability of highwaymen to ply their trade due to the increasing popularity of the automobile."

"Then we shall join the circus," Lucie suggested.

"Regrettably, I have a terror of clowns and broad stripes."

"Then we shall hop aboard a steamer bound for Europe," Lucie said, suddenly quite enthusiastic about the idea, "and become itinerant musicians on the Continent."

"I cannot carry a tune," Jesse said. "Lucie—"

"What is it *you* think we ought to do?"

He took a deep breath. "I think you should return to London without me."

Lucie took a step back. "No. I won't do that. I—"

"You have a family, Lucie. One that loves you. They will never accept me—it would be madness to imagine it, and even if they did—" He shook his head in frustration. "Even if they did, how would they *explain* me to the Enclave without bringing trouble down on themselves? I don't want to take them away from you. You must return to them. Tell them whatever you need to, make up a story, anything. I will stay away from you so that no blame accrues to you for what you have done."

"What I have done?" she echoed, in a near whisper. She had thought, of course, so terribly often of the horror her friends and family would feel if they knew the extent of her power. Knew that she could not just see ghosts, but control them. That she had commanded Jesse to come back, back from the shadowy in-between place where Tatiana had trapped him. That she had *dragged* him back, over the threshold between life and death, thrust him back into the bright world of the living. Because she had willed it.

She had feared what they would think; she had not thought Jesse would fear it too.

She spoke stiffly. "I am the one who brought you back. I have a responsibility to you. You can't just stay here and—and be a fisherman in Cornwall—and never see Grace again! I am not the only one with family."

"I have thought of that, and of course I will see Grace. I will write to her, first, as soon as it is safe. I spoke to Malcolm. He thinks my best course of action would be to Portal to a faraway Institute and present myself as a Shadowhunter there, where no one knows my face or my family."

Lucie stopped short. She had not realized Malcolm and Jesse had been talking about plans, about her, while she was not there. She did not much like the idea. "Jesse, that's ridiculous. I do not want you to live a life of such—such exile."

"But it is a life," he said. "Thanks to you."

She shook her head. "I did not bring you back from the dead so that—" *So that you could go away from me*, she almost said, but cut herself off. She had heard a noise—something at the front door. She and Jesse looked at each other in consternation. "Who could it be?" she whispered.

"Probably nothing. A villager, perhaps, looking for Malcolm. I'll answer it."

But he seized up the poker from where he'd left it and stalked out of the room. Lucie hurried after him, wondering what it was that made the Blackthorns so fond of using fireplace tools as weapons.

Before he could reach the door, she stepped in front of him, her instinct always to protect Jesse even if he didn't need protection. She jostled him out of the way and threw the front door open. She stared, halfway between horror and relief, at the three figures on the doorstep, wrapped in winter coats, flushed from the cold and the long walk up the hill.

Her brother. Her father. And Magnus Bane.

Cordelia dreamed that she stood upon a great chessboard that stretched out infinitely beneath an equally infinite night sky. Stars spangled the blackness like a scatter of diamonds. As she watched, her father staggered out upon the board, his coat torn and bloody. As he fell to his knees, she raced toward him, but as fast as she might run, she seemed to conquer no distance. The board still stretched between them, even as he sank to his knees, blood pooling around him on the black-and-white board.

"Baba! *Baba!*" she cried. "Daddy, *please!*"

But the board spun away from her. Suddenly she stood in the drawing room at Curzon Street, light from the fire spilling over the chess set she and James had played upon so often. James himself stood by the fire, his hand upon the mantel. He turned to look at her, achingly beautiful in the firelight, his eyes the color of molten gold.

In those eyes was no recognition at all. "Who are you?" he said. "Where is Grace?"

Cordelia woke gasping, her covers tangled tightly around her. She fought her way free, almost retching, her fingers digging into her pillow. She longed for her mother, for Alastair. For Lucie. She buried her face in her arms, her body shaking.

The door to her bedroom swung open, and bright light spilled into the room. Framed in the light was Matthew, wearing a dressing gown, his hair a wild tangle. "I heard screaming," he said urgently. "What happened?"

Cordelia let out a long exhale and unclenched her hands. "Nothing," she said. "Just a dream. I dreamed that . . . that my father was calling to me. Asking me to save him."

He sat down beside her, the mattress shifting under his weight. He smelled comfortingly of soap and cologne, and he took her hand and held it while her pulse slowed its racing. "You and I are the same," he said. "We are sick in our souls from old wounds. I know you blame yourself—for Lilith, for James—and you must not, Daisy. We will recover together from our soul-sickness. Here, in Paris, we will conquer the pain."

He held her hand until she fell asleep.

James wasn't sure how he'd expected Lucie to respond to their arrival, but he was startled nonetheless at the fear that flashed across her face.

She took a step back, nearly knocking into the boy standing next to her—*Jesse Blackthorn, it was Jesse Blackthorn*—and flung her hands up, as if to ward them off. As if to ward off James, and her father.

"Oh, dear," Magnus muttered.

This struck James as an understatement. He was exhausted—nightmare-plagued sleep interrupted by uncomfortable carriage rides, the unburdening of his soul to Magnus and his father, and a long, wet walk up a slippery cliff path to Malcolm Fade's house had worn him down to the bone. Still, the look on Lucie's face—worry, fear—sent protectiveness shooting through his veins.

"Luce," he said, stepping into the cottage's entryway. "It's all right—"

Lucie looked at him gratefully for a moment, then flinched as Will, unsheathing a blade from his weapons belt, strode into the cottage and seized hold of Jesse Blackthorn by his shirtfront. Dagger in his fist, fury in his blue eyes, Will shoved Jesse hard against the wall.

"Foul spirit," he snarled. "What have you done to my daughter to force her to bring you here? Where is Malcolm Fade?"

"Papa—no, *don't*—" Lucie started toward Will, but James caught at her arm. He rarely saw his father angry, but Will had an explosive temper when roused, and threats to his family galvanized his rage more quickly than anything else.

"*Tad,*" James said urgently; he only used the word for *father* in Welsh when he was trying to get Will's attention. "Wait."

"Yes, please wait," Lucie broke in. "I'm sorry I left as I did, but you don't understand—"

"I understand that this was a corpse possessed by Belial," Will said, holding his blade level with Jesse's throat. Jesse didn't move; he hadn't moved, in fact, since Will had grabbed him, nor had he spoken. He was very pale (well, he *would* be, wouldn't he, James thought), his green eyes burning. His hands hung carefully loose at his sides, as if to say, *See, I present no threat*. "I understand that my daughter is softhearted and thinks she can save every fallen sparrow. I understand that the dead cannot live again, not without exacting a terrible price on the living."

James, Lucie, and Magnus all started to speak at once. Will said something, angrily, that James could not quite hear. Looking exasperated, Magnus snapped his fingers. Blue sparks leaped from them, and the world went utterly quiet. Even the sound of the wind was gone, swallowed up in Magnus's spell.

"Enough of this," the warlock said. He was leaning in the embrasure of the door, hat tipped over his forehead, his posture a study in exaggerated calm. "If we are discussing necromancy, or possible necromancy, that is *my* area of expertise, not yours." He looked closely at Jesse, his gold-green eyes thoughtful. "Does he speak?"

Jesse raised his eyebrows.

"Oh, right," Magnus said, and snapped his fingers again. "No more Silence spell. Proceed."

"I speak," Jesse said calmly, "when I have something to say."

"Interesting," Magnus murmured. "Does he bleed?"

"Oh no," said Lucie. "Don't encourage my father. Papa, don't you dare—"

"Lucie," Jesse said. "It's all right." He raised his hand—the one with the stolen Voyance rune slashed across the back. He brought his palm up and pressed it to the tip of Will's dagger.

Blood welled, red and bright, and spilled down his hand, reddening the cuff of his white shirt.

Magnus's eyes narrowed. "Even more interesting. All right, I'm tired of freezing in this doorway. Malcolm must have some sort of sitting room; he likes his creature comforts. Lucie, lead us to it."

Once they had piled into the parlor—quainter and prettier than James would have guessed—Will and James sank down onto a long sofa. Lucie, on her feet, watched as Magnus placed Jesse in front of the roaring fire and commenced some kind of full magical examination of him.

"What are you looking for?" Jesse said. James thought he sounded nervous.

Magnus looked up at him briefly, his fingers dancing with blue sparks. Some had caught in Jesse's hair, bright as scarab beetles.

"Death," he said.

Jesse looked grimly stoic. James supposed he would have learned to endure unpleasant things, given the life he'd led—or was it a life? It had been once; but what would one call what he'd experienced since? A sort of nightmare life-in-death, like the monster from the Coleridge poem.

"He is *not dead*," Lucie said. "He never was. Let me explain." She sounded weary, as James had felt when spilling his own secrets at the wayside inn. How much trouble could have been avoided if they'd only all trusted one another in the first place? he thought.

"Luce," James said gently. She looked so tired, he thought, at the same time both younger and older than he'd remembered. "Tell us."

Much of Lucie's story James could have guessed, in its broad strokes if not in its details. First came Jesse's tale: the story of what Belial, and his own mother, had done to him. Much of it James already knew: how Belial had used the corrupt warlock Emmanuel Gast to seed a bit of Belial's demonic essence inside Jesse when he was just a baby; how that essence had destroyed Jesse when the time came for his first Marks to be placed upon him. How Tatiana had turned her dying son into a sort of living specter: a ghost during the nights, a corpse during the days. How she had preserved his last breath in the gold locket that

Lucie now wore about her neck, hoping one day to use it to bring Jesse back to life.

How Jesse had sacrificed that last breath, instead, to save James.

"Really?" Will sat forward, frowning in that way of his that suggested careful thought rather than displeasure. "But how—?"

"It's true," James said. "I saw him."

A boy leaning over him: a boy with hair as black as his own, a boy with green eyes the color of spring leaves, a boy who was already beginning to fade around the edges, like a figure seen in a cloud that disappears when the wind changes.

"You said, 'Who are you?'" Jesse said. Magnus seemed to be done examining him; Jesse was leaning against the fireplace mantel, looking as if Lucie's telling of her story—which was his, too—was draining him as well. "But—I couldn't answer you."

"I remember," James said. "Thank you. For saving my life. I didn't get to say it before."

Magnus cleared his throat. "Enough sentimentality," he said, obviously wishing to forestall Will, who looked as if he were considering leaping up and folding Jesse into a fatherly embrace. "We have a good understanding of what happened to Jesse. What we do not understand, dear Lucie, is how you brought him back from the state he was in. And I am afraid we must ask."

"Now?" said James. "It's late, she must be exhausted—"

"It's all right, Jamie," Lucie said. "I want to tell it."

And she did. The story of her discovery of her powers over the dead—that she could not only see them when they wanted to remain hidden, as James and Will could, but could command them, and they were compelled to obey her—reminded James of the discovery of his own power, of the combined sense of strength and shame that it had brought.

He wanted to stand up, wanted to reach out to his sister. Especially as her story went on—as she told how she had raised an army of the drowned and dead to save Cordelia from the Thames. He wanted to tell her how much it meant to him that she had saved Cordelia's life; wanted to tell her how much bleak horror he felt at the thought that he might have lost Cordelia. But he kept his mouth shut. Lucie had no reason to believe he wasn't in love with Grace, and he would only look to her like an awful hypocrite.

"I am somewhat insulted," Magnus said, "that you went to Malcolm Fade to seek his advice on what to do about Jesse, and did not come to me. Usually I am the warlock you annoy first, and I consider that a proud tradition."

"You were in the Spiral Labyrinth," Lucie reminded him. "And—well, there were other reasons for asking Malcolm, but they don't matter now." (James, who felt he had become an unwilling master of the ability to tell only as much of a story as was required at the time, suspected they mattered quite a bit, but said nothing.) "Malcolm told us, told *me*, that it was like Jesse was stuck at the threshold between death and life. Which is why you couldn't see him like you can normal ghosts." She looked over at Will. "Because he wasn't really dead. What I did to bring him back wasn't necromancy. I just—" She interleaved the fingers of one hand with the other. "I commanded him to live. It would not have worked if he were truly dead, but since I was only uniting a living soul with a living body—from which it had been improperly separated—it did."

Will pushed a lock of black hair, threaded with strands of gray, back from his forehead. "What do you think, Magnus?"

Magnus looked at Jesse, still tensely propped against the mantel, and sighed. "There *are* a few blotches of death energy on Jesse." He held up a finger before anyone could speak. "*But* they are only at the sites of the runes that Belial placed on him."

So James had told Will and Magnus the full extent of what Belial had done to Jesse, Lucie thought. Jesse himself looked as if he were about to be sick.

Magnus added, "Otherwise, as far as I can tell, this is a healthy, living human being. I've seen what happens when someone raises the dead. This . . . is not that."

James said, "I was present when Lucie told Jesse to cast out Belial. And he did it. It is not easy to battle a Prince of Hell for your own soul. To win the fight—" James met Jesse's gaze directly. "It takes courage, and more than that. It takes goodness. Lucie trusts him; I believe we should too."

A little of the tension seemed to leave Jesse, a loosening of the tightness that wrapped him like invisible chains. He looked at Will—they all looked at Will, Lucie with a desperate hope in her eyes.

Will rose to his feet and crossed the room to Jesse. Jesse did not cringe away, but he looked visibly nervous. He stood still and watchful, not dropping his gaze, waiting for Will to make the first move.

"You saved my son's life," said Will. "And my daughter trusts you. That's good enough for me." He held out a hand to Jesse to shake. "I apologize for having doubted you, son."

At that last word, Jesse lit up like the sun coming out from behind a cloud. He had never had a father, James realized. The only parent he had had was Tatiana; the only other adult force in his life had been Belial.

And Will seemed to be thinking the same thing. "You really are the spitting image of your father, you know," he said to Jesse. "Rupert. It's a pity you never knew him. I'm sure he would have been proud of you."

Jesse looked as if he had actually grown taller. Lucie beamed over at him. *Ah,* James thought. *This is not some sort of crush. She is truly in love with Jesse Blackthorn. How did I never guess any of this was happening?*

But then, he had kept his own secrets about love, too well. He thought of Matthew, who would be with Cordelia now in Paris. He tried to breathe around the pain of the thought.

"Now," said Will, and with a decided air, clapped Jesse on the shoulder. "We can stand around blaming Tatiana, and believe me, I do, but it won't help the present situation. It seems you are our concern, young Jesse. What are we going to do with you?"

Lucie frowned. "Why don't we just go back to the Clave? And explain what happened? They already know Tatiana was up to dark doings. They wouldn't blame Jesse for what was done to him."

Magnus rolled his eyes to the ceiling. "No. Terrible idea. Certainly not."

Lucie glared at him.

Magnus shrugged. "Lucie, your heart is in the right place." Lucie stuck out her tongue at him, and he smiled. "But it would be quite dangerous to start involving the Clave on a large scale. There are some who have every reason to believe this story, but just as many, if not more, who would strongly prefer to disbelieve it."

"Magnus is right," said Will. "Unfortunately. This is a question of nuance. Jesse was not brought back from the dead; he was never truly dead to begin with. Still, he was possessed by Belial. And during that possession he did—"

The light had gone out of Jesse's face. "I did terrible things," he said. "They will say, 'Well, if he was alive, then he was responsible for the things he did; if he was dead, then this is necromancy.'" His gaze flicked to Lucie. "I told you I could not return to London," he said. "Mine is a complicated story, and people do not want to hear complicated stories. They want simple stories, in which people are either good or evil, and no one good ever makes a mistake, and no one evil ever repents."

"You have nothing to repent," said James. "If there is anyone who knows what it is like to have Belial whispering in their ear, it is me."

"Ah, but you have never done his bidding, have you?" said Jesse, with a bitter smile. "I think there is nothing to be done here save for me to go away. A new identity—"

"Jesse, *no*." Lucie started toward him, then swayed back. "You deserve to have *your life*. The one Tatiana tried to steal from you."

Jesse said nothing. James, reminded of his sister's admonition to treat him like a person, said, "Jesse. What would you *want* to do?"

"What do I want?" said Jesse with a sad smile. "I want four impossible things. I want to join the Enclave in London. I want to be a Shadowhunter, as I was born to be. I want to be accepted as a normal, living person. I wish to reunite with my sister, the only real family I've ever had. But I don't see how any of that is possible."

A silence came over the room as they pondered this; it was interrupted by a sudden loud creak that made them all jump. It was coming from the direction of the entryway, and after a moment Malcolm Fade came into the room, stamping his feet on the stone floor to remove the snow from his boots. He was hatless, white flakes of snow caught in his already white hair. He looked thinner, James thought, than the last time he'd seen him; his look was intense, and peculiarly faraway. It took him a long moment to notice that his sitting room was full of visitors. When he did see them, he froze in place.

"Thought we'd pop by, Malcolm," said Magnus airily.

Malcolm looked as if he wanted nothing more than to flee through the night, winding up in the morning perhaps in Rio de Janeiro or some other far-flung locale. Instead he sighed and resorted to the last bulwark of an Englishman under stress.

"Tea?" he suggested.

It was late, and Anna Lightwood was getting tired. Unfortunately, the party in her flat showed no signs of slowing. Nearly all her Shadowhunter friends were out of town for a variety of silly reasons, and she had taken the opportunity to invite over some of those Downworlders she wished to know better. Claude Kellington, the master of music at the Hell Ruelle, had a new composition to debut, and he wished to do so before an intimate audience. Anna's flat, according to him, was the perfect spot.

Kellington's new composition involved a lot of singing, never Claude's strongest talent. Nor had Anna realized that it was a song cycle adapted from an epic poem also of his composition. The performance had now entered its fourth hour, and Anna's guests, however well disposed toward the artist, had long ago become bored and drunk. Kellington, whose usual audience were the bored and drunk denizens of the Hell Ruelle, hadn't even noticed; he also, Anna noted, had apparently never heard of the word "intermission."

Now a vampire and werewolf whose names Anna did not recall were entangled passionately on her sofa, a positive step for Downworlder relations, at least. Someone in the corner by the china cabinet had gotten into the snuff. Even Percy the stuffed snake looked worn-out. Every now and again Anna took a discreet glance at her watch to note the hours ticking by, but she had no idea how to stop Kellington politely. Every time he paused for a moment she stood to interject, but he would only barrel right into the next movement.

Hyacinth, a pale blue faerie in the employ of Hypatia Vex, was here and had been sending suggestive glances in Anna's direction all evening. She and Anna had a history, and Anna did not like to repeat a reckless debauch from her past; still, Kellington's performance would have normally driven her into Hyacinth's arms before the first hour was up. Instead she had been carefully avoiding the faerie girl's gaze. Looking at Hyacinth only reminded Anna of the last words Ariadne had spoken to her. *It is because of me that you have become what you are. Hard and bright as a diamond. Untouchable.*

The same words repeated themselves in her mind every time she thought about romance these days. What had once interested her—the purr of petticoats falling to the ground, the whispering fall of loosened hair—no longer did, unless it was Ariadne's hair. Ariadne's petticoats.

She would forget, she told herself. She would make herself forget. She had thrown herself into distractions. This performance of Kellington's, for instance. She had also held a life-drawing class with Percy as the subject, she had attended a number of shockingly dull vampire dances, and she had played cribbage with Hypatia until dawn. She missed Matthew more than she had thought possible. Surely he would have been able to distract her.

She was shaken from her reverie by a sudden knocking at the door. Startled, Anna rose. It was quite late for an unanticipated visitor. Perhaps—hopefully—a neighbor come to complain of the noise?

She threaded her way across the room and threw the door open. On the threshold, shivering with cold, stood Ariadne Bridgestock.

Her eyes were red, her cheeks blotchy. She'd been crying. Anna felt her stomach drop; whatever she might have rehearsed to say the next time she and Ariadne spoke disappeared from her mind instantly. Instead she felt a prickle of fear—what had happened? *What was wrong?*

"I'm sorry," Ariadne said. "For bothering you." Her chin was raised high, her eyes bright with defiance. "I know I shouldn't have come. But I've nowhere else I can go."

Wordlessly Anna stepped aside to let her into the flat. Ariadne came inside; she was carrying a small holdall, and the coat she wore was far too thin for the weather. Her hands were bare. Anna's alarm ticked up a notch. Something was certainly wrong.

In that moment, though Ariadne had said nothing, Anna made a decision.

She strode over to the piano, which Kellington was playing *fortissimo* while singing something about a lonely wolf in the moonlight, and closed the fallboard on his hands. The music stopped abruptly, and

Kellington looked up at her with a hurt expression. Anna ignored him. "Thank you all so much for coming tonight," she said loudly, "but alas, pressing Nephilim business has arisen. I'm afraid I must ask you all to depart."

"I'm only halfway through," protested Kellington.

"Then we shall gather at some other time to hear the second half," Anna lied, and in a few minutes she had managed to herd the dozen or so guests out of the flat. A few grumbled, but most only looked puzzled. As the door closed on the last of them a silence settled, the uncanny stillness that always followed the end of a party. Only Ariadne remained.

A few minutes later found Ariadne perched uneasily on Anna's settee, her legs curled under her, her coat drying by the fire. She had stopped shivering once Anna had gotten some tea into her, but the look in her eyes was grim and faraway. Anna waited, lounging with a false casualness against the back of the settee.

As she sipped, Ariadne looked around the flat slowly, taking it in. Anna was puzzled by this until she realized with a start that Ariadne had never actually been here before. Anna had always arranged to meet her elsewhere.

"You're probably wondering why I'm here," Ariadne said.

Oh, thank the Angel, she's going to bring it up herself, Anna thought. Anna had always welcomed those in distress to her flat—Eugenia, weeping over Augustus Pounceby; Matthew, full of sorrows he could not name; Christopher, fretting that his science would come to nothing in the end; Cordelia, desperately in love with James but too proud to admit it. She knew how to talk to the heartbroken; she knew it was always best not to push for information, and to wait for them to speak first.

But with Ariadne, things were different; Anna knew she could not have held back a moment longer from asking her what had happened. It mattered too much. That was the problem. With Ariadne, things had always mattered too much.

Ariadne began to speak—slowly, and then faster. She explained that earlier that day the Consul had come to seek news of her father, and that she had gone into his office afterward and found a file full of information about the Herondales and the Lightwoods, and all the times any of them had perhaps bent a small law, or caused a problem in the Enclave through an error. None of it, she said, rose to a level of significance such that the Inquisitor should take interest.

Anna did not, as she wanted to, immediately ask whether Ariadne had seen any entries about her specifically. Instead she only frowned and said, "Well, I don't like the sound of that. What could he hope to accomplish by such a record?"

"I don't know," Ariadne said. "But that wasn't the worst of it. The worst of it was that in the fireplace, partly burned, I found this."

From the pocket of her coat, she withdrew a sheet of paper, crumpled and black at its edges, and handed it to Anna. It was obviously a letter, with the Inquisitor's sign-off and messy signature halfway down the page, but it was singed with small holes and its first page was missing.

> *—and I have always considered you to be one of the brightest [blotch] in the Shadowhunter firmament. I have found us to be aligned in our views as to the proper behavior of a Shadowhunter and the importance of the Law and strict adherence to it. Therefore I have watched with growing concern, as it seems to me your sympathy and even preference has increased toward the Herondales and some of the more scandalous Lightwoods with whom they consort. I have reasoned with you and argued with you, all, it seems, to no avail. Therefore I have decided to take the step of letting you know that the secrets which you believe well hidden are known to me. There is such in your history as I might be willing to overlook, but I can assure you the rest of the Clave will not. You should be aware that I intend to [blotch] the Herondales and have them removed from [blotch]. With your help, I believe I could also make charges stick against certain of the Lightwoods as well. I expect resistance from the Enclave, as some people are sentimental, and this is where your support of me will be key. If you back me in my actions to prune the more corrupt branches of the Nephilim tree, I will overlook your indiscretions. Your family has benefited*

from the spoils of—here the letter became illegible, marred by a huge inkblot—*but it could all be lost if your house is not in order.*

I remain,
Inquisitor Maurice Bridgestock

Anna looked up at Ariadne. "Blackmail?" she said. "The Inquisitor—your father—is blackmailing someone?"

"It certainly looks that way, doesn't it," Ariadne said grimly. "But it's impossible to tell whom he is blackmailing, or why, or what about. I only know my mother was furious when she realized what I'd found."

"It might not be what it looks like," Anna offered. "He didn't send this, for one thing."

"No," said Ariadne slowly, "but do you see this blotch? 'Your family has benefited from the spoils of—something.' I think this must have been an early draft and he discarded it in the fire."

Anna frowned. "Without the first page, it is hard to even guess who the target might be. It does seem the person is neither a Herondale nor a Lightwood—they are both mentioned as separate from the recipient." Anna hesitated. "Did your mother really throw you out just because you found these papers?"

"Not . . . entirely," said Ariadne. "I was greatly distressed when I found the files and the letter. She said it was none of my business. That it was my concern only to be an obedient and dutiful daughter, and to make a good marriage. And when she said that, well . . . I may have lost my temper."

"Oh?" said Anna.

"I told her I would not make a good marriage, I would not make *any* marriage, that I would never get married, because I had no interest at all in men."

The air seemed to have been sucked from the room. Anna said quietly, "And?"

"She fell to pieces," Ariadne said. "She begged me to say it wasn't true, and when I wouldn't, she said I could not let such impulses ruin my life." She scrubbed impatiently at her tears with the back of her hand. "I could see in her eyes that she had already known. Or at least suspected. She told me to think of my future, that I would be alone, that I would never have children."

"Ah," Anna said softly. She ached inside. She knew how badly Ariadne had always wanted children, that that desire had been at the heart of what had ended their relationship two years ago.

"I went to my room, threw a few things into a holdall—I told her I would not live under the same roof as her and Papa if they would not accept me as I truly was. As I *am*. And she said—she said she would promise to forget everything I had told her. That we could pretend I had never spoken. That if I were to tell Papa what I had told her, he would throw me out onto the street." Anna did not breathe. "And so I fled," Ariadne finished. "Left the house and came here. Because you are the most independent person I know. I cannot go back to that house. I *will* not. My pride and my . . . my *self* depend on it. I need to learn how to strike out on my own. To live independently, as you do." Her expression was determined, but her hands trembled as she spoke. "I thought . . . if you could show me how . . ."

Anna gently took the rattling teacup from her. "Of course," she said. "You shall be as independent as you wish. But not tonight. Tonight you have had a shock, and it is very late, and you must rest. In the morning you will start a new life. And it will be wonderful."

A slow smiled bloomed across Ariadne's face. And for a moment, Anna was undone by her sheer beauty. The grace of her, the way her dark hair glowed, the line of her neck and the soft flutter of her lashes. An impulse to take Ariadne in her arms, to cover her eyelids and her mouth with kisses, came over Anna. She curled her hands into fists behind her back, where Ariadne would not see them.

"You take the bedroom," she said evenly. "I will sleep here on the chaise longue; it is quite comfortable."

"Thank you." Ariadne rose with her holdall. "Anna—the last time I saw you—I was angry," she said. "I should not have said you were hard. You have always had the biggest heart of anyone I have known, with room in it for all manner of waifs and strays. Like me," she added, with a sad little smile.

Anna sighed inwardly. In the end, Ariadne had come to her for the same reason Matthew did, or Eugenia: because Anna was easy to talk to, because she could be depended on for sympathy and tea and a place to sleep. She did not blame Ariadne, or think less of her for it. It was only that she had hoped that perhaps there had been a different reason.

A little while later, after Ariadne had gone to bed, Anna went to bank up the fire for the night. As she turned back, she caught Percy's disapproving scowl.

"I know," she said quietly. "It is a terrible mistake, letting her stay here. I shall come to regret it. I know."

Percy could only agree.

No one, as it turned out, wanted tea.

"Malcolm Fade," Will said, advancing on the warlock. His anger, which had dissipated quickly enough on hearing Lucie's story, seemed to have returned along with Malcolm. James stood up, ready to intervene if needed; he knew the tone in his father's voice. "I should have you hauled in front of the Clave, you know. Put on trial, for breaking the Accords."

Malcolm walked past Will and threw himself into the chair next to the fireplace. "On what charges?" he said, sounding tired. "Necromancy? I didn't perform any necromancy."

"Well," said Magnus, folding his arms, "you *did* take a Shadowhunter child to a secret location without her parents' knowledge. That's frowned on. Oh, and you stole the corpse of a Shadowhunter. I'm pretty sure that's frowned upon as well."

"*Et tu*, Magnus?" Malcolm said. "Have you no solidarity with your fellow warlocks?"

"Not when they kidnap children, no," said Magnus dryly.

"Malcolm," Will said, and James could tell he was trying to keep his voice down, "you're the High Warlock of London. If Lucie came to you with this forbidden business, you should have said no. You should have come to me, in fact."

Malcolm sighed, as though the whole situation exhausted him. "A long time ago, I lost someone I loved. Her death—her death almost destroyed me." He looked at the window, at the gray sea beyond. "When your daughter came to me for aid, I couldn't help but sympathize. I couldn't turn her away. If that means I must lose my position, then so be it."

"I won't let Malcolm lose his position because of me," snapped Lucie, putting her hands on her hips. "I went in search of him. I *demanded* his help. When I restored Jesse to life, Malcolm didn't even know I was doing it. When he arrived, I—" She broke off. "I insisted on being taken to Cornwall. I feared what the Clave would do to Jesse. I was trying to protect him, and so was Malcolm. This is all my doing. And I am happy to go before the Clave and say so."

"Lucie," James said. "That's not a good idea."

Lucie gave him a look that reminded him of certain scenes from Lucie's first novel, *Secret Princess Lucie Is Rescued from Her Terrible Family*. If he recalled correctly, the brother of the main character, Cruel Prince James, had a habit of putting vampire bats in his sister's hair, and later died a much-deserved death when he fell into a barrel of treacle.

"James is right. The Clave is brutal, ruthless," said Malcolm in a grim tone. "I would not wish you to be questioned by them, Lucie."

"The Mortal Sword—" Lucie began.

"The Mortal Sword will force you to reveal not just that you raised Jesse, but that you were able to do it because of Belial," said Magnus. "Because of the power that comes from him."

"But then James—and Mama—"

"Exactly," said Will. "Which is why involving the Clave in any aspect of this is a poor idea."

"Which is why I remain a problem," said Jesse. "In terms of my returning in any way to the world of Shadowhunters."

"No," said Lucie. "We will think of something—"

"Jesse Blackthorn," said Malcolm, "with his mother and his heritage and history, cannot return to Shadowhunter society, at least not in London."

Lucie looked stricken; Jesse had the grim expression of someone already resigned.

Magnus narrowed his eyes. "Malcolm," he said, "I feel you are trying to tell us something."

"*Jesse* Blackthorn cannot join the London Enclave," said Malcolm.

"But—because of my history, my research, nobody knows more about the Blackthorn family than I do. If I can find a means by which Jesse can be returned to Shadowhunter society, without suspicion . . . could we then consider this whole matter put behind us?"

Will looked at Lucie for a long time. Then he said, "All right." Lucie exhaled, her eyes closing in relief. Will pointed at Malcolm. "You have until tomorrow."

5
Realms Above

Alas! they had been friends in youth;
But whispering tongues can poison truth;
And constancy lives in realms above;
And life is thorny; and youth is vain;
And to be wroth with one we love
Doth work like madness in the brain.
—Samuel Taylor Coleridge, "Christabel"

James couldn't sleep. It was the first time he'd had a bedroom to himself in five days; he no longer had to contend with his father's snoring and Magnus smoking his terrifying pipe, and he was exhausted. But still he lay awake, staring at the cracked plaster ceiling and thinking of Cordelia.

Will had managed to turn the conversation to the question of where the three of them would sleep, in the process—rather deftly, James thought, a reminder of why his father was good at his job—getting Malcolm to think of them less as invaders and more as houseguests.

The little cottage turned out to be much larger on the inside than the outside, and the upstairs corridor was lined with simple, clean rooms on both sides. Magnus magicked their things up from the carriage, and that was that.

Now that James was alone, though, thoughts of Cordelia came crowding back into his mind. He had thought he missed her before, had thought he had been tormented with regret. He realized now that having had his father and Magnus always present, having had a mission on which to focus, had blunted his feelings; he had not even begun to imagine the pain he *could* feel. He understood now why poets damned their hearts, their capacity for desolation and want. Nothing in the false enchantment of love he had felt for Grace had come near this. His mind had told him that his heart was broken, but he had not *felt* it, not felt all the jagged pieces of shattered hope, like shards of glass inside his chest.

He thought of Dante: *There is no greater sorrow than to recall in misery the time when we were happy*. He had never realized before how true that was. Cordelia laughing, dancing with him, her intent gaze as she held an ivory chess piece in her hand, the way she had looked on their wedding day, all in gold—all these memories tormented him. He feared he would hurt her if he begged her to understand what had truly happened, that he had never loved Grace. He feared even more not trying, condemning himself to a life utterly without her.

Breathe measured breaths, he told himself. He was grateful for all the training Jem had given him through the years: practice in controlling himself, controlling his emotions and fears. It seemed to be all that was keeping him from flying apart into pieces.

How had he not known? Matthew's letter to him—much folded, much read, tucked in the pocket of James's coat—had struck him like a bolt of lightning. He'd had no idea of Matthew's feelings, and still did not know Cordelia's. *How* had he been so oblivious? He knew some of it had been the spell of the bracelet—but in the parlor, he'd seen the way Lucie looked at Jesse, and known that she had been in love with him for a long time. Yet he'd had no inkling of anything going on with his sister—nor, it turned out, his *parabatai* or his wife. How were the people he loved the most in the world the ones he seemed to know the least?

Having thrashed the covers into an untenable knot, James flung the wool blanket off and got up. There was bright moonlight coming in the window, and in its pale glow he made his way across the room to where his jacket hung on a peg. In its pocket, still, were Cordelia's gloves. He drew one of them out, running his fingers over the soft gray kidskin with its tracery of leaves. He could see her resting her chin on her gloved hand—he could see her face before him, her eyes shining, dark and fathomless. He could see her turning that gaze up to Matthew, cheeks flushed, lips parted. He knew he was torturing himself, as if he'd been running the fine, sharp edge of a dagger across his skin, and yet he could not stop.

A sudden flicker of motion distracted him. Something interrupting the moonlight, a break in the silvery illumination. He replaced the glove in his coat pocket and went over to the window. He had a view of the jagged rocks of Chapel Cliff from here, of wind-sculpted boulders tumbling down to a silver-black sea.

A figure stood at the edge of the cliffs, where the stone was rimed with ice. The figure was tall, slender; he wore a white cloak—no, not white. The color of bone or parchment, with runes inked at the hem and sleeves.

Jem.

He knew it was his uncle. It could be no one else. But what was he doing here? James had not summoned him, and if Jem had wished them all to know that he was present, surely he would have knocked and roused the house? Moving silently, James took his coat off the peg, put on his shoes, and slipped downstairs.

The cold hit him the moment he went out the door. There was no snow falling, but the air was full of stinging particles of frost. James was half-blinded by the time he circled the house and reached the cliffside where Jem stood. He wore only his thin robes, and his hands were bare, but cold and heat did not touch Silent Brothers. He glanced over as James appeared but said nothing, apparently content for the two of them to stand and look out across the water.

"Did you come searching for us?" James asked. "I thought Mother would have told you where we'd gone."

She did not need to. Your father sent a letter, the night you departed London, Jem said silently. *But I couldn't wait for your return to speak with you.* He sounded serious, and though Silent Brothers always sounded serious, there was something in Jem's manner that made James's stomach lurch.

"Belial?" James whispered.

To his surprise, Jem shook his head. *Grace.*

Oh.

As you know, Jem went on, *she has been in the Silent City since shortly after you departed.*

"She is safer there," James said. And then, with a rancor he hadn't planned, he added, "And the world is safer with her there. Under careful observation."

Both those things are true, said Jem. After a brief silence, he said, *Is there a reason you haven't told your parents what Grace did to you?*

"How do you know I haven't?" James said. Jem regarded him silently. "Never mind," James said. "Silent Brother powers, I gather."

And a general knowledge of human behavior, said Jem. *If Will had known what Grace did to you before he left London, his letter would have sounded quite different. And I rather suspect you have not told him since.*

"Why do you suspect that?"

I know you well, James, said his uncle. *I know you do not like to be pitied. And you imagine that is what would happen if you spoke the truth about what Grace—and her mother—did to you.*

"Because it's true," James said. "It's exactly what would happen." He stared out at the ocean; in the far distance, sparks against the darkness, were the lights of distant boats. He could not imagine how lonely it must be, out there in the darkness and cold, alone on the waves in a tiny craft. "But I suppose I'm not to have much choice. Especially if Grace is to stand trial."

Actually, said Jem, *the Silent Brothers have decided that Grace's power should remain a secret, for now. We do not yet wish Tatiana Blackthorn to know that her daughter is no longer allied with her, nor do we wish her to be aware of what we know. Not until she can be questioned with the Mortal Sword.*

"How convenient for Grace," James said, and was surprised at the bitterness in his own voice.

James, Jem said. *Have I asked you to conceal the truth of what Grace and Tatiana did to you? The Silent Brothers want the truth withheld from the Clave, but I understand that you may need to tell your family, to ease your mind and theirs. But I trust that if you do, you will emphasize that it should not become widely known as yet.* He hesitated. *It was my impression that perhaps you did not want anyone to know. That you would be relieved that it remained a secret.*

James held his tongue. Because he *was* relieved. He could imagine the pity that would fall upon him, the desire to understand, the need to discuss it, when the truth came out. He needed time before then—time to become accustomed to the truth—before everyone knew. He needed time to accept that he'd lived a lie for years, to no purpose.

"It is strange to me," he said, "that you are speaking with Grace. That you may be the only person in the world to really have an honest conversation with her about what—what she did." He bit at his bottom lip; he still had trouble calling it "*the enchantment*," or "*the love spell*"; it was more bearable to say "*what she did*," or even "*what she did to me*," knowing Jem would understand. "I do not think she even told her brother. He seems to know nothing of it."

The sharp wind lifted James's hair, flung it into his eyes. He was so cold he could feel the shivery brush of his own eyelashes against his skin, damp as they were with sea spray. "He has certainly never mentioned anything about Grace's power to Lucie—of that I am absolutely sure." Lucie would not have been able to help herself; she would have flung herself at James the first moment she saw him, railing against Grace, furious on his behalf.

He does not know. At least, Grace has never told him. She has never told anyone, in fact.

"No one?"

Until her confession, no one but her mother knew, Jem said. *And Belial, of course. I believe she was ashamed, for whatever that's worth.*

"It's not worth all that much," said James, and Jem nodded as if he understood.

It is my task as a Silent Brother, said Jem, *to gain greater understanding. Whatever Belial's plan is, I do not believe he is done with us. With you. He has reached for you in many ways. Through Grace, but when he finds that door is closed, it would be better to know where he will turn next.*

"I doubt Grace knows," James said in a leaden voice. "She didn't know about his plan with Jesse. To be fair to her, I don't think she would have gone along with it. I think Jesse might be the only thing in the world she actually cares about."

I agree, said Jem. *And while Grace may not know Belial's secrets, knowing hers may yet help us find gaps in his armor.* He tipped his head back, letting the wind stir his dark hair. *But I will not speak to you of her again, unless I must.*

"As you say," said James carefully, "there are a few who I feel I must tell. Who deserve to be told." Jem didn't respond, only waited. "Cordelia is in Paris. I would like to tell her first, before anyone else knows. I owe her that. She was—more affected than anyone else but myself."

It is your story to tell, said Jem. *Only—if you do tell Cordelia, or . . . others, I would be grateful if you would let me know you have done so. You can reach me whenever you desire.*

James thought of the box of matches in his pocket, each one a sort of signal light that, when struck, summoned Jem to his side. He did not know how the magic of it worked, nor did he think Jem would tell him even if he asked.

It is not easy for me, Jem said. His expression had not changed, but his pale hands moved, knotting together. *I know I must listen dispassionately to Grace's testimony. Yet when she speaks of what was done to you, my silent heart cries out: this was wrong, it was always wrong. You love as your father loves: wholly, without conditions or hesitancy. To use that as a weapon is blasphemy.*

James glanced back at Malcolm's house, and then at his uncle. He had never seen him so agitated. "Do you want me to wake up my father?" James said. "Did you want to see him?"

No. Don't wake him, Jem said, and even though his speech was silent, there was a gentleness in the way he *thought* about Will that was for Will alone. James thought of Matthew, no doubt asleep somewhere in Paris, and felt a terrible admixture of love and anger like a poison in his blood. Matthew *had* been to him what Will was to Jem; how had he lost him? How had he lost him without even knowing it?

I am sorry to have told you all that. It is not a burden you should have to shoulder.

"It is not a burden to know there is someone in the Silent City who listens to all this, and thinks of it not just as a peculiarity of magic, but as something that had a true cost," said James softly. "Even if you pity Grace, even if you must be unsentimental as a judge, you will not forget me, my family. Cordelia. That means a great deal. That you will not forget."

Jem brushed James's hair from his forehead, a light benediction. *Never,* he said, and then, in-between one crash of a wave and another, he was gone, melting into the shadows.

James returned to the house, crawling into bed with his coat still on. He felt cold down in the center of his being, and when he slept, it was restlessly: he dreamed of Cordelia, in a bloodred gown, standing upon a bridge made of lights, and though she looked directly at him, it was clear she had no idea who he was.

There was a splotch on the ceiling above Ariadne's head that was shaped somewhat like a rabbit.

Ariadne had thought she would fall instantly into an exhausted sleep the moment she lay down. Instead here she was, still awake, her mind racing. She knew she ought to be thinking about her father's disturbing papers. About her mother, in tears, telling her that if she would only admit it wasn't true, if she would only take her words back, she wouldn't have to leave. She could stay.

But her mind was on Anna. Anna, who lay sleeping a few feet away, her long, elegant body draped across the violet chaise longue. She could picture her so clearly: her arm behind her head, her dark hair curling against her cheek, her ruby necklace winking in the sculpted hollow of her throat.

Or perhaps Anna was not asleep. Perhaps she was awake, just as Ariadne was. Perhaps she was rising to her feet, tightening the belt of her dressing gown as she stepped silently across the floor, her hand on the bedroom door . . .

Ariadne closed her eyes. But her whole body remained awake. Tense and waiting. She would feel Anna sit down on the bed beside her, feel it sink under her weight. She would feel Anna lean over her, the heat of her body, her hand on the strap of Ariadne's nightgown, sliding it slowly down her shoulder. Her lips on Ariadne's bare skin . . .

Ariadne rolled onto her side with a muffled gasp. Of course, nothing of the sort had happened. She had firmly told Anna to stay away from her the last time they had seen each other, and it was not like Anna to ever place herself where she was not wanted. She stared glumly around the bedroom: it was a small space, containing a wardrobe spilling clothes, and shelves and shelves of books.

Not that Ariadne could imagine reading right now, not when every cell of her body seemed to cry out Anna's name. She had told herself she had purged her desire for Anna, that she understood that Anna could never give her what she wanted. But at the moment, all she wanted was Anna: Anna's hands, Anna's whispered words in her ears, Anna's body molded against hers.

She turned on her elbow and reached for the jug of water on the nightstand. There was a shallow wooden shelf on the wall above it, and her sleeve caught against an object perched there, which tumbled to the nightstand next to the jug. Picking up the object, she saw that it was a palm-sized doll. She sat up, curious; she would not have thought of Anna, even as a child, as a one for dolls. This one was of the sort often found in dollhouses, its limbs stuffed with cotton, its face blank porcelain. It was the gentleman doll, the kind that usually came with a wife and a tiny porcelain baby in a miniature cradle.

Ariadne had owned similar dollhouse inhabitants when she was a child: nothing really differentiated the male dolls and the female dolls save the carefully sewn tiny clothes they wore. Ariadne imagined Anna playing with this little toy, in its natty striped suit and top hat. Perhaps, in Anna's mind, the doll *had* been the lady of the house, only in the sort of outfit Anna felt the lady would prefer; perhaps the doll had been a rakish bohemian, composing infinitesimal poems with a miniature pen.

With a smile, Ariadne set the doll carefully back on its shelf. Such a tiny thing, yet a reminder that here she was, for the first time in Anna's house, among Anna's things. That even if she did not have Anna, her feet were set now on the same path of independence that Anna had chosen for herself years ago. It was Ariadne's turn to seize that freedom and choose what to do with it. She curled up on the bed and closed her eyes.

* * *

Cornwall Gardens was not a short walk from Thomas's house—easily forty-five minutes, an hour if one stopped to enjoy the park along the way—but Thomas didn't mind. It was a rare sunny winter's day in London, and even though it was still cold, the air was clear and bright, seeming to throw every tiny detail of the city into relief, from the colorful advertisements on the sides of omnibuses to the darting shadows of tiny sparrows.

The darting shadows of tiny sparrows, he thought. *Thomas, you sound like an idiot.* Blast. What would Alastair think if he turned up at Cornwall Gardens with a ridiculous smile on his face, twittering about birds? He would send Thomas away, sharpish. Sadly, even that thought did not break Thomas's good mood. His thoughts seemed all awhirl; it was necessary to go back to the beginning to sort them out.

At breakfast—where he had been calmly, innocently eating toast—a runner had come for him with a message; his parents had been surprised, but not nearly as surprised as Thomas.

The message was from Alastair.

It took a full five minutes for Thomas to digest the fact—*the message was from Alastair, Alastair Carstairs, not some other Alastair*—and it contained the following information: Alastair wanted to meet with Thomas at Cornwall Gardens, as soon as possible.

Message digested, Thomas bolted upstairs so quickly he knocked over a teapot and left his confused parents staring at Eugenia, who merely shrugged as if to say one could never truly hope to unravel the beautiful mystery that was Thomas. "More eggs?" she suggested, holding out a plate to her father.

Thomas, meanwhile, had worked himself into a panic over what to wear, despite the fact that it was difficult finding clothes that fit someone of his height and breadth, and that as a result, he possessed a fairly dull wardrobe of browns and blacks and grays. Remembering that Matthew had said that a particular green shirt brought out the color in Thomas's hazel eyes, Thomas put it on, brushed his hair, and left the house—only to return a moment later, due to having forgotten his scarf, his shoes, and his stele.

Now, as the clay-red brick of Knightsbridge, crowded with shoppers, slowly melted into the quiet streets and dignified white edifices of South Kensington, Thomas reminded himself that just because Alastair had sent him a message did not necessarily mean anything. It was possible that Alastair wanted something translated into Spanish, or needed a very tall person's opinion on a matter. (Though Thomas could not imagine why this would be the case.) It was even possible he wanted, for some reason, to talk about Charles. The thought made Thomas's skin feel as if it were tying itself into knots. By the time he arrived at the Carstairs' house, he was subdued—or he was, at least, until he turned onto the walk and caught sight of Alastair, messy-haired and in shirtsleeves, standing outside his front door and holding a very recognizable sword.

Alastair's expression was a grim one. He looked up as Thomas approached. Thomas noticed two things immediately: firstly, that Alastair, with his smooth, light brown skin and graceful build, was still vexingly beautiful. And secondly, that Alastair's arms were covered in vicious-looking scratches, his shirt stained with black, acidic-looking patches.

Demon ichor.

"What happened?" Thomas stopped in his tracks. "Alastair—a demon? In the middle of the day? Don't tell me—" *Don't tell me that they're back.* They'd been plagued some months ago with demons that had possessed the ability to appear in daylight, but that had been because of Belial's meddling. If it was happening again . . .

"No," Alastair said quickly, as if he sensed Thomas's alarm. "I had, rather stupidly, gone into the mews house to look for something. It was dark in there, and one of the demons had apparently decided to lurk in wait."

"One of *what* demons?" Thomas said.

Alastair waved a vague hand. "It was a good thing I had Cortana with me," he said, and Thomas, surprised all over again, said, "Why *do* you have Cortana with you?"

Cortana was Cordelia's sword, passed down through generations of the Carstairs family. It was a precious heirloom, forged by the same Shadowhunter smith who had created Durendal for Roland, and Excalibur for King Arthur. Thomas had rarely seen Cordelia without it.

Alastair sighed. Thomas wondered if he was cold standing about with his sleeves rolled up, but decided not to mention it because Alastair had lean, muscular forearms. And maybe the cold didn't bother him anyway. "Cordelia left it behind when she went to Paris. She thought she should give it up because of the paladin business."

"It's odd," Thomas ventured, "isn't it, Cordelia going to Paris with Matthew?"

"It's odd," Alastair allowed. "But Cordelia's business is her own." He turned Cortana over in his hand, letting the watery sunlight spark off the blade. "Anyway—I've been keeping the sword close to me as much as I can. Which is fine during the day, but not so much once the sun sets. Bloody demons seem to swarm to it like a beacon every time I step outside."

"Are you sure they're attacking you *because* of the sword?"

"Are you suggesting it's my personality?" Alastair snapped. "They weren't attacking me like this before Cordelia handed the sword off to me, and she gave it to me because she didn't want anyone to know where it was. I suspect these ratty demon creatures are intended as spies, sent by someone looking for Cortana—Lilith, Belial, there's really an appalling pantheon of villains to choose from."

"So whoever it is—whoever's looking for it—they know you have it?"

"They certainly suspect I have it," said Alastair. "I *think* I've killed all the demons before they could report back definitively. Nothing nastier has shown up to attack me yet, in any case. But it's not a sustainable way to live."

Thomas shifted his feet. "Did you, ah, ask me here to help?" he said. "Because I'd be happy to help. We could put a guard on you. Christopher and I could take it in turns, and Anna would surely help—"

"No," said Alastair.

"Just trying to be helpful," said Thomas.

"I didn't ask you here for help. You just happened to turn up right after—" Alastair made a gesture apparently intended to encompass demons hiding in stables, and slid Cortana back into its scabbard at his hip. "I *asked* you here because I wanted to know why you sent me a note calling me stupid."

"I didn't," Thomas began indignantly, and then recalled, with a moment of freezing horror, what he had written in Henry's laboratory.

Dear Alastair, why are you so stupid and so frustrating, and why do I think about you all the time?

Oh *no*. But how—?

Alastair produced a burnt piece of paper from his pocket and handed it to Thomas. Most of the paper had been charred beyond legibility. What was left read:

Dear Alastair,
why are you so stupid
I brush my teeth
don't tell anyone
—Thomas

"I don't know *why* you don't want anyone to know you brush your teeth," Alastair added, "but I will, of course, keep this news in strictest confidence."

Thomas was torn between a feeling of terrible humiliation and a strange excitement. Of *course* this would be the one time Christopher's ridiculous experiment would partially work, but on the other hand—it had partially worked. He couldn't wait to tell Kit.

"Alastair," he said. "This writing is just nonsense. Christopher had me scribble some words down for an experiment he was doing."

Alastair looked dubious. "If you say so."

"Look," said Thomas. "Even if you didn't ask me here to help, I do want to help. I—" *I hate the idea of you being in danger.* "I don't think it's a good idea for you to be constantly attacked by demons, and I doubt Cordelia would have left the sword with you if she thought that would happen."

"No," Alastair agreed.

"Why don't we hide it?" Thomas suggested. "Cortana, I mean."

"I know, that's the sensible solution," said Alastair. "But it's felt safer to keep it with me, even though I keep being harassed. If it were hidden, I would just constantly worry that whoever's looking would *find* it, and then what would I tell Cordelia? And also what if the demon who wanted it used it to destroy the world, or something? I would be mortified. I just can't think of a hiding place safe enough."

"Hm. What if I had a hiding place that *would* be safe enough?"

Alastair raised his dark, arched eyebrows. "Lightwood, as always, you are full of surprises. Tell me what you're thinking."

Thomas did.

Cordelia emerged from her bedroom, wearing her striped walking dress, to find Matthew buttering a croissant at the breakfast table. The day was bright, daisy-yellow sunshine spilling in through the high, arched windows, turning Matthew's hair to a halo of spun gold.

"I wasn't going to wake you," he said, "as we *were* up rather late last night." He leaned back in his chair. "Breakfast?"

The table was covered in a daunting spread of croissants, butter, marmalade, fruit jams and jellies, porridge, bacon and fried potatoes, crumpets, kippers, buttered eggs, and tea. "What army are we feeding?" she inquired, sliding into the chair opposite him.

He lifted his shoulders in a slight shrug. "I wasn't sure what you wanted to eat, so I got everything."

Cordelia felt her heart soften. She could tell Matthew was nervous, though he hid it well. She had been badly shaken last night. She remembered his arms around her as she stood under the gaslight on the Boulevard de Clichy, *fiacres* rumbling by like trains. She had told him he had been nothing but kind to her, and it was true.

As she poured out a cup of tea, Matthew said, "I thought today we could visit the Musée Grévin? It has wax sculptures, and a hall of mirrors that resembles the inside of a kaleidoscope—"

"Matthew," she said. "Tonight I would like to return to the Cabaret de l'Enfer."

"I didn't think—"

"That I enjoyed myself?" She fiddled with her spoon. "I suppose I didn't, exactly, but if—if that was truly my father—I want to know the truth. I would like to ask Madame Dorothea a question to which only my father would know the answer."

He shook his head, disarranging his blond curls. "I can't say no to you," he said, and Cordelia felt herself flush. "But—only as long as we can spend today just enjoying ourselves. And *not* thinking about ghosts, or dire warnings. Agreed?"

Cordelia agreed, and they spent the day sightseeing. Matthew insisted on taking the little Brownie camera he had bought, so in the Musée Grévin, Cordelia obligingly posed with wax versions of the pope, Napoléon, Victor Hugo, Marie Antoinette, and various figures in rooms set with scenes from the French Revolution, some of which were so lifelike it felt very strange to walk into the midst of them.

Matthew declared himself in need of fresh air, so they flagged down a *fiacre* to take them to the Bois de Boulogne. "Everything is better in Paris," he said as they rolled past the Opéra and slowly made their way down the Rue Saint-Lazare, "except, perhaps, the traffic."

Cordelia had to agree: as they passed the Arc de Triomphe and approached the Bois de Boulogne, what seemed like hundreds of carriages poured in a flood toward the entrance, mingled with cars tooting their horns, riders on horseback, groups of bicyclists, and crowds and crowds of people on foot. The *fiacre*, trapped in the throng, was buffeted slowly down an *allée* lined with trees, which ended at the edge of a lake, where a cheerfully rowdy group of young students were determinedly having a picnic despite the cold weather.

As they crawled gratefully out of the cab, Cordelia could not help but think about the picnic in Regent's Park that had been her early introduction to the Merry Thieves. She thought of Christopher eating lemon tarts, of Thomas's easy smile and Anna's laughter, of Lucie's inquisitiveness, of James—

But she would not think of James. She could not help a wistful glance at the picnicking students, though they seemed to her so very young—younger than herself and her friends, though they were likely in university. They did not know of the Shadow World, did not see it, did not imagine what lurked beyond the thin scrim of illusion separating them from a darker universe.

She envied them.

Eventually, she and Matthew found an unoccupied park bench and settled on it. Matthew tipped his face up to the pale winter light; in its glare, Cordelia could see how tired he looked. Matthew had the delicacy of extremely pale skin, to go with his fair hair; it showed every bruise and shadow, and right now the crescents below his eyes were dark, as if they had been painted on. Of course, he *had* been up half the night, Cordelia reminded herself with a pang of guilt, holding her hand as she drifted in and out of restless sleep.

"Matthew," she said.

"Hmmm?" he asked, not opening his eyes.

"I thought perhaps we should discuss," she said, "my brother and your brother."

Matthew did not open his eyes, but he went still. "Alastair and Charles? What about them?"

"Well," said Cordelia, "it cannot have escaped your notice—"

"It hasn't." She didn't think she'd heard Matthew's voice so cool before, certainly not when directed at her. She remembered the first time she'd really met him, how she'd wondered if he disliked her, how he'd charmed her anyway. *Fair hair, sideways looks, a blur of a smile.* "I am not an idiot. I have seen the way Charles looks at your brother, and the way your brother does not look at him. Love, unrequited." Now he did open his eyes. They were a very light green in the sunlight. "And to be fair, I doubt my brother did anything to deserve the kind of love he clearly felt himself."

"Really? You think Charles felt so much as all that for Alastair? He was the one who wanted it kept secret."

"Ah, because of his *career*, I'm sure." Matthew bit off the words. "I suppose it depends on your definition of love. Love that will give up nothing, love that one is willing to sacrifice for a more comfortable life, is not love, in my opinion. Love should come above all other things."

The intensity of his words startled Cordelia. She felt them as a sort of accusation: Should she have been willing to give up more, sacrifice more for James? For Lucie? For her family?

"Never mind," Matthew said, in a gentler tone. "I believe Alastair's affections no longer rest with Charles, so the whole business will fade away in time. I find I have a bit of a headache. We should talk about something else."

"I'll tell you a story, then," Cordelia said. "Maybe something from the *Shahnameh*? Would you like to hear about the defeat of Zahhāk, the evil Serpent King?"

Matthew's eyes lit up. "Absolutely," he said, settling back against the bench. "Spin me a tale, my dear."

* * *

James rose feeling still tired, as if he'd barely slept at all. He went to the washstand and splashed ice-cold water on his face, which woke him up promptly. He took a moment to look at himself in the mirror—tired eyes, drooping at the corners; wet black curls; a sharp downturn to the corner of his mouth he didn't recall having before.

No wonder Cordelia doesn't want you.

He told himself, savagely, to stop it, and went to get dressed. As he was buttoning his cuffs, he heard a rustle in the hall outside his room, as if a curious mouse was in the corridor. He reached the door in two strides and threw it open. With no surprise whatsoever, he found Lucie—in a lace-trimmed blue dress, looking unseasonably summery—standing right behind it, glaring at him.

"If it isn't Secret Princess Lucie," he said mildly. "Come to visit her terrible family."

Lucie put her hand on his chest and walked him back into the bedroom. She kicked the door shut behind her. "We need to talk, before we go downstairs."

"Be careful," said James. "You sound just like Mother used to before she gave us a scolding about something or other."

Lucie dropped her hand with a little shriek. "I do *not*," she said. "Though, speaking of parents, do you remember when we bought that enormous guinea pig? And then when Mama and Papa found out, we told them it was a special gift from the Lima Institute?"

"Ah yes, Spots," said James. "I remember him well. He bit me."

"He bit everyone," said Lucie dismissively. "I'm sure he intended it as a compliment. My point is, that story worked because you and I had the *same* story and were working from the *same* information."

"So true," said James. He was pleased to realize that as low as he felt, he could still wind his sister up. "Halcyon memories of a golden past."

"*And*," went on Lucie impatiently, "I have no idea how much you've said to Father—about anything—even though you know everything I've told, and anyway, it isn't fair. Or a good idea."

"Well, I told them—Magnus, too—most everything, I think." James sat down on the bed. "Everything I knew, anyway. Whatever gaps

I might have left in their knowledge, I expect they've been filled in by the events of last night."

"*Everything?*" Lucie demanded.

"Nothing about Cordelia," James allowed. "Nothing about Lilith, or paladins, or—any of that."

"Good." Lucie relaxed a fraction. "I don't think we can tell them, can we? It's Cordelia's secret. It wouldn't be fair to her."

"Agreed," said James. "Look, Luce—why did you never tell me about Jesse? I don't mean about trying to raise him," he said quickly, as Lucie began to protest. "I understand not telling me about that. You knew I wouldn't like it, and you knew I wouldn't like that you were working with Grace."

"You wouldn't," Lucie said.

"I still don't," James admitted, "but I understand why you felt like you had to do it. But why did you never tell me you could see Jesse, or that he existed at all?"

Lucie, with an uncharacteristic shyness, kicked at a dust ball with the toe of her shoe. "I suppose . . . I knew there was something strange about being able to see him. Something dark and uncanny. Something people wouldn't like."

"Luce, I know better than anyone else what it means to have a power other people find unsettling. Even grotesque."

She looked up quickly. "You're not *grotesque*, Jamie, or horrible, or anything like that—"

"Our powers come from the same place," James said. "Belial. Who would understand better than I would, how one struggles with that? I have to believe I can do good even with a power that comes from darkness. I believe that for myself, and I believe it for you, too."

Lucie blinked quickly, then sat down beside James on the bed. They remained there for a moment in comfortable silence, their shoulders touching. "James," she said at last. "Jesse is going to need you. There are things you can help him with that—that I can't. Being possessed by Belial, having the Marks of dead Shadowhunters on his skin. It's hurting him. I can see it in his eyes."

So can I, James thought. "I can talk to him. When we get back to London."

Lucie smiled. It was a quiet sort of grown-up smile, a bit sad, a smile James did not associate with his little sister. But she had changed, he supposed. They all had. "Papa told me," she said. "About Cordelia. And Matthew. That they went to Paris together. He seemed to think you didn't mind, but I—" She turned to look at him. "*Do* you mind?"

"Desperately," James said. "More than I ever thought I would mind about anything."

"So you don't love Grace?"

"*No.* No," James said. "I don't think I ever did. I—" For a moment, he stood on the precipice, wanting to tell his sister the truth. *It was a spell, I never cared for her, those feelings were forced upon me.* But it would not do to tell Lucie before he had told Cordelia. Cordelia had to know first. "Do you think Cordelia loves him? Matthew, I mean. If she does . . ."

"I know," Lucie said. "If she does, you'll go away quietly and leave them to their happiness. Believe me, I am well acquainted with the self-sacrificing nature of Herondale men. *But*—if she feels anything for Matthew, she's never given a sign of it to me, or said anything about it. Still . . ."

James tried to look politely inquiring.

"Still," Lucie said. "Paris is a romantic place. I'd get myself over there and tell Cordelia what you really feel, posthaste." To make her point, she punched him in the shoulder. "*Don't* dawdle."

"You hit me," James said. "*Must* you hit me for emphasis?"

There was a knock, and Magnus leaned in through the open doorway. "I hate to interrupt this moment of beautiful sibling amity," he said, "but Malcolm would like to speak with all of us downstairs."

Malcolm was sitting on a chair by the fireplace when Lucie and James came downstairs. He had an enormous book on his lap, bound in black leather with hammered metal reinforcements along the corners. He was still wearing the same clothes he'd been wearing the night before.

Magnus and Jesse were on the sofa, while Will paced slowly back and forth behind them, his brow crinkled in thought. Jesse gave Lucie a tight smile; she knew he meant to be reassuring, but his own worry showed through clearly. She wished she could cross the room and hug him but knew it would only scandalize her brother, her father, and the two warlocks in attendance. She would have to wait.

When they were all settled, Malcolm cleared his throat. "I have spent the night looking into the question posed last night, and I believe I have an answer. I believe that Jesse should return to London, and that he should do so as a Blackthorn."

Will made a surprised noise.

"He is unmistakably a Blackthorn in his appearance," Malcolm added, "and I don't think he will be able to pretend to be anything else. He looks as much like his father as if he were an artist's copy."

"Indeed," said Will impatiently, "but we've already discussed that it will be a problem for him to reappear as himself. Not only does it bring up issues of necromancy, but the last anyone in the Clave heard of him, he was a dead body possessed by a demon in order to murder Shadowhunters."

Jesse looked down at his hands. At the Voyance rune that had once belonged to Elias Carstairs. He moved his left hand away, as if he could hardly bear to look at it.

"Yes, we've been through all that," said Malcolm tightly. "I am not suggesting he present himself as *Jesse* Blackthorn. How many people saw him, actually saw him as he is now, after he was possessed?"

There was a short silence. James said, "Lucie, of course. I did. Matthew, Cordelia—the Silent Brothers who prepared his body—"

"Most of the Enclave heard the story of what had happened," said Malcolm. "But they did not *see Jesse*."

"No," Will said. "They didn't."

"You must understand, I have ties to the Blackthorn family that none of you share," said Malcolm. "I was their ward—the ward of Felix and Adelaide Blackthorn—a hundred years ago."

"They raised you?" said James.

Malcolm's mouth set in a hard line. "I wouldn't call it that. To them, I was their property, and for the privilege of being fed and clothed and housed by them, I was obliged to perform magic at their command."

Will said, "Some Shadowhunters have always been bastards. My family has good cause to know it."

Malcolm waved this off. "I don't hold the Nephilim at large responsible for the actions of the Blackthorns. They are the only ones who should ever have to answer for those actions. For the purposes of *this* discussion, what is important is only that Felix and Adelaide had four children: Annabel, Abner, Jerome, and Ezekiel."

"Terrible names they had in olden times," Lucie murmured, "simply terrible."

"The children had . . . different attitudes from their parents," Malcolm went on, "regarding the treatment of Downworlders. Ezekiel, especially, found their bigotry and cruelty as unpleasant as I did. When he reached the age of majority, he renounced the family and struck off on his own. You will find in the Silent City no record of Ezekiel leaving any children after him, but I know that not to be the case."

Jesse looked up.

"I happen to know," said Malcolm, "that Ezekiel *did* have children. That he went to America, then a very new nation where Shadowhunters were few and far between, and married a mundane woman. They raised their children as mundanes, but of course, Nephilim blood breeds true, and his descendants are Shadowhunters just as much as any of you.

"I propose, then, that Jesse present himself as one of Ezekiel's grandchildren, come to rejoin the Nephilim and seek out his cousins. That when he learned the truth of his heritage, he wished to be a Shadowhunter and presented himself to Will at the Institute. After all, Will has a not dissimilar history."

It was true enough, Lucie thought; her father had thought himself a mundane until he learned the truth, whereupon he had walked all the way from Wales to London to join the Enclave. He had only been twelve years old. "An excellent plan," she said, though Will and Magnus still looked dubious. "We shall call Jesse Hezekiah Blackthorn."

"We shall not," said Jesse.

"What about Cornelius?" said James. "I've always fancied Cornelius."

"Definitely not," said Jesse.

"It should be something with a J," Will said, his arms folded. "Something it will be easy for Jesse to remember, and to respond to. Like Jeremy."

"Then you agree with Malcolm?" Magnus said. "This will be the scheme? Jesse is to be Jeremy?"

"Have you a better plan?" Will looked tired. "Other than letting Jesse fend for himself in the world? At the Institute, we can protect him. And he *is* a Shadowhunter. He is one of our own."

Magnus nodded thoughtfully. James said, "Can we at least tell the Lightwoods the truth? Gabriel and Gideon, Sophie and Cecily? They are Jesse's family, after all, and he doesn't even know them."

"And my sister," Jesse said. "Grace must know the truth."

Lucie saw James's face tighten.

"Of course," said Will. "Only Jesse . . . I don't know if you've been told, but . . ."

"Grace is in the Silent City," said James, in a stony voice. "In the custody of the Silent Brothers."

"After the discovery of what your mother did to you, she took herself there," Will said swiftly. "The Silent Brothers are making sure that no similar dark magic was worked upon her."

Jesse looked stunned. "In the Silent City? She must be terrified." He turned toward Will. "I have to see her." Lucie could tell he was expending effort to seem calmer than he was. "I know that Silent Brothers are our fellow Shadowhunters—but you must understand, our mother raised us to think of them as fiends."

"I'm sure a visit can be arranged," said Will. "And as for thinking of the Silent Brothers as fiends—if a Silent Brother had done your protection spells, and not Emmanuel Gast, you would not have been harmed as you were."

"His protection spells!" Lucie sat up straight. "They must be done again. Until they are, he will be vulnerable to demonic possession."

"I will arrange for it with Jem," said Will, and Lucie saw an odd look flash across James's face. "We cannot carry out this deception without the cooperation of the Brothers; I will make it known to them."

"Malcolm, is there anyone else besides you who has access to this information about the American branch of the Blackthorns?" said Magnus. "If anyone were to suspect—"

"We should organize this plan," said James. "Sit down and think of every objection, every question anyone might have about Jesse's story, and come up with answers. This must be a complete deception, with no weak spots."

There was a chorus of agreement; only Jesse did not join it. After a moment, when it was quiet again, he said, "Thank you. Thank you for doing this for me."

Magnus mimed raising a glass in his direction. "Jeremy Blackthorn," he said. "Welcome, in advance, to the London Enclave."

That night Cordelia put on her red velvet dress and her fur-trimmed cloak, along with a pair of elbow-length silk gloves, and joined Matthew in a *fiacre* bound for Montmartre. Paris slid by outside the windows as they rode, passing up the Rue de la Paix, lights glimmering from the rows of shopwindows, squares of illumination in the darkness.

Matthew had matched his waistcoat and spats to Cordelia's dress—scarlet velvet, which flashed like rubies as they passed beneath the light of intermittent gas lamps. His gloves were black, his eyes very dark as he watched her. "There are other clubs we could investigate," he said as the carriage rattled past the church of Sainte-Trinité with its great rose window. "There is the Rat Mort—"

Cordelia made an amused face. "The Dead Rat?"

"Oh, indeed. Named after and featuring the mummified body of a rodent put to death for annoying the customers." He grinned. "A popular place to eat lobster at four in the morning."

"We can certainly go—*after* L'Enfer." She raised her chin. "I am quite determined, Matthew."

"I understand." His voice was level. "We all have those we wish to reach, by any means possible. Some are separated from us by death, some by their refusal to listen, or our inability to speak."

Impulsively, she took his hand, threading her fingers through his. His black gloves were striking against her scarlet ones. Black and red as the pieces on a chessboard. She said, "Matthew. When we return to London—for someday, we will—you *must* talk to your parents. They will forgive you. They are your family."

His eyes seemed more black than green. He said, "Do you forgive your father?"

The question hurt. "He never asked for my forgiveness," she said. "Perhaps, if he had—and perhaps that is what I want to hear, why I wish I could speak to him one more time. For I wish I could forgive him. It is a heavy weight to bear, bitterness."

His hand tightened on hers. "And I wish I could take the weight for you."

"You carry enough already." The carriage began to slow, rolling to a stop before the cabaret. Light spilled from the open doors of the demon's mouth. Cordelia squeezed Matthew's hand and drew her own back. They were here.

The same bearded, heavy-shouldered guard stood beside the cabaret door as Cordelia approached; Matthew was a few steps behind her, having paused to pay the driver. As she drew near the entrance, Cordelia saw the guard shake his head.

"No entrance for you," he said, in heavily accented English. *"Paladin."*

6
Through Blood

Whose hearts must I break? What lie must I maintain?
Through whose blood am I to wade?
—Arthur Rimbaud, "A Season in Hell"

Cordelia's blood turned to ice. *But no one knows,* she thought. *No one knows.* It was a secret, that she was bound to Lilith. She and Matthew had spoken of Cortana here, last night, but they had not mentioned the Mother of Demons, nor the word "paladin." She said, "You must be mistaken. I—"

"Non. Je sais ce que je sais. Vous n'avez pas le droit d'entrer," the guard snapped. *I know what I know. You cannot come inside.*

"What's going on?" Matthew asked in French, approaching the door. "You are refusing us entrance?"

The guard retorted; they raced ahead so quickly in French that Cordelia had trouble keeping up. The guard was still refusing; Matthew was telling him there had been a mistake, a misidentification. Cordelia was a Shadowhunter in good standing. The guard shook his head stubbornly. *I know what I know,* was all he would say.

Cordelia pressed her palms together, trying to still the trembling in her hands. "I wish only to speak to Madame Dorothea," she said, her voice cutting through the men's argument. "Perhaps you could bring a message to her—"

"She is not here tonight." A young man entering the club indicated the program affixed to the door; indeed, Madame Dorothea's name was not on it. Instead, a snake charmer was advertised as the amusement for the evening. "I am sorry to disappoint such a beautiful *mademoiselle.*"

He tipped his hat before entering the club, and Cordelia saw the moonlight gleam gold off his eyes. *Werewolf.*

"Look here," Matthew said, about to start in on the guard again—he was waving his walking stick about, in a dramatic manner he probably enjoyed at least a little bit—but Cordelia put her hand on his arm.

"There is no point," she said. "Not if she is not here. Matthew, let's go."

Paladin. The word echoed in Cordelia's ears, long after Matthew and she had climbed into a *fiacre.* Even as they rattled quickly away from Montmartre, she still felt as if she were standing in front of the cabaret, hearing the guard refuse her entrance. *I know what I know. You cannot come inside.*

Because you are corrupted within, said a small voice inside her. *Because you belong to Lilith, Mother of Demons. Because of your own foolishness, you are cursed. No one should be around you.*

She thought of Alastair. *We become what we are afraid we will be, Layla.*

"Cordelia?" Matthew's worried voice seemed to come from far away. "Cordelia, please. Talk to me."

She tried to look up, to look at him, but the darkness seemed to swirl around her, visions of accusing faces and disappointed voices echoing in her head. It was as if she had been flung back to that night in London, that night her heart had broken into a thousand pieces, driving her out into the night and the snow. The terrible feeling of loss, of crushing disappointment in herself, rose like a wave. She raised her hands as if she could ward it off. "The carriage—stop the carriage," she heard herself say. "I can hardly breathe. Matthew—"

The window opened, letting in cold air. She heard Matthew rap on the driver's window, bark out instructions in French. The horses came to a hasty stop, setting the *fiacre* to swaying. Cordelia threw the door open and almost leaped out, nearly tripping over the heavy hem of her gown. She heard Matthew scramble down after her, hastily paying the driver. *"Ne vous inquiétez pas. Tout va bien." It's all right, everything is fine.* He hurried to catch up with her as she took a few steps before fetching up blindly against a lamppost.

"Cordelia." He laid his hand on her back as she struggled to catch her breath. His touch was light. "It's all right. You've done nothing wrong, darling—"

He broke off, as if he hadn't meant the endearment to come out of his mouth. Cordelia was past caring. She said, "I have. I chose to become her paladin. They'll all find out—if that guard knows, everyone will know soon enough—"

"Not at all." Matthew spoke firmly. "Even if there is a rumor in Downworld, that doesn't mean it will spread to Shadowhunters. You've seen how little interest Nephilim take in Downworlder gossip. Cordelia, *breathe.*"

Cordelia took a deep breath. Then another, forcing the air into her lungs. The spots that had dotted her vision began to fade. "I can't keep it from them for all time, Matthew. It's lovely to be here with you, but we can't stay forever—"

"We can't," he said, sounding suddenly weary, "and just because I don't want to think about the future doesn't mean I don't know there *is* a future. It will come to us soon enough. Why run to embrace it?"

She gave a dry little laugh. "Is it so terrible? Our future?"

"No," he said, "but it isn't Paris, with you. Here, come with me."

He held out his hand and she took it. He led her to the center of the Pont Alexandre—it was past midnight, and the bridge was deserted. On the left bank of the Seine, she could see Les Invalides, with its gold dome, rising against the night sky. On the right bank, the Grand and Petit Palais glowed richly with electric light. Moonlight poured over the city like milk, making the bridge shimmer, a bar of white gold laid across the river. Gilt-bronze statues of winged horses, supported on tall stone pillars, watched over those who crossed. Below the span of the bridge, the river water sparkled like a carpet of diamonds, touched by starlight along its wind-whipped currents.

She and Matthew stood, hand in hand, watching the river flow beneath the bridge. The Seine rolled on from here, she knew, piercing the heart of Paris like a silver arrow just as the Thames did London. "We are not here just to forget," Matthew said, "but also to remember that there are good and beautiful things in this world, always. And mistakes do not take them from us; nothing takes them from us. They are eternal."

She squeezed his gloved hand with her own. "Matthew. Do you listen to yourself? If you believe what you say, remember that it is true for you, too. Nothing can take the good things of the world from you. And that includes how much your friends and family love you, and always will."

He looked down at her. They stood close; Cordelia knew any passersby would assume they were lovers, seeking a romantic spot to embrace. She didn't care. She could see the pain in Matthew's face, in his dark green eyes. He said, "Do you think James—"

He broke off. Neither of them had mentioned James's name since they had come to Paris. Quickly, he went on, "Would you care to walk back to the hotel? I think the air would clear our heads."

A set of stone steps led from the bridge down to the *quai*, the riverfront walkway that followed the Seine. During the day, Parisians fished off the edges; now, boats were tied up along the side, bobbing gently in the current. Mice darted back and forth across the pavement, looking for scraps; Cordelia wished she had some bread to scatter for them. She said as much to Matthew, who opined that French mice were probably terrible snobs who only ate French cheeses.

Cordelia smiled. Matthew's jokes, the views of Paris, her own good sense—she wished any of it could lighten the weight on her heart. She could not stop imagining what it would be like when her mother found out the truth about her compact with Lilith. When the Enclave found out. When Will and Tessa found out. She knew they were not destined to be her in-laws for much longer, but she found that she cared terribly what they thought of her.

And Lucie. Lucie would be the most affected. They had always planned to be *parabatai*; she was abandoning Lucie now, without a warrior partner, a sister in battle. She could not help but feel it would be better if Lucie had never known her—what a different life she might have had, a different *parabatai*, different chances.

"Daisy." Matthew spoke in a low voice, his hand tightening on hers. "I know you are lost in thought. But—*listen*."

There was urgency in his voice. Cordelia closed off thoughts of Lilith, of the Herondales, of the Enclave. She turned to look behind them, down the long tunnel of the *quai*—the river on one side, the stone retaining wall rising on the other, the city above them as if they had retreated underground.

Shhhh. Not the wind in the bare boughs, but a hiss and a slither. A bitter smell, carried on the wind.

Demons.

Matthew stepped back, placing himself in front of her. There was the sound of a weapon being drawn, the spark of moonlight on metal. It seemed Matthew's walking stick had a blade cleverly hidden within the hollowed-out wood. He kicked the empty stick aside just as the creatures emerged from the shadows, sliding and slithering over the pavement.

"Naga demons," Cordelia whispered. They were long and low, bodies whiplike, covered in black, oily scales, like giant water snakes. But when they opened their mouths to hiss, she could see that their heads were more like a crocodile's, mouths long and triangular and lined with jagged teeth that glowed yellow in the streetlight.

A gray tide surged past her, a skitter of tiny, racing feet. The mice she had seen earlier, fleeing as the Naga demons advanced on the Shadowhunters.

Matthew shrugged off his overcoat, let it drop to the pavement, and lunged. Cordelia stood frozen, watching, as he sliced the head off one demon, then another—her hands curled into fists. She *hated* this. It ran counter to everything in her nature to hang back while a fight was going on. But if she were to pick up a weapon, she would be vulnerable to Lilith—to Lilith working her will through Cordelia.

Matthew plunged his blade down—and missed. A Naga demon lunged, closing its sharp-toothed jaw around his ankle. Matthew yelled, "My *spats*!" and stabbed downward. Ichor splashed up and over him; he spun, his blade whirling. A demon hit the pavement with a wet smack, bleeding, its tail lashing. With a yell of pain, Matthew staggered back; his cheek was bleeding from a long cut.

Everything about this was wrong. Cordelia should be there, at Matthew's side, Cortana in her hand, scrawling its blood-and-gold signature across the sky. Without being able to stop herself, she tore off her cloak, seized up the walking stick Matthew had dropped, and leaped into the fray.

She heard Matthew call out to her, even as he backed up—there must have been ten Naga demons left. He couldn't possibly kill them all, she thought, even as he shouted at her to get back, to protect herself. *From Lilith,* she thought, but what use would protecting herself be if she let something happen to Matthew?

She slammed the runed cane hard into a Naga demon's head, heard its skull shatter, the crumpling as its body vanished, sucked back to its home dimension. Matthew, giving up on stopping Cordelia, cut a wide arc with his blade, slicing a Naga demon neatly in two. Cordelia stabbed down with the cane, punching a hole through another demon's body. It, too, vanished, a tide of ichor spilling across the ground. Cordelia struck out again—and hesitated. The Naga demons had begun skittering backward, away from the two Shadowhunters.

"We did it," Matthew panted, touching a hand to his bloody cheek. "Got rid of those bastards—"

He froze. Not because of surprise, or even watchfulness. He simply froze, blade in hand, as if he had been turned to stone. Cordelia looked up, her heart beating wildly, as at her feet the Naga demons bent their heads, their chins scraping the ground.

"*Mother,*" they hissed. "*Mother.*"

Cordelia's heart turned over in her chest. Walking toward her along the quai, dressed in a gown of black silk, was Lilith.

Her hair was loose and unbound, the wind catching it, unfurling it like a banner. Her eyes were flat black marbles, with no white visible. She was smiling. Her skin was very white, her neck rising like an ivory column from the collar of her gown. Once she had been beautiful enough to seduce demons and angels. She looked as youthful as ever, though Cordelia could not help but wonder if she had changed through the ages, with bitterness and loss. Her mouth was hard, even as she looked at Cordelia with a deadly pleasure.

"I knew you could not stop yourself, little warrior," she said. "It is in your blood, the need to fight."

Cordelia flung the stick she'd been holding. It bounced across the pavement, fetching up at Lilith's feet. The wood of it was stained with ichor. "I was protecting my friend."

"The pretty Fairchild boy. Yes." Lilith flicked a glance at him, then snapped her fingers; the Naga demons slithered away, back into the shadows. Cordelia wasn't sure whether to be relieved. She was far more afraid of Lilith than of the demons in her command. "You have many *friends*. It makes you simple to manipulate." She cocked her head to the side. "But to see you, my paladin, fighting with this—this bit of wood." She kicked contemptuously at the walking stick. "Where is Cortana?"

Cordelia smiled. "I don't know."

She didn't. She had given Cortana to Alastair and told him to hide it. She trusted that he had. She was glad not to know more.

"I made sure I wouldn't know," she added, "so that I couldn't tell you. No matter what you do to me."

"How brave," Lilith said, with some amusement. "That is, after all, why I chose you. That brave little heart that beats inside your chest." She took a step forward; Cordelia held her ground. Any fear she felt was for Matthew. Would Lilith harm him, just to show Cordelia her power?

She vowed to herself that if Lilith did, she, Cordelia, would dedicate her life to finding some way to hurt Lilith back.

Lilith looked from Matthew to Cordelia, and her smile widened. "I will not hurt him," she said. "Not yet. He does well in that area himself, don't you think? You are loyal, faithful to your friends; but sometimes I think you are too clever."

"There is nothing clever," said Cordelia, "in my doing what *you* want. You wish to have the sword so you can slay Belial—"

"Which you also desire," Lilith pointed out. "You will be glad to know those two wounds you dealt him pain him still. He is in agony without respite."

"We may desire the same thing," Cordelia conceded. "But that does not make it *clever* to give you what you want—a paladin, a powerful weapon. You are not *better* than Belial. You simply also hate him. And if I accepted you, became your true paladin, that would be the end of me. The end of my life, or any part of it that is worth living."

"And otherwise a long and happy life will be yours?" Lilith's hair rustled. Perhaps the serpents she liked so much, slithering among the dark mass of her locks. "You think danger is behind you? The greatest danger lies ahead. Belial has not stopped his planning. I, too, have heard the whispers on the wind. '*They wake.*'"

Cordelia started. "What—?" she began, but Lilith only laughed, and vanished. The quai was empty again, only the stains of ichor, and her and Matthew's fallen coats and weapons, to show anything had occurred.

Matthew. She whirled, and saw him on his knees. She darted to his side, but he was already rising, his face white, the cut on his cheek standing out stark and red. "I heard her," he said. "I couldn't move, but I could see—I heard all of it. '*They wake.*'" He stared down at her. "Are you all right? Cordelia—"

"I'm so sorry." She fumbled off her gloves, reached for her stele. She was already starting to shiver, with reaction and with cold. "Let me—you need an *iratze*." She pushed up the cuff of his shirt, began to scrawl the healing rune with the tip of her stele. "I'm so sorry you're hurt. I'm so—"

"Do not say you are sorry again," Matthew said in a low voice. "Or I will begin shouting. *This is not your fault.*"

"I let myself be fooled," she said. The inside of Matthew's forearm was pale, blue-veined, marked with white, lacelike patterns where old runes had faded. "I wanted to believe that Wayland the Smith had chosen me. I was a fool—"

"Cordelia." He caught hold of her with such force that her stele clattered to the ground. The cut along his cheek was already healing, his bruises fading. "I am the one who believed a faerie who told me that what I was purchasing was a harmless truth potion. I am the one who nearly murdered my own—" He inhaled, as if the words hurt to speak. "Do you think I don't understand what it is to have made a wrong decision, believing you were making the right one? Do you think anyone could imagine what that is like better than I could?"

"I should cut my own hands off so that I can never pick up a weapon again," she whispered. "What have I done?"

"Don't." The agony in his voice made her look up. "Don't talk about hurting yourself. What wounds you wounds me. I love you, Daisy, I—"

He cut himself off abruptly. Cordelia felt as if she were floating in a dream. She knew she had dropped her cloak, that cold air was cutting through the fabric of her dress. She knew she was in a sort of shock, that despite all she knew, she had not truly expected Lilith to appear. She knew despair was there, reaching out long, dark fingers for her like a siren, desperate to draw her under, to drown her in misery, in the whisper of voices that said, *You have lost James. Your family. Your name. Your* parabatai. *The world will turn its back on you, Cordelia.*

"Cordelia," Matthew said. "I'm sorry."

She put her hands flat against his chest. Took a deep breath, air stuttering in her chest. She said, "Matthew. Hold me."

Without a word, he pulled her close. The future was cold and dark, but Matthew was warm against her, a shield against shadow. He smelled of night air, of sweat and cologne and blood. *You are all I have. Hold the darkness back. Hold the memories back. Hold me.*

"Matthew," she said. "Why have you not tried to kiss me, since we came to Paris?"

His hands, which had been stroking her back, stilled. He said, "You told me you considered me only a friend. You remain a married woman, at that. I may be a drunk and a wastrel, but I do have my limits."

"Surely we are already a deplorable scandal in London."

"I don't care about scandal," Matthew said, "as should be obvious from every single thing I do. But I have my limits for . . . myself." His voice shook. "Do you think I have not wanted to kiss you? I have wanted to kiss you every moment of every day. I have held myself back. I always will, unless . . ." There was a hunger in his voice. A desperation. "Unless you tell me I need no longer do so."

She let her fingers fold themselves into the fabric of his shirt. Pulled him closer. Said, "I would like you to kiss me."

"Daisy, don't joke—"

She raised herself up on her toes. Brushed her lips across his. For a moment, memory flashed against the darkness in her mind: the Whispering Room, the fire, James kissing her, the first kiss of her life, kindling an unimaginable blaze. *No,* she told herself. *Forget. Forget.*

"Please," she said.

"Daisy," Matthew whispered, in a strangled voice, before control seemed to desert him. With a groan, he gathered her up against him, ducking his head to cover her mouth with his own.

When Brother Zachariah came to tell her that she had a visitor, Grace felt her heart begin to race. She could not think of anyone who might visit her who would bring good news. It could not be Jesse; if it were public knowledge that Lucie had brought him back, if he were in London, surely Zachariah would have told her so? And if it were Lucie . . . Well, James would have told Lucie the truth of the bracelet by now. Lucie would have no reason to see her save to berate and blame her. No one would.

Then again . . . she had lost track of how many days she had been in the City of Bones. She thought it had been about a week, but the lack of sunlight, and the irregularity of the Brothers' demands on her time, made it hard to know. She slept when she grew tired, and when she was hungry, someone would bring her something to eat. It was a comfortable prison, but a prison nonetheless. A prison where no human voice broke the silence; sometimes Grace wanted to scream, just to hear *someone*.

By the time she saw the shadow coming down the corridor toward her cell, she was resigned: it would likely be an unpleasant encounter, but it would be a break in the numbing tedium. She sat up on her narrow bed, patting down her hair. Steeling herself for . . .

"Christopher?"

"Hullo, Grace," Christopher Lightwood said. He wore his habitual ink- and acid-stained clothes, and his light brown hair was windblown. "I heard you were here. I thought I ought to see how you've been."

Grace swallowed. Didn't he *know*? Hadn't James told him what she'd done? But he was looking at her with his customary mild curiosity. There was no anger on his face.

"How long," Grace said, in almost a whisper, "have I been here?"

Christopher, to her surprise, flushed. "A week, or thereabouts," he said. "I would have come earlier, only Jem said I ought to give you some time to adjust."

He was standing just in front of the barred door. Grace realized with a shock that he thought she was *accusing* him of some sort of neglect, for not having come earlier. "Oh," she said, "no, I didn't mean—I'm glad you're here, Christopher."

He smiled, that kind smile that lit up his unusually colored eyes. Christopher was not handsome in an ordinary way, and Grace knew perfectly well that there were plenty of people, her mother included, who would have thought him not attractive at all. But Grace had known handsome men in abundance, and she knew outward beauty did not ensure kindness, or cleverness, or any kind of a good heart.

"I am too," he said. "I'd been wanting to see how you were. I thought it was awfully brave of you to give yourself up to the Silent Brothers and let them study you. To see if your mother—had done anything awful to you."

He really doesn't know. And Grace knew, in that moment, that she was not going to tell him. Not now. She knew it was dishonesty, that it ran counter to her promise to herself to be more truthful. But hadn't Zachariah said they were planning to keep the information about her power a secret? Wasn't she doing what the Silent Brothers would have wanted?

Christopher shifted his feet. "All right," he said. "I *did* come because I wanted to see if you were well. But not *only* because of that."

"Oh?"

"Yes," said Christopher. Abruptly he dug his hand into his trouser pocket and withdrew a sheaf of pages, carefully folded into quarters. "You see, I've been working on this new project—a kind of amalgam of science and Shadowhunter magic. It's meant for sending messages at a distance, you see, and I've made progress, but now there have been some snags, and I'm rather at an impasse, and—oh dear, my metaphors are getting all muddled now."

Grace's anxiety had quickly faded as soon as she saw the pages, covered in Christopher's unreadable scrawl. Now she found she was smiling a bit, even.

"And you've got a scientific mind," Christopher went on, "and so few Shadowhunters *do*, you know, and Henry's been too busy to help, and I think my other friends are weary of their things catching on fire. So I was wondering if you would read these over? And give me the honor of your opinion on where I might be going wrong?"

Grace felt a smile spread over her face. Probably the first time she'd really smiled since—well, since the last time she'd seen Christopher. "Christopher Lightwood," she said, "there is absolutely nothing I would like to do more."

As they touched, everything fell away for Cordelia—worries, fears, frustrations, despair. Matthew's mouth was hot against hers; he staggered back against a lamppost. He kissed her feverishly, over and over, lacing his fingers into her hair. Each kiss hotter, harder than the last. He tasted sugar-sweet, like candy.

She let her hands run over him, over his lean body, the arms she had admired before, the planes of his chest through his shirt, his skin burning feverishly at her touch. She sank her fingers into his thick hair, rougher than James's, cupped his face in her palms.

He had discarded his gloves and was touching her, too, hands against the thick velvet of her dress, a finger tracing her collarbone, the neckline of her dress. She moaned softly and felt his whole body shudder. He buried his face in the side of her neck. His pulse was racing like wildfire.

"We have to get back to the hotel, Daisy," he whispered, kissing her throat. "We have to get back, my God, before I disgrace myself and you in front of all Paris."

Cordelia barely remembered the trip. They retrieved their coats, left Matthew's weapon, and made their way back in a sort of dream state. They paused several times to kiss in shadowed doorways. Matthew held her so hard it hurt, his hands in her hair, winding the strands around his fingers.

It *was* like a dream, she thought, as they passed the clerk at the hotel's front desk. He seemed to be trying to flag them down, but they ducked into one of the gilt-and-crystal lifts and let it carry them upward. Cordelia could not stop an almost hysterical giggle as Matthew pressed her back against the mirrored wall, kissing her neck. Fingers in his hair, she looked at herself in the glass opposite. She looked flushed, almost drunk, the sleeve of her red gown torn. In the fight, perhaps, or by Matthew; she wasn't sure.

The room, when they came into it, was dark. Matthew kicked the door shut, tearing off his coat with shaking hands. He, too, was flushed, his spun-gold hair disarrayed by her fingers. She drew him toward her—they were still in the entryway, but the door was locked; they were alone. Matthew's eyes were their darkest green, nearly black, as he pushed the cloak from her shoulders. It fell in a soft, whispering heap at her feet.

Matthew's hands were skilled. Long fingers curled around the back of her neck; she raised her face to be kissed. *Let him not think James has*

never kissed me, she thought, and kissed him back, willing thoughts of James out of her head. She looped her arms around Matthew's neck; his body was slim and hard against hers, his mouth soft. She flicked her tongue across his lower lip, felt him shiver. His free hand drew down the sleeve of her dress, baring her shoulder. He kissed the uncovered skin, and Cordelia heard herself gasp.

Who was this, she thought, this bold girl kissing a boy in a Parisian hotel? It couldn't be her, Cordelia. It had to be someone else, someone carefree, someone brave, someone whose passions were not directed at a husband who did not love her back. Someone who was *wanted*, truly wanted; she could feel it in the way Matthew held her, the way he said her name, the way he trembled when he gathered her closer, as if he could not believe his good fortune.

"Matthew," she whispered. Her hands were under his jacket; she could feel the heat of him through the thin cotton of his shirt, feel the flutter in his stomach when she brushed it with her palm. "We can't—not here—your room—"

"It's a mess. We'll go to yours," he said, and kissed her hard, swinging her up in his arms. He carried her through the French doors into the living room, the only light a spill of illumination through the window. A mix of moon and streetlight, turning the shadows a dark gray. Matthew stumbled against a low table, swore, and laughed, setting Cordelia momentarily down.

"Does it hurt?" she whispered, holding tightly to his shirtfront.

"*Nothing* hurts," he assured her, pulling her close for a kiss so yearning, so hot with desire, that she felt it down to her toes.

It was such a relief to *feel*, to lose herself in sensation, to let the weight of memory drop from her shoulders. She reached to touch his face, a shadow in the darkness, just as the lights went on.

She blinked for a moment, her eyes adjusting to the new illumination. Someone had switched on the Tiffany lamp in the reading corner. Someone who was sitting in the plush velvet armchair beneath the lamp, someone in a black traveling suit, pale face a smudge of white between his shirt and his crow-black hair. Someone with eyes the color of lamplight and fire.

James.

7
Bitter Fruit

Am I mad, that I should cherish that which bears but bitter fruit?
I will pluck it from my bosom, tho' my heart be at the root.
—Alfred, Lord Tennyson, "Locksley Hall"

Thomas had never masterminded a secret mission before. Usually it was James who planned the secret missions (at least, the important ones; Matthew often planned secret missions that were entirely frivolous). It was a mixed experience, he decided as he and Alastair trotted down the steps outside the Institute doors. On the one hand, he felt guilty that he had misled his kind aunt Tessa as to the reason for their visit. On the other hand, it was satisfying to have a secret, especially a secret shared with Alastair.

Especially, Thomas thought, a secret that was not weighted with emotion, with longing and jealousy and family intrigues. Alastair seemed to feel that as well; while he was not exactly buoyant, he was quiet, without his usual snappishness. That snappishness, Thomas had always thought, came reflexively to Alastair, as though it were necessary to punctuate anything good with some bad temper, to maintain balance.

Alastair stopped at the bottom of the Institute steps and stuffed his hands in his pockets. "It's a good hiding place, Lightwood," he said, without the gruff tone that he normally used to disguise being in good spirits. "I would never have thought of it."

They were both bundled against the cold, Thomas in a tweed overcoat given to him years ago by Barbara, and Alastair in a fitted dark blue paletot that showed off the lines of his shoulders. Knotted around his neck was a dark green scarf. Due to the winter and the vanishing English sun, Alastair's skin was a few shades lighter than usual, which made his eyelashes look even darker. They framed his black eyes like the petals of a flower.

Petals of a flower? SHUT UP, THOMAS.

Thomas looked away. "So what happens if demons come looking for it now? You tell them you don't have it and they go away?"

Alastair chuckled. "I think they can sense where it is, sense its presence somehow. If they keep turning up at my house and don't sense it, they'll stop. That's my theory, anyway. Which is good," he added, "because the last thing my mother needs right now is demons frolicking in her herbaceous borders."

Thomas could also hear the genuine current of worry in Alastair's voice, under the easy dismissiveness. Sona Carstairs was pregnant, due to have her child very soon. It had been a difficult pregnancy, not helped by the death of Alastair's father only a few weeks past.

"If there's anything else I can do to help," Thomas said, "do please tell me. I like to be of use." *And at the moment, there's no one to be of use to besides Christopher, who considers me another lab implement.*

Alastair frowned at him. "That coat is huge on you," he said. "Your neck must be absolutely freezing."

To Thomas's surprise, Alastair drew off his own scarf and looped it around Thomas's neck. "Here," he said. "Borrow this. You can give it back to me next time I see you."

Thomas smiled without being able to help it. He knew this was Alastair's way of saying *thank you.* The scarf smelled of Alastair, of expensive triple-milled soap. Alastair, who was still holding the ends of the scarf, and looking Thomas directly in the eyes, his gaze unwavering.

A light flurry of snow drifted around them. It caught in Alastair's hair, his lashes. His eyes were so black that the pupils almost lost themselves in the soft darkness of the irises. He smiled a little, a smile that made desire beat through Thomas's blood like a pulse. He wanted to pull Alastair against him, right here in front of the Institute, and wind his hands into the clouds of Alastair's dark hair. He wanted to kiss Alastair's upturned mouth, wanted to explore the shape of it with his own, those little curls at the corners of Alastair's lips, like inverted commas.

But there was Charles. Thomas still had no idea what was going on between Alastair and Charles; hadn't Alastair been visiting Charles just this past day? He hesitated, and Alastair—sensitive as always to the slightest hint of rejection—dropped his hand, catching his lower lip between his teeth.

"Alastair," Thomas said, feeling hot and cold and vaguely sick all at once, "I have to know, if—"

A cracking noise split the air. Thomas and Alastair leaped apart, reaching for their weapons, just as a Portal began to open in the center of the courtyard—a massive one, much larger than the usual. Thomas glanced in Alastair's direction and noted that Alastair had dropped into a fighting stance, a short spear held out before him. Thomas knew they were both thinking the same thing: the last time something had appeared suddenly in the Institute courtyard, it had been a tentacled Prince of Hell.

But there was no sudden rush of seawater, no howl of demons. Instead Thomas heard the stamping hooves of horses, a shout of warning, and the Institute carriage came crashing through the Portal, barely remaining on all four of its wheels as it came. Balios and Xanthos looked very pleased with themselves as the carriage spun in midair and landed, with a jarring thud, at the foot of the steps. Magnus Bane was in the driver's seat, wearing a dramatic white opera scarf and holding the reins in his right hand. He looked even more pleased with himself than the horses.

"I *wondered* if it was possible to ride a carriage through a Portal," he said, jumping down from the seat. "As it turns out, it is. Delightful."

The carriage doors opened, and rather unsteadily, Will, Lucie, and a boy Thomas didn't know clambered out. Lucie waved at Thomas before leaning against the side of the carriage; she was faintly green about the gills.

Will went around the carriage to unstrap the luggage, while the unfamiliar boy—tall and slender, with straight black hair and a pretty face—put a hand on Lucie's shoulder. Which was surprising—it was an intimate gesture, one that would be considered impolite unless the boy and girl in question were close friends or relatives, or had an understanding between them. It seemed, however, unlikely that Lucie could have an understanding with someone Thomas had never seen before. He rather bristled at the thought, in an older-brother way—James didn't seem to be here, so someone had to do the bristling for him.

"I told you it would work!" Will cried in Magnus's direction. Magnus was busy magicking the unfastened baggage to the top of the steps, blue sparks darting like fireflies from his gloved fingertips. "We should have done that on the way out!"

"You did *not* say it would work," Magnus said. "You said, as I recall, 'By the Angel, he's going to kill us all.'"

"Never," said Will. "My faith in you is unshakable, Magnus. Which is good," he added, rocking back and forth a little, "because the rest of me feels quite shaken indeed." He turned to Thomas, looking as if he'd entirely expected to find him loitering about the Institute steps. "Hello, Thomas! Good to see you're here. Someone ought to run up and tell Tess we've arrived."

Thomas blinked. Will hadn't greeted Alastair, which Thomas thought was rather rude until he looked around and realized that Alastair was no longer there. He'd slipped away, sometime between the arrival of the carriage and now.

"I will," Thomas said, "but—where's James?"

Will exchanged a look with Magnus. For a moment, Thomas felt a spasm of real terror. He did not think, after Barbara, after everything that had happened, that he could bear it if James—

"He's all right," Lucie said quickly, as if reading the look on Thomas's face.

"He's gone to Paris," said the strange boy. He too was looking at Thomas sympathetically, which Thomas found a bit much. He didn't even know who this stranger *was*, much less desire his concern.

"Who are you?" he demanded shortly.

There was a moment's hesitation, shared by Magnus, Will, Lucie, and the stranger—a hesitation that seemed to close Thomas out. He felt his stomach knot, just as Will said, "Thomas. I see we owe you an explanation; I think we owe one to all those close to us. Come into the Institute. It's time we called a meeting."

Cordelia froze. She thought for a moment she was still in the dream, that James was a vision, a horror her mind was conjuring up. But no, he was here, impossibly, he was here in their suite, his face blank but hell burning behind his gold eyes. And Matthew had seen him too.

Matthew let go of Cordelia. They stepped away from each other, but Matthew didn't hurry; he wasn't trying to pretend something else had been happening. And indeed, what would have been the point? It was humiliating; Cordelia felt foolish, exposed, but surely James didn't *care*?

She put her hand out and took Matthew's, curling her fingers around his. He was ice-cold, but he said, cordially enough, "James. I didn't think to see you here."

"No," James said. His voice was even, his face expressionless, but he was white as chalk. His skin looked as if it had been stretched too tightly over his bones. "Clearly not. I had not thought—" He shook his head. "That I would be interrupting anything."

"Did you get my letter?" Matthew said. Cordelia looked at him sharply; it was the first she'd heard of a letter to James. "I explained—"

"I got it. Yes." James spoke slowly. His coat had been thrown over the chair behind him. He was in his shirt and trousers, one of his braces slipping off one shoulder. Part of Cordelia longed to step forward and fix it for him, to brush back the messy hair from his forehead. He was holding something—a green bottle, which he was turning over and over in his hands.

"Has something happened?" Cordelia asked. She thought suddenly, with a spasm of fear, of her mother. Of the baby due any day now. But surely she would have heard from Alastair if anything had happened? He knew where she was staying. "For you to journey all the way to Paris—"

"I would have come earlier," James said, his voice low. "I would have come the night you left, if it were not for Lucie."

"Lucie?" Cordelia's mouth went dry. "What could possibly—is she all right?"

James sat forward. "She left London, the same night you did," he said carefully, "because of Jesse Blackthorn. My father fetched me to help bring her home. She is quite all right," he added, holding up a hand, "and eager to see both of you. As I have been."

"Ran off because of Jesse Blackthorn?" Cordelia demanded. "Because of his death? Where did she go?"

James shook his head. "I cannot say. It is Lucie's story to tell."

"But I don't understand," Matthew said, a furrow appearing between his brows. "You said you would have come here the night we left, if not for Lucie—but we assumed—"

"That you would be with Grace." It hurt to say it; Cordelia breathed around the invisible spike in her heart.

James smiled. Cordelia had never seen him smile like that before: a smile that was all bitterness, all inward-turning loathing. "*Grace,*" he said. "I have no desire to spend even a moment with her. I despise her. I shall endeavor never to see her again. Cordelia, Effie told me what you saw—"

"Yes," Cordelia said. She felt as if she were some distance outside her body, looking down. Matthew, beside her, was taking short, shallow breaths. "You did not seem as if you hated Grace then, James. You took her in your arms. You said—"

"I know what I said."

"That was the night I left," Cordelia cried, "*the same night*. You cannot say you would have followed me here."

James's voice sounded scorched, bleak as Belial's land. "I came as soon as I could. For both of you. I thought, if I could explain—"

"James," Matthew said. His voice shook. "You didn't *want* her."

"I was a fool," James said. "I freely admit that. I was wrong about my own feelings. I was wrong about my marriage. I didn't think it was real. It *was* real. The most real thing in my life." He looked directly at Cordelia. "I wish to repair the broken things. To put them back together. I wish—"

"Does it not matter what *I* wish?" Cordelia tightened her grip on Matthew's hand. "Does it not matter, all the times we went to parties, to gatherings, and you stared at Grace instead of looking at me? That you kissed her while we were married? If I have hurt you by coming here, with Matthew, I am sorry. But I did not think you would care."

"That I would not care," James repeated, and looked down at the bottle in his hand. "I was here for hours, you know, before you came in. I thought I might try getting myself drunk on this stuff, thinking it would keep my courage up, but it does taste like the vilest poison. I could only manage a mouthful. How you can stand it, Math, I've no idea."

He set the half-empty bottle on the table next to him, and Cordelia, for the first time, saw the green label: ABSINTHE BLANQUI.

Matthew's hand, in Cordelia's, was like ice.

"That's not Matthew's," Cordelia said.

James looked surprised. "It was in his room—"

No, Cordelia thought, but James only looked puzzled.

"You went into my room?" Matthew demanded, and any thought Cordelia had had that this was a mistake, that the bottle wasn't his, vanished with his words.

"I was looking for you," James said. "I saw this, and the cherry brandy—I suppose I shouldn't have taken it, but it seems I'm not much good at Dutch courage. I . . ." He looked between Matthew, white as a sheet, and Cordelia. He frowned. "What is it?"

Cordelia thought of the way Matthew had tasted when she kissed him. Sweet, like candy. *Cherry brandy*. She let go of Matthew's hand, drew her own in front of her. Laced her shaking fingers together. She was a fool. A fool who had learned nothing from the life and death of her own father.

She could lambast Matthew now, she supposed. Shout at him in front of James for lying to her. But he looked so stunned and fragile, his eyes fixed on some point in the distance, a muscle in his jaw working.

"I should not have come," said James. He was looking at both of them, at Matthew and Cordelia, rage and love and hope and despair all in his eyes, and Cordelia wished she could comfort him, and hated that she wished it. "Cordelia, tell me what you want. If it's Matthew, I'll go—I'll take myself out of your life. I never intended to hurt either of you—"

"You *knew*," Matthew whispered. "I told you in the letter that I loved Cordelia. And yet you come here like this dark angel, Jamie, telling Cordelia you *do* want her—"

"You said what you felt," James said, white as a corpse. "I need only to hear from Cordelia, too."

"By the Angel," said Matthew, his head thrown back. "There is not, never will be, any escape, will there? Never anything better—"

"Stop." Cordelia was suddenly exhausted. It was the kind of exhaustion that sometimes fell upon her after a battle, a dark wave rolling over her, as if she had fallen far below the sea and drifted there, unable to raise herself to the surface. "I will not be the cause of fighting between the two of you. I do not want that. Whatever argument you have between you, settle it. I am going to pack my things, and tomorrow I will return to London. I am sorry you made this journey for no reason, James. And Matthew, I am sorry I came with you to Paris. It was a mistake. Good night."

She walked out of the living room. She had just stepped into her bedroom when she heard Matthew say, sounding more defeated than she had ever heard him, "Damn you, James."

A moment later, the door to the suite slammed closed. Matthew had left.

It took James several moments to summon up the courage to knock on Cordelia's door.

When he had first arrived at the hotel, it had been easy enough to get the number of Matthew and Cordelia's hotel room from the clerk by claiming he wished to leave a message. A trip up in the lift, an Open rune, and he was inside, pacing from room to room, checking to see if they were there.

He had gone to Matthew's room first: Matthew had not even tried to hide the brandy and absinthe bottles—most empty, a few full. They were lined up along the windowsill like green glass sentries. His clothes were everywhere: over the backs of chairs, on the floor, waistcoats and spats abandoned carelessly.

He had spent only a moment in Cordelia's room. It held the scent of her perfume, or her soap: spice and jasmine. It brought the memory of her back too painfully. He escaped to the living room with one of Matthew's absinthe bottles, though he could take no more than a single swallow. Bitter fire, it scorched his throat.

He recalled being relieved that Matthew and Cordelia had two separate rooms. He told himself he should not be surprised. Matthew was a gentleman, however strongly he felt for Cordelia. He could talk through this with them, explain his feelings. Things could be all right.

Then he had heard the door open. He had heard them before he saw them—soft laughter, the sound of falling fabric. The moonlight had turned them into moving shadows as they came into the room, neither of them realizing he was there. Matthew setting Cordelia down, his hands on her, roaming over the curves of her body, and she had been kissing him back, her head tilted, hands in his hair, and James could remember, painfully, what kissing Cordelia was like, hotter and better than any fire. He had felt sick and ashamed and desperate and did not even remember reaching for the cord of the lamp.

But he had, and here they were. Matthew had gone, and James knew he needed to talk with Cordelia. Needed to tell her the truth, no matter how awkward the circumstances. They would not become less awkward if he withheld the reason he was here.

He knocked, twice, and opened the door. The room was decorated in pale pastels that reminded James of the sort of dresses Cordelia had worn when she'd first come to London. The wallpaper and bed hangings were celadon green, the rug striped sage and gold. The wallpaper was a repeating pattern of fleur-de-lis and ivory ribbons. The furniture was gilded; a small writing desk stood by the large, arched window through which he could see the lights of the Place Vendôme.

In the center of the room was Daisy, in the process of carrying a striped dress from the wardrobe to the bed, where the rest of her clothes were laid out. She stopped when she saw him, arrested in mid-motion.

She arched her eyebrows at him but said nothing. Her hair had been done up in some sort of complicated knot, which had come very loose. Long strands of flame red spilled down around her face. She wore a dress of almost the same flame red; James had never seen it before, and he'd thought he knew most of her clothes. This one was velvet, clinging to her breasts and waist, flaring out from her hips and thighs like an upside-down trumpet.

A thread of desire unfurled in his stomach, curling around the knot of anxiety there. He had not been this close to her since he had realized the truth about how he felt. He wanted to close his eyes against the pain-pleasure of it—his body, it seemed, was too foolish to know when he wasn't precisely welcome. It was reacting as if he'd been starving and had just had a plate of the most delicious food placed in front of him. *Go on, you idiot*, it seemed to be saying. *Take her in your arms. Kiss her. Touch her.*

Like Matthew did.

He took a ragged, deep breath. "Daisy," he said. "I wanted to say—I never apologized."

She turned, laid the striped dress on the bed. Stayed there, fiddling with its buttons. "For what?"

"For all of it," he said. "For my stupidity, for hurting you, for letting you think I loved *her*, when it was never love. It was not my intention."

She did look up, at that. Her eyes were very dark, her cheeks flushed. "I know it was not your intention. You never thought about me at all."

Her voice was low, husky; the voice that had read *Layla and Majnun* to him, so long ago. He had fallen in love with her then. He had loved her ever since, but had not known it; even in his blindness, though, her voice had sent disconcerting shivers up his spine.

"I thought of you all the time," he said. It was true; he *had* thought of her, dreamed of her. The bracelet had whispered to him that none of it meant anything. "I wanted you with me. All the time."

She turned to face him. Her dress had slipped partway off one shoulder, baring the skin, a soft gold-brown against the crimson of her dress. It had a sheen like satin, and a softness he recalled with an almost painful sensation of wanting. How had he lived with her, in the same house, for weeks, and not kissed her, touched her, every day? He would die for that chance again.

"James," she said. "You had me. We were married. You could have said any of this at any time, but you did not. You said you loved Grace; now you say you want me. What am I to make of that, other than that you want only what you cannot have? Grace came to you, I saw her, and—" Her voice shook slightly. "And now you have decided you feel nothing for her, but you do want me. How am I to imagine that you mean what you say? Tell me. Tell me something that would make me feel this is real."

This is the moment, James thought. This was when he should say, *No, you see, I was ensorcelled; I thought I loved Grace but it was just dark magic; I couldn't tell you earlier because I didn't know; but now all of that is behind me and—*

He could hear how it sounded. Unbelievable, for one thing, though he knew he could convince her eventually, especially once they had returned to London. It wasn't that he couldn't make her believe him. It was more than that.

The image of Cordelia and Matthew in their embrace came back to him. It had wrenched at him with an awful sort of shock to see them like that. He did not know what he had been expecting, and some part of him had felt a blind sort of happiness in seeing them—he had missed them both badly—quickly swamped by a deep and terrible jealousy. It had frightened him with its intensity. He had wanted to break something.

He thought of Matthew slamming his way out the door. Maybe he *had* broken something.

But there was more to the memory. It hurt to call it back up, like slicing one's own skin with a razor. But he did it, and in the memory he saw past his anger, his misery, and he saw how they had *looked*—happier than he had seen either of them in a long time. Even when he and Cordelia had been happy together, in the memories he had clung to this past week, there had been a melancholy in her dark eyes.

Perhaps she did not feel that melancholy with Matthew. Perhaps, having been sure James would never love her, that their marriage would never be anything but a lie, Cordelia had found joy with someone who could tell her straightforwardly that he loved her, without caveats or denials.

James had come to Paris determined to tell Cordelia the truth—about Grace, about the bracelet. To tell her she had his whole heart and soul and always had. He realized now that this would be binding her with chains. She was kind, his Daisy, the sort to weep over an injured kitten in the street. She would pity him and his chained love, pity him for what Grace and Belial had done to him. She would feel obligated to stay by his side, return to their marriage, because of that pity and that kindness.

For a moment, the temptation was before him. Tell her the truth, take her kindness and her pity and let it chain her to him. Let it bring her back to Curzon Street with him. It would be like before: they would play chess, they would walk and talk and dine together and eventually he would win her back, with gifts and words and devotion.

He let the image hover in his mind, of the two of them in the study, before the fire, Cordelia smiling through the fall of her unbound hair. His fingers under her chin, turning her face toward him. *What are you thinking about, my love?*

He pushed the thought away, sharply, as if he were puncturing a soap bubble. Pity and kindness were not love. Only free choice was love; if he had learned nothing else from the horror of the bracelet, he had learned that.

"I love you," he said. He knew it wasn't enough, knew it even before she closed her eyes, as if terribly weary. "I may have believed I loved Grace, but she was not the person I imagined. I think also I did not want to believe I could have been so wrong, especially about something so important. The time I have been married to you, Daisy, has been—the happiest of my life."

There, he thought wretchedly. It was some of the truth, if not the whole of it.

She opened her eyes slowly. "Is that all?"

"Not quite," he said. "If you love Matthew, then tell me now. I will stop importuning you. I will leave you two to be happy."

Cordelia shook her head slowly. For the first time, she looked a little uncertain as she said, "I don't—I don't know. James, I need time to think about all this. I cannot give you any sort of answer now."

She had put her hand to her throat, an unconscious gesture, and James realized suddenly what lay there above the neckline of her dress: the gold pendant he had given her, in the shape of the globe.

Something lit within him. A small, insane spark of hope. "But you are not leaving me," he said. "You do not want a divorce?"

She gave the ghost of a smile. "Not yet, no."

More than anything else, he wanted to pull her toward him, to crush his mouth to hers, to show her with lips and hands what words were inadequate to prove. He had fought Belial, he thought, had twice faced down a Prince of Hell, yet this was the hardest thing he had ever done: to nod, to back away from Cordelia, to leave her without another question or another word.

He did it anyway.

8
Against Peace

Once for all; I knew to my sorrow, often and often, if not always, that I loved [Estella] against reason, against promise, against peace, against hope, against happiness, against all discouragement that could be. Once for all; I loved her none the less because I knew it.
—Charles Dickens, *Great Expectations*

Ariadne had never awoken in another person's bed before, and as she blinked sleep from her eyes, she wondered if it was always so strange. She was disoriented, first by the shafts of light through the windows, at different angles and different shades than the light into her own bedroom. And then the thought that she was in *Anna's* bedroom came to her, and for a moment she allowed herself to simply be in the place, in the moment. She was sleeping where Anna slept, where she put her head down every night, where she dreamed. She felt a sort of intimate separation from Anna, as if they were two hands pressed to opposite sides of the same glass. She remembered their hands intertwining in the Whispering Room, Anna slowly threading Ariadne's hair ribbon through her fingers . . .

And then of course reality came crashing down, and Ariadne scolded herself for allowing this much romantic feeling. It was only because she was just awake, she told herself.

Anna had sworn off love, so she had said, and Ariadne had to believe her. She had cut away a part of herself, for protection, and

Ariadne could not rescue that part of her, could not bring it back.

The water in the jug on the washstand had a thin scrim of ice on it. Ariadne washed her face hurriedly, plaited her hair, and pulled on the dress she'd been wearing when she arrived; it was rumpled and stale, but she hadn't brought anything else with her. She'd have to buy some new things.

Cautiously she emerged into the living room, not wanting to wake Anna if she was still asleep. Not only was Anna not asleep, she had company. At the breakfast table sat Anna's brother Christopher, and, of all people, Eugenia Lightwood. The three of them appeared to be in the final throes of breakfast. Eugenia, who Ariadne thought of as pleasant, but not someone in whom she would necessarily confide, gave her a little wave and a smile. Whatever Anna had told her about the circumstances of Ariadne's presence, she seemed unbothered.

"Ah, Ariadne. I didn't want to wake you," Anna said, her voice bright. "Do you want a bit of breakfast? It's only tea and toast, I'm afraid. Christopher, shove over and make some room."

Christopher dutifully did so, scattering crumbs as he shifted sideways on a tufted sofa that had been drawn up to make one side of the table's seating. Ariadne sank down next to him, took a slice of toast from the rack, and began to butter it. Anna, looking placid, poured her a cup of tea.

"I've never understood toast racks," murmured Eugenia. "All they do is make sure one's toast gets cold as soon as possible."

"Anna," Christopher said, "I've been doing some work lately and—well, with your permission, I'd like to inscribe just a couple of small runes onto the bottom of your kettle before you put it on the fire, in order to—"

"No, Christopher," Anna said, patting him on the shoulder. "Ariadne, as you can see, I have assembled a team for our mission today."

Ariadne blinked. "What mission?"

"The mission to gather your things and move you out of your parents' house, of course."

Ariadne blinked a few more times. "We're doing that *today*?"

"It's so exciting," Eugenia said, her dark eyes sparkling. "I do love a mission."

"Your mother, as we all know," said Anna, "will be very distraught at her only daughter moving away, and so we will be there to soften the transition. Eugenia, you see, is inherently trusted by Mrs. Bridgestock"—Eugenia put a hand to her chest and bowed—"and will put her at ease. I, on the other hand, am a destabilizing presence and will throw your mother off her game so that she cannot begin copiously weeping, or reminiscing about your early childhood, or both."

"Both seem likely," sighed Ariadne. "And Christopher?"

"Christopher, apart from providing the reassurance of an authoritative male presence—"

"What ho!" put in Christopher, looking pleased.

"—is my little brother and must do what I say," Anna finished.

Ariadne ate some toast thoughtfully. It was a clever plan, really. Her mother was nothing if not fastidious in her observation of etiquette and would be polite to a fault to unexpected visitors. Between them, the assembled Lightwoods would keep her busy such that, even if she noticed Ariadne removing her things from the house, she would never be so rude to guests as to make a scene while they were present.

The other cleverness about the plan, she thought, was that it prevented Anna and Ariadne from having to think about Ariadne's waking up in Anna's bed, or how either Anna or Ariadne felt about any of that.

"Unfortunately," Christopher said, "we will have to be quick about it. All three of us are expected at the Institute later this morning."

Eugenia rolled her eyes. "It's only Uncle Will wanting to assign us tasks for the Christmas party."

"Is that still happening?" Anna said, surprised. "With all that's been going on?"

"Nothing will stop the Herondales' Christmas party," Christopher said. "Even a Prince of Hell would balk before Uncle Will's capacity for making merry. Besides—it's good for everyone to have something to look forward to, isn't it?"

Ariadne could not help but wonder what Eugenia thought about that. It was at an Institute party, during the summer, that Eugenia's sister, Barbara, had collapsed, and not long after she had died, the victim of demon poison.

But if Eugenia's mind was on that, she did not show it. She remained cheerful and determined all the way out of the flat and down into the Lightwoods' carriage.

It was once in the carriage, jouncing along Percy Street toward Cavendish Square, that Ariadne realized that if they were going to retrieve her things today, there would be no place she could bring her trunks other than back to Anna's flat. But that must surely have occurred to Anna already? Ariadne tried to catch her eye, but Anna was caught up in a conversation with Eugenia about neighborhoods where Ariadne might find the right sort of flat for a single young woman to occupy.

So Anna did not expect Ariadne to keep her things at Anna's for long. Certainly not long enough for the situation to become awkward. Though Anna showed no signs of awkwardness; she was lovely and bright as ever. She wore a spectacular waistcoat, striped pink and green like ribbon candy, which Ariadne felt sure she'd nicked from Matthew. Her eyes were as dark blue as pansy flowers. *And soon you'll be telling yourself the angels sing when she laughs,* Ariadne thought to herself sternly. *Be less sentimental.*

Soon enough they had arrived at the Bridgestock house. At the front door Ariadne hesitated, thinking of a thousand things that could go wrong with their plan. But Anna was looking at her expectantly, apparently with full confidence that Ariadne was capable of handling the situation. It was a look that stiffened Ariadne's spine and hardened her resolve. With a smile plastered on her face, she used her key to open the door, stepped into the entryway, and called out with forced cheerfulness, "Mother, just *look* who I ran into this morning!"

Her mother appeared at the top of the stairs. Flora wore the same dress she had worn the day before, and had clearly spent a sleepless night; her eyes were deeply shadowed, her face lined with tension. As her gaze fell upon her daughter, Ariadne thought she saw a flash of relief on her features.

Could she have been worried *about me?* Ariadne wondered, but her mother had caught sight of Anna, Christopher, and Eugenia spilling into the entryway, and was already forcing her expression into a smile.

"Eugenia, dear," she said warmly, descending the stairs. "And young Master Lightwood, and Anna, of course—" Was it Ariadne's imagination that there was a certain coldness in the way Flora Bridgestock looked upon Anna? "How are your dear parents?"

Eugenia launched immediately into a long story involving Gideon and Sophie's search for a new housemaid after the last one had been discovered to be wildly riding omnibuses all around town while a group of local brownies did all the tidying up.

"Dreadful," Ariadne heard Flora say, and, "What trying times," as Eugenia herded her skillfully into the drawing room, Anna and Christopher in her wake. She had underestimated Eugenia, Ariadne thought. She would make an excellent spy.

Ariadne exchanged a quick look with Anna and then hurried up the stairs to her room, where she seized a trunk and began to fill it with her possessions. How hard, she thought, to pack away a life, so quickly! Clothes and books, of course, and old treasures: a sari that had been her first mother's, a *pata* that had belonged to her first father, a doll her adoptive mother had given her, one of its button eyes missing.

From downstairs, she heard Anna say loudly, "Christopher has been entertaining us all morning with his latest work in science! Christopher, tell Mrs. Bridgestock what you were telling us earlier."

That meant Flora was getting fidgety, Ariadne knew. She had only a little more time.

She had just finished folding her gear and was placing the *pata* on top of the pile of clothes in her trunk when Anna appeared at her door. "Almost ready?" she said. "Eventually your mother will try to get a word in edgewise around Christopher, you know."

Ariadne stood up, dusting her hands off on her skirt. She determinedly did not look around at her room, at the familiar furniture, the blanket her mother had knitted for her before she had even arrived from India. "I'm ready."

Together, they carried the trunk down to the entryway, managing not to thump it against *every* stair. As they passed by the doorway to the drawing room, Ariadne saw her mother, looking up from the sofa at Christopher, glance over at her. Her face was pale and strained. Ariadne had to fight the urge to go to her, to ask if she was all right, to fetch her a cup of tea as she was used to doing in difficult times.

The carriage driver came rushing up the steps to take the trunk, and

Ariadne headed back into the house. She could hear Eugenia regaling her mother with another domestic tale and wondered if it was possible that the Lightwoods could keep her distracted long enough for Ariadne to dart down to the conservatory and snatch up Winston's cage.

Technically, he was hers, after all—a gift from her parents. And while Anna had not specifically *agreed* to house a parrot in her small flat, Ariadne—and therefore Winston—was only meant to be a temporary guest there, until she found her own place.

She was about to make a run for Winston when there was a loud screech from outside. Anna cried out a sharp warning. Ariadne spun back to the door to see a hansom cab, being driven hell-for-leather, come to a stop inches away from crashing into the Lightwoods' carriage. The cab's door opened, disgorging a man in a filthy traveling coat, a bent hat jammed sideways on his head. He flung a handful of coins at the cabdriver before heading straight for the Bridgestocks' front door.

Ariadne did not recognize the coat, the hat, or the staggering limp, but she recognized the man, though there was half a week's white stubble on his face, and he looked years older than the last time she'd seen him.

"Father?" she whispered. She had not meant to speak; the word had left her mouth on its own.

Anna looked at her in surprise. It was clear she, too, had not recognized the Inquisitor.

"Maurice?" Ariadne's mother had raced to the door, Eugenia and Christopher behind her, wearing matching looks of surprise and concern. She caught at Ariadne's hand—squeezed it once, hard—and flew down the steps to throw her arms around her husband, who stood stock-still, motionless as a gnarled old tree, even as his wife sobbed, "What *happened*? Where have you been? Why didn't you let us know—"

"Flora," he said, and his voice was harsh, as if he had worn it out by shouting or screaming. "Oh, Flora. It's worse than you could imagine. It's so much worse than any of us imagined."

The next morning Cordelia's greatest fear was having to encounter either James or Matthew upon emerging from her bedroom. She delayed as long as she could, fussing over getting dressed, though she could tell by the angle of the sun through the windows that it was already late morning.

She had slept poorly. Over and over, when she closed her eyes, she saw James's face, heard his words. *I was wrong about my marriage. I didn't think it was real. It was real. The most real thing in my life.*

He had told her he loved her.

It was all she thought she had ever wanted. But she found now that it rang hollow in her heart. She did not know what was driving him—pity, perhaps, or even a regret for the life they had shared together at Curzon Street. He *did* say he had been happy. And she had never thought Grace made him happy, only miserable, but it was a misery he seemed to have relished. And feelings showed themselves through actions; Cordelia believed James liked her, desired her even, but if he had *loved* her . . .

He would have sent Grace away.

After lacing up her boots, she went out into the suite, only to find it empty. The door to Matthew's room was closed, and James was nowhere to be seen.

The green absinthe bottle was still on the table. Cordelia thought of Matthew—of his mouth on hers, and then the way he had whitened when he asked if James had gone into his room.

There was a tight feeling in the pit of her stomach as she went out into the blue-and-gold hall. She spied the hotel porter, just departing another room. "*Monsieur!*" she called out, and hurried over to him. At least she could try to eat something before she had to start her journey. "I wanted to ask about breakfast—"

"Ah, *madame*," the porter exclaimed. "Do not trouble yourself. Your companion has already called for breakfast and it should be delivered very soon."

Cordelia was not sure which companion he meant, James or Matthew. She wasn't sure she wanted to breakfast with either of them, and certainly not both, but it seemed too much to explain *that* to the porter. She thanked the man and was about to turn away when she hesitated. "May I ask you one other question?" she said. "Did you bring a bottle of absinthe to our suite last night?"

"*Non, madame.*" The porter looked puzzled. "I brought one bottle yesterday morning. Six o'clock."

Now Cordelia was the one puzzled. "Why would you do that?"

The porter looked even more surprised. "I bring a bottle every morning, just after sunrise. By request of Monsieur Fairchild. Brandy, or absinthe." He shrugged. "When he was here before, he wanted it in the evening. This visit, early morning. No difference to me, I said, six o'clock every morning."

"Thank you," Cordelia managed to get out, and left the porter staring after her as she stumbled down the hall.

Once inside the suite door, she leaned against the wall, her eyes closed. Matthew had indeed lied to her. He had sworn not to drink, and he had not—in front of her. But the porter had brought him a new bottle of liquor *each morning*. Had he been drinking, then, at every moment that he wasn't in her sight? It certainly seemed like he had been.

It was one lie too many, she thought; now she was truly broken beyond repair. She'd been lied to over and over again, by everybody she cared about. Her family had lied about her father's drinking. James had lied—about Grace, about her, about the very premise of their marriage. Lucie, who was supposed to be her closest friend, who she knew better than anyone, had kept her relationship with Jesse Blackthorn hidden, and had fled London without a word or a warning to Cordelia.

She had thought Matthew would be different—precisely because he believed in nothing, because he had already given up on morality as most people saw it, on virtue and high-mindedness. He cared only about beauty and art and meaning, as bohemians did; this was why she had believed that he would not lie to her. Because if he were going to drink, *he would say so*.

But he had looked her in the eye and promised her that if she came to Paris with him, he would drink only lightly; he had allowed her to believe he had not touched drink at all. Yet the porter had been delivering brandy daily since the day they arrived. Cordelia had thought that even if Paris could not save her, at least it might save Matthew. But it seemed that one could not change oneself by changing one's place, as much as one might dream of it; neither of them had left their troubles behind. They had only carried those troubles along with them.

* * *

When he came back into the suite, James found it undisturbed, as though no one had woken yet. The doors to both bedrooms were still closed. Shaking his head, he went and banged on Matthew's door. When nothing happened, he banged on it again, a bit harder, and was rewarded with a low groaning noise from somewhere within.

"Breakfast," he called. There was another, even lower groan from inside. "Get up, Matthew," he said, his voice harsher than even he expected. "We need to talk."

There was a series of thumping and crashing sounds, and after about a minute Matthew yanked the door open and blinked at James. He looked completely exhausted, and James wondered how late he had gotten back last night; he'd only known Matthew had returned at all because of his coat crumpled on the floor of the suite and another couple of empty bottles next to it. Certainly whenever Matthew had come back, it had been after James was asleep, which would have been very late indeed. James himself had lain on the couch, awake, for what felt like hours, staring into the dark in a state of utter despair. Magnus had slapped him on the back and wished him good luck before sending him through the Portal to get here—but no amount of luck, it turned out, would have helped.

In the space of what felt like a moment, he had lost not one but two of the most important people in his life.

When he finally did nod off, his sleep was strange and disturbed. He had had no dreams at all, that he could remember; there had been only a kind of harsh blank white noise. Strange, he thought, even stranger than the dark dreams Belial had sent him in the past. It had been a sound like the roar of the ocean but unpleasant and metallic, a sound that made him feel as if his heart had broken and poured out a shrill scream only he could hear.

Matthew was still wearing his clothes from the night before, even the red velvet waistcoat that matched Cordelia's dress, but the clothes were crumpled and stained now. Behind him, the bedroom was a disaster. His trunk had been turned over, spilling out clothes, and empty plates and bottles lay scattered about like the bits of glass and crockery that washed up on the banks of the Thames.

Matthew's eyes were red-rimmed, his hair a mass of tangled curls. "I," he said, "was asleep."

His voice was flat.

James counted to ten silently. "Math," he said. "We have to go back to London."

Matthew leaned against the doorway. "Ah. You and Cordelia are returning to London? Safe travels to you, then, or should I say, *bon voyage*? You do work quickly, James, but then, I suppose I rather ceded the battlefield to you, didn't I?" He scrubbed at his eyes with a lace-cuffed sleeve, blinking the sleep out of his eyes. "I will not fight you for her," he said. "It would be undignified."

This, James thought, was the point at which Christopher or Thomas or Anna would have walked away. When Matthew was in a rare quarrelsome mood, it was generally best to let him settle on his own. But James never walked away, no matter how sharp Matthew's words became.

He could see, even now, the faint tremble in Matthew's hands, the hurt at the back of his eyes. More than anything he wanted to put his arms around Matthew, hug him tightly, tell him he was loved.

But what could he really say to comfort him now? *Cordelia loves you?* Three words that felt like spikes driven into his own heart. Three words whose truth he could not be sure of. He did not know what Cordelia felt.

He rubbed his temple, which had begun to throb. "It's not like that, Math," he said. "There is no battlefield. If I had had any idea before last week that you had feelings for Cordelia—"

"What?" Matthew broke in, his voice harsh. "You would have what? Not married her? Married Grace? Because Jamie, that's what I don't understand. You've loved Grace for years—loved her when you thought it was hopeless. Loved her—what does Dickens say? '*Against reason, against promise, against peace, against hope, against happiness, against all discouragement that could be.*'"

"I never loved her," James said. "I only thought I did."

Matthew slumped in the doorway. "I wish I could believe that," he said. "Because what it looks like is that the moment Cordelia left you, you decided you couldn't bear being left. I suppose no one ever has, have they? Everyone's always loved you." He said it with a flat matter-of-factness that was startling. "Except perhaps Grace. Perhaps that's why you wanted her in the first place. I don't think she's capable of loving anyone."

"*Matthew—*" James could feel the weight of the silver bracelet as though it circled his wrist still, though he knew perfectly well it was broken and back at Curzon Street. He wanted to protest, to explain his own innocence, but how could he do so when he hadn't yet told Cordelia? Surely she was owed the truth first. And the thought of telling her, of garnering her pity, was still unbearable. Better to be hated than pitied—by Daisy, by Matthew, though the thought of being hated by his *parabatai* made him sick—

Something crashed loudly in the room behind him, as if a lamp had fallen and smashed. James turned around, in time to see a Portal open in the wall of the living room.

Magnus stepped through into the suite. He, of course, was perfectly dressed in a striped suit, and as he took James and Matthew in, he brushed a speck of dust off his immaculate shirtfront.

On the other side of the suite, the door flew open, and Cordelia appeared, already fully dressed in traveling clothes. She stared at Magnus in astonishment. "*Magnus,*" she said. "I wasn't expecting—I mean, how on earth did you know where we were staying?"

"Because he sent me through the Portal last night," said James. "I know where Matthew likes to stay when he's in Paris."

Matthew shrugged. "I am nothing if not predictable."

"And the night manager here is a warlock," Magnus noted. "I mean, who else could have picked out those curtains?" When no one replied, he gazed from James to Cordelia, both of them, James imagined, clearly strained with tension, and then at Matthew, rumpled and wine-stained.

"Ah," Magnus said, rather glumly. "I see there are some interpersonal dramatics taking place here." He held up a hand. "I do not know what they are, nor do I wish to know. James, you arrived last night, did you not?"

James nodded.

"And have you already told Cordelia and Matthew about Lucie—and about Jesse?"

James sighed. "Just that they were all right. The chance to elaborate did not present itself."

Both Cordelia and Matthew began to ask about Lucie; Magnus raised his hand again, as if he were the conductor of a wayward orchestra. "You'll hear the whole story back in London," he said. "It's imperative that we return now—"

"My mother." Cordelia braced herself against the doorway. "Is she all right? Is the baby—"

"Your mother is well," Magnus said, not ungently, but his expression was grim. "But the situation in London is serious, and likely to grow more so."

"Is there another Prince of Hell with tentacles threatening the Institute, then?" Matthew asked wearily. "Because I have to say, if so, my instinct is to sit this one out."

Magnus gave him a stern look. "The Inquisitor has returned, and the news he has brought is bleak. Tatiana Blackthorn has escaped from the Adamant Citadel and joined forces with Belial. You must return with me to London posthaste; there is much to be discussed."

9
If Gold Rust

If gold rust, what then can iron do?
—Geoffrey Chaucer, *The Canterbury Tales*

Given the grim way Magnus had delivered his news, Cordelia had half expected the Portal he created to open onto a scene of chaos—a battle, a crowd, frightened people shouting at each other.

Instead it opened onto a cool darkness, and the smell of chilled stone. She blinked away her dizziness, knowing they were underground: this was the Institute's crypt, where a permanent Portal resided.

She looked quickly at her companions. The last time she had been here, she and Matthew were arguing with James as he prepared to pass through the Portal into Idris to foil Tatiana's plans. *And because of Grace*, said a small voice in her head. *He did it for Grace.*

This had been the turning point, she thought, in her life: James had gone through, and she and Matthew had followed. Blackthorn Manor had burned; James had been accused, Cordelia had spoken up to defend him; James had proposed to save her reputation, and everything had changed forever.

She was not the same person she had been then, she thought, as Magnus made a gesture, and the brass lamps lining the walls lit, casting the stone walls in eerie gold. She had learned so much since then, of what people were capable of—of what she herself was capable of—and she had learned that things could not be changed by willing them to be different. Dreams, hopes, wishes, were just that. Strength lay in keeping tight hold of reality, even if it was like grasping a stinging nettle in her hand.

The four of them made their way up the stone steps to the Institute's ground floor. Through the windows, London welcomed them back with a gray snow, gusting in swirls and eddies against the glass, and a washed-out steel sky.

Neither James nor Matthew would look at her or at each other. James wore the expression she had dubbed the Mask—blank and unmoving, he adopted it when he wanted none of his feelings to show—and Matthew, she thought, possessed a mask just as sturdy in its own way: a distant, faintly amused look, as if he were watching a not very well-written play. She felt the force of their determined silence like the pressure drop before a storm.

Her saving grace was Magnus, who came to walk beside Cordelia the moment they exited the Portal. He did it so gracefully that Cordelia thought at first that he was merely being polite. She realized a moment later that of course he had recognized the awkwardness of the situation when he'd arrived at Le Meurice. *Dramatics*, he'd said in a bored tone, but the sympathy in his eyes when he looked at her was genuine.

She was not sure why. Soon enough everyone would know she had run off to Paris with Matthew, and that James had not known of it. When she had fled, she had not thought about coming back, save that she would return, move back in with her mother, and try to rebuild her life. Atone for the foolish mistakes she had made by taking care of her little sister or brother. She had not considered how it would look—not just to the whole gossiping Enclave, but to her friends: to Lucie and Thomas, Christopher and Anna.... They had been James's friends first, and Lucie was his sister. They would be loyal to him, disgusted with her.

She wondered if the same thoughts had occurred to Matthew. If he was worried what his friends would say, would think. But he was a boy. People treated boys differently.

"Here we are," Magnus said, snapping Cordelia out of her reverie. "Here" was Will's office. That is to say, it was a room with fewer books than the Institute library, more books than most other rooms, and a tall slatted chair that could roll around the shelves on wheels. It also had a number of comfortable chairs scattered about, and just rising from those chairs were Will, Tessa, Charles, and the Inquisitor.

Cordelia stood back as Will and Tessa came to embrace James. If Tessa noticed that he looked disheveled and unkempt, she did not show it, only kissed him on the forehead in a way that made Cordelia miss her own mother, and Alastair.

"Matthew," Charles said, without crossing the room to meet his brother. "Late as usual, I see. Did it take you that long to get across town?"

"I was in *Paris*, Charles," said Matthew tightly.

"Were you?" Charles said vaguely. "I'd forgotten. Well, you've missed Mother; she was here earlier, but she went home feeling unwell. And you've all missed Maurice's tale. I'm sure Will and Tessa will fill you in on any details you need to know."

"Surely it would be better for them to hear it from the Inquisitor himself," said Magnus mildly.

"The Inquisitor has already told the story several times today," said Charles. "After his ordeal, he needs to rest. As none of you are upper members of the Enclave—and you, warlock, are not even a Shadowhunter—that does not seem necessary." He turned to the Inquisitor. "Would you agree?"

"Indeed," said Maurice Bridgestock. He *did* look a bit battered, Cordelia had to admit, with healing bruises on his face; he was holding his right arm gingerly, as if it had been injured, though surely he'd been given healing runes? "Will, I trust you will take all the measures we have discussed. Tessa—" He nodded stiffly in her direction, and walked out of the room without a word to anyone else, Charles at his heels.

Magnus closed the door behind them. His expression was stony; Cordelia could hardly blame him.

"How nice that Charles has found someone new to adopt him," said Matthew. He was flushed with anger; Cordelia suspected there was some surprise and hurt there too. He and his brother had a complex, often antagonistic relationship, but they had left things on a better note, she'd thought. Charles seemed back to his old, unpleasant self now—but why?

"All of you," added Will, flopping into an armchair, "sit down. You're hovering, and I loathe hovering."

Once seats were taken, Will looked them over. "Alas," he said, "I am tasked with relaying to you an exciting and drama-filled tale. A terrible responsibility to have fallen upon me."

James snorted. "Please, you are barely concealing your delight. Go on, then. Tell us."

Will rubbed his hands together and began. "As you know," he said, "traveling to the Adamant Citadel is not easy, and it took Bridgestock a full day via the Reykjavík Institute to get there. Once he did arrive, he signaled to the Sisters for an audience, and several of them came out to meet him on the tableland that leads down to the Citadel itself, since as you know, only women can pass through its doors. They told him that Tatiana was not there, but when he protested, they explained that this was not unusual: that she often went for long walks alone across the volcanic plains."

"Why on earth did they let her do that?" Cordelia said in astonishment.

Will shrugged. "The Adamant Citadel is not a prison. There is nothing but empty rock for miles around, and nowhere for Tatiana to go, nothing for her to do, no one she could meet. The Iron Sisters hoped that she was using these walks to think upon her choices and meditate upon her new role as a member of their order."

James made a scoffing sound.

"Bridgestock seems to have demanded that the Iron Sisters bring him something of Tatiana's he could use to Track her. They found a sash from one of her robes. He was able to use it—to a point." Will frowned thoughtfully. "He claims he could very clearly sense that the rune was connected to her. It was not like Tracking someone who has died, where there is only a blankness. The Tracking rune sent him urgently after her, but in circles—telling him often that he was close, but never close enough, and changing its direction from time to time, faster than any person could have moved. It was as though the rune was not working at all, though this seemed impossible, especially so close to one of the Nephilim's main strongholds.

"Bridgestock made camp out on the plains, which I personally cannot imagine, but apparently it was so. Perhaps he pitched a tent.

He could not stay at the Citadel itself, although they did provide him with an Icelandic horse that could handle the rough terrain.

"In the dark of night, he heard a voice that came in on the cold wind and told him to go home, to stop seeking what he sought. He ignored this and continued the search the next day, across the volcanic plains, although the voice came to harry him several times. Then, that night, as the sun set behind the mountains, he found himself outside the golden gates to the Iron Tombs."

Cordelia was well aware of the Iron Tombs. They were the burial ground of the Iron Sisters and Silent Brothers, who did not die as ordinary Shadowhunters, but lived for centuries before their souls voyaged out of their bodies. These bodies did not decay, but remained intact, and were preserved in the Iron Tombs, a place forbidden to most Shadowhunters.

"Bridgestock rattled at the gates," Will said, "but nobody came to answer him, because no one in the Iron Tombs is alive, which you'd think he would have gathered from the name of the place. Anyway, he had himself a nice tantrum until he was yanked from his saddle by an invisible hand. But rather than colliding with the ground, he found himself surrounded by swirling darkness. A terrible, depthless darkness, the kind that stretches beyond imagination, the kind that might drive a man mad with a single glimpse—"

"Will," said Tessa. "Do not editorialize."

Will sighed and went on. "He heard a terrible sound like a saw grinding through wood, or bone. Through the shadows, he could see barren land; he suspected he was no longer in Iceland, or even in our world, but he could not be sure. And then . . . a monstrous figure rose in front of him, twice the height of a man, with eyes like burning coals. It spoke to him."

Cordelia waited for Tessa to chide Will, but she stayed silent. Apparently there was no exaggeration here.

"A demon? Did it identify itself?" James asked intently, leaning forward in his chair.

"According to Bridgestock," Will said slowly, "he has always thought that an angel would be a being of such beauty and infinitude that he would barely be able to comprehend its presence.

Yet he always longed to see one. We are, after all, their servants."

"Are you saying Bridgestock saw an angel?" Matthew said.

"A fallen one," said Tessa, a tremor in her voice. "A Prince of Hell in all his glory. He was both beautiful and hideous. Darkness streamed from him like invisible light. He seemed clothed in darkness, yet Bridgestock could see two great wounds in his chest, from which blood poured steadily, though it did not seem to bother him."

"Belial," Cordelia breathed. Not that there had ever been much doubt, but there was only one Prince of Hell who she had twice wounded with the blade of Cortana.

"He told Bridgestock who he was. Announced himself, and demanded that Bridgestock stop the search for Tatiana. He made threats, which Bridgestock would not share. I imagine they were of the general sort—rain of fire, destruction of the Enclave—but also likely personal, having to do with Bridgestock's family."

"He did say one perplexing thing," Tessa said.

"Ah, yes, I nearly forgot," said Will. "The last thing he said before he vanished. I jotted it down. 'If you have any thought of sending your paladin after me, you will bring great doom upon the world.'"

A terrible spear of ice pierced Cordelia's spine. She felt the blood drain from her face and wondered if anyone noticed. James and Matthew, to their credit, did not so much as glance at her. Magnus raised his eyebrows; Will and Tessa only seemed puzzled.

"And after that, Bridgestock fled home?" Magnus inquired.

"One cannot really blame him," said Will. "And believe me, I speak as one who holds no great fondness for the man. But he is no match for Belial. And there is the matter that when he awoke, he found the sigil of Belial burned into his right forearm."

No wonder he was holding his arm strangely, Cordelia thought.

"He *did?*" said James. "Have you seen it?"

"I have. A nasty thing," said Will. "I expect the man was terrified. He spends most of his time punishing other Shadowhunters, not facing Princes of Hell upon a blasted plain."

"*Was* it a blasted plain?" asked James.

"In my mind, yes," said Will, "probably covered in rocks that had been twisted into sinister shapes. One can but dream."

"What happened to the horse?" said Matthew.

"Ran off," said Will. "Probably back to the Adamant Citadel. Horses have sense. Balios would never have put up with that nonsense going on."

Tessa sighed. "Charlotte already drafted an order to be sent out to all Institutes, that they should be on the lookout for Tatiana."

"I doubt she will be found," said Magnus. "She has all the realms of Hell to hide in."

"And if she stays in them, that would be fine," said Will. "If she returns with Belial, or if she is hoping somehow to ease his passage into this world . . ."

"I don't see how she can," said Cordelia. "She is still just a woman. Her power comes from Belial himself. She cannot do what he himself lacks the power to do."

"Belial cannot come into this world, not for very long," said James. "He must possess a living person to do so, but his presence would destroy any ordinary human body. He could possess my body without destroying it, as we share blood, but I would have to be willing to let him—and I am not. He has the same problems he always has. I don't see how Tatiana can help him."

"Still," said Magnus, "it is no good thing that he has returned so soon. He placed his sigil on Bridgestock's arm not because he cares about Bridgestock, but to send the message that he was here. That we should fear him. Last time he stayed away for months; now it has only been a week or so. And what is all this about a paladin? What paladin? There hasn't been a paladin among the Nephilim since the days of Jonathan Shadowhunter."

"It's hard to swear yourself to the service of an angel," Tessa said, "when there never seem to be any around."

"Princes of Hell aren't like people," James said. "For him it's probably only been a short time since paladins were around. We'd be wise not to read too much into it."

"We will make sure the Clave is on high alert for a sighting of Tatiana," said Will. "There is not much else we can do. Still—" He pointed at James, Cordelia, and Matthew. "You, who are not yet adults, though you may feel you are. The three of you must stay close to your homes. Preferably, we'd like you to stay here at the Institute, at least at night."

"I won't go out after dark, if that's the issue," said Matthew. "But I will stay in my flat."

"I'll stay here," James said, making no mention of Cordelia. "And Lucie too, I assume?"

"Yes, of course, and—" Will glanced over at Tessa. "We have to tell them, my dear. About Jesse."

Cordelia exchanged a puzzled look with Matthew. "Jesse?" she said, into the silence. "Jesse *Blackthorn*?"

"I can't believe you didn't *tell* us," Matthew said as he, Cordelia, and James left Will's office, with instructions to find Lucie and Jesse in the ballroom.

"You might as well get used to him," Will had said. "I'm fairly sure he's here to stay."

"There wasn't really time, was there," James said, rather tightly.

"There really wasn't," Cordelia said quickly, hoping to defuse the situation. "It's quite an odd tale, with quite a lot of explaining needed. I—" She shook her head. "I had no idea about any of it."

"Lucie kept it a close secret," said James. "It seems she feared rejection if the extent of her powers was discovered. And even warlocks look darkly on death magic."

"Understandably," Matthew said as they went up the stairs. "Necromancy often has very unpleasant results."

"Well," said James, in a tone that suggested he did not want to discuss the matter, "not in this case."

Matthew shrugged. "By the Angel, Charles is loathsome. I know that a week ago I was concerned about whether he lived or died, but I certainly can't remember *why*."

James smiled a little. "He does seem to have rather attached himself to Bridgestock. Raziel knows why. Since he ended his engagement to Ariadne, I thought Bridgestock despised him."

"Bridgestock likes his boots licked," said Matthew harshly. "And Charles is good enough at that—"

He broke off. They were approaching the ballroom door, and from the other side, Cordelia could hear bright, familiar laughter.

Lucie. When was the last time she'd heard Lucie laugh like that?

Even James paused at the door, before looking at Matthew and Cordelia with a wry twist to his mouth.

"Lucie and Jesse," he said. "It's—a strange situation. Very strange. But she's happy, so . . ."

"Try not to look shocked?" Cordelia said.

"Exactly," said James, and swung the door open.

The ballroom was full of light. It had been stripped bare of decorations, ready for the next event: the curtains were flung wide, and no furniture remained in the room save a large grand piano, lacquered as black and shiny as a new hansom cab.

At the piano sat Jesse Blackthorn. His fingers rested lightly on the keys: he did not touch them as someone who was an expert, but Cordelia guessed he'd had a little instruction, no doubt when he was very young.

Lucie was leaning against the piano, smiling at him. Neither of them seemed to notice that anyone had joined them in the room. Lucie seemed to be reading from a piece of paper.

"Jeremy Blackthorn," she said. "When was it that your family returned with you to Merry England?"

"I was quite young," Jesse said, tapping out a quick flight of high notes. "Seven, perhaps. So that would have been—1893."

"And what happened to your parents?"

"A circus tent collapsed on them," said Jesse immediately. "It is why I am afraid of stripes."

Lucie smacked him lightly on the shoulder. He sounded a low note of protest on the piano. "You *must* take this seriously," she said, but she was laughing. "You'll be asked all sorts of questions, you know. A new addition to the Clave—that's unusual."

They sound so happy together, Cordelia thought wonderingly. *As James and I used to—and yet I knew nothing of this side of Lucie. I did not know this was happening.*

"Jeremy Blackthorn," said Jesse, in a portentous tone. "*Who* is the prettiest girl in the Enclave? It's a very important question . . ."

At that, before the flirting could escalate, Cordelia loudly cleared her throat.

"The ballroom looks lovely!" she exclaimed. "Is it to be decorated for the Christmas party?"

"Very subtle," said Matthew, with a quirk at the corner of his mouth.

Both Jesse and Lucie turned around. Lucie beamed. "James, you're back! Cordelia and Matthew, come and meet Jesse!"

Cordelia could immediately see that this Jesse was very different from Belial-possessed Jesse. As he rose to his feet and came to greet them, Cordelia thought he seemed somehow *clearer* than he had when she had seen him before, like a painting that had been restored. He wore clothes that were a little short on him, his jacket clearly strained across his shoulders, his ankles visible between his shoes and the hem of his trousers. But he was undeniably handsome, with a sharp, articulate face, and long-lashed green eyes several shades lighter than Matthew's.

As they exchanged introductions and greetings, Cordelia saw Lucie glance back and forth between Matthew and James, and frown. Of course; she knew them so well, she would be attuned to any oddness between them. Still, a little frown line appeared between her eyebrows, and stayed.

It was Matthew who said, "What is this Jeremy business, then?"

"Oh, right," Lucie said. "After we got back from Cornwall, we had a meeting with Charlotte and all the aunts and uncles, and decided—we will introduce Jesse as Jeremy Blackthorn, distant cousin of the Blackthorns, part of the branch that broke off and went to America a hundred years ago."

Cordelia frowned. "Don't the Silent Brothers have records of who belongs to what family?"

"They tend not to keep particularly accurate ones for those who have left the Clave," said Jesse. "As my grandfather Ezekiel did. And besides, a very helpful fellow called Brother Zachariah was also at the meeting."

"I ought to have seen his hand in all this," said Matthew. "Well, never let it be said we are not, as a group, up for a deception. Does the Inquisitor know?"

Lucie shuddered. "Gracious, no. Can you imagine? Especially after he apparently just encountered Belial out in the wilds near the Adamant Citadel. He can't be feeling kindly toward Blackthorns, or, well, Shadowhunters doing magic of any sort."

They had all refrained from asking Lucie exactly *how* she had raised Jesse from the dead; James seemed to know it, but Cordelia realized it was simply another thing about Lucie she'd been ignorant of. She felt a hollow sadness at her center. It was not distant from the sadness she felt over James—here she was, so close to someone she loved, and yet she felt a million miles away.

"It's rather too bad we can't tell the truth," said Matthew, "as it's quite an exciting tale. Having someone who returned from the dead among our number seems a feather in the cap for the Enclave, if you ask me."

"I wouldn't mind for me," said Jesse. He had altogether a calm, mild manner, though Cordelia guessed there were deeper currents running beneath it. "But I would hate for Lucie to be punished for all that she did for me, or Grace, either. Without the two of them, I wouldn't be here now."

"Grace?" said Cordelia, in confusion.

Lucie flushed and held her hands out to Cordelia. "I ought to have told you. I was afraid you'd be upset with me—"

"You worked with Grace?" James said sharply. "And didn't tell any of us?"

Jesse looked back and forth between them—at James's ashen face, and Cordelia, who had still not taken Lucie's hands. At Matthew, whose smile had vanished. "Something's wrong," he said. "Something about my sister—?"

"She did not entirely endear herself to the Enclave when she was among us. For example, she broke up my brother Charles's engagement to Ariadne, seemed to wish to marry him, then dropped Charles in a letter from the Silent City with no explanation," said Matthew.

It was a small part of the story. But Jesse's eyes darkened with worry. "I cannot apologize for what my sister has done," he said. "She will have to do that herself. I do know that it was at my mother's insistence that she pursued Charles. My mother has always seen Grace as a path to power. And I believe that in turning herself over to the Silent Brothers, my sister has shown that she no longer wishes to be my mother's tool. I hope that will count for something when she returns to the Enclave."

For a moment there was quiet. Cordelia glanced at James; she saw with despair that he had retreated behind the Mask. It was his armor, his protection.

Lucie has been in love with Jesse all this time, and I never knew, Cordelia thought. *Now they are more firmly together, and that will only bring her closer to Grace. Perhaps Grace will be her sister-in-law someday, and meanwhile I cannot even be her* parabatai. *I will lose Lucie to Grace, just as I lost James to her.*

"I am happy for you, Lucie," she said. "And for you, Jesse. But I find I am very tired and must return home to see my mother. She is not entirely well, and I have left her for too long."

She turned to leave.

"Cordelia," Lucie said. "Surely we could at least have time for a moment alone together—just to talk—"

"Not now," Cordelia said as she walked away from the group of them. "It seems there is much I did not know. Forgive me, if I require some time to consider the nature of my own ignorance."

James caught up with Cordelia on the front steps of the Institute.

He'd hurried after her without a moment's thought—rude, he knew, but all he'd seen was that Cordelia was unhappy, and leaving, and he had to do something about it, immediately.

The snow outside had stopped, though it had left a thin icing-sugar scrim of white on the front steps and the flagstones of the courtyard. Cordelia stood on the top step, her breath puffing around her in white clouds, her hands—gloveless—folded together. Her hair was a bright flame against the whiteness of winter, like a poppy among a field of lilies.

"Daisy—" he started.

"Don't," she said, softly, looking at the Institute gates with their Latin script, PULVIS ET UMBRA SUMUS. "Don't call me that."

He could see where her fingertips were reddened with cold. He wanted to wrap her hands in his, fold them inside his coat the way he had seen his father do with his mother's hands. With the self-control that years of Jem's training had instilled in him, he held himself back.

"Cordelia," he said. "Would you have told Lucie? I know you couldn't have, you didn't have a chance, but—would you have? That you saw me . . . with Grace, before you left for Paris?"

Cordelia shook her head. "I wouldn't have, no. I never told her anything about our discussions of Grace or about our . . . arrangements regarding her." She lifted her chin and looked at him, her dark eyes shining like shields. "I would not be pitied. Not by anyone."

In that, we are alike, James wanted to say; he couldn't bear to tell anyone about the bracelet, the spell. Couldn't bear to be pitied over what Grace had done to him. He had intended to tell Cordelia, but he had imagined a very different sort of reunion for them.

He pushed thoughts of her in Matthew's arms away. "I'm sorry," he said. "I never thought about putting you in a position where you had to lie to Lucie. I see now it's put distance between you two. I never wanted that. My pride was never worth that." He allowed himself to look at Cordelia. Her expression had softened slightly. "Let's just go home."

Unable to hold back, he reached out to move a wayward lock of scarlet hair away from her face. His fingertips grazed the soft skin of her cheek. To his surprise, she did not reach up to stop him. But neither did she say, *Yes, let's go home to Curzon Street*. She said nothing at all.

"That house is our home," he said in the same quiet tone. "*Our* home. It isn't anything to me without you in it."

"It was to be your home with Grace," she said, shaking her head. "You never pretended that it wouldn't eventually be hers. We were only to be married a year, James, you and I—"

"I never thought of living there with her," James said. It was true; he hadn't. The spell hadn't worked like that. It had forced his mind away from thoughts of the future, from any examination of his own feelings. "Cordelia," he whispered. He cupped her cheek in his hand. She closed her eyes, her lashes fluttering down, a fringe of dark copper. He wanted to kiss her so badly it hurt. "Come home. It doesn't mean you forgive me. I'll apologize a hundred times, a thousand times. We can play chess. Sit in front of the fire. We can talk. About Paris, about Matthew, Lucie, anything you want. We've always been able to talk—"

At this Cordelia's eyes opened. James felt his stomach drop; he couldn't help it. Even melancholy and low-lidded, the depths of her dark eyes never failed to utterly undo him. "James," she said. "We've never *really* talked about anything."

He pulled back from her. "We—"

"Let me finish," she said. "We've talked, but we've never told each other the truth. Not the full truth, anyway. Only the parts that were easy."

"*Easy?* Daisy—Cordelia—I told you things I've never told anyone else in my life. I trusted you with everything. I still do."

But he could see her momentary softening had gone. Her face was set, again, into determined lines. "I don't think it would be a good idea for me to return to Curzon Street," she said. "I am going home to Cornwall Gardens. I need to see my mother, and Alastair. After that . . ."

James felt as if he'd swallowed boiling lead. She had called Cornwall Gardens *home*; had made it clear she did not think of their house in Curzon Street that way. And yet, he could not blame her. No part of this was her fault. They had both agreed: a marriage in name only, to last for one year . . .

One year. They'd barely had a month. The thought of that being all the time he ever had with Cordelia was like a wound. He said, mechanically, "Let me get the carriage. I can take you to Kensington."

Cordelia took a step back. For a moment, James wondered if he'd said something to upset her; then he followed her gaze and saw Matthew, closing the front doors of the Institute behind him. He wore no coat, only his velvet jacket, torn at the wrist. He said, to Cordelia, "The Consul's carriage is also at your disposal, if you'd prefer. I won't be in it," he added. "Just Charles. Come to think of it, that's not a very attractive offer, is it?"

Cordelia looked at him solemnly. James could not help but think of the expression on her face when she'd realized Matthew had been drinking in Paris. He knew how she felt; he felt the same way.

"It's kind of both of you," she said. "But there's no need. Alastair's come to bring me back. Look."

She pointed, and indeed, a hansom cab was just rolling in through the Institute's gates. It bumped across the flagstones and came to a stop in front of the gates, steam rising from the horses' blanketed flanks.

The door opened and Alastair Carstairs swung himself down. He wore a thick blue greatcoat, his hands swaddled in leather gloves. He marched up the steps to his sister and said, without looking at either James or Matthew, "Where are your things, Layla?"

Layla. The sound of that name hurt, brought back the poem, the story whose thread had bound James and Cordelia, invisibly, over the years. *That heart's delight, one single glance the nerves to frenzy wrought, one single glance bewildered every thought. . . . Layla, she was called.*

"Magnus says he sent them on," said Cordelia. "Some sort of spell. My trunk ought to turn up at the house. If it doesn't . . ."

"It had better," Matthew said. "It has all your nice things from Paris in it."

All your nice things. Things like the red velvet gown she'd worn the night before. Things Matthew had no doubt gone with her to buy. James's stomach twisted.

"Come on, let's go, *shoma mitavanid tozieh bedid, che etefagi brayehe in ahmagha mioftad vagti ma mirim,*" Alastair said. *You can explain what's going on with these idiots when we leave.* Apparently it had slipped his mind that James had been learning Persian.

"Go on ahead of me. I'll join you in a moment," Cordelia said. Alastair nodded and withdrew to the carriage. Cordelia turned to face Matthew and James.

"I don't know how I feel," she said. "There is too much going on—too many complications. In some ways, I am angry at you both." She looked at them steadily. "In others ways, I feel I have hurt you both, been unfair to you. These are things that must be settled with my own conscience."

"Cordelia—" Matthew began.

"Don't," she said wearily. "I am *so tired.* Please, just understand. I care about you both."

She hurried down to the carriage and held out her hand, and Alastair took it to help her up the steps. As the door closed, James could hear Alastair asking Cordelia if she was all right, or if he was required to hit anyone for her. The carriage rattled off, leaving Matthew and

James alone with each other, and a silence where Cordelia had been.

James turned to look at Matthew. His *parabatai* was almost bloodlessly pale, his eyes like dark green smudges of paint in his white face. "Math," he said. "We shouldn't fight."

"We are not fighting," Matthew said, still looking at the spot where the carriage had been. "I told you already I would cede the field to you."

"But that isn't your choice to make," said James. "Or mine. It is Cordelia's. It will always be Cordelia's."

Matthew rubbed at his eyes with a gloved hand. "I think she hates us both," he said. "Perhaps that puts us on equal footing." He looked at James. "I didn't know," he said quietly. "I had no inkling when I went to Paris with Cordelia that you would mind. I did not think you loved her. I would never have gone, if I had thought that."

"A reasonable enough thing to think, given my behavior," said James. "Though—I wish you had asked me."

"I should have. I was angry. I was about to leave on my own, and then Cordelia was in my flat and she was in tears, and—" He shook his head. "I thought you had hurt her callously. Now I do not know what to think. Grace is in jail; you seem pleased about it. I can't say I'm sorry she's there, but I'm puzzled."

"Grace did come to my house that night you left for Paris," said James. "I turned her over to the Silent Brothers. When I realized Cordelia was gone, I ran after her. All the way to your flat, and then to Waterloo. I was on the platform as your train pulled away."

Matthew slumped back against the door. "James . . ."

"*Mathew,*" James said quietly. "I am in love with Cordelia, and she is my wife. You must understand, I will do whatever I can to mend things between us."

"Why did you never tell her?" Matthew said. "Why did she have to run away for that?"

"I should have," James said. "I wish I had." He hesitated. "Why did you never tell me *you* loved her?"

Matthew stared at him. "Because she is your wife, and I do have *some* scruples, you know. What you saw—the kissing—that was the extent of it. Of anything—physical—between us."

James felt a wave of shameful relief. "And if I hadn't interrupted you?" He held up a hand. "Never mind. You believed my marriage to Cordelia was a sham. I understand that."

"But I knew—" Matthew stopped himself from whatever he was going to say next, and let out a long breath instead. "I knew that once you lived together, once you spent all your time with her, you would come to love her too. And besides—when you find you're in love with your best friend's wife, you don't *tell* anyone. You drown yourself in drink, alone in London or in Paris, until either it kills you or the feelings go away."

James knew he shouldn't say it, but he couldn't stop himself. "But you weren't alone in Paris, were you?"

Matthew sucked in his breath. "It is a sickness. I thought if Cordelia was with me, I would not require the bottle. But it seems too late for that. The bottle requires me."

"I require you more," James said. "Math, let me help you—"

"Oh, dear God, James," Matthew said, with a sort of passionate despair. "How can you be so *good*?" He pushed himself away from the door. "I couldn't bear it, right now," he said, "to be helped by you."

Before James could say anything more, he heard Charles call out, in his booming voice: "*There* you are, Matthew! Do you want a ride back to your flat? Or you could come back to the house and see the parents. I'm sure they'd love to hear about Paris."

Matthew made a face that James knew well: it meant *give me patience*. "Just one moment," he called. He turned back to James and put a hand on his shoulder. "Whatever else happens, don't hate me, James. Please. I don't think I could bear it."

James wanted to close his eyes. He knew that behind them he would see two boys running across a green lawn in Idris, one fair-haired and one dark. "I could never hate you, Math."

As Matthew went to join his brother, leaving James alone on the steps, James thought, *I could never hate you, for all my hate is reserved for myself. I have none left over for anyone else.*

10
Wanderer

He saw a black shadow: a big raven squatted motionless,
staring at Majnun, eyes glowing like lamps. "Dressed in
mourning, he is a wanderer like myself," thought Majnun,
"and in our hearts we probably feel the same."
—Nizami Ganjavi, *Layla and Majnun*

It always surprised Cordelia, how London could be at once overcast and even rainy, and yet also bright enough to sting her eyes. From inside the carriage with Alastair, she blinked against the glare of the milk-white sky, and thought about the clear sunshine in Paris. Her time there was already beginning to seem removed and distant, like the memory of a dream.

They sat in silence as the driver navigated traffic on the Strand. Alastair, even a year ago, would have had a torrent of questions. He now seemed content to wait for Cordelia to speak.

"Alastair," she said as they swung onto the Mall, with its terraced white facades. "I assume Magnus let you know to come and fetch me?"

Alastair frowned at her. "Cordelia, put gloves on. It's cold. And yes, Magnus told me you'd just Portaled back. He said that you seemed exhausted after your travels and that you might appreciate being retrieved."

"*Retrieved,*" Cordelia muttered. "Makes me sound like luggage. And I haven't got gloves with me. I must have left them back at the hotel."

With an exaggerated sigh, Alastair removed his own gloves and began to jam them onto Cordelia's hands. They were comically too big, but very warm, especially since he'd just been wearing them. She flexed her fingers gratefully.

"I was surprised," Alastair said. "I would have thought you'd be returning to your house on Curzon Street. You might recall it? The house in which you reside with James Herondale? Your husband?"

Cordelia looked out the window. Carriages, omnibuses, and the like were snarled up around a large stone arch ahead—some sort of monument, though she couldn't recall which one. Up above, the driver was complaining loudly about the traffic. "I was worried about *Mâmân*," she said. "I oughtn't to have left with the baby due so soon. In fact, I think I shall stay in Cornwall Gardens at least until the baby is born."

"Your devotion to family is admirable," Alastair said dryly. "I'm sure it is unrelated to your having just run off to Paris with your husband's *parabatai*."

Cordelia sighed. "I had my reasons, Alastair."

"I'm sure you did," he said, surprising her again. "I wish you'd tell me what they were. Are you in love with Matthew?"

"I don't know," Cordelia said. Not that she didn't have thoughts on the matter, but she didn't feel like sharing them with Alastair at the moment.

"Are you in love with James, then?"

"Well. We *are* married."

"That's not really an answer," said Alastair. "I don't really like James," he added, "but on the other hand, I also don't like Matthew very much. So you see, I am torn."

"Well, this must be very difficult for you," Cordelia said crossly. "I cannot imagine how you will find it within yourself to go on."

She made a dismissive gesture, which was spoiled when Alastair burst out laughing. "I'm sorry," he said. "But those gloves are *enormous* on you."

"Humph," said Cordelia.

"About James—"

"Are we the sort of family that discusses our intimate relationships now?" Cordelia interrupted. "Perhaps you would like to talk about Charles?"

"Generally not. Charles seems to be healing up, and beyond him surviving, I have no further interest in what happens to him," said Alastair. "In fact, there have been a few touch-and-go moments with my caring about whether he survives. He was always demanding that I adjust his pillows. 'And now the *foot* pillow, Alastair,'" he said, in a squeaky voice that, to be fair, sounded nothing like the actual Charles. Alastair was terrible at impressions.

"I wouldn't mind a foot pillow," said Cordelia. "It sounds rather nice."

"You are clearly in an emotional state, so I will ignore your rambling," said Alastair. "Look, you need not discuss your feelings about James, Matthew, or whatever other harem of men you may have acquired, with me. I merely want to know if you're all right."

"No, you want to know if either of them has done something awful to me, so you can chase them around, shouting," said Cordelia darkly.

"I could want both," Alastair pointed out. They had made it out of the traffic finally and were rattling through Knightsbridge, past Harrods, bright with Christmas decorations, and streets crowded with barrow boys selling chestnuts and hot pies.

"I really have been worried about *Mâmân*," Cordelia said.

Alastair's expression softened. "*Mâmân* is fine, Layla, other than weariness. She sleeps a great deal. When she is awake, she grieves for our father. It is her grief that wearies her, I think, not her condition."

"Is she angry at me?" Cordelia hadn't realized she was going to say such a thing until it was already out of her mouth.

"For going to Paris? No, not at all. She was quite calm when we got your note; calmer than I'd expected, I must say. She said that if your dreams had taken you to Paris, then she was happy. I don't recall anyone ever saying that about *me* when I went to Paris," he added. "It is a dreadful chore, being the eldest."

Cordelia sighed. "I oughtn't to have gone, Alastair—if it hadn't been for *her*, for Lilith, I don't think I would have. But I am *useless*. I cannot protect anyone. I cannot even pick up my sword."

"Cortana." He looked at her, a strange expression in his dark eyes. She knew they had the same eyes—black, only a shade lighter than the pupil—but on Alastair, she recognized that their light transformed his face, softening its severity. That they were striking. She had never thought that about her own eyes; she supposed people didn't consider themselves that way. "Layla, I have to tell you something."

She tensed. "What is it?"

"I couldn't keep Cortana in the house," he said, "or with me, due to some rather—unfortunate visitors."

They were passing Hyde Park; it was a green blur outside Cordelia's window. "Demons?"

Alastair nodded. "Raveners," he said. "Spy demons. I could have managed them myself, but with *Mâmân* . . . Don't worry," he added hastily, seeing her expression. "Thomas helped me hide it. I won't tell you where, but it's safe. And I haven't seen a Ravener since I locked it away."

She wanted desperately to ask him where he had hidden it, but knew she couldn't. It was silly, but she missed Cortana terribly. *I've so changed myself*, she thought, *that I do not know if Cortana would choose me again, even if I were no longer Lilith's paladin.* It was a miserable thought.

"Thomas helped you?" she said instead. "Thomas Lightwood?"

"Oh, look, we're here," said Alastair brightly, and threw the door of the carriage open, leaping from it before it had quite stopped rolling.

"Alastair!" Cordelia hopped down after her brother, who seemed none the worse for his plunge and was already paying the driver.

She looked up at the house. She was fond of it—fond of the calm white front, the shiny black 102 painted on the rightmost pillar, fond of the quiet, leafy London street. But it was not *home*, she thought, as she followed Alastair up the front path to the door. This was her mother's house—a refuge, but not home. Home was Curzon Street.

Cordelia suspected Risa had been peering out a window, as she appeared immediately to whisk the front door open and usher them inside. She pointed accusingly at Cordelia's trunk, which sat in the middle of the entryway.

"It just appeared," she complained, fanning herself with a dish towel. "One moment not there, then *poof!* It gave me quite a *turn*, I tell you. *Tekan khordam.*"

"Sorry, Risa dear," said Cordelia. "I'm sure Magnus didn't mean for it to startle you."

Risa muttered as Alastair lifted the trunk and began heaving it up the stairs. "What did you buy in Paris?" he complained. "A Frenchman?"

"Be quiet, he's asleep," said Cordelia. "He speaks no English, *but* he can sing 'Frère Jacques' and he makes excellent *crêpes suzette*."

Alastair snorted. "Risa, are you going to help me with this?"

"No," Risa said. "I am going to take Layla to *khanoom* Sona. She will be much happier once she has seen her daughter."

Cordelia slipped out of her coat and waved a guilty goodbye to Alastair before following Risa down the corridor to her mother's bedroom. Risa put a finger to her lips before glancing in; a moment later, she was ushering Cordelia into the dimly lit space and closing the door behind her.

Cordelia blinked, her eyes adjusting to the faint light of the fire and the bedside lamp. Sona lay in bed, propped up in a sitting position against a mountain of colorful pillows, a book in her hands. Her belly looked rounder than when Cordelia had seen her only a week before, and her face was sallow and tired, although she smiled at Cordelia brightly.

Cordelia felt a terrible rush of guilt. "*Mâmân*," she cried, and hurried to the bed to carefully embrace her mother.

"Welcome back," her mother said, brushing her hand through Cordelia's hair.

"I'm sorry, *Mâmân*. I oughtn't to have gone—"

"Don't fret." Sona set her book down. "I told you that the most important thing was to do what would make you happy. So you went to Paris. What's the great harm?" Her dark eyes searched Cordelia's face. "I used to think that it was most important to endure, to stay strong. But unhappiness, over time . . . it poisons your life."

Cordelia sat down in the chair by the bed and took her mother's hand. "Was it really so terrible, with Baba?"

"I had you and Alastair," Sona said, "and that always made me happy. As for your father . . . I can only mourn the life we never had, that we could have had, if he—if things had been different. But you cannot fix someone, Cordelia," she added. "In the end, if they can be fixed at all, they must do the repairs themselves."

She sighed and looked at the flames dancing on the hearth.

"When I brought us to London," Sona went on, "it was to save our family. To save your father. And we did. *You* did. And I will always be proud of you for that." She smiled wistfully. "But what brought us here is over. I think perhaps it's time we consider leaving London."

"Return to Cirenworth?" Cirenworth was their country house in Devon, now closed up and uninhabited, with sheets over the furniture and blackout curtains at the windows. It was odd to think of going back there.

"No, Layla, to Tehran," Sona said. "I've been estranged from my aunts and cousins there for too long. And since your father is gone . . ."

Cordelia could only stare. Tehran, where her mother had been born; Tehran, whose language and history she knew as she knew her own hands, but a place she had no memory of living, whose customs she was not wholly familiar with.

"Tehran?" Cordelia echoed. "I—but we live *here*." She was nearly too shocked to speak. "And we could not go *now*. The Enclave needs us—"

"You have done enough for the Enclave," said her mother. "You can be a powerful Shadowhunter in Persia, too, if that is what you desire. Such are needed everywhere." *Spoken like a true parent*, Cordelia thought. "Layla, I am not saying you must come to Tehran. You have a husband here; of course it would be reasonable for you to remain."

Cordelia sensed that her mother was treading lightly, delicately, around the topic of her marriage. She wondered dismally what her mother *thought* had gone wrong between her and James. Or perhaps she only sensed some sort of trouble? She was offering Cordelia an escape, either way.

"Alastair has already said he will come," Sona said. "Risa, too, of course. With the new baby, I will require both their help."

"Alastair said he will go?" Cordelia was astonished. "To Tehran? And take care of the baby?" She tried to imagine Alastair burping a baby and sweepingly failed.

"There is no need to repeat everything I say, Layla. And you need not decide this moment." Sona patted her belly; her eyes were closing in tiredness. "I'm in no state to move thousands of miles away tonight. First I must bring this one into the world. Then you can decide what it is you want."

She closed her eyes. Cordelia kissed her mother's forehead and went out into the hall, where she found Alastair lurking in the corridor. She narrowed her eyes at him. "You knew about all this? You *agreed* to move to Tehran without saying a word to me?"

"Well, you were in Paris. Besides, I thought *Mâmân* should tell you, not me." Cordelia could not see his expression in the darkness of the corridor. "I don't have anything to stay here for—not really. Perhaps you do, but our situations are different."

Cordelia could only look at him silently. She could not bring herself to tell him how she felt it all slipping away from her: James, Matthew, Lucie. Her purpose as a Shadowhunter, the wielder of Cortana. What would it be like for her, to lose all that, and her family too, and still remain in London?

"Maybe not," she said finally. "Maybe they are more similar than you think."

The moment the Consul's carriage vanished, James set off for Curzon Street, the cold wind like a knife that cut through his coat.

It was fully two miles' walk between the Institute and his house, but James wanted the time to himself. London swirled around him, in all its vivid life. Fleet Street itself, with its journalists and barristers and businessmen, on to Leicester Square, where hundreds were queuing outside the Alhambra Theatre for tickets to the winter ballet. Tourists raised glasses to each other in the glowing windows of the brasserie of the Hotel de l'Europe. By the time he reached Piccadilly Circus it was growing dark, and the lights around the statue of Eros were haloed in clouds of dancing snowflakes. The traffic was so busy it had come to a standstill; a raging sea of Christmas shoppers poured past him from Regent Street, laden with brown-paper parcels. A red-faced man who was carrying a giant stuffed giraffe and had clearly been to Hamleys bumped right into him, seemed about to say something rude, then saw his expression and backed away hastily.

James had not glamoured himself, as his winter clothes covered his runes. He could hardly blame the man for rushing off, though; when he caught glimpses of his reflection in the shopwindows as he passed, he saw a young man with a white, stony face who looked as if he had just received some kind of terrible news.

The house on Curzon Street felt as if it had been abandoned for months, rather than days. James kicked the ice and snow off his boots in the entryway, where the bright wallpaper reminded him of the first time he'd brought Cordelia here. *So pretty*, she'd said. *Who chose it?*

And he'd felt a moment of pride when he told her he'd been the one to pick it out. Pride that he'd chosen something she liked.

He moved through the rooms, turning up the gas lamps, through the dining room and past the study, where he and Cordelia had played so many games of chess.

Out of the corner of his eye, he noticed a flicker of light. Still in his coat, he headed downstairs to the kitchen, where he was utterly unprepared to be greeted by a bloodcurdling scream.

A moment later he had a dagger in his hand and was facing off with Effie over the kitchen counter. She was wielding a wooden spoon like a gladiator, her gray pompadour trembling.

"Cor," she said, relaxing as she recognized him. "I wasn't expecting *you* back."

"Well, I'm not back for long," said James, putting the dagger away. "As it happens, I'm going to be staying at the Institute for at least a few days. Shadowhunter business."

"And Mrs. Herondale?" said Effie, looking curious. She was still holding the spoon.

"She's gone to her mother's. Until the baby is born."

"Well, nobody told *me*," Effie said crossly. "Nobody tells me anything."

James had begun to develop a headache. "I'm sure she'd appreciate it if you'd pack some of her things in a trunk for her. Someone will be along to fetch it tomorrow."

Effie hustled out of the kitchen; James thought she seemed relieved to have a specific task to accomplish, or perhaps she was just happy to get away from her knife-wielding employer. He was really winning over the populace today.

James continued through the house, lighting lamps as he went. It had grown dark outside, and the light glowed against the windowpanes. He knew he ought to pack his own trunk, though he had clothes and weapons at the Institute, things he had left there in his old bedroom. He couldn't decide if he should bring a few items with sentimental value; he both didn't want to be without them, and didn't want to contemplate the idea that he would not be returning soon to Curzon Street, to live here with Cordelia.

Everything here reminded him of her. He had known it before, in the back of his mind, but now it was obvious that every decision he'd made in the decorating of the house had been made in the hope of pleasing Cordelia, imagining what would bring her delight. The chessboard in the study, the Persian miniatures, the carved panel over the fireplace that incorporated the Carstairs crest. How could he not have known this at the time? From the beginning they had only agreed to be married a year; he had believed himself in love with Grace, but in the design of the house he'd supposedly hoped they would share someday, he had given Grace no thought at all.

The bracelet's work had been subtle. It was likely that he *had* wondered at the time why Grace was not more at the forefront of his mind. But the bracelet would have made sure such thoughts flickered briefly and were quickly extinguished. He could not now re-create the way he had thought of things then. It was strange, not to have been aware of his own feelings, and so infuriating, to be aware of them now, when it was too late.

He found himself standing at the fireplace in the drawing room. Atop the mantel were the broken pieces of the silver bracelet. Effie must have picked them up from the floor where James had left them.

He could not bring himself to touch them. They lay where they were, dull gray in the candlelight. The inscription written on the inside—LOYAULTÉ ME LIE—had been cut in half along with the band. The two matched crescents seemed only a broken trinket, not capable of destroying anyone's life.

And yet it had destroyed his. When he thought of what he'd *felt* for Grace—and there had been feelings, physical and unnatural, and even worse, what he'd *believed* he felt—it made him nauseated, deep down, in a way that was both violent and violating. His feelings, twisted; his love, directed wrongly; his innocence, turned to a weapon against him.

He thought of Grace, in the Silent City. In the dark, alone. *Good. I hope she rots there,* he thought, with a bitterness that was utterly unlike him. A bitterness that would, under other circumstances, have made him ashamed.

An orange glow like a candlelight suddenly appeared and drifted in through the open window. It was a sheet of paper, folded like a letter, but on fire and rapidly being consumed. It landed gently atop the piano, where the lace doily under it immediately caught fire as well.

Christopher, James thought immediately.

He put the fire out and brushed the ashes from the edges of the paper. When he turned it over, only two words were still readable. James was fairly sure they said *front door.*

Curious, he went to the front door and opened it. There he indeed found Christopher, lurking on the steps and looking sheepish.

"Is this yours?" James asked, holding up the burnt scrap. "And what've you got against doorbells?"

"What I do," Christopher said, "I do in the name of the advancement of science. How did it work, by the way?"

"Well, most of the message is burnt away, and you owe me one lace doily," James said.

Christopher nodded solemnly and withdrew a small notebook and a pencil from his jacket. He began to make a note. "It will be added to the list of friends' possessions that I must replace, due to the exigencies of—"

"Science. I know," James said. "Well, come in then." He couldn't help smiling as Christopher came in and hung up his coat—a little ragged around the cuffs where it had been burned and stained with various acidic compounds. His light brown hair stuck up around his head like duckling fluff. He seemed absolutely familiar and unchanged in a way that felt like a bit of light in a dark world.

"Is Cordelia here?" Christopher asked as James led him into the drawing room. They both sprawled into armchairs, Christopher tucking his little notebook back into his jacket.

"No," James said. "She has decided to remain at her mother's house for the time being. Until the baby is born, at least."

He wondered how many times he was going to have to say those same sentences. They were already beginning to drive him mad.

"Of course," Christopher said firmly. "That makes complete sense. It would be strange, in fact, if she was *not* staying with her mother, so close to the birth of her new sibling. It is my understanding that when a baby is to be born, as many people as possible must gather around to, ah, well. You know."

James raised an eyebrow.

"Anyway," Christopher went on before James could reply, "I was speaking with Thomas and we were wondering . . . I mean to say *he* thought, and *I* agreed, that . . . well, Matthew had sent a note saying he was in Paris and having a fine time with Cordelia and he'd explain when he returned. And now you and Matthew and Cordelia are *all* back from Paris, but Cordelia isn't here and . . ."

"Christopher," said James calmly. "Where is Thomas?"

Christopher's ears turned pink. "He went to talk to Matthew."

"I see," James said. "You got me, and Thomas got Math. The better for wheedling information out of at least one of us."

"It's not like that," Christopher said, looking miserable, and James felt like a cad. "We're the Merry Thieves—one for all, and all for one—"

"I think that's the Three Musketeers," said James.

"There *were* four Musketeers, if you count D'Artagnan."

"Christopher . . ."

"We've never had a fight," Christopher said. "I mean, none of us with each other, at least nothing serious. If you've had a falling-out with Math . . . we want to help repair it."

Despite himself, James was touched. As close as he and Christopher had been for years, he'd understood that Christopher would rarely, if ever, be willing to discuss something as irrational as *feelings*.

"We need each other," Christopher said simply. "Especially now."

"Oh, Kit." James felt a pressure at the back of his eyes. A yearning came over him to seize Christopher and hug him, but knowing that would merely alarm his friend, he stayed where he was. "Math and I are not at each other's throats. It's not like that. Nor are either of us angry with Cordelia, or she with us. Things between us are just—complicated."

"We need Cordelia, too," said Christopher. "And Cortana. I've been reading about paladins—"

"You heard about the Inquisitor, I assume? What happened to him when he went after Tatiana?"

"I am fully informed," said Christopher. "It seems Belial may soon make his next sally, and without Cordelia, or her sword . . ."

"Lilith also hates Belial," said James. "She would not prevent Cordelia from wielding Cortana against him, if it came to that. Still, Cordelia does not want to act while Lilith holds the reins, and I do not blame her."

"No," Christopher agreed. "At least Belial does not have a body to possess, as he did with Jesse Blackthorn."

"You know about Lucie and Jesse, I assume . . . ?"

"Oh, yes," said Christopher. "I met him at the family meeting last night. He seems a nice enough chap, though he won't let me run experiments on him, which is unfortunate."

"I can't imagine why."

"Maybe when things calm down, he'll reconsider."

"Maybe," said James, who doubted it. "In the meantime, we must have a meeting—those of us who know about Cordelia and Lilith—and discuss what can be done."

Christopher frowned. "Does Jesse know about Cordelia and Lilith? Because Lucie will want him to come to any meeting we have."

"And he should," said James. "He knows Belial in a way none of the rest of us do. Even me." He rubbed at his eyes. He felt exhausted, as if he had traveled back from Paris via train instead of Portal. "I'll tell him."

"And I shall send a bevy of my new fire-messages to everyone coming to the meeting," Christopher said, excited.

"No!" James protested, and then, as Christopher blinked worriedly, he said, "We can just send runners."

"*And* fire-messages," said Christopher.

James sighed. "All right. I shall notify the runners. And the fire brigade."

Thomas had no trouble finding Matthew's flat. He had been there before, but even if he had not, anyone who knew Matthew, had they been asked to guess which building in Marylebone he would have chosen to live in, would have picked the Baroque pink monstrosity on the corner of Wimpole Street.

The porter let Thomas in and told him that Mr. Fairchild was indeed at home, but he didn't like to disturb him. Thomas revealed his spare key and was duly sent up the gilded birdcage of a lift to Matthew's flat. He knocked at the door a few times and, not receiving any answer, let himself in.

It was cold in the room, cold enough to send goose bumps flooding across Thomas's skin. There were lamps lit but only a few, and those quite dim—Thomas almost fell over Matthew's trunk as he made his way into the parlor.

It took him a moment to spot Matthew, who was sitting on the floor in front of the fireplace, hatless and shoeless, his back against the sofa. He was gazing at the cold grate, where the ashes were piled in soft gray drifts.

Matthew held a wine bottle in one hand, cradled against his chest; Oscar lay next to him, whining and licking Matthew's other hand, as if he could tell something was terribly wrong.

Thomas crossed the room; he took a few logs from their holder, opened the fireplace grate, and began to build a blaze up. Once it was roaring, he turned to look down at Matthew. In the firelight, he could see that Matthew's clothes were crumpled; his scarlet velvet waistcoat was unbuttoned over a shirt that bore what Thomas at first thought were bloodstains, before realizing they were splashes of wine.

Matthew's eyes were rimmed with red, the green of his irises almost black. Another wine bottle, this one empty, was shoved between the sofa cushions behind him. He was clearly quite drunk.

"So," Thomas said after a long moment. "How was Paris?"

Matthew remained silent.

"I've always liked Paris myself," Thomas went on, in a conversational tone. "Lovely old city. I had a meal at Au Chien Qui Fume I'll not soon forget. Best duck I've ever had."

Without looking away from the fire, Matthew said slowly, "I don't want to talk about bloody ducks." He closed his eyes. "But next time you're there, if you like duck—eating them, I mean—you must go to La Tour d'Argent. Even better, I think. They give you a card commemorating the particular duck you have devoured. It is deliciously morbid." He opened his eyes again. "Let me guess," he said. "Christopher was assigned to James, and you assigned to me."

"Not at all," Thomas protested. Matthew raised an eyebrow. "All right, yes." He sat next to Matthew on the floor. "We drew straws."

"You lost, I suppose." Matthew took a long, deep breath. "Did Lucie talk to you?"

Thomas said, "She let us know you had returned. And she may have spoken a few words of concern related to your well-being, but the idea to speak to you both was our own."

Matthew tossed back his head and took a swallow from the bottle in his hand. It was half-empty. Thomas could smell the vinegary tang of the wine.

"Look," said Thomas, "whatever it is you feel, Math, I want to help you. I want to understand. But above all else, you must preserve your friendship with James. Or repair it, or whatever is necessary. You are *parabatai*, and that is so much more than I can ever understand. If you lose each other, you will be losing something you can never replace."

"*'Entreat me not to leave thee,'*" Matthew said, his voice weary. "Tom, I'm not angry at James." He reached out and scratched Oscar's head for a moment. "I am in love with Cordelia. I have been for some time. And I believed—truly, I believed, and I think you did as well—that her marriage to James was a sham, and that James's love was only and ever for Grace Blackthorn."

"Well, yes," said Thomas. "Isn't that the case?"

Matthew gave a dry laugh. "Cordelia came to me to say she was done with it all, that she could no longer stand the pretense, that it had grown unbearable. And I thought—" He choked out a sarcastic chuckle. "I thought perhaps this was a chance for us to be happy. For *all* of us to be happy. James could be with Grace as he'd always wanted, and Cordelia and I would go to Paris, where we would be happy. But then James came to Paris," Matthew went on, "and as per usual, it seems, I was wrong about everything. He does not love Grace, he says. He never did. He loves Cordelia. He does not want to give her up."

"That's what he said?" asked Thomas. He kept his voice calm, although inside he was reeling. It was astounding what people could hide from one another, even from their closest friends. "Did Cordelia know any of that?"

"She doesn't seem to have," said Matthew. "She seemed as astonished as I was. When James arrived, we were—"

"I'm not sure I want to know," said Thomas.

"We kissed," said Matthew. "That is all. But it was like alchemy, but with misery changed to happiness, instead of lead to gold."

Thomas thought that he knew exactly what Matthew meant, and also that he could not possibly say so.

"I know Cordelia well enough," he said, "to know she would not have kissed you if she did not want to. It seems to me, if you both love her—"

"We have agreed to abide by any decision she makes," said Matthew dully. "At the moment, her decision is that she doesn't wish to see either of us." He set down the bottle and looked at his hand. It was shaking visibly. Emotion and drink, Thomas thought with a terrible sympathy. He himself would have tamped down his passions, but Matthew had never been able to do that. Feelings spilled from him like blood from a cut. "I have ruined everything," he said. "I truly thought James did not love her. I truly thought my decision was the best for all of us, but I have only hurt them both. Cordelia's face when she saw him in the hotel room—" He winced. "How could I have gotten it all so wrong?"

Thomas slid over to Matthew so that their shoulders were touching. "We are all wrong sometimes," he said. "We all make mistakes."

"I seem to make especially terrible ones."

"It seems to me," Thomas said, "that you and James have been hiding parts of yourselves from one another for some time now. Both of you. And more even than the matter of Cordelia, that is what you need to discuss."

Matthew fumbled for the wine bottle, but Oscar whined loudly, and he drew his hand back. "It's just hard to know, when you have a secret . . . will telling it bring healing? Or just more hurt? Isn't it selfish, to unburden myself just to relieve my own conscience?"

Thomas was about to protest, *No, of course not*, but he hesitated. After all, he himself had a secret that he had kept from Matthew and James and Christopher. If he unburdened himself of *his* secret to Matthew, would it make things better? Or would Matthew think of the hurt that Alastair had caused him, had caused his friends, and think Thomas indifferent to it?

Then again, how could he exhort Matthew to tell the truth, if he wasn't going to tell it himself?

"Math," he said. "I have something I want to tell you."

Matthew looked over at him. As did Oscar, who seemed equally curious. "Yes?"

"I don't like girls," Thomas said. "Well, I *like* them. They're lovely people, and Cordelia and Lucie and Anna are excellent friends—"

"*Thomas,*" said Matthew.

"I am attracted to men," said Thomas. "But not like you. *Just* men."

Matthew smiled at that. "I rather guessed," he said. "I wasn't sure. You could have told me earlier, Tom. Why would I ever have minded? It isn't as if I was sitting about, waiting for you to write a handbook entitled *How to Seduce Women*."

"Because," Thomas said, rather wretchedly, "the first boy I ever—the one I still—" He took a deep breath. "I'm in love with Alastair. Alastair Carstairs."

Oscar growled. It appeared he did not approve of the word "Alastair."

"Ah." Matthew closed his eyes. "You—" He hesitated, and Thomas could tell that Matthew was trying to think carefully through the fog of alcohol. Struggling not to react impulsively. "I cannot judge you," he said at last. "The Angel knows, I've made enough mistakes, hurt enough people. I'm not sure I am fit to judge anyone. Even Alastair. But—does Alastair know how you feel?"

"He does," Thomas said.

"And he has been kind to you about it?" Matthew's eyes opened. "Is he—are you two—?"

"He won't agree to be with me," said Thomas quietly. "But not out of unkindness. He thinks he would be bad for me. I think . . . in some way . . . he believes he does not deserve to be happy. Or perhaps it is that he is unhappy, and he believes it is a sort of contagion that might spread."

"I understand that," Matthew said, a little wonderingly. "How much love people have denied themselves through the ages because they believed they did not deserve it. As if the waste of love is not the greater tragedy." His eyes were a very dark green as he looked at Thomas. "You love him?"

"More than anything," Thomas said. "It's just—all very complicated."

Matthew gave a little laugh. Thomas edged closer and pulled Matthew's head down onto his shoulder.

"We'll work it out," he said. "All our troubles. We're still the Merry Thieves."

"That's true," Matthew said. After a long silence, he said, "I probably need to stop drinking so much."

Thomas nodded, staring into the blazing fire. "That, also, is true."

11

Devil's Paladin

Au gibet noir, manchot aimable,
Dansent, dansent les paladins,
Les maigres paladins du diable,
Les squelettes de Saladins.
—Arthur Rimbaud, "Bal des Pendus"

"Alastair," Cordelia said. She had her hands flat on her brother's back and was pushing him, or at least trying to, toward the carriage. Unfortunately, it was like trying to dislodge a boulder. He didn't budge from the doorway. "Alastair, *get* in the carriage."

Her brother's arms were folded, his look stormy. *In a world of chaos,* thought Cordelia, exasperated, *at least some things remain consistent.* "I don't want to," he said. "Nobody wants me at this harebrained confabulation anyway."

"I do," Cordelia said patiently, "and also, *they* do, and the proof is here in writing." She brandished a folded page at him. It had been delivered that morning after breakfast by a messenger boy named Neddy, the Merry Thieves' most regular Irregular.

It requested both Cordelia's and Alastair's presence at the Devil Tavern that afternoon, on behalf of the Merry Thieves, "to discuss the developing situation." Cordelia had to admit she'd been relieved to receive it—she hadn't realized until that moment how worried she'd been that she'd be cut out of her friends' activities. For the crime of mistreating James, or mistreating Matthew, or snapping at Lucie. But no—she had been invited, and quite cheerfully, with Alastair also requested by name.

"I can't imagine why any of them would want me there," Alastair grumbled.

"Maybe Thomas convinced them," Cordelia said, which caused Alastair to forget that he was supposed to be resisting her attempts to drag him outside. He let go of the doorframe, and they both nearly toppled down the stairs. Cordelia heard Risa, wrapped up in fur blankets and perched on the driver's seat of the carriage, chuckle to herself.

They clambered into the carriage and started off, Alastair looking a little stunned, as if he couldn't quite believe he was going. He had his spears with him, and his favorite dagger—as Cordelia remained unarmed, lest she forget herself and accidentally summon Lilith. She hated it. She was a Shadowhunter, and going out weaponless felt like going out naked, only more dangerous.

"Why do you keep mentioning Thomas to me?" Alastair said. They were passing row upon row of white houses, many with holly wreaths pinned to their front doors. Risa had clearly decided to take smaller roads to reach the Devil Tavern, avoiding the traffic of Knightsbridge at peak Christmas shopping time.

Cordelia raised an eyebrow at him.

"Thomas Lightwood," he clarified, tugging on his scarf.

"I didn't think you meant Thomas Aquinas," said Cordelia. "And I keep mentioning him because I am not a complete idiot, Alastair. You did turn up rather suddenly at the Institute the moment he was arrested to tell everyone you knew he was innocent because you'd been following him about for days."

"I didn't realize you knew all that," Alastair grumbled.

"Matthew told me." She reached out to pat her brother on the cheek with a gloved hand. "There is no shame in caring about someone, Alastair. Even if it hurts."

"'*The wound is the place where the light enters you,*'" Alastair said. It was her favorite Rumi quote. Cordelia looked quickly out the window.

She told herself not to be foolish, not to cry, no matter how kind

Alastair was being. Out the window, she could see the crowded streets of Piccadilly, where sellers pushed barrows of holly and ivy wreaths and wooden toys. Omnibuses rolled by, their sides advertising tins of holiday biscuits and Christmas crackers.

"You're not going to mind seeing James, will you?" Alastair said. "It won't bother you?"

Cordelia tugged at the lace on her skirt. She was wearing a pale lavender dress that her mother had gotten her when they first arrived in London, with far too many ruffles and frills. Her only other choices had been the elegant gowns she'd gotten in Paris, but when she'd opened the trunk and touched the silk and velvet, so carefully packed with tissue paper, she'd felt only a wave of sadness. Her time in Paris now seemed tinged with shadow, like the darkening of an old photograph.

"I left him, Alastair," she said. "Not the other way around."

"I know," he said, "but sometimes we leave people to protect ourselves, don't we? Not because we don't want to be with them. Unless, of course," he added, "you are in love with Matthew, in which case, you had better tell me now, and not spring it on me later. I'm braced, I think I can bear up."

Cordelia made a face. "I told you," she said. "I just don't know what I feel—"

The carriage came to a jouncing stop. They had made good time through the park and across Trafalgar Square; here they were at the Devil Tavern. As Cordelia and Alastair clambered out of the carriage, Risa called down that she'd be waiting for them around the corner on Chancery Lane, where the traffic was quieter.

The ground floor of the Devil was as bustling as ever. The usual assortment of regulars filled the high-ceilinged space, and a brief cry of welcome from Pickles, the drunken kelpie, came from the far corner as they closed the door behind them. Alastair looked astonished when Ernie the barkeep welcomed Cordelia by name. Cordelia felt a little surge of pride at that; it was always gratifying to surprise Alastair, no matter how old she got.

She led them through the crowd to the staircase at the back. On the way they passed by Polly, who was carrying a precariously full tray of drinks above her head. "All your Thieves are already upstairs," she said to Cordelia with a nod, and then turned to take in Alastair with wide eyes. "Cor, who knew the Shadowhunters have been hidin' their handsomest away until now. What's *your* name, love?"

Alastair, shocked into silence for a change, let Cordelia pull him past and up the stairs. "That was—did she really—"

"Fret not," Cordelia said with a grin. "I shall keep a weather eye out lest she assail your virtue."

Alastair glared. They had reached the top of the staircase, and the familiar door, above which was carved, *It matters not how a man dies, but how he lives. S.J.*

Alastair read this with some interest. Cordelia poked him in the side. "I want you to be nice in there," she said sternly. "I don't want to hear any comments about how the furniture is shabby and the bust of Apollo has its nose chipped."

Alastair arched one eyebrow. "My concern is never with the shabbiness of the furniture," he said loftily, "but the shabbiness of the company."

Cordelia made a frustrated noise. "You are *impossible*," she said, and swung the door open.

The little room inside was crowded. It seemed everyone else had already arrived: James, Matthew, Thomas, and Christopher, of course, but also Lucie and Jesse, Anna, and even Ariadne Bridgestock. All the available furniture from the adjacent bedroom had been dragged in so that there was a seat for everyone (counting the window ledge, where Lucie had perched), but it was a tight squeeze. James and Matthew weren't sitting next to one another, but Cordelia decided to be relieved that they had both come and didn't seem to be exchanging glares.

A chorus of greetings rose up as Alastair and Cordelia came in. Thomas detached himself from the arm of Anna's chair and came over to them, his hazel eyes bright. "You came," he said to Alastair.

"Well, I was invited," Alastair said. "Was that your doing?"

"No," Thomas protested. "Well, I mean, you are the current holder of Cortana—you *ought* to be here, and you're Cordelia's brother; it wouldn't make any sense to leave you out—"

Cordelia decided it was time to make herself scarce. She smiled awkwardly at Lucie, who smiled equally awkwardly back, and went to sit on the sofa, where she found herself next to Ariadne.

"I heard you were in Paris," Ariadne said. There seemed something different about Ariadne, Cordelia thought, though she could not have put her finger on what it was. "I've always wanted to go. Was it wonderful?"

"Paris is lovely," Cordelia said. It was true enough—Paris was wonderful. Nothing that had happened there had been the city's fault.

She caught Matthew's eye. He smiled a little sadly. Cordelia noticed with a pang at her heart that he looked awful—well, awful for Matthew. His waistcoat didn't match his jacket, a lace had broken on one of his boots, and his hair was untidy. This was the Matthew equivalent of turning up at a party with a dagger protruding from his chest.

Thoughts Cordelia hated crowded her head—was he drunk? Had he been drinking that morning? He had kept up appearances in Paris; what did it mean that he wasn't doing it now? At least he was *here*, she told herself.

As for James—James looked his ordinary self. Orderly, calm, the Mask firmly in place. He did not look at her, but Cordelia knew him well enough now to sense his tension. He did not wear his anguish plainly, as Matthew did, if indeed he felt anguish at all.

"And you," Cordelia said, to Ariadne, "are you all right? And your parents? I am so terribly sorry to hear of what befell your father, though at least he is unharmed."

Ariadne said calmly, "I think my parents are well enough. I am not staying with them at the moment, but with Anna."

Oh. Cordelia glanced over at Anna, who was laughing at something Christopher had said. Ariadne had been pursuing Anna, Anna resisting—did this mean that Anna had finally given in? What on earth was going on with the two of them? Maybe Lucie knew.

Thomas reappeared to retake his place on the arm of Anna's chair; Alastair had stationed himself by the disused fireplace. Cordelia did not fail to notice that Thomas was wearing something new—a long green scarf she recognized as Alastair's. Had Alastair made Thomas a present of the scarf?

A loud *crack* silenced the room, and Cordelia jerked her head around to see that it was Christopher, pounding a small hammer against the table.

"I call this meeting to order!" he cried.

"Is that a *gavel*?" Thomas said. "Don't judges only use those in America?"

"Yes," said Christopher, "but I found it in a knickknack shop, and as you see, it has already proven highly useful. We have gathered here this afternoon to discuss—" He turned to James and spoke in a quieter voice. "What is the order of discussion again?"

James gazed around the room with dark golden eyes. Those eyes had once been able to melt Cordelia's bones inside her body and turn her stomach to a mass of knots. *Not anymore,* she told herself firmly. *Certainly not.*

James said, "First, we are discussing the problem of Lilith. Specifically, that she has tricked Cordelia into becoming her paladin, and that for her own good and for all of ours, we need to find a way to break the connection between them."

Cordelia blinked in surprise. She'd had no idea that the meeting would be focused at all on her, rather than Tatiana or Belial.

"To be honest," Ariadne said, "I'd never even heard of a paladin until Anna told me what happened. Apparently it's a terribly ancient term?"

Christopher banged his gavel again. When they looked over at him, he reached under the table and brought out a huge old tome, its covers elaborately carved wood. He dropped it onto the table with a crash.

Matthew said, "So you brought a gavel *and* the book?"

"I believe in thorough preparation," Christopher said. "I had heard the term 'paladin' before, at the Academy, but only in passing. So I looked it up."

They all waited expectantly. "And then what happened?" Alastair demanded finally. "Or is that the entire story?"

"Oh, yes, sorry," said Christopher. "A *paladin* is simply a name for a warrior sworn to the service of a powerful supernatural being. There are stories of Shadowhunter paladins—pledged to Raziel or sometimes to other angels—that go back to the time of the very first Shadowhunters. But there hasn't been one for hundreds of years. In fact, the most recent reference I found, already five hundred years old, refers to paladins as 'of an earlier time' and 'no more to be found among us.'"

Lucie frowned. "Were there paladins sworn to demons?"

"Not among Shadowhunters," Christopher said, "at least not in the records we have."

"It must have happened," Alastair offered. "But they were probably too embarrassed to record it." Cordelia gave him a cold look. "What?" he demanded. "You know I'm right."

Christopher cleared his throat and said, "There *are* records of a few mundanes who have become the paladins of Greater Demons. Usually they are described as fearsome warriors who killed for pleasure and knew nothing of mercy."

"And they remained paladins until they died?" James said.

"Yes," said Christopher slowly, "but these weren't the kind of people who died in their beds. Almost all of them died violently in some battle or other. The problem, you see, is that all of them very much *wanted* to be a demon's paladin."

"Were any of them sworn to Lilith specifically?" Cordelia said.

"I don't think so," Christopher said. "I believe you said Lilith sought you out as a paladin because she has lost her realm—Edom. It is a terrible place, reportedly, a scorched desert with a burning sun."

"So why does she want it back so badly? What's important about it?" asked Ariadne.

"Demons are very attached to their realms," said James. "They function as a source of power, with the realm being almost an extension of the demon itself." He frowned. "If only we could figure out a way to drive Belial from Edom, perhaps Lilith would release Cordelia."

"I doubt it would be easy to do that," said Christopher glumly. "Although I like the epic nature of your thinking, James. Edom is a world that was not unlike ours once. It even had Shadowhunters and a capital city, Idumea, much like our own Alicante. But the Nephilim there were destroyed by demons. Some of the old texts speak of the Princes of Hell referring to Edom as a site of great victory, where Raziel's hopes were dashed. I imagine as realms go, it's a sort of trophy, and—I see your minds are wandering, so I'll just say I intend to do more research on the subject. *And* I intend to make all of you help me," he added, brandishing the gavel at them.

Everyone seemed to be waiting for Cordelia to say something. She said, "I understand why you all think ending Lilith's hold on me should be our focus. If I could wield Cortana again, it remains our best defense against Belial."

"Don't be ridiculous," Lucie said loudly. "It is our focus because you are in danger, and we care about you."

Cordelia felt herself flush, painfully pleased.

James said, "If I may . . . Lucie is right, but Cordelia is also right. It has become clear that Belial will never leave us alone. Perhaps if my family were dead—"

"James," Lucie murmured, her face pale. "Don't even think it."

"—but even then, Tatiana would remain at large, causing trouble. With Cortana, it might be possible to end Belial's life."

"That is something I do not understand," said Anna. "Princes of Hell are meant to be eternal, is that not true? Yet we have been told many times that Cortana can kill Belial. Can he be killed, or not?"

"Much of the language regarding Belial, Lilith, and the Princes of Hell is poetic. Symbolic," said Jesse, and the rich, soft timbre of his voice struck Cordelia. He sounded very confident for someone who'd spent so many years half-alive and hiding. He smiled at the surprised looks he was being given. "I read a great deal, when I was a ghost. Especially when I realized my mother was being drawn in deep with powerful demons. There was a time," he went on, "when research into the Princes of Hell and their powers was quite popular. Unfortunately, the monks and magicians and others doing the research had a nasty habit of turning up dead, nailed to tree trunks."

Everyone winced.

"As a result, the books containing such information are few, and old. And they do not solve the paradox. They are full of such riddles. Lucifer lives, but does not live. Belial cannot be killed, but Cortana can end Belial with three mortal blows." He shrugged. "Belial certainly seems *afraid* of Cortana. I think we must trust that means something."

"Perhaps a third blow from the sword will put him into a deep and permanent sleep?" suggested Thomas.

"From which he will be awakened by a kiss from Leviathan's sticky tentacles?" suggested Matthew, and there was a chorus of groans.

"What about your dreams, James?" said Anna. "You've always had some power to see what Belial's up to, in the past."

James was shaking his head. "There's been nothing," he said. "In fact, there's been so much nothing that it's begun to worry me. No dreams, no visions, no voice. No hint of Belial in my mind at all since—well, since I was in Cornwall." He frowned. "I dreamed I saw a long blank road, with demons rushing by above, and I heard Belial's voice. Nothing since then. It's as if I used to be able to see through a doorway and now—the door is closed."

"You heard his voice?" said Anna. "What did he say?"

"'They wake,'" said James.

Cordelia felt as if she'd been walking down a flight of stairs and missed a step; the same flinch, the same drop in her stomach. Her eyes met Matthew's; he, too, looked startled, but when she shook her head, he nodded. They were not going to say anything yet.

"But what does it mean?" Anna mused aloud. She turned to Jesse. "Did Belial ever say anything like that to you? 'They wake'?"

Jesse spread his hands wide. "I don't think my possession was like the possession of a living person. During the time Belial was inhabiting my body, I had no awareness of his presence, or any memory of my body having been away from Chiswick. Whenever you might have encountered him while he was in me . . . I was fully unconscious of any of it. And I've had no awareness or image of him or anything since."

"Maybe this is good news?" Thomas offered. "Maybe he's been set back on his heels for the moment, and we have some time?"

"Maybe," James said doubtfully. "But I'm not saying things have been *normal*. I'm not dreaming about Belial, but I'm not dreaming of anything else at all. In recent nights, no dreams at all, just a blank white void where dreams should be."

"There's also the matter of Tatiana," Lucie said. "Belial appeared before the Inquisitor to warn him off finding her."

Christopher said, "James, do you think Belial is hiding from you on purpose?"

James shrugged. "It could be."

Matthew gave a hollow laugh. "Very frustrating, what? All you want is for Belial to leave you alone and now he is, just when we want to see what he's up to."

"All of that considered," Anna said, "we may have to pursue

the questions of Lilith and Belial on parallel tracks. Let's get back to Cordelia. Our best weapon against Belial, should he show up, is Cortana, and who wields Cortana? You do, darling. We need you."

Cordelia glanced over at Alastair, worried, but Alastair was nodding. "It's true," he said. "Cortana chose Cordelia a long time ago. I didn't become its wielder when Cordelia handed it to me. I used it, as one might use any sword, but it did not kindle in my hand as it does in my sister's."

"So," Christopher said, "to sum up: Cortana is hidden. Cordelia remains bound to Lilith, though only us ten know that."

"And Belial," James said quietly. "He told Bridgestock we should keep our paladin away from him, though of course the Inquisitor didn't know what he meant." His eyes fixed briefly on Ariadne, then looked away.

Anna, however, caught his look. "Ariadne is no longer on speaking terms with the Inquisitor," she said primly. "She is part of our group now." She looked around as if to challenge anyone to deny this, but no one did.

"If Bridgestock pursues the question of what Belial meant," said Cordelia, "it'll only be a matter of time before it comes out."

"Belial may know that you are a paladin of Lilith, but he cannot know you will not raise a weapon in her name," said James. "If Belial is telling Bridgestock to keep you away from him, he likely fears Cortana more than ever."

"Do you think Tatiana knows?" Thomas said. "About Cordelia being a paladin?"

"I wouldn't be surprised if he hadn't told her," said James. "She is not his confidante, his partner. Belial doesn't have those. He has dupes and minions—" He hesitated.

"Oh dear," said Christopher. "I'm sorry, Jesse. Perhaps this is awkward for you."

Jesse waved this off. "Not at all."

"You could wait in the stairwell," Christopher suggested magnanimously, "while we talk about how to defeat your mother and crush her plans. If you like."

Thankfully, Jesse smiled at this. "I know it would be helpful if I had any idea where my mother was. She kept most of this from me while I was with her—both when I was fully alive, and after—though I did what I could to piece things together. I'm going to speak to Grace in the Silent City tomorrow, but I doubt she'll have any better guess than I do where she—our mother—is."

"Jesse," Lucie said, nudging his shoulder with hers. "Tell them your idea."

Jesse said, "I was going to suggest that while it remains empty, we should perform a thorough search of Chiswick House. I may not know where my mother is right now, but I do know many of her hiding places in the house."

Matthew said wearily, "The Enclave has been over Chiswick House at this point. Many times. If they haven't found anything—"

"Maybe it's because there's nothing to find," Jesse said. "But maybe it's because my mother hides things *well*. I saw her do it; she was often unaware of when I was watching."

"All right," said James, "then we'll go tomorrow. There are enough of us to make a significant search party." He hesitated. "After you see Grace, of course."

Ariadne said, "We could go right now. I'm eager to do something. Aren't all of you?"

"I can't," said James. "Nor Lucie, nor—more crucially—Jesse. We were only able to convince my parents to let us come here because it's still daytime. If we aren't back for dinner, they'll send their own search party after us."

"And while Chiswick won't be the *first* place they look," Lucie put in, "it'll probably be the third or fourth. Searching Chiswick *is* a good idea," she added. "But there must be something we can do to try to help Cordelia, too. I don't expect to find anything about Lilith, or paladins, among Tatiana's things."

Cordelia took a deep breath. "She is still very much watching me. She sent demons to attack us, in Paris. So that I would fight back and summon her."

"*What?*" said Alastair and James at the same time. They glared at each other for a moment, before Alastair demanded, "For what purpose? What did she want?"

"She assumed I'd still have Cortana," she said. "Once she realized I didn't, it was mostly taunting and threats."

"Do we know of anything that can hurt Lilith?" Thomas said. "Cortana could, of course, but . . . it's not an option."

Lucie brightened. "Why, James's revolver, of course. That's how we sent her away last time."

"It only seemed to damage her temporarily," Cordelia pointed out. "She left, but she didn't appear wounded at all when I saw her in Paris."

Christopher said, "The revolver was blessed with the names of three angels—Sanvi, Sansanvi, and Semangelaf. They are enemies of Lilith. I mean, I suppose *all* angels are enemies of Lilith. But they are particularly her enemies. Perhaps we could make use of the power of those angels in some other fashion to dispatch her?"

To Cordelia's surprise, Alastair spoke up. "Or what if we tried to find, or summon, the real Wayland the Smith? He must be one of the most powerful beings alive, *if* he's still alive. Surely he'd be vexed to learn that a demon had impersonated him?"

"A good thought," said James, and Alastair looked a little surprised to have James's approval. Thomas smiled at him, but he was looking down at his feet and didn't appear to notice.

"And we must keep in mind," said Jesse, "that Belial and my— that Belial and Tatiana are using each other. She is using him that she might find a way to have revenge against those she hates: Herondales, Lightwoods, Carstairs, Fairchilds. Even the Silent Brothers. What he is using her for, we do not yet know. But I expect it will be an important part of his plan."

There was a short silence. Then, "I think," Christopher cried, "that this will call for some *significant research*!"

This seemed to punctuate the meeting in some way, and immediately the larger conversation broke down into chatter. Christopher began trying to recruit fellow researchers, whereas Lucie began organizing who would go to Chiswick House and when they would meet. Only Matthew sat where he was, his eyes closed, looking green around the gills. Hungover, Cordelia thought sadly. She wished—but it didn't matter what she wished. She'd learned that again in Paris.

As discreetly as she could, she slipped out of her seat to approach

James. He was standing by one of the shelves of books, running a finger along the spines, clearly looking for something.

"James—I need to speak to you in private," she said quietly.

He looked down at her. His golden eyes seemed to burn in his pale, intent face. For a moment there was no one in the room but the two of them. "Really?"

She realized, belatedly, that what she'd said must have seemed to him as if she were saying she wished to speak to him about their marriage. She could feel her cheeks turning pink. "It's about something I heard," she said. "In Paris. I thought we'd better talk at the Institute before alarming everyone. Lucie ought to be there too," she added.

He remained motionless for a moment, his hand on a thick book of demonology. Then, "Of course," he said, turning away from the shelves. "We can speak at the Institute. And if you like, you can stay for supper."

"Thank you." Cordelia watched as James stepped away to say something to Christopher and Matthew. She felt stiff, uncomfortable, and it was nearly unbearable feeling uncomfortable around James—James, of all people.

Her heart felt like a rag, wrung out but still saturated with stubborn, ineradicable love. She could not help wondering: If there had never been a Grace, would James have fallen in love with her? Would she and James have found happiness together, a simple, direct happiness that was now forever out of reach? Even in her wildest dreams, she found it impossible to picture what that happy ending would have been like. Perhaps she ought to have learned something from that before all this, she thought; if one could not even imagine something, surely it indicated that thing was never meant to happen?

12

The Seeing Ones

And you have known him from his origin,
You tell me; and a most uncommon urchin
He must have been to the few seeing ones—
A trifle terrifying, I dare say,
Discovering a world with his man's eyes,
Quite as another lad might see some finches.
—Edwin Arlington Robinson, "Ben Jonson
Entertains a Man from Stratford"

As they walked back to Anna's flat, their boots kicking up slushy snow, Anna kept a weather eye on Matthew.

Matthew had always been her companion in mischief. She swore she could remember the day when she was two years old, when gurgling baby Matthew had been plonked into her lap and she had decided then and there that they would be the best of friends.

There had been a time, two years ago, when a darkness had taken up residence at the backs of Matthew's eyes. A shadow where there had always been sunshine. He had never been willing to speak of it, and after some time it had gone away, replaced by a slightly wilder and more brittle cheerfulness. She had put it down to the oddness of boys growing up—after all, had James not grown odd and distant around the same time?

Today, in the Devil Tavern, Anna had seen that the shadow was back in Matthew's eyes. She was not so foolish as not to assume it had something to do with the awful situation regarding Cordelia and James. If Matthew was unhappy—and that was clear—he was unhappy enough to have made himself ill over it. The shadows under his eyes looked like a boxer's fading bruises.

So she had invited him home with her for tea. He'd seemed agreeable enough, especially once it was clear that Cordelia was returning to the Institute with James and Lucie. He spoke little on the walk to Percy Street: he was hatless and gloveless, as if taking some pleasure from the bitingly cold air.

Once inside the flat, Ariadne excused herself to change her dress, a carriage on Tottenham Court Road having splashed muddy slush all over its hem. Anna offered Matthew food, which he refused, and tea, which he accepted. His hands shook as he lifted the teacup to his mouth.

Anna scolded him out of his damp coat and handed him a flannel to dry his wet hair. He'd finished his tea, so she poured him another cup and added a capful of brandy. Matthew almost looked as if he were going to protest—odd, he'd never protested against brandy in his tea before—but stopped himself. His hair sticking up in soft gold spikes, he took the cup and flicked his eyes to the door of Anna's bedroom. "So Ariadne is living with you now?"

Trust Matthew to want to gossip regardless of the circumstances.

"Temporarily," Anna said. "She couldn't remain with the Bridgestocks."

"Even as a temporary measure," Matthew said, a swallow of the brandied tea seeming to have steadied his hands, "do you think that's a wise idea?"

"And who are you, exactly, to have anything to say about wisdom?" Anna said. "*Your* most recent idea was to run away to Paris with James's wife."

"Ah, but I am already well known for having only terrible ideas, whereas you are regarded as possessing good judgment and common sense."

"Well, there you go," said Anna. "If this was not a good idea, I would not be doing it, since I have only good ideas."

Matthew began to protest, but Anna shushed him with a warning finger; Ariadne had come bustling back into the sitting room in a peach-colored day dress. There were few people Anna knew who could have carried off that shade of coral, but it seemed to make Ariadne's skin glow from within. Her hair was down, a mass of black silk about her shoulders.

There was worry in Ariadne's eyes as she glanced at Matthew, but wisely she said nothing, only took a seat beside him on the purple tufted sofa.

Good, don't show him you're worried, Anna thought. *He'll only dig his heels in like a stubborn pony.*

But Ariadne had been well trained by her mother in etiquette. She could probably carry on a conversation about the weather with someone whose head was on fire. "I understand, Matthew," she said, accepting a cup of Earl Grey, "that you have your own flat. That you, like Anna, prefer to live on your own. Is that true?"

"I'm not sure it was down to preference, but rather necessity," said Matthew. "But I *do* like where I am living," he added, "and you might like it as well; the flats are serviced, and I am fairly sure I could battle a demon in the lobby and the porter would be too polite to have any questions." He glanced at Anna. "Is that why you asked me here? Advice over flats?"

Anna said nothing; the thought of Ariadne leaving unsettled her in a way she could not define. Surely she wished her privacy back, she thought, the calm and comfort of her flat, the refuge it provided, uninhabited by anyone but herself . . .

Ariadne set her teacup down. "Not at all. We wanted your advice on something I found."

Matthew raised his eyebrows, clearly curious now. Ariadne fetched the letter from atop the mantelpiece and passed it over. Matthew unfolded it and read it quickly, eyes widening.

"Where did you find this?" he asked when he was done. Anna was pleased to see that he seemed sharper, more focused.

"My father's office," Ariadne said. "And it's obviously his. His handwriting, his signature."

"But he didn't send it," said Matthew. "So either your father is blackmailing someone, or he is *planning* to blackmail someone but didn't get around to it before he left for the Adamant Citadel. Did he notice it missing?"

Ariadne bit her lip. "I—don't know. I think he meant to burn it—I found it in the fireplace, so I wouldn't think he'd be looking for it. But we haven't spoken since he got back."

"The question," said Anna, "is who the Inquisitor would want to blackmail, and over what."

"I can't imagine," said Ariadne. "He's already in such a position of power. Why would he need to hold something over someone? If a Shadowhunter was violating the Law, he would have every authority to confront them directly."

Matthew was silent for a moment. "Is this letter why you feel you must move away?" he asked finally. "Why it is a . . . necessity for you to go?"

"I've always been raised to be a model Shadowhunter," Ariadne said softly. "I'm the daughter of the Inquisitor. It is my father's job to hold all the Nephilim to the impossibly high standard of Raziel's Law, and he holds his family to no less a standard. I was raised to be an obedient daughter, in training to become an obedient wife. I would do what they said, marry who they wanted—"

"Charles, for instance," Matthew said.

"Yes. But it was all rubbish in the end, wasn't it? My father apparently doesn't hold *himself* to his high-minded standards." She shook her head and looked out the window. "It was the hypocrisy that was the last straw, I suppose." She looked directly at Matthew, and as she spoke Anna felt, against her will, a surge of pride in Ariadne. "I told my mother that I would not marry whatever man they chose for me. That, in fact, I would not marry any man at all. That I did not love men, but women."

Matthew wound a curl of his fair hair around his forefinger, a nervous gesture left over from childhood. "Did you know," he said slowly, "that you were saying something she did not want to hear? Something you thought might cause her to cut you off? Even to—hate you?"

"I knew," Ariadne said. "Yet I would do it again. I am sure my mother is mourning the daughter that she never had. But if she loves me—and I believe she does—I think she must love the reality of me."

"What about your father?"

"He was in shock when he came back from Iceland," Ariadne said. "I did not hear from him for nearly a day, and then it was a letter—clearly he knew I have been staying with Anna—saying that I could come home if I apologized to my mother and took back what I had said."

"Which you will not do," said Matthew.

"Which I will not do," Ariadne agreed. Her smile was sad. "It may be hard for you to understand. Your parents are so remarkably kind."

Matthew seemed to flinch. Anna thought with a pang of the time when the Fairchilds had been one of the closest families she knew, before Charles had grown so cold, before Matthew had become so sad.

"Well, they certainly aren't blackmailing anyone," Matthew said. "I noted something here in the letter: 'Your family has benefited from the spoils of—giant ink blot—but it could all be lost if your house is not in order.' What if it means 'spoils' quite literally?"

Ariadne frowned. "But it has been illegal to take spoils from Downworlders since the Accords were first signed."

Anna shuddered. *Spoils.* It was an ugly word, an ugly concept. Spoils had been the practice of confiscating possessions from innocent Downworlders: common before the historic peace treaty between Downworlders and Shadowhunters that was now called the Accords. Common, and usually unpunished. Many old Shadowhunter families had enriched themselves that way.

"It may not refer to crimes being committed now. When the Accords were signed in 1872," Anna said, "Shadowhunters were meant to return the spoils they had taken. But many did not. The Baybrooks and the Pouncebys, for instance. Their wealth came from spoils originally. Everyone knows it."

"Which is dreadful," Ariadne said, "but not an excuse for blackmail."

"I doubt the blackmail springs from moral outrage," said Matthew. "More convenience. He wishes to blackmail this person, and has found an excuse to do so." He rubbed at his eyes. "It could be anyone he seeks to control. It could be Charles."

Ariadne looked startled. "But my father and Charles have always been on good terms. Even after our engagement ended, they righted things quickly. Charles has always wanted to be just the sort of politician that my father is."

"What do you think it is Charles has done that could render him vulnerable to blackmail?" Anna said.

Matthew shook his head. His hair, dry now, was beginning to fall into his eyes. "Nothing. Just an idea. I wondered if the spoils could be considered the spoils of political power, but I agree—let's look into Baybrook and Pounceby first." He turned to Ariadne. "Would you mind lending me the letter? I'll confront Thoby—I know him best. And he has never been good at standing up to interrogation. Once he pilfered someone else's food hamper at the Academy but folded like cheap paper under questioning."

"Of course," Ariadne said. "And I'm friendly with Eunice. I think she'll be open to meeting with me, and she won't even notice she's being questioned. She's too self-absorbed."

Matthew rose to his feet, a soldier bracing for a return to the field. "I ought to go," he said. "Oscar will be howling for my return."

Anna walked him down to the front door. As Matthew opened it, he glanced up the stairs where Ariadne remained.

"She is brave," he said. "Braver than either of us, I think."

Anna laid a hand against his cheek. "My Matthew," she said. "What is it you fear so much to tell your parents?"

Matthew closed his eyes, shaking his head. "I—I can't, Anna. I do not want you to despise me."

"I would never despise you," Anna said. "We are all flawed creatures. As diamonds are flawed, each distinct imperfection makes us unique."

"Perhaps I don't wish to be unique," Matthew said. "Perhaps I wish only to be happy and ordinary."

"Matthew, darling, you are the least ordinary person I know—besides myself—and that is part of what *makes* you happy. You are a peacock, not a duck."

"I see you have inherited the Herondale hatred of ducks from your mother," said Matthew, with the faintest of smiles. He looked up at the sky, deep black, spangled with stars. "I cannot help but feel something terribly dark is coming. Even in Paris, we could not escape the warnings. It is not that I fear danger, or a battle. It is a greater shadow than that, casting itself across all of us. Across London."

Anna frowned. "What do you mean?" she said, but Matthew, seeming to feel he had said too much, would not elaborate. He only straightened his jacket and set off, a slim figure making its way down Percy Street, unobserved by passersby.

"You could stay the night at the Institute, Daisy," Lucie said as she, Jesse, Cordelia, and James made their way along Fleet Street. The streetlamps had been lit, each illuminating a circle of light where tiny flakes of snow swirled like swarms of icy gnats. The wind had picked up, and again blew flurries of ice in misty eddies around the four of them, which Jesse alone seemed to enjoy, his face upturned to the night as they walked. He had not been able to feel hot or cold for years, he had pointed out, and extremes of temperature still delighted him. Apparently he had once gotten close enough to the fireplace in the Institute drawing room to singe his jacket before Lucie pulled him away. "I mean, look at all this snow."

"Perhaps," Cordelia said. She cast a sideways glance at James, who had been quiet through the walk, his hands plunged deep into the pockets of his coat. Pale flakes were caught in the darkness of his hair.

She did not finish the thought; they had reached the Institute. Once inside, they stomped the snow off their shoes in the entryway and hung their clothes up next to gear jackets and an assortment of weapons on pegs near the front door. James rang one of the servants' bells—presumably to let Will and Tessa know they had returned—and said, "We should go to one of the bedrooms. For privacy."

If they had been at Curzon Street, of course, there would be no need to worry about Will and Tessa overhearing them. But James had promised to stay at the Institute while Tatiana was at large, and anyway Cordelia didn't think she could have faced Curzon Street.

"Yours," said Lucie promptly. "Mine is a mess."

James's bedroom. Cordelia had not been in it often—she had a blurred memory of arriving to see James, a copy of *Layla and Majnun* in her hand, and finding him in his room with Grace. If only she had given up on him then—not let this farce play out as long as it had. She was silent as they passed through the chapel: it was unlighted now, stripped of decorations. Only a few weeks ago she and James had gotten married here, wreaths of pale flowers garlanding the pews, spilling into the aisle. She had walked on crushed petals as she approached the altar, so that they released their perfume in a cloud of cream and tuberose.

She glanced sideways at James, but he appeared lost in thought. Of course she could not expect him to feel about this place as she did. It would not be a knife to the heart for him.

James led them to his bedroom. It was much neater than it had been when James had lived here before—probably because it was mostly bare, other than the open trunk at the foot of the bed. In the trunk Cordelia recognized James's clothes, brought from their house, and a few knickknacks—was that a flash of ivory? Before she could look more closely, James had kicked the trunk shut. He turned to Jesse. "Lock the door, would you?"

Jesse hesitated before turning to Cordelia, to her surprise. "Cordelia," he said. "I've heard so much about you from Lucie I feel as if I know you. But in truth—I'm nearly a stranger to you. If you'd prefer to speak to James and Lucie alone . . ."

"No." Cordelia slipped off her gloves, tucking them into her pockets. She looked from Lucie's worried face to James's set one, and back to Jesse. "We have all been touched by Belial in some way or another," she said. "Lucie and James, because they share his blood. You, because of the monstrous way he controlled you. And I, because I bear Cortana. He fears and hates us all. You are as much a part of this as any of us."

Jesse met her gaze. She could certainly see why Lucie had been drawn to him, Cordelia thought. He was attractive, but that was not all of it; there was an intensity to him, a focus, as if everything he saw, he carefully considered. It made one wish to be considered by him. "All right," he said. "I'll lock the door."

They settled themselves somewhat awkwardly around the room: James on the trunk, Cordelia in the chair, Lucie on James's bed, and Jesse sitting atop the windowsill, his back against the cold glass. Everyone looked expectantly at Cordelia.

"It was what you said about your dream," she explained. "That you heard Belial say, 'They wake.'"

"I've no idea what he meant," said James. "But Grandfather does like a puzzle. Whether it has a solution or not."

"Ugh," said Lucie. "Don't call him Grandfather. It makes it sound as if he carried us piggyback when we were children."

"I'm sure he would have," said James, "as long as he was piggybacking us up a volcano to sacrifice us to Lucifer."

"He'd never sacrifice you," Lucie said tartly. "He needs *you*."

Jesse cleared his throat. "I think," he said, "Cordelia was trying to tell us something?"

James turned his eyes on her, though Cordelia noticed they slid away, as if he could not bear to look directly at her. "Daisy?"

"Yes," she said, and told them quickly about the Cabaret de l'Enfer, Madame Dorothea, and the words that had come, in theory, from her father. "'They wake,'" she said, and shivered. "And I might have thought it was nonsense, except that when we were attacked by Lilith, she repeated the same words. I'm not sure she even knew what they meant," Cordelia added. "She said, 'Belial has not stopped his planning. I, too, have heard the whispers on the wind. They wake.'"

When she finished, Lucie sighed. "Why are prophetic pronouncements always so *vague*? Why not a bit of information about who wakes, or why we should care?"

"Yet Belial wanted me to hear it," said James. "He said, 'Do you hear that, grandson? They wake.' And I am fairly sure he was not referring to a litter of puppies somewhere in Oxfordshire."

"It is meant to make you afraid. The fear is the point," said Jesse. They all looked at him. "It is a method of control. My mother used it often—do this or that, or fear the consequences."

"But there are no orders here, no demands," James said. "Only the warning."

"I do not think Belial feels fear," Jesse said. "Not as we do. He wishes to grasp and to possess. He feels rage when his will is thwarted. But to him, fear is a human emotion. He knows it makes mortals behave in irrational ways. He may feel that by striking fear into us, we will run in circles, making it easier for him to do"—Jesse sighed—"whatever it is he plans to do."

"Belial is afraid of one thing," said James. "He is afraid of Cordelia."

Jesse nodded. "He does not wish to die, and so if he fears anything, I suppose it is Cortana, in Cordelia's hand."

"Perhaps he merely means a horde of demons has awoken," said Lucie, "as one might expect. Demons he intends to send against us."

"He could have whipped up an army of demons at any point," James pointed out. "Why now?"

"Maybe they needed military training," Lucie suggested. "They're not really *disciplined*, are most of them? Even with a Prince of Hell ordering them about."

Cordelia tried to imagine Belial putting a horde of demons through basic military exercises, and failed. "Lucie," she said, and hesitated. "With your powers, we could . . . well, do you think it would be wise to . . . try to reach my father through you? To find out if he knows more?"

Lucie looked discomfited. "I don't think we ought. I've summoned an unwilling ghost before, and it is . . . unpleasant. Like torturing them." She shook her head. "I wouldn't want to do that to your father."

"It may not have been your father who spoke to you at all," Jesse said. "The words 'they wake' certainly indicate it was a spirit who knew who you were. But that spirit could have been impersonating your father."

"I know," Cordelia said. *But I so much want it to have been my father. I was never able to bid him goodbye, not properly.*

"If you could reach out, Lucie," she said. "Not to draw him back, but just to see if he is a spirit, hovering somewhere in the world . . ."

"I *have*, Cordelia," Lucie said. "I *did* look—and no, I didn't sense anything. Your father didn't seem to be anywhere I could . . . reach him."

Cordelia felt startled, and a little as if she'd been slapped. Lucie's tone was so cold—though no colder, she supposed, than her own when she'd snapped at Lucie in the ballroom. The boys, too, looked startled, but before anyone could speak, there was a sudden loud knock on the door—less a knock than a sound as if someone had bashed the door with a hammer. They all jumped, save James, who rolled his eyes.

"Bridget," he called. "I've *told* you—"

"Your parents sent me to fetch you for supper," Bridget snapped. "I see you've locked your door. Lord knows what you're up to in there. And where's your sister?"

"Lucie's in here as well," James called. "We are having a *private* conversation."

"Humph," said Bridget. "Have I ever sung you the song about the young prince who wouldn't come to dinner when his parents requested it of him?"

"Oh, dear," murmured Lucie. "Not a song."

A bonny young man was young Edward the prince
In his finest always dressed.
But one dark day he would not come to dinner
Even at his parents' request.

Jesse raised his eyebrows. "Is this a *real* ballad?"

James waved a hand. "You'll get used to Bridget. She is . . . eccentric."

Bridget continued to sing:

His father did weep, his mother did moan
But Edward he would not hear.
That night a highwayman did waylay him
And cut off both his ears.

Cordelia couldn't help but laugh, even amid her fretting. James looked over at her and smiled, that real smile of his that melted her insides. *Bother.*

"I think you would look fine without your ears, James," said Lucie as Bridget stomped off down the hallway. "You could just grow your hair long and cover up the holes."

"Wonderful advice from my loving sister," said James, springing off the trunk. "Cordelia, did you want to stay for supper?"

Cordelia shook her head; it would only be painful being around Will and Tessa. And there was the tension with Lucie, which would hardly be solved when they were surrounded by others. "I had better get back to my mother."

James only nodded. "I'll walk you out, then."

"Good night," said Lucie, not quite directly to Cordelia. "Jesse and I shall hold the fort in the dining room."

After a careful look up and down the corridor, James ushered Cordelia down the stairs. But their covert escape was not to be: Will appeared suddenly on the landing, in the midst of fixing his cuff links, and beamed with delight to see Cordelia. "My dear," he said. "A pleasure to see you. Have you come from Cornwall Gardens? How is your mother?"

"Oh, very well, thank you," Cordelia said, then realized that if her mother really *were* in peak condition, she had little excuse for staying away from James and the Institute. "Well, she has been very tired, and of course we are all concerned that she get her energy back. Risa has been trying to build her back up again with many . . . soups."

Soups? Cordelia was not at all sure why she'd said that. Perhaps because her mother had always told her that *ash-e jo*, a sour barley soup, could cure anything.

"Soups?"

"Soups," Cordelia said firmly. "Risa's caretaking is very thorough, though of course, my mother wishes me by her side as much as possible. I have been reading to her—"

"Oh, anything interesting? I'm always seeking a new book," said Will, having finished with the cuff links. They were studded with yellow topaz. The color of James's eyes.

"Ah—no," Cordelia said. "Only very boring things, really. Books about . . . ornithology." Will's eyebrows went up, but James had already thrown himself into the fray.

"I really must get Cordelia back home," he said, laying a hand on her back. It was an entirely ordinary husbandly gesture, not at all remarkable. It felt to Cordelia like being struck by lightning between her shoulder blades. "I'll see you in a moment, Father."

"Well, Cordelia, we all hope you'll be back before too long," Will said. "James is positively pining away without you here. Incomplete without his better half, eh, James?" He went away up the stairs and down the corridor, whistling.

"Well," said James after a long silence. "I thought, when I was ten years old and my father showed everyone the drawings I'd made of myself as Jonathan Shadowhunter, slaying a dragon, that was the most my parents would ever humiliate me. But that is no longer the case. There is a new champion."

"Your father is something of a romantic, that's all."

"So you've noticed?" James still had his hand on her back, and Cordelia did not have the willpower to ask him to remove it. She let him guide her downstairs, where she fetched her coat in the entryway while James went to ask Davies, one of the Institute's footmen, to bring the carriage around.

She joined him on the front step. He had not put on a jacket, and the icy wind stirred the locks of his dark hair where they kissed his cheeks and the back of his neck. When he saw her come outside, he exhaled—a plume of white—and reached into his pocket.

To Cordelia's surprise, he drew out a pair of gloves. *Her* gloves. Pale gray kidskin with a tracery of leaves, though they were now very crumpled, and even a bit spotted, as if drops of rain had fallen on them.

"You left these," James said, his voice very calm, "when you went to Paris. I wanted to return them to you. My apologies—I've been carrying them around all this time and meant to give them to you earlier."

Cordelia took the gloves from him, puzzled. "But—why have you been carrying them around?"

He ran his hands through his hair, a characteristic gesture. "I want to be honest with you," he said. "Very honest, because I think it is the only hope we have to come out of this. And I do still hope, Daisy. I will not bother you about it—about you and me—but I will not give up on us either."

She looked at him in surprise. For all he had joked on the stairway about being humiliated, there was only a quiet determination in his face, his eyes. Even a sort of steely pride. He was not ashamed of anything he felt, that much was clear.

"I went after you that night," he said. "The night you left. I followed you to Matthew's, and then to the train station. I was on the platform—I saw you board the train. I would have gone after you, but my father had Tracked me to Waterloo. Lucie had disappeared, and I had to go after her."

She looked down at the gloves in her hand. "You were there? On the train station platform?"

"Yes," James said. He reached out and folded her hand over the gloves. His own was reddened with cold, his fingernails bitten down to the quick. "I wanted you to know. I went after you the moment I knew you'd left. I didn't wait until hurt pride settled in or anything like that. I realized you were leaving and I ran after you, because when someone you love is leaving, all you think about is getting them back."

Someone you love. His face was inches from hers. She thought, *I could raise myself up on my toes and kiss him. He would kiss me back. I could put down the dreadful weight I've been carrying, this weight of caution that says: Be careful. You could be hurt again.*

But the image of Matthew flashed across her field of vision then. Matthew and the lights of Paris, and all the reasons she had run away in the first place. She heard the creak of the wheels of the carriage as it rolled into the courtyard, and like Cinderella's midnight clock, the spell was broken.

"Thank you," she said. "For the gloves."

She turned to descend the steps; she didn't look back to see if James watched her depart.

As the carriage rumbled away from the Institute and into the purple-and-gray London dusk, she thought, *If James saw me get on that train, he can't have spent more than an hour with Grace, and probably less. And then—he fled from her? But what could possibly have caused his feelings to change so suddenly as that?*

Would anything ever feel familiar again? James was not sure. Here he sat, eating supper with his family in the dining room where he'd eaten thousands of meals before, and yet the experiences of the past weeks had made everything strange. Here was the china cabinet with the glass-paneled doors and delicate inlaid floral marquetry; he remembered his mother ordering it from Shoolbred's to replace the hideous Victorian monstrosity that had been there before. Here were the slim and elegant dining chairs with their backs carved in the shape of ferns that Lucie, when younger, had liked to pretend were warring pirate ships, and the pale green wallpaper, and the white glass lily-shaped lamps on either side of the fluted porcelain vase on the mantel that Tessa kept filled with fresh flowers every week, even in winter.

None of this had changed. But James had. He had left, after all; he had gotten married, moved into his own house. Very soon he would reach the age of majority, and the Clave would acknowledge him as an adult. But now he felt as though circumstance had forced him back into ill-fitting children's clothes, a costume he had long outgrown.

"And what do you think, James?" said his mother.

James looked up, feeling guilty. He hadn't been paying any attention. "Sorry, what was that?"

Lucie said, "We were talking about the Christmas party. It's only three days away." She gave James a beady look, as if to say, *I know perfectly well you weren't paying attention, and weren't we just talking about this earlier?*

"Really?" James frowned. "Is everyone still planning to attend?"

His parents were extremely dedicated to the tradition of the Institute Christmas party. It had started under Charlotte and Henry, who, his parents had explained, had decided that it didn't matter that Shadowhunters didn't celebrate the mundane holiday. It was so pervasive in London, present in every corner of the city through all of December, that they had realized the value of having something festive for the Enclave to look forward to during the long, cold winter months. The Herondales had continued the tradition of a ball in late December; in fact, James knew that it was at one of the Institute Christmas parties that his parents had become engaged to be married.

"It *is* odd," Tessa said. "But the invitations were all sent at the beginning of the month, before any of the troubles we've been having. We thought perhaps guests would cancel, but they haven't."

"It's important to the Enclave," Will said. "And the Angel knows, it's not a bad thing to keep up morale."

Lucie moved her doubtful look to her father. "Yes, a completely selfless act, holding the party you love more than all other parties."

"My dear daughter, I am offended by the insinuation," Will said. "Everyone will be looking to the Institute to set the tone and demonstrate that as the chosen warriors of the Angel, the Shadowhunters will carry on, a united front against the forces of Hell. 'Half a league, half a league, half a league'—"

"Will!" Tessa said reproachfully. "What have I said?"

Will looked chastened. "No 'Charge of the Light Brigade' at the table."

Tessa patted his wrist. "That's right."

Jesse said, "Is there anything particularly dangerous about holding the party?"

It was a sensible question. James had noticed this was Jesse's way generally: he tended to be quiet and offer thoughts rarely, but when he did, they cut to the heart of things.

"Not where Belial is concerned," said James. "The Institute's the safest place in London when it comes to demons; if he did somehow attack, the whole Enclave would retreat here as a matter of policy."

"I suppose," said Jesse, still in the same calm voice, "I was thinking of my mother. A party like that, with so many of you collected in one place—it might attract her. Draw her here."

Will regarded Jesse thoughtfully. "And then she would do what?"

Jesse shook his head. "I don't know. She is unpredictable, but certainly she hates you all, and she has a special loathing for these Christmas parties—she spoke often to me of having been humiliated at one once, and the Enclave not caring."

Will sighed. "That was me. I read her diary out loud at a Christmas party, long ago. I was twelve. And I was quite severely punished, so in fact, the Enclave *was* on her side."

"Ah," said Jesse. "When I was a child, I thought it was terrible that she had been so often wronged. Later I came to understand that my mother saw everything as a wrong undertaken against her. She *collected* grievances, as if they were china figurines. She liked to take them out and speak about them, examining them over and over for new facets of evil and betrayal. She held them closer to her than she ever held her children."

"The next time she acts, the Clave will not be so lenient with her," said Will tightly. "This time her Marks will be stripped."

"Father," said Lucie, looking pointedly in Jesse's direction.

"It's all right," Jesse said. "Believe me. After what she did to me—" He put down his fork, shaking his head. "I try not to think about revenge. I take no pleasure in it, but I know that what is necessary must be done. She has done too much to me, to my sister, to be given another chance."

Grace. For a moment, James could say nothing; his throat had closed up. The thought of Grace was like falling down an endless black hole, a pit lined with mirrors, each of which reflected back a vision of himself cringing, foolish, filled with shame.

He saw Lucie look at him, her blue eyes wide with worry. He knew she could not understand, but it was clear she sensed his distress. She said loudly, "I was thinking, since we *are* having the party, that it would be the best opportunity to introduce Jesse to the rest of the Enclave. As Jeremy Blackthorn, of course."

She had successfully drawn off James's parents attention. Will drew a lazy circle in the air with the tip of his spoon. "Good thought, *cariad*."

"I am sure he will be instantly beloved," Lucie said.

Jesse smiled. "I would settle for not being left to rot in the Silent City."

"Oh, nonsense," Tessa said kindly. "The Clave accepted me, and they'll accept you as well."

"He needs something new to wear," Lucie said. "He can't go on in James's old clothes; they're too short." This was true; Jesse was taller than James, though thinner as well. "And half of them are fraying, and they all have old lemon drops in the pockets."

"I don't mind the lemon drops," said Jesse mildly.

"Of course," Will exclaimed. "A new wardrobe for a new man. We must take you to Mr. Sykes—"

"Mr. Sykes is a werewolf," Lucie explained.

"He does excellent work," Will said. "Twenty-seven out of thirty days. The others, he gets a bit wild with his colors and cuts."

"We needn't depend on Sykes," Lucie stage-whispered, patting Jesse's arm. "We'll get in touch with Anna. She'll sort you out."

"If I am going to be presented to the Enclave . . ." Jesse cleared his throat. "I'd like to make use of the training room. I know very little of fighting, and I could be much stronger than I am. I need not master every skill; I know I am old to begin learning. But—"

"I'll train with you," James said. The black pit had receded; he was back at the table with his family again. Relief and gratitude made him sympathetic. He wanted to help Jesse. And if part of it was wanting someone to train with who was not Matthew, he did not admit it to himself at the moment.

Jesse looked pleased. Will was gazing at them both with an expression that seemed to portend a Welsh song on the horizon. Thankfully for everyone present, Bridget appeared suddenly, scowling as she slammed the door behind her. She approached Will and murmured something in his ear.

Will's eyes lit up. "My goodness. We have a call."

Tessa looked puzzled. "A call?"

"A call!" confirmed Will. "On *the telephone*. Bring it in, Bridget."

James had forgotten about this. A few months before, Will had had one of the new mundane "telephones" installed in the Institute, although James knew that Magnus had done quite a lot of fiddling with magic in order to get it to work. But now it could be used for Institutes to call between one another. James was fairly sure that mundane telephones were usually connected to something by a wire, which this one was not, but he hadn't wanted to bring it up.

Bridget came in holding a heavy wooden machine. She held it at arm's length, as though it might explode, while from somewhere within a bell rang continuously, like an alarm clock.

"It just keeps clanging on," Bridget complained, setting it down on the table with a thump. "I can't get it to stop."

"It's supposed to do that," Will said. "Just leave it there, thanks."

He lifted a sort of black cone attached to the wooden box. Immediately a voice, sounding as though it were yelling from the far end of a tunnel, bellowed, "Identify yourself!"

Will held the cone away from his head, looking pained.

James and Lucie exchanged a look. The voice was immediately identifiable: Albert Pangborn, the head of the Cornwall Institute. Lucie gleefully mimed her hands sticking together, to Jesse's puzzlement and a disapproving look from Tessa.

"This is Will Herondale." Will spoke into the mouthpiece slowly and clearly. "And *you* telephoned *me*."

Albert shouted back, "This is Albert Pangborn!"

"Yes, Albert," said Will in the same careful tone, "from the Cornwall Institute. There is no need to shout."

"I wanted! To tell you!" Albert shouted. "We found that lady! Who went missing!"

"Which lady was that, Albert?" said Will. James was fascinated. It was a rare circumstance to witness a conversation in which his father was the calm, quiet participant.

"The ONE WHO WENT MISSING!" Albert yowled. "From the Adamant Citadel!"

Jesse froze as if his blood had turned to ice. Out of the corner of his eye, James saw Lucie blanch. Will was suddenly all attention, hunched over the receiver of the telephone. "Albert," he said. "Say that again. You found *which* missing woman?"

"Titania Greenthorpe!" shouted Albert.

"Do you mean Tatiana Blackthorn, Albert?"

"Whatever her name is!" Albert said. "She can't answer to it herself, you see!"

"What?" said Will. "What do you mean?"

"We found her out on the moors!" Albert said. "One of us, I mean, not myself! It was young Polkinghorn found her!"

"On the moors?" said Will.

"On Bodmin Moor!" Albert said. "During patrol! She was out like a light when we found her! Still hasn't woken up! Injured pretty badly, I daresay!"

It must be very strange, James thought, a little dazed, to patrol empty moors, rather than city streets full of mundanes. Albert was still shouting: "We thought she was dead at first, truth be told! She'd been slashed up pretty badly! Didn't even want to put *iratzes* on her! Not sure she could take it!"

"Where is she now?" Will said.

"Sanctuary," said Albert, calming down slightly. "Thought that was best."

Will nodded, though of course Pangborn couldn't see him. "It is. Keep her there, Albert." Tessa was frantically miming drawing on her arm. Will added, "Don't put any runes on her, though. We don't know how much demonic magic there might be in her."

"Amazing what young people get up to today, eh, Will?" Pangborn said. "You know what I mean! The young people! Running wild!"

"I'm one year older than Tatiana," Will pointed out.

"Why, you're but a boy!" Albert shouted. "Look, I've no idea how you do things in London, but I prefer not to harbor criminals in the Sanctuary of my Institute! Is anyone going to come get this woman?"

"Yes," Will said. "The Silent Brothers will be on their way shortly, to examine her. Keep her in the Sanctuary until then. No runes, and minimal contact. Stay away from her if you can."

"Give her what in a can?" Albert shouted, but Will was already hanging up. Without another word, he bent to kiss Tessa, who looked as astonished as everyone else, and walked out of the room.

To contact Jem, of course; James did not have to wonder. He knew his father.

There was a silence. Jesse sat like a statue, his face white, staring at the opposite wall. At last Tessa said, "Perhaps she broke with Belial. She may have—resisted him, or disagreed with him, and he abandoned her."

"It would be very unlike her to do that," said Jesse, and there was bitterness in his voice. James could not help but think it would also be very unlike *Belial* to do that: If Tatiana turned against him, surely he would kill her without a second thought?

"There's always hope for people, Jesse," Tessa said. "No one is a lost cause, not even your mother."

Jesse looked at her, bemused, and James thought, *Jesse has never had a kind motherly figure in his life*. He'd never known a mother who gave him hope, rather than despair or fear. Now he pushed his chair away from the table and stood up with a small bow. "I think I'd better be alone for a little while," he said, his voice calm. "I will need to tell Grace this news when I see her tomorrow. But I do very much appreciate the dinner. And the kind words," he added, and departed.

Lucie said, "Should I go after him, do you think?"

"Not right this moment," Tessa said. "Sometimes people just need to be by themselves. Poor Tatiana," she added, to James's surprise. "I can't help but wonder if Belial simply took what he wanted from her, all these years, and when he was done, left her to die."

James wondered if Tessa would still think "poor Tatiana" if she knew what Tatiana had wrought on her own son through Grace. What would she think of how James felt now—the acid burn of bitterness in his throat, the terrible sense of near pleasure in Tatiana's suffering, which shamed him even as he felt it?

He grabbed for his empty wrist with his hand and held it. No matter how much he wished, he could not tell his parents about the bracelet. His mother always thought the best of everyone, and looking at her face, full of compassionate concern for a loathsome woman who had only ever wished her ill, he could not bring himself to ruin that.

13
Angels Alone

Stone walls do not a prison make,
Nor iron bars a cage:
Minds innocent and quiet take
That for an hermitage.
If I have freedom in my love,
And in my soul am free,
Angels alone, that soar above,
Enjoy such liberty.
—Richard Lovelace, "To Althea, from Prison"

Cordelia squinted at the page in the fading candlelight.

She was tucked up in her bed in Cornwall Gardens, under the eaves, reading some of the paladin books Christopher had given her. The soft thump of snowdrifts against the roof made the room feel cozier, but it still didn't feel like home. Rather like a room in the house of a kind relative that one was visiting.

Cordelia was not unaware that she hadn't entirely unpacked—not her clothes from Paris, and not the things James had sent over to her from Curzon Street. She was living in a sort of limbo, not quite here or there, a space where she did not yet have to make a firm decision.

She wondered a bit about the baby, soon to be born. Not *too* soon, she hoped. Not while she, its big sister, was undecided about every aspect of her life—and worse, while she was cursed to be a demon's paladin. She turned back to her book—in the combined light of the fire and the taper on her nightstand, she could just make out the words.

The words were not encouraging. Most paladins wanted to be paladins and would never seek to break the bond with their masters. There was much a paladin could *do* that seemed appealing: fight harder, jump higher, survive wounds that would kill another. She had even found an account of a paladin who had stabbed his friend due to a case of mistaken identity, but was then able to magically heal him with his "paladin's blade," all of which seemed unlikely—what did that even mean, *healed him with his blade?* But it was only an anecdote, sandwiched between another one in which a single paladin had defeated an advancing army, and yet another in which two *parabatai* had become paladins together.

Thump, went the snow at her window. It almost sounded like a bird hitting the glass. She couldn't help but remember when Matthew had tumbled through her window in orange spats, bearing alarming insights. *This may be a false marriage,* he'd said, *but you're truly in love with James.*

She thought of James, and what he'd said that night, about following her to Waterloo; the thought that he'd been on the train platform was nearly too much to bear—

Thump. This time louder, more insistent. *Thump, thump, thump,* and the window came open, along with a puff of white snow. Cordelia bolted up in bed, dropping her book, about to shout for Alastair, when she realized that the person clambering through her window, all snowy boots and undone brown hair, was Lucie.

She sat back down on her bed, speechless, as Lucie shut the window behind her and hurried over to the fire. She wore a heavy cloak over gear, and her hair had come out of its fastenings and was halfway down her back, threaded with strings of ice.

"Lucie," Cordelia said, finding her voice, "you must be *freezing.* What on earth are you doing coming through the window? Risa would have let you up—you could have used the front door—"

"I didn't want to," Lucie said crossly. She was holding out her hands to the fire, letting the heat turn the white tips of her fingers back to pink.

"Well, come here, then," Cordelia said. "I can't wield a weapon, but I can still manage a stele. You could use a Heat rune—"

Lucie whirled around. Her hair flew dramatically as she said, "Things cannot go on as they have been."

Cordelia was fairly sure she knew what Lucie meant. Still, she said, "What do you mean?"

"When you married James," Lucie said, "I thought it would bring us closer together. But it has driven us further apart."

"Lucie." Cordelia clasped her hands in her lap. She felt underdressed—Lucie was in gear, and here she was in a nightgown with a slightly ragged hem and her hair in plaits. "The distance between us—it's not James's fault. It's not the fault of our marriage—"

"You don't think so? Cordelia, he's breaking his heart over you. He's so miserable—"

"Well, I suppose it could cause discord," Cordelia said coldly, "if you take a side. I know you adore your brother. I also know you're aware that he's been in love with Grace Blackthorn until last week. And this is exactly the kind of conversation we should *not* be having. I don't *want* to hurt James, but I don't want to be hurt myself, either, and James only feels guilty—"

"It's not just guilt," Lucie protested. "I know the difference—"

"Did you know the difference when you chose to secretly befriend Grace behind my back, and never tell me about it at all?"

It was most likely the harshest thing Cordelia had ever said to her best friend. Lucie looked shocked.

"I did it to save Jesse," Lucie said in a whisper.

"I know what it's like to be in love," said Cordelia. "You think I wouldn't have understood? You didn't trust me."

"What I was doing," Lucie fumbled, "it was so forbidden, so dreadful, I didn't want to pull you into any of the trouble I'd be in if I was found out."

"Nonsense," Cordelia said. "You wanted to do what you were doing and not have me fuss at you about Grace." Some part of her seemed to have detached itself and was watching in horror as she struck at Lucie with words like knives, intended to slice and cut. Part of her felt a sort of desperate relief that as much as she had been hurt, she no longer had to hold it in—she could say: *You hurt me. You never thought about me at all, and that hurts the most.*

"*Parabatai* are supposed to tell each other everything," Cordelia said. "When I was in the worst trouble of my life, finding I was sworn to Lilith, I *told* you."

"No, you didn't," said Lucie. "I found out when you did. You couldn't have hidden it."

"I told you the whole story—"

"Oh, really?" Lucie's blue eyes filled with tears. Cordelia had hardly ever seen her cry, but she was crying now, and yet she sounded furious. "We're supposed to tell each other everything? Well, I have a few questions for you about the fact that the moment my brother came looking for me in Cornwall, you ran off to Paris with his best friend! You never said anything to me about Matthew—"

"That," said Cordelia in a voice as cold as the snow outside, "is not exactly the order of events as they took place. And your brother is not blameless, but I will leave it to him to tell you how that night unfolded."

"I don't know what you think he did," said Lucie, dashing her tears away with her hands. "But I know how he looks. Like he wants to die without you. And you expect me to believe you ran off with Matthew in a purely friendly way, and nothing romantic passed between you?"

"And you would blame me if it did?" Cordelia felt a white fire of rage and pain blaze up under her ribs, nearly choking off her breath. "Do you know what it's like to be in a marriage that's a lie, where you're the only person who feels anything? James never felt a thing for me—he never looked at me the way Matthew has—he was too busy looking at Grace, your new best friend. Why don't you ask him if he kissed Grace while we were married? Better, why don't you ask him *how many times* he kissed Grace while we were married?"

"You're still married." Lucie was shaking her head. "And—I don't believe you."

"Then you're calling me a liar. And perhaps that is the distance between us. It is the same as the distance between myself and James. It has a name: Grace Blackthorn."

"I didn't know how much my working with her would hurt you,"

Lucie said. "I doubt James knew either. You never let on that you felt anything for him. You—you're so *proud*, Cordelia."

Cordelia raised her chin. "Maybe I am. What does it matter? We aren't going to be *parabatai* after all, so we don't need to know each other's secrets. That's not in our future."

Lucie caught her breath. "You don't know that. Or are you saying you don't want to be *parabatai* with me, even if you break your bond with Lilith?"

"Oh, Lucie," Cordelia said in despair. "It's like you don't live in the real world. You live in a world of stories. The beautiful Cordelia, who can do anything she likes. But in the real world, we don't get everything we want. Maybe—we shouldn't."

In that moment, Cordelia saw Lucie's heart break. Her whole face crumpled, and she turned away, as if she could hide her reaction from Cordelia, but it was in every line of her shaking shoulders, her arms wrapping around herself as if she could hold in the hurt.

"Luce." Cordelia's voice shook. "I didn't—"

But Lucie had darted to the window. She threw it open and practically hurled herself outside. Cordelia cried out and jumped to her feet, racing to follow her—Lucie should not be climbing about on icy rooftops, not in the state she was in—but when she reached the window, she saw only darkness outside, and the swirling snow.

Lucie had cried enough on her way back to the Institute that when she had finally crept back inside, and upstairs to her room, she found her hair frozen to her cheeks by crystalline tracks of salt.

She had cleaned herself up as best she could, put on a clean nightgown, and sat down at her desk. Her tears were spent; she felt only an awful hollowness, a terrible missing of Cordelia and a knowledge of her own guilt. She *had* concealed her relationship—friendship, whatever it was—with Grace; she had concealed Jesse's whole existence.

But. Cordelia had hidden things too. How she felt about James, for one thing—which normally wouldn't have been Lucie's business, but now, she felt, very much was. She loved her brother. Every time

Cordelia turned away from him, and the anguish on his face was clear, Lucie wanted to jump up and down and scream.

In the past, she would have poured out her feelings with her pen, but since Jesse's return she hadn't been able to write a word. And now it was worse: she kept hearing Cordelia's voice in her head. *It's like you don't live in the real world. You live in a world of stories.* As if that were a terrible thing.

She slumped back in her chair. "I don't know what to do," she said aloud, to no one. "I just don't."

"You could command the dead to solve your problems," said a familiar, waspish voice. Jessamine, the Institute's resident ghost, was seated atop Lucie's wardrobe, her long skirts trailing off into indistinct translucence. "It's what you always do, isn't it?"

Lucie sighed. "I've already apologized to you, Jessamine." This was true. When Lucie had first returned to her room after getting back from Cornwall, she had delivered an extensive and sincere apology for having controlled the dead against their will. There had been quite a lot of rustling, and she was sure Jessamine had heard her.

Jessamine folded her transparent arms. "Your power is much too dangerous, Lucie. Even in the hands of someone sensible, it would cause trouble, and you are the least sensible person I know."

"Then you'll be happy to know I have no plans to use it again."

"Not good enough." Jessamine shook her head. "It is one thing to plan not to use your power again, but that's the problem with power, isn't it? There's always some reason to make an exception, just this once. No, you must get rid of it."

Lucie opened her mouth to protest, but closed it again before she spoke. Jessamine was, she thought with an uncomfortable pang, probably right.

"I wouldn't know how," she said truthfully.

Jessamine turned up her nose and began to make a dramatic exit through the wall. "Wait," said Lucie. "If I said to you, 'They wake,' would that mean anything to you?"

"Of course not." Jessamine sniffed. "What do I know about anyone waking? What kind of fool question is that?"

Lucie doused her witchlight, stood up, and reached for her dressing gown. "I've had enough of this," she said. "I'm going to see Jesse."

"You *can't*!" Scandalized, Jessamine followed Lucie out of the room and down the hall. "This is disgraceful!" she cried, doing somersaults near the ceiling. "A young lady should *never* see a young gentleman in his bedroom, alone!"

Crossly, Lucie said, "From what I hear from my parents, you snuck out *repeatedly* to see a single gentleman when you were an unmarried girl, *at night*. And he turned out to be my evil uncle. Which is certainly not going to happen with Jesse."

Jessamine gasped. She gasped again when Jesse's door opened, and he stepped out into the hall, apparently alerted by the ruckus. He wore only trousers and a shirt with the sleeves pulled up, putting a great deal of his admirable forearms on display.

"You were a *ghost*," Jessamine said, sounding a little amazed, though Lucie was sure she'd already been aware of Jesse's return. Still, it must be very odd for Jessamine to see him standing directly in front of her, so entirely alive.

"People change," said Jesse mildly.

Jessamine, apparently realizing that Lucie meant to carry out her scandalous plan of entering Jesse's room, gave a squawk and vanished.

Jesse had been holding the door open; Lucie ducked under his arm and immediately realized she hadn't been in here, not since the moment Jesse had picked the room out, alongside her and her whole family.

It was still spare, as there had not been much time to decorate it—a standard Institute bedroom, with a wardrobe, a desk, a bookshelf, and a four-poster bed. Little bits of Jesse were visible, though. The jacket he had worn at dinner, hung over a chair back. The books on his nightstand. The Blackthorn sword, which had been retrieved from the Sanctuary, was propped against the wall. Lucie's gold hair comb that he'd purloined on the night of Anna's party, what felt like so long ago, had pride of place atop the dresser.

She sank down onto his bed as he went to bolt the door. Of course he did—he always seemed to sense when Lucie needed to be alone, or alone together with him, in order to feel safe. "What's wrong?" he asked, turning back to her.

"I had an awful fight with Cordelia."

Jesse was silent. She wondered if—compared to everything else—her problem sounded silly. He stayed by the door, clearly anxious—she supposed it *was* the first time she'd ever been in his room alone with him, and she'd given him no warning.

She had expected that when she and Jesse returned to the Institute, to live there together, they would be in and out of each other's bedrooms all the time. But Jesse had been relentlessly, scrupulously polite, bidding her goodbye every evening, and never coming to knock on her door. She'd seen more of him at night when he was a ghost.

She sat up straight, realizing as well that she was wearing only a nightgown of white batiste, with a transparent lace dressing gown. The sleeves of the nightgown were loose and tended to slip down her shoulders. She looked at Jesse. "Am I making you uncomfortable?"

He exhaled. "I'm glad you're here. And you look . . ." His gaze lingered on her. Heat sparked in her chest. "But I keep thinking about . . ."

"Yes?"

"Your parents," he said apologetically. "I would not want them to think I was taking advantage of their hospitality. Their very extreme kindness."

Of *course*. Her lovely, caring, pesky family. She had already seen the way that Jesse was brightening under the attention from Will and Tessa, becoming more himself. Jesse had never experienced a family where people were fond of each other and loved each other; now that he was in such an environment, he had become paralyzed by the fear of ruining it. And while she could recognize that this was good for Jesse, it did mean that he did everything in his power to assure Will—even when Will wasn't there—that his attentions toward Lucie were honorable. Which she didn't entirely want them to be.

"My parents," she said, "got up to the most scandalous stuff you can imagine when they were our age. Believe me when I say they will not reject you out of hand if they find out I came to you for sympathy and sat on the end of your bed."

He still looked worried. Lucie wound a strand of her hair around a finger and looked at him with her largest eyes. Turning a little to the side, she let one of her sleeves slip down her shoulder.

Jesse made an incoherent sort of noise. A moment later he sank down on the bed beside her, though not *too* close. Still, a small victory.

"Luce," he said. His voice was warm and rich and kind. "What happened with you and Cordelia?"

She told him quickly: everything from her visit to Cordelia to her silent ride home in a hansom cab after nearly falling off the Carstairs' roof. "It's like she never wanted to be *parabatai* at all," Lucie finished. "There's nothing more important to me in all the world, and she's just—throwing it away."

"It might be easier," Jesse said, "to behave as if she wants to throw it away than to acknowledge that it's being taken from her against her will."

"But if she wanted it—if she wanted to be my *parabatai*—"

"She can't, Lucie. As long as she's the paladin of Lilith, she cannot be your *parabatai*. So, like you, she shares the loss of the *parabatai* bond, but unlike you, she knows it's her fault."

"If she cared," Lucie said, knowing she was being stubborn, "she would fight for it. It's like she's saying we were never special to each other. We were just ordinary friends. Not like—not like I thought."

Jesse stroked her hair back from her face, his fingers gentle. Careful. "My Lucie," he breathed. "You know it's the people who we love the most who can hurt us the most."

"I know she is upset." Lucie pressed her cheek into his hand. They had moved closer to each other, somehow; she was almost in his lap. "I know she feels I kept secrets from her, and I *did*. But she kept secrets from me. It's hard to explain, but when someone is your *parabatai*, or nearly, and you feel distant from them, it is like a piece has been cut out of your heart." She bit her lip. "I don't mean to be dramatic."

"It's not dramatic." As if mesmerized, Jesse trailed his fingers along her cheek, to her lips. He touched her mouth with his fingertips, and she saw his eyes darken. "That's how I feel when I am away from you."

She lifted her hand to the ribbon that held her dressing gown closed. Her eyes fixed on Jesse, she drew slowly on the ribbon until it came undone, until the dressing gown slipped down her shoulders and fell to the bed, a pool of lace and satin. She was only in her nightgown now, her skin flooded with goose bumps, all her thoughts a silent whisper: *I want to forget. Take it all away, all the pain, all the loss.*

It was as if he could hear her. Jesse cupped her face in his hands and brought her mouth to his—carefully, reverently, as if he were drinking from the Mortal Cup. Their lips touched lightly at first, and then with increasing pressure, he kissed her over and over as his breathing sped up, his heart racing. She could feel it against her, his live and beating heart, and it made her want to feel even more.

She threw decorum to the winds. She opened her mouth to his, traced his bottom lip with a pointed tongue, caught at the front of his shirt, her body arching into his until he melted into her. Until she was sure no fear of her parents, no misguided sense of duty, was going to tear him away.

She sank back against his pillows and he rose over her. The look on his face was wondering, hungry. She was trembling: she could not imagine what this flood of sensation was like for him, who had felt so little for so long. "Can I touch you?" she whispered.

He squeezed his eyes shut. "Yes. Please."

She ran her hands over him, his arms and shoulders, the wiry length of his torso. The heat of him, feverish under her touch. He shivered and kissed her throat, making her gasp like a heroine in a novel. She was beginning to understand why heroines in novels did the things they did. It was all rather worth it for experiences like this.

"My turn," he said, stilling her hands. "Let me touch you. Tell me to stop"—he kissed the corner of her mouth—"if you want me to."

His fingers, long and pale and clever, traced the lines of her face, over her mouth, down her throat, danced along her collarbones, cupped her bare shoulders. The green of his eyes had burned away to black. He shaped her body under his hands, over the slight curves of her breasts, the dip of her waist, until his hands were bunched in the fabric at her hips.

"I dreamed of this," he said. "Of being able to touch you. Really touch you. I could always only half feel you—and I imagined what it would be like—I tortured myself with it—"

"It is it like what you thought?" Lucie whispered.

"I think it might break me," he said, and stretched out above her. "You might break me, Lucie," and he drove his mouth against hers, hot and demanding. Parting her lips with his, his tongue stroking along hers, making her arch up against him in her desperation to feel his heartbeat close to hers.

"Oh God," he whispered against her mouth, and she thought, *Of course, he's never learned to call out to the Angel, like we do.* "Oh God, Lucie," and she wanted to fall apart in pieces so that he could fit more closely with her, wanted to break so she could be joined back together with him.

And then the darkness came down. That same darkness she had felt before, the feeling of losing her footing, of falling away from the world. An uncontrolled descent, her stomach dropping, her struggle to surface through a sea of utter darkness. All around her were voices wailing in despair, ragged shadows reaching out to her, crying out because they had been lost, somehow exiled and wandering. Something had been taken from them, something precious. She seemed to see the gleam of a familiar shape, but it had been wrenched out of recognition—

"Lucie! *Lucie!*" She sat up, gasping, her heart pounding. She was on Jesse's bed, and he was kneeling over her, his face white with fear. "Lucie, what happened? Please tell me I didn't hurt you—"

"No," she whispered. "It wasn't you—not anything you did—"

"It has to be," Jesse said, a sudden wrench of self-loathing in his voice. "Because I'm unnatural, because I was dead—"

She caught at his hand. She knew she was probably crushing his fingers, but she couldn't help it. "*No,*" she said again, in a stronger voice. "It's something in *me*. I can feel it." She looked at him anxiously. "When I kiss you, I hear—" She shook her head. "Voices crying out. They seem to be telling me of something terrible, something awful that is happening far away, perhaps in another world." Her eyes burned. "Somewhere beyond where I, or anyone, should be able to see."

"Malcolm told me that you walked in shadow when you raised me," Jesse said softly. "It is possible, I suppose, that some of that shadow still clings to you. But it cannot only be you. I lived very close to the edge of death for a long time, and you have always been able to cross that border. It has to be the two of us combined, somehow. Something amplified when we touch."

"Then I had better contact Malcolm." Lucie felt unutterably weary. She had so hoped that part of her life was behind her—bargains with warlocks, desperate conversations about Jesse, the shadow of death touching everything she did or was. "He may know if there's some way to make it go away." She flung her head back fiercely. "Because I am not letting you go. Not now."

"No." Jesse pressed his lips to her hair. "I do not think I could bear to be let go by you, Lucie Herondale. I think I would follow you, even if you ordered me away. I am alive because of you, but not only because you commanded me to live. I am alive because my life has you in it."

Lucie's eyes burned, but tears seemed pointless. Useless. Instead she kissed Jesse—quickly, on the cheek—and let him wrap her in her dressing gown, his arms lingering around her, before she crept back out into the corridor.

She barely recalled returning to her room. It was nearly dark, the fire burning low in the grate. Still, there was some dim moonlight coming through the panes of her windows. It was enough. Sitting down at her desk, she took up her pen and began to write.

14

NEVER SIMPLE

The truth is rarely pure and never simple.
—Oscar Wilde, *The Importance of Being Earnest*

In between interrogation sessions, Grace read Christopher's notes.

His handwriting was cramped, careful, a mix of thoughts and equations that blazed across the loose-leaf pages like a shower of falling stars. In reading them, Grace felt as if she were reading a book in another language, one she *almost* spoke fluently. There were moments where she sat up, elated at understanding, and moments where she despaired of ever understanding at all.

Brother Zachariah had been kind enough to bring her a workbook and a pen, that she might make her own notes. She found herself distracted enough that she was often surprised when it was time to be taken from her cell to the Speaking Stars for her questioning by the Brothers.

There was no torture, no torment. Only the endless whispering voices inside her head, forcing her to unearth memories long buried and long ignored. *When did your mother first take you to the forest? When did you become aware of your power and what it could do? When did you realize you were doing the bidding of a demon? Why did you not run away?*

And since Tatiana had escaped from the Adamant Citadel, it had been worse. *Where do you think your mother might have gone? Do you know if your mother had a hiding place? Is she with the demon Belial?*

There was no response Grace could give, nothing in her mind save that she didn't know, that her mother had never considered her worthy of confiding in. That she wished more than anyone else that her mother could be caught and punished, penned up somewhere safe where she could never hurt anyone again.

After each interrogation, which left Grace as limp as a rag, Brother Zachariah would escort her back to her cell. He would sit, silently, on a chair outside the barred door, until Grace was no longer huddled on her bed, shuddering. When she could breathe again, he would go—leaving her alone, as she preferred.

Alone, to think about magical equations and chemical weights, about mathematics that bent the laws of physics, and charts that seemed to hover above her bed as she waited for sleep, traced against the stone walls in brilliant lines.

She was at her desk, struggling with a particularly stubborn calculation, when Brother Zachariah appeared at her door. He moved soundlessly through the City, but for her benefit tended to knock at the bars to warn her he was there before startling her by speaking.

You have a visitor, Grace.

She sat up, nearly dropping the pen. Quickly inventoried what she was wearing—a plain ivory dress, her hair tied back with a ribbon. Presentable enough. Grace said, "Is it Christopher?"

There was a momentary pause. Zachariah said, *It is your brother, Grace. It is Jesse. He came here from the London Institute.*

Grace found that she was cold all over, despite the shawl. *It cannot be*, she thought. *I have been so careful not to ask. . . . Not about Lucie, and not about—*

"Jesse?" she breathed. "Please—oh, please, bring him here."

Zachariah hesitated, then was gone. Grace rose shakily to her feet. *Jesse.* He had been real to her, and only her, for such a long time. Now Jesse was alive, someone who had been in the London Institute, someone who could travel from *there* to *here*.

Witchlight danced along the walls, illuminating her cell. A moment later, following the light, came Jesse.

Grace caught at the edge of her desk to keep herself from falling. She had hoped that Lucie had brought him back. She'd had faith. But to see him like this—just as he'd been the day before his awful runing ceremony, young and tall and healthy and *smiling* . . .

She stared at him as he came over to the door, settling the witchlight torch he carried into a holder on the wall. He was the same, and yet different—she did not remember such curious eyes or such a wry, thoughtful turn to his mouth.

He put his left hand through the bars of the door. A hand marked with a wide black Voyance rune. "Grace," he said. "Grace. It's me. It *worked*."

Grace Blackthorn did not cry, or at least, she did not *truly* cry. This was one of the earliest lessons her mother had imparted to her. "The tears of a woman," she'd said, "are one of the few sources of her power. They should not be freely shed any more than a warrior should throw his sword into a river. If you are to shed tears, you should know, from the first, your purpose in doing so."

So when she tasted salt in her mouth now, it surprised her. It had been so long. She caught her brother's hand and held it tightly, and when he said, "Grace, it will all be all right, Grace," she let herself believe it.

It was nice, Ariadne couldn't help but notice, coming up the steps of Anna's building to her flat door, taking Anna's key from her beaded bag, letting herself into a cozy, charming space that smelled of leather and roses. *Don't get used to it*, she reminded herself as she came into the building's entryway from the cold. That way lay only madness. She knew well enough by now the danger of allowing herself to fall into another fantasy about a life with Anna. She was returning from looking for her own flat, after all, and that was what was best for both of them.

Finding a suitable flat in central London was turning out to be harder than finding a Naga demon hiding in a drainpipe. Nothing affordable was livable, and nothing livable was affordable. She received the same stipend as any other Shadowhunter, but since she'd been living with her parents, she'd given it all to them for house expenses; she had nothing saved up.

As for the flats she *could* afford—if she sold her jewelry—they were uniformly awful. There was the flat in the cellar of a house whose owner announced breezily that he would frequently be passing through the parlor in the nude and did not expect to have to knock or make himself known beforehand. There was the one full of rats—which were, the landlady informed her, pets. The others she saw were all mold and mildew, broken faucets and cracked plaster. Worse, whatever mundanes thought of a woman Ariadne's age—and complexion—looking for her own flat, it was not complimentary, and most had no qualms about making that clear.

"I shall have to go to Whitechapel," she murmured to herself as she went up the stairs. "I shall find a band of knife-wielding gangsters and join them in order to make some money. Perhaps I shall rise to the top and become a criminal mastermind."

She plastered a bright smile on her face and pushed the door of the flat open. Inside, she found Anna gazing at her half-cleared bookshelf, books piled on all nearby surfaces. She was balanced on a dangerously tilting chair, wearing a loose white shirt and a silk waistcoat with gold buttons. "I'm arranging them by color," she said, gesturing at the books. "What do you think, darling?"

"How will you find anything?" Ariadne said, knowing better than to be affected by that casual *darling*; Anna called everyone that. "Or do you remember the colors of all your books?"

"Of course I do," said Anna, hopping down from her chair. Her black hair was flyaway and mussed, her pin-striped trousers clinging to her hips—they had clearly been tailored for her slim curves. Ariadne sighed inwardly. "Doesn't everyone?" Anna peered more closely at Ariadne. "What's wrong? How goes the flat hunt?"

Half of Ariadne wanted to spill all her troubles at Anna's feet. If nothing else, they could have had a laugh about the naked landlord in Holborn. But she had promised she'd be out of Anna's flat as soon as was possible; surely Anna was looking forward to having it back?

"It went very well," she said, going to hang up her coat. *Can't I just stay here?* she did not say. "I found a lovely little place in Pimlico."

"Splendid!" Anna shelved a green book with a loud *thunk*, a bit more forcefully than Ariadne would have expected. "When will they let you have it?"

"Oh," said Ariadne, "the first of the month. New year, new start, as they say."

"Do they say that?" Anna asked. "Anyway, what's it like?"

"It's very nice," Ariadne said, aware she was digging herself in ever deeper but now unable to stop. "It has a light, airy feel and, er, decorative sconces." So now she had to find not only a flat in Pimlico in the next ten days, it had to be "light" and "airy." With "decorative sconces." She wasn't even sure she knew what sconces were. "Winston will love it."

"Winston!" said Anna. "Why didn't we retrieve him when we went to your parents' house?"

Ariadne sighed. "I tried, but there wasn't any chance. I do feel awful. As if I've abandoned him. He won't understand at all."

"Well, he's *yours*," said Anna. "Winston was a gift, wasn't he? You have every right to take that parrot back."

Ariadne sighed and sat down on the settee. "My parents' letter said they've changed the locks. I can't even get into the house. At least Mother is fond of Winston. She'll take good care of him."

"That is terribly unfair to Winston. He will be missing you. Parrots become very attached to their owners, and they can live more than a hundred years, I've heard."

Ariadne raised an eyebrow. "I didn't realize you were such a defender of the feelings of birds."

"Parrots are very sensitive," Anna said. "It's not all pirates and biscuits. I know we're meeting the others at Chiswick this afternoon, *but* I also happen to know your parents will be at the Consul's tonight. Which provides a perfect opportunity to liberate Winston so that he may join you in your new life."

"Did you just come up with this idea on the spot?" Ariadne said, amused.

"Not at all," Anna said, tossing a volume of Byron's poetry into the air. "I've given it at least two or three hours of consideration over the past few days. And I have devised a *plan*."

"They didn't want to let me see you at first," Jesse said, smiling. He'd pulled the corridor chair up to the cell door, as close as he could get, and Grace had dragged her desk chair over to the other side. She sat holding Jesse's fingers as he told her everything that had happened since he had left London with Lucie and Malcolm, up until this very moment. As he spoke, she marveled at how ordinary and alive he felt. "But I refused to have my protection spells done unless they let me see you at the same time. I mean, it would hardly make sense if I came to the Silent City and *didn't* see you, wouldn't it?"

"Sometimes I wonder if *anything* makes sense," said Grace. "But—I am so glad you're here. And glad Lucie did what she did."

"I'll thank her for you." He smiled a little at the thought of Lucie, that besotted smile that Grace had often seen on the faces of her own suitors. She had to push away a small pang. So often her mother had told her that if Jesse ever fell in love, he would have no further time for his mother and sister. But her mother had been wrong about so many things. And it wasn't as if the clock could be turned back, either, and undo what he felt. And he seemed *happy*. She would not want to undo it if she could.

"And you're both safe," Grace said. "The Clave doesn't suspect Lucie of—anything?"

"Grace," Jesse said. "Don't worry."

But she couldn't help it. The Clave was unlikely to understand, or care about understanding, the distinction between necromancy and what Lucie had done. Jesse would need to pretend to be this obscure Blackthorn cousin, and she would need to pretend that too, for now. Maybe forever. It would still be worth it.

"Last night," Jesse said, "Mother was recaptured. She was found on Bodmin Moor. I assume Belial tired of her and abandoned her." His lip curled. "It was bound to happen. She was looking for loyalty from a demon."

"Recaptured?" Grace was almost too stunned to speak. "So—will they take her to Idris? Try her by the Mortal Sword?"

Jesse nodded. "You know what that means, don't you? You don't have to stay here, Gracie. It was brave of you to bring yourself to the Silent Brothers, to see if Mother had done anything to you like she did to me, but surely they would have discovered it by now if she had? And I'm sure it felt safer here, as well," he added, lowering his voice, "but if you come back to the Institute with me—"

"But you are Jeremy Blackthorn now," said Grace, her mind whirling. "Surely you are not meant to even know me."

"Within the walls of the Institute, I am still Jesse," he said. "Still your brother. And I want you with me. You'll be safe there—"

"I'll be whispered about," said Grace. "Tatiana's daughter. Everyone in the Enclave will stare."

"You cannot spend the rest of your life in the Silent City because you are worried about vicious gossip," said Jesse. "I know there are things Mother forced you to do that you're ashamed of, but people will understand—"

Grace felt as if her heart had begun to pound in her stomach. Her mind was full of a hot, twisting horror. To go to the Institute—to see James every day, James who had looked at her as if she were the worst monster he had ever seen—James, who she had wronged beyond belief. And there were Cordelia, Charles, Matthew . . . and Lucie . . .

Perhaps they did not know the truth yet. It seemed James was keeping the secret. But they would know soon enough.

"I can't," Grace said. "I need to stay here."

"Grace, I too bear the marks of the terrible things our mother forced me to do. Quite literally. But this is Lucie's family. They *will* understand—"

"No," Grace said. "They won't."

Jesse's intelligent green eyes narrowed. "Did the Silent Brothers find something?" he said quietly. "Did *she* do something to you—?"

Grace hesitated. She could lie to him, she thought. She could hide the truth just a little bit longer. But Jesse was the most important person in her life. She needed him to know who she really was. All of it. If he did not understand not just what she had gone through, but what she had done, he would never really know her.

"It's worse than that," she said.

And she told him. All of it, sparing no details, from the forest to the bracelet to Charles to James's demand that she be arrested. She spared him only one thing: her mother's last request of her, that she use her power to seduce Jesse, too, and bend him to Belial's will.

As she spoke, Jesse sat back slowly in his chair, withdrawing his hand from hers. Shivering, she clenched her fists in her lap, as her voice finally trailed off. The story was done. She felt as if she had cut her wrists in front of her brother, and poison had poured out instead of blood.

"You," Jesse said, and cleared his throat. He was shaking—she could see it, though he had jammed his hands into the pockets of his coat. "You did those things to James? And others, too, Matthew and Charles and—Christopher?"

"Not Christopher," Grace said. "I never used my power on him."

"Really." There was a coldness in Jesse's voice she had never heard before. "Lucie said you had grown friendly with him; I don't see how else that could have happened. How could you, Grace? How could you have done all that?"

"How could I not?" she whispered. "Mother told me it was a great gift. She said I was a weapon in her hand, that if I only did what she said, together we would bring you back—"

"Don't use me as an excuse," Jesse snapped.

"I felt I had no choice."

"But you did," he said. "You had a choice."

"I know that now." She tried to look into his eyes, but he would not meet her gaze. "I wasn't strong enough. I am trying to be strong enough now. That is why I'm here. And why I won't leave. I told James the truth—"

"But you haven't told anyone else. Lucie is unaware of this. And Cordelia—what you've done to their *marriage*, Grace—"

James hasn't told her? Grace thought in surprise, but she was barely able to feel it. She was numb, as if a limb had been severed and she was in the first shock of the wound. "I can't tell anyone," she said. "I shouldn't have told you. It's a secret. The Silent Brothers wish to keep it hidden so they can use the information to deceive our mother as to what they know—"

"I don't believe you," Jesse said flatly. "You are trying to make me a party to your deception. I won't have it."

Grace shook her head wearily. "Ask James," she said. "He will tell you just what I have. Talk to him before you speak with anyone else—he has a right—"

Jesse stood up, knocking over his chair. It clattered to the stone floor. "You are the last person," he said, "to lecture me about James's rights." He snatched the witchlight torch off the wall. His eyes glittered in its light—surely those were not tears?

"I must go," he said. "I feel sick."

And without another word, he was gone, taking the light with him.

Thomas would have preferred going to Chiswick House to helping Christopher in the Institute library, fond as he was of Kit. He had a mad curiosity about the abandoned place that had once belonged to his family, of course, but also he felt that James and Matthew both needed his emotional support more than Christopher did. (Christopher seemed sanguine as always.) Though he did sometimes wonder if he were providing the strong, silent emotional support that he intended, or if he were merely staring fixedly at his friends in an alarming manner that they probably discussed when he was not there.

In the end, the deciding factor was—as it often seemed to be these days—Alastair. He had come straight over to Christopher after the Devil Tavern gathering and said, "I'll help you in the library with research, if you like."

Christopher's eyebrows had gone up, but he'd only said, "You read Persian, don't you?"

"And Sanskrit," Alastair said. "Urdu, some Malay, Tamil, Greek, and a bit of Coptic. If that would be useful."

Christopher looked as if someone had given him a box of kittens with bows on. "Wonderful," he said. "We'll meet in the library tomorrow morning." His eyes darted over to Thomas, who tried to school his expression into complete blankness. "Thomas, are you still on for joining me, as well?"

And then Thomas could not say anything but yes; it was one thing to disappoint Christopher, another to make it seem as if he had changed his mind about assisting Christopher in the library simply because Alastair was going to be there.

Thomas was not someone who normally paid that much attention to his clothes. If they were not bizarre, and did not have holes or burns in them, he was happy. Yet he changed his jacket at least six times that morning before finding a dark olive one that brought out the green in his eyes. He brushed his sandy hair four or five different ways before coming downstairs to find Eugenia, alone in the breakfast room, buttering toast.

She eyed him. "You're going out wearing *that*?" she said.

Thomas stared at her in horror. "What?"

She chuckled. "Nothing. You look fine, Tom. Go have fun with Alastair and Christopher."

"You are a fiend," he said to her. "A fiend from the deep."

Thomas was running through various cutting remarks he could have made to Eugenia, had he thought of them at the time, when he arrived at the Institute and took the stairs two at a time to reach the library. It was immediately evident that he was the last to arrive; as he was making his way down the library's central aisle of heavy oak study tables, he caught sight of Christopher down the stacks, where he had carefully arranged a pile of books as a stepstool so he could reach something else on a top shelf. He turned when he heard Thomas's footsteps, nearly toppled off the stack, rescued himself with a heroic waving of arms, and jumped down to greet Thomas.

Alastair was somewhat farther into the room, sitting at one of the study tables, green lamp burning and a fearsome stack of leather-bound volumes next to him. Christopher led Thomas over to him.

"Lightwood," Alastair said, nodding to Christopher, and then to Thomas, "Other Lightwood."

"Well, that *is* going to be very confusing," Christopher said, while Thomas fumed silently at being referred to as Other Lightwood. "But no matter. We are here to find out about paladins."

"And more specifically," Alastair said, "to help my sister stop being one." He sighed. "I've been going through these," he said, patting the stack of books on the table, a patchwork of volumes in languages familiar to Thomas—Greek, Latin, Spanish, Old English—and many that were not.

"You're a braver man than I," Christopher said. To Thomas's quizzical expression he added, "Books of Deeds. The Shadowhunters used to record notable demon fights for their records. Extensively."

"Or, more often," Alastair said, "highly boring, completely ordinary demon fights engaged in by notable *persons*. Heads of Institutes, that sort of thing. And, long ago, paladins."

"What have you found?" Christopher said.

"A fat lot of nothing," Alastair said briskly. "All the paladins I've found stay paladins until they die in their beds."

Thomas said, "I wouldn't think Shadowhunter paladins would *want* to stop being paladins."

Alastair grimaced. "It's not only that. Do you think if a Shadowhunter stopped being the paladin of an angel—and the angel didn't smite them dead—they'd stay a Shadowhunter? The Clave would surely strip their Marks and cast them out."

"Because a Shadowhunter paladin is bound to an angel," Thomas said. "So those vows are holy. To leave the angel's service would be unholy." Alastair nodded. "What if they violate their vows? Do something that makes the angel break the connection with *them*?"

"What are you getting at?" Alastair looked at him, dark eyes curious. They were a velvet-dark, a softer sort of shade than black. For a moment Thomas forgot what he was supposed to be saying, until Christopher poked him in the ribs.

"I mean," said Thomas, "that if you're the paladin of an angel, but you do terrible things—commit terrible sins—the angel might reject you. But what if Cordelia does lots of good deeds? Very good deeds, I mean. Feeds the sick, clothes the needy . . . washes the feet of beggars? I can tell from your faces that you don't see much merit in the idea, but I think we should consider it."

"Cordelia already only does good and kind things," Alastair said testily. "Well," he added, "the last week excluded, I suppose."

Christopher looked alarmed, an expression Thomas strongly suspected was mirrored on his own face.

"Oh, what?" snapped Alastair. "Are we all supposed to pretend that Cordelia didn't run off to Paris with Matthew because James made her miserable, always gazing after that vacuous Grace Blackthorn? And now they're all back, and they all look miserable. What an appalling mess."

"It's not James's fault," Thomas said hotly. "He and Cordelia had an agreement—she knew—"

"I don't need to listen to this," said Alastair ferociously. Thomas had always secretly loved Alastair's god-damn-you expression, with his dark eyes snapping and that hard twist to his soft mouth. At the moment, though, he wanted to snap back—wanted to defend James—and at the same time, he couldn't help but understand what Alastair felt. Eugenia might be a toast-eating fiend, but Thomas had to admit he would not think much of any man marrying her and then mooning about over someone else.

But Thomas never got to say any of this, of course, because Alastair had already snatched up a volume from his table and was striding away toward the privacy of the stacks.

Thomas and Christopher looked at each other gloomily. "I suppose he has a point," Christopher said. "It is a mess."

"Did you learn anything from talking to James the other night?" Thomas said. "About Grace, or . . ."

Christopher sat down on the table Alastair had abandoned. "Grace," he said, in an odd sort of voice. "If James loved her once, he doesn't now. He loves Cordelia, and I think for him, not being with her is like it would be for me if I had to give up science and learning things." He looked at Thomas. "What did you find out from Matthew?"

"He also loves Cordelia, unfortunately," said Thomas. "And he is also miserable, just like James; in part he is miserable *because* of James. He misses him, and he feels like he has wronged him, and at the same time he feels wronged—he feels like if James had ever told him that he loved Cordelia, he would never have let himself fall in love with her. And now it's too late."

"I wonder," said Christopher. "Do you think Matthew really loves Cordelia?"

"I think for him Cordelia is a sort of absolution," said Thomas. "If she loved him, he imagines it would fix everything broken in his life."

"I don't think love works that way," said Christopher, with a frown. "I think some people are suited for each other, and others aren't. Like Grace and James weren't suited. James and Cordelia are a much better match." He lifted a heavy Book of Deeds, holding it up so he could examine the faded gilt spine.

Thomas said, "I suppose I never gave much thought to whether James and Grace were well suited. I barely know her at all, to be honest."

"Well, she was shut up like Rapunzel in a tower by her mother for all those years," said Christopher. "Yet despite all that, she is possessed of a fine scientific mind."

"*Is* she," Thomas said, arching an eyebrow.

"Oh, yes. We have had some excellent conversations about my work on the fire-messages. And she shares my views on activated moth powder."

"Christopher," said Thomas. "How do you know so much about Grace?"

Christopher's eyes widened. "I am observant," he said. "I am a scientist. We *observe*." He squinted again at the book in his hand. "This will not be useful. I must return it to the shelf from which it was taken."

With which unusually formal pronouncement, he sprang off the table and disappeared into the shadows at the east end of the library.

Thomas struck off toward the other end of the library, where Alastair had vanished among the shadows between the white-flickering lamps placed at intervals on the tables. The curving stained-glass windows threw diamonds of scarlet and gold at Thomas's feet as he turned a corner and found Alastair sitting on the floor, his head thrown back against the wall, a book dangling from his hand.

He started when he saw Thomas but made no move to relocate as Thomas sat down beside him. For a long moment they simply sat together, side by side, looking out at the painted angel on the library wall.

"I'm sorry," Thomas said, after some time had passed. "The business between James and Cordelia—I oughtn't to have inserted my opinion into it. James has been my friend for a long time, but I've never fathomed his interest in Grace. None of us have."

Alastair turned to look at Thomas. His hair had grown long since he had come to London; it fell over his eyes, soft and dark as a cloud of smoke. The desire to touch Alastair's hair, to rub the strands between his fingers, was so strong that Thomas clenched his hands into fists. "I'm sure they would say the same about you and me," Alastair said, "if they knew."

Thomas could only stammer. "You—and me?"

"Grace is a mystery to the Merry Thieves, it seems," said Alastair, "but I am a known and disliked quantity. I am only saying they would no doubt find it just as puzzling that you and I had—"

Thomas could stand it no more. He caught hold of Alastair's collar and drew him in to kiss him. Alastair had clearly not been expecting it; the book he had been holding fell, and he laid an unsure hand on Thomas's arm, steadying himself.

But he did not pull away. He leaned into the kiss, and Thomas unclenched his hands and let them find their way into Alastair's hair, which was rough silk against his fingers. He felt an exquisite sense of relief—he had wanted this for so long, and what had happened between them in the Sanctuary had only made it worse—and then the relief melted away into heat, traversing his veins like liquid fire. Alastair was kissing him hard, each kiss opening his mouth a little wider, their tongues touching in a flickering dance. In between kisses, Alastair murmured soft words in Persian. *"Ey pesar,"* he whispered, *"nik ze hadd mibebari kar-e jamal."* His tongue swept Thomas's lower lip; Thomas shuddered, pressed into him, his breath catching with every kiss, every movement of Alastair's body. *"Ba conin hosn ze to sabr konam?"*

And then, just as abruptly as it had started, it was over. Alastair pulled back, his hand still on Thomas's arm, his face flushed. "Thomas," he breathed. "This isn't something I can do."

Thomas closed his eyes. "Why not?"

"The situation hasn't changed," Alastair said, in a voice closer to his usual tone, and Thomas could feel the spell broken, dissipating as though it had never been. "Your friends hate me. And they are right to do so—"

"I told Matthew," Thomas said.

Alastair's eyes widened. "You what?"

"I told Matthew," said Thomas. "About me. And that I—that we—that I cared about you." He cleared his throat. "He knew about you and Charles already."

"Well, Charles is his brother," said Alastair, in an oddly mechanical voice. "And Matthew is himself—different. But your other friends . . ."

"Christopher won't care. As for James, he is married to your *sister*. Alastair, you are already part of us, part of our group, whether you like it or not. You cannot use my friends as an excuse."

"It's not an *excuse*." Alastair was still holding on to Thomas's jacket, still leaning toward him. Thomas could smell Alastair's scent of smoke and spice and leather. Desire burned deep in his belly like a swallowed coal, but he knew it made no difference. Alastair was shaking his head. "I learned—with Charles—things cannot be all stolen moments. But neither can we hurt others by blindly pursuing what we want—"

"So you do want me," Thomas said, and felt a bitter sort of gladness.

Alastair's eyes darkened. "How can you even ask—"

There was a *bang* and both of them looked up to see Christopher, carrying a tall stack of books, one of which had just fallen loudly to the ground. He seemed delighted to see them, as if it were perfectly normal for Thomas and Alastair to be sitting on the floor, with Alastair clutching Thomas's sleeve.

"Enough shilly-shallying, you two," Christopher exclaimed. "I've had an idea. We must go immediately to Limehouse."

15

Old Voices

All day within the dreamy house,
The doors upon their hinges creak'd;
The blue fly sung in the pane; the mouse
Behind the mouldering wainscot shriek'd,
Or from the crevice peer'd about.
Old faces glimmer'd thro' the doors
Old footsteps trod the upper floors,
Old voices called her from without.
—Alfred, Lord Tennyson, "Mariana"

Cordelia had been late getting out of the house, and she found herself at Chiswick House after the others had already arrived. She climbed out of the carriage, waving at Anna and Ariadne, who were waiting by the steps; the Institute carriage had already pulled up in the circular drive. Cordelia could see a few figures in the distance where James, Jesse, and Lucie seemed to have gone to look at the gardens.

It was a bracing day, cold enough to sting her chest when she breathed. She glanced around as she pulled on her gloves. At night, the house and its grounds had the feel of a classical ruin, like a Roman villa gone to seed—marble and brick chipped and unrepaired, paint peeling, formal gardens now a shaggy war of briars and hedges invading each other's space. She remembered the effect as quite Gothic, with Grace very much the pale maiden languishing behind the dark walls.

But here in the white winter sun the house looked merely shabby and squalid. Nothing romantic lurked here, she thought. Only the end result of decades of domestic horror, negligence, and cruelty.

As she went to join Ariadne and Anna, the others approached—James, pale but calm, Jesse, seemingly distracted, and Lucie, brightly friendly as she greeted Ariadne and Anna, but careful not to look at Cordelia.

Cordelia had not expected anything different—it was probably why she had dawdled getting started that morning—but it still hurt to have Lucie ignore her. Not, she thought, that she didn't deserve it.

At least all of them were wearing ordinary clothes, not gear, which was a relief to Cordelia—she had wondered about it herself and finally decided on a simple dress and sturdy boots. It was not as if she could fight anyway, she thought bitterly, if the situation arose. She would have to fling herself behind someone else for protection, like the sort of Victorian heroine she particularly disliked.

Anna glanced around with a languid blue gaze. "I believe that's all of us," she said. She wore a Norfolk hunting jacket over a pair of trousers tucked into boots; around her neck was a brightly patterned silk scarf, tucked into the collar of her shirt. Below it dangled the ruby necklace she always wore, which detected the presence of demons. On anyone else the combination would have been odd; on Anna it was dashing.

Cordelia said, without thinking, "What about Matthew?" and saw James glance quickly away.

"He hasn't come," said Ariadne. "He's doing a favor for me today, I'm afraid."

That was a bit surprising, but, Cordelia reminded herself, Ariadne *had* been engaged to Matthew's brother. And Matthew and Anna were very close. She felt a bit left out—she had been missing Anna lately, and even more now that she and Lucie had fallen out.

"I daresay six of us should be more than enough," James said. "I would suggest we divide into two equal groups."

"Capital," said Anna. "Cordelia, would you be kind enough to join Ariadne and me?"

Cordelia felt a rush of gratitude. Anna was being kind, drawing

Cordelia away from any potentially awkward interaction with James.

"Of course," Cordelia said.

"Jesse," said Ariadne, and Jesse looked surprised. She hesitated. "I just wanted to make sure—I mean, we all know it's for the greater good, but are you all right with us, you know . . . ransacking your house?"

Jesse looked at the sky. James said, in some surprise, "*Do* you mind?"

"It's not that," Jesse said. "I was only going to say—you might as well look through my house, because I've been in all of yours."

"Scandalous!" Anna said, delighted. "But why?"

"Nothing indecent," Jesse said. "I've never looked in on any of you in the bath, or anything like that. It's just, ghosts, we tend to drift about. We don't really obey property laws. I obey them *now*, of course," he added, "and I am perfectly fine with you pillaging this wretched pile. I can't imagine I'd ever want to live here, even if I do inherit it. Given that I'm Jeremy Blackthorn these days, who knows who will end up with it? I'd say it ought to go back to the Lightwoods, but I doubt you want to be cursed with the place."

"Do you think there are likely to be any demons or such about?" Lucie said curiously.

"It seems unlikely," said James, "given how many times the Enclave has been over this place. I suppose one can never be entirely sure."

"Not where my mother is concerned," said Jesse. "I can think of a few places she might have hidden things—I'd suggest Anna, Ariadne, and Cordelia search inside, and the rest of us take the gardens and greenhouse area. When we're finished, we can meet back on these steps."

James nodded. His dark gold eyes scanned the horizon. "Hard to imagine your mother enjoyed living here, with the place in this state," he said.

"She liked it like this," said Jesse. "She's the one who smashed all the mirrors and stopped the clocks. It was a reminder to her every time she set foot here that she was a victim, and your families were to blame."

"Some people like being miserable," said Lucie, staring off above Cordelia's head. "Some people won't do things that would make them, and other people, happy, just because."

"Lucie," said Anna, "I have no idea what you're on about. What are we meant to be looking for?"

"Anything that looks off—disturbed dust on the floor, pictures hanging oddly, any hint of demonic activity that might activate your necklace," said Jesse.

Those who had watches—James, Anna—checked them to set the time, and they were off. Lucie turned away without a glance at Cordelia, following her brother and Jesse into the gardens. She put her hand on James's elbow to steady herself as they went down a cracked flight of stone steps—a friendly, affectionate gesture—and Cordelia felt an awful jealous pang in her chest. Whether she was jealous of Lucie or of James she was not sure; somehow, that made it worse.

Even on a bright afternoon, the greenhouse at Chiswick House was still a dim, gloomy place. When last James had been here, he had passed through Belial's realm and arrived choking on ashes in the middle of a fight between Cordelia and a Cerberus demon. Today the dust was gone, and no sign remained of any demonic activity. Whatever had been grown here had long ago been taken over by the briars and the hedges of the gardens outside, which slowly extended their branches and vines a little more every year, to eventually draw the greenhouse itself back into wildness.

James didn't think Tatiana had hidden anything here; everything was so damp and overgrown that she would never be able to find anything a second time, if it wasn't destroyed by the plants and the rain and the insects first. But they were gamely searching; Jesse especially thought that the gardens might hold some secrets.

At the other end of the greenhouse James saw the flash of Lucie's witchlight rune-stone as she and Jesse emerged from behind a crumbling wall. Jesse had been silent and uneasy-looking since he'd come back from seeing Grace in the Silent City that morning.

Part of James was desperate to know what Jesse had discovered. Had Grace told him the truth about her power, about what she'd done? Though James would have expected Jesse to look at *him* differently if he knew, and he didn't seem to be doing that. He seemed rather to have retreated inside himself, however hard he was trying to put a good face on things.

Perhaps it had simply been seeing his sister in the Silent City prison that had affected him. For Jesse, Grace represented hope—the hope of family, the hope of orphans clinging together when their parents were dead or lost. But for James, still, thoughts of Grace meant thoughts of darkness, a forever fall into shadow, like Lucifer falling from heaven. From grace itself.

He could not bring himself to ask. And so he schooled his expression into a calm neutrality as Jesse and Lucie approached. There were streaks of dirt on Jesse's face; he looked discouraged. "There's nothing here," he said.

"Or rather, there *was* a Cerberus demon here," said Lucie, "until a few months ago, when James killed it."

"You killed Balthazar?" Jesse said in horror.

"It was a *demon*," James began, and broke off as Jesse smiled. He wasn't doing a bad job pretending things were all right, James had to admit.

"Sorry," Jesse said. "Just a joke. Never been friends with a demon. Didn't know the, ah, former . . . occupant."

Lucie looked at Jesse. Carefully, she said, "Shall we try the . . . other structure?"

Jesse's smile faded immediately. He glanced over at a squat brick building a little way away, difficult to see behind all the overgrowth of the gardens. It looked like a potting shed, and might have been once, but now its roof was gone. A rickety wooden door hung open on one side.

"Yes," Jesse said. "I suppose we have to, don't we?"

Lucie took his hand. James noted the gesture but said nothing. There was no shame in needing support, but not all Shadowhunters—male ones, especially—were brought up to think so. James had been raised by Will, whose central tenet in life was that he would have been dead in a ditch at age fourteen had it not been for Jem. He had always encouraged James to rely on his friends, to depend on his *parabatai*. It was something James loved about his father, but it also meant he could not approach him to talk about Matthew and Cordelia. He could not admit to his father that he was angry with Matthew. James was sure Will had never been angry with Jem in his life.

James followed Lucie and Jesse through the overgrowth to the brick shed. Jesse went inside first, and the others next; the moment James was inside the place, he froze. The room was empty but for a table in its center, on which sat a carved wooden casket. Suddenly James knew what this place was, and why Lucie had only called it the *other structure*.

The casket—open now, gaping like a slack mouth—was Jesse's. This was his tomb.

James could see where rain and damp had warped the wood of the casket over the years, a consequence of the building having no roof. Prongs jutted out from one wall, as if something—a sword, perhaps—had hung there once. One of the walls was smoke-blackened, ashes scattered across the frozen ground.

"Bleak, isn't it," said Jesse, with a tight sort of smile. "My mother seemed to feel this was the safest place to leave me; she was always afraid the Enclave would search the house."

"But not the grounds?" James said quietly. He could not have described the look on Jesse's face—half pain, half horror; this place must remind him of all he had lost. All the years and time.

"I suspect, though she said otherwise, that she wanted me far away from her," said Jesse. "I suspect the presence of my . . . corpse . . . made her feel guilty. Or perhaps just horrified."

"She *ought* to feel guilty," Lucie said fiercely. "She ought to never have another moment of peace, after what she did to you."

"I don't think she has much in the way of peace," James said, thinking of Tatiana's wild eyes, of the hatred burning in them. "Do you?"

Jesse seemed about to reply, but before he could, James gasped. Something arrowed across his vision—a slice of darkness, as if he were gazing through a cracked window at Belial's shadow realm. Something was terribly wrong; something nearby.

Cordelia, he thought, and bolted back toward the house without another word.

The upper floors of Chiswick House were emptier than Cordelia would have expected. Most of the rooms were without pictures, rugs, or furniture. Cordelia knew Tatiana had smashed every mirror in the house when Rupert Blackthorn had died; she had not realized they still hung on the walls, ruined frames of jagged glass.

There was a training room, in which there were no weapons, only cobwebs and mice. And there was one bedroom, plain but furnished, which had a small vanity table, with a silver-backed brush set still laid out on it. There was one hard-looking chair, and a nearly bare iron bed, with torn sheets still on it. On the nightstand was a mug, at whose bottom something ancient—chocolate? milky tea?—had hardened into a moldy green scum.

With a start, Cordelia realized this cheerless place must have been Grace's bedroom. What kind of dreams had she dreamt, on that plank of a bed? Surrounded by the darkness of this moldering, bitter house?

Surely I cannot be pitying Grace, Cordelia thought, and started when she heard someone cry out. She reached for Cortana—her hand slapped against fabric. Her blade was not there.

She pushed through the hurt, running out into the corridor and up a flight of stairs, following the sound of the cry. She burst into a large ballroom, where the remains of a massive chandelier, easily eight feet across, lay in the middle of the room where it had crashed to the ground at some point. It looked like a massive, jeweled spider that had lost a fight with a much larger spider.

Ariadne, in the center of the room, shot Cordelia a guilty look. "Oh, bother," she said. "I didn't mean to make you come running."

"Ariadne may have thought it was a real spider," Anna said. "A real, giant spider."

Anna meant to be teasing, Cordelia knew, but the tone of her voice was . . . fond. Fonder than either Anna or Ariadne were aware of, Cordelia suspected. They were both smiling as Ariadne teased Anna about whether the spider chandelier might look nice in her flat, and perhaps even make a friend for Percival the stuffed snake.

Cordelia went to examine the rest of the room. There were broken floorboards aplenty, each of which she tested to see if it was loose and perhaps hiding something beneath it. Having made herself sneeze several times by disturbing the dust, she went over to a window to catch her breath.

A moment later Anna joined her. Ariadne was at the other end of the room, examining the dumbwaiter, whose door she had managed to wrench open with a puff of dust and broken paint. For a long moment, Anna and Cordelia stood together, looking out the cracked window at the once-green lawns sloping down toward the River Thames.

"Anna," Cordelia said, in a small voice. "Is Matthew really doing an errand for Ariadne?"

"Indeed he is," Anna said. She touched a long finger to the window glass, making a spot in the dust. "Why do you ask?"

Cordelia felt herself flush scarlet. "I suppose I was worried. And there's no one else I can ask. Is he all right?"

Anna paused in the act of drawing back a curtain. "Does he have a reason not to be?"

"I just thought," Cordelia said, "since you are close to him, you might know something of his state of mind."

"My dear," Anna said gently. "His state of mind is that he loves you. He loves you and he mourns that love as impossible. He fears that you despise him, that everyone does. That is his state of mind, and it is a difficult one indeed."

Cordelia shot a quick look at Ariadne, who thankfully had her head half-stuck in the dumbwaiter and couldn't possibly have heard. Then she felt foolish for worrying. *My fraught love life is evidently the worst-kept secret in the Enclave, so perhaps I should give up trying to maintain my dignity.*

"I do not hate Matthew," Cordelia whispered. "I regret going to Paris—and yet I cannot regret all of it. He held out a hand to me when I was desperate. He took me out of my despair. I could never, ever despise him."

"He needs help now," Anna said, half to herself. "The sort I am afraid I cannot give him, because he will refuse it. I worry—" She broke off, shaking her head. "Cordelia, what happened in Paris?"

"It was lovely at first. We went to museums, dressmakers, the theater. It was a sort of game of pretend, as children play. We pretended we were other people, without troubles, people who could do as they liked."

"Ah," said Anna delicately. "You . . . there isn't a chance you are with child, is there, Cordelia?"

Cordelia nearly fell out of the window. "*No,*" she said. "None—we kissed, that's all. And then James showed up in the middle of it, and saw everything."

"A very romantic gesture, his rushing to Paris," Anna noted, "but his timing leaves something to be desired."

"Except," said Cordelia, "that James has been in love with Grace for years, before I ever came to London. He was in love with Grace through all of our marriage. He was very plain about it."

"People's feelings change."

"Do they?" Cordelia said. "I didn't run away to Paris on a lark, you know. I left our house because Grace appeared at our door. And though James didn't know I could see, I found him in the vestibule, holding her close. As in love as ever, by all appearances."

"Oh, my poor darling," Anna said. "What can I say? That must have been dreadful. Only—things are not always as they first appear."

"I know what I saw."

"Perhaps," Anna said. "And perhaps you should ask James what truly happened that night. It may be as you fear. But I am an excellent reader of faces, Daisy. And when I see James looking at Grace, I see nothing at all. But when I see him looking at you, he is transformed. We all carry a light inside ourselves. It burns with the flame of our souls. But there are other people in our lives who add their own flames to ours, creating a brighter conflagration." She glanced quickly at Ariadne, and then back at Cordelia. "James is special. He has always burned bright. But when he looks at you, his light blazes up like a bonfire."

"Really?" Cordelia whispered. "Anna, I don't know—"

Anna jolted, putting her hand to her chest, where her ruby necklace was flashing like a winking eye. At that moment, Ariadne shrieked, reeling back from the dumbwaiter, which had begun to tremble and rattle within the wall. "*Demon!*" she cried. "*Look out!*"

The shed appeared untouched since the day Lucie and Grace had found the coffin open and Jesse gone, little knowing the night would end with his resurrection and Grace turning herself in and so much else. Strange—she would have expected the Clave to seek it out, or Tatiana at least, but if anyone had come, they had left no trace; they had not even closed the coffin lid. Lucie found it distressing to be back here; had she really spent so much time in this awful, morbid room?

Despite the sun and the missing roof, the high brick walls cast shadows over the room, which felt dark and small now that Jesse was standing in it, his face tipped up to the sky. When Lucie and Grace had been working to bring him back, it had seemed dramatic to her—a secret crypt from a Gothic novel, the dungeon of a castle. Now she recognized it as a place where Jesse had been imprisoned, where he had been dreadfully controlled. She was grateful that James had ducked out, sensing that being back here would be fraught for Jesse, and even for her.

"Is it hard to be here?" she asked.

Jesse looked around: at the small space, the damp walls, the ashes where she and Grace had burned so very many ineffective ingredients for useless spells. With a visible effort, he turned to Lucie and said, "I was never even aware of being here, really. So what it reminds me is how much work you did, to bring me back."

"Grace helped," Lucie said, but Jesse's expression only hardened. He turned and went over to the coffin. Taking off his glove, he reached inside. Lucie moved to join him. There was nothing inside; Jesse seemed to be running his bare hand over the black velvet lining, now beginning to spot with mold from exposure to the elements. "Jesse," Lucie said. "Something happened when you went to see Grace in the Silent City, didn't it?"

He hesitated. "Yes. She told me something that—that I didn't want to hear, or know."

Lucie felt a grim little twist of cold at her spine. "What was it?"

"I . . ." Jesse looked up from the coffin, his green eyes dark. "I will not lie to you, Lucie. But the whole of what I can tell you is that it is not my secret to tell."

"But if there is a danger . . . to the Enclave, or to anyone—"

"It's nothing like that. And the Silent Brothers know it; if there were a danger, they would share it."

"Oh," Lucie said. The curious part of her wanted to stamp her feet and demand to be told. The part of her that had been changed by everything that had happened in this past year, the part that had begun to understand patience, won out. "I trust you will tell me when you can."

Jesse did not reply; he was leaning into the coffin, tearing at the velvet lining—"Aha!" He turned to her, holding up a small wooden box. "I knew it," he said, almost savagely. "There's a false bottom in the coffin, under the lining. Where else would my mother hide something than with her most precious possession?"

"You were not her possession," Lucie said. "You never belonged to her."

"That's not what she believed." Jesse frowned as he opened the box and withdrew an object. He held it up to show her: a hand mirror. Its handle was cut glass, but black—not black *adamas*, she didn't think, but it was hard to tell—and around the octagonal looking glass itself she could see tiny carvings that seemed to twist and writhe in the light.

"What is it?" Lucie said. "Do you recognize it?"

"Yes." Jesse nodded. "It's the only remaining mirror in Chiswick." There was an odd look on his face. "And—I believe I know where else we ought to be searching . . ."

Cordelia whipped around to see something the size of a small dog explode from the dumbwaiter, shattering it—and a good portion of the wall—apart. The demon had a ratlike face, with long yellow teeth. It was covered in scales and too many skinny limbs, whipping around in a fury, each one tipped with a hooked claw. A Gamigin demon, Cordelia thought, though she'd never seen one in person before.

Ariadne drew a blade from her belt, but it was too fast. One of its skinny limbs shot out, the hook at the end of its claw sinking into the back of Ariadne's jacket. It flung her away; she skidded across the dusty floor as Anna screamed, "*Ari!*"

And Anna sprang into motion, racing across the room, her whip suddenly in her hand. The demon was crouched over Ariadne, its yellow-toothed mouth opening wide. She screamed as black demon saliva spattered her neck and face. Then Anna was there, her whip arcing through the air, a wire of golden flame.

With a shriek, the demon sprang away. Anna dropped to her knees—Ariadne was convulsing on the floor—and the demon, hissing, shot across the floor toward Cordelia.

Time seemed to slow. Cordelia could hear Anna, begging Ariadne to hold still, hold still, and the demon was hurtling across the room toward her, leaving a trail of black ichor, and Cordelia knew that if she so much as lifted a broken floorboard to defend herself it would bring Lilith, but she had no choice—

The demon was on her. It lunged, and Cordelia kicked out as hard as she could, her boot colliding with its dense, springy frame. It yowled like a cat, rolling onto its back, but the yowls weren't just noise, Cordelia realized. They were words.

"They rise," it hissed. *"Soon they will be invincible. No seraph blade will harm them."*

"What?" Throwing caution and sense to the winds, Cordelia ran toward the demon where it crouched on the floor. "Who is rising? Tell me!"

The demon looked up at her—and went limp. Its fanged mouth trembling, it cringed away from her, covering its body with some of its legs. *"Paladin,"* it rasped. *"Oh, forgive me. Thine is the power, thine and thy Lady's. Forgive me. I did not know—"*

A sharp *crack* sounded. Something punched into the demon's body—Cordelia thought she saw a hole open between its eyes, a black hole rimmed with fire. The demon spasmed, legs curling in. Then it melted away into smoke.

The stench of ichor on the air was mixed with the sharp smell of cordite. Cordelia knew what she would see even before she looked: James, white-faced, pistol in hand. It was still pointed unerringly at the spot where the demon had just been.

"Daisy." Lowering his arm, he moved quickly to her side. His gaze raked her, searching for injuries, bruises. "Are you hurt? Did it—"

"You needn't have shot it," Cordelia snapped. "I was questioning it. It said, 'They rise,' and I—"

His hands still on her shoulders, James's expression turned incredulous. "You can't question a demon, Daisy. It'll just lie."

"I was *managing*." Shock had turned to a hot fury in Cordelia's veins, a fury that seemed to have a tight hold of her, even as a small part of her mind looked on, appalled. "I didn't need your help—"

His golden eyes narrowed. "Really? Because you can't wield

a weapon, Cordelia, in case you've forgotten—"

"Stop it. Both of you." It was Anna, speaking more sternly than Cordelia had imagined she could. She and Ariadne had crossed the room to them; Cordelia, intent on James, had not noticed. She wondered how much they had overheard. Anna held her stele in her hand; Ariadne, beside her, sported red welts on the left side of her face, where the demon's acid saliva had touched her. There was a freshly applied healing rune on her throat. "Whatever's happening between you may be none of my business, but I won't have you arguing in the middle of a mission. It puts us all in danger."

Cordelia felt wretchedly ashamed. Anna was right. "James," she said, looking at him directly. It hurt to do that; it was like pressing a sharp pin into her hand. He was beautiful, just as he was—breathing hard, his black hair in his eyes, a sheen of sweat along his collarbones. She wished she could make herself immune to his beauty, but it seemed impossible. "I'm sorry, I—"

"Don't apologize." The Mask had gone up; he was expressionless. "In fact, I'd rather you didn't."

A crash came from downstairs, and a shout. *Lucie*, Cordelia thought, and a moment later they were all bolting down the steps toward the main floor of the house.

Cordelia, James, Anna, and Ariadne raced back downstairs, only to find Jesse and Lucie in the parlor. More specifically, Lucie was in the parlor: Jesse was halfway up the fireplace, getting covered in soot.

"What happened?" James demanded. "What was that crash?"

Lucie, also streaked with soot, said, "Something fell out of the fireplace into the grate. Jesse?" she called. "Jesse, did you get them?"

A moment later Jesse emerged, the top half of his body nearly caked with soot. He looked as if it had been raining black paint on him. In one hand he held a dirty mirror; in the other, what seemed to be a book with a leather cord wrapped around its binding, which held a number of loose papers.

"Notes," he said, coughing. "My mother's notes and bits of old diaries. I remembered seeing her peering up the chimney with this"—he held up the mirror, which James realized was not dirty so much as made of a shiny, reflective black material—"and I realized, she had a hiding place up there you could only see if you shone the mirror up the chimney. Some kind of magical signal beacon. That's why the Enclave didn't find it."

"Does it do anything else?" Anna asked, peering at the mirror curiously. "Besides pointing the way to the chimney hiding place?"

"Might I see it?" James asked, and with a shrug, Jesse handed it over. James could hear the others discussing the demon they'd found upstairs, Jesse wondering aloud how long it had been living in the dumbwaiter, but James's concentration was all on the mirror.

Before he even touched the mirror's handle, he felt as though it were in his hand: smooth and cool to the touch, humming with power. It seemed made of black *adamas*, or something very close to it, surrounding a circle of dark glass. And around the edge of the glass were runes, obviously demonic, though not in a language James recognized.

He touched the glass. When his finger made contact, though, there was a sudden flash, like an unexpected leaping ember from a fire. He sucked in his breath.

"Belial," he said, and everyone seemed to jump. He was conscious of Cordelia looking at him with wide eyes, darker than the mirror's glass. He forced himself not to stare at her. "I—cannot tell you what the mirror does; I've no idea. But I would swear on my life that Belial gave it to Tatiana. I can feel his touch on it."

"It looks just like the *pithos*," Lucie observed. "Belial's stele-thingy that he used to steal runes from his victims' bodies. Maybe Belial gave Tatiana a whole vanity set?"

"Try touching it yourself, Luce," Anna suggested, and after a moment, Lucie reached out her hand and skated it across the mirror's surface.

This time, there was a flicker from within the mirror, like a dancing flame. It was faint, but it continued to glow as long as Lucie was touching it.

She drew her hand back, biting her lip. "Indeed," she said, her voice subdued. "It has Belial's aura."

"I doubt it was just a gift," said Cordelia. "I don't think Belial would have given it to Tatiana unless it had some darker purpose."

"More than just looking up chimneys," Ariadne agreed.

"We should bring the book and the mirror back to the Institute," Jesse said. "Have a closer look at both. And I'll start trying to decipher my mother's notes; they are written in a sort of code, but not a complicated one."

James nodded. "And I agree about returning to the Institute. It's warded, for one thing, and I would also rather we not remain at Chiswick after dark, all things considered. Who knows what else might be roaming the grounds?"

16
Chimes at Midnight

We have heard the chimes at midnight, Master Shallow.
—Shakespeare, *Henry IV, Part 2*

Cordelia had been nervous about approaching the Hell Ruelle, given what had happened at the cabaret in Paris, but the doorman (a squat, broad-shouldered fellow with a square jaw and lidless toad's eyes) gave her only a cursory glance before allowing her in. It seemed she was a known visitor, a fact that Cordelia was not sure whether she should be pleased about. She hadn't visited the Ruelle *that* many times, she thought, but it appeared she'd left an impression.

This was the first time she'd ever come to the Downworlder salon alone. She had not told anyone what she was planning. She felt a little guilty about it—Anna had been so kind to her, and Alastair had spent all day with Christopher and Thomas in the Institute library, searching out ways to help her. When she had returned to the Institute from Chiswick House with the others, they had found the boys waiting for them in the chapel. Apparently Christopher had only just returned from Limehouse, where he had purchased an amulet from Hypatia Vex's magic shop.

"It seems there are loads of these," he'd said, passing it over to her. It was silver, round like a coin, with a pin on the back that allowed it to be worn as a brooch. "Protective amulets against Lilith specifically. Even mundanes used to wear them, and Shadowhunters did before the protection rituals were invented. It has the names of the three angels who oppose Lilith etched on it, the ones who blessed James's gun. Sanvi, Sansanvi, Semangelaf." He traced the Hebrew letters with his fingers before handing the amulet to Cordelia. "It won't make you not a paladin anymore, but it may discourage Lilith from approaching you."

That night, after dinner, she'd pinned it to the sleeve of her dark blue dress before clambering out her window—with a silent apology to Alastair, but there was no point telling him where she was going; he would only worry—and hurrying to hail a hansom cab on the street.

She had been too worried about Matthew to sleep. Anna's words kept echoing in her head: *He needs help now. The sort I am afraid I cannot give him, because he will refuse it.* Did Anna know about Matthew's drinking? And regardless of whether she did or not, Cordelia *did* know—and had not spoken to him about it since they'd returned to London. She'd been too angry, too caught up in protecting herself against the kind of pain her father had caused her.

But Matthew deserved—needed—friends. And instinct told her that if she were to find him, it would be here.

The place was bustling, as usual. Tonight the main salon was done in a kind of deep winter theme, with walls of deep blue, and papier-mâché sculptures of snow-burdened trees dangling in midair. The floor was covered with a sort of brilliant false snow, made of what looked like tiny pearls. The tips of Cordelia's black velvet boots scattered them as she walked; they turned colors as they rose into the air, reflecting miniature rainbows. Everywhere were stamped images of the moon, in various phases—full, half, crescent—in gold paint.

Cordelia was surprised; it did not seem long since she had last been here, and the theme had been a celebration of Lilith, which she had braced herself to endure. She was relieved to see the change and tried to look about unobtrusively, seeking a glimpse of a familiar head of blond curls.

As always, there were sofas and low divans scattered around the salon, and Downworlders crowded onto them, most deep in conversation. There were vampires with powder-white faces, and werewolves in sack suits; faeries dressed as parlormaids, with seaweed curls peeking out from under their mobcaps, moved among the guests, carrying trays of drinks. An unfamiliar warlock with cat's ears sat across from a round gnome in a pin-striped suit, arguing about the Boer Wars.

But she did not see Matthew. Cordelia blew out a frustrated breath, just as Hypatia Vex herself glided up to her. She wore a silver gown that spread in a pool around her feet, but somehow did not catch on things as she walked—magic, surely—and, atop her head, a massive midnight-blue headdress into the center of which was set a white pearl, the size of a dinner plate and etched to resemble the moon.

"Shadowhunter," Hypatia said pleasantly, "if you must insist on attending my salon, I'd thank you to take a seat. I cannot tell you how much having Nephilim hovering about unnerves my guests."

The first time Cordelia had met Hypatia, she had found her terrifying. Now she just smiled politely. "Good evening, Hypatia. Your hat matches your eyes."

Hypatia's eyes, whose pupils were the shape of stars, sparkled a bit. Cordelia had known Hypatia long enough to recognize that a bit of flattery was helpful when speaking with her. "Thank you. It was a gift from a sultan. I don't recall which one."

"I haven't any intention of staying and disturbing your guests," Cordelia said. "I only came to see if Matthew Fairchild was here."

Hypatia's perfectly plucked brows rose. "It distresses me that Shadowhunters have decided the place they are most likely to find wayward members of the Enclave is in my salon."

"He's not some wayward member of the Enclave," Cordelia said. "He's *Matthew*."

"Humph," said Hypatia, but Cordelia thought she saw a flicker of sympathy in Hypatia's spangled eyes. "Well, it's likely a good thing you came, regardless. I'd been hoping to speak to you."

"To me?" Cordelia was astonished. "What about?"

"A private matter. Come with me," Hypatia said, in a tone that brooked no argument. "Round Tom can look after the salon while we're gone."

With no idea who Round Tom might be, Cordelia followed Hypatia from the room, trying not to trip on her silver train as it slipped and slid over the false snow.

Hypatia led Cordelia through an arched door and into a small, circular room, in which two plush chairs faced each other across a table inlaid with a chessboard. A rosewood box for the chess pieces had been set to the side, and a tall bookshelf, which oddly held no books, rested against the far wall.

Hypatia sat down and motioned for Cordelia to be seated across the table. Cordelia hoped very much that Hypatia did not want to play a game of chess. Chess was something Cordelia associated with James: with cozy domestic evenings at Curzon Street, where they sat together on the sofa in the light of the fire . . .

"Stop daydreaming, girl," said Hypatia. "Good gracious, you'd think you'd have heard me. I said, 'So, you've become a paladin?'"

Cordelia sat down hard enough to jounce her spine. Oh, Raziel. She'd been a fool, hadn't she? "The Cabaret de l'Enfer," she said. "They told you, didn't they?"

Hypatia nodded, the pearl in her headdress gleaming. "Indeed. There is quite a gossip network among Downworlders, as you should well know." She gave Cordelia an appraising look. "Does Magnus know of this paladin business?"

"He does not. And I would ask you not to tell him, but I know you may, regardless. Still. I am asking."

Hypatia did not respond to Cordelia's request. Instead, she said: "There have been Shadowhunter paladins before, of course, but—"

Cordelia raised her chin. Might as well make Hypatia say it. "But I'm different?"

"There is no holy light about you," said Hypatia. She gazed at Cordelia, her starry eyes fathomless. "I have seen the voids between the worlds, and what walks there," she said. "I have known the fallen angels of the heavenly war, and admired them for their steely pride. I am not one to turn away from shadows. One finds beauty in the darkest of places, and Lucifer was the most beautiful of all Heaven's angels, once." She leaned forward. "I understand the urge to reach for such dark beauty, and such power. I have not brought you here to sit in judgment upon you."

Cordelia said nothing. Far away, she could hear faint laughter from the salon, but she felt as if it were happening on another planet. This *was* a sort of chess, she realized—a chess game without pieces, played with words and insinuation. Hypatia had not mentioned Lilith by name, yet Cordelia knew Hypatia to be very interested in Lilith indeed.

"You are correct. I am not sworn to an angel," Cordelia said. "But you do not know who it is I *am* sworn to, and I am not inclined to say."

Hypatia shrugged, though Cordelia suspected she was, at the least, disappointed. "So you do not wish to name names. I will find out eventually, I suspect. For when the Shadowhunters discover what you have done, it will be a scandal that rocks the foundations of their world." She smiled. "But I imagine you know that, and do not care. As a paladin, you are more powerful than any of them now."

"It was not a power I wanted," said Cordelia. "I was tricked into taking the oath. Deceived."

"An *unwilling* paladin?" Hypatia said. "That's rather unique."

"You don't believe me," Cordelia said. "Yet I am desperate to sever this bond. There is much I would do for anyone who could tell me how to cease being a paladin."

Hypatia sat back in her chair, her gaze thoughtful. "Well," she said. "Ceasing to be a paladin is easy enough. The trick is to do so and survive. A paladin can be rejected by the one she serves, of course. But whether that rejection would leave you alive afterward . . . well, I would not bet money on it."

Cordelia let out a long breath. "I do not think the one to whom I am bound would reject me," she said. "My master knows I did not seek this out. That I serve unwillingly. That I go unarmed, that I might not even in error lift a weapon in the service of the demon who tricked me."

"*My*," said Hypatia. She seemed, somewhat despite herself, interested in the drama of the situation. "That *is* commitment. A Shadowhunter who will not fight." She shook her head. "Most paladins of demons have served enthusiastically. And the ones who refused to serve were torn apart by their masters, as a warning. You have been lucky, so far."

Cordelia shuddered. "So, what you're saying is that it can't be done?"

"I am saying it is a waste of time to pursue it. Pursue instead the idea of turning your power toward something good."

"No good can come from an evil power."

"I disagree," said Hypatia. "You took on, what, a dozen Naga demons in Paris? And more demons here in London. You truly could become the greatest, most effective Shadowhunter that has ever been known."

"Even if I were willing to lift my sword in a demon's name," Cordelia said, "other demons recognize me as a paladin. They flee from me. It happened just today."

"So summon them. Then they can't flee." Hypatia sounded bored. "You are a paladin. Simply find a place—it's best if it has a dark history, a place of death or horror, scarred by tragedy—and say the words *cacodaemon invocat*, and—"

"Stop!" Cordelia held up her hands. "I'm not going to do it. I'm not going to do anything that will summon up *demons*—"

"Well, all right," said Hypatia, clearly affronted. "It was just an *idea*." She looked at Cordelia narrowly, but before she could say anything, the bookcase slid aside like a pocket door, and Magnus emerged, looking elegant in royal blue.

"Hypatia, my sweet," he said. "It's time for us to leave, if we wish to arrive in Paris in time for the evening performance." He winked at Cordelia. "Always a pleasure to see you, my dear."

"Paris?" Cordelia echoed. "I didn't realize you were going—I mean, I'm sure you'll have a lovely time."

"I thought I'd have a word with Madam Dorothea at the Cabaret de l'Enfer," he said. "A warlock who claims they can communicate with the dead . . . well. So many of them are charlatans or fakes."

"You will never find me near such a grubby place," Hypatia said, and stood up from her chair. "But there are many other things in the City of Lights to tempt me." She inclined her head in Cordelia's direction. "Take care, little warrior." She gestured toward the main room of the salon. "Your boy is here. He arrived some moments ago, but I was enjoying our discussion too much to mention it. My apologies."

With that, Hypatia turned and followed Magnus back through the gap of the bookshelf, which slid closed behind them. Cordelia hurried into the main room, where she spotted Matthew at a table by himself, wearing dark green velvet and drinking something fizzy from a tall glass.

He was staring down at his drink, turning the glass around and around, as if it were a scrying bowl and he could see the future in it. Only when Cordelia approached him did he raise his head.

She could see immediately why Anna was worried. There were dark yellow-green circles under his eyes, and bruises at the corners of his mouth. His hands shook as he reached for his glass; his nails were bitten, which she had never seen before—Matthew usually kept his hands immaculate.

"Cordelia?" he said wonderingly. "What are you doing here, in the Ruelle?"

She took the seat across from him. Somehow he had gotten gold paint on his hands, from the glass he was holding, and a little had smeared on his cheekbone as well. It seemed strangely festive, at odds with how unwell he looked. "I came because I thought you would be here."

"I thought you didn't want to see me."

He was right, of course. She *had* said that, because it was the sensible thing, because not seeing him or James was the sensible path. But nothing in her life was sensible right now. "I was worried about you," she admitted. "When you didn't come to Chiswick today. Ariadne said you were doing her a favor, but I wondered . . ."

"I *was* doing her a favor," said Matthew. "A bit of investigative work. I am not entirely useless, you know."

"I suppose I was worried—not just about you, but that you didn't want to see me. That that's why you didn't come."

"Surely," he said, "we are not going to have an argument about which of us doesn't want to see the other one. It does not seem productive."

"I don't want to have an argument at all," said Cordelia. "I want—" She sighed. "I want you to stop drinking," she said. "I want you to tell your family the truth about what happened two years ago. I want you to reconcile with your parents, and with James. I want you to be brilliant and wonderful, which you are, and *happy*, which you are not."

"Just another way that I've failed you," he said quietly.

"You must stop thinking about it that way," Cordelia said. "You're not failing me, you're not failing your family. You're failing yourself."

Impetuously, she held out her hand. He took it, closing his eyes as he threaded their fingers together. He was biting his lower lip, and Cordelia remembered in that moment what it was like to kiss him, the taste of cherries and the softness of his mouth. How it had made her forget everything else; how she had felt like the beautiful Cordelia, a princess in a story.

He pressed his thumb into the center of her palm. Circled it there, the pad of his fingertip against the sensitive skin sending a jolt up her arm. Cordelia shivered. "Matthew . . ."

He opened his eyes. The velvet jacket turned them to a very dark green, the color of fern leaves or forest moss. *My beautiful Matthew*, she thought, all the more beautiful for being so broken. "Raziel," he said, his voice ragged. "This is torture."

"Then we should stop," Cordelia said in a low voice, but she did not draw back her hand.

"It is a torture I like," he said. "The best kind of pain. I felt nothing for so long, held every experience and every passion at arm's length. And then you—"

"Don't," Cordelia said softly.

But he went on, looking not at her but inward, as if at an imagined scene. "They used to make a sort of flat dagger, you know, a narrow thing that could slide through the gaps in armor."

"A *misericorde*," said Cordelia. "Meant to deliver the death stroke to a wounded knight." She looked at him in some alarm. "Are you saying . . . ?"

Matthew laughed a little breathlessly. "I am saying that with you, I have no armor. I feel everything. For better or worse."

"We should not be talking like this," Cordelia said. She squeezed his hand, hard, then drew hers back, clasping her own hands together to prevent herself from reaching out to him again. "Matthew, you must tell James—"

"Tell him what?" said Matthew. He was pale, a sheen of sweat across his forehead and cheekbones. "That I love you? He knows that. I've told him. There's nothing to be gained there."

"I meant, tell him about what happened," said Cordelia. "At the Shadow Market. The faerie, the potion—it will be easier to tell him than your parents, and then he can help you tell *them*. Matthew, this secret is like poison in your blood. You have to draw it off. You told me; you must be able to—"

"I told you because you were a stranger to the situation," Matthew said. "James has known my mother all his life. She is his godmother." His voice was flat. "I honestly don't know whether he could truly forgive me for hurting her."

"I think he would forgive you for anything."

Matthew rose to his feet, nearly knocking over his glass. He stood for a moment, holding on to the back of his chair; his hair was stuck to his forehead with sweat, and his eyes looked glazed.

"Matthew," Cordelia said in alarm. "Matthew, what—"

He bolted from the room. Gathering up her wool skirts, Cordelia raced after him, not bothering to retrieve her coat.

She found Matthew outside the Ruelle, on Berwick Street. Bright light from naphtha torches stabbed at her eyes, throwing him into sharp relief against the snow-frosted carriages rattling by. He was on his knees, being sick in the gutter, his shoulders shaking.

"*Matthew!*" Cordelia started forward in horror, but he waved her back.

"Stay away," he said hoarsely. He was shivering, his arms wrapped around himself as his body spasmed. "Please—"

Cordelia hung back as passersby swirling around her, none of them giving Matthew a second look. He wasn't glamoured, but a gentleman being sick in the gutters of Soho was hardly a rare sight.

At last he clambered to his feet and went over to a lamppost; he leaned his back against it, and with shaking hands, he slipped a flask from inside his jacket.

"Don't—" Cordelia started toward him.

"It's water," he said hoarsely. He drew a linen handkerchief from his breast pocket and cleaned his hands and face. His sweat-damp hair hung into his eyes. There was something intensely painful about watching him, Cordelia thought. About the contrast between his expensive clothes and monogrammed handkerchief and his bruised eyes and trembling hands.

He put the flask away, balled up the handkerchief, and hurled it into the gutter. He raised his bloodshot green eyes to hers. "I know what you said inside. That you wanted me to stop drinking. Well, I've been trying. I haven't had alcohol since—since yesterday."

"Oh, Matthew," Cordelia said, wanting to go to him, to put her hand on his arm. But something about his posture—spiky, defensive—held her back. "I don't think it's quite that simple. One cannot just *stop*."

"I always thought I could," he said emptily. "I thought I could stop anytime I liked. Then I tried, in Paris, our first day. And I was vilely sick."

"You hid it well," she said.

"I could barely manage twelve hours," he said. "I knew—in that state—I could be of no use to you. It's not an excuse, but it is why I lied about stopping. I had not brought you to Paris so you could spend time watching me convulse and clutch the floor."

Cordelia knew she could tell him how foolish that had been, how she would have preferred to hold his hand as he screamed out for brandy than to be lied to. But now did not seem the time; it would be like kicking Oscar.

"Let us get you back to your flat," Cordelia said. "I know things that can help—I remember, the times my father tried to stop—"

"But he never did succeed, did he?" Matthew said bitterly. The cold air ruffled his hair as he let his head fall back against the lamppost. "I'll go home," he said wearily. "But—alone."

"Matthew—"

"I don't want you to see me like this," he said. "I never did." He shook his head, his eyes closed. "I can't bear it. Cordelia. Please."

In the end, all he would allow her to do was flag down a hansom cab and watch while he climbed inside. As it drove off, she saw, illuminated by gaslight, that he was hunched over, his face in his hands.

Cordelia turned back toward the Hell Ruelle. She needed to find a runner who could deliver a message—several messages—as quickly as she could.

Jesse was not at dinner that night. Which, Will and Tessa said, was entirely to be expected: he'd had his protection ceremony done that day, in the Silent City, and though Jem had said everything had gone well, it was natural for him to be tired.

But Lucie still looked worried, though she tried to hide it, and James was even more sure that Jesse's mood had something to do with Grace. He picked listlessly at his food as his family's voices rose and fell around him: the Christmas tree had been misplaced by Bridget and she and Tessa were checking every closet in the Institute one by one; also, Tessa and Will agreed that Alastair Carstairs was a very well-mannered young man; also, remember when he and James had to deal with the unpleasantness at James and Cordelia's wedding, hurrying a drunk Elias away from the reception party before he made a scene. Which only reminded James of Cordelia, as everything did these days.

When dinner had ended, James retreated to his room. He shucked off his dinner jacket and was in the process of unlacing his boots when he saw a piece of paper stuck into the corner of his mirror.

He plucked it up, frowning. Someone had scrawled the word *ROOF* on it in capital letters, and he had a fairly good idea who. James caught up a wool coat and headed for the stairs.

To reach the roof of the Institute required climbing up through the attic and unlatching a trapdoor. The roof was steeply slanted in most places; only here, at the top of the stairs, was there a flat, rectangular space surrounded by an iron fence, whose finials ended in pointed fleur-de-lis. Leaning against the dark fence was Jesse.

It was a clear night, the stars glittering like diamonds made of frost. London lay spread out under a silvery moon, the smoke from chimneys rising in black columns to stain the sky. Rooflines were crusted in sugary white.

Jesse wore only his dinner jacket—an old one of James's, it was much too short on him, the sleeves coming only halfway down his forearms—and no coat or scarf. Here, the wind blew off the Thames, bringing with it an icy chill, but if Jesse noticed, he gave no sign.

"You must be freezing," James said. "Do you want my coat?"

Jesse shook his head. "I am freezing, I think. It is still hard for me to tell, sometimes, exactly what my body is feeling."

"How did you know about the roof?" James asked, coming to stand beside Jesse, next to the fence.

"Lucie showed me," Jesse said. "I like to come up here. It makes me feel as if I'm as I once was—traveling freely through the air above

London." He cast a glance at James. "Don't misunderstand me. I don't wish I were a ghost again. It's the loneliest thing you can imagine. The whole city beneath your feet, swirling around you, yet you cannot touch it, affect it. You cannot speak to the people you pass. Only the dead answer and those few, like your sister, who can see the dead. But most are not like Lucie. Most fear and shun us. The sight of us is, to them, a curse."

"And yet you miss this one bit of it," James said. "That's understandable. It used to be that when I slept, I would sense Belial. See the shadowy realms he inhabits. Now, when I sleep, I see nothing. And it frightens me, that nothing. One should dream."

Jesse looked off toward the river. There was something contained about him, James thought, as if he had been through so much that it would take a great deal to shock or upset him now. "I saw Grace this morning," Jesse said. "She told me everything."

James felt his hands grip the railing hard. He had guessed, and yet . . . "Everything?" he said quietly.

"About the bracelet," Jesse said. "Her power. About what she did to you."

The metal of the fence was icy, but James found he could not let go of it. He had worked so hard to control who knew what had happened to him. He knew it would happen someday—knew any relationship he could have with Cordelia depended on her knowing—and yet when he thought of saying the words *Grace controlled me, made me feel things, do things*, he wanted to retch. How pitiable Jesse must think he was—how weak.

He heard his own voice as if from a distance. "Have you told anyone?"

"Of course not," Jesse said. "It's your secret, to share as you wish." He looked back out at the city. "I considered not telling you," he said. "That Grace confessed to me. But that seemed like another betrayal, even of a small kind, and you deserve the truth. You must decide how to tell your friends, your family, in your own time."

With a great effort, James unclenched his fists from around the iron railing. He shook them, trying to restore feeling to his fingertips. "I have told no one," he said. "I suppose Grace told you that the Silent

Brothers wish to keep this fact a secret—"

Jesse nodded.

"—but that will only be a temporary reprieve for me."

"A reprieve?" Jesse looked surprised. "You don't wish to tell your friends, your family?"

"No," James said quietly. "It feels to me as if telling them would be like reliving every moment of what happened. They would have questions, and pity, and I could bear neither."

There was a long silence. Jesse looked at the face of the moon, visible through a break in the clouds. "Belial used my hands to kill people. To kill Shadowhunters. I tell myself over and over there was nothing I could have done, but I still believe somehow, in my heart, I could have stopped it."

"Of course you couldn't," said James. "You were being controlled."

"Yes," Jesse said, and James heard his own words again, echoed back to him. *You were being controlled.* "Do you pity me?"

"No," James said. "At least—it isn't pity. I feel anger that you were wronged. Sorry for the hurt caused to you. Admiration for the way in which you have faced it."

"Do not think so little of your friends," said Jesse, "and of Cordelia, as to imagine they will feel differently than that." He looked down at his hands. "I know they will be angry," he said. "With Grace. I am furious at her. Sickened by what she did. And still . . ."

"Still she is your sister. No one would blame you if . . . you forgave her."

"I don't know," Jesse said. "For so many years, she was the only person in my life who loved me. She was my little sister. I felt as if I had been born to protect her." He gave the faintest of smiles. "You must know what I mean."

James thought of all the scrapes Lucie had gotten into over the years, the many times he'd had to rescue her from tree-climbing adventures gone too far, overturned rowboats, and warlike ducks, and nodded.

"But how can I forgive Grace for doing to you what Belial did to me?" Jesse said wretchedly. "And when Lucie finds out—she adores you, you know. She has always said she could not have asked for a better brother. She will want to kill Grace, and will not thank me for standing in her way."

"The Clave's laws against murder will stand in her way," said James, finding that despite everything, he could smile. "Lucie is tempestuous, but she has sense. She will know that you would never have approved of what Grace did."

Jesse looked out toward the silver ribbon of the Thames. "I had hoped we would be friends, you and I," he said. "I had imagined us training together, perhaps. I had not imagined this. And yet . . ."

James knew what he meant. It was something of a bond, this peculiar connection: both of them had had their lives warped and twisted by Belial and Tatiana. Both bore the scars. He almost felt as if he should shake Jesse's hand; it seemed the manly sort of thing to do, to seal the agreement that they were to be friends from this moment on. Of course, if it had been Matthew, he would not have cared at all about manly agreements—Matthew would simply have hugged James or wrestled him to the ground or tickled him until he was breathless.

But Jesse was not Matthew. No one was. Matthew had brought anarchic joy into James's life, like light into a dark place. With Matthew, James felt the unspeakable happiness that came from being with one's *parabatai*, a happiness that transcended all other things. Without Matthew . . . the image of Chiswick House came unbidden into his mind, with its smashed mirrors and stopped clocks. The symbol of sadness frozen in time, never-ending.

Stop, James told himself. *Focus on the present. On what you can do for Jesse.*

"Come with me, tomorrow," he said, rather suddenly, and saw Jesse raise an eyebrow. "I won't tell you where—you'll have to trust me—but I think you will find it rewarding."

Jesse laughed. "All right," he said. "I trust you, then." He frowned down at his own hands. "And I believe you were right. I *am* freezing. My fingers are turning quite blue."

They scrambled back through the trapdoor and made their way through the attic, which James suspected had not changed much since his parents had been young. Jesse returned to his room, and James to his, only to discover that Bridget had slid a slightly crumpled envelope halfway under his door. It seemed that while he had been on the roof, Neddy had come to the Institute with a message for him.

A message from Cordelia.

It turned out that Anna's plan, which Ariadne had assumed involved a complex series of maneuvers that would somehow produce Winston the parrot, consisted of them using an Open rune to get into the Bridgestocks' house through a back entrance and commencing a lightning raid on the home Ariadne had lived in since she'd moved to London.

She found she rather enjoyed it. She led Anna immediately to the conservatory, where Winston's gold cage usually held pride of place. Her stomach swooped when she saw that it was not there. What if her parents, in their anger at her, had sold Winston or given him away?

"He's likely just in another room," Anna whispered. They had both been whispering since they entered the house, though Ariadne knew it was empty and the servants, in their quarters downstairs, would be unlikely to hear anything. *And* they were both wearing Soundless runes. Still, there was something about the dark house that invited whispering.

They searched through the ground floor, Anna shining her witchlight rune-stone into every corner. Having found nothing, they moved upstairs, creeping along the carpeted floors to Ariadne's bedroom.

Ariadne noticed several things the moment she stepped into her former room. First was Winston, perched in his cage, which had been placed on her desk. A small dish of nuts and seeds sat beside it. Winston flapped his wings happily at the sight of her.

"*There* you are," Anna said, glancing over at Ariadne, who *was* relieved, but . . . The second thing she'd noticed was the state of her bedroom. She had expected it to be stripped down, removed of everything that might remind her parents of her. Instead everything was in its place, pin straight. The jewelry she had not taken with her was in an open velvet box on the dresser, along with her cosmetics and comb. The remainder of her clothes hung pressed in the wardrobe. Her bed was neatly made.

They are keeping up appearances, she realized. *For themselves, not for anyone else. They are keeping up the fiction that I might return at any moment*. She could imagine the scenario they envisioned—Ariadne fleeing back to Cavendish Square, the tears of regret on her cheeks, her mother fussing over her as she told them of the wide world and its cruelties, of the beliefs she'd entertained that she knew now were wrong. Why, she couldn't *imagine* how she'd *ever* come to think that she loved—

"Pretty bird," called Winston hopefully.

"Oh, Winston," Ariadne murmured, and passed a shelled peanut through the bars of his cage. "Never fear, I hadn't forgotten you. You're coming with us." She looked around; ah, here was her purple afghan, folded at the foot of the bed. She picked it up to unfold it.

Winston glanced over at Anna, who had flung herself on Ariadne's bed and was watching their reunion with amusement. "Anna," he said.

"That's right," Ariadne said, pleased. Usually when Winston looked at people he said, "Brazil nut?"

"Trouble," said Winston, now gazing askance at Anna. "Anna. Trouble."

"Winston," Ariadne said, and now she could see that Anna was trying hard not to laugh, "that is a very rude thing to say. She is helping me rescue you so we can be together again. It's her flat we're taking you to, so you had best behave yourself."

"Ariaaaadne," Winston said in an almost frighteningly perfect imitation of her mother calling for her. "Pretty bird? Brazil nut?"

Ariadne rolled her eyes and tossed the afghan over his cage. "Bird," Winston said thoughtfully from beneath it, and then fell silent.

She shook her head ruefully as she turned back to Anna, and then stopped as she realized that Anna's expression had lost its mischief. She seemed quietly serious now, as if lost in thought.

"What is it?" Ariadne said.

Anna was quiet a moment, and then said, "I was only wondering—do you still want to be called Ariadne? It's the name that your . . . well, you know, Maurice and Flora gave you. And you were also Kamala. Which is quite a lovely name. Not that Ariadne is not also a lovely name." Her mouth quirked again. "It ought to be your choice, I think. What you wish to be called."

Ariadne was touched, and a little startled. It was something she herself had been considering, but she would not have expected Anna to have thought of it. "It is a good question," she said, leaning against the dresser. "Both names were given to me. As names are, of course; they represent a sort of gift, but also, I think, a set of expectations. My first family thought I would be one sort of girl, but I am not that girl. My second also had expectations of who I would be, and I am not that girl either. Yet those names are still a part of who I am. I think I would like to be named something new, that binds the two together. I thought," she said shyly, "Arati. It was my first grandmother's name. She always said it referred to divine fire, or to praising the Angel with a lamp in hand. It makes me think of being a light in darkness. And that is something I would like to be. I would ask to be called Ari," she added, "for that honors the name I have had for the past twelve years."

"Ari," Anna said. She was leaning back on her hands, looking up at Ariadne, her blue eyes very intent. Her collar was loose, her dark curls just touching the back of her neck. The line of her body was graceful, her back slightly arched, the curves of her small, high breasts just visible beneath her shirt. "Well. That name should not be hard to remember, given that I've been calling you by it for quite some time. *Ari*," she said again, and the sound was different than it had been before—a caress.

A future seemed to open before Ari in that moment. A more honest future, one in which she was who she wished to be. Right now she knew she was crossing a sort of bridge, from her old life to the new one, and Anna was in that in-between place with her. A place of transformation, where there was no commitment, no vows or promises, only an understanding that everything was changing.

She sank down on the bed beside Anna, who turned to her, a question in her eyes. Ari reached out and stroked her hand along the curve of Anna's cheekbone. She had always loved the contrasts of Anna's face: her sharp, angular bones, her lush red mouth.

The blue of Anna's eyes darkened as Ari traced the line of her jaw, then her throat, coming to rest on the top button of her shirt. Ari leaned forward and kissed Anna's neck—kissed her fluttering pulse point, daringly licked the hollow at the base of her throat. She thought Anna tasted of tea, dark and bittersweet.

Anna caught at Ari's waist, her hips, pulled her closer. Said, her breath uneven, "Ari, should we—?"

"It need not mean anything," Ari whispered. "It need only be because we want to. Nothing more."

Anna seemed almost to flinch—and then her hands buried themselves in Ari's hair, her mouth finding Ari's, nipping at her lower lip, their tongues curling together. Ari had always let Anna take the lead before, but now they sank onto the bed together, Ari undoing Anna's shirt, her hands smoothing across soft, pale skin, the rise and fall of slim curves, Anna gasping into her mouth.

Anna's arms rose to twine about her, and everything else—Ari's parents, her future in the Enclave, her imaginary flat—was forgotten in the tide of fire that swept across her skin as she luxuriated in the touch and feel of Anna, of Anna's clever hands, of the pleasure given and received between them, as strong and shining and delicate as flame.

17

Lamp of Night

Deep in her eyes the lamp of night
Burns with a secret flame,
Where shadows pass that have no sight,
And ghosts that have no name.
—James Elroy Flecker,
"Destroyer of Ships, Men, Cities"

Outside the Whitby Mansions, that big pink wedding cake of a building which housed Matthew's flat, James looked up at its turrets and curlicues and felt a stabbing reminder of the last time he had been here. He had come racing in, sure Cordelia was here, only to be told by the lobby porter that Matthew and Cordelia had already left for the train station. To go to Paris.

And his whole world had broken apart, shattering like his cursed bracelet. Though it had not broken into two neat halves—rather a sort of pile of ragged bits, which he had been trying to put back together ever since.

This time the porter barely took any notice of him, only waved a hand when James announced he was here to see Mr. Fairchild. James took the lift up and, on a hunch, tried the doorknob before even bothering to knock. It was open, and he went inside.

To his surprise, the first thing he saw was Thomas, kneeling in front of the fireplace. The fire was burning high and the flat was hotter than was comfortable, but Thomas only set another log on the fire and shrugged at James.

In front of the fireplace had been laid a pile of thick eiderdowns. Curled on the blankets was Matthew, in an untucked shirt and trousers, his feet bare. His eyes were closed. James felt a pain at his heart—Matthew looked so young. His chin was on his fist, his long eyelashes feathering down against his cheeks. He seemed asleep.

"Cordelia summoned you as well, I see," James said to Thomas in a low voice.

Thomas nodded. "All of us, I think. Your parents were willing to let you out of the house?"

"They understood it was important," James said absently. He went to sit down on the sofa. Matthew had begun shivering, burrowing down into the blanket as his body shook. "He can't be cold."

Thomas glanced at Matthew. "It's not the temperature. He's . . . not well. He won't eat—I tried to get some beef tea into him but it didn't stay down. He drank a bit of water, at least."

There was a scuffling noise, which James realized after a moment must be Oscar, shut into Matthew's bedroom. As if he knew James was looking in his direction, the dog whined sadly from behind the closed door. "Why is Oscar in there?" James demanded.

Thomas sighed and rubbed his hand across his forehead. "Matthew asked me to shut him in. I don't know why. Perhaps he's worried about Oscar making noise and bothering the other tenants."

James doubted Matthew was concerned about the other tenants, but he said nothing. Instead he got up, kicked off his shoes, and crawled onto the blanket with Matthew.

"Don't wake him up," Thomas warned, but James could see the thin crescent of green visible beneath Matthew's eyelids.

"I think he's awake," James said, knowing Matthew *was* awake, but wishing to let him keep pretending if he liked. "And I was thinking—sometimes an *iratze* can be good for a hangover. It might be worth trying here. Since I'm his *parabatai* . . ."

Matthew thrust his arm out from the blanket pile. His sleeves were already unbuttoned at the cuffs, and the loose material flapped dramatically around his wrist. "Have at it," he said. His voice was raspy, although considering how hot and dry it was in the flat, that wasn't surprising.

James nodded. Thomas poked at the fire, watching curiously as James drew Matthew's arm across his lap. He took his stele from his jacket, and carefully applied the healing rune to the blue-veined skin of Matthew's forearm.

When he was done, Matthew exhaled and flexed his fingers. "Does it help?" said James.

"My head pounds with slightly less intensity," Matthew said. He pushed himself up on his elbows. "Look—I didn't ask Cordelia to dispatch you here. I don't want to be a burden."

"You're not a burden," James said. "You can be an ass, but you're not a burden."

There was a scuffling sound at the doors. Christopher had arrived, carrying a black doctor's bag and wearing a determined expression. "Oh, good," he said without preamble. "You're all here."

"Well, where else would I be?" Matthew said. His fair hair was stuck to his forehead and cheeks with sweat. He stayed propped up on his elbows as Christopher came and knelt on the eiderdown near James. He set his black bag down and began rummaging through it.

"Why is the fire built up so high?" Christopher asked.

"I was cold," Matthew said. He looked on the verge of pushing his bottom lip out, like a defiant child.

Christopher straightened his crooked spectacles. "It is possible," he began, "that this is something the Silent Brothers could assist with—"

"No," Matthew said flatly.

"I'd drag him to the Silent City myself if I thought it would help," said James. "But they weren't able to do anything for Cordelia's father."

"I am not—" Matthew broke off, plucking at the eiderdown. James knew what he wanted to say: *I am not like Cordelia's father.* Perhaps it was for the best that he couldn't finish the sentence, though; perhaps he was beginning to understand that Elias Carstairs was not his present, but would be his future if things did not change.

"I am a scientist and not a physician," said Christopher. "But I have read about . . . dependence."

He glanced at Thomas, and James could not help but wonder

how much Thomas and Christopher had discussed this before, when Matthew and James were not with them. Whether they had thought James, too, needed protection from the truth. "One cannot simply stop drinking all at once. It's a noble endeavor, but it's dangerous," Christopher said. "Your body believes it needs alcohol to survive. That's why you feel so rotten. Hot and cold and sick."

Matthew bit his lip. The shadows under his eyes were bluish. "What can I do?"

"This is not just about discomfort or pain," Christopher said. "The alcohol has made itself necessary to you. Your body will fight for it, and perhaps kill you in the process. You will shake, be sick, your heart will beat too fast. You will be feverish, which is why you feel cold. You could have seizures—"

"Seizures?" echoed James, in alarm.

"Yes, and even heart failure, which is why he should not be alone." Christopher blinked owlishly. "I cannot emphasize enough, Matthew. You must stop trying to do this on your own. Let us help you."

In the flickering light of the fire, the hollows of Matthew's face looked cavernous. "I don't want that," he said. "I did this to myself alone. I ought to be able to undo it alone."

James rose to his feet. He wanted to scream, wanted to shake Matthew, shout at him that he wasn't just hurting himself, he was hurting all of them, that in risking himself he was risking James, too.

"I'm going to let Oscar out," he said.

"Don't," said Matthew, rubbing at his eyes. "He was whimpering. He doesn't understand what's wrong."

"He wants to help you," James said, heading to the bedroom door. The moment the door was open, Oscar shot across the room to Matthew; for a moment, James was worried he'd try to jump up and lick his owner's face, but he only lay down next to Matthew and panted quietly. "See?" James said. "He feels better already."

"He's going to take all the blankets," Matthew complained, but he reached out a free hand to scratch Oscar behind the ears.

"He loves you," James said, and Matthew looked up at him, his eyes very dark in the sallow pallor of his face. "Animals are innocent. To have their trust is an honor. He will be miserable unless you let him stay with you, help you. You are not saving him from a burden by keeping him away. Only breaking his heart."

Matthew looked at James for a long moment before turning to Christopher. "All right, Kit," he said in a subdued tone. "What do you need me to do?"

Kit rummaged in his bag. "When was the last time you had a drink, Matthew?"

"This morning," Matthew said. "Only some brandy."

"Where is your flask?"

"I've lost my silver one," Matthew said. "Might have left it in Paris. I've been keeping water in this."

From his pocket, he withdrew a simple tin flask with a cork stopper. He handed it to Christopher, who unscrewed the top, reached into his doctor's bag, and brought out a bottle. He began to pour the contents of the bottle into Matthew's flask, frowning as he did so, as if he were measuring amounts in his head.

"What *is* that?" Thomas asked, staring; the liquid was a pale tea color.

"Water and alcohol, mixed with sedative herbs. The sedatives will prevent seizures, most likely."

"Most likely?" Matthew muttered. "This is why no one likes scientists, Christopher. Too much accuracy, not enough optimism."

"Everyone likes scientists," said Christopher with supreme confidence, and handed the now-full tin flask to Matthew. "Drink."

Matthew rather gingerly took the flask from Christopher and brought it to his lips. He swallowed, coughed, and made a face. "Awful," he proclaimed. "Like a mixture of licorice and soap."

"That's good," Christopher said. "It's not supposed to be pleasant. Think of it as medicine."

"So how does this work?" said James. "Does he just drink this muck whenever he feels like it?"

"It's not muck, and no," Christopher said. He turned to Matthew. "I'll bring you a new flask every morning, with less in it each time. You'll drink a little in the morning and a little in the afternoon, and each day less, and eventually you will feel better and won't want the flask anymore."

"How long will this take?" Thomas said.

"About a fortnight."

"And that's it?" said Matthew. He already looked better, James thought. Some color had come back to his face, and his hands were steady when he set the flask aside. "It'll be over?"

There was a short silence. Christopher looked unsure; here, where the subject was no longer dosages and timing, he was on more unsteady ground. James could only think of Elias, and what Cordelia had said about him: the many times he'd tried to stop, the way he'd relapsed after months had gone by without a drink.

It was Thomas who broke the silence.

"Whatever in your mind made you drink in the first place," said Thomas. "That will still be there."

"So you're saying I will still *want* to drink," Matthew said slowly, "but I will not *need* to drink."

James reached out and ruffled Matthew's damp hair. "You should rest," he said.

Matthew leaned into James's touch. "I would. But I don't want all of you to leave. It's selfish, but—"

"I'll stay," said James.

"As will I," said Thomas.

Christopher closed his doctor's bag with a snap. "We'll all stay," he said.

Which was how they ended up sleeping curled on the eiderdown before the fire, like a litter of puppies. Matthew fell asleep almost immediately, and the others shortly after; James, back-to-back with Matthew, had not thought he would sleep, but the crackle of the logs in the fire and the soft breathing of the other Merry Thieves quieted him into an exhausted slumber. Only Oscar did not sleep: he padded a slight distance away and sat down, watching over them throughout the night.

Cordelia lay awake, tossing and turning on her bed. She missed Curzon Street; she missed her bed there, missed knowing James was only a room away. Here, she had Alastair and her mother, but it was not the same. Returning to Cornwall Gardens felt like trying to turn a key in a lock it no longer fit.

Over and over she heard Hypatia saying, *You truly could become the greatest, most effective Shadowhunter that has ever been known.* But at what a price! The price of embracing darkness, of accepting Lilith as her master. And had it not been a desire for greatness that had led her down this path? But then, how could it be wrong to want to be an excellent Shadowhunter? How could it be wrong to want to protect the world from Belial?

And not just the world, she knew. Lucie and James. They were targets; their vulnerability pierced her heart. Perhaps Lucie hated her now, and perhaps she had lost James, but everything inside her wanted to protect them.

She wondered what James had thought when he had gotten her message asking him to go to Matthew's. She hoped he had done it. He and Matthew needed each other desperately, however stubborn they both might be.

She flopped over, knocking her pillow to the floor. Her hair was tangled, her eyes aching with tiredness. Hypatia had told her to fight in Lilith's service. But that she would never do. Still—the memory of the Gamigin demon in Chiswick returned to her. She was sure that if she'd been able to question it longer, she would have learned more about Belial's plans.

She sat up, staring sightlessly into the dark. Surely *questioning* a demon didn't require lifting a weapon. And as long as she was Lilith's paladin, she could take advantage of the demons' fear of her. It would be a way to wrest something good out of her horrible binding to Lilith. A way to help Lucie, James, and the others.

Simply find a place of death or horror, scarred by tragedy, Hypatia had said. And Cordelia knew just the location.

Thomas was woken at dawn, by Oscar.

The other boys were still asleep, sprawled in a pile on the rug before the now-cold fireplace. Fingers of dawn light crept through the windowpanes, illuminating the curve of James's shoulder, the glint off Christopher's glasses, and Matthew's bright hair.

Oscar was whimpering and fussing, darting between the door and Matthew, his nails clicking on the wood floor. Thomas bent over

Matthew; he was fast asleep but breathing regularly, his hand clamped over James's wrist. If he had not been so exhausted, he would certainly have been awakened by Oscar, which didn't seem ideal.

Leaving Matthew to rest, Thomas rose to his feet. He glared down at Oscar—who looked up at him with wide brown eyes—said, "Why me?" under his breath, and went to get his coat.

Oscar happily snapped to his leash, they headed downstairs, passing the empty porter's desk. Outside, Thomas gazed industriously into the distance while Oscar did what he needed to do under a plane tree.

Dawn was just beginning to illuminate the sky. It was a dusky-pink sort of dawn, with streaks of darker red cutting lengthwise through the lower clouds. Marylebone had not yet begun to awaken; there was not even the sound of a distant milk cart rattling along the streets to disturb the quiet.

In the reddish dawn, Whitby Mansions looked even pinker. Around its corner, Thomas noted, quite out of place, a dark shadow lurked.

"Alastair?" Thomas called, and the dark shadow started and turned toward him. Alastair was leaning against the building and appeared to have partially fallen asleep; he rubbed at his eyes, stared at Thomas and Oscar, and muttered something under his breath.

"Alastair." Thomas approached him, Oscar trotting happily at his side. "What on earth are you doing?"

"I don't think that dog likes me," Alastair said, eyeing Oscar suspiciously.

"That doesn't really answer the question, does it?"

Alastair sighed. He was wearing his dark blue paletot and a gray scarf. His thick black hair touched his collar, and his dark eyes were tired, the lids hanging heavy in a way that was almost seductive, though Thomas knew perfectly well it was only exhaustion. "All right," he said. "Cordelia told me what happened. And believe it or not, I was worried."

"About Matthew?" Oscar bounced at his owner's name. "I'm not sure I do believe you."

"Thomas," Alastair said, with exaggerated patience, "I have a great deal of experience with drunks. I know what it means when they stop drinking suddenly. How ill they get. My father nearly killed himself a few times."

"Oh," Thomas said. "Well, why didn't you ring the bell, then? Come up?"

"I arrived," Alastair said, "and realized my presence might not be entirely welcome. I had been rather impulsive." He looked surprised as Oscar sat on his feet. "Why is he doing that?"

"Because he *does* like you. He likes everybody. He's a dog. So you decided you didn't want to come in, and you'd just stand out here all night?"

"I thought I'd stand out here until one of you came out, and I'd ask how Matthew was. I could at least bring the information back to Cordelia. She's sick with worry." He patted Oscar's head tentatively. "I admit I hoped it would be you. There's something I've been meaning—needing—to tell you."

Thomas's heart gave a treacherous thump. He looked around, and then reminded himself they were both glamoured. No mundane could see them, and Shadowhunter patrols had ended with the sunrise. He moved a step closer to Alastair, and then another step, until he, Oscar, and Alastair were crowded together under the arch of a false doorway.

"All right," Thomas said. "What is it?"

Alastair looked at him, his eyes sleepy, sensual. His licked his lips, and Thomas thought of their kiss in the library, the delicious friction of their mouths sliding together, and Alastair said, "I'm leaving London soon. I'm moving to Tehran."

Thomas took a step back, accidentally putting a foot on Oscar's paw. Oscar yelped resentfully, and Thomas bent to lay a hand on the dog's head. It provided a blessed opportunity to hide his expression.

"My mother is going to move to Tehran with the baby," Alastair said, "and I cannot let her go alone. If I don't accompany her, Cordelia will volunteer, but Cordelia needs to stay here. She is the one with friends, a future *parabatai*, and a husband here. All I have is you."

Thomas straightened up. His heart felt as if it had frozen in his chest. "And I am not enough?"

"You can't be my only reason to stay," Alastair whispered. "I can't expect you to carry that weight. It isn't fair to you."

"I wish," Thomas said, surprised at the coldness in his own voice, "that you would stop telling me what the best thing for me is. You tell me over and over that there are all these reasons why you think my loving you would be bad for me."

Alastair's chest was rising and falling quickly. "I didn't say anything about love."

"Well, I *did*," Thomas said. "You came *here*; you even said it was because you hoped to talk to me. You're the one chasing me around, telling me to leave you alone."

"Don't you see? It's because I am a wretched, selfish person, Thomas. It's not good for you to see me, for us to meet, but I *want* to see you. I want to see you every damned moment of every day, and so I spent the night standing outside this ugly pink building in hopes of seeing you, and now that I have seen you, I am reminded of all the reasons this is a bad idea. Believe me," he said, with a bitter laugh, "if I were a better person, I would have just sent you a note."

"The only reason you've given me that this is a bad idea," said Thomas stubbornly, "is because you believe yourself to be a wretched and selfish person."

"Isn't that *enough?*" Alastair said, in an agonized voice. "You're the only person who thinks I'm not, and if we were in a relationship, I would disappoint you, and you would stop being the one person who thinks well of me."

"Don't go to Tehran," said Thomas. "I don't want you to go."

They stared at each other, and for a moment Thomas thought he saw something he knew to be an impossibility—the bright glint of tears in Alastair's eyes. *I cannot get through to him*, he thought miserably. *If only I had Matthew's charm, or James's gift with words, perhaps I could make him understand.*

"Alastair," he said softly, and then Oscar whimpered, moving restlessly beside Thomas's leg. A precursor, Thomas knew, to the retriever setting up a mournful howl.

"He's missing Matthew," Thomas said. "I'd better get him back. I'll tell Matthew you stopped by," he added, but Alastair, twisting the material of his scarf in one hand, only shook his head.

"Don't," he said, and after a moment, Thomas shrugged and headed back inside.

* * *

Cordelia had done enough planning; she was ready to act. Still, she had to wait for sunset. She knew she should be reading the books on paladins and bonding magic Christopher had given her, but she could not concentrate.

It was always like that when she'd come up with a plan; as the hour of action grew near, her thoughts went around in a whirl, stopping intermittently to concentrate on this or that aspect of her scheme. *First go here, then there; this is what I will tell Alastair; here is how I will return without being noticed.*

Enough. She visited with her mother, until Sona fell asleep; she bothered Risa in the kitchen while she was making *khoresh-e fesenjoon*, and she even went to see what Alastair was doing, which turned out to be reading in the armchair in his bedroom. He looked up when Cordelia came in. "Oh no," he said. "Please tell me you're not coming to demand I participate in some harebrained scheme your friends have come up with. *Kachalam kardan*." *They drive me crazy.*

"Not at all," Cordelia said, and thought she saw a flicker of disappointment on her brother's face. There was a time, not long ago, when Alastair would never have tolerated his sister invading his room, and she would never have thought to seek out his advice. They had both guarded their privacy so carefully; she was glad that some of that had fallen away. "I just wanted to see you."

Alastair closed his book, marking his place with a slim finger. "What is it, *moosh?*" Which meant *mouse*; it was something he hadn't called Cordelia since she was quite small. He looked tired; there were shadows under his eyes, and a slump to his shoulders that wounded Cordelia's heart. "If you're wondering about Matthew, all his friends *did* stop by his flat yesterday. In fact, they spent the night."

Cordelia exhaled a deep breath of relief. "Really? James, too? I'm so glad."

"Yes." He looked at her soberly. "Do you think Matthew will be angry at you? For telling them?"

"I don't know," Cordelia admitted. "But I would do the same again. He needed them. He wasn't willing to be desperate or sick in front of me. But in front of them, I think he knows it is not weakness, or shameful. I hope so."

"I hope so as well." Alastair looked over at the wall where his daggers were displayed; one was missing, which was odd. Alastair was particular about his things. "The disease he has, that our father had—it is a disease of shame, as well as of addiction and need. Shame poisons you. It makes you unable to accept help, for you do not believe that you deserve it."

"I think that is true about many things," Cordelia said softly. "Turning away love because one believes one does not deserve it, for instance."

Alastair looked at her beadily. "You are simply not going to stop bothering me about Thomas, are you?"

"I just don't understand it," Cordelia said. "Ariadne is living with Anna—surely it would not be the end of the world if you and Thomas were to love each other?"

"Ask *Mâmân*," said Alastair grimly.

Cordelia had to admit she'd no idea how her mother would react to finding out that Alastair's romantic love was for men.

"Our deepest illusions, and the most fragile, are the ones we hold on to about our friends and families. Thomas believes our families would be happy as long as we were happy; I look at the Bridgestocks and know that is not always the case. Thomas believes his friends would accept me with open arms; I believe they would sooner abandon *him*. And what a terrible situation that would be for him. I could not allow it."

"That," Cordelia said, "is beautifully noble. And also very stupid. And you are not the one who is going to *allow* Thomas to do anything; he has the feelings he has, and they are his business."

"Thomas could have anyone," said Alastair, with a righteously moping air. "He could choose better than me."

"I am not sure we choose who we love," said Cordelia, turning toward the door. "I rather think love is something like a book written just for us, a sort of holy text it is given to us to interpret." She paused in the doorway, looking back over her shoulder. "And you are refusing to read yours."

"Oh?" said Alastair. "What does *yours* say?" Cordelia glared at him, and he relented, waving a hand in apology. "Are you off somewhere, Layla?"

"Just to Curzon Street," Cordelia said. "Most of my clothes are still there—I need to fetch something I can wear to the Christmas party tomorrow."

"I can't believe they're still holding that," Alastair said, opening his book. "Just—be back before full dark, all right?"

Cordelia only nodded before slipping out the door. Of course she had no intention of returning before nightfall—her plan required her to be out after the sun set. But a nod wasn't precisely a lie, now, was it?

Letty Nance had been employed by the Cornwall Institute since she was twelve years old. The Sight ran in her family, which to her parents, who had both worked for the Cornwall Institute before her, had always been an honor. To Letty it seemed a cruel joke that the Lord had chosen to allow her to see that the world contained magic, but not to allow her to be part of it.

She had thought the Institute would be an exciting, wonderful kind of place to work. Unfortunately, it wasn't. Over the years she had come to understand that not all Nephilim were like the ancient Albert Pangborn, too cranky to be kind to the help, and too cheap to even keep the wards up around the Institute properly. Local piskies were always wandering onto the property, and about the only contact with real magic she had most weeks was chasing them out of the garden with a rake while they yelled filthy oaths at her.

Some excitement had come to her at last, though, with the events of two nights before. Pangborn often patrolled the area with a group of younger Shadowhunters—as far as Letty could tell, patrolling meant riding about on horses looking for Downworlders, seeing if they were up to no good, and returning to the Institute to drink when it turned out they weren't. Some of the Shadowhunters, like Emmett Kelynack and Luther Redbridge, weren't half bad-looking, but none of them would look at a mundane girl twice, not even one with the Sight.

But two nights ago they'd brought in the old woman. Or at least she seemed old to Letty—not as old as Pangborn; nobody, after all, was as old as Pangborn—but she was scrawny, her light brown hair streaked with gray, and her skin sickly pallid.

The odd thing was that the woman was a Shadowhunter. She had Marks on her, like the others did, black printings of angelic script. And yet they brought her right quick to the Sanctuary and locked her in.

The Sanctuary was a great big stony crypt of a place, where Downworlders came sometimes when they wanted to speak to Pangborn. It doubled, as well, as a makeshift prison. After the old woman was locked up, Pangborn took Letty aside, saying, "Check in on her twice a day, Ms. Nance, and make sure she's fed. Don't speak to her, even if she speaks to you. With any luck, she'll be gone out of here in a day or two."

Now that, Letty thought, was a bit exciting. A Nephilim who'd done something bad enough to get themselves tossed in prison, and she, Letty, had the keeping of them.

She'd tried to bring her supper in the Sanctuary, and breakfast the next day, but the woman remained insensible, sprawled on the bed and unresponsive to any of Letty's entreaties or even finger pokes. She had left the food on the table and then come and taken it away again hours later; the woman slept on. Letty hoped that this morning would be better—surely it was not good to sleep for a night and a day—and that the woman would wake and eat. She had to keep up her strength, considering her wounds.

Letty used the largest of the keys on the ring at her waist to open the Sanctuary. Inside the door, four steps led down to the stone floor, and as she descended she saw that the woman—Tatiana Blackthorn, that was her name—was awake, perched on the bed, her legs sprawled out in front of her in a most indecorous way. She was muttering to herself, in a voice too low for Letty to make out words. The supper from last night remained on the table, untouched.

"I've brought you some porridge, missus," Letty said, taking care to make her voice slow and clear. Tatiana's eyes followed her as she went over to the table. "Just simple porridge with some milk and a bit of sugar."

Letty almost jumped and spilled her tray when Tatiana spoke. Her voice was raspy, but clear enough. "I was . . . betrayed. Abandoned by my master."

Letty stared.

"He promised me everything." The rasp became a low wail. "Power, and revenge. Now I have nothing. Now I must fear him. What if he comes after me?"

"I wouldn't know about any of that," Letty said sympathetically as she set the breakfast tray down. "But it's my understanding that the safest place around is this here Sanctuary. That's why they call it that, after all."

The woman's tone altered, and when she spoke again, there was a kind of cunning in it. "I would see my children. Why can I not see my children?"

Letty blinked. She didn't look much like someone who *had* children. Not what Letty imagined a mother to be. But clearly she was half out of her head. Perhaps she'd been different once.

"You must ask Mr. Pangborn about that," she said. "Or—I know a Silent Brother is coming soon. Perhaps one of them can help you see your children." *Through bars*, she thought, but there was no point saying that.

"Yes." The woman smiled at that, a peculiar, unsettling smile that seemed to stretch across half her face. "A Silent Brother. I would very much like to see him when he comes."

Cordelia hadn't been looking forward to going to Curzon Street. She had imagined something dim and ghostly, a shadow of the place it had been, with dustcloths over the furniture.

But it was nothing like that. It felt like stepping back into the house as she'd left it. Lights were on—Effie's doing, no doubt—and it was clean and swept. As she wandered through the rooms, she saw that fresh flowers had been placed on the tables in cut-crystal vases. The chess table was set up in the study, as if waiting for a game, though she could not bear to look in the room for very long. A fire burned low in the hearth.

Perhaps this was worse than dustcloths, she thought, passing into the dining room. On the walls hung the Persian miniatures: one depicted a scene from *Layla and Majnun*, with Layla standing in the doorway of a tent, gazing out. Cordelia had always liked her expression—yearning, seeking. Looking for Majnun, perhaps, or looking for wisdom or answers to her troubles.

She could feel Layla's yearning in her own longing for this home. She stood here inside it, and yet it was as if it were a lost place. Everything within it called to her; everything had been selected by James with such care and attention, such determination that she would like it.

What had he been *thinking*? Cordelia wondered, as she went up the stairs to what had been her room. Had he been planning to get rid of it all when Grace became mistress of the house? The miniatures, the chess set, the Carstairs panels over the fireplace? Or could it be true, what he'd said—that he'd never really planned a life with Grace at all?

But that was a dangerous road to go down. Cordelia found the bedroom, like everything, much as she'd left it; she caught up a champagne-colored silk dress from the wardrobe—she'd have to return with *something*, to bolster the story she'd told Alastair. She carried it downstairs before realizing that hauling around a heavy, beaded dress was not going to help her in her next endeavor. She'd leave it here, on the table near the door, and return for it when she was done.

The cold outside seemed more bitter compared with the warmth inside the house. She wondered idly where Effie had been—asleep downstairs, perhaps, or even out; it might well be her day off.

She touched the Lilith-protection amulet at her throat for reassurance as she reached the end of the street and ducked through an alley, which took her to the brick-lined narrow lanes of Shepherd Market. All was quiet, unusually so: too late for any shopping, too early for the mundanes who prowled this lane at night. Ahead of her rose Ye Grapes, light spilling from its windows. Within the pub a few regulars sat and drank, unaware that just outside was the place her father had been murdered.

A place of death or horror, scarred by tragedy.

She knew where it had happened. James had told her; he had seen the whole thing. She ducked down a narrow street alongside the pub. It was dark here, no gas lamps to pierce the night. Only a milky-colored moon, brushed by threaded clouds, just beginning to rise over the buildings.

She half expected to see her father's ghost, but that was not unusual. Every once in a while she imagined herself turning and seeing him, smiling at him, saying, *Baba joon*, as she had when she was very young. To think he had died here, in this dark place that stank of human misery.

She straightened her back. Narrowed her eyes. Thought of Rostam, who had slain the Div-e Sepid, the White Demon.

With a deep breath, she said out loud, her voice echoing from the surrounding stone, "*Te invoco a profundus inferni. . . . Daemon, esto subjecto voluntati meae!*"

She said it again, and then again, calling on the deepest Hell, until the words began to blur together and lose their meaning. She became aware of a strange, muffling silence—as if she had been placed for a moment beneath a glass jar and could no longer hear the ordinary sounds of London: the rattle of carriage wheels, the tramp of feet on snow, the jingle of horse bridles.

And then, cutting through the silence, came the hissing.

Cordelia whirled around. It stood before her, grinning. The demon was humanoid, but both taller and skinnier than any human. It was wearing a long, ragged cloak the color of soot. Its skull was egg-shaped, with burned, puckered skin stretched over it; its eye sockets were skin-covered hollows, and its mouth was a slash, a wound in its face lined with pin-like scarlet teeth.

"*My, my,*" said the demon in a voice like metal scraped against stone. "*You haven't even drawn a pentagram, nor bear you a seraph blade.*" As it spoke, gray liquid drooled from its mouth. "*Such a foolish mistake, little Shadowhunter.*"

"It is no mistake." Cordelia spoke in her haughtiest tone. "I am no mere Shadowhunter. I am a paladin of Lilith, Mother of Demons, bride of Sammael. If you lay a hand upon me, she will make you regret it."

The demon spat, a pellet of gray *something*. The stench in the alley was sickening. "*You lie.*"

"You know better," Cordelia said. "You can surely sense her, all around me."

The demon's mouth opened, and a purple-gray tongue resembling a calf's liver emerged from between its red teeth. The tongue slurped at the air, as if tasting it. Cordelia held still; she had not realized how revolting this would be. Her urge to lay hands on a blade, to slay the *thing* in front of her, was primal, bred in her blood. She felt her hands clench.

"You are a paladin," it said. *"Well then, paladin, why have you summoned me up from Hell? What does the Mother of Demons wish?"*

"She seeks knowledge of the doings of the Prince of Hell Belial," Cordelia said, which was true enough.

"I would be a fool to betray Belial," the demon said. Cordelia was not sure she had ever heard a demon sound *hesitant* before.

"You would be a fool to cross Lilith," she said. She folded her arms and stared the demon down. It was all she could do, of course; she didn't have so much as a knitting needle on her with which to fight the demon if it came to that. But the demon didn't know that. "And Belial does not know I am asking you this. Lilith *does.*"

After a moment, the demon said, *"Your mistress rages at Belial because he occupies her realm of Edom. 'There shall Lilith repose, and find for herself a place to rest,'"* it said in a high voice; it was unnerving to hear a demon quote a holy text. *"But Edom is not his goal. He is moving, ever moving. He builds an army."*

"They wake," Cordelia said, and the demon hissed through its scarlet teeth.

"Then you know," the demon said. *"Belial found them, empty vessels. He has filled them with his power. They wake and rise and do his bidding. And the Nephilim will be ended."*

A cold shiver went up Cordelia's spine. "Empty vessels? What do you mean?"

"The dead," said the demon, looking amused, *"who are not dead. I will not say more."*

"You will answer—" Cordelia cut herself off. She caught up her witchlight rune-stone from her pocket and raised it, light spilling out between her fingers. In its illumination, she saw a score of slinking shadows. Small demons, perhaps twice the size of a typical cat. Each had a hard-shelled body, with sharp, protruding mandibles. They scuttled along on razored claws. One was an annoyance, but a group could de-flesh a human being in less than a minute.

Paimonite demons.

They had blocked the mouth of the street. Cordelia began to regret not having brought any weapons. She very much did not want Lilith to appear, but it was probably a preferable result to being torn apart by Paimonites.

The larger demon laughed. *"Did you really think you'd only summoned me?"* it purred. *"You called out into Hell, and Hell will answer."*

Cordelia held out a hand as if to hold back the Paimonites. "Stop," she commanded. "I am a paladin of Lilith, Mother of Demons—"

The larger demon spoke. *"These are too stupid to understand you,"* it said. *"Not every demon plays the great Game, you know. Many are simply foot soldiers. Enjoy your battle."*

Its mouth stretched impossibly wider, grinning and grinning as the Paimonites scuttled forward. More were joining them, clambering over the neighboring wall, spilling into the alley like blackbeetles through a filthy hole in the ground.

Cordelia tensed. She would have to run. She had no choice. Either she would outrace the Paimonite demons, or she would die; there were simply too many of them to fight.

A Paimonite broke free of the pack and lunged at her. She darted aside, dealing it an almighty kick. It flew against the wall as the larger demon laughed, and Cordelia began to run, even as the other Paimonites closed in like a dark and moving river—

A gunshot rang out, tremendously loud. A Paimonite blew apart, spattering green and black ichor. A second shot, and this time Cordelia saw the force of it fling one of the smaller demons backward, where it smashed against the window of Ye Grapes and disintegrated.

The other small demons began to panic. Another shot, and another, smashing the Paimonites apart like stepped-on bugs. They began to scatter, chittering in terror, and Cordelia raised her witchlight.

Out of the shadows came James, an avenging angel with pistol in hand. He was coatless, and his gun seemed almost to glow in the clear cold, the inscription on its side shining: LUKE 12:49. She knew the verse by heart. *I have come to bring a fire on the earth, and how I wish it were already kindled.*

James held the pistol trained now on the tall demon, who moved quickly to put Cordelia between itself and James. James looked past it, at Cordelia, his eyes communicating a silent message.

Cordelia dropped to the ground. She fell as she'd been trained to do, letting her legs drop out from beneath her, catching herself on her feet and hands, twisting, poised to spring. She saw the demon open its red-toothed mouth in surprise, just as James pulled the trigger. The look of surprise remained as a bullet shot straight into the demon's mouth; it blew apart, vanishing into ashes.

Silence. Not the silence that had descended after Cordelia had spoken the summoning spell; she could hear the sounds of London again. Somewhere in the distance were three mundanes, already quite drunk, calling out in rowdy voices their intention to get "bloody pissed" at Ye Grapes.

But James was utterly silent. When she rose to her feet, he made no move to help her, only stared with blazing eyes. His face was white; his jaw was set in an expression Cordelia recognized as a rare emotion for James: absolute, incandescent rage.

18

One False Glass

But now two mirrors of his princely semblance
Are crack'd in pieces by malignant death,
And I for comfort have but one false glass,
That grieves me when I see my shame in him.
—William Shakespeare,
Richard III

James stalked ahead of Cordelia, back through Shepherd Market, down the alley, along Curzon Street to their house—or whoever's house it might be now. Cordelia hurried after him, feeling annoyed that she had to race behind him, but it was an annoyance that was mixed with guilt. He *had* saved her life, she *had* done something incredibly risky. If she could just explain—

James swept up the steps, letting her pass by him into the entryway. When they were inside, he slammed the door behind him, shoving his pistol into a holster on his belt.

"Hello?" Effie's voice drifted up from downstairs, sounding querulous. Well, that answered *that* question.

"It's nothing, Effie!" James shouted. He caught hold of Cordelia's arm—his grip was firm, but not painful—and half herded her down the hall to the study.

Once inside, he flung the study door shut behind them. There was no other light in the room but the fire Cordelia had noticed earlier, and the shadows in the corners were deep and black. James rounded on Cordelia, his face white with fury. "What," he said, between gritted teeth, "the bloody *hell* did you think you were doing?"

Cordelia was stunned. She had never seen James like this. He looked as if he wanted to tear something apart with his bare hands; the pulse at his throat showed the battering of his heartbeat. "I—"

"I *heard* you," he said tightly. "It wasn't as if you just wandered out at nightfall, which would have been foolish enough, and happened to encounter a group of demons. *You summoned them.*"

"I had to," Cordelia gasped. She took a step back, nearly knocking into their chess table. "I had to ask them—about Belial—"

"Are you mad? Do you think you're the first Shadowhunter to think of capturing and questioning demons? They *lie.* And they'll attack if they have the slightest opportunity."

"But I am a *paladin,*" Cordelia cried. "It's awful, I loathe it—don't imagine that I feel anything other than hatred for this thing that binds me to Lilith. But they *fear* me because of it. They dare not touch me—"

"Oh?" snarled James. "They dare not touch you? That's not what it bloody looked like."

"The demon at Chiswick House—it was about to tell me something about Belial, before you shot it."

"Listen to yourself, Cordelia!" James shouted. "*You are without Cortana!* You cannot even lift a weapon! Do you know what it means to me, that you cannot protect yourself? Do you understand that I am *terrified*, every moment of every day and night, for your safety?"

Cordelia stood speechless. She had no idea what to say. She blinked, and felt something hot against her cheek. She put her hand up quickly—surely she was not *crying*?—and it came away scarlet.

"You're bleeding," James said. He closed the distance between them in two strides. He caught her chin and lifted it, his thumb stroking across her cheekbone. "Just a scratch," he breathed. "Are you hurt anywhere else? Daisy, tell me—"

"No. I'm fine. I promise you," she said, her voice wavering as his intent golden gaze spilled over her, searching her for signs of injury. "It's nothing."

"It's the furthest thing from nothing," James rasped. "By the Angel, when I realized you'd gone out, at night, weaponless—"

"What were you even doing at the house? I thought you were staying at the Institute."

"I came to get something for Jesse," James said. "I took him shopping, with Anna—he needed clothes, but we forgot cuff links—"

"He did need clothes," Cordelia agreed. "Nothing he had fit."

"Oh, no," said James. "We are not *chatting*. When I came in, I saw your dress in the hall, and Effie told me she'd caught a glimpse of you leaving. Not getting into a carriage, just wandering off toward Shepherd Market—"

"So you Tracked me?"

"I had no choice. And then I saw—you had gone to where your father died," he said, after a moment. "I thought—I was afraid—"

"That I wanted to die too?" Cordelia whispered. It had not occurred to her that he might think that. "James. I may be foolish, but I am not self-destructive."

"And I thought, had I made you as miserable as that? I have made so many mistakes, but none were calculated to hurt you. And then I saw what you were doing, and I thought, yes, she does want to die. She wants to die and this is how she's chosen to do it." He was breathing hard, almost gasping, and she realized how much of his fury was despair.

"James," she said. "It was a foolish thing to do, but at no moment did I want to die—"

He caught at her shoulders. "You cannot hurt yourself, Daisy. You *must not*. Hate me, hit me, do anything you want to me. Cut up my suits and set fire to my books. Tear my heart into pieces, scatter them across England. But do not harm yourself—" He pulled her toward him, suddenly, pressing his lips to her hair, her cheek. She caught him by the arms, her fingers digging into his sleeves, holding him to her. "I swear to the Angel," he said, in a muffled voice, "if you die, I will die, and I will *haunt you*. I will give you no peace—"

He kissed her mouth. Perhaps it had been meant to be a quick kiss, but she could not help herself: she kissed *back*. And it was like breathing air after being trapped underground for weeks, like coming up into sunlight after darkness.

James caught at her waist, pulled her tight against him, his mouth slanting over hers. She had kissed him before, and it had always been overwhelming, an experience that shattered all her senses. But there was something different in this kiss—never had she felt such unbridled desperation in him, such a consuming blaze of need and fury and love, a whirlwind that seemed to spin her high into the upper atmosphere, where she could barely breathe.

They fell back against the wall. Her hands threaded themselves into his dark hair, soft and familiar. He bit at her lower lip, sending a shudder of exquisite sharpness through her before he soothed the sting with his tongue. She delved into his mouth; the sweet heat of him was like hot honey, and the moan she wrung from him was pure gratification. Kissing him was like traveling, exciting and unfamiliar, and at the same time it was coming home. It was everything.

"Daisy," he whispered against her mouth, sending delicious shivers through her, a chorus of cascading sparks. "Do you have any idea what it would do to me if something happened to you? Do you?"

"Oh, my *goodness*!" It was Effie, her gray pompadour wobbling with shock. Cordelia and James sprang apart; James's expression was composed, but Cordelia was sure she was blushing scarlet.

"Effie," James said. "The door was *closed*."

"Well, I'm *sure*," Effie snapped. "I thought you meant to keep out a draft. Besides, there's someone at the front door." She snorted. "Married folk, carrying on like this. Well, I *never*, in all my born days, I haven't. *Humph!*"

She stalked off. James turned to Cordelia—he looked a mess, flushed and disheveled, his mouth red from kisses. "Daisy—don't go—I'll get rid of whoever it is, you can wait upstairs—"

But she was already backing away, shaking her head. She had held everything she felt for James locked away for so long, and now she had opened that door just a crack and already waves of emotion were battering at her.

"I need to tell you something," he said, his voice shaking. "To show you something."

"It's too much," she whispered. "Too much right now—I can't—" His face fell. She sucked in a breath; she so desperately wanted to tell him she would wait for him upstairs, she so desperately wanted *him*, it felt like a sort of insanity. Her whole body screamed at her: *Be with him, touch him, let him love you.*

But upstairs waiting was where she had been when she had seen him with Grace. She could not relive that experience. And she could not trust her body. She knew that well enough.

"Tomorrow," she said. "At the party—we'll talk then."

He only nodded; Cordelia caught up her skirts and ran from the room, nearly knocking down a very surprised-looking Jesse Blackthorn in the entryway as she fled the house.

"Jesse," James said. "I, ah—well. Hello. I hadn't been expecting you."

Jesse only raised his eyebrows. James had hung back for several moments before leaving the study, composing himself. He could still feel Cordelia in his arms, still smell the scent of her spice and jasmine perfume. He felt exhausted, wrung through with layers of emotion: fear, then anger, then desperation, then desire. And hope, dashed quickly. Hope wore out the soul, more than any other feeling.

He let the control Jem had taught him take over, before he left the study and strode down the hall to find Jesse looking bemused in the foyer. Effie had taken herself off to continue her hysterics elsewhere, which was probably all to the good. Jesse was wrapped in the new olive-green coat Anna had helped him choose, and in his hand, he clutched a sheaf of yellowing parchment sheets bound in fragile leather. James recognized them immediately: Tatiana's notes from Chiswick House.

"Is this a bad time?" Jesse said.

Yes, James thought, but it wasn't as if he was going to be able to get Cordelia back now. And Jesse looked intensely worried. James felt suddenly cold, and not only from the night air. "Is Lucie all right?"

"Yes," Jesse said. "This isn't about her."

James smiled. "Aren't you supposed to stay in the Institute at night?"

Jesse said, "Aren't *you*?"

"I only came to fetch some cuff links," James said.

"Well, I came to talk to you," said Jesse, "where we could not be overheard. About my mother's papers."

"Oh!" said Effie, who had, it seemed, not vanished in hysterics after all, but rather come up behind James with little warning. And was staring past him, at Jesse. "Good *evening*, sir."

Was Effie . . . blushing? Certainly James had never seen her look like that before. She was close to twittering. "I'm so sorry, sir, I only ran to fetch you a towel for the snow in your hair. I should have taken your coat and scarf first—of course—lose track of my own head next. Such a lovely coat, too, and so suitable for such a handsome young man."

As Jesse handed over the coat and scarf, Effie clutched them to her like treasures. She gazed at Jesse, who looked back with mounting puzzlement.

"Effie," James said. "Perhaps some tea?"

"Oh! Yes, of course. I'll lay it on in the drawing room, and build up the fire there as well." She bustled off, still clutching Jesse's coat.

"She seems nice," Jesse said as James led him down the hall to the drawing room. James thought to himself that Effie had never before demonstrated the slightest interest in any of his visitors. It seemed she liked the look of Jesse. After all, Effie must like the look of *someone*. Didn't everybody?

In the drawing room, they settled into armchairs, Jesse still clutching the sheaf of old papers; they gave off a sooty, sour smell, like embers and rot.

"I've been going through them," he said, without preamble. His expression was grim. "All of them. They took a little decrypting, but it wasn't much of a code. The key was my father's name—Rupert."

"I'm guessing from your expression that you didn't much like what you found," said James.

"I always knew my mother was bitter," Jesse said. "I assumed that she'd struck out at you purely because of her hatred of your parents. But it seems you've been central to Belial's plans—to Belial and my mother's plans—all along."

"I know," James said. He'd never been quite sure how much *Jesse* knew, but the notes seemed to be providing a quick and harsh education. "Belial's goal has always been to possess me, to live in my body, since it can sustain him on Earth without burning away."

"He nearly managed with mine, but it meant he had to give up half the day," agreed Jesse. "I don't know if my mother reached out to Belial first, or he to her, but either way, their interests are far more aligned than I had realized. But it's more than that. Possessing you isn't the end of his plan. It is a stepping-stone to wreaking much larger destruction. But what kind of destruction, what form it will take, I cannot say."

James made a frustrated noise in the back of his throat. "In the past, I had this bond with Belial. Since the first time I fell into shadow. It was wretched, but at least I could see through his eyes, catch glimpses of his realm, his actions. Now I feel as though I've been blindfolded. I'm feeling around in the dark, searching for any sign of the next step in his plans."

"I know," Jesse said reluctantly. "That's why I wanted to show these to you. In the notes, I discovered how my mother was able to communicate with Belial for all those years. She used the mirror we found."

"She used the mirror? And you're implying we could use it the same way?" James demanded, sitting forward, and then shook his head before Jesse could respond. "I don't think *communication* with Belial would be a good idea. In the past, he was unaware of my presence. And"—he smiled wryly—"I'd prefer to keep it that way."

"I think you're right. But there's more to it. At some point, Belial told my mother to destroy the mirror. He didn't want there to be evidence tying the two of them together that could be found by the Clave."

"But she didn't destroy it."

"No." Jesse's face twisted with an intense disgust. "She kept it—she would look through it, and watch Belial without his knowledge. It brought her some kind of . . . enjoyment. I—can't think about it too much."

"Like the Wicked Queen in 'Snow White.'" James said. He put his elbows on his knees; his whole body felt tense. "Did she explain how it functioned? How she was able to spy upon Belial without him realizing it?"

Jesse nodded. "Yes. It's detailed in her notes."

"And it's something we could do?"

"Maybe. It's something we *shouldn't* do—"

But James had already sprung up out of his seat and made for the nearest desk. He needed pen and paper, needed a few pennies for Neddy, needed to think of what to say. Jesse watched him quietly, with the air of someone who has delivered a piece of news he wished he did not know.

Having located a pen, James began to scribble three notes. "Jesse, will you come to the Devil Tavern tomorrow? To discuss all this with the Merry Thieves?"

"Are we really going to discuss it?" Jesse said. "Or are you just going to go ahead and use the mirror?"

James looked at Jesse over his shoulder. "And here you were worried about fitting into the London Enclave." Despite himself, despite everything, he felt himself smile. "It's like you've known us for years."

The day broke sunny and very cold. The fire in Letty's room had gone out sometime in the night, and she woke to find herself curled into a ball under the thin wool blanket. She shivered, not only with the chill. The evening before, a Silent Brother had arrived, and his presence unnerved her beyond her expectations. The Shadowhunters had told her what to expect, but it wasn't even the sewn-shut mouth and eyes that had most distressed her; it was a terrible uncanny feeling, like falling, that hung about him.

He had arrived on a blast of cold air, and stood motionless in the chilly foyer while Pangborn explained what had been going on, and that Tatiana Blackthorn was imprisoned in the Sanctuary.

Letty knew that the Shadowhunters could hear the Silent Brothers speak in their minds, but that mundanes could not. She assumed Pangborn could hear Brother Lebahim in his odd, silent way; Pangborn shrugged and pointed the way to the Sanctuary, and the Silent Brother vanished without a sound down the hall.

Letty looked shyly at Mr. Pangborn. "What did he say? In your head, I mean?"

"Nothing," the old man said. "Nothing at all." He looked sternly at Letty. "Keep away from this," he added. "It's Shadowhunter business."

Odd, Letty thought. Odd enough that an hour later, she crept down to the Sanctuary and put her ear to the thick oak door. Through it, she could hear muffled noises: it must be the old woman speaking, she thought, rambling on as she had the day before.

But the closer she listened, the stranger the noises were. They didn't seem like the sounds a human voice would make. They were rough, guttural, and they seemed to *pulse*—as if every word was the beat of an exposed heart.

Shivering and nauseated, Letty retreated as fast as she could to the safety of her bedroom. Mr. Pangborn was right. Better to keep away from the whole business and let the Shadowhunters do whatever they thought best. Yes. Better to keep away.

That morning James and Jesse walked from the Institute to the Devil Tavern together, under a sky heavy with the promise of thunder. Mundanes hurried to and fro, hats pulled low over their eyes, shoulders hunched against the gathering storm. Patches of blue sky were just visible between mountainous black clouds, and the air tasted faintly of ozone and soot.

"How is Matthew . . . ?" Jesse asked delicately as they made their way into the tavern. A werewolf sat at the bar looking gloomy, all his hair standing on end thanks to the static electricity in the air. Pickles drifted half-asleep in his vat of gin.

"I haven't seen him since the night before last—we've been trading off looking after him," James said. Anna, Ariadne, and Lucie had taken shifts at Whitby Mansions too, which was doubtless how Jesse knew about Matthew's condition. Only Cordelia had not; Matthew had requested, flatly, that she not see him in the state he was in.

"It's brave of him to address his illness. Many would not," Jesse said as they reached the scratched old door that guarded the inner sanctum of the Merry Thieves.

James had no opportunity to reply or agree, as the door was already half-ajar; he pushed it open to find Christopher and Thomas sitting on the worn sofa by the fireplace. Matthew sat in one of the threadbare armchairs, which had once been expensive brocade.

He looked up and met James's eyes. Weary, James thought—Matthew looked weary, something deeper than tired. His clothes were clean and unwrinkled, but plain: gray and black, the tarnished bronze flask protruding from his breast pocket the only color in his outfit.

James remembered suddenly a summer night, the windows of this room flung open, the air soft as kitten's paws, and Matthew laughing, colorful, reaching for the wine: *Is that a bottle of cheap spirits I see before me?*

It seemed a chasm had opened between that Matthew and Matthew now: James could not bear to think on it, but only turned as Jesse brought out the stack of his mother's papers and laid them out on the round table in the center of the room. Christopher got up immediately to examine them, and Thomas followed a moment later, pulling out a chair and sitting down. James watched them, but went over to lean against Matthew's chair. Jesse, for his part, went to the window and glanced out it, as though he wished to put physical distance between himself and the proof of his mother's actions.

"Time to defeat evil, I see," Matthew said. "Let us have at it."

"Matthew," said Thomas, looking up. "How are you *feeling*?"

"Well," Matthew said, "each morning I feel as though I have been put into this flask here, and then shaken vigorously. And then each evening, the same. So overall, I would say things are up and down."

"He's better," Christopher said, not looking up from the papers. "He may not want to admit it, but he's better."

Matthew smiled up at James, who restrained the urge to ruffle his hair. It was a thin reflection of the Smile for which he was famous, but it was there. "Do you hear that?" said Matthew, nudging James with his elbow. "A scientist says I'm better."

"You are," James said quietly. "Are you coming to the Christmas party tonight?"

He had wondered, and not wanted to ask, and wanted to ask at the same time. A Christmas party meant mulled wine and spiced brandy; it meant people toasting each other's health. It meant drink. It meant temptation.

A veil came down over Matthew's expression. If the eyes were the windows of the soul, he had drawn the curtains tightly over his. He turned away from James, saying lightly, "I'll be fine. I am not so under the command of the cursed bottle that I cannot stand to see a punch bowl without flinging myself into it."

"Jesse, I hope you'll forgive me for saying so." Christopher had sat down beside Thomas at the table and was peering at Tatiana's papers through his spectacles. "But I'm afraid your mother is not a very good person."

"Of that," said Jesse, "I am keenly aware." He looked over at James. "Did you bring them?"

James had worn his most voluminous coat; Oscar used to hide in the pockets when he was a puppy. He drew out the hand mirror they had taken from Chiswick, and then a pair of handcuffs he'd located that morning in the Sanctuary.

"Handcuffs," Matthew observed as Thomas and Christopher exchanged a look of alarm. "This would seem to portend something very dangerous, or very scandalous. Or both?"

"The handcuffs are to protect me," James said. "From—"

Christopher frowned. "It says here that Tatiana used the mirror to contact Belial. You're not—"

"He *is*." Matthew sat up straight, his green eyes flashing. "James, you're going to try to contact Belial?"

James shook his head and shrugged off his coat, tossing it onto the sofa. "No. I'm going to try to *spy* on Belial."

"What on earth makes you think that's going to work?" Thomas asked.

Jesse sighed and crossed the room to lean against the mantel. James had already talked him around the night before, though Jesse had pointed out that he'd had enough of people meddling with Belial in his lifetime.

"My mother did use this mirror to speak with Belial," Jesse said, and went on to explain that after Belial had instructed her to destroy it, she had kept it instead, using it as a sort of scrying glass to spy on the Prince of Hell.

Thomas looked baffled. "She liked watching him? Just . . . watching him?"

"My mother is a very strange woman," said Jesse.

"Catoptromancy," said Christopher brightly. "The use of mirrors in magic. Dates back to the ancient Greeks." He nodded thoughtfully. "Mirrors were the way Tatiana used to contact Grace."

"It's strange that you know that," Matthew said.

Christopher busied himself flicking through the papers. Matthew was not incorrect, James thought, but it did not seem the line of questioning they ought to go down just now.

Thomas frowned. "It still seems dangerous. Maybe Tatiana believed that Belial didn't know she was watching, but we have only her word on that. And she isn't reliable."

"You're not wrong, Tom," James said. "This is a desperate measure. But these are desperate times." He looked around the room at the Merry Thieves. At Jesse, who had brought him this information against his own better judgment, against even his own will not to be reminded of his mother's actions. "I never realized the significance of my connection to Belial before. I was so focused on controlling it, keeping it at a distance. It was only when it was gone that I realized: if it were not for the knowledge I gained through that connection, each of our previous confrontations with him would have ended in ruin. If Belial has severed this bond we had, it must be because it is better for him for it to be cut. Which means that it would be better for *us* if we could at least *see* what he was doing."

Thomas rubbed the back of his neck. "Have you *tried* turning into a shadow lately?"

"I have," said James, "but it doesn't work. I think whatever Belial has done to shut me out also prevents me from going into shadow. There has to be something he doesn't want me to see—if I can get sight of it, it would be worth the effort."

"Is he always this reckless?" Jesse said to Thomas.

"You get used to it," said Thomas.

"I've always thought of it," Christopher said loyally, "as admirably heroic."

James nodded. If he was only going to get support from someone who regularly blew himself up, he would take it. "Thank you, Christopher."

Thomas rested his big hands on the table. "So," he said. "I assume you know how the mirror works?"

"Yes," James said. "There are instructions among Tatiana's notes."

"I suppose—it does seem worth a try," Thomas said.

"*No!*" said Matthew sharply. James turned, surprised. Matthew was upright, his arms crossed, his pale cheekbones stained with red blotches of anger. "Why are we even entertaining this mad idea? James, you can't risk yourself like this. If Belial is leaving you alone, then *let him leave you alone*!"

There was a startled silence. Of them all, James was likely the most surprised. He would have expected a protest from Matthew a few months ago, even a few weeks ago, but the sheer fury and denial in Matthew's voice shocked him now.

"Math," James said. "Belial will come for me—perhaps not today, but soon. Wouldn't it be better to *see* him coming, and have some inkling of his plans?"

"When he comes for you, we'll protect you," Matthew said. "We're not going to let him have you."

"It's not only me. Lots of people stand to suffer if he succeeds."

"Lots of people suffer all the time," Matthew said. "But they aren't *you*."

"I know," James said. "But I am the only one who can do this. The only one who has a chance of making it work. I don't *wish* it were that way, Math. It just is."

Matthew took a deep, ragged breath. "Explain it, then. How you use the mirror."

"I put my back to the wall," said James quietly. "We handcuff me to something fairly intractable—I'd suggest the fireplace grate; it probably hasn't moved in centuries. I gaze into the mirror and picture Belial's sigil in my head. I don't *know* if the handcuffs will be necessary, but I don't want to be drawn into the shadow realms. They're a precaution."

"Fine," said Matthew. "Fine—on one condition."

"All right—what is it?"

"I will be holding on to you," Matthew said, "for the entire duration."

He stood straight, not leaning against the chair, color blazing in his face. He reminded James of the Matthew he had tied himself to at their *parabatai* ceremony so long ago: a Matthew who seemed to fear nothing: not shadow, not fire.

"Yes," James said. "That, we can do."

In the end, James ended up sitting on the floor by the fireplace, his legs crossed awkwardly. Matthew sat next to him, his hand looped through James's belt. Jesse held the mirror while Thomas fixed the handcuffs so one cuff went around James's wrist, and the other through the fireplace grate.

Jesse took one last look at the mirror before he leaned forward to pass it over to James. Their hands touched; Jesse looked into James's eyes, his own very dark. He was showing immense strength, James thought, in being willing to take part in a ritual that involved the demon who had once possessed him.

Jesse sat back with Thomas and Christopher, who were on the floor facing James and Matthew. Christopher gave a slight nod, as if to say, *Begin.*

James gazed down at the mirror. It was heavy, heavier than metal and glass should have been. It seemed to weigh down his hand as if his arm were being forced down by an iron grip.

It was not without beauty, though. The dark metal that surrounded the glass had its own somber glow; it gathered in light and held it, and the inscriptions carved into it shone like glass.

The glass reflected his own face, darkly, a shadowy version of himself with a harsh curve to his mouth. As he gazed at the reflection of his face, he thought of Jem, of what Jem had taught him about controlling his thoughts. He pictured Belial's sigil, the sign of his power; he concentrated on it, giving it all his attention, letting the image fill the glass.

The mirror began to hum and buzz in his hand. The glass seemed to turn to mercury, a liquid, silvery substance. Shadow poured from it, expanding and rising, until James could still feel Matthew's hand gripping his belt but could no longer *see* Matthew at all. He could see only shadows, ever growing, until he gazed on a world of shadow, illuminated by the light of alien stars.

And in the shadows was Belial. He sat upon a throne James had seen before; a throne of ivory and gold, massive in size, so even Belial was dwarfed by it. Though it had clearly been created for an angel, Belial had bastardized it with his sigil: the symbol, spiky and vicious-looking, was scratched all over the ivory and marble, and down the gold steps that led up to the seat.

James drew in a sharp breath and felt Matthew's hand tighten at his side. What was Matthew seeing? he wondered. What did this look like, to the others? James was still in the Devil Tavern, still chained, yet in Belial's realm at the same time.

Belial was not the only demon in the shadows. Surrounding him—crawling about at his feet, pawing at the foot of his throne—were a swarm of piglet-sized demons: wormlike, humped and creeping, their skin gray and almost featureless save for a pair of glowing green eyes.

Chimera demons.

Belial rose and came down the steps of his throne. It seemed he could not tell James was watching—he winced as he walked, his hand pressed over his left side, where the wounds Cortana had dealt him still bled. Raising a hand stained with his own blackish blood, Belial sketched an archway on the air.

It was as if he had sliced a piece out of the night. Dim light shone through the arch, and the Chimera demons leaped and frolicked excitedly. James could hear no sound, only a sort of roaring in his ears like the crash of waves, but he saw Belial's lips move, saw Belial ordering the demons through the open arch, and then Belial turned, a frowning sneer on his face, and looked toward James—

Darkness swallowed him. He was falling, though he could still feel Matthew's grip. He was caught in a whirlwind of unfamiliar stars, the air ripped from his throat, tearing away his voice. He was no longer in silence. He could hear screaming—the terrible screaming of someone, something, that was being *invaded*, taken over—

James gasped for breath. He would lose his mind soon, he knew, if he did not break free of the shadows: he forced himself to concentrate, to think of Jem's lessons, Jem's voice, calm and steady, training him to regain control of himself. *You must find the place within that nothing outside can reach. The place beyond senses, beyond even thought. You don't need to learn how to get there; you are already there, always. You only need to learn to remember you are there. You are within yourself. You are James Herondale, fully and only.*

And with a wrench that seemed to tear at every muscle in his body, James hit the ground. The floor, in fact, of the Devil Tavern. He gasped, taking gulps of familiar, musty air as though he'd been rescued from drowning. He tried to move, to sit up, but he was wrung out: his shirt was plastered to him with sweat, and his hands—

"Are you bleeding?" Christopher demanded. They were all around him, he realized: Thomas and Jesse, Christopher and Matthew, surrounding him, their faces stunned and disbelieving.

"The mirror," Jesse said. James glanced down to see that the glass had fragmented into a thousand pieces, and his hands were snowflaked with tiny cuts like spiky red lines.

"Just scratches," he said breathlessly. Through sheer exhaustion he was aware of Matthew at his side, of Matthew taking his arm, of the touch of Matthew's stele. "I saw . . ."

"It's all right, James," Jesse said, working to undo the cuff around James's left wrist. "You don't have to talk. Just breathe."

But the pain was fading, energy surging back into James's veins as Matthew drew rune after rune on his skin. He let his head fall back against the wall and said, "I saw Belial. He was—surrounded by demons. Chimera demons. He was giving them orders, sending them through some kind of Portal. I couldn't tell where."

He closed his eyes, as Christopher said, in a puzzled tone, "But Chimera demons are symbiotic. They need to possess someone in order to come into their full power."

"They're easy to defeat on their own," said Thomas. "Why create an army of *them?*"

James thought of the screaming he had heard in the void: the agony of it, the terrible sense of invasion. "I think he *is* sending them to possess someone," he said. "It felt like a great many someones." He looked up at his friends. "But who could they be?"

It had been a whole day since the Silent Brother had arrived, and Letty Nance couldn't sleep.

Her room was a small one, up under the eaves of the Institute, and when the wind blew, she could hear it whistle through the broken roof tiles. Her small fireplace was often choked with soot, and smoke puffed into the room like dragon's breath.

But none of that was the reason she was awake. Every time she shut her eyes, she heard the voices she had discerned through the Sanctuary door. The soft, sibilant, pulsing words she didn't understand. *Ssha ngil ahrzat. Bhemot abliq ahlel. Belial niquaram.*

She rolled over, pressing her hands over her eyes. Her head throbbed.

Belial niquaram.

The floor under her feet was cold. She found herself walking to the door, turning the handle. It creaked open, and the cold air from the corridor hit her.

She didn't feel it. She went down the stairs, which curved in a circle. Down and down, into the dark and unlit nave of the old church. Down the steps to the crypt.

Belial niquaram. Letty niquaram. Kaal ssha ktar.

Come, Letty. I call you, Letty. The door is open.

And indeed, the door of the Sanctuary was unlocked. Letty swung it wide and stepped inside.

A strange tableau met her eyes. The Silent Brother stood below the light of a tallow lamp, his head tilted back at an unnatural angle. His mouth was as open as it could be, straining against the threads that held it sewed shut, and from it emanated more of those *words*, those grating, terrible words that stuck and *pulled* her closer, as if she were imprisoned in tar.

Ssha ngil ahrzat. Bhemot abliq ahlel. Belial niquaram. Eidolon.

At his feet lay the body of Albert Pangborn. He had died in his nightclothes, the front of his shirt torn open, showing red flesh and white bone, like a gaping mouth. Blood pooled beneath him.

And still Letty could not run.

On the metal bed sat the old woman, Tatiana Blackthorn. Her eyes, gone dark as ink, fixed on Letty, and she began to grin. Letty watched as Tatiana's mouth opened—and opened, distending well beyond any human jaw.

From the old woman now came a low, creaking sound. It sounded like she was laughing, deep in her chest.

I must run, said some small, buried part of Letty. *I must get out of this place.*

But she couldn't move. Not even when the old woman's skin split, her body shifting and changing so rapidly it was as if she were melting and re-forming into something else. Something pale and tall, skinny-limbed, bald and hairless, with skin like a puckered burn. Something that hunched its back, and hopped and crawled. Something slimy and pale white that came at Letty so fast that she had no time even to cry out.

19

Marks of Woe

I wander thro' each charter'd street,
Near where the charter'd Thames does flow.
And mark in every face I meet
Marks of weakness, marks of woe.
—William Blake, "London"

Grace suspected it was evening. She had no real way of telling, save by the changing nature of the meals she was brought—oatmeal for breakfast, sandwiches for luncheon, and supper, which tonight had been mutton with currant jelly. It was all rather better than her mother's usual fare.

She had also been provided with two plain linen dresses, in a sort of bone color, not unlike the robes the Brothers wore. She supposed she could sit about the cell stark naked for all they really cared, but she dressed carefully each day and plaited her hair anyway. It seemed like giving up something not to do it, and this evening she was glad she had, as soft footsteps heralded a visitor.

She sat up on her bed, heart pounding. *Jesse?* Had he forgiven her? Returned? There was so much she wanted to say, to explain to him—

"Grace." It was Christopher. Gentle Christopher. The torches burning in the corridor—Brother Zachariah had put them there for her, since the Brothers did not need light—showed her that he was alone, coatless, and carried a leather satchel over his shoulder.

"Christopher!" she whispered loudly. "Did you sneak in?"

He looked puzzled. "No, of course not. Brother Zachariah asked me if I knew the way and I said yes, so he went to attend to other business." He held up something that glittered. A key. "He said I could come into the cell and visit with you. He says he trusts you not to try to escape, which is rather nice."

Into the cell? Grace hadn't been near another human being without bars between them for what felt like forever. It *was* kind of Zachariah to let a friend come into her cell, she thought, as Christopher unlocked the door and pushed it open, the hinges squeaking. Kindness still knocked her off guard, leaving her feeling confused and almost uncomfortable.

"I'm afraid that there's only the one chair," Grace said. "So I'll remain sitting on the bed, if that's all right. I know it isn't proper."

"I don't think the usual rules of British etiquette hold here," Christopher said, sitting down with his satchel in his lap. "The Silent City isn't in London—it's everywhere, isn't it? We could walk out the doors and be in Texas or Malacca. So we can cobble together any rules of politeness we like."

Grace couldn't help but smile. "That makes a surprising amount of sense. But then, you often do. Have you come to discuss the notes you left? I've had some thoughts—ways the process might be refined, or experiments that could be tried—"

"We needn't talk about the notes," said Christopher. "It's the Institute's Christmas party tonight, you see." He began rooting around in his satchel. "And I thought, since you couldn't go, I might try to bring some of the party to you. To remind you that even though you are here, it is not forever, and soon enough you will again be someone who goes to parties." As though performing a magic track, he drew out a green glass bottle. "Champagne," he said. "And glasses for champagne." These too he drew out of the bag and set on the small wooden table next to Grace's bed.

There was a feeling in Grace's stomach that she didn't recognize, a sort of fizziness like champagne itself. "You are a very strange boy."

"Am I?" said Christopher, sounding legitimately surprised.

"You are," said Grace. "You turn out to be very sensitive, for a scientist."

"One can be both," Christopher said mildly. His kindness, like Zachariah's, left her almost worried. She would never have expected it, not from one of James's friends, who had every reason to dislike her, but he seemed steadfast in his desire to make sure she did not feel utterly abandoned or forgotten.

And yet it was all built on deceit. She knew that now, from Jesse's reaction to what she had told him. He would have found out on his own, anyway, she was sure; but if she had not told him, every part of their relationship would have been a lie. Now at least, if he forgave her . . .

With a loud *pop*, Christopher removed the cork from the top of the bottle. He poured two glasses, set the bottle on a shelf, and held a glass out to her: it was an oddly pretty thing in the dreary cell, the gold-colored liquid shining.

"Christopher," she said, taking the glass. "There is something I must tell you."

His lavender eyes—so beautifully odd, the color—widened. "What's happened?"

"It's not quite that." Solemnly Christopher clinked his glass against hers. She took a long drink from the glass, and it tickled her nose; she had to hold back a sneeze. It was better than she remembered. "It's something I've done . . . to someone. Something terrible, in secret."

His brow furrowed. "Is this something you did to me?"

"No," she said hurriedly. "Not at all. Nothing to do with you."

"Then probably," he said, "it's not me you need to confess to, but rather the person you did it to."

His voice was solemn. Grace looked at him, at his gentle serious face, and thought, *He suspects. I don't know how, and perhaps he only speculates, but—he guesses something very close to the truth.*

"Grace," he said. "I'm sure whomever you have wronged, he will forgive you. If you explain how it happened, and why."

"I have confessed already," she said slowly. "To the one I wronged. I cannot say that he has forgiven me, nor that I deserve his forgiveness." She bit her lip. "I have no right to ask," she said slowly. "But if you could help me . . ."

Christopher looked at her, with his steady scientist's gaze. "Help you with what?"

"There is someone else," she said, "who has been harmed greatly by my actions, through no fault of their own. Someone who deserves to know the truth." She took a deep breath. "Cordelia. Cordelia Carstairs."

Lucie would never have admitted it out loud, but she was pleased that the Christmas party was going forward. She had become reacquainted with Jesse at a ball at the Institute, but he had been a ghost and she the only one who could see him: it had been startling, but not, perhaps, *romantic*. This was her first chance to dance with him as a breathing, living man, and she was filled with nervous excitement.

The weather outside had been electric all day, heavy with the promise of a storm that had not yet broken. Lucie sat at her vanity table as the sun dipped low outside her window, firing the horizon with scarlet while her mother put the finishing touches on Lucie's hair. (Tessa had grown up without a maid and had learned early on to do her own hair; she was excellent at helping Lucie with hers, and some of Lucie's best memories were of her mother plaiting her hair while reciting to her the plot of a bad novel she'd just read.)

"Could you pin my hair with this, Mama?" Lucie asked, holding up her gold comb. Jesse had given it to her earlier that day, saying only that he would like to see her wear it again.

"Of course." Tessa deftly smoothed a coil of Lucie's French pompadour into place. "Are you nervous, kitten?"

Lucie tried to convey a negative response without moving her head. "About Jesse? I think he'll be fine being Jeremy. He's had to pretend a great deal in his life. And he'll still be a Blackthorn."

"Luckily," Tessa said, "the Blackthorns have a long-standing reputation for all looking alike. Dark hair, green or blue eyes. Honestly, I imagine everyone will simply be delighted to have someone new to bother and gossip about." She slid a few gold-and-ivory pins into Lucie's hair. "He's a lovely boy, Lucie. Constantly asking what he can do to help. I think he's not used to kindness. He's downstairs in the ballroom now with your father, assisting with the tree." She winked. "He looks very handsome."

Lucie giggled. "I hope you mean Jesse, and not Papa."

"Your father also looks very handsome."

"You are allowed to think so," said Lucie. "I am allowed to find the idea horrifying."

"Why didn't you tell us about Jesse? Before, I mean?" Tessa picked up a pair of Lucie's earbobs—ice-gray drops set in gold—and passed them over to her. Lucie's only other jewelry was the gold Blackthorn locket around her neck.

"You mean when he was a ghost? Because he was a ghost," Lucie said with a smile. "I thought you would have disapproved."

Tessa gave a small chuckle. "Lucie, my love, I know that to you I am your boring old mother, but I had my share of adventures when I was younger. And," she added, in a more serious voice, "I know that there is no way for me to wrap you in cotton wool and protect you from all danger, much as I wish I could. You are a Shadowhunter. And I am proud of you for that." She pinned the final shining coil of Lucie's hair with the gold comb and stood back to admire her handiwork. "There. All done."

Lucie looked at herself in the mirror. Her mother had left the pompadour loose, with curls falling on either side of Lucie's face. Near-invisible ivory pins held the whole structure in place and matched the ivory lace trim on Lucie's lavender silk dress. Her Marks stood out black and stark against her skin: Agility against her collarbone, her Voyance rune on her hand.

Lucie got to her feet. "It's one of my favorite parts of the Christmas party, you know," she said.

"What is?" asked Tessa.

"The part when you do my hair beforehand," Lucie said, and kissed her mother on the cheek.

Thomas glared at the fruit basket, and the fruit basket glared back.

He had been standing on the pavement in front of Cornwall Gardens for nearly ten minutes and had long ago run out of excuses for his failure to knock on the front door. Also, he had stepped in a cold puddle while exiting the carriage and his socks were wet.

The fruit basket was for Alastair's mother, Sona. Eugenia had been meant to deliver it, but some kind of emergency had occurred in which hair had been burnt in an attempt to curl it, and chaos had taken the reins at his house. Somehow, Thomas—only half-dressed for the party himself—had found himself being shoehorned into a carriage by his father, with the basket following. Gideon Lightwood had leaned into the carriage and said solemnly, "It is a far, far better thing that you do, than you have ever done before," which seemed to Thomas quite unfunny. After which his father had closed the carriage door.

Thomas looked down at the basket again, but it persisted in offering him no advice. It seemed to have some oranges in it, and a biscuit tin and some nicely wrapped holiday sweets. It really was a kind gesture from his family, he reminded himself, and nothing he should be worried about. And he'd checked already to make sure that the Carstairs carriage was gone, which meant Alastair and Cordelia had already left for the party. Telling himself that he was being ridiculous, he raised a hand and knocked firmly on the door.

Which was answered immediately by Alastair.

"What are you *doing* here?" said Thomas indignantly.

Alastair looked at him with his dark eyebrows peaked. "I *live* here," he pointed out. "Thomas, have you brought me a fruit basket?"

"No," Thomas said crossly. He knew it was unfair, but he could not help but feel Alastair had played a sort of trick on him by being home when Thomas had not expected it. "It's for your mother."

"Ah. Well, come in, then," Alastair said, and swung the door wide. Thomas staggered inside and set the basket down on the entryway table. He turned back to Alastair, and immediately launched into the speech he'd prepared on his way over:

"The basket is from my mother and my aunt Cecily. They were concerned that your mother would feel forgotten, since everyone will be at the party tonight. They wanted her to know they were thinking of her. Speaking of which," he added before he could stop himself, "why aren't you at the Institute?"

He looked Alastair up and down: Alastair was certainly not dressed like someone planning to attend a party. He was in shirtsleeves, his braces hanging down around his hips, his feet in slippers. He looked sulky and bitten-lipped and ferocious, like a Persian prince from a fairy tale.

A Persian prince from a fairy tale? SHUT UP, THOMAS.

Alastair shrugged. "If I'm leaving for Tehran soon, it hardly seems worth socializing with the Enclave. I thought I'd spend a productive evening at home. Go through some of Cordelia's books about paladins. See if I could find anything helpful."

"So Cordelia went to the party on her own?"

"With Anna and Ari. She left a bit early to pick them up."

An awkward pause fell over the foyer. Thomas knew that the correct thing to say was something along the lines of, *Well, I should be off*. Instead he said, "So your plan is to brood at home by yourself all night? Rather than going to a party with your friends?"

Alastair gave him a sour look. "They're not my friends."

"You say that kind of thing often," Thomas said. "Almost as though if you repeat it enough, it will become true." He crossed his arms over his broad chest. He was wearing his best black jacket, which strained at the seams over his shoulders. "If you don't go, I won't go either. I will stay home, and mice will nibble on me in my despair."

Alastair blinked. "There's no reason for that," he said. "You've got every reason to go—"

"But I won't," Thomas said. "I will remain at home, despairing, being nibbled upon by mice. It's your choice."

Alastair held up one finger for a moment as though to speak, and then let it drop. "Well. Damn you, Lightwood."

"Alastair?" came a light voice from the parlor. Sona; of course they would have brought her down here, to keep her from having to climb the stairs every day. "*Che khabare? Che kesi dame dar ast?*" *What's going on? Who was at the door?*

Alastair looked darkly at Thomas. "All right," he said. "I'll go to your stupid party. But you have to amuse my mother while I get dressed."

And with that, he turned and stalked upstairs.

Thomas had never been alone with Alastair's mother. Before he could lose his nerve entirely, he snatched up the fruit basket and brought it into the parlor.

Sona was sitting up, propped on a chaise longue by about a thousand pillows of various rich colors. She was wearing a brocade dressing gown and wrapped in a thick blanket, which rose like a mountain over the hill of her stomach. Not knowing where to look, Thomas carefully put the basket on the table next to her. He explained the nature of the gift while Sona smiled delightedly.

"Oh my," she said. "That's so very thoughtful of them. I *do* feel thought of, and that is a lovely gift in itself."

"Ghâbel nadâre," said Thomas. *Don't mention it.* It was a gamble—he'd studied Persian on his own, and helped James with the language as well. He knew the phrase meant, *It's not worthy of you*, and was a common thing to say when giving a gift. He also wasn't sure he was pronouncing it properly, and he was fairly sure the tops of his ears were turning red.

Sona's eyes sparkled. "So many young people learning Persian these days," she said, as if highly entertained. She leaned forward. "Tell me, where is my son? I do hope he didn't abandon you at the front door."

"Not at all," Thomas said. "I managed to talk him into coming to the Christmas party. He went to change clothes."

"You *managed to talk him into it*," Sona repeated, as if Thomas had claimed that he had sailed around the world in a canoe. "Well, I"—she looked at Thomas closely—"I am delighted that Alastair has a friend who will look out for his best interests, even when he does not. Not like that *ahmag* Charles," Sona added, as if to herself. But she was looking at Thomas even more closely than before.

"Charles?" Thomas echoed. Surely Sona had no idea—

"Charles never cared for Alastair," Sona said. "Not the way he deserves to be cared for. Alastair deserves to have someone in his life who understands how truly wonderful he is. Who suffers when he suffers, and is happy when he is happy."

"Yes," Thomas said, "he does," and his mind raced. Did Sona know he wanted to be that person for Alastair? Did she know that Alastair and Charles had been romantically entangled? Was she giving Alastair and Thomas her blessing? Was he inventing things in his fevered mind? "I think," he said at last, hardly realizing he was saying it, "that the person most standing between Alastair and happiness is Alastair himself. He is brave, and loyal, and his heart—" He found himself blushing. "I suppose I wish Alastair would treat *himself* as he deserves to be treated."

Sona was smiling down into the fruit basket. "I do agree. As a child, Alastair was always gentle. It was only when he went away to school—"

She broke off as Alastair stalked into the room. No one would have guessed he had gotten dressed in a hurry: he was starkly elegant in black and white, his eyes luminous and deep. The curve of his throat was as graceful as a bird's wing. "All right, Thomas," he said. "If you're quite done assaulting my mother with fruit, we might as well be on our way."

Thomas said nothing as Alastair went across the room to kiss his mother on the cheek; they spoke together in Persian too rapid for Thomas to understand. He only watched Alastair: Alastair being gentle, Alastair being loving, the Alastair Sona had known, but Thomas so rarely ever saw. As Alastair bid goodbye to his mother, Thomas could not help but wonder: If Alastair was so utterly determined to hide that part of himself from Thomas, did it *matter* that Thomas knew it existed at all?

The ballroom had become a forest of fairy-tale winter, of garlands of holly and ivy, red berries against dark green, and white mistletoe hanging above every doorway.

To Lucie this seemed only fitting. After all, she and Jesse had met in a forest—the forest of Brocelind, in Idris, where faeries laid clever traps, and white flowers that shone at night grew among the moss and the bark of the trees.

The party had not yet started, officially; the rush to get everything ready before guests arrived was ongoing. The problem of the missing Christmas tree had been solved by Tessa, who had talked Magnus into creating a tree-shaped sculpture out of a variety of weapons before he left for Paris. The trunk of the tree was made of swords: hook swords and falchions, longswords and katanas, all held together by demon wire. At the top of the tree was a golden starburst, from which dangled smaller blades: daggers and *zafar takieh*, *bagh nakh* and *cinquedeas*, *jambiyas* and *belawas* and jeweled stilettos.

Bridget and a smaller crew of maids and servants were rushing to and fro, setting up the refreshment tables with their silver bowls of punch and mulled wine, dishes of gooseberry and bread sauces next to plum puddings and roast goose stuffed with apples and chestnuts. Candles glowed from every alcove, illuminating the room with soft light; gold ribbons and paper chains hung from hooks in the walls. Lucie could see her parents over by the ballroom doors, deep in conversation: Will's hair was full of pine needles, and as Lucie watched, her mother reached up and drew one out with an impish smile. Will rewarded her with a gaze so adoring Lucie looked swiftly away.

Next to the weapon tree was a tall ladder upon which Jesse was perched, trying to put a figurine of Raziel atop the gold starburst. When he caught sight of her, he smiled—his deep, slow smile that made her think of dark chocolate, rich and sweet. "Wait," he said. "I'm coming down, but it's going to take me a moment—this ladder is held together with old runes and a spirit of optimism."

He descended and turned to Lucie. He was not smiling now, though her mother had not been wrong. He *did* look handsome in his new, Anna-and-James-provided clothes. They actually fit him, following the lines of his slender body, the emerald velvet collar of his frock coat darkening the green of his eyes and framing the elegant shape of his face.

"Lucie," he said, drawing her a little bit behind the weapons tree. He was looking at her in a way that made her feel hot all over, as if her whole body was blushing. A way that said he knew he shouldn't be looking at her like that, but that he could not prevent himself. "You look . . ." He raised a hand as if to touch her face, then dropped it quickly, his fingers clenching in frustration. "I want to make a romantic speech—"

"Well, you should," said Lucie. "I firmly encourage it."

"I can't." He leaned in close; she could smell Christmas on him, the scent of pine and snow. "There is something I must tell you," he said. "You reached out to Malcolm, didn't you? About what was happening when—with us?"

She nodded, puzzled. "How did you know?"

"Because he sent me a message," Jesse said, glancing at Will and Tessa as if—though they were a good distance away—they might overhear. "He's in the Sanctuary, and he wants to see you."

* * *

Going into the Sanctuary had not been part of Lucie's plan for the evening, and she was even more unhappy to be there when she realized that it was still arranged for Jesse's funerary rites. There was the bier his body had been laid upon, with its muslin shroud and the ring of candles. There too was the white silk blindfold that had been tied around his eyes, discarded on the floor next to the bier. She was sure nobody in the Institute, staff or resident, knew what to do with the blindfold. She had never before heard of one that had been used on a body, but not cremated along with it.

Malcolm, dressed all in white, was perched on a chair near an unlit candelabra. His suit seemed to glow in the sparse light from the high windows. "Nephilim never clean up after themselves, it seems," he said. "Very fitting, I think."

"I take it you got my message." Lucie cocked her head to the side. "Though there's no need for this kind of subterfuge. You could simply drop by. You're the High Warlock of London."

"But then I would have had to pay my respects, chat with your parents. Pretend I had other business that needed attending to. In this case, I only came to speak with you." Malcolm rose to his feet and made his way over to the bier. He laid a long hand on the muslin shroud crumpled atop it. "What you did here," he said, his voice low. "Truly marvelous. A miracle."

And suddenly Lucie saw it as if it were happening again: Jesse sitting up, his chest hitching as he took his first breaths in seven years, his eyes rolling to look at her in shock and confusion. She could sense the gasp of his desperate, hungry breaths; she could smell the cold stone and candle flames; she could hear the clatter on the floor as—

"There's something wrong," she said. "When I am close to Jesse, when we kiss or touch—"

Malcolm looked alarmed. "Perhaps this would be a conversation better had with your mother," he said. "Surely she has, ah, told you how these things work—"

"I know about *kissing*," Lucie said crossly. "And this is not at all normal. Unless normal is touching your lips to someone else's and feeling as if you are falling . . . faster and faster toward an endless, yawning darkness. A darkness that is full of shining outlines like foreign constellations, signs that seem familiar, but are changed in odd ways. And voices crying out . . ." She took a sharp breath. "It only lasts until the contact with Jesse ceases. Then I am back on solid ground again."

Malcolm bent down to pick up the silk blindfold. He drew it through his fingers, saying nothing. He probably imagined she was being ridiculous, Lucie thought, some silly girl who got the vapors when a boy came near her.

In a low voice, he said, "I don't like the sound of this."

Lucie felt her stomach swoop and fall. Perhaps she had *hoped* Malcolm would dismiss the issue as nothing.

"I suspect," went on Malcolm, "that in raising Jesse, you drew on your power in a way you never have before. And that power is of the shadows in origin, you know that as well as I do. It is possible that in pushing it to its limit, you may have forged a channel between yourself and your demon grandfather."

Lucie found she was breathless. "Would my—would Belial know that?"

Malcolm was still looking down at the blindfold in his hands. "I cannot say. Does it seem to you that he is trying to communicate?"

Lucie shook her head. "No."

"Then I think we can assume he is not yet aware of it. But you should avoid attracting his attention. There may well be a way to sever this connection. I will set myself to finding out. In the meantime, not only should you avoid kissing Jesse, you should refrain even from touching him. And you should avoid any summoning or commanding of ghosts." He looked up, his dark purple eyes nearly black in the dimness. "At least you need not worry that I won't be motivated to help you. Only once it is safe for you to engage with the magic of life and death again can you call Annabel forth from the shadows."

"Yes," Lucie said slowly. It was better for him to be personally invested, surely. And yet she did not like the look in his eyes. "I will help you say goodbye to Annabel, Malcolm. I promised, and I intend to keep that promise."

"Say goodbye," Malcolm echoed quietly. There was a look on his face Lucie had not seen before; it vanished quickly, though, and he said calmly, "I will consult my sources and return the moment I have any answers. In the meantime . . ."

Lucie sighed. "Avoid touching Jesse. I know. I ought to get back," she added. "If you'd like to come to the party, you'd be welcome."

Malcolm cocked his head, as if he could hear the music through the walls; perhaps he could. "The Blackthorns had a yearly Christmas party, when I was a boy," he said. "I was never invited. Annabel would creep out during the festivities, and we would sit together, overlooking the ocean, sharing the iced cakes she'd smuggled out in her coat pockets." He closed his eyes. "Try not to collect any painful memories, Lucie," he said. "Do not get too attached to anything, or anyone. For if you lose them, the memory will burn in your mind like a poison for which there will never be any cure."

There seemed nothing to say to that. Lucie watched Malcolm wend his shadowy way out of the Sanctuary, and she composed herself to go upstairs. She felt cold all over. It was bad enough just knowing that touching the boy she loved might connect her more strongly to Belial, the demon who had once tortured him; how on earth would she explain it to Jesse?

By the time James made his way to the ballroom, a good number of the guests had already arrived. There was family—his aunts and uncles, though he did not see his cousins yet, or Thomas. Eugenia was there, looking furious and wearing a yellow velvet cap over what seemed to be slightly charred hair. Esme Hardcastle was lecturing the Townsends about the difference between mundane and Shadowhunter Christmases, and the Pouncebys were admiring the weapons tree, along with Charlotte, Henry, and Charles. Thoby Baybrook and Rosamund Wentworth arrived together, wearing matching outfits in rose-colored velvet, which oddly suited Thoby better than Rosamund.

Those who *were* there were outnumbered by those—Cordelia, Anna, Ari, Matthew—who had not yet arrived; what was puzzling, though, was Lucie's absence. Jesse was at the doorway with Will and Tessa, presumably being introduced to arriving partygoers as "Jeremy

Blackthorn," but Lucie was nowhere to be seen, and it was not like her to have left Jesse to face the party alone.

James wondered if he should get himself a glass of champagne. Under normal circumstances, he would have, but with everything that had happened with Matthew recently, the idea of taking the edge off his nerves with alcohol had lost its appeal. And he *was* nervous—each time the ballroom doors opened, he turned his head, hoping for a glimpse of scarlet hair, a flash of dark eyes. Cordelia. He had something he desperately needed to tell her, and though it was not quite the core of his secret, it was very close.

He knew perfectly well that he ought to be thinking about what had happened that afternoon. The mirror, the vision of Belial, the Chimera demons. The question of who Belial was possessing—mundanes? It would be a fool's errand, though, to send even possessed mundanes against Shadowhunters. But the last time he'd seen Cordelia, she'd said, *Tomorrow, at the party—we'll talk then*, and regardless of any number of Princes of Hell, it was nearly all he could think about.

Nearly. The ballroom doors swung open; this time it was Matthew, wearing a frock coat that put biblical Joseph's to shame. There was brocade of violet, green, and silver, and a tasseled gold fringe. On anyone else it would have looked like a costume; on Matthew, it seemed avant-garde. There appeared to be shining leaves in his hair; he looked a bit as if he were about to appear as Puck in *A Midsummer Night's Dream*.

James started to smile, just as his aunt Cecily swept up to him. She had three-year-old Alex by one chubby hand; he wore a blue velvet sailor suit, with a matching hat complete with white ribbon.

"His debut, I see," James said, eyeing Alexander, who was scowling. He did not seem to like the sailor suit, and James did not blame him.

Cecily swung Alex up into her arms with a smile. "Speaking of debuts, I do think that Blackthorn boy you've all adopted may need saving."

This turned out to be true. The musicians had arrived, which had required that Will and Tessa show them where to put their instruments; in the resulting confusion, Jesse had been trapped in an alcove by Rosamund Wentworth. She had obviously been introduced to Jesse already, or at least, James hoped she had been, given how intently she was speaking to him. As James approached them, Jesse shot him a beseeching look.

"Jeremy, Rosamund," said James. "Lovely to see you. Jeremy, I was wondering if you'd be interested in a hand of cards in the games room—"

"Oh, don't be a *stick*, James," said Rosamund. "It's much too early for the gentlemen to retire to the games room. And I've only just met Jeremy."

"Rosamund, he's now part of the London Enclave. You'll meet him again," said James, as Jesse mimed what James thought was someone being saved from a sinking ship.

"But look at his *eyes*." She sighed, as if Jesse were not, in fact, present. "Couldn't you just *die*? Isn't he *divine*?"

"Excruciatingly so," said James. "Sometimes it pains me just to gaze upon him."

Jesse shot him a dark look. Rosamund tugged at Jesse's sleeve.

"I thought it was only going to be the same old soggies as always, so what a pleasant surprise you are!" Rosamund said. "Where did you say you grew up?"

"When my parents returned to England, they settled in Basingstoke," said Jesse. "I lived there until I found out I was a Shadowhunter, and decided to rejoin the ranks."

"A tragic backstory indeed," said Matthew, who had appeared at James's side.

"It isn't tragic at all," said Rosamund.

"Being from Basingstoke is a tragedy in itself," said Matthew.

James grinned. They *had* chosen Basingstoke because it was a dull enough place not to inspire much questioning.

"Rosamund," Matthew said, "Thoby has been looking all over for you."

This was a clear and blatant lie; Thoby was poking at the weapons tree, a mug of cider in hand, and chatting with Esme and Eugenia. Rosamund frowned suspiciously at Matthew but took herself off to join her fiancé.

"Are people always like that at parties?" Jesse asked as soon as she'd gone.

"Rude and peculiar?" said James. "In my experience, about half the time."

"Then there are those who are charming and spectacular," said Matthew, "though I'll admit there are fewer of us than the other kind." He winced, then, and touched his head as if it hurt; James and Jesse exchanged a worried glance.

"So," said James, trying to keep his voice light, "I suppose the question is, who do you wish to meet first: the more pleasant people or the unpleasant people or a mixture of both?"

"Is there a need to meet unpleasant people?" Jesse asked.

"Unfortunately, yes," Matthew said. He was no longer holding his head, but he looked pale. "So you can be better prepared to guard yourself against their wiles."

Jesse did not reply; he was looking out at the crowd. No, James realized, he was looking at someone making their way through the crowd: Lucie, looking elfin in a pale lavender dress. The gold locket around her throat shone like a beacon. She smiled at Jesse, and Matthew and James exchanged a look.

A moment later they had made themselves scarce, and Lucie and Jesse were whispering together in the alcove. James had every confidence that Lucie could easily show Jesse around *and* fend off the Rosamund Wentworths of the world.

He was less confident that Matthew was all right. James led him toward one of the tinsel-encircled pillars at the edge of the room, trying to peer into his face. He looked pinched, and there was a greenish cast to his skin; his eyes were bloodshot.

"I assume you are not staring at me because you are riveted by my beauty or my *haute couture*," Matthew said, leaning back against the pillar.

James reached up and plucked one of the leaves from Matthew's hair. It was pale green, edged with gold: not a real leaf, but enamel. Painted beauty taking the place of a living thing. "Math. Are you all right? Have you got the stuff Christopher gave you?"

Matthew tapped his breast pocket. "Yes. I've been doling it out as instructed." He looked out across the room. "I know what I'd be doing at an ordinary party," he said. "Floating about, being entertaining.

Scandalizing Rosamund and Catherine. Joking with Anna. Being witty and charming. Or at least, I *thought* I was witty and charming. Without the alcohol, I . . ." His voice sank. "It's like I'm watching clockwork dolls in a child's dollhouse, acting out their parts. Nothing seems real. Or perhaps I am the one who is not real."

James was aware that Thomas and Alastair had arrived—interestingly, together—and that Alastair was looking over at them, his eyes narrowed.

"I've known you a long time, Matthew," said James. "You were witty and charming long before you began drinking. You will be witty and charming again. It's too much to ask it of yourself at this very moment."

Matthew looked at him. "James," he said. "Do you know when I started drinking?"

And James realized: he did not. He had not seen it, because of the bracelet; he had not felt the changes in Matthew, and then it had seemed too late to inquire.

"Never mind," Matthew said. "It was a gradual process; it's unfair to ask." He winced. "I feel as if there's a gnome inside my head, banging away at my skull with an axe. I ought to give him a name. Something nice and gnomish. Snorgoth the Skullcrusher."

"Now," said James, "*that* was witty and charming. Think of Snorgoth. Think of him taking an axe to people you don't like. The Inquisitor, for instance. Perhaps that can help you get through the party. Or—"

"Who is Snortgoth?" It was Eugenia, who had come up to them, her yellow cap askew on her dark hair. "Never mind. I am not interested in your dull friends. Matthew, will you dance with me?"

"Eugenia." Matthew looked at her with a weary affection. "I am not in a dancing mood."

"*Matthew.*" Eugenia looked woebegone. "Piers keeps stepping on my feet, and Augustus is lurking about as if he wants a waltz, which I just *can't* manage. One dance," she wheedled. "You're an excellent dancer, and I'd like to have a bit of fun."

Matthew looked long-suffering but allowed Eugenia to lead him out onto the floor. As they took up the positions for the next dance, a two-step, Eugenia glanced over at James. She cut her eyes toward the ballroom doors as if to say, *Look there,* before letting Matthew sweep her into the dance.

James followed Eugenia's glance and saw that his parents were greeting Anna and Ari, who had just arrived, Anna in a fine blue frock coat with frogged gold clasps. With them was Cordelia.

Her fiery hair was pinned in braided coils around her head, as if she were a Roman goddess. She wore a dress of stark, satiny black, the short sleeves baring her long brown arms to the elbow, the front and back cut so low it was clear she was not wearing a corset. No fashionably pallid dress, covered in lace or white tulle, could hold a candle to hers. A snatch of a poem James had read once flashed through his mind: *viewing the shape of darkness and delight.*

She glanced over at James. Her dress set off the depth of her eyes. Around her throat gleamed her only jewelry: the globe necklace he had given her.

She seemed to see that he was alone and raised her hand to beckon him to join her and his parents at the door. James crossed the room in a few strides, his mind racing: it only made sense that he should join his wife when she arrived. Perhaps Cordelia was merely thinking of appearances.

But, said the small, hopeful voice that still lived in his heart, the voice of the boy who had fallen in love with Cordelia during a bout of scalding fever, *she said we would talk. At the party.*

"James," Will said cheerfully, "I'm glad you've turned up. I require your help."

"Really?" James glanced around the room. "Everything seems to be going well."

"*Will,*" Tessa scolded. "You haven't even let him greet Cordelia!"

"Well, they can *both* help," announced Will. "The silver trumpet, James, the one that was given to your mother by the Helsinki Institute? The one we always use as a centerpiece at Christmas? It's gone missing."

James exchanged a mystified look with Tessa. He was about to ask his father what on earth he was on about when Will said, "I'm quite sure it was left in the drawing room. Can you and Cordelia fetch it for me?"

Cordelia smiled. It was a thoroughly expert smile, the sort that showed nothing at all of what she was thinking. "Of course we can."

Well, James thought as he and Cordelia crossed the ballroom, *either she believes the story about the trumpet or has accepted that my father is a mad person and needs to be humored.* Most likely, he had to admit, it was the latter.

He followed Cordelia into the drawing room and closed the pocket doors behind them. He had to admit he rarely gave much thought to the drawing room; it tended to be used at the end of parties, when the ladies who were too tired to dance but not tired enough to go home sought a place to talk and gossip and play cards while the men retired to the games room. It was old-fashioned, with heavy cream-colored curtains, and delicate, spindly gilt chairs surrounding small tables set up for whist and bridge. Cut-glass decanters gleamed on the mantelpiece.

Cordelia turned to face James. "There is no silver trumpet," she said, "is there?"

James smiled wryly. "You know my family well."

Cordelia tucked a stray lock of hair behind her ear. The gesture sent a bolt of heat through James. Such a small gesture, one he wished he could make himself; he wished he could feel the softness of her hair, her skin.

"It is sweet that your father wants us to be alone together," she said. "But it is also true that we ought to talk." She tipped her head back to look up at him. "At the house—you said you had something to show me."

And she blushed. Only slightly, but it was encouraging nonetheless. She seemed so calm, armored in her elegance, almost untouchable. It was a relief to know she also felt unease.

"Yes," he said, "only for me to show you, you will have to come closer."

She hesitated for a moment, then took a step toward him, and another, until he could smell her perfume. She was breathing quickly, the jet beads edging the neckline of her dress gleaming as her breasts rose and fell. His mouth was dry.

He reached out, capturing the gold pendant that hung around her neck, the tiny globe he had given her. The one she still wore, despite everything.

"I know you believe that I only want you now that I cannot have you," he said. "But it is not true."

He tapped the pendant with his thumb. There was a faint click and the globe popped open; her eyes widened. From inside he drew a small slip of paper, carefully folded. "Do you remember when I gave this to you?"

She nodded. "Our two-week anniversary, I believe it was."

"I didn't tell you then what was inside," he said, "not because I did not want you to know, but because I could not face the truth of it myself. I wrote these words down and folded them up and put them where they would be near you. It was selfish. I wanted to speak them to you, but not to face the consequences. But here." He held out the slip of paper. "Read them now."

As she read, her expression changed. They were familiar, lines from Lord Byron.

> *There yet are two things in my destiny—*
> *A world to roam through, and a home with thee.*
> *The first were nothing—had I still the last,*
> *It were the haven of my happiness.*

"'*A world to roam through*,'" Cordelia whispered. "That is why you chose this necklace. The shape of the world." She fixed her gaze on his. "It means . . ."

Her eyes were deep and wide, and this time he let himself touch her cheek, his palm against her soft skin, his whole body burning at even that little touch. "It means I would rather have a home with you than all the world," he said fiercely. "If you cannot believe me now, believe the James who gave you that necklace, long before you left for Paris. My God, what other reason could I have for placing those verses there, save that I loved you, but was too much a coward to say it?"

Cordelia leaned her cheek against his hand and looked up at him through the dark fringe of her lashes. "So you loved me and you loved Grace at the same time. That is what you are telling me?"

He felt his heart tighten in his chest. She was offering him a way out, he knew, a way to explain his past behavior. A way to say, *Yes, I loved you both, but then I realized I love you more.*

It was a story that made sense, in a way that the story he had offered her so far did not. And perhaps she would even accept it, forgive it. But it would never be something he could accept for himself. He dropped his hand from her face and said, "No. I *never* loved Grace. Never."

Her expression changed. It had been questioning, curious; now it seemed to close like a fan. She nodded once and said, "All right. If you will excuse me, James. There is something I must do."

And she walked out of the room, sliding open the pocket doors as she went. James followed her but hesitated in the doorway. He could see Cordelia, who had paused to speak to her brother and Thomas; he could not stop himself from staring after her, at the elegant line of her back, the crown of her flame-red hair. *Why couldn't you just lie?* he asked himself savagely. *If you can't bring yourself to tell her the truth—*

But there had been enough lies between them. He had given Cordelia one more piece of the truth, a piece he could bear to give. It was in her hands what she would do with it.

"James?" He nearly jumped out of his skin; lurking next to the drawing room door was Esme Hardcastle, a pen and notepad in hand. She peered at him owlishly. "I'm sorry to interrupt you, James," she added, tapping the pen against her front teeth, "but as you know, I'm working on a family tree, and it would be awfully helpful to know: Are you and Cordelia planning to have children, and if so, how many? Two?" She tilted her head to the side. "Six or seven?"

"Esme," James said, "that family tree is going to be very inaccurate if this is the way you're going about things."

Looking highly offended, Esme sniffed. "Not at all," she said. "You'll see."

Events like the Christmas party were Anna's ideal milieu. She liked nothing better than to observe the peculiarities of people's behavior: the ways they made small talk, their gestures, the way they stood and laughed and smiled. She'd started when she was small, trying to guess what the grown-ups were feeling while she watched them talk at parties. She'd quickly discovered she was quite good at it, and often made Christopher laugh by telling him what this or that person was secretly thinking.

Sometimes, of course, her subjects made it easy, as in this moment, when she was watching James as he looked at Cordelia as if he were longing for the moon. Cordelia *did* look stunning—she must have gotten her dress on her ill-judged trip to Paris; it had the hallmarks of a more daring fashion than was usually seen in London. Instead of boasting ruffles, it curved in swirls around Cordelia's hips; instead of lace, the deep neckline was edged with jet beads that glimmered against her light brown skin. She was talking to Alastair and Thomas now, as Thomas tossed a delighted and giggling Alex into the air; though Anna knew perfectly well that Cordelia had a great deal on her mind, one could certainly not tell it by looking at her.

Beside Anna, Ari chuckled. They were both at the refreshment table, shamelessly eating the miniature iced queen's cakes. Each was decorated with the crest of a Shadowhunter family. "You *do* enjoy people-watching, don't you?"

"Mm," Anna said. "It's always so deliciously telling."

Ari cut her eyes around the room. "Tell me a secret about someone," she said. "Tell me what you've deduced."

"Rosamund Wentworth is thinking of leaving Thoby," said Anna. "She knows it will be a scandal, but she cannot bear that he's really in love with Catherine Townsend."

Ari's eyes were like saucers. *"Really?"*

"You just wait—" Anna began, and broke off at Ari's expression. She had gone very still and was looking past Anna, her expression flat and strained. Anna turned toward the door to see who had just arrived, though she had already guessed. Of course. Maurice and Flora Bridgestock.

Anna curled her hand around the crook of Ari's elbow; it was an automatic gesture, a need to help brace Ari on her feet. "Remember," she said, steering her gently away from the refreshment table. "If they want to make a scene, that is their decision. It does not reflect on you."

Ari nodded but didn't take her eyes off her parents, and Anna could feel her hand trembling slightly. It was Flora who caught sight of her daughter first. She started in their direction, looking hopeful. Before she could get within twenty feet, Maurice had swept up behind her, put his hand on her waist, and firmly steered her away. Flora said something to her husband, who looked irritated as he replied; Anna thought they were arguing.

Ari watched them with a look that cut at Anna's heart. "I don't think they will make a scene," she said softly. "I don't think they care enough to do that."

Anna swung around so she was facing Ari. Ari, who had been her first love, who had opened and then broken her heart. But also Ari who slept in her bed, who liked to do the washing-up but put all the dishes away in the wrong places, Ari who sang to Percy the stuffed snake when she thought no one was listening, Ari who used her hairpins as bookmarks and put too much sugar in her tea, so that when Anna kissed her, she always tasted sweet.

"Dance with me," Anna said.

Ari looked at her in surprise. "But . . . you've always said you don't dance."

"I like to break rules," Anna said. "Even ones I have set myself."

Ari smiled and held out her hand. "Then let us dance."

Anna led her out onto the dance floor, knowing full well that Ari's parents were watching. One hand on Ari's shoulder, another on her waist, she led her into the steps of the waltz. Ari began to smile as they whirled around the dance floor, her eyes glowing, and for once, Anna's need to observe the rest of the party—the interactions, gestures, conversations—fell away. The world shrank down to only Ari: her hands, her eyes, her smile. Nothing else mattered.

20
Iron Heart

By thy leave I can look, I rise again;
But our old subtle foe so tempteth me,
That not one hour I can myself sustain;
Thy grace may wing me to prevent his art,
And thou like adamant draw mine iron heart.
—John Donne, "Thou Hast Made Me,
and Shall Thy Work Decay?"

Cordelia was looking for Matthew.

Every once in a while, she would reach up and touch the necklace around her throat. Now that she knew its secret, it felt different, as if the metal were hot against her skin, though she knew that was ridiculous—the necklace had not changed. Only her knowledge of it had.

She kept seeing James, standing over her, his dark gold eyes fixed on hers. The feeling when he opened the necklace, his fingers brushing her throat. That breathless, shivery feeling that sent goose bumps flooding across her skin.

So you loved me and you loved Grace at the same time, she had said to James, thinking he would take hold of that, nod gratefully at her understanding. But the look that had flashed across his face—bitter despair, self-loathing.

I never loved her. Never.

It made no sense, not when matched with his behavior, and yet she felt as if her reality had tilted on its axis. James did love her; he *had* loved her. Whether that was enough, she did not know; but she knew the depth of her own reaction, reading the words he had written inside her necklace. She had felt as if her heart were pumping light, not blood, through her veins.

Her stomach churned now: confusion, mixed with a hope she had not dared to feel before. If someone—if Lucie—had asked her that moment what she felt, she would have said, *I don't know, I don't know*, but she knew enough: her own feelings were too strong to be ignored any longer. There were things that could go no further, before real damage was done.

She found Matthew at last on the dance floor, being flung about energetically by Eugenia. She hung back among the crowd waiting for the next dance and saw Eugenia look over at her and smile sadly. To Cordelia, the smile said, *Please don't hurt him*, though perhaps it was her own imagination. Her own dread.

When the song was over, Eugenia tapped Matthew on the shoulder and pointed to Cordelia; his face lit up, and he walked off the dance floor to join her, rubbing his shoulder. He had grown thinner, she thought with a pang, and that, combined with the bright coat and the enamel leaves in his hair, made him look like a faerie prince.

"Are you rescuing me from Eugenia?" he said. "She's a good girl, but she does toss one around like a rag doll. I swear I saw through the wards of London to a new and terrible world."

Cordelia smiled; he *sounded* all right, at least. "Can we talk?" she said. "Perhaps in the games room?"

Something lit in his eyes: guarded hope. "Of course."

The games room had been readied: it was a tradition, as a party came to a close, for some of the guests—mostly the men—to retire here for port and cigars. The room smelled of cedar and pine, the walls hung with red-berried holly wreaths. Upon the sideboard had been set bottles of sherry, brandy, and all manner of whiskies. The windows were silvered with ice, and a high fire burning in the grate illuminated the framed portraits on the walls.

It was cozy, and still Cordelia wanted to shiver. Everything in her wanted to avoid hurting him now, tonight. The rest of her knew this wasn't going to get easier, and the longer she waited, the worse it would be.

"Thank you for sending the Thieves to look after me the other night," Matthew said. "It was a true act of kindness. And—" He looked at her closely. "I am getting better, Daisy. Christopher has me on this regimen, a bit less every day, and soon enough he says my body will no longer depend on the stuff. I will be able to stop."

Cordelia swallowed. In all that speech, she thought, he had not once said the words "alcohol" or "drink." She wanted to say: *It will be good when your body no longer wants the stuff, but you will still want it. Every time you are unhappy, you will want to blunt that pain with alcohol; every time you are bored, or feel empty, you will want to fill that hollow, and that will be the hard part, so much harder than you think.*

"I remember this dress," Matthew said, touching her sleeve lightly. There was a little unease in his voice, as if he wondered at her silence. "You worried it was so plain that it wouldn't suit you, but it does," he said. "With your hair, you look like a dark flame, edged in fire."

"You talked me into it," Cordelia said. She let herself remember the gilded shop, the streets of Paris, the elegant rooftops rising and falling like musical notes. "And I am glad you did. You have Anna's skill; you see the beauty in potential."

Matthew closed his eyes. When he opened them again, they were fixed on her; she could see every detail in his irises, the bits of gold mixed among the green.

"Do you think of Paris, as I do?" His voice was a little rough. "Even now, when I open my eyes in the morning, I briefly imagine a whole day lies ahead of adventures in Paris with you. There is so much we did not get a chance to do. And after Paris, we could have gone to Venice. It is a palace of water and shadow. There are masked balls—"

She laid her hands against his chest. She could feel his sharp intake of breath. And, this close to him, she could smell his cologne, clean as ocean water, unmixed for once with brandy or wine. "We cannot always be traveling, Matthew," she said. "We cannot always be running away."

In answer, he kissed her. And for a moment she let herself be lost in the kiss, in the tender gentleness of it. There was nothing of the fire that there had been the first time, born out of desperation and yearning and incoherent need. There was *Matthew* in the kiss, who she loved: his bright cutting mind, his vulnerability, his beauty and fragility. There was love, but not passion.

Raziel, let her not hurt him. Not badly. She stood with her hands against his chest, feeling the beat of his heart, his lips brushing hers with the softest pressure, until he drew away, looking at her with confusion in his eyes.

So he had felt it too, the difference.

"Cordelia? Is something wrong?"

"Matthew," she said. "Oh, my dear Matthew. We must *stop*."

He went rigid under her hands, his graceful body suddenly stiff as wood. "Stop what? Stop traveling? I understand," he added, more calmly. "I did not mean we abandon the fight here in London. We must stay, defend our friends and our city, separate you from Lilith—"

"And then what? What if it were all dealt with? Then what happens?"

In a halting voice, he said, "I know I seem—awful now. But Christopher says I will be well in a fortnight. This will be behind me, I can move forward—"

"Stopping the physical craving isn't enough," said Cordelia. "You will still want to drink."

He flinched. "No. I hate it. I hate what it makes me. *You* know," he added, "the reason I started in the first place. You can help me, Daisy. You can go with me to tell my parents what I did. I know it won't fix everything, but it is the wound at the heart of all that has happened since."

He was almost breathless; she could feel his heart racing. After a moment, almost impatiently, he said, "What's wrong? Please, say something."

There was a brittleness to the question that terrified Cordelia. She had to comfort him, she thought. She had to let him know she would never abandon him. "I will go with you to speak to your parents, Matthew," she said. "Whatever happens, I will be there every time you feel guilty, to remind you that you are a good person who is worthy of forgiveness and love."

"Then—" His eyes searched her face. "If you will always be with me—"

"When I married James, it was only supposed to be for a year. It was all I thought I could have," Cordelia said. "Everyone thought I was being selfless, but I was not. I told myself if I could just have a year with James, just a year, it would be something I could hold on to for the rest of my life, and treasure, that time with the boy I had loved since I was fourteen years old—"

"*Daisy*." She could see the words had hurt him, wished she had not had to say them. But he had to see, to understand. "You should never—you are worth more than that. Deserve more than that."

"And so do you," Cordelia said in a whisper. "Matthew, what I feel for James hasn't changed. It has nothing to do with you. You ought to be adored above all things, for you are wonderful. You ought to have someone's whole heart. But I do not have a whole heart to give you."

"Because you still love James," Matthew said flatly.

"I always have loved him," Cordelia said, with the ghost of a smile. "I always will. It is not a choice; it is part of me, like my heart or my soul or . . . or Cortana."

"I can wait for you to change your mind." Matthew sounded as if he were drowning.

"No," Cordelia said, and felt as if she were breaking something, some fragile, delicate thing made of ice or glass. "I cannot and never will love you in the way you wish to be loved, Math. The way you *deserve* to be loved. I do not know what I will do about James. I have no plan, have made no decision. But I do know this. I know I must not"—and there were tears in her eyes—"let there be false hope between us."

Matthew raised his chin. There was a terrible look in his eyes, the sort of look her father had when he had lost a great deal at the gambling table. "Am I so hard to love?"

"*No*," Cordelia said, in despair. "You are so easy to love. So easy that it has caused all this trouble."

"But you don't love me." There was real bitterness in his voice now. "I understand, you've made it clear enough; I'm a drunk and always will be—"

"That is *not* true, and not what this is about," Cordelia said. "My decision has nothing to do with your drinking, nothing at all—"

But he was already backing away from her, shaking his blond head.

Scattering green-gold leaves. "This is unbearable," he said. "I can stand it no longer."

And with a few strides, he was gone through the door, leaving Cordelia alone, her heart hammering in her chest as if she had just run a hundred miles.

Thomas had expected that the moment they arrived at the party, Alastair would peel away to join his usual cohort: Piers Wentworth, Augustus Pounceby, and the other boys who had graduated with him from Shadowhunter Academy.

To his surprise, Alastair stayed by his side. He did not devote his entire attention to Thomas—they stopped repeatedly to greet everyone from James to Eugenia, who looked from Thomas to Alastair and grinned maniacally, to Esme Hardcastle, who had a long list of questions for Alastair about his Persian relatives. "My family tree must be *thorough*," she said. "Now, is it true that your mother was married to a French Shadowhunter?"

"No," Alastair said. "My father was her first and only husband."

"So she didn't poison the Frenchman for his money?"

Alastair glowered.

"Did she murder him for a *different* reason?" Esme inquired, pen hovering.

"He asked too many questions," said Alastair darkly, after which he was dragged away by Thomas, who, to his own surprise, was able to convince Alastair to join in playing with his cousin Alex. Alex had always enjoyed being put on top of Thomas's shoulders, as it afforded an excellent view. It turned out he also liked it when Alastair picked him up and tickled him. When Thomas raised his eyebrows, Alastair said, "I might as well practice, oughtn't I? I'll have my own baby brother or sister soon." Alastair's dark eyes sparked. "Look at that," he said, and Thomas turned to see that Anna and Ari were waltzing on the dance floor, arms around each other, seemingly oblivious to the world. A few of the Enclave were staring—the Baybrooks, the Pouncebys, Ida Rosewain, the Inquisitor himself, glaring from the sidelines—but most were simply going about their business. Even Ari's mother was looking over at them wistfully, with no anger or judgment on her face.

"See," Thomas said, in a low voice. "The sky has not fallen."

Alastair set Alex down, and Alex toddled on chubby legs to his mother, pulling at her blue skirts. Alastair indicated that Thomas should come with him, and Thomas, wondering if he had annoyed Alastair and if so, how much, followed him behind a decorative urn that was exploding yew branches covered in red berries. From behind it, Thomas could catch only glimpses of the ballroom.

"Well, all right," Thomas said, squaring his shoulders. "If you're angry at me, say so."

Alastair blinked. "Why would I be angry at you?"

"Perhaps you're annoyed that I made you come to the party. Perhaps you'd rather be with Charles—"

"Charles is here?" Alastair looked honestly surprised.

"He's been ignoring you," Thomas noted. "Very rude of him."

"I hadn't noticed. I don't care about Charles," said Alastair, and Thomas was surprised at how startlingly relieved he felt. "And I don't know why you want him to speak to me either. Perhaps you need to figure out what you *do* want."

"Alastair, you are the last person—"

"Do you realize we're under the mistletoe?" Alastair said, his dark eyes sparking with mischief. Thomas glanced up. It was true; someone had hung a bunch of the waxy white berries from a hook in the wall overhead.

Thomas took a step forward. Alastair instinctively retreated a step, his back against the wall. "Would you like me to do something about it?" Thomas said.

The air between them suddenly seemed as heavy as the air outside, weighted with the promise of a storm. Alastair laid a hand on Thomas's chest. His long lashes swept down to hide his eyes, his expression, but his hand slid down, over Thomas's flat belly, his thumb rubbing small circles, setting every one of Thomas's nerves alight. "Right here?" he said, hooking his fingers into Thomas's waistband. "Right now?"

"I'd kiss you right here," Thomas said in a harsh whisper. "I'd kiss you in front of the Enclave. I am not ashamed of anything I feel about you. You are the one, I think, who doesn't want it."

Alastair tipped his face up, and Thomas could see what his lashes had been hiding: the slow-melting desire in his eyes. "I want it," he said.

And Thomas was about to lean forward, he was about to crush his lips to Alastair's, was about to suggest that much as he wanted to claim Alastair as his in front of the whole Enclave, they had to go somewhere, anywhere, where they could be alone, when a scream split the air. The scream of someone in anguished pain.

Alastair jerked bolt upright. Thomas reeled back, his heart slamming in his chest. He knew that scream. It was his aunt Cecily.

James paused halfway down the corridor, his heart pounding. He had not meant to follow Cordelia and Matthew to the games room; he'd gone there to retrieve a cheroot Anna had good-naturedly demanded, but as he'd approached the door, he'd heard their voices. Matthew, low and intense; Cordelia, obviously distressed. The pain in her voice kept him nailed in place, even as he knew he should back away. He had *started* to back away, when he heard Cordelia say, "I cannot and never will love you in the way you wish to be loved, Math. The way you *deserve* to be loved. I do not know what I will do about James. I have no plan, have made no decision. But I do know this. I know I must not let there be false hope between us."

He would have thought he would be relieved. But it had felt like a thorn driven into his heart: he felt Matthew's pain, nearly choked on it. He walked away then, not staying to hear what Matthew said. He could not bear to.

He found himself walking mechanically back into the ballroom. He could barely even perceive the other partygoers, and when his father tried to get his attention, he pretended he didn't notice. He slipped into one of the alcoves and stared across at the Christmas tree. He could barely breathe. *I do not know what I will do about James,* she had said. Perhaps they would both lose her, he and Matthew. Perhaps it would be better that way; they could share their pain, repair each other. But a small and treacherous pulse beat inside his chest, repeating over and over that she had not said she was done with him, only that she did not know what she would do. It was enough for hope, a hope that warred with guilt, and a darker feeling that seemed to tighten like a band around his chest, cutting off his breath.

The party whirled on in front of him, a torrent of color and sound, and yet through it, he seemed to see a spill of shadows. Something dark, rising like smoke: a threat he could taste on the air.

This was not sorrow or worry, he realized. This was danger.

And then he heard the scream.

Lucie knew she should have taken Jesse aside immediately to tell him what Malcolm had said to her, but she hadn't had the heart.

He appeared truly to be enjoying himself at this, the first social occasion he had ever attended as a living adult. The admiring glances shot his way nonplussed him, but Lucie glowed with happiness for him. She was proud of the way he held himself, and the real interest he showed in people, and she couldn't bear to ruin it.

She'd once read in an etiquette book that when one introduced two people, one should add a small detail about one of them that might spark a conversation. So she told Ida Rosewain, "This is Jeremy Blackthorn. He collects antique cow-creamers," while she informed Piers that Jeremy was an amateur astronomer, and told the Townsends that he had spent fourteen days living in the basket of a hot-air balloon. Jesse quite calmly went along with all the fibs, and even embroidered on them: Lucie had nearly choked when he'd told the Townsends that all his meals in the balloon had been brought to him by trained seagulls.

Eventually, as guests ceased arriving and more people joined the dancing, Lucie squeezed Jesse's hand (she was wearing gloves, as was he; surely it did not count as *touching*) and said, "There's only a few people left you haven't met. Do you want to brave the Inquisitor and his wife? You'll have to meet them eventually."

He looked down at her. "Speaking of inquisitions," he said, with a slightly self-mocking turn to his mouth, "I note that you have been avoiding telling me what Malcolm said in the Sanctuary."

"You are too clever for your own good."

"If you'd rather tell me later, we could dance—"

She bit her lip. "No," she said quietly. "Come with me. We should talk."

She glanced around to see if anyone was watching—no one seemed to be—before leading him to the French doors that gave onto the long stone balcony outside the ballroom. She slipped through them, Jesse on her heels, and went to the railing.

The snow had not been cleared, and it chilled her feet through her slippers: it was not expected that anyone would come out here during the coldest time of the year. Beyond the railing was a London gripped by cold, a Thames sluggish with chill water, the constant smell of burning wood and coal. The rooflines of distant houses resembled an Alpine ridge, dusted with snow.

"Can't we just have one lovely night?" Lucie said, gazing out at the city from the chilly stone balustrade. "Can't I refuse to tell you what Malcolm said?"

"Lucie," Jesse said. He had joined her at the railing; the cold had already whipped color into his pale cheeks. She knew he liked it, liked the extremes of heat and cold, but he did not seem to be enjoying it now. "Whatever it is, you must tell me. I am not used to having a mortal heart, one that beats; it is out of practice. It cannot sustain this kind of panic."

"I did not mean to make you panic," Lucie murmured. "Only—Jesse—I cannot touch you. And you cannot touch me."

She quickly summarized what Malcolm had told her. When she was done, Jesse rested a hand on the cold stone of the railing and said, "For so long, as a ghost, you were the *only* one I could touch. And now I am alive, and you are the only one I cannot." He looked up at the stars in the clear sky above them. "It hardly seems worth the return."

"Don't say that," Lucie breathed. "There is so much to being alive, and you are wonderful at it, and Malcolm *will* find a solution. Or we will. We have found solutions to worse problems."

He almost smiled. "Wonderful at being alive? That *is* a compliment." He raised a hand as if to touch her cheek—then drew it back, eyes darkening. "I don't like to think that raising me made you more vulnerable to Belial."

"I raised you," Lucie said. "I did not ask you. I commanded you. The responsibility lies with me."

But she could tell that had not comforted him; his gaze had turned inward, dark. The gaze of the boy who withdrew easily into himself,

because for so long he had not been seen, not been heard. "Jesse," she said. "The shadow of Belial has always hung over myself and my brother. You did not bring that upon us. It has become clearer and clearer over the past year that it was always his plan to turn his attention to us—that whatever his goal is, his blood descendants are a part of it."

"So what you are saying is that the only thing to be done is to end Belial. Even though they say he can't be killed."

"But they also say that Cortana can kill him." She thought, with a piercing loneliness, of Cordelia. "We have to believe it is true."

He looked down at her. He looked like Christmas and winter: dark green eyes, snow-white skin, hair as black as coal. "Then what do we do?"

"We think about it tomorrow," Lucie said softly, "but not tonight. Tonight is a Christmas party, and you are alive, and I am going to dance with you in the only way we can." She held out her hands. "Here. Let me show you."

She stepped in closer to him. Close enough that she could feel the warmth of him, though they were not touching; she raised her hand, and he raised his so that they stood with their palms facing each other, separated by an inch of cold winter air. He curved his other arm around her waist, careful not to make contact, not to even brush her skin.

She turned her face up to his. She could have raised herself up on her toes and kissed his mouth. Instead she caught his gaze with her own. Their eyes held each other's, as their bodies could not, and together they began to dance. There on the balcony, under the stars, with the rooftops of London the only witnesses. And though Lucie could not touch him, Jesse's presence warmed her, surrounded her, calmed her. She felt a pressure in her throat: Why had no one ever told her how close happiness was to tears?

And then there was a crash, a sound like a chandelier falling to burst apart in fragments upon the floor. And from inside the ballroom, a scream.

Cordelia's hands were wet with tears.

She had lingered in the games room as long as she could after

Matthew left. She had been aware she was crying—making hardly any noise at all, but the hot tears kept coming, spilling down her cheeks, spotting the silk of her dress.

Hurting Matthew had been one of the hardest things she had ever done. She wished she had been able to make him understand that she did not regret their time in Paris, that much of what had happened was good, even wonderful. That Matthew had taught her that there was life for her even if she were not a Shadowhunter. That even in the darkest moments, humor and light could shine through.

Part of her wanted to run after him and take it all back, but then they would only be exactly where they were before. She had told him the truth. She had been honest when she'd said she didn't know what she would do about James.

But the necklace. The necklace had changed things. She touched it now, with damp fingers. Realized there were no longer hot drops of salt water splashing onto her collarbone. There was only so long she could hide in here; Anna and Ari would come looking for her, as would Alastair. With a quick glance in the mirror over the fireplace, she tucked her hair into place and returned to the ballroom.

She scanned the room quickly—if she had been worried that anyone would have noticed her disappearance with Matthew, it seemed not—before realizing who she was looking for. Lucie. Who she did not see anywhere, or Jesse, but even if Lucie *had* been there, Cordelia could not simply have gone to her for comfort. Things were too complicated for that.

The party was a torrent of color and brightness and warmth, and then the sound of breaking glass tore through it all.

She remembered the loud crash at her wedding when her father had crumpled drunkenly to the floor, knocking over plates and dishes as he fell, and thought, *Someone has broken something.*

And then came the scream. An awful, heartrending scream. A flash of movements. The crash of instruments as the musicians fled their small stage; the twang of a violin string breaking. A scramble as Shadowhunters retreated from the dance floor, some reaching for weapons, though most would have come unarmed.

The blade of a sharp, familiar voice, cutting through the noise and motion like a knife.

"STOP," Tatiana Blackthorn cried. She stood atop the stage, wearing a faded, bloodstained dress, her hair wild, a bundle cradled against her chest. Her voice carried as if supernaturally amplified. "You will stop this instant—stop moving, stop speaking, and drop every weapon—or the child dies."

By the Angel. The bundle was a child. The scream had been Cecily Lightwood's. Gripped in Tatiana's arms was tiny Alexander Lightwood, his blue velvet suit crumpled, a sharp silver blade at his throat.

Utter silence descended. Cecily shuddered silently in Gabriel Lightwood's arms, her hand clamped over her mouth, her body shaking violently with the effort not to scream. Anna stood white-faced on the dance floor, Ari's hand on her arm, holding her back.

James, Thomas, Alastair. The Lightwoods, the Fairchilds, the Herondales. The Inquisitor and his wife. All stood staring, helpless as Cordelia was helpless. She still could not see Lucie or Jesse anywhere. *Good,* she thought. Better that Tatiana not lay eyes on Jesse.

Everyone was silent. The only sound in the room was Alexander's crying, until—

"Tatiana!" cried Will, in a ringing voice. "Please! We will listen to whatever you have to say, only put down the child!"

Cordelia's mind raced. Hadn't Tatiana been found, bleeding and injured, in Cornwall only a few days ago? Hadn't the Silent Brothers said she was too weak to risk moving her? And yet here she was, not just healed but looking as though she had never been hurt at all; there wasn't so much as a scratch on her face. And the bloody dress, while torn, was her old costume; it was what she preferred to wear.

"None of you have ever listened!" Tatiana shouted, and Alexander began sobbing. "Only by taking something of yours can I even get your attention!"

"Tatiana," said Gideon, loudly but calmly. "We are your brothers. Your friends. We will listen to you now. Whatever it is you need, we can help—"

"Help?" Tatiana shouted. "None of you have ever helped. None of you *would* ever help me. Here gathered together are Lightwoods, Herondales, Carstairs, none of whom have lifted a hand to help me in my direst times of trouble—"

"That's not true!" came a voice, and Cordelia turned in surprise to see that it was James, his golden eyes flashing like fire. "You think we haven't read your notes? That we don't know how often help was offered to you? How often you scorned it?"

"It was always *poison*," she hissed. "When my son died, I hoped that in recognition of the loss I had sustained, the terrible tragedy of his loss, my fellow Shadowhunters might support me. Might *help*. But if it had been up to you all, his body would have been burned in days! Before anything could be done!"

The answer to this—that death did not give back what it had taken—was so obvious that nobody even bothered to speak it.

"I sought help in the places you forbid to me," Tatiana said. "Yes. You cast me out to look among demons for help." She swept her gaze across the whole Enclave assembled before her. "Eventually the Prince Belial heard my pleas, and when I begged for my son's life back, he promised it to me. But still the Nephilim resented that I might have anything—*anything* but failure in this life. And when you discovered my poor attempts to help my son, you threw me in the Adamant Citadel, to make the very weapons by which you keep me held down.

"And all this time!" Tatiana shot out a finger, pointing it directly at . . . Tessa. All eyes turned to regard her; she stood unmoving, meeting Tatiana glare for glare. "All this time these Herondales have been the allies of Belial. All along, since long before I ever knew him. *Tessa Gray is his daughter*," she cried, her voice rising to a triumphant climax, "and while I am punished for merely *talking* to him, the Herondales prosper!"

There was a terrible silence. Even Alexander had stopped crying; he was only making breathless choking noises that were somehow worse than sobs.

Someone—Eunice Pounceby, Tessa thought—said in a quiet voice, "Mrs. Herondale, is this true?"

Will looked over with exasperation. "Are you truly asking? No, of course the Herondales have never been *allied* with any demon, the whole notion is—"

"Is it true," interrupted the Inquisitor, in a voice that reminded everyone present that he *was* the Inquisitor, "that Tessa is the daughter of the Prince of Hell Belial?"

Will and Tessa looked at each other; neither spoke. Cordelia felt sick. Their silence was as damning as any confession could be, and here it was, witnessed by the whole Enclave.

To Cordelia's relief, Charlotte stepped forward. "It has never been a secret," she said, "that Tessa Gray is a warlock, and any warlock must have a demon parent. But neither has it been a secret, or a question, that she is equally a Shadowhunter. Those issues were debated, and resolved, *years* ago, when Tessa first came to us. We are not about to reconsider them again now just because a madwoman demands it!"

"The spawn of a Prince of Hell," jeered Tatiana, "running the London Institute! The fox in the house of the chicks! The viper in the bosom of the Clave!"

Tessa turned away, her hands over her face.

"This is ridiculous." Gideon spoke up. "Tessa is a *warlock*. She is no more *allied* with her demon parent than any other warlock. Most warlocks never know, and do not want to know, what demon is responsible for their birth. Those who do know *despise* that demon."

Tatiana laughed. "Fools. The Angel Raziel would turn his face in shame."

"He would turn his face in shame," snapped James, "if he saw *you*. Look at you. A knife to the throat of a baby, and you dare to throw accusations at *my* mother—my mother, who has only ever been good and kind to everyone she has ever known?" He whirled on the assembled Shadowhunters. "How many of you has she helped? Lent you money, brought medicine when you were sick, listened to your troubles? And you doubt her now?"

"But," said Eunice Pounceby, her eyes troubled, "if she's known all these years that her father was a Prince of Hell, and not said it—then she's lied to us."

"She hasn't known all these years!" It was Lucie. Cordelia felt a wave of relief at the sight of her. Lucie was alone—Jesse was nowhere in sight. "She only just found out! She didn't know what to say—"

"More lies from those who have deceived you!" Tatiana retorted. "Ask yourself this! If the Herondales are so innocent, why would they have kept this lineage a secret from all of you? From the whole Clave? If they truly had no relationship with Belial, why would they have feared to speak of him? Only to hide behind closed doors, chortling with Belial and taking orders from him. And the Lightwoods and the Fairchilds are no better," Tatiana went on, apparently relishing her captive audience. "Of course they've known the truth all this time. How could they not? And they have hidden the secret, protected the Herondales—lest they be tainted and their careers and influence harmed by the knowledge of the infernal spawn they have put in charge of all of you. The warlock shape-shifter and her children—who have their own powers, you know! Oh yes! The children too have inherited dark powers from their grandfather. And they roam free, while my own daughter rots in the Silent City, imprisoned though she has done nothing wrong—"

"Nothing wrong?" It was James, to Cordelia's surprise; there were scarlet spots burning on his cheeks, a deadly intensity to his voice. "Nothing wrong? You know better than that, you monstrous, vicious—"

Tatiana screamed. It was a wordless noise, a long terrible howl, as if perhaps some part of her realized that the person speaking to her had more reason than anyone else alive to know what she truly was. She screamed—

And Piers Wentworth rushed toward Tatiana. *"No!"* Will shouted, but it was too late, Piers was blustering forward, flinging himself up onto the stage; he reached for Tatiana, whose mouth was open like a terrible black hole, his fingers were inches from Alexander—

Cordelia felt a rush of something cold go through the room. Behind Tatiana, the ballroom windows swung open, dangling on their hinges; Piers fell to his knees, shouting in rage, his hands closing on empty air.

Tatiana had vanished, and Alexander with her.

Lucie saw it as if it were happening in slow motion: that idiot Wentworth lunging at Tatiana. The explosion of glass as a window blew outward. The terrible sound made by Cecily as Tatiana vanished with Alexander. Anna pushing through the crowd, racing to her mother. The motionless Enclave jerking into movement again.

And Jesse—Jesse had come in from the balcony, where Lucie had pleaded with him, cajoled and demanded that he stay out of the ballroom. If Tatiana caught sight of him, she'd said, she might do anything; she might harm Alexander. Reluctantly, he'd agreed to remain outside, but he had clearly seen everything that had happened. He was nightmare-pale, his hand cold where it encircled Lucie's.

"I thought she was in Cornwall," he said. "She was meant to be imprisoned. She was meant to be kept away."

"It wasn't her," Lucie whispered. She did not know why she felt it so strongly, only that she did. "It was never her in Cornwall. It was a distraction. She knew about the party. She planned this. She and Belial planned this."

"To kidnap your cousin?" Jesse asked.

"To tell everyone," Lucie said. She felt numb. It had finally happened: everyone in the Enclave knew the truth about her family. About Belial. "About us."

She had half expected that the moment Tatiana vanished, the Enclave would turn on her and her family. But Tatiana had made a tactical error: in taking Alexander with her, she had delayed even the Inquisitor's interest in anything other than tracking her down and getting the child away from her. It was as if a silent agreement had been reached between them all: the issue of Belial would have to wait. Rescuing Alexander came first.

The adults began to move in a sort of wave. They descended on the weapons tree and began to pull it apart, everyone seizing up a blade—Eugenia claimed a three-pointed *fuscina*, while Piers took a longsword, Sophie seized a crossbow, and Charles a brutal-looking war hammer. They began to pour out of the ballroom, through the doors, some even through the broken window, into the streets outside, spreading out to search for Tatiana.

Before James and Lucie could even start toward the weapons tree, Will stepped in front of them. He held a curved blade in one hand. "Go upstairs," he said. He was pale, his jaw set. "Both of you. Take your friends and go upstairs."

"But we want to help," Lucie said. "We want to go with you—and Anna is old enough, and Thomas—"

Will shook his head. "They may be old enough," he said. "But Cecily has just had one of her children kidnapped. She cannot also be panicking over her daughter. Anna should stay with you. Thomas, as well." He looked around. "Where is Christopher?"

"He doesn't like parties. He told Anna not to expect him because he 'had science to do'; I imagine he's in Henry's lab," said Lucie. "But, Father, please—"

It was clear there was no begging, no wheedling, that would change his mind. "No," he said. "I have too much to think about already, Lucie. Your mother's with Cecily, trying to hold her together. I know you want to help. I would want to do the same, in your place. But I need you to stay here, stay safe, or you and your mother will be all I can think about. Not Tatiana. Not getting Alexander back."

"How did she get here?" James said. "Tatiana. I thought she was in the Cornwall Sanctuary."

"We'll discuss that later," said Will. There were dark lines at the sides of his mouth. "Go upstairs. Stay there. Do you understand me?"

"We understand," James said calmly. "We'll take care of the situation."

And he did. Lucie saw why the Merry Thieves had always called him the leader of their group. With a calm that brooked no argument, he gathered them all—Alastair and Cordelia, Anna and Ari and Matthew, Thomas and Jesse—and even though each one of them objected, herded them out of the (now nearly empty) ballroom and up the stairs. They had reached the second floor when Anna began to protest.

"James," she said, her voice a harsh rasp. "I ought to be with my mother—"

"I understand," James said. "And if you choose to be there, you should be. But I thought you might want the chance to go after Alexander."

Anna sucked in a breath. "James? What do you mean?"

James took a left off the landing and began to lead them down the hall; Lucie could hear the others muttering in puzzlement, but she was beginning to have an inkling of where her brother was taking them. James said, "Jesse, tell them what you told me."

"I think I know where my mother will have taken the child," said Jesse.

"Alexander," Anna said, a savage edge to her voice. "His name is Alexander."

"Anna," said Ari gently. "Jesse is trying to help."

"Then why not tell everyone?" Thomas asked Jesse. He did not sound hostile, only puzzled. "Why not tell Will, let him spread the word that you know what your mother would have done?"

"Because nobody knows who Jesse really is," said Alastair as James paused in front of a large iron door. "They think he's *Jeremy* Blackthorn."

"Indeed," said Matthew. "If Will claims to have knowledge gained from Tatiana's son, it will blow up the whole enterprise."

"It's not only that," Jesse said quickly. "I would sacrifice my identity happily. But I could be wrong. It's a guess, a feeling, not a surety. I cannot send everyone in the Enclave off after a *belief* I have—what if they all descend on one location, but it's the wrong one? Then who would be looking for Alexander elsewhere?"

He's right, Lucie wanted to say, but that would be seen as mere partisanship. Everyone knew how she felt about Jesse.

It was Cordelia who spoke.

"Jesse is right," she said. "But James—you did swear to your father that we'd stay here, didn't you?"

James's face was set like iron. "I'll have to beg his forgiveness later," he said, and swung the doors open. Beyond it was the weapons room. It had only grown since Will had taken over the Institute, and now spread over two chambers of axes and longswords, hammers and quoits and shuriken that gleamed like stars, runed bows and arrows, whips and maces and polearms. There was armor: gear and chain mail, gauntlets and greaves. On the wide table in the center of the room, seraph blades were lined up like rows of icicles, ready to be named and used.

"Everyone who wants to come—and there is no shame in remaining here—arm yourselves," James said. "Your preferred weapon might not be available," he added, looking at Thomas, "but we have no time to gather those. Take something you think you'll be able to use, and whatever gear you need. Do it quickly. We have little time to lose."

"So you think that she would go to Bedford Square?" Anna said, as they set off through the darkened streets. James had brought them out of the Institute through a back way and looped around the narrow streets carefully so as to minimize the chance of running into an Enclave patrol. They could not afford to be immediately sent back. "To my parents' house?"

The note of fear in her voice made Ari's heart ache. Not that Anna would *show* her fear. She usually lounged like a purring cat, but she was stalking along the streets now like a tiger in the Odisha forests, elegant and deadly.

"Yes," said Jesse. He had armed himself with the Blackthorn sword. It was strapped to his back in a tooled leather sheath and made him look as if he had been a practicing Shadowhunter for years, rather than days. "I can't be absolutely certain, but it is my instinct, after years of knowing her, of listening to her."

"How can you not know—" Anna began, but Ari caught her hand and squeezed it.

"He is being honest, Anna," she said. "That is better than false hope."

But Anna did not squeeze back. Ari could not blame her; she could only imagine the terror that was in Anna now, the terror that she was only barely holding back. She wished she could take some of it into her own heart, that she could bear that fear for Anna, share it with her that the burden might be lessened, even a little bit.

"But why?" said Thomas. He shifted his shoulders; the gear jacket he wore was too small, but there had not been one in the weapons room to fit him. "Why Uncle Gabriel's house? Wouldn't she expect to be caught there?"

"Not before—" Jesse broke off, but Thomas could guess at what he had almost said. *Not before she kills Alexander.* "Not immediately," Jesse said. "I doubt anyone is going to look there first, other than us."

They were on High Holborn; it was quiet at this hour, though no street in London was ever entirely deserted, no matter how late it became. At night, the damp patches on the pavement froze, and their boots crunched on ice as they walked. Hansom cabs rolled by, spraying them with filthy gutter-ice; they tried to stay well back from the curbs, since they were invisible to drivers.

Jesse said, "My mother will want to inflict the most hurt possible. She'll want her revenge symbolic and visible."

"So she's going to bring Alexander to his own house?" Lucie said.

"Everything that happened to me when I was a child," said Jesse, "happened in my own house. That was where my mother gave me to Belial. Where the rune ceremony almost killed me. She spoke often to me of how she had been violated in her own home, my father and grandfather killed on the grounds of the house she grew up in. It will seem, to her, to have a certain awful kind of balance."

Thomas's grip on the *Zweihänder* he held had grown damp. He felt sick to his stomach. *I am so sorry,* he wanted to say. *I am sorry for anything my family, or any of our families, may have done to cause this.*

But he did not say it; nearly all of them there came from families that Tatiana believed had authored her misery, and while he could assume guilt on his own part, he could not assume it on theirs. He knew, logically, that James—walking ahead of them all, bareheaded, determined—could not be blamed for this, nor Anna, nor Matthew or Cordelia or—

"It is not your fault," said Alastair. He was walking beside Thomas; Thomas wondered how long he had been there. Alastair had not bothered to change into gear, though he wore gauntlets on his hands, and his favorite spears were secured inside his coat. "None of this is your fault. Benedict Lightwood brought down vileness upon his own family, and Tatiana could not accept either his culpability or her own."

"You sound very wise," Thomas said. For a moment, it was as if he and Alastair were alone on the street, surrounded by the icy sheen of London in winter, the cold itself a sort of protective circle around the two of them.

"Guilt is one of the most sickening feelings there is," Alastair said. "Most people will do anything to avoid feeling it. I know I—" He took a deep breath. "One can either refuse to accept it, push it away and blame others, or one can take responsibility. One can bear the unbearable weight."

He sounded exhausted.

"I have always wanted to bear it with you," said Thomas quietly.

"Yes," Alastair said. His eyes were bright with cold. "Raziel knows, perhaps that is the reason I have not become like Tatiana myself. You keep me human, Tom."

"Matthew," James said, softly. "Math. Come here."

They were nearing the Lightwoods' house, passing darkened mundane homes whose doors were brightened with wreaths of holly and yew. James could see Bedford Square up ahead; most of the houses had curtains pulled across the windows, and the small park in the center, its winter greenery surrounded by an iron fence, was dark and unlit.

Matthew had been walking on his own, silent. He had shucked off his brocade coat and put on a gear jacket and leather fighting gloves. A half-dozen *chalikars* were looped over his forearm like bracelets, gleaming in the icy moonlight.

Still. As they had all prepared in the weapons room, James had watched his *parabatai*. Had watched as he stumbled against the table, holding himself there by gripping its edge, breathing hard as if he were trying not to be sick or to faint.

And he had watched Matthew as they left the Institute. He had kept himself a little away from the group, even from Lucie and Thomas. James could not help but feel that this was because he did not want anyone to see that he was walking *too* carefully, every step deliberate to the point of exaggeration.

Matthew drew close to him. And James knew—knew from his own observations, and also simply from the feeling in his chest. It was as if a tiny barometer had been inserted there during their *parabatai* ceremony, one that measured Matthew's state of being.

"James," Matthew said, a little warily.

"You're drunk," James said. He said it without accusation or blame; Matthew started to protest, but James only shook his head. "I am not going to be angry at you, or blame you, Matthew."

"You could if you wanted," Matthew said bitterly. "You thought I'd have trouble with the party, and I waved it away."

James did not, could not, say what he was thinking. *I did not know what would happen with Cordelia. I know you were sober when you spoke to her. But if she had said to me what she said to you, and I had afterward found myself thrust into a party surrounded by alcoholic merriment, I doubt I could have held back either.*

"If I'd known I'd have to fight," Matthew said, "I would never—"

"I know. Math, it's not a question of being perfect. What you are trying to do is incredibly difficult. You may falter at times. But I do not believe a moment of weakness is failure. Not as long as you keep trying. In the meantime—let me help you."

Matthew exhaled a soft white cloud. "What do you mean?"

"We may be about to go into battle together," James said. He showed Matthew his right hand, in which he held his stele. "I am your *parabatai*; it is my duty to protect you, and yours to protect me. Now give me your hand. While we're walking—I don't want to stop and have the others staring."

Matthew made a choked noise and pulled the glove off his left hand. He thrust the hand at James, who slashed an *iratze* across Matthew's palm, followed by two Energy runes. He would not normally give Matthew, or anyone, more than one, but they would act as knives, cutting through any fog in Matthew's brain.

Matthew swore under his breath, but kept his hand steady. When James was done, he wrung it out as if it had been scalded by hot water. He was breathing hard. "I feel like I might be sick," he said.

"That's what city pavement is for," said James unrepentantly, putting the stele back in his pocket. "And you're already steadier on your feet."

"I really do not know why people say you are the nicer one of the two of us," said Matthew. "It is clearly untrue."

Under other circumstances, James would have smiled. He almost smiled now, despite everything, at hearing Matthew sound like himself. "No one says that. What they say is that I am the handsomer one."

"That," said Matthew, "is also clearly untrue."

"And the better dancer."

"James, this terrible habit of lying seems to have come on you suddenly. I am concerned, very concerned—"

Behind them, Anna called out. James whirled to see her standing with her hand at her chest; her Lightwood pendant was pulsing in flashes of bright red, like intermittent fire.

It could mean only one thing. *Demons.*

21
Under a Dragon Moon

Do you remember when we went
Under a dragon moon,
And 'mid volcanic tints of night
Walked where they fought the unknown fight
And saw black trees on the battle-height,
Black thorn on Ethandune?
—G. K. Chesterton, *Ballad of the White Horse*

Mantid demons, Cordelia saw, seven or eight of them, chittering as they sprang over the metal fence surrounding the square's central garden. They kept their jagged forelegs folded against their chests, though Cordelia knew they could whip out with shocking speed, slashing anything in their path like straight razors. Their heads were triangular, with long mandibles clicking to either side, their eyes blank, ovoid and white.

James slid his pistol from his belt. Cocked and aimed it. "Cordelia, Jesse, Anna," he said in a low, calm voice. "Get to the house. We'll deal with these."

Cordelia hesitated. Part of her suspected James was just trying to get her out of the way of the fight. She'd been the only person in the weapons room at the Institute not to pick up equipment. She knew she couldn't risk it, couldn't risk summoning Lilith, however much she hated to duck away from a fight.

And Jesse, of course, for all that he was armed, wasn't trained. He didn't seem bothered, though. He glanced once at Lucie, already swinging her axe, before he turned and ran silently alongside Cordelia and Anna toward the Lightwoods' house.

At first it seemed that all the windows were dark, but a faint glow showed around one side of the house, like a spark of reflected moonlight. Anna tensed, and gestured for Jesse and Cordelia to follow her quietly.

As they slipped around the house, keeping to the shadow of the wall, Cordelia could hear the noises of fighting from the square. Metal scraping stone, grunts and hisses, the thick sound of a blade colliding with demon flesh, all of it punctuated every few minutes by the sharp report of a gun.

They turned a corner. They were behind the house now, almost up against the fence that divided the Lightwoods' property from the one next door. An arched window here was lit with a soft radiance; in its glow, Cordelia could see the harsh fury on Anna's face. Her parents' home, the place she had grown up, had been invaded.

The three Shadowhunters gathered at the edge of the window and peered inside. There was Gabriel and Cecily's sitting room, as it always was, with blankets folded in a basket near the comfortable-looking couch, and a Tiffany lamp casting a warm glow over the room.

Before the cold fireplace, Tatiana sat in an armchair, Alexander cradled in her arms. Her lips were moving. Cordelia's stomach turned. Was she *singing* to him?

Alexander was struggling, but feebly; Tatiana's grip on him seemed to be iron-hard. With one hand, she pulled up the jacket of his little suit, and then his shirt, while with the other—with the other, gripping a stele, she *began to draw a rune on his bare chest.*

Cordelia stifled a moan of horror. You simply couldn't put runes on a three-year-old; it would be traumatic, painful, very likely dangerous to the child's survival. It was an act of brutal cruelty: pain for the sake of its own infliction.

Alexander screamed. He twisted and thrashed in Tatiana's grasp, but Tatiana held him down, her stele slicing like a scalpel across his skin, and Cordelia, without thinking, formed her gloved hand into a fist and punched the window with every bit of her strength.

Her hand slammed into the glass, which cracked and spiderwebbed, a few shards splintering outward. Pain shot up her arm, and Jesse caught hold of her, yanking her aside as Anna, her face like stone, bashed the rest of the window out with her elbow. Cracked as it was, it fell apart in enormous shards; Anna swung herself up onto the sill and dove through the jagged hole.

Jesse followed, turning to pull Cordelia up after him. He caught at her hands, lifting her, and she bit her lip to keep from screaming out in pain. Her glove had not been designed to withstand being driven through a pane of glass; it had torn wide open across her knuckles, and her lacerated hand was bleeding freely.

She landed on a worn Persian carpet. In front of her was Anna, swinging a long blade. She struck Tatiana in the shoulder, and Tatiana cried out, flinging the screaming Alexander away from her.

Anna dropped her sword, diving to catch her little brother. Tatiana bared her teeth, turned, and fled through the nearest open door.

Anna, on her knees, cradled the sobbing Alexander against her chest, frantically stroking his hair. "Baby, baby boy," she soothed, before turning a wild look on Jesse and Cordelia. "Go after Tatiana! *Stop her!*"

Cordelia raced through the house with Jesse. It was nearly too dark to see; she fumbled a witchlight from her coat pocket, letting its white glow illuminate the space. Jesse followed her in a mad dash down hallways, past an empty kitchen, and into a library. He stopped to peer into the shadows while Cordelia raced through the next doorway and into a dimly lit music room—where she found Tatiana sitting blank-faced on the bench in front of the piano.

Tatiana was bleeding from the wound Anna had given her. Scarlet drenched the shoulder of her already bloodstained dress. She did not seem bothered by it. She held her pointed silver dagger in her hand and was humming quietly to herself, a soft and eerie tune.

Cordelia sensed Jesse at her side. He had come into the room after her, moving soundlessly, and was staring at his mother in the glare of Cordelia's witchlight.

Tatiana raised her head. She glanced at Cordelia before turning her attention to Jesse.

"So she raised you," said Tatiana. "That little Herondale bitch. I thought she might try. I never thought you'd allow it."

Jesse went rigid. Cordelia bit her tongue before she could say, *She did it with Grace's help*. That would make the situation better for no one.

"I thought it was what you wanted, Mother," Jesse said. Cordelia sensed he was controlling his voice with an effort. Stalling for time until the others could arrive and surround Tatiana. "Me, alive again."

"Not if it means you are in the thrall of these wretched people," Tatiana snarled. "The Herondales, the Carstairs—you know better than anyone how badly they have treated us. How they betrayed me. Don't you know it, my sweet and clever son?"

Her voice had gone sickly sweet; Jesse looked nauseated as she turned her malevolent gaze on Cordelia. *If you move toward me, you witch, I will attack you with a broken piano leg and manage whatever Lilith does to me for it*, Cordelia thought.

There was a soft *hiss*. Jesse had drawn his sword—the Blackthorn sword. The thorns on the cross guard gleamed in the witchlight.

Tatiana smiled. Was she *pleased* to see her son holding the family blade? After all she had just said?

"You are sick, Mother," said Jesse. "You are sick in your mind. All your beliefs that you are being persecuted, that these people, these families, are trying to harm you, are the refuges you have found in which you can bury your grief over my father's death. Over your own father—"

"Those are *lies*," Tatiana hissed. "I am not sick! They have tried to ruin me!"

"Not true," said Jesse quietly. "I have come to know them now. There is a truth much harsher. One I think you know. They have not tried to ruin you over all these years. They have not plotted your downfall. *They have barely ever thought of you at all.*"

Tatiana flinched—a true, unguarded movement, and in that moment Cordelia saw something real in her expression, something unalloyed by delusion or falsehood. A profound bitter hurt, almost savage in its intensity.

She began to rise from the bench. Jesse tightened his grip on his blade. Then quick steps in the hall: the door flew wide, and James came in, longsword in hand.

He was bruised and bleeding, a bad cut over his left eye. He must have found the tableau before him bizarre, Cordelia thought—she and Jesse, unmoving, facing down Tatiana in her bloody dress. But he did not hesitate. He raised his blade and pointed it directly at Tatiana's chest.

"Enough," he said. "It's done. I've sent for Brother Zachariah. He'll be here any moment to complete your arrest."

Tatiana looked at him with an odd little smile. "James," she said. "James Herondale. So like your father. You are just the one I wanted to talk to. You still have a chance to earn your grandfather's support, you know."

"That," said James, "is the last thing I want."

"He has set his sights on his desires," she said, "and he will have them. They march, you know. Even now, they march." Her smile widened. "Your only choice will be whether to show your loyalty, or whether to be trampled beneath him, when the time comes." An ugly look of cunning passed over her face. "I think that you will be clever enough, when the choice is forced, to show your loyalty. Loyalty, after all, binds us."

James winced, and Cordelia recalled the engraving on the inside of the bracelet Grace had given him. *Loyalty binds me.* If Tatiana had hoped to endear herself to James by reminding him of it, it did not work. He took two breathless steps forward and set the tip of the sword to the base of her throat.

"Drop the weapon and put out your hands," he said, "or I'll slit your throat in front of your son and gladly pay the cost of my sins to Hell when the time has come."

Tatiana dropped the knife. Still smiling, she held out her arms to James, her palms turned up to show she held no weapon. "You are my master's blood," she said. "What choice have I? I will surrender, then, only to you."

As James bound her wrists with demon wire, Cordelia exchanged a puzzled look with Jesse. It was over, it seemed, and yet she could not shake the feeling that something was wrong. After all that, why had Tatiana not put up more of a fight?

* * *

Grace had worried that Christopher would leave after she'd told him she needed to confess to Cordelia. But he didn't—he remained, and seemed pleased when she handed over the notes she had taken regarding his experiments in sending messages through the application of runes and fire. She had watched him as he read, concerned that he would be offended—she was not a scientist, and having never been educated properly as a Shadowhunter, she knew only the most basic runes, while Christopher's knowledge of the Gray Book seemed comprehensive.

But, "This is interesting," he said, pointing to a note she had made about the application of a new kind of metal to steles. It turned out that what he found helpful was not intricate knowledge, but the willingness to sit with an idea, to turn it over in her mind and examine it from all angles. At some point she realized that it was not only Christopher's curiosity and imagination that made him a scientist: it was patience. The patience to keep pressing against a problem until it yielded, rather than giving in to the frustrations of failure.

And then, as Christopher was jotting down a summary of their most recent idea, a knock came at the barred door, and suddenly Brother Zachariah was there, his parchment robes flowing silently around him.

And he was speaking in both their heads, and the words were a jumble of nightmare images. The Christmas party, invaded. Grace's mother, bearing a sharp silver dagger, the blade to the throat of a little boy. The little boy who was Christopher's brother. Tatiana vanishing, taking Alexander with her, the whole of the Enclave in pursuit.

There was a crash as Christopher shot to his feet, sending his glass of champagne flying. Without stopping to gather up his notes, or even to look at Grace, he bolted from the room. Zachariah regarded Grace for a moment in silence, then followed Christopher, closing the door behind him.

Grace sat on the bed, her blood turning to ice. *Mother,* she thought. *I had made a friend. I had . . .*

But that was just it, wasn't it? Her mother would never allow Grace to feel anything, to *think* anything, to have anything that wasn't about her. Grace was sure Tatiana had no idea that she'd ever spoken to Christopher Lightwood—but even so, Tatiana had made certain that she never would again.

* * *

"It was too easy," Cordelia said in a low voice.

"I'm not sure I can agree with that," Alastair replied. They were sitting in the drawing room at the Institute. Alastair was industriously applying a second *iratze* to Cordelia's hand, though the first one had already caused Cordelia's cuts to scab over. He did not seem to have minded Cordelia getting blood all over his new jacket, and he held Cordelia's hand with gentle care. "Being attacked by Mantids, which are quite revolting up close, and barely getting there in time to stop Tatiana from putting a rune on the child that would have killed him—" He finished her *iratze* and held out Cordelia's hand to examine his work. "It wasn't *easy*."

"I know." Cordelia looked around the room—everyone was milling about, talking in low voices: Will and Tessa, Lucie and Jesse and Thomas, Matthew and James. Only Ari sat by herself in an armchair, looking down at her hands. Anna had run back to the Institute with Alexander, not waiting for Tatiana to be dealt with, and was in the infirmary with him and her parents. He was being looked after by Brother Shadrach, who had said that while the injury might heal slowly, the rune had not been completed: no lasting harm had been done.

Cordelia knew Will would have preferred to have Jem looking after his nephew, but James had summoned Jem to arrest Tatiana at the house on Bedford Square and escort her to the Silent City, and Jem was busy with that. Meanwhile, Bridget had put out rather mad sandwiches (mince pie and pickle, sugar icing and mustard) and a great deal of very hot, very sweet tea, which she seemed to feel was the cure for shock, but nobody was eating or drinking much.

"But how did she get out? I don't understand what happened," Thomas was saying. "Tatiana was found barely alive on Bodmin Moor. She was awaiting transport at the Cornwall Institute. In the Sanctuary. How did she get to London so quickly, and without any sign of being hurt?"

"It wasn't Tatiana," Tessa said. "I mean, in Cornwall. It was never her."

Will nodded wearily. "We heard from the Silent Brothers—too late, alas. It was all a trick." He drew a hand across his eyes. "The thing Pangborn found on the moors was an Eidolon demon. Brother Silas was sent to retrieve Tatiana, but when he arrived at the Cornwall Institute, all he found was a bloodbath. The demon slaughtered everyone in the place before it fled. A reward for its service to Belial, no doubt. It did not spare even the mundane servants. The body of a young girl was found on the front steps, horribly mutilated—she had crawled there, no doubt trying to summon help." His voice shook. "Awful stuff, and all simply to fool us into believing Tatiana was not at large."

Silently Tessa took Will's hand and held it in her own. Will Herondale was like his son, Cordelia thought; both felt things strongly, however they might try to hide it. When they had all returned to the Institute, bloody and scratched but with the news that Tatiana had surrendered, Will had rushed over to make sure Lucie and James were all right. Once he had reassured himself, he looked down at James and said in a flat, humorless voice, "You did good work, James, but you broke a promise to do it. This night's events may have worked out, but they very easily could have gone terribly wrong. You might have been hurt, or your sister, or you might bear the responsibility for someone else's death or wounding. *Don't* do something like this again."

"Forgive me," James had said, standing very straight, and Cordelia recalled him saying to her, *I'll have to beg his forgiveness later.* He could have protested, she had thought; he could have told Will that they could not in good conscience have failed to act on Jesse's convictions. But he said nothing. He was proud and stubborn, Cordelia thought, just as she herself was. And she thought of Lucie.

You—you're so proud, *Cordelia.*

It had not been a compliment.

Will had only touched James on the cheek, still frowning, and led them all upstairs to the drawing room. Cordelia glanced over at Lucie now, but she was in quiet conversation with Jesse and Thomas.

"But what about the wards?" Ari asked. "At the Cornwall Institute. I understand that they let the demon into the Sanctuary, but shouldn't the wards have prevented it, or sent up some kind of warning?"

"It seems Pangborn had let the wards around his Institute lapse." Will shook his head. "We all knew he was old, probably too old to have the job he did. We should have done something."

"It was a clever trick," said Matthew, who was leaning back in an armchair. He had used all his *chalikars* in the Mantid battle, and there were bruises on his neck and collarbones. "But if it had not been Pangborn's weakness, Belial would have found some other way to play it."

"It meant we let our guard down," said Tessa. "At least where Tatiana was concerned. The Institute is well warded against demons, but not against Shadowhunters."

"Even really evil Shadowhunters," added Lucie fiercely. "They should have stripped her Marks at the Adamant Citadel."

"I'm sure they will now," said James, "since the Mortal Sword will drag the truth out of her and reveal all her past crimes. Perhaps we'll finally discover something useful about Belial's plans as well. I am sure they do not end here."

"Speaking of Belial," Will said in a heavy voice, "the Inquisitor has called a meeting for tomorrow. To discuss the issue of our family."

"I do not see how our family is *any* of his business," James began hotly, but to Cordelia's surprise, Lucie cut in.

"He is going to make it his business, James," she said. "The Institute may be the only home we've ever known, but it doesn't belong to us. It belongs to the Clave. Everything we have and everything we are is subject to the Clave's approval. Think how many of the Enclave have always been awful to Mother just because she was a warlock—because she has a demon parent. Before they ever knew he was a Prince of Hell to boot." Her voice was tight, lacking any of Lucie's usual optimism; it hurt to hear. "We should have known that they would turn on us the moment they found out about Belial."

"Oh, Lucie, *no*." Cordelia bolted to her feet before she could stop herself. Lucie looked at her in surprise. In fact, Cordelia could feel every eye in the room on her. "The Inquisitor can fuss and fume all he wants," she said, "but the truth is on your side. The *truth* matters. And the Enclave will see it."

Lucie looked at Cordelia calmly. "Thank you," she said.

Cordelia's heart sank. It was the sort of *thank you* that you'd offer to someone you didn't know very well after they'd apologized for stepping on your foot at a party. But before she could reply—or even sit down in embarrassment; everyone seemed to be staring at them—the drawing room door flew open, and Christopher came in.

He looked as if he had run halfway across London. He was coatless, his boots and trousers splashed with icy mud, his bare hands red from the cold. His eyes, behind his glasses, were wide and stunned. Cordelia was reminded for a moment of someone else—and then realized it was Alexander, as Tatiana tormented him, his eyes full of a terrible confusion that anyone could wish to cause him pain.

"What happened?" he said, in a half whisper, and then Thomas, James, and Matthew were surging over to him, hugging him tightly, their voices overlapping as they explained that Alexander was fine, that Tatiana had been caught, that his little brother was being taken care of in the infirmary. That he would be all right.

"I just don't understand," Christopher said, the color coming back slowly to his face. He was clinging to Matthew's sleeve with one hand, his shoulder touching James's. "Why Alexander? Who would want to hurt a baby?"

"Tatiana wants to hurt *us*, Kit," Tessa said. "She knows the best way to do it is through our families. It's the worst pain she can think of to inflict. Any of us would gladly suffer in place of our children, but to have them suffer in our place is . . . horrifying."

"She has been brought to the prisons of the Bone City," said Will. His voice was cold. "So we will have ample opportunity to ask her."

Christopher's eyes widened. "They're holding her in the Silent City?" he said, sounding inexplicably unhappy with this development.

Jesse appeared disturbed as well. As if he had suddenly realized something, he said sharply, "They keep the prisoners apart from each other, right? They must. She must not get near Grace."

"They would never let that happen," Will began, and then Cecily appeared at the door and flew to hug Christopher. "Come upstairs, darling," she said. "Alexander is sleeping, but he might wake at any time, and he will want to see you." She turned to Ari with a warm smile. "And Anna asks that you come as well, my dear. We would love to have you with us."

Ari's face lit up. She rose to her feet and joined Christopher and Cecily as they left the room. Jesse watched them go, a grim look on his face. Thinking about Grace? Cordelia wondered. Or more likely, about Tatiana, and what would happen now.

"All my life my mother has told me how much she hates you, all of you," Jesse said. He was leaning against the wall, as if he required it to hold him up. "Now that she knows I have joined with you, fought beside you against her—she will see it as a betrayal even more profound."

"Does it matter?" said Matthew. "She is mad; if she does not have a reason to be full of hate, she will invent one."

"I am only thinking," Jesse said, "she knows who I am, that I am among you. Nothing will stop her from telling the Clave once she is questioned. Perhaps I could help you, if I told the Enclave first. If I confessed who I truly am—Jesse Blackthorn—I could testify to my mother's madness and lying, her hate for you, her need for revenge."

"No," James said, very gently. "That is a generous offer, considering what it would mean for you, but it would only further darken the Enclave's view of us, if they believed Lucie had engaged in necromancy." He held up a hand as Lucie began to protest. "I know, I know. It wasn't necromancy. But they will not see it that way. And there is every chance Tatiana will not immediately spill the truth about you, Jesse; it reveals too many inconvenient facts about her own crimes. About her relationship with Belial."

"Speaking of Belial," Will said. "It is kind of you to try to spare us, Jesse, but it is past time for us to face all this, rather than leaving it hanging like a sword over our heads. We have kept this secret too long—forgetting, I think, that secrets give others power over you."

Tessa nodded. "I wish we'd simply told everyone the moment we learned. Now we have to separate the truth from the fiction that we are in league with Belial." She snorted, which made Cordelia smile; it was a very unladylike gesture for Tessa. "'In league.' The notion is medieval and thoughtless. Is Magnus 'in league' with his demon parent? Is Ragnor Fell? Is Malcolm Fade? No, no, obviously no: that's been settled business for hundreds of years."

"At least it's only your word against Tatiana's," Cordelia said, "and I think most people know her word isn't worth very much."

"What will happen at the meeting tomorrow, do you think?" Alastair said.

Will spread his hands. "It's hard to say. This is exactly the kind of thing the Mortal Sword is for, and of course Tessa and I would hurry to Idris at any moment to testify to the truth. But it would be extreme even of Bridgestock to push the issue that far. I suppose it depends how much annoyance Bridgestock feels like causing us."

Matthew groaned. "He *loves* causing annoyance."

"Good gracious," said Tessa, glancing at the clock over the mantel. "It's one in the morning. We must all get some rest before tomorrow, which promises to be rather unpleasant." She sighed. "Cordelia, Alastair, I shall walk you downstairs to your carriage."

Alastair and Cordelia exchanged a glance. This was an odd offer. They could manage to find their way to the front door themselves, of course; or Will or James would be the usual ones to offer. Tessa, however, seemed firm in her resolve.

Alastair went to say something quick and quiet to Thomas. Wanting to give him a moment, Cordelia took her time putting away her ruined gloves and tying her scarf around her neck. As she dusted herself off, she felt a gentle touch on her shoulder.

It was James. The cut over his eye had mostly healed, though she thought he might have a scar through his eyebrow. It would look rather dashing, of course; that always seemed to be the way of things. "You're right," he said, in a low voice.

"Probably," Cordelia said. "But—about what, exactly?"

"It was too easy," James said. "Tatiana wanted to be caught. She snatched Alexander, ran a little distance away, and waited to be arrested. I could not for the life of me say *why*, however." He hesitated. "Daisy," he said. "The thing you said you had to do, earlier—did you do it?"

She hesitated. It felt a thousand years since she had stood in the games room with Matthew, a thousand lifetimes ago that they were all at a party together. It seemed as though she had been a different person entirely then, though only a few hours had passed.

"I did," she said. "It was awful."

James looked as if he very much wanted to ask something else. But then Tessa came up to them, and with her usual deftness had in moments drawn Cordelia away and was leading her, along with Alastair, downstairs.

The cold air outside was a shock after the warmth of the drawing room. The carriage was brought round quickly, and Alastair clambered in. He seemed to sense that Tessa wanted a moment to speak to his sister alone, and perhaps sensed as well that it might be awkward. He drew the curtains of the carriage closed, giving Cordelia and Tessa as much privacy as could be managed.

"Cordelia," Tessa said gently, "there is something I had to say to you."

Cordelia took a deep breath of icy air. She felt the loneliness she associated only with London: of being both one of millions together in the dark of the city, and of being utterly alone in that same dark.

Tessa said, "I know it is reasonable that you should be with your mother now. But I am not entirely oblivious. I know it is not *only* that. Things are not well between you and James. Or between you and Matthew, for that matter."

"Or between James and Matthew," Cordelia said. "I am so sorry. You trusted in me to make James happy, and I am doing exactly the opposite."

After a moment Tessa said, "I know people hurt one another. I know relationships are complicated. Believe me. But it's been my experience that—well, that when everyone loves one another enough, there will always be a way for things to come out all right in the end."

"That's a lovely thought," Cordelia said. "I hope you're right."

Tessa smiled. "I have been so far."

And with that, she ducked back into the Institute. Cordelia was just reaching for the handle of the carriage when she heard the sound of running feet behind her. Perhaps Tessa had forgotten to tell her something else, or Thomas—

But it was Lucie. Lucie, in her gear jacket and lavender dress, the ruffles on the hem flying around her like sea-foam. She hurtled down the steps and flung herself into Cordelia's arms, and Cordelia could feel that she was shaking as if with a terrible chill.

Cordelia's whole heart melted. She tightened her arms around Lucie, rocking her a little, as if she were a child.

"Thank you," Lucie whispered, her face buried in Cordelia's shoulder. "For what you said."

"It was nothing," Cordelia said. "I mean, it was true. It was a true nothing."

Lucie sniffled an almost-laugh. "Daisy," she said. "I'm so sorry. And I'm so awfully scared." Her breath hitched. "Not for me. For my family. For Jesse."

Cordelia kissed the top of Lucie's head. "I won't ever leave you," she said. "I will always be right beside you."

"But you said—"

"It doesn't matter what I said," Cordelia said firmly. *"I will be there."*

The door of the carriage cracked open, and Alastair glared out peevishly. "Really," he said. "How many meetings are you planning to have on these steps, Layla? Should I be preparing to spend the night in this carriage?"

"I think that would be very gracious of you," said Cordelia, and though it wasn't terribly funny, she and Lucie both laughed, and Alastair grumbled, and for just those few moments, everything felt as if it were going to be all right.

22
Deep Malice

Artificer of fraud; and was the first
That practiced falsehood under saintly show,
Deep malice to conceal, couched with revenge.
—John Milton, *Paradise Lost*

The last thing in the world Cordelia wanted to do the next morning was attend a meeting at the Institute in which awful accusations were launched at the Herondales.

Despite her more friendly parting with Lucie, she had barely slept through the night, awakened often by terrible dreams in which people she loved were threatened by demons, but she was unable to lift a blade to help them. Either the weapon would skitter away from her grasp, leaving her crawling after it on her hands and knees, or it would crumble to dust in her hand.

And each dream ended the same way—with Lucie, or James, or Matthew, or Alastair, or Sona, choking in their own blood on the ground, their eyes fixed on her, wide and accusing. She woke with the words of Filomena di Angelo ringing in her ears, each syllable a stab of pain in her heart.

You are the bearer of the blade Cortana, which can slay anything. You have spilled the blood of a Prince of Hell. You could have saved me.

"I can't go," she said to Alastair, when he came to her room to see why she had not yet come down to breakfast. Their mother, it seemed, had joined them—a rare occurrence these days—and, though she was not herself attending the meeting, was anxious that her children go—Cordelia to support her husband, of course, and both of them to repay all the kindness shown to them by the Herondales since they had arrived in London. "I can't bear it."

"Layla." He leaned against her doorway. "I agree it will be miserable. But you are not going for yourself; you are going for James and Lucie. They will bear it better if you are there." He flicked his eyes over her; she was wearing an old dressing gown that Risa had patched several times. "Put on one of the dresses you bought in Paris. Look magnificent and unassailable. Stare down your nose at anyone who insults the Herondales or offers support to the Inquisitor. You are James's wife—if you do not go, people will whisper that you doubt him and his family."

"They wouldn't *dare*," Cordelia gasped in fury.

Alastair grinned. "There you go. There is the blood of Rostam in your veins." He glanced over at her wardrobe, which was standing open. "Wear the brown silk," he said, and with that, brushed dust from his cuffs and headed downstairs.

The thought that her absence might be used as ammunition against the Herondales sent Cordelia shooting out of bed. She put on her coffee silk dress, with its gold embroidery, and wheedled Risa into putting up her hair with topaz pins. She dabbed a bit of rouge on her cheeks and lips, seized up the gloves James had returned to her, and walked downstairs with her head held high. If she could not bear a weapon, then this, at least, would do for armor.

Her despair was already beginning to turn into a far more bracing emotion—anger. In the carriage, on the way to the Institute, she fumed aloud (in between bites of an Eccles cake Alastair had thoughtfully smuggled from the breakfast table) that she could not believe *anyone* would truly credit the idea that the Herondales were in league with a Prince of Hell. It was an accusation wielded by Tatiana Blackthorn, of all people, and most of the Enclave had known Will and Tessa for decades.

Alastair was not impressed by this reasoning. "Your faith in the goodness of humanity is very admirable. But misplaced. Plenty of people resent the Herondales for their position. Charlotte was a controversial choice for Consul, and there's a widespread belief, even among those who like them, that the Herondales got the London Institute position because of her."

"You only know this because you have associated with low and resentful sorts of people like Augustus Pounceby," Cordelia pointed out.

"True," Alastair said, "but if not for my vile friends of yesteryear, I would not have the keen and penetrating insights into their thoughts that I do now. The point is, never underestimate people's desire to make trouble if they think they might get something out of it."

Cordelia sighed, brushing crumbs from her lap. "Well, I do hope you're wrong."

Alastair was not wrong. By twenty minutes into the meeting, with Bridgestock and Charlotte glaring at one another and the whole Enclave in an uproar, Cordelia had to admit that he might have downplayed things.

The meeting was held in the chapel, which already made Cordelia feel grim. Up on the altar stood Bridgestock, Charlotte, and Will. The Enclave filled the pews: Cordelia had scanned the room for her friends the moment they arrived, and cast as reassuring a glance as she could at Lucie and James, who sat in the front pew with Tessa and Jesse. Everyone else was there was well, even Anna, looking stern and furious between her father and Ari. (Cecily, it was to be presumed, was in the infirmary with Alexander.)

"The events in Cornwall have obviously disturbed me greatly," Bridgestock declaimed, "and in combination with the claims of Tatiana Blackthorn, I must say that the failure to protect us from Belial has greatly shaken my trust in the Herondales' leadership." He cast a dark glance at Will. "Now, I am not necessarily saying that you *are* in league with demons," said Bridgestock.

"What a compliment," said Will coldly.

"But," the Inquisitor went on smoothly, "Tatiana Blackthorn certainly told one truth—that Belial is Tessa's father. A truth that has been concealed from all of us, all these years. Well," he added with a sarcastic nod at Charlotte, "from *most* of us."

"This was all settled years ago," Charlotte said. "Tessa is a Shadowhunter in good standing, in addition to being a warlock. It is a situation unique to her, caused by a mundane with a specific ill intent, unlikely to ever be repeated. The identity of the demon who fathered her was not known to anyone, even to Tessa, until recently. And regardless, we do not believe warlocks to be in league with their demon parents."

"With all due respect," said Bridgestock, "most warlocks' demon parent is an anonymous, minor demon, not one of the Nine Princes. Most Shadowhunters have never faced a Prince of Hell. But *I have*," he thundered, which made Cordelia feel cross. He hadn't so much faced Belial, had he, as passed out in his presence. "I cannot tell you of the depth of his vile evil. To think he is the parent of Tessa Herondale makes me shudder."

"I remember these discussions," said Charlotte. "Twenty-five years ago. I was there. So were you, Maurice. The ravings of Tatiana Blackthorn, who is by her own admission an ally of Belial, should not disinter this debate from its long-ago burial."

After a moment of silence, Eunice Pounceby piped up, the flowers on her hat trembling with her agitation. "Perhaps they shouldn't, Charlotte. But . . . they do."

"What are you saying, Eunice?" Tessa asked. Though Cordelia knew her real age, Tessa still looked only about twenty. She was dressed plainly, her hands folded in front of her. Cordelia felt the sort of desperate pity for her she would have felt for a girl her own age, staring down the barrel of the Enclave's anger.

"What Eunice is saying," said Martin Wentworth, "is that while it may be true that we have all known Mrs. Herondale to be a warlock, for many years now, the fact that her demon parent is a *Prince of Hell*, and that you have all known and concealed it—well, it might be within the letter of the Law, but it does not inspire trust."

A murmur went through the crowd. Bridgestock said, "It seems the London Enclave has lost faith in the Herondales to run our Institute. Indeed, had they but spoken earlier, I might not bear now the terrible branded sigil upon my arm." He scowled.

"You do not speak for the Enclave," said Esme Hardcastle

unexpectedly. "Perhaps Tessa did know that her father was Belial. Why *would* she tell anyone, when the result would be this—this tribunal?"

To Cordelia's surprise, Charles rose to his feet. "This is not a tribunal," he said. His face looked strained, as if some unseen force were pulling his skin too tight. "This is a meeting we are holding to decide what our next steps will be."

"*We?*" said Will. He was looking at Charles with a sort of hurt bewilderment—was Charles trying to be helpful? Cordelia wondered herself. . . . But the look on Charles's face was so awful.

And he had not stopped speaking. He turned to look around the room, his mouth a hard line. "I'm the only one of my family who will have the courage to say it," he said. "But the Inquisitor is right."

Cordelia's gaze shot to Matthew. His eyes were squeezed tight, as though he were trying to shut out everything around him. Henry, beside him, looked as if he were going to be sick. Charlotte stood motionless, but the effort it took her was clear.

"I have known the Herondales all my life," Charles said. "But the revelation of this terrible secret has shaken us all. I wish to assure you all, I was not made aware of it, even if my mother knew. I believe the Herondales had a duty to share it, and that my mother had the same duty. My loyalty to family cannot account for this unconscionable omission."

There was a terrible silence. Cordelia stared at Charles. What *was* he doing? Was he truly so loathsome that he would betray his own family? She glanced over at Alastair, who she expected to be glowing with rage, but he wasn't even looking at Charles. He was looking across the room at Thomas, who sat with his fists clenched at his sides, as if he were barely holding himself back from lunging at Charles.

"Charles," Gideon said wearily. "You speak to protect your own ambition, though the Angel knows what has so corrupted your heart. There is no evidence whatsoever to indicate any alliance between the Herondales and Belial, though you are trying to imply otherwise—"

"I am *not* saying that," Charles snapped.

"But you are implying it," Gideon said. "It is a cynical ploy. At a time when the Enclave must come together, to defeat the threat Belial still poses, you are trying to divide us."

"He speaks for those who did not know until *yesterday*," Bridgestock cried, "that the Institute was inhabited by the offspring of a Prince of Hell! Has he truly never made an overture, never reached out to his blood—"

James shot to his feet. He looked as he did when he held his pistol in his hand, an avenging angel, with eyes like chips of gold. "If he were to reach out," he snarled, "*we would refuse him.*"

Cordelia began to rise to her feet as well. She would defend them, she thought. She would swear up and down that no one had more cause to hate Belial than the Herondales did—she would speak out for James and Lucie—

A hand touched her arm. For a moment, she thought it was Alastair, urging her to sit back down. But to her surprise, it was Christopher. Christopher, who she had assumed was in the infirmary. He was looking at her with an uncharacteristic seriousness, his eyes dark purple behind his owlish glasses.

"Come with me," he said quietly. "Quickly. No one will notice in all this fuss."

Alastair, looking over at the both of them, shrugged as if to say he had no more idea than she did what Christopher wanted. "Christopher," Cordelia whispered. "I must speak for them—"

"If you truly wish to help James," Christopher said, and there was an intensity in his voice that Cordelia had rarely heard, "come with me. There is something you must know."

Ari sat through the meeting in a state of numb shock. She already knew her father did not like the Herondales; his strange note-keeping had made that clear. Yes, they had saved London, and perhaps the whole Shadow World, but to Maurice Bridgestock this only made them celebrities who had been rewarded with a cushy position. Not, like him, dedicated public servants devoted to the needs of the Clave.

It seemed to her that Will and Tessa had had twenty years of showing themselves to be fine stewards of the London Institute, and her father's resentment struck her as petty and small, unworthy of him. But it turned out it hadn't been small at all: it had instead loomed so large that when he espied weakness in their position, he moved against them.

She had been sitting with the Lightwoods, of course, tucked in among them, with Gabriel on her left and Anna on her right. When her father thrust his finger at those he was accusing, he was pointing at Ari. (Her mother, interestingly, was not there; Ari wondered at her absence.)

She would have taken Anna's hand, but Anna sat tensed, her arms folded tightly against her chest. As always, in the face of a threat, she turned to stone.

Eventually, as the shouting reached a fever pitch, a recess was called for everyone to calm down. As people began to cluster into small groups—the Herondales and Lightwoods together, Matthew moving to join his parents—she saw Alastair (though where was Cordelia?) cross the room to Charles, who was standing obstinately alone, and fall into conversation with him. Well, it wasn't quite a conversation—whatever Alastair was saying, it was low and furious, accompanied by urgent gestures. Charles stood looking off into the air, as if Alastair was not there. *By the Angel,* Ari thought. *How could I even have pretended to be engaged to that man?*

And then she saw her father. As he stepped down from the altar and ducked through a side door, she rose to her feet. With a light touch to Anna's shoulder, she darted into the aisle between the pews and hurried out of the room, taking the same side door.

Beyond it was a stone-bound corridor, in which her father was pacing. He looked smaller than he had up on the altar, the focus of all eyes. He muttered as he paced, though she could catch only a few of the words—"Belial" and "have to see the truth" and, one of his favorite words, "unfair."

"Father," she said. "What have you done?"

He looked up. "This isn't any of your concern, Ariadne."

"You must know that none of what you have said is true."

"I know no such thing," he snapped.

"If there is a lack of faith in the Herondales, it is only because *you* have created it."

He shook his head. "I would have thought you would give me more credit than that," he said. "I am not the villain in a play where the

Herondales are the heroes. Tessa Herondale is the child of a Greater Demon. *And they lied about it.*"

"In the face of blind prejudice, one curls in on oneself," Ari said quietly. "It is not something you would understand. Will acted to protect his wife, James and Lucie to protect their mother. Against the hatred you are whipping up *right now*. A hatred born out of fear, out of the blind belief that the blood in Tessa's veins, in her children's veins, matters more than every act of heroism or kindness she has ever performed."

His face crumpled into a look that mixed fury with a terrible sort of pity. "They have drawn you in," he rasped. "The Herondales, who came from nowhere to rule over us, magic users all. And the Lightwoods, the children of Benedict, who *famously* consorted with demons, so much so that eventually it killed him. Whatever was twisted up in his heart is there, you know, in the blood of his children and his grandchildren. Including that half-woman who has taken you under her wing—"

"Don't speak about Anna in that way," Ari said in a clear and calm voice. "She has shown me more kindness of late than any of my own family."

"You left," he said. "You took your things, the things we have given you over the years, and you went to live with that Lightwood creature. You could still come home, you know." His voice had taken on a wheedling quality. "If you swear you will never see any of these people again. The Herondales, the Lightwoods—they are a sinking ship. It would be wise for you to disembark while you still can."

Ari shook her head. "Never."

"It's a dangerous path you're on," her father said. "One that ends in ruin. It is out of kindness that I wish to save you—"

"Kindness?" Ari said. "Not love? The love you owe a daughter?"

"A daughter is not defiant. A daughter is obedient. A daughter cares for her parents, protects them—"

"As James and Lucie are protecting Tessa?" Ari shook her head. "You cannot see it, Father. You are too blinded by your hatred. The Herondales are not criminals. They are not, for instance, *blackmailers*."

It was an arrow shot blindly, but Ari saw it hit its mark. Her father flinched and stared at her in horror.

"The letter," he whispered. "The fireplace—"

"I don't know what you mean," Ari said blandly. "I only know this. The further you push this, Father, the more you, too, will come under scrutiny. Only be sure you can bear such scrutiny of your every action. Most men could not."

Grace sat shivering against the wall of her cell. She had wrapped the blanket from her bed around her, but it had not stopped the shaking.

The tremors had begun that morning, when Brother Zachariah had come to her cell, after her breakfast of porridge and toast. She had sensed the concern in him, a pity that had terrified her. In her experience, pity meant scorn, and scorn meant that the other person had realized how horrible you were.

"The baby," she whispered. "Christopher's brother. Is he—"

He is alive and healing. Your mother has been found. She is in custody now. I would have told you last night, but I feared to wake you.

As if she had slept, Grace thought. She was glad Alexander had been found but doubted it would make a difference to Christopher. She had still lost him, forever. "She did not—damage him?"

The rune she put upon him burned him badly. Luckily, it was incomplete, and we were able to get to him in time. He will have a scar.

"It's because that's how Jesse died," Grace said numbly. "Having runes put on. It's her idea of poetic justice."

Zachariah said nothing, and Grace realized with a jolt that there was more he had come to tell her. And then, with a sense of sick horror, what that more must be.

"You said my mother was in custody," she said. "Do you mean—she is here? In the Silent City?"

He inclined his head. *Given her history, it seemed crucial to keep her where all the exits are known, and guarded, and where no Portals can be opened.*

Grace felt as if she were going to be sick. "No," she gasped. "No. I don't want her near me. I'll go somewhere else. You can lock me in somewhere else. I'll be good. I won't try to get out. I swear it."

Grace. She will only be here one night. After that she will be moved to the prisons of the Gard, in Idris.

"Does—does she know I'm here?"

She does not seem to. She has not spoken at all, said Zachariah. *And her mind is closed to us. Belial's doing, I would guess.*

"She will find a way to get to me," Grace said dully. "She always does." She raised her head. "You have to kill her," she said. "And burn the body. Or she will never be stopped."

We cannot execute her. We must know what she knows.

Grace closed her eyes.

Grace, we will protect you. I will protect you. You are safest here, warded by our protections, closed behind these doors. Nor can your mother escape her cell. Not even a Prince of Hell could break out of that cage.

Grace had turned her face to the wall. He would not understand. He could not understand. She still possessed her power; therefore she was still of value to her mother. Somehow her mother would get her back. The Adamant Citadel had not held her. She was a great dark blight across Grace's life, and she could no more be separated from Grace than venom from a body it had poisoned.

After some time, Brother Zachariah had gone away, and Grace had retched dryly into her empty bowl from breakfast. Then she had closed her eyes, but that only brought visions of her mother, of the forest in Brocelind, a dark voice in her ears. *Little one. I've come to give you a great gift. The gift your mother asked for you. Power over the minds of men.*

"Grace?" The hesitant voice was as familiar as it was impossible. Grace, hunched in her corner, looked up—and to her disbelief, saw Christopher standing at the barred door of her cell. "Uncle Jem said I could come and see you. He said you weren't feeling well."

"Christopher," she breathed.

He looked at her, worry plain on his face. "Are you all right?"

It's nothing, she wanted to say. She wanted to force a smile, not to burden him, for she knew men did not like to be burdened by women. Her mother had told her.

But she could not make the smile come. This was Christopher, with his blunt honesty and kind smile. Christopher would know she was lying.

"I thought you hated me," she whispered. "I thought you would never be able to stand to see me again, because of my mother. Because of what she did to your family."

He did not laugh at her, or recoil, only looked at her with a level gaze. "I suspected you might think something like that," he said. "But Grace, I have never blamed you for your mother before. I will not start now. What she did was vile. But you are not vile. You have done wrong, but you are trying to make it right. And such trying is not easy."

Grace felt tears burn against the backs of her eyes. "How are you so wise? Not about science, or magic, I mean. About people."

At that, he did smile. "I am a Lightwood. We are a complicated family. Someday I shall tell you all about it." He reached a hand through the bars, and Grace, relieved beyond measure that there might be a *someday*, took hold of his hand. It was gentle and warm in her own, scarred by acid and ichor, but perfect. "Now, I want to help you with your trying." He looked down the hallway outside the cell.

"Cordelia?" he called out. "It's time."

Thomas felt his heart sinking lower and lower with each minute of the Enclave meeting. He hadn't expected it to go well, but neither had he expected it to go quite this badly. Once Charles had announced that he was standing with Bridgestock against his own family, the debate quickly deteriorated into a screaming match.

Thomas longed to get to his feet, to shout out something cutting, something that would shame and damn Charles for his betrayal, something that would make the Enclave *see* how ridiculous, how vicious this all was. But words had never been his strength; he sat, with Eugenia white-faced and incredulous beside him, his head aching with the strain of it all. He felt clumsy and oversized and utterly useless.

As the adults around him muttered among themselves, Thomas tried to catch Matthew's eye. Matthew, he imagined, must be sickeningly shocked by Charles's words, but he seemed determined not to show it. Unlike James, or Anna, who sat stone-faced and unmoving, Matthew had flung himself back in his chair as if he were posing for a louche Parisian artist. He had his feet up on the back of the chair in front of him and was examining his cuffs as if they held the secrets of the universe.

Matthew, turn around, Thomas thought urgently, but his attempt at Silent Brother–like communication failed him. *Alastair* glanced over, but Thomas's view of him was cut off by Walter Rosewain, who had risen to his feet (almost knocking off his wife Ida's hat) and begun shouting, and by the time Rosewain sat down again, Matthew had slipped out of his pew and was gone.

Quickly, Thomas caught James's eye. Despite the strain of the situation, James nodded, as if to say, *Go after him, Tom.*

Thomas didn't need to be told twice. Anything was better than sitting here, helpless to change the course of events. Thomas would always rather have something to do, some tool in his hand, some path to follow, no matter how narrow or dangerous. He rose and hurried out of the pew, stepping on several feet as he did so.

He raced through the Institute to the foyer, not bothering to pause and catch up his coat. He pushed his way out into the cold, only to see Matthew's borrowed carriage already rolling out the Institute gates. *Bloody hell.*

Thomas wondered if his parents would mind if he helped himself to their carriage and gave chase. They probably would, if he was being honest with himself, but—

"We can take my carriage." Thomas spun in surprise to see Alastair standing behind him, calmly holding Thomas's coat. "Don't look at me like that," he said. "Clearly I was going to follow you. There's nothing I can do in *there*, and Cordelia's already gone."

Gone where? Thomas wondered, but there was no time to process the thought: he took his coat from Alastair and shrugged it on, grateful for the warmth. "I'm going after Matthew," he said, and Alastair gave him a dark look that clearly said, *Yes, I knew that.* "And you don't like Matthew."

"After what Charles has just done, your friend Matthew will be desperate for a drink," Alastair said. There was nothing accusing or contemptuous in his tone; it was matter-of-fact. "And I have much more experience looking after drunks than you do. Even talking them out of drinking, sometimes. Shall we go?"

Thomas started to object, though he wasn't entirely sure what he was objecting to, but the Carstairs carriage had already rolled into the courtyard, the driver swaddled against the cold in a thick blanket. Alastair had hold of Thomas's sleeve and they were marching down the steps; a moment later, they were in the carriage as it began to lurch across the ice-slippery courtyard.

On the way to the terrible Christmas party at the Institute, Thomas had told himself to enjoy the time he had in the carriage with Alastair. Though Alastair had been in an odd mood that night, with a sort of suppressed excitement to him, as if he were considering whether or not to spill a secret.

He hadn't, of course, spilled anything; still, Thomas had enjoyed being in such an intimate space with him. And, he had told himself, it was all right to enjoy it, as long as he kept in mind that Alastair was not going to be a permanent fixture in his life. That Alastair was most likely leaving as soon as his sibling was born.

He tried to enjoy it now, but his stomach was too knotted up over James and his family, over Matthew, over everything that had happened. The carriage bounced over a rut in the road; Thomas steadied himself and said, "He's stopped drinking, you know."

Alastair looked out the window. He blinked against the wintery light and said, "He's still a drunk. He'll always be a drunk, even if he never drinks again." He sounded weary.

Thomas stiffened. "If you're going to say that sort of thing to him—"

"My father stopped drinking a dozen times," said Alastair. "He would go weeks, months, without a drink. Then something would happen—a disappointment, a minor setback—and he would begin again. Have you ever wanted something," he said, looking at Thomas with a sudden directness, "something you knew you should not have, but that you could not keep away from? Something that occupied all your waking and dreaming thoughts with reminders of how *much* you wanted it?"

Thomas was once again conscious of the intimacy of the space he shared with Alastair. He remembered Barbara giggling about kissing Oliver Hayward in his carriage: the shared private space of it, the pleasure of misbehaving. He was also sure he was probably turning tomato red above his collar. "Matthew needs to hear that there is hope."

"I didn't say there was no hope," Alastair said quietly. "Only that it is a difficult journey. It's best for him to know that, so he can be prepared for it." He rubbed at his eyes with a gesture that made him seem younger than he was. "He needs a plan."

"He has one," said Thomas, and he found himself explaining Christopher's treatment plan, weaning Matthew off alcohol gradually and deliberately. Alastair took this in with a thoughtful look.

"It could work," he said. "If Matthew abides by it. Though I gather you fear he won't, or we wouldn't be following him with such urgency."

Thomas could hardly argue that point; besides, they'd arrived at Matthew's address. Leaving the carriage, they headed upstairs, where Thomas used his key to let them into Matthew's room, praying to the Angel as he did so that Matthew had not yet done anything dangerous, self-destructive, or embarrassing.

He was surprised to find Matthew sitting in an armchair by the fire, one hand on Oscar's head, his legs crossed, reading a letter. He looked mildly over at Thomas and Alastair as they spilled into his flat.

"Thomas," Matthew said. "I see you've come to discover whether I have or have not plunged myself into a hogshead of brandy. And you've brought Alastair, noted handler of drunks."

"*Well?*" said Thomas, who saw no point bluffing. "Have you been drinking?"

Matthew looked at Alastair. Thomas had known Matthew might see his bringing Alastair here as a betrayal of sorts, and he'd been braced for it. But Matthew looked rather more like a general who had finally met his enemy on the battlefield only to discover that they both agreed the long years of bloodshed had not been worth it.

"Only what Christopher has given me," Matthew said. "I suppose you will have to take my word for it. Or decide if I seem drunk to you."

"It isn't really about seeming drunk, though, is it?" said Alastair, unbuttoning his coat. "My father had to drink, in the end, simply to seem normal."

"I am not your father," said Matthew frostily.

"You are much younger. You have been drinking a much shorter time. Your chances are much better," said Alastair, rolling up his sleeves. Thomas did not have time to ponder how Alastair's forearms looked as if they belonged on a statue by Donatello, because Alastair was already striding across the room to the shelves where Matthew's bottles of spirits were kept.

"Thomas says you have given up drinking for good," Alastair said.

"Yet you still have all this booze here, I see." He selected a bottle of whiskey and uncorked it thoughtfully.

"I haven't touched it since I came back from Paris," said Matthew. "But I do still have visitors. For instance, the two of you, although I'm not sure if this is a visit or a rescue mission."

"Visitors don't matter," Alastair said bluntly. "You need to get rid of this stuff. All of it." Without warning, he strode to the open window and began emptying the bottle out of it. "Free liquor for the mundanes," he added. "You'll be popular."

Matthew rolled his eyes. "Yes, I hear mundanes prefer their drinks poured on their heads from four stories up. What exactly do you think you're doing? Thomas, make him stop."

Alastair was shaking his head. "You can't have this stuff around you all the time. It will just make every moment a battle, where you *could* have a drink but must, over and over, choose not to."

"You think I have no willpower at all?" Matthew said. "That I cannot withstand a little temptation?"

"You will withstand it," said Alastair grimly, "until you don't." He went back to the shelf to collect a second bottle. At the window, he turned to look at Matthew. "Having all this here is like asking an addict to live in an opium den," he said. "You are never going to be able to drink casually. Alcohol will always mean something to you that it does not mean to other people. Getting rid of this stuff will make it easier. Why not have it be easier?"

Matthew hesitated a moment, and Thomas knew him well enough to read the look in his eyes: *Because I do not deserve to have it be easy, because the suffering is part of the punishment*. But Matthew would not say such things in front of Alastair, and perhaps it was better that he did not.

"Math." Thomas sat down in the chair opposite Matthew's. Oscar thumped his tail on the ground. "Look, I understand wanting to flee that foul meeting—after Charles said the things he said, I—"

"I think the Inquisitor is blackmailing Charles," Matthew said.

Alastair (who had made it through the whiskey and was on to pouring out gin) and Thomas exchanged a look of surprise.

"I just assumed Charles was being his usual lickspittle self today,"

Alastair said. "You don't need to make excuses for him. We all know what he's like."

Matthew waved the paper he'd been reading. "The Inquisitor is blackmailing *someone*. Ari found this in his fireplace. Read it, Tom."

Thomas took the letter from him. He looked up after a quick skim to find Alastair peering at him. "Well, all right," Thomas said. "So the Inquisitor is blackmailing someone. But Charles isn't named."

"I've been trying to figure out who the letter was for," Matthew said. "Well, Anna and Ari and I. The wording of it has led us to a few possibilities: Augustus, Thoby . . ." He sighed. "I didn't want to think it was Charles. But now I'm sure of it." He looked over at Alastair. "I ought to have gotten up in the middle of the meeting. Denounced him. But—he is my brother."

"It's all right," Thomas said. "If Bridgestock's blackmailing him into voicing support, that means Charles doesn't actually believe what he's saying in the first place. It's Bridgestock and a few cronies who are trying to lay blame on Uncle Will and Aunt Tessa. Denouncing Charles wouldn't fix the root of the problem."

Alastair, standing by the window, said, "I just—"

Thomas looked up. "What is it?"

"Should I assume," Alastair said, "that Charles is being blackmailed about . . . me?"

"Not specifically," Matthew said, and Thomas saw Alastair relax minutely. "But it would be, more generally, because he loves men, rather than women."

"Bridgestock is foul," said Thomas furiously. "And Charles—is his shame so all-consuming as that? He couldn't possibly believe that your parents would care, or that the Enclave who have known him all his life would shun him."

"He thinks it would ruin his political career," said Alastair. "He is meant to be the next Consul. I don't know if you knew that."

"I, for one, hadn't heard," said Matthew dryly.

"It was his dream," Alastair said, "and I suppose it is hard to give up on one's dreams." Thomas sensed that Alastair was doing his best to be fair. "He thinks that without his career, he would be purposeless. He believes he cannot be a family man, cannot have children, that his only legacy will be as Consul. He fears to lose that. I believe a blend of shame and fear drives him." He sighed. "I'd honestly *like* to believe Charles was being blackmailed. Rather than that he would turn on his own family for Bridgestock's approval. He can be an insufferable weasel, but I never believed him a monster."

"I have to believe he can be reasoned with," Matthew said. "It is why I came here. To get the letter. To be sure." He sighed. "I'll talk to Charles as soon as I can."

Alastair folded his arms. "If you like, when you do, we'll come with you."

Matthew looked over at Thomas, surprised. Thomas nodded his agreement: of course they would go with Matthew. "That might be best," Matthew said, pushing past a clear reluctance. "It is unlikely Charles will listen just to me. But you, Alastair—you have insight into him that we do not."

"You know," Thomas said, feeling bold, "you two think you have nothing in common, but here, we've found something. You're both experts on the same pompous git."

Matthew chuckled quietly. Alastair gave Thomas a wry look, but Thomas thought he seemed a little pleased.

It was a bad situation, surely, he thought, and he didn't think Charles would respond well to the three of them confronting him. But if it could bring Matthew and Alastair together, then perhaps another miracle was also possible.

James was alone in his room, and evening was coming on. The time just after the meeting had been excruciating. He and Will and Lucie and Tessa all gathered in the parlor (Jesse had gone back to his room, giving them space to be together), where the Herondales had spent so many happy evenings reading and chatting or just being quiet in each other's company. They were quiet now, too, with Lucie curled up at Will's side, as she had when she was a little girl, and Tessa gazing blankly into the fire. Will did his best to reassure them all, but he could hardly hide his anger and uncertainty. And James—James sat closing and unclosing his hands, yearning to do something for his family, utterly unsure of what it might be.

He had excused himself to his room eventually. He wanted desperately to be alone. Actually, he wanted desperately to be with Cordelia. She had an uncanny ability to inject reason and even humor into the darkest situation. But Cordelia was no doubt back at Cornwall Gardens. He did not think she had stayed until the end of the meeting. He supposed he could not blame her, and yet—

I do not know what I will do about James.

He had felt a flicker of hope, after overhearing her conversation with Matthew, that at least *I do not know what I will do* was not *I do not love him at all.* And yet—Cordelia was a steadfast friend. He had truly expected, after the horror of the meeting had ended, to see her there among the crowd; surely she would be there in friendship, in fellowship, even if not as a wife.

Her absence had been like a blow. He wondered now if it had been the blow of realization, of acceptance. That he had really lost her. That it was over.

There was a knock on the door. James had been pacing back and forth; he turned now and went to answer it. To his surprise, Jesse stood in the doorway.

"A runner came, with a message," he said, holding out a folded paper to James. "I thought I would bring it to you. God knows I'd like to be of some sort of use in this nightmare."

"Thank you," James said hoarsely. He took the paper and unfolded it, aware of Jesse's eyes on him.

James—I must see you at Curzon Street immediately on a matter of great urgency. I will await you there. Cordelia.

He stood motionless. The words seemed to dance on the page in front of him. He read the note again; surely it could not say what it seemed to say.

"Is it from Cordelia?" Jesse asked—alerted, no doubt, by the look on James's face.

James closed his hand over the letter, the paper crumpling in his fist. "Yes," he said. "She wants to see me at Curzon Street. Immediately."

He waited for Jesse to say something about curfew, or about how

James ought to remain at the Institute with his sister and parents, or about the danger that lurked in the dark streets of London.

But Jesse said none of those things. "Well, then," he said, and stepped aside. "You had better go—hadn't you?"

Lucie had to knock on Jesse's door several times before he opened it. When he did, it was apparent he'd fallen asleep in his clothes: he was barefoot, his shirt wrinkled, his hair an untidy mess.

"Lucie." He leaned wearily against the doorway. "Not that I'm not glad to see you. But I assumed your parents would be needing you this evening."

"I know," she said. "And they did for a bit, but—" She shrugged. "They went off to bed. I think they rather wanted to be by themselves, at the end of it. Not that they wanted to get rid of me, just that they have their own little world that's just them, and they retreat into it every now and then. I suppose that's true for every couple," she added, finding the thought rather surprising, "even if they are very old and one's parents."

Jesse laughed softly and shook his head. "I didn't think anything could make me laugh tonight, but you do have a particular talent."

Lucie closed the door behind her. The room was cold; one of the windows was propped slightly open. Jesse's bed was scattered with papers—his mother's papers from Chiswick, and his own scrawled notes on how to decode them.

"I cannot help feeling as if somehow this is my fault," Jesse said. "As if I have brought you bad luck. This information about Belial has gone unknown by the Enclave for so long, and then, the moment I arrive—"

"The two things have nothing to do with each other," said Lucie. "Your mother didn't tell the world about my demonic grandfather because of you; she did it because she hates us. She always has. And because Belial decided it was time for it to be known," she added. "You always say it's Belial's bidding she's doing. Not the other way around."

"One does wonder," said Jesse. "What good does it do him, having everyone know your mother's parentage? Why now?"

Lucie clasped her hands in front of her. She was wearing a very plain, light tea dress, and the cold from the open window was making her shiver. She said, "Jesse. I want—I'd like you to put your arms around me."

A light flared in his dark green eyes. He looked away quickly. "You know we can't," he said. "I suppose—if I put on gloves—"

"I don't want you to put on gloves," Lucie said. "I don't want to fight off what happens when we kiss. Not this time. I want to follow it as far as I can go."

Jesse looked stunned. "Absolutely not. Lucie, it could be dangerous—"

"I realized something," she said. "Belial has always focused his attention on James. Pushed him to fall into shadow, forced him to see things he would never have wanted to see, feel what he would never have wanted to feel. I have been protected from Belial for all these years, because my brother stood in the breach." She took a step forward. Jesse did not move away, though he stood rigid, his hands at his sides. "Now James cannot see Belial. All that effort with the mirror, the danger he undertook—it was to catch a glimpse of my grandfather's doings. If there is a chance I can catch such a glimpse, I should try. I cannot let my brother shoulder all the risk."

"I want to say no," Jesse said roughly. "But if I do—you'll find some other way to try, won't you? And I won't be there to protect you."

"Let us protect each other," she said, and put her arms around him. He stiffened but did not pull away. She wrapped her arms around his neck, looking up at him. At a new bruise on his cheek, at his untidy hair. He had never been messy when he was a ghost—he had always been perfectly put-together, not a hair out of place. Not a scratch on his paper-pale skin. She had not imagined he would be so much more beautiful when he was alive, that it would seem the difference between a living rose and one made from porcelain or glass.

His body was warm against hers. She rose up on tiptoe and kissed the bruise on his cheekbone. Lightly, so it wouldn't hurt, but he made a low noise and his arms came up to wrap around her.

And it was heavenly. He was warm and smelled of soap and Jesse. Wool, ink, winter air. She burrowed into him, kissed the side of his jaw. Slid her bare foot along his. As experiments went, this one was delightful, but—

"Nothing's happening," she said, after a moment.

"Speak for yourself," Jesse muttered.

"I mean it. I don't feel like I'm about to faint." She raised her chin. "Maybe we need to be touching a bit more intensely. It could be more than just touching. It could be . . . desire." She laid her hand against his cheek; his green eyes flared darkly. "Kiss me."

She had thought he would object. He didn't. He closed his eyes before he kissed her, and she felt the harsh intake of his breath. She had feared it would feel like something other than a real kiss, like an experiment or a test. But his lips on hers swept away self-consciousness and thought. He was practiced at kissing her now: he knew what she responded to, where she was sensitive, where to linger and where to press. Her lips parted: her fingers stroked his neck as his tongue stroked the inside of her mouth. It was not just her body, but her mind and soul that were lost in the kiss, lost in Jesse.

And she began to fall.

She clung to the feel of his body against hers as a lighthouse in a storm, something to keep her anchored. Her vision darkened. She seemed to be in two places at once: in the Institute, kissing Jesse, and somewhere between worlds—somewhere where points of light raced around her, swirling like paint on a palette.

The points of light began to resolve themselves. They were not stars, as she had thought, but grains of dark gold sand. They swirled, blown by an invisible wind, half-concealing what stood in front of her.

High walls. Towers that pierced the sky, shimmering like crystal. *The demon towers of Alicante?* Was she seeing Idris? Gates wrought from silver and iron rose up; they were covered with a strange calligraphy, like Marks rendered in an alien script.

A hand, long and white, reached out. It was not her own hand—it was massive, inhuman, like the hand of a marble statue. It laid itself against the gates, and rough words scored the inside of Lucie's mind:

Kaal ssha ktar.

A grinding, wrenching sound. Images flashed through her head: an owl, with glowing orange eyes; a sigil, like Belial's, but with something oddly different about it; the statue of an angel holding a sword, standing above a dying serpent.

Belial's face, turned toward hers, his mouth stretched wide in a grin, his eyes the color of blood.

With a gasp, Lucie wrenched her gaze away. Light flared and died; she was back in Jesse's room; he was holding her, his eyes panicked as they searched her face. "Lucie!" His fingers tightened on her arms. "Are you all right, did you—"

"See anything?" she whispered. "Yes—I did—but I don't know, Jesse. I don't know what any of it means."

23

A Single Chant

Thus many a melody passed to and fro between
the two nightingales, drunk with their passion. Those who
heard them listened in delight, and so similar were the two
voices that they sounded like a single chant. Born of pain
and longing, their song had the power to break
the unhappiness of the world.
—Nizami Ganjavi, *Layla and Majnun*

Cordelia ran.

It had begun to snow, and the wind whipped tiny ice crystals against her skin. The hansom cab had only been willing to bring her as far as Piccadilly because of roadwork, and so she was running up Half Moon Street, almost tripping over her skirts, heavy with wet snow along the hem. But it didn't matter.

She ran, hearing Grace's words in her head, explosive fragments that had blown her whole world apart like one of Christopher's experiments.

He never loved me. Not really. It was a spell, administered through the bracelet. It was always you he loved.

Cordelia was hatless, and every once in a while a topaz pin would whip free of her hair and rattle to the sidewalk, but she did not stop to pick them up. She hoped someone found them and sold them and bought a Christmas goose. She could not slow down.

Belial gave me this gift, this power. I can convince any man to do anything I like. But it didn't work on James. The bracelet had to be invented to keep him in line. He and I were still friends when I gave it to him. I recall snapping it onto his wrist and seeing the light go out in his eyes. He was never the same again.

Cordelia had been glad Christopher was there too; otherwise it might have seemed too much like a strange dream to have really happened.

Grace had been icily calm as she recounted what had happened, though she had not met Cordelia's gaze, instead staring down at the floor. Under other circumstances Cordelia might have been furious. What Grace was telling her was a story of terrible cruelty and violation, but Cordelia sensed that if Grace showed anything of what she felt about it, she would come apart completely, and Cordelia could not risk that. She needed to know what had happened.

Cordelia had reached Curzon Street. She ran along the icy pavement, up the curve of the street, toward her house. Christopher had told her James would be there. She had to believe he would.

He loved you, Grace had said. *Even the bracelet could not contain it. My mother moved us to London that I might be closer to him, exert more power over him, but ultimately it failed. All Hell's power could not extinguish that love.*

Cordelia had whispered, "But why didn't he tell me?"

Grace had looked at her then, for the first time. "Because he didn't want your pity," she said. "Believe me, I understand. I understand all desperate, self-defeating thoughts. They are my specialty."

And then Grace's voice faded. The smell of the Silent City, the feeling of dazed, sickening shock, all of it fell away, because Cordelia had reached her house, and the lights were on inside. She raced up the front steps, thanking Raziel for her balance runes—her heeled boots had never been meant for running in—reached the front door, and found it unlocked.

She threw it open. Inside, she flung her damp coat in a heap on the floor and raced through the house—the dining room, the drawing room, the study—calling out for James. What if he wasn't there? Cordelia thought, stopping at the foot of the steps. What if Christopher had been wrong?

"Daisy?"

She looked up. And there was James, coming down the steps, a look of surprise on his face. Cordelia did not hesitate. She bolted up the stairs, taking them two at a time.

James, too, began to run.

They collided on the landing. They tumbled into a heap, rolling over, skidding down several steps until James arrested their fall. And somehow Cordelia was underneath him, and she could feel the slamming race of his heartbeat, see the look in his eyes—bewilderment and hope and pain—even as he started to get up, to ask if she was all right.

She caught at the lapels of his jacket. "James," she said. "Stay."

He froze, looking down, his dark gold eyes searching her face. He was braced over her, but she could still feel the weight of his body against hers.

"I love you," Cordelia said. She had never said it to him before, and she sensed somehow now was not the time for flowery phrases or shy deflections. He needed to know. "*Asheghetam.* I love you. I love you. Without you, I cannot breathe."

Wild hope flashed across his face, chased by a wary disbelief. "Daisy, what—"

"Grace." She felt him flinch, held on to him tightly. She had to keep him close, keep him from recoiling away from the truth. "She confessed to me. About the spell, the bracelet. James, why didn't you tell me?"

As she had feared, the Mask covered his expression quickly. He still held her, arms under her, cradling her, cushioning the harsh angles of the stairs. But he was motionless. "I could not bear your pity. If you knew what had happened, you would have felt obligated to me. You are kind, Cordelia. But I did not want your kindness, not at the sacrifice of your true feelings."

"My true feelings?" she said. "How could you know them? I have hidden them, all this time." It was dark outside, and the lamps in the entrance hall burned low; in the dimness, the angles of James's face appeared more acute. For the first time since she had fled the Silent City, Cordelia began to fear it would not be enough to tell him she loved him. He might withdraw regardless. She might lose him, no matter how fast she had run. "I have hidden them for *years.* All the years that I have loved you. I fell in love with you when you had the scalding fever, when we were both children, and I never stopped."

"But you never said—"

"I thought you were in love with Grace," she said. "I was too proud to tell you I loved you, when I thought you had given your heart to someone else. We have both been too proud, James. You feared I would *pity* you?" Her voice rose, incredulous. "Belial wove an enchantment, a band of silver and the darkest magic, to bind you. Most would have crumbled. You fought it. All this time you have been fighting a silent battle entirely alone, while nobody knew. You fought it and you *broke* it, snapped it in half, the most incredible thing. How could I ever pity that?"

She felt his chest rise and fall against hers with his quick breaths. He said, "I did not break that enchantment knowingly. Yes, I fought it, without knowing I was fighting. But what snapped that band was the force of what I felt for you." He gathered up a handful of her tumbling hair, let the strands slip through his fingers. There was wonder in his eyes as he looked at her. "If it were not for you, my Daisy, I would have belonged to Belial long ago. For there is no one else in this world, my most beautiful, maddening, adorable wife, that I could ever have loved half as much as I have loved you. My heart beats for you," he said. "Only ever you."

Cordelia burst into tears. They were tears of relief, happiness, joy, even desire. There might not have been anything else she could have done that would have so thoroughly convinced him she meant what she said.

"Daisy—Daisy—" He began to kiss her, wildly—her bared throat, the tears on her cheeks, her collarbone, returning over and over to her mouth. She arched up against him, kissing back as hard as she could, as if the motion of her lips against his were words, as if she could speak to him through kisses.

She tugged his jacket off—he was wearing his pistol in a holster at his side, and it dug into her, but she didn't much mind. She pulled at the buttons on his shirt, tearing it, kissing the bare skin at his throat, tasting the salt of his skin.

When she licked his throat, he groaned. "You have no idea how much I have wanted you," he said. "Every moment of being married to you has been bliss and torture." He dragged up her skirts, ran his hands up the sides of her legs, his fingertips skating over the silk of her stockings. "The things you did to me—when you came to me wanting help with your corset, on our wedding night—"

"I thought you were embarrassed," she said, biting gently at his jaw. "I thought you wished I would go away."

"I *did* want you to go away," he murmured against her neck. His hands were behind her now, cleverly undoing the hooks at the back of her dress. "But only because my self-control was hanging on by the thinnest thread. I pictured myself lunging at you, you absolutely horrified by what I wanted to do to you—"

"I would not have been horrified," Cordelia said, looking at him steadily. "I *want* you to do things to me. I want to do things to *you*."

He made an inarticulate noise, as if she had shot him. "*Cordelia*," he gasped raggedly. His hands grasped her hips; he rocked against her—and a moment later he was rising to his feet, sweeping her up into his arms. "I will not despoil you on the staircase," he said, "though Effie has the night off, and believe me, I want to."

"Why not?" she giggled. She had not imagined she could feel so happy, so light. He carried her up the steps. When he reached the door of her room, she wrapped her arms around his neck; he struggled with the doorknob for a moment—it was either jammed or locked—before muttering something that sounded a great deal like "Sod *that*" under his breath, taking out his pistol, and firing it at the lock.

The door blew open. Cordelia gasped with astonishment and laughter as James carried her over the threshold of her—their—bedroom, deposited her on the bed, and hurled the pistol into the corner of the room.

He crawled onto the bed after her, tearing at his clothes. She watched in fascination as his boots flew off, and then his shirt, and then he was lowering himself on top of her and kissing her hungrily, which allowed her to run her hands all over him. All over his bare skin, which was hot and smooth, all up and down his sides, and over the planes of his chest, which made him growl against her mouth and stirred a dark, hot feeling in her belly.

"*Please*," she said, not really knowing what she was asking for, but James sat back, so he was straddling her, and looked down at her with eyes that seemed wildly golden, like a tiger's.

"How much do you like this dress?" he asked. "Because I can take it off you slowly, or I can take it off you fast—"

"Fast," she said, and caught her breath as he took hold of the fabric at her neckline and, with a quick movement, ripped it apart. It was not a matter of tearing something fragile, like a ribbon—the dress was of stout construction, with corseting and buttons and hooks, but James simply tore it open as if he were freeing her from a chrysalis. Cordelia was gasping and laughing as he ripped the skirt into two pieces and flung the whole mass of the dress aside, and then her laughter vanished as he looked down at her and his whole expression changed.

She knew she was nearly naked—she had a light cambric chemise on, which barely brushed the tops of her legs, and he could certainly see through the thin material. See the exact shape of her breasts, the precise curve of her hips and thighs. She fought the urge to put up her hands, to shield herself against his staring. Because he was staring. And he looked *starving*. It was the only word she could think of: he looked as if he wanted to pin her down and devour her.

He was braced over her on his hands. She reached up and encircled his upper arms, as much as she could, with her fingers. She could feel the tension in his muscles, stone-hard under her touch. He was holding himself back, she knew. This was their wedding night, terribly delayed, and he wanted what happened in books. Wanted her to *give herself to him*, wanted to *take her*, and though she did not know precisely what that meant, she wanted it too. She ached for him, but he was holding back for her, and it gave her the courage to say:

"James. Have you ever before—with Grace—?"

He looked puzzled for a moment; his face darkened. "No. We kissed. I never wanted anything beyond that. I suppose the bracelet kept me from noticing how strange that was. I thought perhaps that it was not in my nature to want." He let his eyes roam over her, making her skin prickle. "That was wildly inaccurate."

"Then this is your first—?"

"I never had anything with Grace," he said gently. "Nothing that was real. You are my first, Cordelia. You are *all* my firsts." He closed his eyes. "We can keep talking, if you desire, but tell me now, because I am going to need to go into the adjoining room and run cold water on myself for at least—"

"No talking," she said, and locked her hands around the back of his neck. She drew him down, so their bodies touched, which made her writhe and squirm against him. He gasped a curse and caught at her hips, stilling her while he bent his head to explore her throat with his lips and tongue. Somehow he kicked his own trousers away, and she realized she was holding him naked in her arms as he slipped the straps of her chemise from her shoulders, his kisses following it as it slid lower and lower, baring her breasts. And when he kissed those, too, she could no longer control herself. She sobbed and she begged him for more, and he gave her more: harder kisses, his hands all over her, touching her where she had expected to be touched, and in some places where she had not imagined it.

And all the time he watched her face, as if he fed off her incredulous delight, her pleasure. He was urgent with her, but careful and gentle, as if terrified of hurting her. In the end, she was the one to urge him on, to kiss him harder, to try to shred his control, until: "Are you ready?" he whispered. His voice was dry and rasping, as if he were choking on his own need for her, and she arched up against him and said yes, she was ready, yes *please.*

She had been told, nebulously, that *something* would hurt, and at first there was a moment of glancing pain. She saw the fear on his face and wrapped her legs around him, whispering for him not to stop. She said things to him that would later make her blush, and he cradled her in his arms and kissed her as they moved together, the brief pain turning into a pleasure that wound tighter and tighter inside her until she was clutching at James's shoulders with desperate, searching hands, until her voice was rising and rising as she begged him incoherently to stay with her, until everything in her head came apart in a kaleidoscope of shimmering fragments more perfect than anything she had ever known.

"Pass me the soap," James said good-naturedly, dropping a kiss on Cordelia's bare shoulder.

"No," Cordelia said. "I'm too comfortable to move."

James laughed, and Cordelia felt it all through her body. They were in the bathtub together—however unsure of his feelings James had been, he had had the foresight to arrange a tub large enough for two people, bless him. James reclined against the wall of the tub, Cordelia leaning against him, her back to his chest. He had put something in the water that made it foam and smell of lavender, and she was happily covering herself with suds.

Lazily, he slid his hands through her wet hair. Outside, snow was falling; lovely sleepy white flakes tumbling past the window.

Cordelia had not, she thought, ever been utterly *naked* with another person who was not her mother, and that not since she was a small child. She'd had a moment of shyness before, in the bedroom, as her chemise had come away and she had lain before James, entirely naked. But the way he'd looked at her dispelled it—as if he had never seen anything so miraculous.

And now, here they were, man and wife in absolute truth. Man and wife in the bathtub, covered in slippery bubbles. Cordelia turned her head against James's shoulder and arched up to kiss his chin.

"There are things we still have to talk about, you know," she said.

James tensed for a moment, before picking up a handful of bubbles. He placed them carefully atop her head. "Like what?"

"What happened," she said. "At the meeting, after I left with Christopher."

James sighed and drew her closer. "My parents are going to Idris. Charlotte and Henry as well, and my aunts and uncles. And Uncle Jem. There will be a trial by Mortal Sword. It will be grim, but it should exonerate them."

"They're all leaving?" Cordelia was startled. "What about Thomas, and Matthew and Christopher—"

"Everyone will gather at the Institute tomorrow," said James. "Thomas and Anna are old enough to be on their own, but they'll likely come as well, as it will be more pleasant if we're all together. They'll put someone in charge of the Institute for the few days they're gone—I'd like it to be Thomas, but more likely some bore like Martin Wentworth."

"Well," said Cordelia. "If everyone's going to be under the same roof, then, it will be easier for you to tell them all about the bracelet. They've all worried about you so much, James. It will be a relief to them, to know what happened, and that you are free."

James leaned forward to run more hot water from the tap. "I know I must tell them," he said. "None of the lies I've been living have brought me anything but misery. But what will they *think?*"

"They will be angry on your behalf," Cordelia said, reaching out to stroke his cheek. "And they will be proud of your strength."

He shook his head. His wet hair made a cap of sleek waves, the ends, just beginning to dry, curling in against his cheeks, his temples. "But the telling of the tale, even knowing I will be glad, once it is done, to have told it—when I speak of what happened, I live it again. The violation of it."

"That is the most terrible part," Cordelia said. "I can understand it only a little, for I felt it when Lilith controlled me. The poisoning of one's own will. The *trespass* of it. I am so sorry, James. I was so ready to believe you loved someone else, so ready to believe you would never love *me*, I saw none of the signs of it."

She turned around so she was facing him. It was slightly awkward until she found the right position, almost in his lap, her knees on either side of him. Her hair was a wet cloak draped over her back, and she could not help but wonder if she had suds on her face.

If so, James gave no sign he noticed. He traced the line of her bare shoulder with a damp finger, as if it were the most fascinating thing he ever examined. "You could not have known, Daisy. The bracelet had its own odd powers; it seemed to prevent not just me, but those around me, from truly seeing its consequences." The water sloshed in the bath as he moved, taking hold of her hips under the water. She leaned into him. She could see desire rising in his eyes, like the first lighting of a fire, the embers beginning to smolder. It made her feel breathless, that she could have that effect on him.

"You look like a water goddess, you know," he said, letting his gaze roam over her, lazy and sensual as a touch. It was rather overwhelming, the manner in which he seemed to admire, even worship, her body. She admitted to herself that she felt rather the same way about his. She had never seen a man naked, only Greek statues, and when she looked at James, she began to see what the point of the statues was. He was lean, hard with muscle, but his skin when she touched it was fine-grained and smooth as marble. "I never want anyone to see you like this but me."

"Well, I can't imagine anyone *would*," Cordelia said practically. "It isn't as if I were about to take up bathing in the Thames."

James laughed. "I've loved you for years without being able to say it," he said. "You will now have to put up with me finally speaking aloud every ridiculous, possessive, jealous, impassioned thought I have ever had and been forced to hide, even from myself. It may take some time to work through them all."

"Constant declarations of love? How ghastly," Cordelia said, running the tips of her fingers down his chest. "Hopefully there will be some other reward for me, to make up for it." She grinned at the look he gave her. "Shall we repair to the bedroom?"

"Much too far away," he said, pulling her closer, into his lap. "Let me show you."

"Oh," Cordelia said. She had not realized quite how portable the act of love was, or what it was like for wet bodies to slide against each other. A great deal of water was sloshed onto the floor that night, and quite a lot of soap and bubbles. Effie would be horrified, Cordelia thought, and found she did not care in the least.

It was a pleasure for Cordelia to wake up the next morning and discover James's arm holding her tight against him as they slept, a thing she had wanted for so long that it was hard to believe it was real.

She rolled over in his embrace, so that she was facing him. The fire in the grate had long since died down, and the room was chilly, but they made a space of warmth together, under the blankets.

Lazily, James stroked her hair, following the strands down over her shoulders, her bare back. "How long can we stay like this?" he said. "Eventually, we would starve to death, I suppose, and Effie would discover our bodies."

"A very great shock for her," Cordelia agreed solemnly. "Alas, we cannot stay here forever, and not because of Effie. Aren't we all meant to gather at the Institute today?"

"Right," said James, kissing her throat. "That."

"And," said Cordelia, "you said everyone will be there. Including Matthew."

"Yes," said James cautiously. He had taken her hand in his and seemed to be inspecting it, turning it over to trace the lines on her palm. Cordelia thought of Matthew at the Hell Ruelle and a wash of sadness rolled over her, a gray wave.

"I suppose we are not planning to conceal from him that—that—"

"Well," said James, "I think we can spare him the details of last night. Which reminds me, where did I throw my pistol?"

"Into the corner." Cordelia grinned. "And we'll need to get a locksmith in, to fix the door."

"I adore discussing domestic details with you," said James, and kissed the inside of her wrist, where her pulse beat. "Talk to me of locksmiths and grocery deliveries and what's wrong with the second stove."

"Nothing, as far as I know. But we *do* have to talk about Matthew."

"Here's the thing." James sighed and rolled onto his back. He put an arm behind his head, which made Cordelia want to run her hands over all the different muscles in his shoulders and chest. She suspected, however, that it would not be conducive to continued discussion. "We find ourselves in an odd position, Daisy. No," he added, at her grin, "not *that* odd position. Unless—"

"No," Cordelia said, with mock severity. "Tell me what's odd."

"That everything changed between us last night," said James. "I think we can both agree on that. Perhaps it has only turned into what it always should have been, what in some ways always was beneath the surface. But it *has* changed—and yet from the outside it will look like nothing is different. We have *already* been married, we have *already* declared ourselves to each other in front of the entire Enclave. It is only now that we know that all the words we spoke then were true, and will always be true. It is a peculiar thing to confess."

"Ah." Cordelia hugged a pillow to her chest. "I see what you mean, but we need not make a great announcement to our friends, James. The story of that cursed bracelet *is* our story, and the truth will come out along with it. It is only that most of our friends will be made happy by the truth. But Matthew—neither one of us wants to hurt him."

"Daisy, darling," said James. He turned his head to look at her, his amber eyes grave. "It may not be possible to prevent him from feeling any pain at all, though we shall certainly try. I should tell you," he said, propping himself up on an elbow, "I heard you. At the Christmas party. Talking to Matthew in the games room."

Cordelia's eyes widened. "You did?"

"I'd gone to get something for Anna when I recognized your voice through the door. All I heard was you saying that you did not love Matthew, and that you did not know what to do about me. Which was not inspiring—but I had not meant to eavesdrop, and I left quickly, without hearing anything else. I swear that," he added, and Cordelia nodded. She had overheard a few conversations herself without intending to; she could hardly sit in judgment. "I would like to think I would not have let things get as far as they did last night if I had not known, with surety, that Matthew knew how you felt. That he did not hold out hope."

"I had to tell him," Cordelia whispered. "But it was awful. Hurting him like that. Matthew does not let many people in, but when he does, he is so very vulnerable to them. We must make him understand that neither of us is going to leave him, and we will always love him and be there for him."

James hesitated, just for a moment. "On the staircase, you spoke to me of pride. It has its downfalls, as we both know. But Matthew will not want to be pitied. He will want us to be blunt and honest, not treat him as an ailing patient. He has enough of that already. I would do anything to spare Matthew pain. I would cut my own hands off if it would help."

"It would be dramatic, but unhelpful," said Cordelia.

"You know what I mean." He reached up to touch her hair. "By all means, let us tell him how important he is to us both. But it would help neither of us to pretend or to lie. We are married, and we will remain married, and in love, until the stars burn out of the sky."

"That is very poetic," said Cordelia. "Rather the sort of thing Lord Byron Mandrake would have said to the beautiful Cordelia."

"I believe she was promised a herd of stallions," said James, "which I cannot provide."

"Well, what use are you then?" Cordelia wondered aloud.

"Is that a challenge, my proud beauty?" he demanded, and drew her toward and under him, until her giggling turned into kisses, and then into gasps, and she wrapped herself around him in the depths of the bed that was theirs now. That would always be theirs.

As they approached the Institute, Cordelia wondered: Would anybody be able to tell that something had changed between her and James? Was there something different now, in the way she looked? In the way James looked? In the way they looked at each other? She touched the globe necklace at her throat; she would never again take it off. Aside from that and her family ring, her only jewelry was the amulet Christopher had given her, which she had pinned to her cuff almost as an afterthought.

They found the Institute in a state of chaos. The Lightwoods—Gabriel, Cecily, Alexander, Sophie, and Gideon—had already departed for Idris. Thomas, Christopher, Ari, and Anna were milling about, choosing which bedrooms they wanted; as far as Cordelia could tell, all the bedrooms were the same, but people seemed to have preferences anyway. Bridget and the other servants were busy stocking the larder with extra food and rushing about making up the new bedrooms. Bridget was singing a song called, ominously, "The Unquiet Grave," which Cordelia took to mean she was in a good mood.

They found Will and Tessa in the drawing room with Jesse and Lucie, who were helping them sort and pack years' worth of Will's meticulous notes on the Institute's stewardship. Cordelia felt a deep sadness that Will and Tessa would have to present *proof* of the years of good they'd done, the Shadowhunters and Downworlders they'd helped, as if the truth of experience didn't matter. Only accusations, fear, and lies.

"It's not just the Mortal Sword," Jesse was saying earnestly, as Will flipped through a leather-bound book of minutes from various meetings. "If you need to tell the truth about me, or my relation to my mother—anything about who I really am—I just want you to know that it's all right. Do what you must do."

"Although," Lucie put in, "it would be better if you didn't."

"Let's hope it doesn't come to that," Will said gently. "What matters to me is that you all stay safe in the Institute while we're gone—"

"Well, we'd be a lot safer if *he* wasn't in charge," Lucie grumbled; she looked up when James and Cordelia came in, glanced from one of them to the other, and raised her eyebrows. "James. Help me make them see sense."

"Sense about what?" said James.

Tessa sighed. "About who will look after the Institute while we're gone."

It was James's turn to raise his eyebrows. "Who?"

"You have to promise," said Will, "not to shout when I tell you."

"Ah," said James, "rather what you said to me when it turned out the puppy you bought me when I was nine was in fact a werewolf, and had to be returned, with apologies, to his family."

"A mistake anyone could make," said Jesse.

"Thank you, Jesse," said Will. "The fact is—it's going to be Charles. Stay strong, James."

"But he's on Bridgestock's side," protested Cordelia. "He said horrible things at the meeting."

"This cannot have been Charlotte's idea," said James.

"No. We needed to put someone in charge who the Inquisitor would agree to," said Will, a rare tinge of bitterness in his voice. "Someone he would trust not to destroy all the evidence of the many times we've had Belial over for tea and croquet."

"I don't like the idea of Charles having access to everything here," said James. "All our records—we can't think of him as an ally—"

"We can't think of him as an enemy, either," said Tessa. "Only as misguided and foolish."

Will said, "As for records, all the most important ones are coming with us to Idris."

"I still don't like it," said James.

"You are under no obligation to like it," said Will. "Only to bear it. If all goes well, we should only be gone for a day or two. Speaking of which, Cordelia, if you'll need to be traveling between Cornwall Gardens and the Institute, we could offer you the use of our carriage—"

"I won't," said Cordelia. "I will remain here with James."

Lucie's eyes widened. She was clearly trying to hold back a look of delight, and doing a poor job of it. "*Really?*"

"You are all my family too," said Cordelia, and smiled at Lucie; she hoped Lucie could read in her smile the thousand things she wanted to say. "I will not leave you at a time like this. Alastair is with my mother, and if I'm required at Cornwall Gardens, I'm sure I'll hear from him right away."

Cordelia *was* sure she'd be hearing from Alastair, quite shortly; after all, she had not come home the night before. She'd sent a message this morning saying all was well, but still. She'd been gone all night without a word. She suspected Alastair would have something to say about that, and that it would not be a brief something.

Tessa smiled demurely. Will seemed not to have noticed anything unusual. "It'll all turn out all right," he said, in his usual cheerful way. "You'll see."

James nodded, but when he looked back at Cordelia, she could see the concern in his face, and she knew it mirrored her own.

Brother Zachariah had not come to see Grace all day, and she had wondered why until Brother Enoch had stopped by her cell with her porridge. Brother Zachariah was in Idris, he had informed her, and it was not known when he would return.

Grace found to her surprise that she felt a small pang upon hearing that. Brother Zachariah was by far the kindest of the Brothers, and the only one who ever attempted to converse with her.

Still, it was far from the most surprising feeling she had had today. She was sitting on the edge of her iron bed, new notes from Christopher in her hand, waiting to be read. But she had not been able to concentrate on them. She kept seeing Cordelia, the look on Cordelia's face as Grace had explained everything. She had not known what Cordelia's reaction would be to the truth. Rage, like James? Cold despair, like Jesse? Perhaps Cordelia would fly at her and hit her. Grace was prepared to accept it if she did.

She knew Cordelia had been incredulous, and horrified. That her eyes had filled with tears when Grace spoke of certain things. *James never loved me. My mother used him. He never knew.*

And yet, at the end of it all, as Cordelia sprang to her feet and rushed to the door of the cell—desperate to get to James, Grace knew—she had made the effort to stop, to pause for a moment. To look at Grace. "I cannot condone what you did," she said. "But it cannot have been easy, telling me all that. I am glad you did."

She had hurt James with the truth, Grace thought, and hurt Jesse perhaps more. But Cordelia—she clung to the thought that in telling Cordelia the truth, she had helped her. That perhaps, after this, Cordelia would be happier.

James loves you, she had told Cordelia. *He loves you with a force that cannot be turned aside, or broken, or made small or insignificant. For these past years Belial struggled against that force, and in the end he lost. And Belial is a power that can move the stars.*

There was something very pleasant about giving people good news, Grace thought. She would very much like to have that feeling again. Specifically, she would like to give Christopher good news about his message experiments. She could imagine his face lighting up, his eyes sparkling behind his spectacles—

"Gracie." A giggle. One so familiar that it sent an arrow of terror through Grace. Her hands released their grip on Christopher's papers; they fluttered to the floor. "Oh, my dear Grace."

Grace turned, slowly. All the blood in her body seemed to have turned solid in her veins; she could barely breathe. There, at the barred door of her cell, stood her mother.

Her hair had lost every last bit of its color. It was bone-white, straggling about her face like a corpse's hair. Her dress was filthy, matted with blood at the shoulder. She was grinning a shark's grin, her mouth like a bloody slash.

"My little daughter," she said. "Shall I come in?"

She put a hand to the cell door, and it swung open; Grace cringed back against the headboard of her bed as Tatiana drifted into the little space where she had been safe. But no space was safe from her mother, Grace thought. She had told Zachariah. He had not believed her.

Tatiana looked down at her. "It is astonishing," she said, "how thoroughly you have failed me."

Grace felt her lips pull back from her teeth. "Good," she said, to her own surprise; the word came out savagely. "Leave me alone. I am no use to you now. They know my power. I can no longer be your tool—"

"Oh, do shut up," said Tatiana mildly, and turned to snap her fingers. "Come along, then," she said to someone in the hall. "We might as well be quick about it."

To Grace's astonishment, a Silent Brother stepped into the room. She did not recognize him as one she'd seen before, even among the group that gathered in the room of the Speaking Stars. He was tall and bony, with scar-like runes, and his face seemed to strain against the threads that closed his mouth and eyes. The hem of his white robe was caked with what looked like soot or ash.

Help me, Grace thought. *This woman is your prisoner. Take her away from me.*

But if the Silent Brother heard her, he gave no sign of it. He stood impassively as Tatiana took a step toward her daughter, then another. "I gave you a great gift, Grace," she said. "I took you in when no one else would have you. And I gave you power, power with which you could attain anything on this earth you wanted. It was one of my most shameful mistakes, one I aim to rectify."

Grace took a step back. "I am your daughter," she said, with what voice she could muster. "I am more than just your instrument. I have feelings of my own, thoughts of my own. Things I wish to do. Things I wish to be."

Tatiana chuckled. "Oh, the naivete of youth. Yes, we all have those at some point, my dear. And then the truths of life come and crush them beneath their wheels."

"And so you ally with a Prince of Hell?" said Grace.

"You owe that prince everything you have," her mother spat. "The power you have squandered. Your place in London society, which you have also squandered. You were never worthy of the gifts you were given," Tatiana went on. "I should never have invested so much effort into you."

"I wish you had not," Grace said. "I wish I had been left alone. I would have grown up in an Institute, and my guardians might not have loved me, but they would not have done to me what you have done to me."

"What I have done to you?" Tatiana echoed in astonishment. "Given you opportunities you could never have had otherwise? The ability to have anyone or anything you wanted, by giving a single command?

Why can you not be more like Jesse? He is loyal in his heart. Recognizing that Herondale witch's connection to our benefactor, becoming her confidant, guiding her toward effecting his resurrection—"

"*That's* what you think?" After all this time, it seemed, Grace's mother could still shock her. "My God. You do not understand Jesse at all."

"Listen to you. Calling upon God," said Tatiana, with derision. "God has no use for you, child. Heaven will not help you. And you will learn the price of spurning Hell."

Grace twisted around to look at the motionless Silent Brother who stood beside Tatiana. Her power was still there, though it felt like years since she had used it. She did not want to use it now, and yet what other choice did she have? "I command you to take hold of my mother," she said, her voice echoing off the cell walls. "I command you to remove her. To take her back to her cell—"

The Silent Brother did not move, as Tatiana laughed out loud. "Grace, you fool. Your power only affects the minds of men, and this one here is not a man. He is not even a Silent Brother."

Not even a Silent Brother? What does that mean?

"And now you wish you could use it, don't you? The gift you spurned," Tatiana hissed. "But it is too late. You have proven yourself unworthy of it, over and over." She turned to the Silent Brother who was not a Silent Brother. "Take it from her. Now."

The Silent Brother's eyes opened. Not like human eyes—they ripped open, leaving dangling threads where they had once been sewn shut. From between his lids shone a terrible light, a light that burned pale green like acid.

He moved toward Grace. Soundless, fast, almost crouching, he came at her, and noise exploded inside her head. It was like the Silent Brothers' unspeaking communication, yet it barely sounded like human speech at all—it was a grinding, scratching roar, as though someone were scraping at the inside of her skull with a fork.

Grace began to scream. She found she could not stop screaming, over and over. But nobody came.

24

Fire Falls Asunder

The fire falls asunder, all is changed,
I am no more a child, and what I see
Is not a fairy tale, but life, my life.
—Amy Lowell, "A Fairy Tale"

Alastair did, in fact, get in touch with Cordelia, even sooner than she had imagined, through the straightforward mechanism of showing up at the Institute.

Will and Tessa had departed through the Portal in the crypt, and the general mood was downcast when the downstairs bell rang. Lucie had been the one to open the front door; she immediately went and got Cordelia, who found her brother in the entryway, stamping snow off his boots. He was carrying a small traveling trunk and wearing a long-suffering expression. "There's a storm brewing," he said, and indeed, Cordelia could see through the open front door that the sky had darkened, thunderclouds like great colliding blocks of smoke roiling across its surface. "This situation," he said, "is utterly ridiculous."

"I don't disagree," Cordelia said, closing the front door and turning to eye Alastair's trunk, "but—have you come to *stay*?"

He stopped in the act of removing his coat. "*Mâmân* told me to stop pacing and join you here. Do you think—they won't let me?" he said, with a sudden hesitation. "I suppose I should have asked—"

"Alastair, *joon*," Cordelia said. "If you want to stay, you will stay.

This is the Institute; they cannot turn you away, and I would not let them. It is only that . . ."

"That they've made Charles temporary Institute head?" Alastair said. "I know." He glanced around, as if to make sure no one else was nearby to overhear him. "It's why I came. I can't leave Thomas alone in close quarters with Charles. There's no telling how unpleasant Charles will decide to be to him, and Thomas is too good-natured to—" He stopped and glared. "Cease looking at me like that."

"You should *talk* to Thomas—"

"*Mikoshamet*," Alastair said, making a fearsome face that would have terrified Cordelia if she were still seven. "Where is everyone, then?"

"Gathering in the library," Cordelia said. "James has something to tell everyone. Come—I'll show you where the rooms are, and you can join me and the others once you're settled in."

"You don't mind, do you?" Cordelia said, her hand on James's shoulder. "If Alastair's there?"

James was sitting in a chair at the head of one of the long library tables. They were alone for now; everyone else was on their way. Everyone but Charles, of course. Charles had arrived just after Will and Tessa had gone, greeted no one, stalked up to Will's office, and shut himself in there. At some point Cordelia had caught sight of Bridget bringing him some tea; even she had a puckered expression, as if she didn't relish the task.

James laid his hand over hers. "He's your brother. Family. I can't imagine how he thinks I've treated you, at that. He should know."

Matthew came in first. And if Cordelia had wondered whether the others would be able to tell something had changed in her relationship with James, she knew immediately that Matthew could and did. She doubted he knew exactly what, of course, but he sat down with a wary look, his shoulders curled in slightly, as if he were awaiting bad news.

We must find a chance to speak with him alone, she thought. *We must.* But it would not be before James told his story; it was too late for that. Everyone was arriving—Anna and Ari, Jesse and Lucie (who looked at James with immense worry, before sitting down at his right hand), Thomas and Christopher, and finally, Alastair, who Thomas clearly had not been expecting. Thomas sat down with a rather sudden thump (he was a bit too big for the library chairs, and his long legs stuck out at all angles) but otherwise restrained himself. Alastair sat beside him with studied nonchalance.

Cordelia tried to catch Christopher's eye across the table. She was not entirely sure why he'd convinced Grace to confess to her, but she was endlessly grateful that he had. He smiled at her, but only in his ordinary, affable, lemon-tarts Christopher way, not in a manner that indicated he knew he'd done something special. She resolved to thank him as soon as she could.

"Well, do tell us what this is about, James," said Matthew, once everyone was seated. "This feels like one of those scenes in a Wilkie Collins novel where the will gets read out, and then the lights go out and someone turns up dead."

"Oh, I *love* those," said Lucie. "Not," she added hastily, "that I want anyone to turn up dead. James, what's going on? Has something happened?"

James was very pale. He folded his hands together, intertwining his fingers tightly. "Something did happen," he said, "though—not today. This is something that happened a long time ago. Something I only became aware of recently myself."

And he told them. Speaking in a monotone, he told it all: from his first meeting with Grace at Blackthorn Manor in Idris, to her arrival in London, to the shattering of the bracelet, to the realization that his mind was being altered against his will. His voice was calm and steady, but Cordelia could hear the anger beneath it, like a river running beneath city streets.

Those present who already knew the story—Cordelia herself, Christopher, Jesse—remained expressionless, watching the reactions of the others. Cordelia, in particular, watched Matthew. This would change so much for him, she thought. Perhaps it would help. Raziel knew, she *hoped* it would help.

He grew more and more still as the story progressed, and more white around the mouth. Lucie looked sick. Thomas began to rock his chair back and forth violently until Alastair laid a hand over his. Anna's eyes snapped like blue fire.

When James was done with the story, there was a long silence. Cordelia yearned to say something, to break the silence, but she knew she could not. James had feared the response of his friends, his family. It had to be one of them who spoke first.

It was Lucie. She had trembled as James spoke, and she burst out now, "Oh—Jamie—I am *so* sorry I ever worked with her, was kind to her—"

"It's all right, Luce," James said gently. "You didn't know. Nobody knew, not even Jesse."

Lucie looked shocked, as if the idea of Jesse having known had never occurred to her. She turned to him. "The last time you went to the Silent City," she said, "you came back upset. Had she told you then?"

Jesse nodded. "It was the first I ever knew of any of it." He looked as ashen as he had when Belial possessed him, Cordelia thought. The usual calm light had gone out of his eyes. "I have always loved Grace. Always taken care of her. She is my little sister. But when she told me—I walked out of the cell. I have not spoken to her since."

Christopher cleared his throat. "What Grace did was unforgivable. But we must remember she was a child when she was given this task. And she was terrified of what her mother would do if she refused."

"That doesn't *matter*," said Thomas. His hazel eyes blazed with a rare fury. "If I murdered someone, and then said it was because I was afraid, would that make me not a murderer?"

"It isn't murder, Thomas—"

"It's just as bad," said Matthew. He held one of the flasks Christopher had given him, but he was not drinking from it. He was running his fingers over the engravings, again and again. "She took the things about James that we know so well, his loving kindness, and his trust, and his idealism, and she turned them against him like knives. Like a faerie curse."

James tried to catch Matthew's eye—Cordelia could see it—but however horrified Matthew seemed to be on James's behalf, he could not meet his *parabatai*'s gaze. He sat with his hand wrapped around the cheap flask as if it were a talisman.

"She stole his choices," Ari said. She, too, looked sick. "I lived with her in my house and I never guessed that she had something like that on her conscience."

"But James is all right," Christopher said gently. "It's come out all right in the end. Things usually do."

"Because he fought back," Matthew snapped. "Because he loved Cordelia enough to crack that foul bracelet in half." Seeming a little surprised at his own outburst, he looked, finally, at James. "You really do love her," he said. "Like you said."

"*Matthew*," said Lucie, looking scandalized.

But James only looked back at Matthew with a steady gaze. "I do," he said. "I always have."

"And Grace?" Thomas said softly.

"I hate her," James said. Christopher flinched; Jesse looked away. "At least—she came to me, at the last, when she was fleeing her mother. Tried to seduce me one last time. She didn't realize the bracelet was broken. It was strange to see her try this game that must have worked every time she'd attempted it in the past. It was as if I were standing outside myself, realizing that every time I'd encountered her before, I had lost myself. That my whole life had been a lie, and she had made it so. I told her I despised her, that I would never forgive her, that there was nothing she could do to make up for her crimes. She is in the Silent City now because I demanded she turn herself in." He sounded a little wondering, as if surprised at his own capacity for anger, for revenge. "I put her there." He looked at Jesse. "You knew that."

"Yes." Jesse sounded wearily despairing. "She told me. I do not blame you at all."

Christopher said, "She did plenty of harm, and she knew the harm she was doing. She hates herself for it. I think all she wants is to live somewhere far away and never bother anyone again."

"That power of hers is too dangerous for that," Alastair said. "It is as if she owned a feral, poisonous snake, or an untamed tiger."

"What if the Silent Brothers take that power from her?" said Christopher. "She will be defanged then."

"Why are you defending her, Kit?" Anna said. She did not sound angry, only curious. "Is it because she will return to the Enclave eventually, and we must learn to live with her? Or simply because she likes science?"

"I suppose," Christopher said, "I have always thought everyone deserves a second chance. We are each given only one life. We cannot get another one. We must live with the mistakes we have made."

"True enough," Alastair muttered.

"Nevertheless," Thomas said, "we cannot forgive her." Alastair flinched and Thomas added, "What I mean is that we cannot forgive her on James's behalf. Only James can do that."

"I'm still angry—very angry," James said, "but I find I don't want to be. I want to look forward, but my anger draws me backward. And"—he took a deep breath—"I know she will return to the Enclave at some point. I do not know how I am meant to treat her then. How I will stand seeing her."

"You won't have to," said Jesse roughly. "There is Blackthorn money. It will come to her, now that my mother is imprisoned. We will get a house for Grace, somewhere in the countryside. I will only ask that she never go near you or anyone close to you again."

"Just don't abandon her entirely," said Christopher. "Jesse—you are the only thing she lives for. The only one who was kind to her. Do not leave her alone in the dark."

"Kit," Anna said, with a regretful sort of love. "Your heart is too soft."

"I am not saying these things because I am naive or foolish," said Christopher. "Only because I do see things that are not in beakers and test tubes, you know. I see how hatred poisons the person who hates, not the person who is hated. If we treat Grace with the mercy she did not show James, and that was never shown to her, then what she did will have no power over us." He looked at James. "You have been terribly strong," he said, "enduring this, all alone, for so long. Let us help you leave anger and bitterness in the past. For if we don't do that, if we are consumed by the need to pay Grace back for what she has done, then how are we any different from Tatiana?"

"Bloody Kit," said Matthew. "When did you get to be so insightful? I thought you were only supposed to be good at putting the contents of one test tube into another test tube and saying, 'Eureka!'"

"That *is* most of it," Christopher agreed. They were in the drawing room, Matthew having had an inexplicable aversion to the idea of retreating to the games room after their long session in the library. In the end, nothing specific had been *decided*, exactly, but Thomas could tell James felt much better than he had. He had been able to smile with a lightness that Thomas had long ago thought gone with his first year at the Academy. Everyone had pledged unwavering support for anything James might choose to do, and of course undying secrecy. James would tell his family, he said, when they returned from Idris; he had not made up his mind about anything else, but he did not need to now. There was time to consider things.

"And let me say it is lovely, James," Ari had said, as they were all standing up, "to see you so happy with Cordelia. A true case of real love winning out."

James and Cordelia had both looked faintly embarrassed, if pleased, but Matthew had looked down at his hands on the table, and Thomas had exchanged a quick signal with Christopher. As the others in the library fell to discussing what could be done to clear the Herondales' names, and again how Cordelia's paladin connection could be severed, Matthew slipped from the room and Thomas and Christopher followed him. Christopher suggested whist, which Matthew agreed to, and Thomas suggested the games room, which Matthew did not.

And to Thomas's great surprise, once they'd made themselves comfortable in the drawing room and Matthew had produced a pack of cards, Alastair had come in.

He had been carrying a thick leather-bound book, and rather than trying to join the game, he'd sat down on a sofa and immersed himself in it. Thomas had waited for Matthew to glare, or say something cutting, but he did neither.

Every once in a while, as they played, Matthew would take out the flask Christopher had given him and run his fingers over the engravings; it seemed a new nervous habit he had formed. Still, he did not drink from it.

When Thomas and Matthew had lost most of their money to Christopher, as was usual, there was a knock on the door, and James poked his head in. "Matthew," he said, "could I speak to you for a moment?"

Matthew hesitated.

"Bad idea," Alastair muttered under his breath, still staring at his book.

Matthew cast Alastair a look, then threw down his cards. "Well, I have lost all I can here," he said. "I suppose I had better see what else there is left for me to lose in this world."

"That's a bit dramatic," said Thomas, but Matthew was already on his feet, following James out into the hall.

Cordelia could tell James had been exhausted by explaining the story of the bracelet. Still, he had had to run the gauntlet of everyone's well-meaning but difficult questions afterward: about his own feelings, then and now, about what would happen with Grace and Tatiana, about whether he was now remembering things he had forgotten before, small details or incidents. And there were apologies from everyone, of course, for not noticing, even though James explained over and over, patiently, that it was the bracelet's magic that made people overlook it. Like a glamour that caused mundane eyes to slide past Downworlders, or Shadowhunters in their gear. They had all been enspelled, at least a little, he had said. They had all been affected.

Through all of this, Cordelia had tried to keep an eye on Matthew, but he had slipped early from the room, with Thomas and Christopher following, and Alastair snatching a book off a shelf before beating a retreat after them.

Once everyone had begun to drift off to various places in the Institute—several of them, along with Lucie, had gathered by the library windows to watch the progress of the storm—James went up to Cordelia and took her hand.

"Where do you think he is?" he said, and he did not have to explain which *he* they were speaking of. She curled her fingers around his, feeling immensely protective—of Matthew and of James in equal measure. If Matthew were angry, if he lashed out at James now that James had opened his heart and spilled his secrets, he could hurt him badly. But Matthew, having learned that what he believed about James when he had gone to Paris with Cordelia had been a lie, could be hurt just as severely.

"Christopher and Thomas will want to distract Matthew," she said. "Matthew won't want to go to the games room—I've an idea where they might be."

She had turned out to be right. All four boys had been in the drawing room; Cordelia waited nervously in the hall with James as Matthew came out to meet them.

He emerged looking tousled, tired, and painfully sober. As if not drinking were like putting down protective armor. Only pride could armor him now—the pride that had kept him upright outside the Hell Ruelle, carefully cleaning his hands with a monogrammed handkerchief as if he had not just been sick in a gutter. Pride that kept his chin up, his eyes steady, as he looked from Cordelia to James and said, "It's all right. I know what you're going to say to me and there's no need."

Hurt flashed across James's face, a sharp, shallow wound. Cordelia said, "It's not all right, Matthew. None of this is the way we would want it to be. What Tatiana did—the effects of the bracelet didn't just change James's life. They changed mine. They changed yours. We've all made choices we wouldn't have made, if we'd known the truth."

"That may be true," Matthew said. "But it doesn't change where we are now."

"It does," said James. "You had every reason to believe I didn't love Cordelia. You couldn't possibly have known what I myself didn't know."

"It doesn't matter," Matthew said, and there was a sharp blade in his voice. Cordelia felt a coldness in her chest. Matthew's moods were mercurial. He could feel one way one moment, and another the next; still, she had never imagined a Matthew who did not think anything mattered.

"It does matter," she said fiercely. "We love you. We know this is a terrible time for these revelations, for any of this—"

"Stop." Matthew held his hands up. They shook slightly in the dim light of the hall. "As I listened to you, James, in the library, I could not help but think I have lived all this beside you. Noticing nothing and knowing nothing."

"I explained," James said. "The bracelet—"

"But I am your *parabatai*," said Matthew, and Cordelia realized the blade in his voice was set against himself. "I was so much in my own misery that I never saw the truth. I knew it made little sense for you to love Grace. I know your heart, your sensibilities. There was nothing about her that would have won your affections in any sensible world, yet I let it pass by, dismissed it as a mystery of human behavior. The mistakes I made, the signs I missed—"

"Math," James said, in despair. "*None of this is your fault.*"

But Matthew was shaking his head. "Don't you see?" he said. "Cordelia told me already, at the party, that she loved you. And I thought, well, I can be disappointed, I can be angry, for some short time. I am allowed that. But now—how can I be either of those things? I cannot be disappointed that you have your life back, and your steadfast love. I cannot be angry when you have done nothing wrong. I cannot be angry at anyone but myself."

And with that, he turned and walked back into the drawing room.

Christopher and Thomas pretended to play cards until Matthew returned to the room. At least Thomas was pretending. He wasn't quite sure what Christopher was doing; he might have invented his own game without mentioning it to Thomas, and be contentedly playing along with its rules.

Alastair continued steadfastly reading his book, at least until Matthew stalked back into the room. Thomas's heart sank—he guessed the conversation with James had not gone well. Matthew looked feverish: there was a high color in his cheeks, and his eyes were bright. "No more cards for me," he announced. "I'm going to go confront Charles about being blackmailed."

Alastair dropped his book with a thump. "I had a feeling you were going to do something like that."

"So you didn't just come in here to read a book about"—Matthew stared—"sixteenth-century warlock burnings? Ugh."

"I did not," said Alastair. "I chose it randomly from the shelves. What a pity so many books are filled with terrible things."

"Why did you think I intended to confront my brother?"

Alastair began ticking off the reasons on his fingers. "Because

Charles is here, because he's shut himself up in the main office, because the other adults are gone, and because he can't do a bolt since he's supposed to look after the Institute."

"Well, you are entirely—correct," said Matthew, rather grudgingly. "You have outlined why it is an excellent plan."

"Math," said Thomas. "I'm not so sure it is—"

"I have outlined the positives," interrupted Alastair. "There are also negatives. We are all stuck in this building with Charles, and he can make life unpleasant for us if you upset him, which you will."

Matthew looked at all three of them in turn. It was a direct look, and also very sober, in both senses of the word. Not just serious—Thomas had seen Matthew serious many times, but there was something different about him now. As if he knew he were shouldering a burden of risk; as if he no longer believed consequences were something that happened to other people: not him, not his friends.

It jolted Thomas a little to realize that this Matthew, this newly considering person, was a different Matthew from the one he'd known for the past three years. *Who have you been*, he thought, *and who are you becoming now?*

"My brother is miserable," Matthew said, "and when he is miserable, he makes life awful for other people. I want to tell him that I know, not only so that he'll stop doing it, but also to take some of the burden away. For all our sakes."

After a moment, Alastair nodded. "All right. I won't stand in your way."

"Well, thank goodness, as I was waiting desperately for your approval," said Matthew, but there was no real malice in it.

In the end, it was decided Matthew would go, and Thomas would accompany him to keep the whole thing from descending into a family squabble. Charles had to understand that this was a serious matter, that not only Matthew knew about it, and that it could not be swept under the rug.

Thomas followed Matthew upstairs, dreading the awkwardness to come. Without knocking, Matthew burst open the double doors of Will's office, where Charles appeared to be deep into a pile of ledger books on the desk.

He looked up blandly when they came in. "Thomas," Charles said. "Matthew. Is anything the matter?"

"Charles," Matthew said, with no further preamble, "you are being blackmailed to ensure your support of Bridgestock, and it must stop. You cannot fear Bridgestock so much that you are willing to sell out everyone who has ever cared for you. Even you cannot be so low."

Charles sat back slowly in his chair. "I suppose I ought to expect this sort of fanciful accusation from you, Matthew," he said. "But I'm surprised he got you to go along with it, Thomas."

Thomas felt suddenly weary. Sick of the whole thing. He said, "He has proof, Charles."

Something flickered in Charles's eyes. "What sort of proof?"

"A letter Bridgestock wrote," said Matthew.

"As usual," Charles sighed, "you have jumped to a conclusion based on nothing but conjecture. May I ask how you came across such a note? Assuming you do have it, and it is from the Inquisitor—which is quite a wild accusation, by the way."

"It is here," Matthew said, drawing the letter from his inside jacket pocket and holding it up. "As to how we got hold of it, Ari found it. That is why she left home. The letter is clearly meant for you. There is absolutely no doubt as to what is going on."

Charles's face had gone sallow. "Then why did you not speak to me about this before?"

"The letter did not make it clear what he wanted you to *do*," said Thomas. "After your performance at the meeting yesterday, we know. You spoke out against Will and Tessa, against your own family, because he threatened you, and you were too afraid to tell him no."

Charles said, with a ghastly sort of smile, "And what do you think *you* can do to fix it?"

"Stiffen your spine," said Matthew. "So Bridgestock plans to tell everyone you love men. So what? Some will understand; those who don't are not worth your knowing."

"You don't understand." Charles put his head in his hands. "If I want to do good in this world, if I want to rise to a position of authority in the Clave . . . I cannot—" He hesitated. "I cannot be like you, Matthew. You've no ambition, and so you can be whomever you want. You can dance with anyone you wish, man, woman, or other, at your salons and your clubs and your orgies."

"You attend orgies?" Thomas said to Matthew.

"Don't I wish," murmured Matthew. "Charles, you're a pillock, but you've always been a decent pillock. Don't throw that away because of bloody Maurice Bridgestock."

"And how, exactly," said Charles, "are you proposing to help? If I reverse my opinion on the Herondales, it will only mean I am condemned with them."

"We will vouch for you," Thomas said. "We will testify that you are being blackmailed and that you were coerced into supporting Bridgestock."

"There is no way to do that," said Charles, "without revealing the blackmail letter and its contents. You understand he is not just threatening to tell people I love men, but that I love—that I loved Alastair. It is Alastair, too, whom I am protecting."

The door burst open. Alastair stalked inside, his black eyes snapping. He looked furious, and also rather—in Thomas's view—glorious. Proud and strong as the Persian kings of old. "Then stop," he said to Charles. "I don't need your protection, not where this is concerned. I'd rather everyone know than that you let a dozen good people be dragged down by lies, just because you fear Bridgestock."

Charles's face appeared to crumple. "None of you can possibly understand what it is like to hold on to this kind of secret—"

"We *all* understand," Thomas said forcefully. "Myself as well. I'm like you, you idiot. I always have been. And Charles, you're right, it isn't as easy as it is for Matthew, who has never cared what anyone thought. Most of us do care. And the secret is your own business, and it is disgusting of Bridgestock to have used it against you like this. But neither can Will and Tessa, and all our parents, pay such a terrible price for his criminality."

"They will be vindicated by the Mortal Sword," Charles said hoarsely. "Then this will all be over."

"Charles," said Alastair. "Don't you know how blackmail works? It's never *over*. It'll never be *enough* for Bridgestock. He'll hold your secret over you for as long as he's able. You think he won't want other things in the future? That he'll simply give up his leverage? He will bleed you *dry*."

Charles looked back and forth between Alastair and Matthew, his expression anguished. Thomas felt for him; Charles was being a coward, but he knew well how difficult bravery could be in such a situation. "If we seek to bring down Bridgestock," Thomas said, "will you help? Even if you cannot disclose the . . . the contents of the blackmail?"

Charles looked at them helplessly. "It would depend on what was being done, and what its consequences might be—" he began.

Matthew shook his head, his fair hair flying. "Charles, you are being a milksop and a blockhead. Let the record show that I tried. I tried, despite how little you deserve it."

With that, he stalked out of the room.

Charles looked at Alastair, as if there was no one else in the room. No one else in the world. "Alastair, I . . . you know I can't."

"You can, Charles," Alastair said tiredly. "And there are people in the world like us who don't have what you do. A family that will never abandon you. Money. Safety. People who could lose their lives for confessing such a thing. All you will lose is prestige. And still you will not do the right thing."

There seemed nothing more to say. Charles seemed visibly shrunken, but he was still shaking his head, as if denial could ward off the truth. Alastair turned on his heel and left; after a moment, Thomas followed.

He found himself alone in the corridor with Alastair. Matthew was already long gone. Alastair was leaning back against the wall, breathing hard. "*Ahmag*," he snarled, which Thomas was fairly sure meant *idiot*; he was also fairly sure Alastair didn't mean him.

"Alastair," he said, meaning to say something vague and kind, something about how none of this was Alastair's fault, but Alastair caught hold of Thomas and pulled him close, his fingers cupping the back of Thomas's neck. His eyes were wide, black, feverish. "I need to get out of here," he said. "Come for a carriage ride with me. I have to breathe." He leaned his forehead against Thomas's. "Come with me, please. I need you."

* * *

"Daisy, you summoned a *demon*? All by yourself?" Lucie exclaimed. "How enterprising and brave and—also a terrible idea," she added hastily, catching James's dark expression. "A very bad idea. But also, enterprising."

"Well, it was certainly *interesting*," Cordelia said. She was perched on the edge of a table, nibbling the corner of a piece of shortbread. "I wouldn't do it again, though. Unless I had to."

"Which you will not," James said. He gave Cordelia a mock-stern look, and she smiled at him, and the stern part of the look melted away. Now they were gazing soppily at each other.

Lucie could not help but be delighted. It was as if James had been going around with something missing, some small piece taken out of his soul, and now it was put back. He was not perfectly happy, of course; being in love did not mean one did not notice anything else going on in the world. She knew he was worried about Matthew—who was currently lounging in one of the window seats, reading a book and not eating—and about their parents; about Tatiana and Belial and what was happening in Idris. But now, at least, she thought, he could face these things with his whole self intact.

They were all gathered in the library, where Bridget had set out sandwiches, game pies, tea, and pastries for them, since, as she loudly complained, she did not have time to put together a real supper for so many people on short notice. (Besides, she had added, the brewing storm was giving her the worriments, and she could not concentrate enough to cook.)

Everyone except Thomas and Alastair—who had, according to Matthew, rather inexplicably gone on some sort of errand in an Institute carriage—had gathered around the food. Even Charles had turned up briefly, taken a game pie, and stormed out, leaving them to an inevitable discussion of Belial's plans.

"Now that we know this whole dreadful bracelet business," Anna said, sitting cross-legged in the middle of a table near a shelf holding books on sea demons, "surely it points toward Belial's goals. Certainly breaking James's heart and tormenting him was *part* of it," she added, "but I do not believe it was a goal in itself. More of a treat to enjoy along the way."

"Ugh." Cordelia shuddered. "Well, clearly he sought to control

James. He always has—he wishes James to collude with him. To offer up his body for possession. He no doubt hoped he could talk him into it using Grace."

Christopher, holding a chicken sandwich as delicately as he might hold a beaker of acid, said, "It is a terrible story, but an encouraging one in a way. The bracelet was Belial's will made manifest. But James matched Belial's will with his own."

James frowned. "I do not feel ready for a battle of wills with Belial," he said. "Though I have wondered if my training with Jem has helped me to hold out against him."

The courtyard below seemed to flash in colors of blue and scarlet as lightning speared through the clouds. And the clouds themselves—Lucie had never seen anything like them. Thick but jagged-edged, as though they had been drawn onto the darkening sky with a razor dipped in melted gunmetal. As they heaved and collided with each other, she felt her skin prickle, as if snapped by a dozen elastic bands.

"Are you all right?" It was Jesse, his look quizzical. He had been quiet since James had told his story. Lucie could understand why; though she had told him over and over that no one could possibly blame him, she knew he did not, could not, entirely believe her.

"I feel awful," Lucie said. "James is my brother, yet I allied myself with Grace, even held secret meetings with her. I did not know what she had done, but I did know she'd hurt him. I knew she'd broken his heart. I just thought . . ."

Jesse said nothing, only leaned against the window, letting her gather her thoughts.

"I suppose I thought it wasn't real heartbreak," she said. "That he didn't really love her. I always thought he'd come to his senses and realize he loved Daisy."

"Well, in a way, that was true."

"It doesn't matter," Lucie said. "She may not have broken his heart in the classic sense, but what she did was much worse. And yet—" She looked up at Jesse. "If I had not done what I did, I don't know if I would have gotten you back."

"Believe me." Jesse's voice was husky. "Where it comes to my sister, I too am torn."

Thunder cracked again outside, loud enough to rattle the windows in their frames. The wind was tearing around the Institute, howling down the chimney. It was the sort of evening Lucie usually enjoyed, curled up in bed with a book while a storm raged. Now, she found it made her uneasy. Perhaps it was the unseasonable nature of the storm—when did snow ever come with thunder and lightning?

The door to the library slammed open. It was Charles, his red hair falling out of its usual cap of stiff pomade. He was pushing someone ahead of him, someone in a torn and wet dress, with straggling hair the color of milk.

Lucie saw James stiffen. "Grace," he said.

Everyone went still, save Christopher, who rose to his feet, his expression hardening. "Charles, what on earth—?"

Charles's face was twisted in a look of fury. "I found her creeping around the entrance to the Sanctuary," he said. "She's broken out of the Silent City, clearly."

Did he know? Lucie wondered. Did he know what Grace had done to him, that she had enspelled him into proposing to her? James had said that his own memories of Grace's past actions were coming back to him; perhaps Charles's were too. He certainly seemed angry enough for it to be possible.

Lucie had always thought of Grace as cold and self-possessed, hard and shining as an icicle. But now she was cringing back—she looked awful; her hair was hanging in wet strings, there were scratches up and down her bare arms, and she was shivering violently. "Let me go, Charles—please, let me go—"

"Let you *go*?" said Charles incredulously. "You're a prisoner. A criminal."

"I hate saying this, but Charles is right," said Matthew, who had put his book away. He, too, was on his feet. "We should contact the Silent City—"

"It's gone," Grace whispered. "It's all gone."

Lucie could not help but look at James. It was clear, when he had told them his story earlier, that he did not expect to encounter Grace again soon, if ever; now he looked frozen in place, staring at her as if she were a dream that had sprung to life, and not the nice kind of dream.

It was Cordelia who, placing a hand on James's arm, said, "Grace, what do you mean? What's gone?"

Grace was shivering so hard her teeth chattered. "The Silent City. It's been taken—"

"Stop lying," Charles interrupted. "Look here—"

Jesse snapped. "Charles, *stop*," he said, stalking across the room. "Let go of her," he added, and Charles, to everyone's surprise, did exactly that, though with a look of reluctance. "Gracie," Jesse said carefully, drawing off his jacket. He flung it over Grace's thin shoulders; Jesse was hardly burly, but his jacket seemed to swallow up his sister. "How did you get out of the Silent City?"

Grace said nothing, only clutched Jesse's jacket around her and trembled. There was a starkness in her eyes that frightened Lucie. She had seen that look before, in the eyes of ghosts whose last memories were of something dreadful, something terrifying . . .

"She needs runes," Jesse said. "Healing runes, warming runes. I don't know how—"

"I'll do it," said Christopher. Ari and Anna rose to help him, and soon enough Grace was seated on a chair, with Christopher drawing on her left arm with his stele. She would not let go of Jesse's jacket, but clutched it around herself with one hand.

"Grace," James said. Some of the color had come back to his face. His voice was steady. "You need to tell us what's happened. Why you're here."

"I hate to say this," said Anna, "but ought she be restrained while we question her? She does have a very dangerous power."

Grace pushed a handful of wet hair back from her face. "My power's gone," she said dully. "It was taken."

"And why should we believe that?" said Charles, frowning.

"Because it's true," said Christopher. "She told you to let her go, Charles. And you didn't."

"He's right," Matthew said. "I've seen her use it before. Charles should have had to do whatever she asked."

Charles looked puzzled. Lucie, too, was puzzled—*when* had Matthew seen Grace use her power? But there was no time to ask.

"Well, that's good, isn't it?" said Cordelia. "The Silent Brothers were supposed to take it away."

"They didn't," said Grace. She began to shake wildly. "It was my mother. They brought her into the Silent City. I told them she would find me *and she did*—"

She lifted her hands, as if she could ward something off, something terrible and invisible. Christopher caught at her wrist as Jesse's jacket slid to the floor. To Lucie's surprise, his touch seemed to calm Grace. She leaned toward him—it seemed instinctive, unconscious—and said, "She ripped the power out of me. Not with her own hands. She had some kind of creature with her, some kind of demon."

"This is nonsense," Charles said. "Tatiana is safely locked in the Silent City, and this is some tale Grace has concocted to explain why she has escaped from prison."

"I don't think it's nonsense," Cordelia said sharply. "If she had truly escaped from the Silent City, this is the last place she'd come."

"There's one way to be sure," James said. "Charles, we must reach the Silent City."

There was a long silence. Then: "Fine," Charles said. "I'll summon the First Patrol. We'll ride out to Highgate; see what's going on. If anything at all," he added, with a tinge of malice.

He left, slamming the library door behind him. Jesse had come to stand on the other side of Grace, opposite Christopher. He put his hand on his sister's shoulder. Lucie could tell it was costing him an effort, to treat her as he always had. But Grace seemed to relax at the touch; she brushed quickly at her face, and Lucie realized she was crying.

"Grace," Christopher said, "it's all right. You're safe here. Just tell us, slowly, what happened."

"I told them," Grace said in a singsong voice. "That she would always find me, my mother. She came to my cell. She had one of them with her. They look like Silent Brothers but they're not. Its eyes were—open. They shone with an awful sort of light."

James straightened up. "Its eyes were alight? Did they shine with a color?"

"Green," Grace said. "An ugly sort of awful green. The Silent Brother, he put his hands on my face, and my mother told him to take away my power, to rip it out of me."

"It hurt?" Jesse asked gently. Lucie could hear the pain in his voice.

And the fear. A sense of dread was growing in him, as it was in her, Lucie guessed. As it was in all of them.

Grace nodded. "She was laughing. She said I didn't matter anymore. That I was nothing now. An empty shell. She turned her back on me, so—I ran. I ran through the Silent City—it was full of those *creatures.*" Her voice rose, her words tripping over each other. "They looked like Silent Brothers and Iron Sisters, but they weren't. They had weapons, and those awful eyes. They were attacking the real Brothers. I saw Brother Enoch stab one of them with a longsword, but it didn't fall down. It didn't die. It should have died. Even a Silent Brother would have died from that. They're not immortal." She clutched her bare, frost-reddened hands together, and Lucie could not help remembering how glamorous she had once found Grace, how perfectly elegant. Her pale hair hung in wet snarls, and her feet, Lucie suddenly realized, were bare—bare and filthy and crusted with dried blood.

"The real Silent Brothers began to move up the stairs. Brother Enoch saw me, and he pulled me along with them. It was like being caught up in a flood. It carried me along. Enoch was trying to shield me. He kept saying I had to tell the Institute something—"

"What was it?" James said. "What did we need to know?"

Grace cringed back. She was *afraid* of James, Lucie realized suddenly. Because he had been angry at her, because he had sent her to the prisons of the Bone City? Lucie knew he would never have laid a hand on Grace. She recalled her father telling her once, *There is no one on earth we recoil from more than those we have wronged.* Perhaps that was what it was. Perhaps Grace had it within her to feel guilt.

"Grace," Ari said. She spoke gently but firmly, like a nanny to a child. "What did Brother Enoch say?"

"He said that my mother must have found the key," Grace whispered. "And taken it from the Citadel." She swallowed. "He said *they* had come from the Path of the Dead. Then he pushed me through a door, and I fell out into the night. I was alone. I was in London, and I was alone in the graveyard."

"What of the other Silent Brothers?" said Matthew. "Jem is in Idris, but Enoch, Shadrach—"

Grace shook her head. "I don't know. I couldn't get back into the City, couldn't even see the door. I ran until I found the road. A hansom cab pulled over, asked if I was all right. He felt sorry for me, the driver. He brought me here—"

She was cut off by the sound of the Institute gate slamming open, a harsh, metallic thud. Lucie turned to the window, peering out through the half-frosted pane. "It's Charles," she said in relief, seeing the redheaded figure on horseback gallop through the gates. "He's riding Balios out to Highgate."

The gate closed behind him. The air was full of flying bits of small debris, snatched up by the wind: twigs and dead leaves and bits of old birds' nests. Above, the clouds seemed to be heaving and surging like the surface of the sea.

"The key," Anna said, frowning. "What does that mean, that Tatiana took the key from the Adamant Citadel?"

"My mother was looking for a key," Jesse said grimly. "She and Belial. It was in her notes."

Matthew said, "A key to the prisons of the Silent City, perhaps? Tatiana must have let herself out of her cell. And let these—these things in. These false Silent Brothers and Iron Sisters."

"We know from what James saw in the mirror that Belial was trying to possess someone," said Jesse. "That he was using Chimera demons. They must have possessed the Silent Brothers, and be acting on Belial's orders—"

"Silent Brothers cannot be possessed," said Cordelia. "They have the same protections we all do. If anything, theirs would be stronger."

Still holding Grace's wrist, Christopher said, "It sounds as if they were fighting with each other, isn't that right, Grace? As if some of them were defending you and the City?"

Grace nodded. "Enoch was still himself. And the others that I recognized. The dark ones, the glowing ones—they were strangers. I'd never seen them before."

"Really," said James. "Were they dressed differently, as well? Try to remember, Grace. It's important."

Lucie gave him a hard look—James had clearly thought of something, but his look was inward. He was caught up in the net of his own thoughts, working through the problem before him as if he were unknotting a ball of string.

Grace looked at her feet. "Yes. Their robes were white, instead of parchment, and they had different runes on them."

"White robes." Lucie exchanged a look with James; she could feel her face growing hot with anxiety. "Burial garments."

"The Iron Tombs," said James. "That's how Belial managed it. Most Silent Brothers would be protected from possession, but *not the ones in the tombs*. Their souls have left their bodies, and those bodies have been taken to rest under the volcanic plains, near the Adamant Citadel. They're empty vessels."

Anna cursed floridly. Ari said, "There *is* a key to the Tombs. I've seen drawings of it. It's kept—oh, it's kept in the Adamant Citadel—" She covered her mouth with her hand.

Jesse said numbly, "My mother must have stolen it. She would have unlocked the tombs for Belial, let him in. He would have brought the Chimeras there. Possessed the bodies of the Iron Sisters and Silent Brothers who were lying there, undefended. And once that was done, marched them to the Silent City to attack."

"'They wake,'" Cordelia whispered. "'They rise.' 'They march.' All those messages, they were *telling* us what step Belial was at in his plan. But we didn't realize."

"We've been outplayed," James said quietly. "That business of Tatiana's, appearing at the Christmas party, throwing out those accusations, even kidnapping Alexander—"

"It was too easy, capturing her," Cordelia said. "She *wanted* to be arrested. She wanted to be thrown into the Silent City so she could do—whatever this is."

"I don't know if it's what she wants, precisely," said Jesse. "All of this is what Belial wants. He used her, as a pawn in his chess game. A piece he could move into the Silent City, a sort of Trojan horse, filled with his evil, his will—"

A massive thunderclap sounded. It shook the Institute: several lamps fell over, and the burning logs tumbled in the grate. Lucie gripped the windowsill as the others gasped—and saw, through the glass, that the Institute gate was open.

But it was far too soon for Charles to have returned from Highgate. She rose up on her tiptoes to look down.

And froze.

In the courtyard below stood Tatiana Blackthorn, a deadly scarecrow in a bloodstained dress. The wind whipped her stark-white hair around her face. Her arms were upraised, as if she meant to call down the lightning.

And she was not alone. Surrounding her in a half circle were just what Grace had described—Silent Brothers, in ice-white robes, their hoods pushed back to show their eyes, which shone with an acid-green fire.

Tatiana threw her head back, and black lightning crackled through the clouds. "Come out!" she called, in a voice that echoed like a massive bell tolling through the Institute, shaking the stone of its foundations. "Come out, Lightwoods! Come out, Carstairs! Come out, Fairchilds! Come out, Herondales! *Come out and meet your fate!*"

25

Vexed with Tempest

Dark, waste, and wild, under the frown of Night
Starless exposed, and ever-threatening storms
Of Chaos blustering round, inclement sky;
Save on that side which from the wall of Heaven,
Though distant far, some small reflection gains
Of glimmering air less vexed with tempest loud.
—John Milton, *Paradise Lost*

"*Laanati,*" Alastair muttered. *Damn it.* He was staring out the window of the carriage, which he had been doing ever since he and Thomas had clattered out of the courtyard. Thomas had heard him tell Davies, the driver, "Just keep going around the streets, I don't much care where," and Davies seemed to have taken the directive to heart. Thomas, who had lived in London all his life, had absolutely no idea where they currently were.

It had been cold in the carriage at first, and both of them had snatched up blankets from a folded pile. After which Thomas had waited expectantly for Alastair to begin a conversation—after all, why would Alastair have requested his company if he didn't have something to *say*?—but Alastair had only slumped back against his seat, occasionally muttering a curse in Persian.

"Look," Thomas said finally, trying not to let disappointment gnaw at him. "We ought to go back to the Institute. The others will worry—"

"I imagine they will worry that I kidnapped you," said Alastair.

Thunder cracked overhead like a whip. The wind was blowing hard enough to rock the carriage on its wheels. Dry brown leaves and flakes of icy snow were swept into small tornadoes, scraping the glass of the windows, rattling down the deserted streets. Even in the carriage, the air felt heavy and pressurized.

"Are you upset because of Charles?" Thomas asked. He worried the question was too blunt, but Alastair was so silent anyway. There seemed nothing to lose.

"That is a part of it," Alastair said. The light coming into the carriage through the window was tinged with red, as if there was fire burning in the storm clouds above. "When I first met Charles, I would look at him and see who I wished to be. Someone confident, who knew his path, his future. I realize now it was a sham. That he feels utterly powerless. He is so overwhelmed with fear and shame that he believes he has no choices." His hand made a fist in his lap. "And I fear that I am doing the same."

Thomas could see row houses outside the window, and London plane trees laden with snow. The wind was a soft howl, the lampposts lining the street tinged with a smoky glow. "Are you saying that you're afraid of what people would think if they knew your true feelings about—"

"About you?" Alastair said. His dark eyes were somber. "No."

Of course not. Of course he doesn't mean you.

"No," Alastair went on. "I have presented this move to Tehran to myself, to you, to my sister, as a chance for a fresh start. They were words my father always spoke, every time we left a place we had made a home and set out for somewhere new. '*A fresh start.*'" His voice was bitter. "It was never the truth. We were moving to get away from the problems my father had created—from his debts, his drinking. As if he could outrun them. And I—" His eyes were haunted. "I *never* wanted to be like him, I fought so hard not to be like him. And yet I find myself planning to run away. To do what he would do. Because I'm afraid."

Thomas kicked the blanket off his lap. The carriage rocked under his feet as he moved to sit on the opposite bench beside Alastair. He wanted to put his hand over Alastair's but held back. "I have never thought of you as afraid," he said, "but there is no shame in it. What are you afraid of?"

"Change, I suppose," Alastair said, a little desperately. Outside, the branches of trees whipped back and forth in the wind. Thomas could hear a dull roaring sound—thunder, he guessed, though it was oddly muffled. "I know that I must change myself. But I don't know how to do it. There is no instruction manual for becoming a better person. I fear that if I remain in London, I will only continue hurting the people I've hurt before—"

"But you *have* changed," Thomas said. "Without being instructed on how to do so. The person you were when we were at school wouldn't have rushed to help me when I got arrested. Wouldn't have followed me in the first place, to make sure I was safe. The person you used to be wouldn't have looked after Matthew. Wouldn't be reading book after book about paladins to try to help his sister." Thomas's hands were shaking. It felt like a terrible risk, saying these things to Alastair. As if he were stripping away protective gear, leaving himself vulnerable. He swallowed and said, "*I* wouldn't feel the way I do about you if you were the same person now that you were last year."

Alastair looked at him. He said, his voice husky, "I thought you liked me last year."

Thomas stared at him. And, unexpectedly, Alastair started to smile. "I was teasing you," he said. "Thomas, you—"

Thomas kissed him. He caught Alastair by the lapel of his coat, and then he was kissing Alastair, and both their mouths were cold and then not cold at all. Alastair arched up against him as the carriage lurched, his hands twining in Thomas's hair. He pulled Thomas against him, hard and then harder.

Thomas's pulse beat hotly in every part of his body. Alastair pressed his mouth against his, his lips finding ways to tease and explore, and then their mouths were open, their tongues sliding against each other, and the carriage lurched hard, throwing them both to the floor.

Neither of them cared. They had landed on Thomas's discarded blanket. Thomas tore at Alastair's coat, yanking the buttons free. He wanted to feel Alastair, feel the shape of him, not just crumpled wool under his hands. Alastair was on top of him; behind Alastair he could

see the sky through the windows. It was riven by storm, the clouds slashed through with a bloody channel of fire.

Thomas struggled out of his own coat. Alastair was leaning over him, his eyes black as a starless night. He opened the collar of Thomas's shirt and kissed his throat. He found the notch of Thomas's collarbone and licked it, making stars explode behind Thomas's eyes.

He tore at Thomas's shirt. The buttons came free, and he shoved Thomas's undershirt up, baring his chest. "Look at you," Alastair said, in a low voice. "Beautiful. You're so beautiful, Tom."

Thomas felt tears burn behind his eyes. He tried to tell himself not to be ridiculous, but that little buzzing voice in the back of his head, the one that mocked him when he was fanciful, was silent. There was only Alastair, who bit and kissed and licked at him until he was writhing and crying out, until he was pulling Alastair's shirt free, running his hands over Alastair's bare skin, silk pulled tight over hard muscle.

He rolled over, pinning Alastair beneath him. His naked skin against Alastair's was driving him out of his mind. He wanted more of it. More of Alastair. Alastair's bare chest was gorgeous, marked with old scars, his nipples peaked in the cold air. Thomas bent his head and circled one with his tongue.

Alastair's whole body arched. He whimpered low in his throat, clawed at Thomas's back. "Tom. *Tom*—"

With a slamming lurch, the carriage struck hard against something. Thomas heard the wheels scream, the whinny of the horses as the whole thing tilted to the side. A clap of thunder, loud as the crack of a whip, sounded overhead as the carriage came to a grinding halt.

Alastair was already sitting up, buttoning his shirt. "Bloody hell," he said. "What was that?"

"We must have hit something." Thomas did his best to put his clothes back as they had been, though half his buttons were torn. "You're all right?"

"Yes." Alastair looked at Thomas, then leaned over and kissed him, hard, on the mouth. A second later he was throwing the carriage door open and leaping out.

Thomas heard him hit the ground, heard him suck in his breath. There was a bitter smell in the air, he thought as he clambered after

Alastair, like charcoal. "Bloody hell," Alastair said. "What *is* all this?"

A moment later, Thomas was leaping out of the carriage after him.

"Well," Matthew said as Tatiana's shriek faded on the air, "I think we can all agree that that's one invitation we should turn down." He looked around the room at the others, all of whom seemed stunned, even Anna. "We should at least wait until Charles gets back with the First Patrol."

"I never thought I'd hear you say we should wait for Charles," said Anna, who was already drawing a seraph blade from her belt.

"Tatiana's a madwoman," said Matthew. "There's no telling what she'll do."

"She'll break the doors down," Jesse said. "Those things with her—they're *Shadowhunters*. Demons in Shadowhunter skin. They can come inside the Institute."

"Jesse's right," said Grace, who had begun to shake again. "Mama's only making it an invitation now because it amuses her to force you to do what she wants."

"So if we don't go down there," said Cordelia, "she and her demon companions will burst in here."

"Then we'll all go," James said, "and hold her off at the front door. The Sanctuary's locked; there's no other way in." He turned to the others, who were busy laying hands on whatever weapons they had. Most had a seraph blade or two; Ari had her *khanda*, Jesse the Blackthorn sword. "I think Jesse and I should go outside and confront her in the yard. The rest of you remain at the entryway, as defense. Keep the false Silent Brothers from trying to creep around and get inside. I'll try to keep her talking, at least until Charles and the First Patrol return—"

"Jesse isn't trained, though," Matthew said, buckling on his weapons belt. "Let me go outside with you. She demanded a Fairchild, didn't she?"

James said, "Jesse's the one of us she's least likely to hurt. The only one who might give her pause."

"I should confront Tatiana," Cordelia said.

James turned to face her. She had her chin up, her gaze fixed unwaveringly on his. "I am a paladin. She should fear me. She should fear Lilith."

"But she won't know that unless you start fighting," Lucie protested. "Unless Lilith is summoned. And I can't imagine summoning Lilith will make the situation better."

"There may be a point where it can't make it worse," Cordelia said quietly. "I promise—I won't lift a weapon unless there's no other choice. But I want to go out there."

James wanted to shake his head, wanted to protest that Cordelia should stay inside, stay safe. But he knew that was a kind of protection Cordelia would never accept. He could ask her to remain inside, and perhaps she would do it because he had requested it, but it would be asking her to be someone other than who she was.

"Come out!" Tatiana shrilled, and Lucie felt the shriek in her bones. "Come out, Herondales! Come out, Carstairs! Come out, Lightwoods! *I will not ask again!*"

"I'm going outside," Cordelia said firmly, and there was no chance for James to protest anyway; they were all headed downstairs, all save Grace, who watched them go, her face blank and sad, as if she had exhausted even her capacity to be afraid.

Tatiana had not moved from her place in the center of the courtyard. As James walked out the front door of the Institute, followed by Cordelia and Jesse, he saw her standing below them, near the foot of the steps. She faced the Institute, grinning, surrounded by demons and shadow.

The sky overhead was a boiling mass of dark gray clouds, laced with black and scarlet. The moon was visible only as a dim and flickering lamp behind a frost of reddish-white, casting the courtyard of the Institute into a bloody light.

Tatiana's white hair streamed around her like smoke. It was as if she had brought storm and darkness with her, as if she had ridden the forked lightning that crackled through the clouds. On either side of her stood three Silent Brothers, in the white robes Grace had described. The runes that edged the cuffs and plackets were runes of

Quietude and Death; Grace would not have recognized them as such, but James did. Each held a staff, as the Silent Brothers usually did, but their staffs crackled with a dark energy, and each wooden tip had been sharpened to a wicked point. They flanked Tatiana like foot soldiers flanking a general.

James held his pistol firmly in his right hand. Cordelia had taken up a place on his left; Jesse stood at his right. The others were inside the entryway, waiting with weapons in hand.

"Tatiana Blackthorn," James said. "What do you want?"

He felt strangely calm. He had faced Tatiana before, when she had surrendered to him at the Lightwoods', but she had been lying and pretending then. Perhaps she intended to lie and pretend again, but now he expected it. Now there was a metallic taste in his mouth, and a hot wire of rage running through his veins. He had been angry at Grace for some time, and still was, but in truth, it was Tatiana who had been the architect of his misery. Grace had only ever been the blade in her hand.

She narrowed her eyes, looking at him. It was clear she'd thought he would be shocked at her appearance, and she was taken aback by his calm. "*Grace*," she hissed. "My traitor daughter came before me, did she not? She told you I had taken the Silent City. That stupid child. I should have ordered my Watchers to kill her when the chance presented itself, but . . . my heart is too soft."

Jesse made a noise in the back of his throat. Tatiana was clearly quite out of her mind at this point, he thought. She had been bitter and falling apart for as long as he had known of her, and then Belial came along, like the spider in the children's rhyme, and offered her power. The power to have the revenge she had only ever dreamed of. She was a shell scraped clean now, her humanity gone, hollowed out by hatred and revenge.

"I want one thing from each of you," she said, her gaze moving restlessly between the three Shadowhunters ranged on the steps. "One thing, or my Watchers"—she gestured at the white-clad figures on either side of her—"will be turned loose upon you." She turned to Cordelia with a sneer. "From you—Cortana. The sword of Wayland the Smith."

"Certainly not," said Cordelia. Her head was held high; she looked at Tatiana as if Tatiana was a bug spitted on a needle. "I am Cortana's rightful bearer. The sword chose me; you have no right to it."

Tatiana smiled as if she had expected, and even welcomed, such an answer. She turned to Jesse. "From you, my son," she said, "I wish for you to drop your ruse. You need not pretend you are one of the Nephilim any longer. Abandon these traitors. Join me. There will be a New London soon, and we will rule it. Your father will be raised, and we will be a family again."

A New London? James turned to Jesse, worried—but Jesse's face was like stone. The Blackthorn sword gleamed in his hand as he raised it, holding it across his body. "I'd rather be dead than join with you, Mother," he said, "and since I've *been* dead already, I can say that with great confidence."

"Belial can give you worse than death," Tatiana murmured. There was an odd light in her eyes, as if she were contemplating the joys of Hell. "You will reconsider, child."

She turned to James.

"And you, James Herondale," she said. "You who consider yourself a *leader*. Give yourself up to Belial willingly. He has given me his word, and I pass it on to you, that he will spare those you love, and let them live, if only you come willingly to him. Even the Carstairs girl he will allow to live; he will *gift* her to you. She left you once, but she will never be able to leave you again. She will have no choice but to remain at your side."

James felt his lip curl. "It says much of you, that you think that would tempt me," he said harshly. "That you think love is the ability to possess another person, to force them to your side, even if they hate you, even if they can hardly bear it. You offer me what Grace had of me—not a partner, but a prisoner." He shook his head, noting that Tatiana looked angry, which was good; they were stalling for time, after all. "Belial cannot understand, nor you, Tatiana. I *want* a Cordelia who can leave me, because then I know that when she stays with me, it is by choice."

"A meaningless distinction," said Tatiana. "You speak of morals that belong to a world that is receding into the past. Belial is coming; there will be a New London, and its denizens will either serve Belial or die."

"Belial will abandon you when he has no further use for you," said James.

"No." Tatiana's eyes glittered. "For I have granted Belial an army, one he could never have had without me." She gestured at the Silent Brothers on either side of her, and James saw with a start that there were more of them now—at least five on either side of Tatiana. Somehow more of the creatures Tatiana had called Watchers had glided into the courtyard without being noticed. Their eyes were sewn shut, but in the darkness James could see the gleam of an ugly green light beneath their lids. "Your own Silent Brothers have abandoned you and joined with Belial—"

"That is a lie." James tried not to look at the gates; surely Charles and the First Patrol had to return soon. "Do you wish me to tell you what we know? You arranged to be sentenced to imprisonment in the Adamant Citadel so you could steal the key to the Iron Tombs. You escaped and gave it to Belial. You opened the Tombs for him. He summoned an army of Chimera demons, and now they possess these bodies—these who were once Silent Brothers and Iron Sisters. Once you were in the Silent City, you let them in, let them take it over. We know our own do not act against us willingly. As always, you and your master must force others to act for you. No one is *loyal* to you, Tatiana. You know only coercion and possession, threats and control."

For barely a moment, something flickered across her face—was she angry? Taken aback? James could not tell—before she forced a nasty smile. "Clever boy," she said. "You discerned our plan. But not, alas, soon enough to stop it." She looked up at the spire of the Institute, piercing the bloodred sky, which rumbled and shook with such force James half expected the ground to rock under his feet. "All of London will soon fall. I have stated the three things I want. Do you still refuse to give them to me?"

James, Cordelia, and Jesse exchanged a look. "Yes," Cordelia said. "We still refuse."

Tatiana looked delighted. "Wonderful," she said. "Now you will have a chance to see what demons in the bodies of Nephilim can do." She turned to the Watchers. "*Show them!*"

The Watchers moved as if they were one being. Gripping their lightning staffs, they began to swarm up the steps of the Institute. James raised his pistol and fired at one of the Watchers; it fell back, but the others kept coming, as Jesse drew his sword and Cordelia raced to fling the entryway door open. The Shadowhunters of the Institute poured out, seraph blades glowing in their hands.

The battle had begun.

The Institute's carriage had run up onto the curb, one wheel on the pavement, the other three still in the road. It was likely due to the horses, still in their harnesses, that it hadn't struck any of the trees lining the street: it certainly wasn't thanks to the driver, who had climbed down from his seat and was wandering along the road ahead of them, seemingly in a daze.

Alastair cupped his hands around his mouth. "Davies!" he called into the shrieking wind. "Davies, what's wrong?"

Davies didn't seem to hear. He kept walking—not in a straight line, but in a dizzy zigzag, lurching from one side of the street to the other. Thomas started forward, worried that Davies would be struck by oncoming traffic—and realized as he did so that there *was* no oncoming traffic. As he and Alastair hurried down the street, Thomas saw other carriages standing abandoned; there was a stopped omnibus, too, and through its windows he could see mundanes milling about in confusion.

They were on Gray's Inn Road, usually a busy thoroughfare. Now there were few pedestrians, and even the pubs, which should still have been open, were dark and lightless. Wind howled down the street as if it were a tunnel, and the clouds overhead seemed to froth and boil like the chaos at the base of a waterfall.

As they reached the intersection with High Holborn, they caught up with Davies, who had sunk to his knees on the icy ground. He appeared to have found a discarded child's hoop toy, which he was rolling back and forth with a blank, perplexed expression.

"Davies!" Thomas shook the driver by the shoulder. "Davies, for the Angel's sake—"

"There's something wrong," Alastair said. "More than with just poor Davies. Look around."

Thomas looked. More mundanes were emerging onto the street, but they were wandering aimlessly, without purpose. All were blank-faced. A costermonger stared vacantly into the distance as a riderless horse, reins dragging, helped itself to the fruit in his barrow. A man in an overcoat was stumbling back and forth across the pavement as if trying to keep his balance on the rolling deck of a ship. An old woman, wearing only a thin dress, stood staring up at the bloodred sky. She was weeping loudly and inconsolably, though none of the passersby seemed to notice, or stopped to help. On the street corner, a young man was hitting out at a lamppost, over and over, as his glove darkened with blood.

Thomas started forward—not sure what to do, but feeling as if he must do something—but was stopped by Alastair's hand on his shoulder. "Thomas," Alastair said. He was gray-faced, the mouth Thomas had kissed mere minutes ago tight with fear. "This is Belial's doing. I'm sure of it. We need to get back to the Institute *now*."

The battle was not going well, Lucie thought grimly.

It had seemed otherwise at first. She and the others who had crowded into the entryway had been listening to Tatiana as she argued with James—listening and growing angrier and angrier. By the time Cordelia reached the door and threw it open, they had burst out with a furious will to fight.

They had been struck first by the wind, tearing at them, distant claps of rumbling thunder like the beating of a vast drum. Lucie was halfway down the steps when she heard James's pistol fire, the crack of it almost lost in the train-like roar of the wind overhead, screaming through the sky above London.

Something white had surged up in front of her—a Watcher, fire crackling along its staff. She had swung her axe with a shriek, burying it in the creature's midsection. It had gone down, silently, without even a look of surprise.

The blood that edged her axe when she pulled it back was a dark, dark red, very nearly black.

Something shot by her head—a *chalikar*; Matthew was throwing them fast, the bladed discs slamming into one Watcher and then another, sending the second tumbling down the steps. Jesse was swinging his sword with admirable skill, nearly severing the arm of the tallest Watcher. Anna plunged her seraph blade into another, leaving a wound in its chest that was rimmed with fire. It went to its knees, its chest burning, its face devoid of expression.

It was Ari, brandishing her bloody weapon with a look of horror, who shouted, *"They're getting back up!"*

And it was true. The Watcher James had shot was on its feet again, starting back toward the Institute. Then the next false Silent Brother rose, plucking Matthew's *chalikars* from its body as if it were ridding itself of fleas. Though their white robes were slashed and stained, their wounds had already stopped bleeding.

Tatiana was laughing. Lucie could hear the sound of her high-pitched giggles as she whirled to look for the Watcher she had wounded. It was already climbing the steps again, swinging its staff toward Christopher, who ducked under it.

Cordelia, behind him, caught the staff between her hands. If it burned, she gave no sign, only gripped the staff and *pushed*, using its own force to drive the creature back down the steps.

But the other wounded Watchers were already rising like a wave. One after another they staggered back to their feet; one after another they returned to assail the Institute, and the small group of Shadowhunters defending its entrance.

After that the battle became a nightmare. Tatiana danced an odd, jerking dance of delight as one by one they beat the Watchers back and one by one the demons rose again. Throwing weapons were abandoned. They would not kill the Watchers, and would only become weapons in the creatures' hands if they chose to use them. Matthew and Christopher drew seraph blades, their glow helping to illuminate the courtyard even through the thickening fog. James kept his gun—it seemed able to put the Watchers down for longer than a blade, though it would not kill them. Nothing seemed to. And worse, they *healed*—Jesse had nearly severed one's arm, but Lucie saw that the arm had been restored, the Watcher seemingly unhurt as it battled Matthew, its staff blazing as it slammed over and over into Matthew's seraph blade.

Matthew had already slipped once on the icy step. He had caught himself and rolled fast away from the downward slice of the Watcher's staff, but Lucie knew that their time was limited. They were Nephilim, but they were human; they would grow exhausted eventually. Even the blood of the Angel could only hold out so long against unstoppable foes.

They were already getting hurt. James had a torn and bleeding sleeve where his arm had been gashed, Ari a bad scrape from a staff that had slammed against her torso. And Cordelia—Lucie was desperately worried about Cordelia. Cordelia was doing what she could, using the Watchers' own staffs to drive them back—apparently this did not count as raising a weapon, as Lilith had not appeared—but there was already a bad burn on her cheek, and it would only be a matter of time—

"Cordelia Carstairs!" Tatiana had stopped dancing; she had her hands clasped under her chin in glee, like a little girl on Christmas morning. "Is this really the great wielder of Cortana? Look at you. Too afraid to even use it in battle, lest my master find you out and take it." She turned to the Watchers at her side. "Capture her. We will get that blade."

Cordelia froze. Two Watchers started up the steps, moving quickly toward her. The next moments were a blur. Lucie began to run toward Daisy and saw that James was doing the same, raising his pistol as he darted down the steps, trying to get a clear shot at the Watchers—

But Christopher got there first. He dashed in front of Cordelia, facing the Watchers, his seraph blade blazing in his hand. For a moment, it illuminated them both like fireworks lighting a dark night: he and Cordelia stood haloed in angelic light. Never had Christopher looked more like a warrior—

Something metal flashed as it left Tatiana's hand and flew through the air. Christopher jerked, cried out, and tumbled backward, landing awkwardly on the steps.

"Christopher!" Cordelia shrieked, and started to go after him, just as James stepped in front of her, pistol in hand. Two loud shots rang out, and then two more; the attacking Watchers were flung back like rag dolls, their bodies pitching headlong down the steps.

Anna darted through the fog, zigzagging up the steps to fall at Christopher's side. "I'm all right," Lucie heard him say, as Anna bent over him. "It's just my shoulder."

And indeed, something sharp and silver was embedded just above his clavicle. A throwing knife. But battle did not stop because a warrior was wounded; something white fluttered at the edge of Lucie's vision, and she was turning to hack and slash at a lunging Watcher, its red-black blood spattering her. As it fell, she saw Jesse's blade through the fog and gun smoke, as he buried it in a demon's shoulder. Ari, Matthew, James, Cordelia, all were fighting too, now not just to protect the Institute but to keep the Watchers away from Anna as she crouched over her brother; she had already pulled the dagger from his shoulder and was drawing healing runes on his arm as he protested; Lucie couldn't hear him, but she knew what he was saying: that he was fine, ready to fight again. That there was no time for him to be injured.

The Watcher at Lucie's feet had begun to stir again. She buried her axe in its spine, pulled it free, and ran up several steps; at least she could avoid being right there when it rose again. Exhausted, she looked down. She felt like she had swallowed a lump of ice. She had been in battles before, they all had, but never one where she couldn't see a way to win, or even a way out. If Charles didn't return soon with the First Patrol—and perhaps, even if he did—she could see no way forward in which they all survived. Perhaps if they ran to the Sanctuary, locked themselves in . . . But one of these creatures had gotten into the Sanctuary in Cornwall. Perhaps all they'd be doing was trapping themselves in a corner . . .

Something cold touched Lucie's arm. She spun, raising her axe—then lowered it again in surprise. Grace stood in front of her. Still barefoot, with Jesse's jacket once more wrapped around her shoulders. Her face was thinner than Lucie remembered it, her huge gray eyes blazing. "Lucie, I want—"

Lucie was too exhausted to be polite. "Go back inside, Grace. You'll just get in the way."

"You have to listen," Grace said, with a ghost of her former forcefulness. "*You can stop this.*"

Lucie glanced around and realized that for the moment, they were alone, or at least out of earshot of the others. The fight was concentrated lower down the steps, where a sort of half circle of Shadowhunters had formed around Christopher and Anna. "What?" she demanded. "Grace, if this is a trick—"

Grace shook her head violently. "They're killing you," she said. "I could see it from the window. My mother won't stop them until you're all dead. She might spare Jesse, but—" She bit her lip, hard. "She might not. And there is only one person she will listen to—"

"Belial?"

"Not him. Someone you can reach. Someone *only* you can reach." Grace leaned up then and whispered in Lucie's ear, as if she were telling a secret. And as Lucie listened, her body growing cold, she realized—with a terrible sense of dismay—that Grace was right.

Without a word, she drew away from Grace and began to walk down the steps. She was conscious of Grace behind her, watching; she was conscious of the flickering light of seraph blades, dancing through the fog; she was conscious of Anna helping Christopher to his feet; she was conscious of Cordelia's blazing hair as she savagely kicked a Watcher's legs out from under it; she was conscious of James and Matthew, fighting side by side.

And yet even as she was conscious of all that, she was reaching inside herself. Into the silence and the dark, through the thin veil that was all that ever separated her from that shadowy place between life and death.

In one world she was surrounded by battle, by Tatiana's laughter, by the gleam of demonic fire as the Watchers wielded their staffs. In the other, darkness rose up around her as if she were looking up from the bottom of a well. When it closed overhead, she was floating, surrounded by shadow on all sides, a darkness illuminated by flickering points of light.

Lucie did not believe this was what death looked like for those who died. This was a translated world, interpreted by her mind in the only way that made sense to her. She could as easily have visualized a great ocean, the hidden recesses of a green forest, a vast and featureless plain. For whatever reason, this was what Lucie saw. A depthless field of stars.

Into that field she reached, steadying her breathing, calling out into the silence. *Rupert Blackthorn?*

She felt something *move*, like the tug of a fish on a line.

Rupert Blackthorn. Father of Jesse. Husband of Tatiana. She held tight to the tenuous connection she felt. Drew it closer, outward. *Come. Your family needs you.*

Nothing. And then, suddenly, the connection exploded into motion, like rope sliding through her hands, fast enough to burn her skin. She held on tight, despite the burning pain. Held on as she opened her eyes wide, willing herself back into the world of wintry London, the world of the battle that roared all around her. A world where she had only been gone a few seconds—gone in her mind, not her body—a world where she could smell blood and cordite on the air, where she could see the white shadow of a Watcher making its way across the steps toward her.

A world where, just in front of her, on the steps of the Institute, Rupert Blackthorn's ghost was beginning to take shape.

Here was no hidden shade, the kind that went unseen. This was the spirit of Rupert Blackthorn, half-translucent but entirely recognizable. As Lucie watched, he began to solidify—she could see his face now, so much like Jesse's, and his old-fashioned clothes, and his pale, half-clenched hands. Even little details—a pair of unlaced boots—had become as clear as if he had been drawn onto the air with shimmering ink.

The Watcher that had been approaching her stopped in what seemed like real confusion, its head tilting, as if to say, *What is this?* The other Watchers were still fighting; Lucie could hear the crash of weapons, the sound of boots on ice, though she did not dare to look away from Rupert's ghost.

The ghost raised his head. His lips parted and he spoke, his voice ringing out even over the storm. "Tatiana?"

Tatiana turned, looked up—and cried out. She had been staring at the unmoving Watcher in puzzlement, no doubt wondering what had given it pause. Now her eyes widened and her mouth fell open.

"Rupert!" she gasped. She took a step forward, as if to rush toward the ghost, but her legs did not hold her. She sank to her knees, her hands clasped together; it looked horribly as if she were praying. "Oh, *Rupert*! You are here! Belial has fulfilled his vow to me!" She made a sweeping gesture, drawing his attention to the Watchers, the fight, the armed Shadowhunters. "Oh, behold, my love," she said. "For this is our revenge."

"Revenge?" Rupert was looking at his wife in what was plainly horror. Because she was so much older, Lucie wondered, or because of the lines of bitterness, rage, and hatred scored into her face?

Lucie could not help but look toward Jesse, who was standing utterly still, the Blackthorn sword lowered at his side. His expression as he regarded the ghost of his father—Lucie could not bear it. She tore her gaze away. She could not see Grace, but the others were still fighting—all save Anna and Christopher, who had retreated to a darker corner of the steps. Even as she watched, a Watcher approached Jesse, no doubt having noticed his stillness; it raised its blazing staff and swung at him. He barely parried, and Lucie's heart thumped with terror.

She wanted to go to Jesse—wanted to race toward him, fight at his side. It was her fault his reaction time was slow; he was likely in a state of shock. But she could not move. She was all that was holding Rupert Blackthorn here on this earth. She could feel the starry void trying to pull him back, trying to fling him out of this world and into the other. It was taking every bit of her will to hang on.

"Rupert?" Tatiana's voice rose to a whine. "Are you not pleased? Did Belial not tell you of our great victory? We will destroy the Nephilim; we will rule London, together—"

"Belial?" Rupert demanded. He had become less translucent; he was still without color, a strange monochrome figure, but Lucie could not see through him, and the expression on his face was easy to read. Anger, mixed with disgust. "I have not returned at the request of a Prince of Hell. I was drawn from my resting place by the cry of a Shadowhunter in battle. One who needed my help."

Tatiana's eyes flicked to Lucie. There was rage in them, and a hatred so intense it was nearly impossible to comprehend. "That's impossible," she snarled. "You cannot be raised, not by some stupid little brat—"

"Put an end to this, Tati," Rupert snapped. "Send these—creatures—away."

"But they are fighting for *us*." Tatiana staggered to her feet. "They are on our side. Belial has promised us a great future. He has sworn *he* will raise you, Rupert, that you will once more be by my side—"

"Tell them to stop before they kill our son!" Rupert roared.

Tatiana hesitated—then flung out her hand. "Stop," she called, as though the word was being dragged out of her. "Servants of Belial. Stop. Enough."

All together, just as they had begun fighting, the Watchers stopped. They stood like frozen soldiers; they could have been made out of tin, but Lucie could see that the eerie green light moved behind their eyelids still.

The Nephilim, still holding their weapons, were staring from Lucie to Rupert in amazement. Anna had her back against a stair railing, Christopher propped against her shoulder. Both were pale. Grace was kneeling at the top of the steps, shivering, her arms wrapped around herself. Lucie thought that she was looking at Christopher, but she couldn't be sure. And Jesse—Jesse was staring at his father, his knuckles white where he gripped his sword's hilt. Lucie could not read the look on his face; too much of her attention was still on Rupert. Some strange magic was present, drawing on him, trying to pull him away from here, away from her.

"My darling," Tatiana crooned, her voice echoing in the sudden stillness, now that the fighting had stopped. "How is this possible? You have been bound, bound for so long, bound in the shadows where even the other dead cannot see you. Belial promised that as long as he kept you there, he could bring you back."

Jesse was shaking his head, in horror and disbelief. "No," he whispered. "No, that can't be."

Bound in the shadows, Lucie thought. What had happened to Rupert? What binding was there on him, that was not present with other ghosts? Was it that binding that now tried to pull him away from the courtyard?

But Rupert did not seem to be wondering what she meant. He was shaking his head slowly. His dark hair was in his eyes—it was the kind of fine, straight hair that seemed to have a mind of its own, just like Jesse's. It made Lucie's heart ache. Rupert had been so close to Jesse's age when he had died. "Do you remember when we met?" Rupert said, his gaze fixed on his wife. "At the Christmas ball? You were so delighted that I only wanted to dance with you. That I snubbed all the others."

"Yes," Tatiana whispered. She wore an expression that Lucie had never seen on her before. Open, loving. Vulnerable.

"I thought your delight was because you were lonely and hurt," Rupert went on. "But I was wrong. I did not understand that in your heart, you were bitter and vindictive. Enough to set a pack of monsters on Shadowhunter children—"

"But these are the children of those who let you *die*, Rupert—"

"Your father murdered me!" the ghost cried, and Lucie thought the ground shook with the force of it. "The Herondales, the Lightwoods—they did not cause my death. They *avenged* it. They arrived too late to save me. There was nothing they could have done!"

"You cannot believe that," Tatiana moaned. "All these years I have worked for your vengeance, as well as mine—" She started up the steps, her arms outstretched, as if she meant to gather Rupert into her arms. She had taken only a few strides when she staggered back, as though she had collided with an invisible wall. She raised her hands, scrabbling against a barrier Lucie could not see.

"Oh, let me in," Tatiana wailed. "Rupert. Let me touch you. Let me hold you—"

Rupert's face twisted in disgust. "*No.*"

"But you love me," she insisted, her voice rising. "You loved me always. You are bound to me forever. When I am gone, we will be together at last. You must understand—"

"Whomever it was that I loved," Rupert said, "that woman is gone now. It seems she has been gone for years. Tatiana Blackthorn, I renounce you. I renounce any feeling that I ever had for one who bore your name." He gazed at her impassively. "You are nothing to me."

At that, Tatiana screamed. It was an unearthly sound, like the howl of the wind. Lucie had heard noises like it before: it was the sound of a ghost who had only just realized it was dead. A scream of loss, of despair. Of defeat.

As she screamed, on and on, the Watchers, one by one, lowered their staffs. They began to march down the steps, passing Tatiana as if she were a lifeless pillar of salt. Their white robes gleaming, they filed out of the courtyard, passing under the Institute gates one by one until the last of them was gone.

It worked, Lucie thought wonderingly, *it actually worked.* And then she realized that her legs had given out from under her, and she was sitting on the steps. Her heartbeat was strong in her ears, and fast, too fast. She knew she should let Rupert go. The effort of keeping him here was wrecking her.

And yet, if there was any chance at all that Jesse could speak to his father, even once—

Lightning blazed across the sky. Rupert turned toward Jesse, looking up at him. He began to reach out his hand, as if to beckon Jesse, to urge him to come closer.

Tatiana, seeing this, gave one more terrible scream and bolted out of the courtyard, disappearing through the iron gates.

To Lucie's utter astonishment, a figure flew down the steps and through the courtyard, and flashed through the gates after Tatiana. A figure in a ragged dress, with long white hair.

Oh no, Lucie thought, struggling to get to her feet. *Grace, no—you cannot hope to fight her.*

But Cordelia had already had the same thought, it seemed. Without a word, she turned and tore after Grace and Tatiana, hurtling through the gates in pursuit.

26
The Remorseful Day

How hopeless under ground
Falls the remorseful day.
—A. E. Housman, "How Clear,
How Lovely Bright"

Cordelia ran.

She ran through the ice-blasted streets, under a red sky streaked with black and gray. The cold air froze her lungs, and she could hear her own breath whistling, the only sound in the noiseless maze of streets around the Institute.

Though she knew they *shouldn't* be noiseless. London never truly went to sleep; there were always late-night wanderers and barrow boys, policemen and lamplighters. But the streets were utterly empty, as if London had been scraped clean of its people.

Cordelia ran, deeper into the tangle of side streets between the Institute and the river. She ran with no clear plan, only the knowledge that Grace could not possibly face down her mother on her own. That she would certainly be killed. That perhaps Cordelia shouldn't care, but she did. Christopher's words echoed in her ears: *If we don't do that, if we are consumed by the need to pay Grace back for what she has done, then how are we any different from Tatiana?*

And then there was Tatiana. She couldn't get away. Not again.

Cordelia ran, and her hair came out of its bindings and flew out behind her like a banner. She turned a corner, nearly skidding on the icy street, and found herself in a cul-de-sac where a short paved lane ended abruptly in a wall. Grace and Tatiana were both there—Grace, a knife in her shaking hand, seemed to have trapped her mother, like a hound trapping a fox. And like a fox, Tatiana bared her teeth, her back against the wall. Her white hair was a startling contrast to the red brick behind her.

"Are you going to attack me, girl?" she said to Grace; if she noticed Cordelia, she gave no indication. "You think I didn't know about your little training sessions with Jesse?" She laughed. "Were you the finest of all the Nephilim, you could not touch me. Belial would strike you down."

Grace shivered—she was still barefoot, still in only a light dress—but did not lower her knife. "You are deluding yourself, Mother," she said. "Belial cares nothing for you."

"It is *you* who care nothing for me," snapped Tatiana, "after all I have done for you, after every advantage I gave you: the clothes, the jewelry, after I trained you in proper manners, after I gave you the power to bring any man to heel—"

"You made me cold and hard," Grace said. "You taught me there was no love in this world, only power and selfishness. You closed my heart. You made me what I am, Mother, your blade. Do not now complain if that blade is turned on you."

"Weak." Tatiana's eyes glowed luminous in the ugly light. "You have always been weak. You could not even peel James Herondale away from *her*."

Grace started, and turned; it was clear she had not realized Cordelia was there until that moment. Cordelia flung her hands up. "Keep the blade trained on her, Grace," she said. "We must bind her hands, get her back to the Institute—"

Grace nodded determinedly. She kept the blade level, as Cordelia moved forward, already thinking about how she could secure Tatiana: if she caught her arms behind her back, she could march her forward—

But as she approached, Tatiana, with the speed of a striking snake, lunged for her with a pearl-handled blade—the twin of the one she had thrown at Christopher. Cordelia ducked out of the way, knocking into

Grace, who dropped her knife. It rolled into the middle of the street, the metal blade striking sparks off the cobblestones.

Cordelia stared at it, her heart beating fast. There was nothing for it. And perhaps, in some dark corner of her heart, she *wanted* what she knew would come next if she touched the weapon at her feet.

"Run, Grace," she said in a low voice, and caught up the knife.

Grace hesitated for a moment. Then the brick edifice that rose before them began to open—somehow, impossibly—the bricks grinding and turning to smoke, and Lilith stepped from the dark doorway, wearing a dress of green overlapping scales, and with black serpents wriggling from her eye sockets.

Lilith smiled. And Grace, wisely, ran. Cordelia did not move, but she heard the rapid patter of Grace's bare feet on stone, mixed with the harsh gasps of Tatiana's breathing.

"My paladin," said Lilith, grinning like a skull. "You have finally come to your senses, I see, and taken up arms in my name." Her serpent eyes darted, looking Tatiana up and down. One of the serpents flicked out a silver tongue. Tatiana did not move, seeming frozen in terror and revulsion. "And how clever, Cordelia," said Lilith. "You've got Belial's little minion at the end of your blade. Now go ahead and cut her throat."

Half of Lucie wanted to bolt to her feet and run after Cordelia, but she knew she did not have the energy—she would collapse halfway to the Institute gates.

What energy she had left was concentrated on Rupert. If she loosed her grip on his spirit, he would be torn back to the darkness she had pulled him from. And Jesse—Jesse was already approaching Rupert's ghost, drawn by his father's beckoning hand.

She was dimly aware of James and the others milling around at the bottom of the steps. She thought she heard Anna's voice, sharply raised, but everything outside the small circle of her and Jesse and Jesse's father seemed as if it were occurring on a shadowy stage. She gripped the edge of the cold stone step tightly as Jesse came to a stop a few feet from Rupert.

His father's ghost regarded him with a calm sadness. "Jesse," he said.

"But how?" Jesse whispered. He had a cut on his cheek, still bleeding; he was shivering with the cold, though Lucie doubted he'd noticed. He had never looked more human and alive than he did standing beside a ghost, a ghost who was nearly the mirror image of Jesse as he used to be. "If you're a spirit—how was I a ghost for so many years and I never saw you?"

Rupert raised a hand as if he could touch his son's face. "Your mother made sure of that," he said. "But Jesse—we have little time."

He was right, Lucie knew. He was slipping away from her, already growing more indistinct around the edges. His fingers were turning pale, translucent, the edges like smoke.

"I was asleep," Rupert said, "and have been awakened, but only for this moment. I died before you were ever born, my child. Yet after death, I have seen you."

"My mother said—you were bound in the shadows—" Jesse said haltingly.

"I could not return as a ghost on this earth," said Rupert gently. He was fading faster now. Lucie could see entirely through him, see the stones of the Institute, see Jesse's stricken face. "Yet I dreamed of you, even in my endless sleep. And I feared for you. But you have proved strong. You have restored honor to the Blackthorn family name." Lucie thought he smiled; it was difficult to tell. He was wisps of smoke now, only the shape of a boy, like a figure seen in a cloud. "I am proud of you."

"Father—" Jesse started forward, just as Lucie cried out—she could feel Rupert torn away from her, out of her grip. She tried to hold on, but it was like holding water. As he slipped away, she saw once again the star-spangled darkness, the world away from this one, the place between.

And he was gone.

Jesse stood shivering, sword in hand, his face a mask of sadness. Now that she was no longer struggling to hold on to Rupert, Lucie was able to catch her breath; slowly she rose to her feet. Would Jesse be furious? she wondered bleakly. Would he hate her for not being able to hold on to his father's spirit—or worse, for drawing him back to this world at all?

"Lucie," Jesse said, his voice rough, and she saw that his eyes were glittering with tears. Forgetting her fear, she ran toward him, slipping on the icy stone, and threw her arms around him.

He put his head down on her shoulder. She held him with care, making sure their skin did not touch. Much as she ached to kiss him, to tell him with her touch that his father was not the only one proud of him, it was too dangerous. The world was coming back to her more clearly now, along with her strength. Over Jesse's bent head, she could see the courtyard, see the unearthly red sky illuminating drops of blood in the dusting of snow that covered the ground. The thunder had stopped; the wind was dying down. It was quiet.

In fact, Lucie realized, the silence was eerie. Her friends were gathered at the foot of the steps, but they were not speaking. No one was discussing what had just happened, or what would have to happen next.

She felt suddenly very cold. Something was horribly wrong. She knew it; she would have known it before had she not been so focused on Rupert. She drew away from Jesse, touching his arm lightly. "Come with me," she said, and together they descended the steps, hurrying when they reached the courtyard.

As they neared the small group gathered at the edge of the steps, she saw who was standing there in a small circle: James, Matthew, and Ari. They were motionless. Her heart lurching, Lucie drew closer, until she could see Anna, sitting on the ground, Christopher's head in her lap.

His body was sprawled across the flagstones, and Lucie thought he could not possibly be comfortable. He was twisted at an odd angle, his shoulder hunched in. His spectacles lay on the ground beside him, the glass cracked. Blood stained the shoulder of his coat, but not much; his eyes were closed. Anna's hand stroked his hair, over and over, as if her body was making the gesture without her mind even being aware of it.

"Kit," Lucie said, and all of them looked over at her, their faces strangely expressionless, like masks. "Is he all right?" she said, her voice sounding too loud in the awful silence. "He was all right, wasn't he? It was just a little wound—"

"Lucie," Anna said, her voice cold and final. "He's dead."

* * *

Tatiana hissed. "Lilith. The bitch of Edom."

The serpents in Lilith's eyes hissed and snapped. "Paladin," said Lilith. "Slay her."

"Wait," Cordelia gasped, feeling the clench of Lilith's will, closing around her like a vise. She pushed back, barely aware of a spark of hot pain at her wrist as she did so. Her voice shook as she said, "Tatiana stands at Belial's right hand. No one is closer to him or knows his plans better. Let me question her, at least."

Lilith smiled. The green scales of her dress flashed under the red light of the sky, a strange chromatic mixture of poison and blood. "You may try."

Cordelia turned to Tatiana. The bone-white strands of her hair snapped in the wind. She looked ancient, Cordelia thought, a sort of crone torn by time, like the witches in *Macbeth*. "Before you stands the Mother of Demons," Cordelia said, "and I am her paladin. Tell me how I can find Belial. Tell me, or Lilith will destroy you. There will be nothing left of you to rule your New London."

Tatiana sneered. "So you are not so righteous after all, Cordelia Carstairs," she said. "It seems we both have our demon masters." She threw her head back. "I will tell you nothing. I will never betray my lord Belial."

"The Blackthorn woman is a thrall," Lilith said dismissively. "She is not negotiating with a will separate from Belial's. She will do what he says and die for him. She is useless to you—and to me. Kill her."

It was as if a steel arm had seized Cordelia's wrist, forcing her own hand, with the blade held in it, up and out, curving her grip around the knife's hilt. Cordelia took a step forward toward the cowering Tatiana—

Heat flared at her wrist. The amulet Christopher had given her, she realized, the one that was meant to protect her from Lilith. She came to a stop as her will slipped free of Lilith's, evading it; she whirled and flung the knife as hard as she could, toward the mouth of the cul-de-sac. It skidded into the darkness.

Pain shot through Cordelia. She gasped, almost doubling over. Lilith's displeasure: twisting her, crushing her. There was a crack at her wrist that she first feared was broken bone, but no: it was her amulet, falling shattered to the ground.

Lilith snorted. "Truly, you thought to hold me back with trinkets? You are a foolish, stubborn girl."

Tatiana cackled wildly. "The reluctant paladin," she said. "What a choice you have made, Mother of Demons. The avatar of your will on the Earth is too weak even to follow your orders." Tatiana turned her gaze on Cordelia with a sneer. "Weak, like your father," she said.

"It is not weakness," whispered Cordelia, rising to her feet. "It is mercy."

"But mercy must be tempered with justice," said Lilith. "I cannot understand you, Cordelia. Even now you stand in a city that rests in the palm of Belial's hand, yet you resist me—the only one who could help you fight back against him."

"I won't be a murderer," Cordelia gasped. "I won't—"

"Please. You know better than anyone how much pain Tatiana Blackthorn has caused, how many lives she has ruined." Lilith's hands moved together in a strange dance, as if she were shaping something between them. Her fingers were long and white as icicles. "She has spent years tormenting the Herondale boy, the one you love." The air between her hands had begun to shimmer and solidify. "Is it not your duty to avenge him?"

Cordelia thought of James. Of his steady gaze, always encouraging, always believing the best of her, always believing *in* her. And the thought of him stiffened her spine, her will. She raised her chin defiantly. "You think James is like Belial, because he is his grandson," she said. "But he is nothing like him. He wants peace, not revenge." She turned to Lilith. "I will not kill Tatiana, not when she is helpless—I have cast away my weapon—"

The shimmer between Lilith's hands solidified. It was a sword, made entirely of ice. The red light of the sky sparked off it, and Cordelia could not help but be struck by its loveliness. Its blade was like quartz, like moonlight hardened into stone. Its hilt resembled rock crystal. It was a thing born out of the chill of winter stars, beautiful and cold.

"Take it," Lilith said, and Cordelia could not stop herself; her hand flew out and seized the ice sword, sweeping it in front of her. It burned

coldly against her hand, a glimmering, deadly icicle. "And kill the thrall. She murdered your father."

"Not I, but I was glad to see him die," Tatiana hissed. "How Elias screamed—how he begged for mercy—"

"*Stop!*" Cordelia screamed; she was not certain at which of them she was shouting. Only that tremors were shuddering through her body as she held herself still; it hurt, and she knew the pain would stop if only she ceased fighting Lilith's will.

"Tsk," said Lilith. "I did not want to have to do this, but look—see what this creature, this thrall, has just done—"

And Cordelia saw a vision of the Institute courtyard. She saw Anna, struggling to hold Christopher. Christopher, who was jerking and twisting in her arms, as if trying to get away from something that had its teeth sunk into him. Anna had her stele in her hand; she was desperately trying to scribble *iratzes* onto her brother's skin, each one vanishing, like a teaspoon of ink spilled into an ocean of water.

Beside Anna lay the pearl-handled knife that Tatiana had thrown. Its blade foamed with blood that was already turning black with venom even as Cordelia watched. A silent scream built in her throat, a desperate need to call out to Anna, even though she knew Anna could not hear her. Knew, even as Christopher's spasming motions ceased, even as he exhaled and went still, his eyes fixed blankly on the sky above him, that there was nothing she could do to save him. Knew, as Anna folded up over his body, her shoulders shaking, that he was gone.

All the breath went out of Cordelia in a rush, as though she had been stabbed in the stomach. And with it went her will to resist. She thought of Christopher, his kindness, his mercy, the way he had smiled at her as he led her through the Silent City to Grace, and she turned toward Tatiana, the ice sword flashing in her grip. In that moment, it did not matter that it was not Cortana. It was a blade in her hand, as with one swift, sure motion she slit Tatiana's throat open from ear to ear.

There was a roaring in Cordelia's mind. She could not think, could not speak, could only watch as Tatiana's blood poured from her throat. She made a noise, a sort of gurgle, as she sank to her knees, clawing at her neck.

Lilith was laughing. "It is too bad for her that you refuse to use Cortana," she said, prodding at Tatiana's spasming body with her toe. "You could have saved her life. A paladin's bonded weapon has the power to heal what it has harmed."

"What?" Cordelia whispered.

"You heard me," said Lilith. "And you have doubtless read it in the legends. A paladin's blade has the power of salvation as well as destruction. But you wouldn't have healed her anyway, would you? You do not have *that* much mercy in your heart."

Cordelia tried to picture herself stepping forward, somehow healing Tatiana, who had sowed so much ruination, so much pain. Even now, she might not be able to save Tatiana's life, but she could kneel beside her, speak a comforting word. She began to step forward—just as Tatiana toppled over, falling facedown into the snow. Her body burst into flames. Cordelia stood motionless as she watched the fire swiftly consume her: her clothes, her skin, her body. Acrid smoke rose from the conflagration, sour with the stench of burning bone.

"Oh, my," clucked Lilith. "Swift action is a paladin's friend." She laughed. "You should really pluck up your courage, my dear. Without Cortana, you are only half the warrior you could be. Do not fear your own destiny. Grasp it."

And with that, she disappeared in a flash of extending wings, an owl darting into the sky, leaving Cordelia to stare in horror at what she had done. The ashes that had been Tatiana Blackthorn rose with the wind and blew in eddies around the courtyard, drifting into the sky until they vanished. The sword in Cordelia's hand slid from her grip, falling away to melt among the ice along the street. Her heart was a bell, tolling for death.

Cordelia ran. But this time, as she ran, the wind whipped tears from her face. Tears for Christopher, for London. For Tatiana. For herself.

The fog that hung over the city had thickened. Lampposts and stopped carriages loomed up out of the mist, as if she were fleeing through a snowstorm. There were other shadows too, moving ones, appearing and disappearing in the fog—mundanes, wandering?

Something more sinister? She thought she saw the flash of a white robe, but when she dashed toward it, it had vanished into the mist.

All Cordelia knew was that she had to get back to the Institute. Over and over she saw the tableau of Christopher lying dead, so vivid in her mind that when she finally reached the Institute gates and the courtyard beyond, she was shocked to find it deserted.

It was clear there had been a battle—the snowy ground was disturbed, spotted with blood and thrown weapons; even ragged chunks of the Watchers' staffs. But the silence that hung over the place was eerie, and when Cordelia went into the cathedral, it held the same tomb-like quiet.

She had not realized how cold she was. As the warmth of the Institute enveloped her, she began shivering uncontrollably, as if her body had finally been given permission to feel the chill. She made straight for the Sanctuary, where the doors were already open. The great, high-ceilinged room yawned beyond.

And inside, silence. Silence and a grief so palpable it was like a living force.

Cordelia was reminded of the awful room in the Silent City where her father's body had been laid out. She recalled Lucie saying that no one had cleared away the bier Jesse had been laid out on, and indeed, here it was, with Christopher stretched atop it. He was on his back, his hands folded across his chest. Someone had closed his eyes, and his spectacles had been laid neatly beside him, as if at any moment he might awake and reach out for them, wondering where they had gone.

Around Christopher's body knelt his friends. James, Lucie, Matthew, Anna. Ari. Jesse. Anna was at the head of the bier, her hand lightly against Christopher's cheek. Cordelia did not see Alastair or Thomas, and she felt a small chill—she had been glad, selfishly, that Alastair had not been there for the battle, that he had been well out of it. But now that she had been out in the city, she had begun to worry. Were they lost in the creeping fog? Or worse, facing whatever creatures were hiding in that fog?

As Cordelia approached, she caught sight of Grace, huddled alone in a corner. Her feet were bare and bloody; she was curled in on herself, her face in her hands.

James looked up. He saw Cordelia and rose to his feet, his hand on Matthew's shoulder. Something in his eyes had changed, Cordelia thought with an awful pang. Changed forever. Something had been lost, as he seemed lost, like a little boy.

Not caring if anyone was watching, she held out her arms. James crossed the room and caught her tightly to him. For a long time he held her, his face pressed against her loose hair, though it was damp with melting snow. "Daisy," he whispered. "You're all right. I was so worried—when you ran—" He took a deep breath. "Tatiana. Did she get away?"

"No," Cordelia said. "I killed her. She's gone."

"Good," Anna said savagely, her hand still against Christopher's cheek. "I hope it was painful. I hope it was agony—"

"Anna," Lucie said gently. She was looking from Jesse, who was expressionless, to Grace, still huddled against the wall. "We should—"

But Grace raised her head from her arms. Her hair was stuck to her cheeks with dried tears. "You promise?" she said, her voice trembling. "You promise me she's dead? Belial cannot raise her?"

"There is nothing to raise," Cordelia said. "She is dust and ashes. I promise that, Grace."

"Oh, thank God," Grace whispered, "oh, thank God," and she began to shake violently, her whole body shuddering. Jesse got to his feet and went across the room to his sister. Kneeling down beside her, he took one of her hands, pressing it between his own, murmuring words Cordelia could not hear.

James's lips brushed Cordelia's cheek. "My love," he said. "I know it is not easy to take a life, even such a life as that."

"It does not matter now," Cordelia said. "What matters is Christopher. I am so, so sorry, James—"

His face tightened. "I can't fix it," he whispered. "That is the unbearable part. There is nothing I can do."

Cordelia only murmured and stroked his back. Now was not the time to speak of how no one could fix this, how death was not a problem to be solved, but a wound that took time to heal. Words would be meaningless against the chasm of the loss of Christopher.

Cordelia looked over at the bier and caught Lucie's gaze. Alone among them all, Lucie was weeping—silently and without movement, the tears trickling down her cheeks one by one. *Oh, my Luce,* Cordelia thought, and wanted to go to her, but there was noise at the Sanctuary door, and a moment later, Thomas and Alastair came in.

"Oh, thank the Angel," James said, hoarsely. "We had no idea what happened to you—"

But Thomas was staring past him. Staring at Christopher and the others. At the bier, the lighted tapers. The scrap of white silk in Matthew's hands. "What . . ." He looked at James, his eyes bewildered, as if James would have an answer, a solution. "Jamie. What's happened?"

James squeezed Cordelia's hand and went over to Thomas. Cordelia could hear him speaking, low and fast, as Thomas shook his head, slowly and then faster. *No. No.*

As James finished the story, Alastair backed away, as if to give James and Thomas privacy. He came to join Cordelia, and he took her hands in his. He turned them over, silently, looking at the red frost burns where she'd held the ice sword. "Are you all right?" he said, in Persian. "Layla, I am so sorry I was not here."

"I am glad you were not here," she said fiercely. "I am glad you were safe."

He shook his head. "There is nothing safe about London now," he said. "What is happening out there—it is Belial's doing, Cordelia. He has turned the mundanes of the city into mindless puppets—"

He broke off as Thomas approached the bier where Christopher lay. As big and broad-shouldered as Thomas was, he seemed somehow shrunken as he stared at Kit's body, as if he were trying to disappear into himself. "It's not possible," he whispered. "He doesn't even look wounded. Have you tried *iratzes*?"

No one spoke. Cordelia recalled her vision of Anna, drawing healing runes on Christopher over and over, becoming more and more frantic as they vanished against his skin. She was not frantic now—she stood like a stone angel at the head of the bier and did not even look at Thomas.

"There was poison on the weapon, Thomas," said Ari gently. "The healing runes could not save him."

"Lucie," Thomas said roughly, and Lucie looked up in surprise. "Isn't there something you can do? You raised Jesse—you brought him back—"

Lucie whitened. "Oh, Tom," she said. "It's not like that. I—I did reach out for Kit, just after it happened. But there wasn't anything there. He's dead. Not like Jesse. He's truly dead."

Thomas sat down. Very suddenly, on the floor, as if his legs had given out. And Cordelia thought of all the times she had seen Christopher and Thomas together, talking or laughing or just reading in companionable silence. It was the natural outcome of James and Matthew being *parabatai* and always together, but it was more than that: they had not fallen together by chance, but because their temperaments aligned.

And because they had known each other all their lives. Now, Thomas had lost a sister and a friend as close as a brother, all in one year.

Matthew stood up. He went over to Thomas and knelt down beside him. He took Thomas's hands, and Thomas, who was so much taller and bigger than Matthew, gripped onto Matthew as if he were anchoring him to the ground. "I shouldn't have left," Thomas said, a hitch in his voice. "I should have stayed—I could have protected him—"

Alastair looked stricken. Cordelia knew that if Thomas blamed himself for Kit's death because he had been with Alastair, it would crush her brother. He already blamed himself for so much.

"No," Matthew said sharply. "Never say that. It was only chance that Kit was killed. It could have been any of us. We were outnumbered, outmatched. There was nothing you could have done."

"But," Thomas said, dazed, "if I'd been there—"

"You might be dead too." Matthew stood up. "And then I would have to live with not just a quarter of my heart cut out, but half of it gone. We were glad you were somewhere else, Thomas. You were out of danger." He turned to Alastair, his green eyes bright with unshed tears. "Don't just stand there, Carstairs," he said. "It isn't me Thomas needs now. It's you."

Alastair looked stunned, and Cordelia knew immediately what he was thinking: *That can't be true, it can't be me Thomas needs, or wants.*

"Go," she said, giving him a little shove, and Alastair put his shoulders back, as if he were readying for a battle. He marched across the room, past Matthew, and got down on his knees beside Thomas.

Thomas raised his head. "Alastair," he whispered, as if Alastair's name were a talisman against pain and grief, and Alastair put his arms around Thomas, with a gentleness Cordelia did not think she had ever seen her brother express before. He pulled Thomas close to him and kissed his eyes, and then his forehead, and if anyone had wondered what their relationship might be before, Cordelia thought, they would not wonder now. And she was glad. It was past time for the end of secrets.

She caught Matthew's eye and tried to smile at him. She did not think she actually managed anything like a smile, but she hoped he read the message in her eyes, regardless: *Good work, Matthew.*

She turned to look at James. He was frowning, but not at Thomas or Alastair. It was as if he heard something—and a moment later, Cordelia heard it too. The sound of hoofbeats in the courtyard.

"That's Balios," James said. "And others. Charles must be back with the patrol."

Matthew nodded. "We'd better go see what they've found," he said, sounding weary unto death. "By the Angel, how is this night not ended yet?"

They made their way out of the Sanctuary, all of them save Anna—who had only shaken her head mutely when James had asked if she wished to come outside—and Ari, who would not leave Anna's side, and Grace, who was in no fit state to go anywhere.

Charles had ridden out alone, but he had returned with about ten members of the First Patrol, all in gear, all on horseback. They crowded the courtyard, steam rising from the horses' flanks, and as the patrol dismounted one by one, Cordelia could not help but stare.

They looked as if they, too, had been in a battle. They were tattered and bloodstained, their gear ripped and torn. A white bandage circled Rosamund's head, soaked through with blood on one side. A large patch along the side of Charles's jacket was blackened with burn marks. Several of the others bore healing runes; Augustus, one of his eyes swelling blue and black, wore a dazed expression, nothing like his usual cocky demeanor.

Charles threw his reins over his horse's neck and stalked over toward James, Cordelia, and the others. There was a grim expression on his scratched face; he looked like a Shadowhunter, for once, rather than a mundane businessman.

"Grace was telling the truth," he said, without preamble. "We went straight to Highgate, but the entrance to the Silent City was surrounded by demons. A swarm of them. We could barely fight our way through—finally Piers broke through the line, but . . ." He shook his head. "It didn't matter. The doors to the City were sealed shut. We couldn't find any way through, and demons just kept coming . . ."

Piers Wentworth joined them. He had his stele out, his gloves off. He was drawing a healing rune onto the back of his left hand. Cordelia couldn't blame him—he had a nasty cut along the side of his neck, and one of his fingers appeared broken. "That wasn't the worst of it, though," he said, looking over at James. "Have any of you been out in the city?"

"Only a little ways," said Cordelia. "It was hard to see anything in the fog."

Piers barked a hollow laugh. "It's much worse than just fog. Something has gone horribly wrong in London."

James glanced back at the others. Matthew, Thomas, Lucie. Alastair. Jesse. They all looked pale and stunned; Cordelia could tell that James was worrying that they could take very little more.

He also hadn't mentioned Christopher. Not yet. Or the Watcher attack. Clearly he wanted Charles and the patrol to speak first. "What do you mean, Piers?" he said.

But it was Rosamund who answered. "It was like riding through Hell as soon as we left Highgate," she said, and winced. She put a hand to her head, and Piers reached over with his stele to mark her with an *iratze*. "We couldn't fight the demons in the cemetery—some of us thought there were too many of them, anyway." She eyed Augustus coldly. "The minute we left, a thick fog came up. We could barely see through it. Lightning was striking everywhere—we had to dodge it, it was hitting the ground all around us—"

"It split a lamp in Bloomsbury in half," put in Esme Hardcastle, "like the blasted tree in *Jane Eyre*."

"Not the time for literary references, Esme," snapped Rosamund. "It nearly set Charles on fire. Whatever it was, it wasn't ordinary lightning. And the storm—it stank of demonic magic."

"None of the mundanes we passed reacted to any of it," said Charles. "Not the storm, not the fires. They were wandering around in a daze."

"We saw a woman crushed by a runaway milk cart and no one stopped to help," Esme said in a wobbly voice. "I ran to her but—it was too late."

"Alastair and I saw the same kind of thing," said Thomas, "when we were out in the carriage. Davies suddenly just—stopped driving. He didn't respond when we called to him. We saw other mundanes too—children, old people—just staring into space. It was as if their bodies were here, but their minds were somewhere else."

Charles frowned. "What on earth were you doing, going for a carriage ride?"

Alastair crossed his arms over his chest. "It was just after we talked to you in the office," he said, a sharp note in his voice. "We didn't know anything had gone wrong."

"So before Grace arrived," said Charles. "We thought Tatiana . . ." He looked around, as if truly seeing the courtyard—the spatters of blood, the discarded weapons—for the first time. And as if he were seeing *them*—Cordelia, James, and the others—for the first time. How miserable they must look, Cordelia thought; miserable and bloody and dazed. "What happened here?"

Rosamund looked uneasy. "Maybe we should go inside the Institute," she said. "We can send a few riders to summon the rest of the Enclave. It clearly isn't safe out here—"

"It isn't safe inside, either," James said. "Tatiana Blackthorn escaped from the Silent City. She tried to take the Institute. She killed Christopher. She had warriors with her, Belial's warriors. Possessed Silent Brothers—"

Charles looked stunned. "*Christopher* is dead? Little Kit?" and for that moment he sounded not like the temporary head of the Institute, or Bridgestock's pawn. He sounded a bit like Alastair did sometimes, as if he still thought of his little sibling as a child. As if Matthew's friends too were children in his mind, Christopher only a little boy, looking up at him with bright and trusting eyes.

"Yes," Matthew said, not ungently. "He's dead, Charles. As is

Tatiana. But it is all very far from over." He glanced at Rosamund. "We can summon the Enclave," he said. "But these creatures of Belial's—they're nearly impossible to defeat."

"Nonsense," said Augustus. "Any demon can be defeated—"

"Shut up, Augustus." James had gone rigid; he was staring at the Institute gates. He put a hand to the pistol in his belt. "They're here. Have a look."

And indeed, pouring through the gates were more Watchers in the form of Silent Brothers; they were joined by Iron Sisters this time, with Death runes the color of flame edging their white robes. They were in two files, walking at a steady stride.

"They're not alone," Jesse said. He had drawn his sword and was staring with narrowed eyes. "Are those—mundanes with them?"

They were walking between one group of Watchers and another, prodded along by the points of sharpened staffs without seeming to notice. A ragtag group of five mundanes, seemingly chosen at random, from a man in a striped business suit to a little girl whose pigtails were tied with bright ribbons. They could have been gathered up from any London street.

Cordelia felt a cold spike of horror, sharp in her chest. The mundanes stumbled as they walked, blank-eyed and helpless as cattle being led to the slaughter. "James . . . ," she whispered.

"I know." She could feel him beside her, his presence solid, reassuring. "We'll just have to see what they want."

The strange parade made their way into the courtyard and came to a stop in front of the assembled Shadowhunters. The Watchers were impassive, holding their staffs level, pointed at the mundanes. Dull-eyed, wordless, the mundanes simply stood where they were, gazing off in different directions.

Charles cleared his throat. "What is this?" he demanded. "What is going on?"

The Watchers didn't move, but one of the mundanes stepped forward. She was a young woman, freckle-faced, wearing a servant's black dress with a white apron over it. Her hair was tucked up under a cap. She could have been a maid in any fine house in London.

Like the rest of the mundanes, she wasn't wearing a coat, but she didn't appear to be cold. Her eyes stared into space, unfocused, even as she began to speak.

"Greetings, Nephilim," she said, and the voice that rumbled from her chest was deep and fiery and familiar. Belial's. "I speak to you from the void between the worlds, from the fiery pits of Edom. You may know me as the eater of souls, the eldest of the nine Princes of Hell, the commander of countless armies. I am Belial, and London is under my control now."

"But Belial can't possess humans," Cordelia whispered. "Their bodies can't sustain it."

"That is why I have gathered so many together," Belial said, and as he spoke, black pits, like scorch marks edged in flame, began to spread across the woman's skin. A streak ran up her jaw, another along her cheekbone. It was like watching acid eat away a photograph. As the rents in her skin widened, her jawbone, exposed to the air, flashed white. "It will take more than one mundane to get—"

Her voice—Belial's voice—choked off in a rush of blood and black, tar-like sludge. She melted like a candle, her body dissolving, until all that was left was a wet, blackened lump of fabric, and the charred edge of a once-white apron.

The second mundane stepped forward. This one was the man in the striped business suit, black hair slick with pomade, his pale eyes wide and dead as marbles. "To get my message across," he finished smoothly, in Belial's voice.

"Oh, this is awful," Lucie whispered, her teeth chattering. "Make it stop."

"I will stop when I am given what I want, child," said Belial. Surely the mundane man's hair had been black a moment ago, Cordelia thought. It was turning white as Belial spoke, the color of dead ash. "The form I am in now will not last long. The fire of a Prince of Hell burns away such clay as this." He raised one of the mundane's hands. The tips of the man's fingers were already beginning to blacken and char.

"*Enough*," James snapped. "Belial. What do you want?"

The mundane's face twisted into a smirk. Belial's smirk. "James, my grandson," he said, "we have come to the end of our long dance."

The char was spreading down the man's hand, to his wrist, and more black patches were visible on his neck, edging up toward his chin. "Tatiana Blackthorn is dead," Belial went on. "She had come to the end of her usefulness, and now she is gone." The mundane man jerked, and green-black fluid spilled from the corners of his mouth. It dripped onto the cobblestones, where it sizzled against the snow. When Belial spoke again, his voice was thick and wet, almost too distorted to understand. "Therefore I have come to tell you as directly as is possible that it . . . is . . . over."

The man gave a low grunt, and his body collapsed in on itself, blackening and curling sickeningly. The man's clothes fell empty to the ground, followed by a trickle of black ash. There was nothing else left.

Cordelia saw Tatiana's body, burning away to ashes as Lilith laughed. It seemed a thousand years ago, yet it was hideously clear in her mind's eye, as if it were still happening now.

"Stop!" It was Thomas, his kind face white with strain. "There must be some other way you can communicate with us. Let the mundanes go. Let one of the Silent Brothers speak to us instead."

James, who knew Belial better than any of them, closed his eyes in pain.

"But that would be much less fun." Belial giggled. A third mundane had stepped forward, with the same wooden, jerky gait as the others. This one was an older woman—someone's grandmother, Cordelia thought, a gray-haired woman in a pale, much-washed flowered dress. She could picture the woman reading aloud by a fire, a grandchild on her lap.

"I have taken the Silent City," Belial said, and it was alien and strange to hear his voice issue from the old woman's lips. "I have taken the bodies of your Silent Brothers and Iron Sisters, and I have made of them an army and marched them down the Path of the Dead into your City of Bones. It was quite thoughtful of you, to keep a whole horde of Shadowhunters around whose bodies do not degrade, but who are no longer protected by your Nephilim spells—"

"Congratulations," said James, looking sick. "You are very clever. But we know all this, and I know what it is you want."

"You can stop this," Belial hissed. "Give yourself up to me—"

"No. If you possess me, you will only wreak more destruction and more ruin."

Augustus, Rosamund, Piers, and the others were staring in amazement. At least they would see now, Cordelia thought. They would all see that James was not in league with Belial; far from it. That he hated Belial, and Belial wished only to possess and destroy him.

"No," Belial snarled. As Cordelia watched, the woman's skin began to sift away like flour, revealing the white bones of her skull. "There can be . . . negotiation. I—"

But the old woman had no more ability to speak. Her skin had crumbled away from her neck, revealing her bare spine and trachea. There was no blood, only ash, as if her body had burned from the inside out. Her empty dress fell to the ground, covered in the gray-white powder of what had once been her bones.

"We have to stop this," Lucie whispered. "There must be something we can do." But Jesse was holding her arm tightly; Cordelia could not blame him.

A fourth mundane stepped forward—a thin young man wearing spectacles and a waistcoat. A student at King's College, perhaps; he looked as if he had once been studious, thoughtful.

"Negotiation?" said James. "You know I will not negotiate with you."

"But perhaps," Belial mused, "you do not yet understand your situation. London is cut off from the rest of the world. A sigil of fire blocks the borders of the city, and none may enter or leave, by means magical or mundane, save at my whim. I have sealed every entrance, every exit, from the Portal in your crypt to the roads that lead out of London. Nor will any telephone or telegraph or other such nonsense function. I control the minds of all within these borders, from the meanest mundane to the most powerful Downworlder. London is locked away from the rest of the world. No help can come for you."

Rosamund gave a little shriek and covered her mouth with her hands. The others were staring. Belial was clearly enjoying himself to the hilt, Cordelia thought; it was sickening, and she resolved to show no emotion. Not even when black lines began to appear on the student's skin, ragged seamlike cuts, as if he were a rag doll that had been stitched together and was now coming undone. "If," Belial said, "you will come with me, James, and listen to my proposition, I will give the Shadowhunters of London a chance to escape."

"Escape?" snapped Charles. "What do you mean, escape?"

A seam split in the student's cheek. It gaped wide, and black flies began to crawl out of the wound. "There is a gate called York," Belial hissed, "down by your River Thames, a gate that comes from nowhere and goes to nowhere. I will give the Shadowhunters of London thirty-six hours to depart London through that gate. No tricks," he said, holding up his hands as James began to protest. The student's hands were seamed with black lines, several of his fingers dangling as if held on by threads. "The Portal will take any who pass through it safely to a spot just outside Idris. It is only London I want, and only London I will take; I have no interest in Nephilim. But the lives of any who remain will be forfeit."

"You will let the other inhabitants of London live?" Jesse asked. "The mundanes, the Downworlders . . ."

"Indeed." Belial grinned, and the student's face split apart and hung in flaps of skin. His hands were peeling away from the wrists, like bloody gloves. "I wish to rule an inhabited city. It amuses me to have them go about their normal lives, knowing nothing—"

There was a wet, squelching noise. Cordelia forced herself not to look away as the student toppled over. What was left of him resembled a raw side of beef stuffed into a suit of clothes. She wanted badly to be sick.

And then the last of the mundanes stepped forward. Cordelia heard Matthew swear softly. It was the little girl, her blank face innocent and clear, her wide eyes a shade of blue that reminded Cordelia of Lucie. "James," Belial said, and the force of his voice seemed to shake the little girl's body.

"Stop," James said. Cordelia could sense him trembling beside her. She felt a cold terror. They were watching murder, murder after murder happening before their eyes, and James would blame himself. "Leave the girl alone—"

Blood flecked the child's lips as she spoke with the voice of a Prince of Hell. "Not unless you will come with me to Edom."

James hesitated. "You will leave Cordelia out of this," he said. "Regardless of Cortana. You will not harm her."

"*No,*" Cordelia cried, but Belial was grinning, the little girl's face twisted horribly into a leer.

"All right," he said. "Unless she attacks me. I will leave her be, if you agree to hear me out. I will lay before you your future—"

"*All right,*" James said desperately. "Leave the girl. Let her go. I will go with you to Edom."

Instantly, the little girl's eyes rolled up in her head. She collapsed to the ground, her small body still and barely breathing. As she exhaled, a plume of dark smoke emerged, rising and diffusing into the air. Rosamund dropped to her knees beside the girl and put her hand against the girl's shoulder. Above them all, the smoke-shadow began to coalesce, spinning like a small tornado.

"James, *no.*" Matthew started toward him, the wind whipping his blond hair. "You can't agree to that—"

"He's right." Cordelia caught at James's arm. "James, please—"

James turned toward her. "This was always going to happen, Daisy," he said, catching urgently at her hands. "You have to believe me, believe in me, I can—"

Cordelia screamed as her hands were torn from his. She was lifted off her feet—it was as if a hand were gripping her, squeezing her. She was flung aside like a doll; she hit the stone steps with a force that knocked the breath from her body.

Shadow swirled around her. As she struggled to sit up, gasping past her broken ribs, she saw James, half-hidden from her by darkness. It was as if she were looking at him through dimmed glass. She saw him turn toward her, saw him look directly at her, even as she tried to get to her feet, tasting bitter blood in her mouth.

I love you, she read in his eyes.

"*James!*" she screamed, as the shadows between them thickened. She could hear Lucie screaming, hear the others shouting, hear the terrible beating of her own terrified heart. Holding her side, she started toward James, aware of the Watchers moving toward the steps, toward her. If she could just reach him first—

But the shadow was everywhere now, cutting off her vision, filling the world. She could barely see James—the smudge of his pale face, the gleam of the pistol at his waist. And then she saw something else—Matthew, moving more quickly than she would have thought possible, shot through a gap in the darkness and flung himself at James, catching hold of his sleeve just as the darkness closed in on them both.

It seemed to boil and churn—there was a flash of bloody gold light, as if Cordelia looked through a Portal—and then it was gone. Gone entirely, not the wisp of a shadow remaining, only empty steps, and a scatter of what looked very much like sand.

Belial was gone. And he had taken James and Matthew with him.

Intermission: Grief

Grief, Cordelia would realize during that night and the next day, was like drowning. Sometimes one would surface from the dark water: a period of brief lucidity and calmness, during which ordinary tasks might be accomplished. During which one's behavior was, presumably, normal, and it was possible to hold a conversation.

The rest of the time, one was pulled deep below the water. There was no lucidity, only panic and terror, only her mind screaming incoherently, only the sensation of dying. Of not being able to breathe.

She would remember the time later as flashes of light in the dark, moments when she surfaced, when the making of memories was possible, if incomplete.

She did not remember getting from the courtyard into her bedroom—James's bedroom—at the Institute. That was a drowning time. She remembered only suddenly being in the bed, a bed that was much too big for her alone. Alastair was leaning over her, his eyes red, drawing healing runes on her left arm with his stele. "*Tekan nakhor,*" he said, "*dandehaat shekastan.*" *Don't move; your ribs are broken.*

"Why are we here?" she whispered.

"The Enclave seems to think we might as well trust Belial's bargain," said Alastair, misunderstanding her. "What other choice do we have?

We have to assume we're safe from the Watchers for the next day and a half. I have to go home," he added. "You know I do, Layla. I have to bring Mother here, to be with us. She'll need help getting out of London."

Make someone else go, Cordelia wanted to say. *Don't leave me, Alastair.*

But the dark was coming down, she was being swallowed up in it. She tasted bitter water, salt on her lips.

"Be careful," she whispered. "Be careful."

She was in the corridor, unable to remember how she got there. The Institute was full of people. The whole Enclave had been notified of what had happened, an emergency meeting called. Many Nephilim were moving to the Institute, not wishing to be alone in their homes. Patrols had searched houses and office buildings for a working telephone or telegraph to no avail: they were, as Belial had promised, entirely cut off from the outside world.

Martin Wentworth came up to Cordelia, shamefaced, as did Ida Rosewain. "So sorry to hear," they said. "About James. About Matthew. About Christopher."

Cordelia nodded, accepted their apologies. Wished they would leave her alone. She looked for Anna but couldn't find her. Couldn't find Lucie, either. She went to her room to sit by the window, waiting for Alastair's return.

The little girl who had been the last mundane possessed by Belial had died. She had been brought into the infirmary by Jesse, and been tended to carefully, but her body had been too damaged to survive. Lucie said that Grace had wept over her; Cordelia could not find it within herself even to be surprised.

Night was day, and day was night. There seemed no difference here in Belial's London: the heavy clouds were constant, and while sometimes strange light shone, it came irregularly, with no notice paid to the time. Watches and clocks were still, or the hands spun unceasingly; the Institute's inhabitants charted the time as best they could using an hourglass taken from Will's office.

Understanding that she might never return to Cornwall Gardens, Sona had not been able to decide what to bring and what to leave behind. Cordelia found herself stacking an odd assortment of ornaments and books, clothes and keepsakes, on a dresser in one of the Institute's spare rooms. When she was done, her mother held out her arms from the bed. "Come here," she said. "My poor baby girl. Come here."

Cordelia wept in her mother's arms, holding on tightly until the waves took her down again.

As she passed through the drawing room, Cordelia saw Thomas. He was with Eugenia, both of them talking intently, yet he seemed alone. He was the last of the Merry Thieves left in this world, Cordelia realized with a dull horror. The last of four. If they did not get James and Matthew back somehow, he would always be alone.

Charles led the meeting. His face was calm, but Cordelia could see he felt utterly unprepared for the situation. His hands shook like fluttering paper, and he was drowned out quickly by a chorus of voices from those in the Enclave who were older, and more determined, than he was.

"We are not remaining in London and endangering our families," roared Martin Wentworth. "We have been given a chance to escape. We should take it."

Cordelia was stunned to find herself objecting loudly during the meeting. She heard her own voice as if from a distance, protesting that they should not leave London. They were Shadowhunters. They could not abandon the city to Belial. But it didn't matter—no matter how vociferously she and her friends protested, the decision was made. Belial could not be trusted, Cordelia argued. And what if James and Matthew escaped, returned to London? How could they be allowed to find it deserted, under demonic control?

"They will not return," Martin Wentworth said somberly. "What a Prince of Hell takes, he does not give back."

Cordelia could not breathe. She looked across the room, met Lucie's eyes. Lucie's gaze held hers, keeping her above the waves.

It was past midnight. They were all in the library, lamps lit but turned low. Maps and books were spread out before them. Anna read fiercely, as if she could burn up the pages with her eyes.

Cordelia lay in the too-big bed again, hating it. Surrounding her were objects that reminded her of James. His clothes, old books, even the carvings he had made in the wood of his nightstand. *TMT at the DT*, he had scratched into the paint. *The Merry Thieves at the Devil Tavern.* A reminder? The title of a play, a poem, a thought?

When the door opened, she was too exhausted even to be surprised as Lucie came in, with Jesse beside her. As Jesse watched from the door, Lucie crossed the room and lay down on the bed next to Cordelia.

"I know you miss them as much as I do," she said.

Cordelia put her head on Lucie's shoulder. Jesse looked at them both, then quietly slipped from the room, closing the door behind him.

"Do you think we can do it?" Cordelia whispered, into the shadowy dark.

"I have to believe we can," Lucie said. "I have to."

Morning was as dark as night. Sona took Cordelia's hand. "You are grieving," she said, "but you are a warrior. You have always been a warrior." She looked over at Alastair, who stood by the window, gazing out at the blackened sky. "You will help her to do what is necessary."

"Yes," Alastair said. "I will."

27
Clouds of Darkness

Horror covers all the sky,
Clouds of darkness blot the moon,
Prepare! for mortal thou must die,
Prepare to yield thy soul up soon.
—Percy Bysshe Shelley, "Ghasta or,
the Avenging Demon!!!"

Belial had given them thirty-six hours; that was thirty-four hours ago. And now Cordelia walked through the cold, dark morning, part of a somber procession of Shadowhunters marching toward the gate that would take them away from London, perhaps forever.

Lucie was nearby, with Jesse, and Alastair accompanied Sona, who was resting in a Bath chair pushed by Risa. Cordelia could see others she knew in the crowd: Anna, her back arrow-straight; Ari, carrying Winston in a cage. Eugenia. Grace, alone and silent, limping slightly—she had refused healing runes for her injured feet. Thomas, who had Oscar on a leash. They were all together, yet Cordelia felt as though each of them made this walk alone, isolated from one another by their sorrow and their worry.

As they neared their destination, more Shadowhunters joined the procession. Mostly families, sticking close together. Cordelia felt a dull horror in her stomach. These were the Angel's chosen warriors, the ones who stood against the dark. She had never imagined that they could be driven from their own city with only the belongings they could carry.

The procession moved in silence, and part of that silence, Cordelia knew, was shame. Once it had been confirmed that Belial was telling the truth—that a wall of magic encircled the borders of the city and could not be crossed, and London was under his complete control—the Enclave had folded like a pack of cards. London was only one city, the older Shadowhunters argued. To stay and fight without the hope of reinforcements, against an enemy whose powers were unknown, was foolish: better to go to Idris, to rally the Clave and try to find a solution.

No solution, Cordelia was sure, began with doing exactly what a Prince of Hell told you to.

Which was what she and her friends had said. Every one of them had protested, and been ignored. They were too young—they had romantic dreams of glory—they did not understand the danger, they were told. Even Charles had spoken up but was outnumbered. Every adult they would have had on their side—the Herondales, the Lightwoods, the Consul—was in Idris now, Cordelia thought bitterly. Belial had planned well.

As though knowing her thoughts, Lucie murmured, "I can't believe they wouldn't stay."

"They wouldn't even *consider* it." Cordelia still felt a bite of anger within her. "But," she added, "at least *we* have a plan."

They were passing St. Clement's church, then turning en masse down Arundel Street toward the Thames. After only a day and a half, Cordelia was still shocked by London's transformation. It was morning, and yet the sky was black with roiling clouds, as it always was now. The only real illumination came from the horizon, where (as a few who had ridden to the outskirts of the city had reported) a dull white glow emanated from the wall of demonic wards that encircled the city.

All around them were the city's mundanes, as always, but they too had been transformed. Mundanes in London always moved urgently when they were out on the street, like they all had important appointments to keep; now there was something eerie and manic about their hurrying. They performed their usual actions without thought, without change. By Temple Station there was a newspaper stand, stacked with papers already beginning to yellow at the edges. The headlines blared the news from two days past. As Cordelia watched, a man in a bowler hat picked one up and held out an empty hand to the vendor, who pretended to count out change. On the other side of the station entrance, a woman stood in front of the darkened, empty windows of a shuttered boutique. As Cordelia passed, she could hear the woman repeating over and over, "Oh my! How delightful! How delightful! Oh, my, my!"

A little way behind that woman, the white-robed figure of a Chimera-possessed Silent Brother glided through the shadows. Cordelia looked away quickly. How strange to feel terror at the sight of a Silent Brother, those who were meant to protect her, to heal her.

Oscar strained against his leash, growling softly.

Cordelia was glad when they reached the Embankment, the fog and the darkness blotting out everything beyond the river wall so that only the lap of water gave any indication that the Thames was there at all. Waterloo Bridge loomed faintly above them, and then they were passing through the entrance to the Embankment Gardens and along a path bordered by bare, wintry trees to an open area of neat lawn, where most of the Enclave had already gathered.

In the center of the lawn, looking bizarrely out of place, was a peculiar structure: an arched gate surrounded by Italianate pillars. Alastair had looked it up; it had been the water entrance to a grand mansion before London built out the Embankment, stranding the gate 150 yards from the river itself, in the middle of the park. There seemed no connection between the York Gate and Belial or anything demonic; Cordelia thought it was just Belial's sense of humor, sending them through a set of doors that led from nowhere to nowhere.

Cordelia could see nothing through the archway, only shadow. A crowd surrounded the water gate: there was Rosamund, with a tremendous trunk of clothes that had been set on a wheeled stand by which she dragged it. Behind her was Thoby, who somehow was pulling an even larger trunk. Martin Wentworth, stone-faced, held a tortoise in a glass cage with surprising gentleness, and Esme Hardcastle was juggling a half-dozen folders stuffed with papers. As Cordelia watched, a gust of wind blew some of the papers out of place, and Esme danced around in a panic, retrieving them. Augustus Pounceby watched her silently—for his part, he had decided to bring armfuls of weapons, though Cordelia could not imagine why. He was going to Idris, where they had plenty of weapons already.

Then Cordelia caught sight of Piers Wentworth and Catherine Townsend. Someone else was carrying their belongings; they instead accompanied a rolling bier on which lay the body of Christopher, sewn into his shroud. Only his head was visible, his eyes bound in white silk.

If any of the Enclave found it odd that Thomas, Anna, and their friends had declined to act as pallbearers, they did not say so. If they noticed at all, they would likely think it to be a silent declaration of protest against abandoning London.

In a way, it was.

Oscar barked. Thomas knelt to hush him, but he barked again, his body rigid, eyes fixed on the gate. The shadow beneath the archway had begun to *move*—it seemed to shimmer, the darkness streaked with lines of color. There were murmurs all around Cordelia as slowly a view took shape through the arch: a wintry meadow, mountains rising in the distance.

Any Shadowhunter would recognize those mountains. They were looking at the border of Idris.

This was their way out, their escape from Belial. Yet nobody moved. It was as if they had all just realized who they were trusting to bring them safely through this Portal to the other side. Even Martin Wentworth, the strongest proponent of leaving London, was hesitating.

"*I'll* go," Charles said, into the silence. "And I'll signal from the other side if—if everything's all right."

"Charles," Grace protested, but it was half-hearted; wasn't passing through the gate what they were all here *for*? And Charles was already striding forward, his back straight. Cordelia realized Charles was carrying nothing—he had brought no belongings with him from London, as if there was nothing he cared about enough to mind its loss—as he approached the York Gate and ducked through the Portal.

He vanished for a moment, before reappearing on the other side, in the middle of the frosted landscape. He turned around, staring back where he'd come from. Though it was clear he could no longer see the Portal, or the Shadowhunters waiting on the other side, he raised one hand solemnly, as if to say, *It's safe. Come through.*

Those waiting on the London side glanced around at one another. After a long moment, Martin Wentworth followed Charles, and he too turned to wave. He seemed to be mouthing, *Idris*, before he walked out of sight.

Now the crowd was moving. They began to arrange themselves in a loose queue, filing toward the gate, stepping through it one by one. Cordelia looked over at Anna as Piers and Catherine passed through, accompanying Christopher's body on its wheeled bier; Anna was utterly motionless, a stone statue.

Eugenia went through, carrying Winston in his cage, which she had taken from Ari. "Farewell! Farewell!" Winston called, until his chirping voice was swallowed up by the Portal. Flora Bridgestock had gone to speak to Ari, who shook her head sternly; Flora went through the Portal alone, casting a despondent glance back at her daughter before she stepped across the threshold.

"Layla," Risa said, laying a hand on Cordelia's arm. "It's time to go."

Cordelia heard Alastair suck in his breath. She looked over at her mother in the Bath chair. Sona had her hands folded in her lap; she was looking at her children with dark, questioning eyes. *She suspects,* Cordelia thought, though she could not prove it, could not be sure. She could only hope her mother would understand.

Risa had begun to push her mother's chair forward, clearly expecting Cordelia and Alastair to follow.

"Oscar!" Thomas shouted. Cordelia whirled to see that Oscar had broken free of his leash and was galloping delightedly in circles.

"Bloody dog," Alastair cursed, and ran to help Thomas catch the wayward retriever.

As Thomas reached out for the dog, Oscar broke to the left and pranced away, yapping merrily. "Bad dog!" Thomas called, as Lucie ran toward him, reaching for Oscar's collar. "This is not the time!"

"Risa—I have to help. Bring *Mâmân* through; I'll see you on the other side in a moment," Cordelia said. With one last look at her mother, she ran to join the others.

Anna, Jesse, Ari, and Thomas had spread out into a circle, trying to trap Oscar inside. Lucie was calling, "Here, Oscar, here," clapping her hands together to catch his attention. Members of the Enclave continued to pass by, giving Cordelia and her friends a wide berth as Oscar frolicked, running up first to Ari, then darting just out of her grip, then doing the same to Grace and Jesse.

"Leave the dog, idiots!" yelled Augustus Pounceby, who was just passing through the Portal. He was nearly the last one going through, Cordelia saw; there were perhaps five Nephilim behind him.

Not long now.

Oscar flung himself down on the ground and rolled, his legs waving. It was Anna who got down on her knees, as the last of the Enclave—Ida Rosewain—passed through the Portal. She laid a hand on Oscar's side. "Good *dog*," she said. "What a very good dog you are, Oscar."

Oscar rose to his feet and nosed gently at her shoulder. The Embankment was nearly deserted now. Cordelia looked around at the group who remained: she and Alastair, Anna and Ari, Thomas, Lucie, Jesse, Grace.

The Portal still beckoned; Cordelia and the others could still see glimpses of the cold plains outside Idris, the milling crowd of Nephilim beginning to regroup on the other side. They could still choose to step through. But to do so would be to abandon not just London, but Matthew and James. And they were none of them going to do that.

Thomas stepped forward to clip Oscar's leash back on. "Good boy," he said, rubbing Oscar gently behind the ears. "You did exactly what you were meant to do."

"Who would have thought Matthew Fairchild's dog would be so well trained?" Alastair said. "I assumed Oscar lived a life of dissipated debauchery at the Hell Ruelle."

"Matthew and James used to train Oscar together," said Lucie. "They taught him all sorts of games and tricks, and—" Her eyes were bright. "Well. It worked. I hadn't thought it would."

Cordelia suspected none of them really had, not when they had come up with the idea in the desperate dead of night, with only hours to go before morning and departure. Yet they had all gone along with it, faithfully; in times like this, it seemed, faith was all one had.

"I feel so guilty," Ari murmured. "My mother—what will she think when I don't join her?"

"Eugenia will explain our plan to everyone," Thomas said. "She promised she would." He straightened up, staring toward the gate. "The Portal's closing."

They all watched, locked in place, as the view through the archway faded. Shadows crowded in, like black paint covering a canvas, erasing first the mountains, then the plains below them, and the distant images of the Shadowhunters who waited on the other side.

The Portal winked out of existence. The archway had gone back to being what it was: *a gate that comes from nowhere and goes to nowhere.* Their way out of London had vanished.

"Now what?" Grace whispered, staring at the darkness below the arch.

Cordelia took a deep breath. "Now we go back to the Institute."

From the York Gate it was only a short walk back, but it had a very different, more dangerous feel than the trip there. Then they had been following Belial's orders; now they were defying them and hoping they weren't noticed.

Lucie felt like they were mice trapped in a basin, and somewhere above hovered a cat. She watched the mundanes move through the streets in their daze. It was not mercy, she knew, that had prevented Belial from killing everyone in the city, or expelling them as he had the Shadowhunters. It was that he wanted to rule over *London*—not an empty shell that had been London, not a ruin of London, but the city as he knew it, complete with bankers walking to work with newspapers under their arms, with women selling flowers outside churches, with tradesmen driving their carts to their next jobs.

When the eight of them had made their plan, after the terrible meeting yesterday, they'd agreed they would stay in the Institute. They were fairly sure that the Watchers, and any other of Belial's demons who might be roaming the streets, would attack them on sight now, and it was easier to secure one house than many. Also, Lucie thought, it was too depressing for them to sleep in their empty houses, and Grace had nowhere else to go.

Even Oscar's expression was grave as he trotted alongside Thomas. The silence weighed on Lucie. She had mostly spent the time since James and Matthew had been taken shut up in her room, often with

Jesse's company. He was—as she supposed ought not surprise her—excellent at providing silent and almost invisible support. He stayed with her quietly as she read her old stories and wondered what she had been thinking, how she could have been so carefree and playful. Sometimes Jesse held her on the bed, stroking his fingers gently through her hair; they were careful not to do much more than that. When alone, she stared at blank pages for hours, sometimes writing a line, then crossing it out in violent slashes of ink.

Christopher was dead. Lucie had reached out for him and felt nothing. She did not want to force it—she knew from experience that calling up spirits that were not already haunting the human world was a violent act, that they came reluctantly at best. Wherever they were, it was better than being a ghost.

James was gone, and Matthew with him. Were they still alive? Belial could only possess James while he lived, and surely if he'd succeeded in that, he would have already come back to taunt them about it. It was bizarre to see that the Merry Thieves, who had been the lifeblood of all her friends, who had been the central ring, strong as steel, to which everyone else could attach themselves securely, had been whittled down to only Thomas.

And now they were back at the Institute courtyard, which was empty and quiet, as it always was. There was no scar here, no sign of the dreadful things that had happened there such a short time ago. Lucie envisioned a plaque: HERE IS WHERE IT ALL BROKE APART. Matthew and James's vanishing, Christopher's death—they seemed both very close, a trauma still ongoing, and yet far away.

On the other hand, she thought, this courtyard had been torn up by Leviathan a couple of weeks ago, and there was no sign of that, either. Perhaps to be a Shadowhunter simply meant drawing runes over one's scars, over and over.

Inside, all was just as silent and empty, an eerie change after the bustle that had filled the place for the last days. Their boots rang loudly against the stone floor and echoed off the walls. As they made their way up the central staircase, Jesse slid his gloved hand into hers.

"Did you notice Bridget leave?" he said in a low voice. "I swear I didn't see her in the crowd."

Lucie was startled. "No—I didn't—but she must have, mustn't she? Probably we were all too busy with Oscar to notice."

"I suppose," Jesse said, though with doubt in his voice.

They had reached the library. Lucie looked around at the results of the planning they'd done secretly in the last day and a half, working in short, feverish bursts whenever they could grab a moment. The table was piled with maps of London, the Silent City, the environs of the Adamant Citadel. There was also an empty chalkboard on wheels off to the side; Thomas had dug it out of some supply closet or other.

"At least we can write our plans down now," Jesse said—they'd been avoiding doing so for fear of detection. "Assuming we all remember what they are."

"Ari, would you write?" Anna said. "You have the best penmanship of all of us, I'm sure."

"Not in *chalk*," Ari protested, but she looked pleased anyway. She took up the chalk and gestured toward them expectantly.

Thomas looked around and, finding no one else wanted to start, cleared his throat. "First priority," he said, "is securing the Institute. Board up the windows of any room we're going to use, and no lights in any room we're not using. We chain up the front doors. From now on we enter and exit only by the Sanctuary. With some luck we can keep Belial from knowing that any Shadowhunters stayed behind at all."

"He'll figure it out eventually," Alastair said. "If we weren't spotted by Watchers on our way back from the water gate already."

Ari pointed her chalk at him. "That's very dark thinking, Alastair, and we won't have it. The longer we can keep our presence hidden, the better."

"Agreed," said Anna. "Next. Ari and I are going to try to find a way in and out of London. There must be some magical gate Belial would have missed. A leftover warlock Portal, a path to Faerie. Something."

"What about trying to get back the way Tatiana and the Watchers got here?" suggested Thomas. "The Path of the Dead."

In the past frantic days in the library, they had learned what the Path of the Dead was—a passageway that led from the Silent City to the Iron Tombs. It seemed that after Tatiana had been imprisoned, she had opened a gate within the City of Bones to allow Belial's army to march from the Iron Tombs, along the Path, and into the heart of the Silent Brothers' stronghold. It was a painful thought.

"I wish we could do that, Tom," said Anna, "but remember what Charles said—not only is the entrance to the Silent City sealed, but we couldn't possibly fight off the demons that would attack if we tried to open it. Especially now, when there is no real daylight, there is no time we would be safe in trying."

"If we had the aid of a warlock, we might be able to try," Lucie said. "Magnus and Hypatia are in Paris, but Malcolm is the High Warlock of London; he must at least know what has happened. And not just warlocks," she added. "We must attempt to make contact with any Downworlders still in London, and see if they can be of help. Belial said they were all under his control, but he lies about everything."

"Fire-messages," said Grace's small voice from the other end of the table, surprising Lucie. "The invention that Christopher was working on. He thought he was very close. If we can get them working, we can perhaps send messages to Idris. Since Belial doesn't know they exist."

Everyone nodded. Cordelia folded her arms. "The Watchers. It's dangerous, but we must learn more about them. What they can do. Whether they have any weaknesses we can exploit." She turned to Lucie. "Luce, have you ever encountered the ghost of a Silent Brother or Iron Sister? I know their bodies do not decay, but what of their souls?"

Lucie shook her head. "I have never seen such a ghost. Wherever the souls of the Iron Sisters and Silent Brothers are voyaging, it is someplace further than I have ever been."

"Figuring out anything about the Watchers is going to be difficult," Alastair said, "given that we are also trying to remain undetected. If we fight a Watcher and run away, it will report us to Belial. If we fight a Watcher and kill it, it will be missed. I'm not saying we shouldn't try," he added, holding up his hands before Cordelia could respond. "Maybe we could drop heavy things on them from above."

"You're on dropping things on Watchers from above," Anna agreed. "Meanwhile, the worst and most important problem remains."

"Saving James and Matthew," said Lucie.

"We'll have to *find* James and Matthew first," Jesse pointed out.

"James will hold out for as long as he can," Cordelia said firmly.

"But we don't know how long that will be, or if Belial will find some means after all of possessing him without his consent."

"And Belial didn't expect to take Matthew at all," Thomas pointed out. "He has no reason to keep him alive. So we have even less time than that."

"He has one reason to keep him alive," Lucie said. "James will never cooperate if Belial hurts Matthew."

Thomas sighed. "We'll have to cling to that, for now. Since we don't even know where to start to rescue them. Edom is another world. We have no way of reaching it. Perhaps with the help of a warlock—it depends on whether Belial was lying about them being in his thrall."

"So," Anna said, sitting up. Lucie felt grateful—even as deep in grief as Anna was, she wasn't going to let them fall into despair now. "Ari and I will be looking for magical ways in and out of London. Grace, you should look into the fire-messages, you know the most about Christopher's work on them so far."

"I'll help Grace," Jesse said.

Anna nodded. "Alastair, you and Thomas are on Watchers and how to fight them. Cordelia—"

"Lucie and I will look into the Downworlders," Cordelia said. She caught Lucie's eye and held her gaze intently. "And we'll figure out how to rescue Matthew and James."

"That's all the tasks and all of us," Ari said. "Funny how quickly things can be accomplished when the rest of the Enclave isn't here to slow us down."

"When everything has gone to Hell," Alastair said, "it focuses the mind rather effectively."

They all began to speak. Lucie looked over at Cordelia, who remained silent, also watching the rest of them. For the first time in a long time, Lucie felt a bit of hope. *Cordelia and I are going to be working together,* she thought. *And we are going to be* parabatai. Even through the chill of the empty city and the daunting tasks ahead, that thought kindled a warmth within her, the first warmth she'd felt since all this business began.

* * *

Cordelia and Lucie stuck close to one another as they made their way down Berwick Street. Cordelia could not help but remember the first time she had ever been here, in Soho, with Matthew and Anna. How she had stared around eagerly, taking it all in: the neighborhood bursting with life, naphtha beacons lighting the faces of customers haggling at stalls over everything from china plates to bolts of shining fabric. Laughter spilling from the lighted windows of the Blue Posts pub. Matthew smiling at her in the moonlight, reciting poetry.

How lively and lovely it had been. Now it was eerie. Though it was midday, it was dark, the gas streetlamps unlit: the night before she had seen lamplighters wandering the streets, going through the motions of their jobs, but there had been no lit flames at the ends of their poles. Figures slumped in doorways, many dressed only in rags: shivering Jemmys, they were called in ordinary times, but now they were not shivering. They seemed not to notice the cold, though their fingers and bare feet were blue. Cordelia wished she could throw blankets over all of them, and knew she couldn't: interfering with the mundanes drew the attention of Watchers, and—as Anna had reminded her and Lucie sternly—the best way to help them was to end Belial's control of London as soon as possible.

Still. Her heart hurt.

Nearing Tyler's Court, they came upon an artist with his easel set up on the pavement. He wore a ratty old overcoat, but his paints and palette were fresh. Lucie stopped to look at his easel and winced—the image there was hellish. He'd painted London in ruins, the city on fire, and in the sky above, leathery-winged demons flapping, some with bleeding humans in their talons.

Cordelia was glad to get off the street. They ducked down the narrow aisle of Tyler's Court, and her heart sank as she saw that the door to the Hell Ruelle hung wide open, like the gaping mouth of a corpse.

"Better draw a weapon," she whispered, and Lucie slipped a seraph blade from her weapons belt, nodding. Cordelia was armed—she knew it was simply too dangerous not to be—but she had not raised a weapon since she had killed Tatiana. She hoped she would not have to; the last thing she needed now was to summon Lilith forth.

She had half expected, after seeing the open door, to find the Ruelle deserted. To her surprise, once inside, she heard voices coming from the inner part of the salon. She and Lucie moved slowly along the corridor toward the main room of the Ruelle, and paused in shock when they entered.

The room was full of Downworlders, and at first glance the Hell Ruelle seemed to be going on as usual. Cordelia looked around in astonishment—there were entertainers on the stage, and an audience seated at tables before it, seeming to watch the performers avidly. Faeries passed among them, carrying trays on which glasses of red wine rested like flutes of rubies.

And yet. Where normally the walls were covered with art and adornments, all of that was gone. Cordelia did not think she'd ever seen the Ruelle so bare of color and decoration.

She and Lucie began walking carefully toward the stage, which brought them among the crowded tables. Cordelia thought of Alice, disappearing down the rabbit-hole. *Curiouser and curiouser.* The Downworlders were not watching the performance: they were staring fixedly ahead of themselves, each lost in a separate vision. There was an acrid smell of spoiled wine in the air. Nobody took any notice of Cordelia and Lucie. They might as well have been invisible.

On the stage a strange sort of performance was unfolding. A troupe of actors had assembled there, in mismatched, moth-eaten costumes. They had placed a chair at the center on which sat a vampire. He was dressed as a mundane's idea of the devil: all red clothing, horns, a forked tail curled around his feet. Before him stood a tall faerie wearing a bishop's miter and holding a circle of rope, caked with dirt, that had been woven to resemble a crown. The faerie did not look at the vampire but only stared into space, but as they watched, he lowered the crown onto the vampire's head. After a moment, he took it back off, and then made to crown the vampire a second time. There was a fixed smile on his face, and he was murmuring, almost too quietly to be heard; as they drew closer, Cordelia was able to make out the words. "Sirs, I here present unto you your undoubted king. Wherefore all you who are come this day to do your homage and service, are you willing to do the same?"

The vampire giggled. "What an *honor*," he said. "What an *honor*. What an *honor*."

The other actors on the stage stood to the side and applauded politely without stopping. From here Cordelia could see their hands, which were red and raw: how long had they been applauding this bizarre coronation? And what was it supposed to mean?

Around the tables, a few Downworlders were upright, but most were slumped over at their seats. Lucie stepped in a puddle of dark liquid and quickly hopped away, but it was too thin to be blood—wine, Cordelia realized, as a faerie waiter wandered by with a bottle, stopping here and there to pour more wine into already-full glasses. The alcohol sloshed and spilled over the tablecloths and onto the ground.

"Look," Lucie murmured. "Kellington."

Cordelia had hoped to encounter Malcolm, or even one of the Downworlders who were friendly with Anna, like Hyacinth the faerie. But she supposed Kellington would do. The musician was sitting by himself at a table near the stage, barefoot, his shirt splashed with wine stains. He didn't look up as they approached. His hair was matted on one side: blood or wine, Cordelia couldn't tell.

"Kellington?" Cordelia said gingerly.

The werewolf looked up at her slowly, his gold-tinged eyes dull.

"We're looking for Malcolm," Lucie said. "Is Malcolm Fade here?"

In a monotone, Kellington said, "Malcolm is in prison."

Cordelia and Lucie exchanged alarmed looks. "In *prison?*" Cordelia said.

"He was caught by the Nephilim when he was only a boy. He will never escape them."

"Kellington—" Lucie started to say, but he droned on, ignoring her.

"When I was a boy, before I was bitten, my parents would take me to the park," he said. "Later they died of scarlet fever. I lived because I was a wolf. I buried them in a green place. It was like a park, but there was no river. I used to make paper boats and float them on the river. I could show you how."

"No," Lucie stammered, "that's all right." She drew Cordelia away, her face troubled. "This is bad," she said quietly. "They're no better off than the mundanes."

"Worse, maybe," Cordelia agreed, glancing around nervously. Kellington had picked up a small knife from his table. Slowly, he cut the back of his hand, watching in fascination as the wound swiftly healed. "Maybe we should go."

Lucie bit her lip. "There's a chance—maybe—that Malcolm is in his office."

Even if he was, Cordelia doubted Malcolm would be in any fit state to help them. But she couldn't say no to the look of hope on Lucie's face. As they left the main room, they passed a table of vampires; here the spilled liquid was blood, dried to brown, and she had to catch herself to keep from retching. The vampires lifted goblets of blood long hardened to their lips over and over, swallowing air.

Malcolm's office seemed undisturbed, though it had the same atmosphere as the rest of the Hell Ruelle: dark, unlit, and damp. Cordelia lit her witchlight and raised it, illuminating the room; it seemed safe enough to use it here. She doubted the Watchers had any interest in the Ruelle.

"No Malcolm," Cordelia said. "Should we go?"

But Lucie was at Malcolm's desk, holding her own witchlight over it, flipping quickly through the papers stacked there. As she read them, her expression changed, from curiosity to concern, and then to anger.

"What is it?" said Cordelia.

"Necromancy," said Lucie, letting the pile of papers she was holding fall to the surface of the desk with a *smack*. "Proper necromancy. Malcolm promised me he wasn't going to try to raise Annabel from the dead. He *swore* to me!" She turned to face Cordelia, her back against the desk. "I'm sorry," she said. "I know it doesn't matter right now. I just . . ."

"I think we both know that when you lose someone you love," Cordelia said carefully, "the temptation to do *anything* to get them back is overwhelming."

"I know," Lucie whispered. "That's what frightens me. Malcolm knows better, but it doesn't matter what he *knows*. It's what he feels." She took a deep breath. "Daisy, I need to tell you something. I . . ."

Oh no, Cordelia thought with alarm. Was Lucie about to confess to something awful? Had Malcolm been teaching her dark magic?

"I have a problem," Lucie said.

Cordelia spoke with great care. "A . . . necromancy problem?"

"No! Honestly. I *haven't* done any necromancy. It's more of a—well, a kissing problem."

"And you want to talk about it *now*?" Cordelia inquired.

"I do, because—well, I suppose it's sort of a necromantic kissing problem."

"Kissing Jesse isn't necromancy," Cordelia said, frowning. "He's alive now. Unless you're kissing someone else."

"I'm not," said Lucie, "but every time I kiss Jesse or touch him, for more than a moment"—she blushed deeply enough for it to be obvious even under witchlight—"anytime my skin touches his, really, I feel as though I am falling into shadow. And . . . I see things."

"What kind of things?"

"Belial's sigil. But changed; it doesn't match up with what's in the books. And I saw towers, gates, like in Alicante, but as if Idris had been possessed by demons." Her voice shook. "I heard an incantation, some kind of demon language saying—"

"Don't speak it aloud," Cordelia said quickly. "Belial might be trying to trick you into doing just that. Oh, Lucie. Did you talk to Malcolm, tell him what was happening?"

Lucie nodded. "He said that in using my power to raise Jesse, I might have forged a channel between myself and Belial." She frowned. "I imagine I'm seeing things he's thinking about, or doing. I wish he would stay out of my mind. As it is, I fear even to touch Jesse's hand."

At least you can see him. At least he is in the same world with you. But that was unfair, Cordelia knew; for such a long time, it had not been true. "I cannot say I know Jesse well yet, but it is apparent that he truly loves you. And that he is patient. He has had to be, considering the life he's had. I am sure he will wait for you—there is nothing he cares about more."

"I hope so," Lucie said. "It's all going to be over soon—one way or another. Isn't it?" She shuddered. "Shall we go? It feels terrible to be out on the street right now, but it's better than the creeping feeling this place gives me."

They left Malcolm's office and made their way back into the main room of the Ruelle. As they headed for the exit, something caught Cordelia's eye: a patch of wall that had been painted with the image of a forest, small owls peeking from between the trees. She recognized it as a piece of the mural of Lilith that had covered the wall during Hypatia's celebration of the Festival of Lamia, now incompletely painted over.

The image of the mural remained with her, and by the time they were back out on Tyler's Court, it had given her an idea. A very, very bad idea. It was exactly the sort of idea that seized the imagination and, against one's own will, took hold, growing stronger by the moment. It was a dangerous idea, perhaps a mad idea. And there was no James around to tell her not to do it.

There had been a long, long time of darkness before James awoke. How long, he could not have said. He had been in London, in the courtyard of the Institute, looking at Cordelia through a mist of shadow. Then he had seen Matthew rush toward him and heard Belial's roar in his ears—and then it was the roar of the wind, a tempest that tumbled him head over heels, and darkness had come down like an executioner's hood.

The first thing he had noticed upon awaking was that he was lying flat on his back, staring up at a sky that was a sickly yellow-orange, roiling with dark gray clouds. He scrambled to his feet, head and heart pounding. He was in a courtyard with a flagged stone floor, surrounded on all sides by high, windowless walls. Above him on one side rose a fortress of gray stone that looked very much like the Gard in Alicante, though this version of it had high black towers that vanished into the low-hanging clouds.

The courtyard looked as if it had once been a sort of garden, a pleasant, enclosed outdoor space meant for the enjoyment of the occupants of the fortress. There were stone walkways, which had probably once bordered a riot of flowers and trees; now, all there was between them was packed dirt, gray and stony; not so much as a single weed poked up from the unfriendly ground.

James whirled around. Cracked, ancient marble benches, the stumps of withered trees, a stone bowl placed precariously atop a broken bit of statuary—and there, a flash of green and gold. *Matthew.*

He took off running across the courtyard. Matthew sat propped against one of the stone walls, in the shadow of the dark Gard. His eyes were closed. He peeled them open slowly as James sank down on his knees beside him, and offered an exhausted-looking smile. "So," he said. "This is Edom. I'm not sure I see what all the fuss"—he coughed and spat black dust onto the ground—"is about."

"Math," James said. "Hang on—let me look at you." He pushed Matthew's hair back from his face, and Matthew winced. There was a jagged cut across his forehead; though the blood had dried, it looked painful.

James fumbled for his stele and took Matthew's arm, pushing his sleeve up. Matthew watched with a sort of distant interest as James drew a careful *iratze* against his friend's forearm. They both stared as the *iratze* seemed to tremble, and then faded, as if it were being absorbed by Matthew's skin.

"Let me guess," Matthew said. "Runes don't work here."

James swore and tried again, concentrating fiercely; the *iratze* seemed to hesitate for a moment this time, before abruptly fading like the other one.

"It feels a bit better," Matthew offered.

"You needn't humor me," James said darkly. He had been kneeling; now he sank down beside Matthew, feeling drained of energy. Overhead, a dark red sun was drifting in and out of the black masses of cloud above the fortress. "You shouldn't have come, Math."

Matthew coughed again. "Whither thou goest," he said.

James picked up a jagged black pebble and threw it at a wall, where it made an unsatisfying plink. "Not if you're following me into death."

"I think you'll find it's *especially* when I'm following you into death. 'And naught but death part thee and me.' No exceptions for demon dimensions."

But there's nothing you can do to help, James thought, and *But Belial will kill you if it amuses him, and I will have to watch.* He said neither of those things. It would be cruel to say them. And there was a part of him, though he was ashamed of it, that was very glad Matthew was here.

"You need water," James said instead. "We both do. It's dry as a bone here."

"And we'll need food soon enough," Matthew agreed. "I assume Belial knows that and will try to starve us out. Well, starve *you* out. You're the one he wants to break. I am an annoyance." He sifted his hand through a pile of dark pebbles. "Where do you think he is?"

"Belial? Anyone's guess," James said. "In the fortress, perhaps. Riding some sort of demonic hell-beast around Edom, chortling to himself. Admiring the wastelands. He'll turn up when he wants to."

"Do you think there are any nice demon dimensions? You know, green lands, fruitful hills, beaches and things?"

"I think," James said, "that demons feel the same way about barren hellscapes as we do about pleasant countryside retreats." He exhaled a frustrated breath. "I know there's no point to it. But I'll feel ridiculous if I don't even *try* to search for a way out of here."

"I won't judge," said Matthew. "I admire a pointless heroic quest."

James laid a hand on Matthew's shoulder before rising to his feet. He paced the perimeter of the yard, finding nothing he didn't expect. The walls were smooth and unclimbable. There was no doorway into the fortress, no gaps in the walls that would suggest a secret panel, no unusually flat piece of ground that might indicate a trapdoor.

He tried not to feel hopeless. There were crumbs of comfort. Belial had sworn he wouldn't hurt the others, the ones they had left back in London. He had even agreed not to target Cordelia. James could not help but recall how happy he had been, only a short time ago, waking up in his bedroom at Curzon Street and realizing Cordelia was there next to him. How he had thought it was the first morning of many, how he had let himself believe this would be the rest of his life. It was so cruel, how little time they had had before he was taken away.

"I don't suppose you have any control over this realm, the way you did the other," Matthew said as James circled back in his direction.

"I don't," James said. "I can tell. In Belphegor's realm, there was something always calling to me, like something just out of earshot that I could hear if I really listened. But this place is dead." He paused. He had reached the broken statuary he'd seen before, and he realized the bowl balanced atop it wasn't empty. It was full of clear liquid.

Water. In fact, next to the bowl, a metal cup rested, placed there by some helpful invisible hand.

James narrowed his eyes. The water could, of course, be poisoned. But was it likely? Belial would be happy to poison Matthew, but poisoning James—well, Belial wanted him alive.

And every cell in James's body was crying out for water. If Belial had decided to poison him, so be it; he'd just kill him another way if this didn't succeed. James took hold of the metal cup and dunked it into the bowl. The water was pleasantly cold against his fingers.

"James—" Matthew said warningly, but James was already drinking. The water tasted cold and clear, surprisingly delicious.

James lowered the cup. "How long do you think we need to wait to see if I dissolve or turn into a pile of ashes?"

"Belial wouldn't poison you," Matthew said, echoing James's own thoughts. "He doesn't want you dead, and if he did, I imagine he'd want to take the opportunity to kill you in a more spectacular fashion."

"Thank you. Very reassuring." James filled the cup again and carried it over to Matthew. "Drink."

Matthew did, obediently, though without the enthusiasm James had expected. He'd drunk only half the water when he pushed the cup away, his hand trembling.

He didn't look at James. But he didn't have to; James realized in that moment that Matthew was shivering all over—shivering violently, despite the heat in the air and the long coat he wore. His blond curls were damp with sweat.

"Math," James said quietly. "Do you have your flask with you? The one Kit gave you. With the sedative."

Matthew flinched; James didn't blame him. It hurt to say Christopher's name.

"I have it," Matthew said quietly. "There's only a bit left in it."

"Let me see," James said, and Matthew handed it over without protest. James unscrewed the top of the flask and peered in, his stomach sinking: there were probably two swallows of the liquid remaining.

Trying to keep his own hands steady, James poured a thimbleful of liquid into the cap of the flask and handed it to Matthew. After a moment Matthew tossed it down his throat, before slumping back against the wall.

When he gave the cap back to James, his hand was steadier, James thought. Or perhaps he just wanted it to be true. He closed up the flask and tucked it back into Matthew's pocket. He let his hand rest there for a moment, feeling the warmth of Matthew's skin through his shirt, the steady beat of his heart.

"They'll come for us, you know," he said, and felt Matthew's heart jump under his hand. "Our friends. They know where we are. Cordelia, Lucie, Thomas, Anna—"

"We haven't just popped round the corner shops," Matthew said wearily, though without any rancor. "We're in another world, James."

"I have faith," James said.

Matthew looked at him, his green eyes steady. "Good," he said, and put his hand over James's, where it rested on his heart. "It's good to have faith."

28
Tides of London

And only the tides of London flow,
Restless and ceaseless, to and fro;
Only the traffic's rush and roar
Seems a breaking wave on a far-off shore.
—Cicely Fox, "Anchors"

Thomas led Jesse and Grace through the streets of Mayfair, feeling as if he were leading untrained hunters through a forest of tigers.

They'd had to find gear in the Institute storerooms, and Jesse had needed to help Grace put it on, as she'd never worn it before. All three of them were armed, as well—Jesse had the Blackthorn sword, and Grace a long silver dagger—but Thomas was very aware of how much they lacked a Shadowhunter's usual training. He knew that Jesse had taught himself years ago, and that he had been working to catch up, but it was a far cry from the years of intensive training a normal Shadowhunter would have had by Jesse's age. Grace, of course, had never been trained at all except for the few things Jesse had taught her, and while she held the silver dagger carefully, Thomas wished she'd had more training with long-range weapons. If she got close enough to a Watcher to use the dagger, he suspected, she would already be as good as dead.

It was midday, though it was hard to tell given the constantly shifting black clouds in the sky. The Watchers were out, though not in force. They seemed to be wandering the streets in a sort of disorganized patrol, keeping an eye on things in a desultory fashion. Luckily, they stood out sharply in their white robes, and Thomas was able to drag everyone safely into doorways each time a Watcher appeared.

The whole business made him grit his teeth. He didn't like hiding from a fight, and they would have to learn to defeat the Watchers to have any hope of survival in the long run. Maybe if it had just been him and Jesse—but it wasn't. And they needed Grace. She was the only one who could understand Kit's work on the fire-messages—their only chance to reach the outside world.

He did have to admit, grudgingly, that she didn't seem afraid. Not of the Watchers, nor of the bizarre behavior of the mundanes, eerie as it often was. The three of them passed a shop with all its front windows smashed, and mundanes—some with bleeding feet—walking through the jagged glass on the pavement without noticing. Inside the shop, a mundane had curled up on a display of coffee tins and was napping, like a cat. At another broken shopwindow a lady primped herself as though she could still see her reflection in the smashed glass. A child tugged at her skirt, over and over, with a mechanical sort of regularity, as if he expected no response.

"I *hate* this," Grace said; it was the first time she'd spoken since they'd left the Institute. Thomas looked over at Jesse, whose expression was bleak. Thomas guessed what he would be thinking in Jesse's place: *Why return from the dead to a world that seems unliving?*

Thankfully, they had reached Grosvenor Square and the Fairchilds' house. It was dark and carefully shut up. It had an air of being long abandoned, though only a few days had passed since Charlotte and Henry had left for Idris, and Charles for the Institute.

Thomas let himself in with his key, and Grace and Jesse followed. Every inch of his skin crawled as they went inside. Each room called to mind the hundreds of times he'd been here, the hours spent with Matthew, with Charlotte and Henry, with Christopher in the lab, laughing and chatting. Those moments felt like ghosts now, as if the past were reaching forward to leave a mournful fingerprint on the present.

Perhaps it would be better in the lab, Thomas thought, and led them all down into the cellar. Jesse looked around in wonder while Thomas activated the large stones of witchlight that Henry had installed to illuminate the work space. "I had no idea Henry Fairchild did this kind of thing," Jesse said, gazing at the lab equipment, the glass flasks and metal ring stands, the funnels and beakers and stacks of notes in Christopher's cramped handwriting. "I didn't think *any* Shadowhunters did this kind of thing."

"Doing this kind of thing invented the Portal, silly," Grace told him, and for the first time, she sounded to Thomas not like the orphaned victim of a madwoman's deal with a Prince of Hell, but like a normal sister enjoying correcting her brother. "If the Nephilim wish to survive in the future, we must be aligned with the rest of the world. It will move forward with or without us."

"You sound just like Christopher," Thomas murmured, but then, why be surprised; she and Christopher had, in an odd way, been friends.

It was harder, much harder, to be in the lab than he'd expected. Of course it was Henry's lab officially, but for Thomas it was so closely associated with Christopher that it was like seeing his body all over again. There was an empty throb in his stomach as he sat down on one of the stools along the worktable that stretched the length of the room. It was unfathomable to be here and to grasp that Christopher was *not* here, that he was *not* about to come down the stairs and demand that Thomas help him with something that would doubtless explode in their faces.

He had half expected that Grace would mope too. Instead she got to work. She took a single deep breath and busied herself, going straight to the shelves and gathering equipment, murmuring almost silently as she chose implements from here and ingredients from there.

Thomas had always thought of Grace as a frivolous sort of girl, with nothing serious on her mind. That was how she carried herself at parties and gatherings. But it was obvious now that this had always been a ruse, as Grace moved with purpose and efficiency around the lab, peering at the labels on flasks of liquid, hunting in Henry's toolbox for a set of measuring spoons. She had the same focus Christopher had had, silent because she was thinking, planning, calculating in her head. He could *see* it in her eyes; he wondered at how well she'd concealed it from everyone.

"Can I help?" Jesse said eventually.

Grace nodded and began to direct Jesse—measure this, trim that, soak this paper in that liquid. Feeling guilty for just sitting there, Thomas ventured that he was also happy to assist. Without looking up from the gas flame she was lighting, Grace shook her head. "You should get back to the Institute; you're needed there more. They'll be wanting you to help protect the place against the Watchers." She looked up then, her brow furrowed as though she'd had a realization. Hesitantly she added, "I could use a Fireproof rune, though, before you go."

"Oh," said Thomas. "You don't know how to make one."

Grace pushed her hair behind her ears, frowning. "I only know the runes I learned before my parents—my birth parents, I mean—died. No one ever taught me beyond that."

"Mother never did think of your education," said Jesse, his calm tone concealing, Thomas thought, a lot of well-justified anger. "But I can do it, Grace. I studied the Gray Book often during . . . well, while I was a ghost."

Grace looked almost tearfully relieved. "Thank you, Jesse." Her brother just nodded and reached for the stele at his side.

Thomas watched as Grace held out her wrist, waiting for Jesse to Mark her. The way she was looking at him—with a hopeless sort of yearning—made it clear: she did not really ever expect to be forgiven, or for her brother to love her again.

Thomas could not blame her. Even now, he could still feel a bitterness toward her, at what she had done to James. Would he ever be able to truly forgive her that? He tried to imagine how he would react if he'd learned Eugenia had done something so terrible.

And yet, he knew the truth—that he would forgive Eugenia. She was his sister.

"I'll be off, then," Thomas said, as Grace, her new rune freshly applied, returned to the worktable. "*Don't* leave the house. I'll come back in a few hours to escort you back to the Institute," he added. "All right?"

Jesse nodded. Grace seemed too deep in her work to respond; as Thomas headed up the stairs, he saw her hand Jesse a beaker of powder. At least they seemed to feel comfortable working together; perhaps that could be a path to forgiveness, in the end.

On the way out, Thomas stopped in the kitchen to fetch a pitcher of water, and went to water the potted plants in the entryway. A show of faith, he thought, that the Fairchilds would return home. That despite Belial's power, all would be right again eventually. He had to believe that.

Perhaps Anna, Ari, Alastair, and Thomas had done their job a bit too well, Cordelia thought; when she and Lucie returned to the Institute, they found it looking as if it had been abandoned for decades. Wide boards had been nailed over the lower windows, and the upper windows were painted black or hung with dark fabrics. Not a hint of light escaped into the smoky glare of London.

The Sanctuary was lit with a few candles burning low, which gave off just enough light to keep Cordelia and Lucie from bumping into the walls. Even though Cordelia knew full well it was the same Institute it had been a few hours ago, the dim amber glow gave the place a somber feeling, and they went up the stairs in silence.

Although it was possible that Lucie's silence was merely a sign of her suppressed excitement. When Cordelia had turned to her in Tyler's Court and said, "I've had an idea, and I need your help," she had fully expected Lucie to reject the entire plan. Instead Lucie had turned the color of a raspberry, clapped her hands, and said, "What a wonderfully terrible idea. I am *entirely* willing to help. And keep it secret. It *is* a secret, isn't it?"

Cordelia had assured her it was, though it would not stay that way for long. She only hoped their observant friends would not note Lucie's suspiciously bright eyes and ask questions. At least the dark would help with that.

Once upstairs, they heard a murmur of voices coming from the library and headed that way. Inside they found Alastair and Thomas and Anna and Ari, stained with paint, dusted in sawdust, and holding a picnic on the floor in the middle of the library. A coverlet from one of the spare bedrooms had been spread out in the space between two of the study tables; on the tables themselves were an assortment of tinned foods from the pantry: canned salmon and baked beans, tins of cherries and pears, even steamed Christmas pudding.

Anna looked up as they came in and beckoned them to join in. "It's all cold food, I'm afraid," she said. "We didn't want to send up any smoke from a fire."

Cordelia settled herself on the coverlet, and Alastair passed her an open tin of apricots. The sweet taste was a relief from the bitter air outside; as she ate, she couldn't help but be reminded of another picnic, the one they'd held in Regent's Park when she first came to London. She thought of the sunlight, the abundance of food—sandwiches and ginger beer and lemon tarts, but lemon tarts only made her think of Christopher, and remembering the picnic made her think of those who were gone. Barbara had been there, with Oliver Hayward. And Matthew and James and Christopher, of course, and they had all vanished along with the summer and the sunlight. She glanced over at Thomas. Who was he, without the company of the other Merry Thieves? She didn't quite know, and she wondered if he did either.

She set down the empty apricot tin with a thump. James and Matthew, at least, were *not* gone beyond reach. They were still alive. And she would not let them be lost.

Lucie was poking at the tinned pudding with a fork. "Other than nailing boards to windows, what have you been up to while we've been gone?"

"Looking for magical exits from London," Ari said. "Ones that Belial might have overlooked."

"There are some old burial barrows, one over at Parliament Hill, that used to be Faerie gates," Anna added. "And some very old wells mentioned in historical texts, that water faeries used to inhabit. Bagnigge Wells, Clerks' Well—we'll be spending tomorrow with our heads down wells, it looks like."

"While Thomas and I will be trying to kill a Watcher," said Alastair.

"Trying to determine *how* to kill a Watcher," Thomas said. "Without the other ones noticing."

"Or being killed by one yourself," said Anna. "How was the Hell Ruelle?"

"Awful," said Cordelia. "The Downworlders are a bit more active than the mundanes, but no less lost in a dreamworld. If you speak to them, they'll look at you, but they don't really know you and they don't really hear you. It's very unsettling."

"So they'll be no help," said Thomas glumly.

"Belial did say they wouldn't be," said Lucie. "I suppose it's now a matter of what Cordelia and I do next. Anna, what would be most helpful?"

"Well, we could always use help looking for a way out of London," said Anna, leaning back on her hands. The gold braiding on her waistcoat gleamed, and even the smudge of dirt on her high cheekbone looked elegant.

"Alastair," Cordelia said in a low voice, "could I talk to you in private?"

Alastair raised his eyebrows but stood up, brushing the crumbs off his trousers, and allowed himself to be led out of the library. It seemed almost silly to seek privacy in the vast emptiness of the Institute, but Cordelia led him to the drawing room anyway. She closed the door behind them and turned to him; he was watching her, his arms crossed over his chest, a frown darkening his expression. Without preamble, he said, "You want Cortana back."

The Alastair of a year ago would not have known her well enough to guess that, Cordelia thought. It was a downside of their improved relationship that he did now. "How did you know?"

"The look in your eye," Alastair said. "I know that look. You have a plan, and if I don't miss my guess, it is both a very big plan and a very bad plan. So I assume it has something to do with Belial. And killing him. Which can only be accomplished with Cortana."

"You don't know that it's a bad plan," Cordelia protested.

"I know that we're desperate," Alastair said, in a quieter voice. "We've assigned ourselves these projects, and perhaps they'll help—but I know that they may not accomplish anything. We may have stayed behind in London only to die here."

"Alastair . . ."

"And I know that when it comes down to it, you and Cortana are our single best hope. It's just . . ."

"What is it?" Cordelia said.

"If you plan to face Belial somehow, let me come with you," he said, to Cordelia's surprise. "I know Belial would be likely to step on me as though I were an ant. But I would stand with you, for as long as I am able."

"Oh, Alastair," Cordelia said softly. "I wish I could have you with me. But where I'm going, you cannot follow. Besides," she added, seeing him start to scowl rebelliously, "I have no choice but to face this fight, this battle with Belial. You do. Think of *Mâmân*. Think of the little brother or sister we have not yet met. One of us must stay safe, for their sakes."

"Neither of us will be safe, Cordelia. There is no safety in London now."

"I know. But this is a Prince of Hell we are speaking of; the only thing that protects me from him at all is Cortana. It would be foolish and—and even selfish—for us both to face him at once."

Alastair gazed at her for a long time. Finally, he nodded. "All right. Come with me."

He led her back out into the hall; it wasn't long before Cordelia realized where they were going. "The weapons room?" she demanded, as they approached its metal doors. "You hid a sword in a room full of weapons?"

Alastair smiled crookedly. "Have you never read Poe's 'The Purloined Letter'?" He pushed the doors open and led her inside. "Sometimes 'in plain sight' is the best place to hide something."

At the far end of the room was a small wooden door, half-hidden behind a display of hand axes. Alastair rolled them aside and threw the door open, beckoning for Cordelia to follow him into a room that turned out to be the size of a large closet. Sagging shelves held battered weapons—a sword with a bent blade, a rusty iron mace, a pile of simple longbows with no strings. Across from the door was a workbench of some kind, with wrought-iron legs and a heavily pitted wooden surface. On it were a number of short wooden rods that she realized after a moment were axe handles, denuded of their blades.

"The repairs room," he said. "This is where broken weapons go—bows that need restringing, blades that need sharpening. It was Thomas's idea," he added, with a slight flush, and knelt down to look under the workbench. "He pointed out that this is the most heavily warded area of the Institute, and hardly anyone ever comes in here. They wouldn't notice—" He grunted. "Give me a hand with this, will you?"

He was reaching for a large oilskin cloth that had been wrapped around a bundle and tucked under the workbench. She grabbed one end of it and he the other, and with some difficulty they dragged it out. Alastair folded back the oilcloth, revealing a pile of swords in scabbards, most of their blades wrapped in cheap, protective leather pouches. Their hilts rattled as Alastair fanned them out, and a dark gold gleam shone from the oilcloth.

Cortana.

There it was, as beautiful and golden as ever, sheathed within the exquisite scabbard that had been a wedding gift from her father. The intricate pattern of leaves and runes carved into its hilt seemed to glow. Cordelia yearned to reach out and snatch it up, but she turned to Alastair instead.

"Thank you," she said, her throat tight. "When I asked you to look after it for me—I knew how much I was asking. But there was no one else I trusted. That *Cortana* trusted. I knew you'd keep it safe."

Alastair, still kneeling, regarded her with thoughtful dark eyes. "You know," he said, "when Cortana chose you as its bearer instead of me, everyone thought I was upset because I had wanted to be the one. The bearer. But—it wasn't that. It was never that." He rose to his feet, laying Cortana atop the workbench. "When you first picked up the sword . . . I realized, in that instant, that being its wielder would mean you were always the one in danger. You would be the one to take the bigger risks, to fight the harder fights. And I would be the one who would watch you, again and again, walk into danger. And I hated that thought."

"Alastair . . ."

He held up his hand. "I should have told you that. A long time ago." His voice carried the weight of a thousand emotions: resignation, loss, anger—and hope. "I know I cannot fight beside you, Layla. I only make one request. Be careful with your life. Not only for your own sake, but for mine."

* * *

James didn't know how much time had passed since they'd come to Edom. Matthew had fallen asleep after his small dose of sedative; James had lain down beside him and tried to rest, but the glaring orange-red of the daytime sky, and his own racing thoughts, had kept him awake.

Eventually he'd given up and circled the courtyard a few more times, searching for anything that might be a means of attack or escape. He found neither.

He *had* discovered, to his surprise, that while his seraph blades and other weapons had been taken away before he'd woken up in Edom, he still had his pistol on him, stuck through his belt. Unfortunately, it didn't seem to fire in this dimension, which was no doubt why Belial had let him keep it.

Eventually, he'd used the barrel of the gun to try digging into the ground beneath the walls, but the soil crumbled into powder to fill in any hole he started.

He'd returned to the stone bowl to drink more water and found that at some point a second bowl had appeared, this one full of hard green apples and stale rolls of bread. James wondered if the apples were meant to be an ironic nod to Lilith, or whether Belial was simply thinking about how to feed James and Matthew without giving them anything they'd actually enjoy eating.

He brought an apple over to Matthew, who was sitting up, having unbuttoned his coat and thrown it off. He was flushed, his hair and collar wet with sweat. When James handed him the apple, he took it with a hand that shook violently.

"Maybe you should drink a little more," James suggested. "The remainder in the flask, at least."

"No," Matthew said shortly. He looked up at the burning orange sky. "I know what you're thinking."

"I doubt that," James said mildly.

"That there was little point in my following you here when I can barely stand up," said Matthew. "It isn't as if I can fight to defend you."

James sat down beside him. "It's Belial we're up against, Math. There isn't a single one of us who could stand against him, no matter how sick or well we were."

"No one," said Matthew, "except Cordelia."

James glanced down at his hands. They were filthy from digging in the dirt, two of his nails bloody. "Do you think they're still there? In London? Or have they gone to Idris?"

Matthew was looking at the sky again. "Our friends? They'd never take Belial's offer. They'll find some way to stay in London, whatever happens."

"I agree," said James. "Although I wish—"

Matthew held up a hand, interrupting James. He narrowed his eyes. "James. Look up."

James looked. A few flying things had passed overhead while he was searching for an exit, too big and misshapen to be birds. It looked as if another was passing, much bigger and closer than the ones he'd seen before. As he watched, he realized with surprise that it was coming closer. And then it was definitely descending toward them.

It was an enormous creature, with feathered black wings, a long insectile body, and a triangular face like an axe-head, with oblong, marble-white eyes and a gaping circle of teeth.

Riding on the bird-demon's back, on a tooled gold saddle, was Belial.

He had abandoned his usual trousers and jacket: he wore instead a silk doublet and a long cloak of white samite, like the angel he had been once. It flapped in the hot wind as the bird-demon alighted on the rocky ground of the courtyard, sending up a small tornado of dust.

James felt Matthew shift beside him, and saw that he had slipped the flask from his pocket. He tipped it back, swallowing hard, staring at Belial as he sprang down from his bizarre-looking mount.

When Matthew replaced the flask into his jacket, his hand no longer shook. He took a deep breath and rose to his feet; James stood up quickly beside him, realizing that this was what Matthew had been saving the last mouthful of Christopher's mixture for: so that when Belial came, they could face him together, on their feet.

Belial walked toward them, a gold riding whip in hand, an amused look on his face. "Aren't you two adorable," he said. "Your *parabatai* wouldn't leave your side, James. Such a very *holy* bond, isn't it, that love that passes all understanding. The very expression of God's love." He grinned. "Only God touches nothing here. This place lies beyond

His sight, His touch. Your runes do not work here; *adamas* is dull in this world. Can your bond survive in such a place?" He slapped his palm with his riding whip. "Pity we'll never know. You won't be here long enough."

"What a shame," said James. "I was finding it all so pleasant here. Food, water, sunshine . . ."

Belial smiled. "Well, I did want you to be comfortable. It would be awfully inconvenient for me if you died of starvation or thirst while I was taking care of London. So fragile, these human bodies of yours."

"And yet you want one," said Matthew. "Isn't that strange?"

Belial looked at him thoughtfully. "You would never understand," he said. "Your world, and all its blessings, are forbidden to me, unless I inhabit a human body."

"I've seen what your presence does to human bodies," said Matthew tightly.

"Oh, indeed," said Belial. "Which is why my grandson is necessary to me." He turned to James. "James, I am going to offer you a deal. You should take it, because the offers will only get worse from here, and you have absolutely no leverage to negotiate." When James didn't respond, only folded his arms in reply, Belial went on. "It's the simplest thing in the world. Beside you is your *parabatai*. The other half of your soul, who has followed you here out of loyalty, in faith that you would keep him safe."

He's manipulating you, James told himself, but still. He wanted to grind his teeth.

"He isn't well," Belial went on mercilessly. "Look at him; he can barely stand. He is sick, in body and soul."

Unexpectedly, Belial's bird-demon, which had been poking at the ground with its sharply angled head, spoke up in a voice like gravel rolling through a cast-iron pipe: "It's true. Your bloke there looks like he just fell from a great height."

Belial rolled his eyes. "Do shut up, Stymphalia. I'll do the talking. You're not here because you're the brains of the operation."

"'Course not," said Stymphalia. "It's my bloody great wings, innit?" It flapped them proudly.

"The bird-demon sounds like a Londoner," Matthew observed.

"Spent some time in London," acknowledged the bird-demon. "Back in the day. Ate a few Romans. Delicious, they were."

"Yes, yes," said Belial. "Everyone loves London. Tea, crumpets, Buckingham Palace. If we may return to the matter at hand, James—agree to be possessed by me, and I will send *him* back to your people unharmed." He pointed at Matthew.

"No," Matthew said. "I didn't come here to abandon James to his fate. I came to save him from it."

"Good for you," said Belial, sounding bored. "James, you must know this is the best thing for everyone. I don't want to have to resort to violence."

"Of course you do," James said. "You love resorting to violence."

"That seems true," said Matthew.

"I only agreed to come," put in Stymphalia, "because I thought there might be violence."

"The birdie and the drunk are right," Belial allowed. "But let me point out—if you refuse, I lose nothing but a bit of time. If you accept, this is all over and both of you survive and go back to your world."

"I don't *survive*," James said. "I let you take over my body, my consciousness. In every meaningful way, I'd be dead. And while I don't care about my life, I care very much about what you'd do if you could freely roam Earth in my body."

"Then you must choose, I suppose," said Belial. "Your life, your *parabatai's* life—or the world."

"The world," said Matthew, and James nodded in agreement.

"We are Nephilim," he said. "Something you would not understand. Every day we risk ourselves in service of the lives of others; it is our *duty* to choose the world."

"Duty," said Belial dismissively. "I think you will find little satisfaction in duty when the screams of your *parabatai* are echoing in your ears." He shrugged. "I've much to do in London to ready it, so I will give you one more day. I imagine you'll see sense by then. If that one"—he looked at Matthew—"even survives the night, which I doubt." He turned, dismissing them both. "All right, you worthless bird, we're leaving."

"Not just a bird. I have a life of the mind too, you know," Stymphalia grumbled as Belial climbed back into the saddle. Sand rose in a dark cloud as Stymphalia's wings beat the air. A moment later Belial and his demon rose into the red-orange sky. Both Matthew and James watched in silence as they flew past the towers of the dark Gard, rapidly vanishing into the distance.

"If it happens," James said. "If Belial possesses me—"

"He won't," Matthew interrupted. His eyes were enormous in his thin face. "Jamie, it can't—"

"Just listen," James whispered. "If it happens, if he possesses me, and snuffs out my will, and my ability to think or speak—then, Matthew, you must be my voice."

"Where are you going this time of night?" said Jessamine.

Lucie, in the middle of buttoning her gear jacket, glanced up to see Jessamine perched on top of her wardrobe, looking half-transparent as usual. She also looked worried, her usual insouciant manner muted. She didn't seem to be asking Lucie where she was going just for the sake of bothering her. There was real worry in her voice.

"Just on a short trip," Lucie said. "I won't be gone long."

She looked over at the small rucksack on her bed, which she'd packed with just what she'd thought was necessary. A warm compact blanket, her stele, bandages, a few flasks of water, and a packet of ship's biscuit. (Will Herondale was convinced that ship's biscuit was the greatest contribution the mundanes had made to the art of survival, and he always kept plenty of it in the Institute stores; for once it seemed they might actually make use of it.)

"I ought to stop you, you know," Jessamine said. "I'm supposed to protect the Institute. It's my job." Her eyes were wide and fearful. "But it's so dark in here now, and I know it's the same outside. There are *things* walking in London that make even the dead afraid."

"I know," Lucie said. Jessamine was the same age as her parents, and yet death had trapped her in a sort of permanent youth; for the first time, Lucie felt almost older—protective, even—of the first ghost she'd ever known. "I'm going to do what I can to help. To help London."

Jessamine's pale hair drifted around her as she inclined her head. "If you must command the dead, I give you my permission."

Lucie blinked in surprise, but Jessamine had already disappeared. Still, Lucie thought. A good sign, considering her plans for the evening.

Shouldering her rucksack, Lucie checked over her gear—gloves, boots, weapons belt—and headed down the hall. It was eerily dark, the only light coming from the dim tapers placed at intervals along the corridor.

She had meant to slip the note under Jesse's door and leave, but in her imagination, the door had been closed. Instead it was propped slightly open. What if Jesse was awake? she thought. Could she justify simply leaving without a word?

She pushed the door open; his room was even darker than the corridor, lit only by a single candle. He was asleep on his narrow bed, the same bed where they'd kissed, what felt like decades ago.

Even now, he slept entirely without moving, turned slightly on his side, his dark hair surrounding his pale face like a reverse halo. In the past, she had watched him as he lay in his coffin and thought he looked as if he was asleep. She wondered now, as she drifted closer to the bed, how she could have been so mistaken: his body had been there, but his soul had not. Now it was, and even asleep he seemed both terribly alive and terribly fragile, the way all mortal creatures were fragile.

She felt a fierce protectiveness flood through her. *I'm not just doing this for James, or Matthew,* she thought, *much as I love them. I'm doing this for you, too.*

She slipped the note under his pillow, then bent to kiss his forehead lightly. He stirred but didn't wake, even when she left the room.

Ari turned over restlessly in bed. She had not been able to sleep well since the night Belial had taken London. Perhaps it was ridiculous to even consider that, as if it were unusual, she thought, flipping over her pillow, which had grown unbearably hot. She doubted *any* of them had slept well since. How could they? They were reminded at every turn of the dire situation they were in: by the blackened sky, the abandoned carriages and motorcars in the middle of empty streets, the blank-faced, wandering mundanes.

She might normally have thrown open a window, despite the cold, just to get fresh air, but there was nothing fresh about the air outside. It was heavy and oppressive and tasted bitter as soot.

When they had first arrived at the Institute, she had felt lost. Surely it would be presumptuous to assume she and Anna would stay in the same room, and yet at the same time, it felt strange to imagine sleeping so apart from Anna. She was used to waking up in the morning to the sounds of Anna making tea or teaching Winston rude words. Used to finding embroidered waistcoats, frock coats, and velvet trousers thrown over every piece of furniture. Used to the faint perfumy fragrance of burning cheroots. A place without those things would not feel like home.

They had ended up, by accident or design, in rooms connected by an adjoining door. Ari had wondered in these last few dark days if Anna would make use of the door to come to her for comfort after Christopher's death, but the door had remained firmly locked, and Ari lacked the nerve to break in on Anna's grief.

Ari had not known Christopher well, but she mourned, of course, not just for him but for Anna. In her darkest moments she worried that even if they made it through their current situation, Anna would still never be the same again. Could she recover her laughter, her mischief, her rebellious joy, after her brother had died while she held him?

Ari had never known anyone to grieve so silently. She had not seen Anna shed a tear. She'd always thought Anna resembled a beautiful statue, with her fine features and balanced grace, but now it was as if Anna had truly turned to stone. She wasn't completely immobilized—she had thrown herself into the plan to stay in London and defeat Belial as much as anyone. She and Ari had spent long hours together, not just boarding up the Institute but looking through old books in the library, too, searching for ways out of London that Belial might have overlooked. But any attempts Ari had made to deepen the conversation, or bring up Christopher or even family, were gently but firmly rebuffed.

Ari closed her eyes and tried counting. She got nearly to forty before she heard an odd, unfamiliar creaking noise. The door between her room and Anna's was slowly cracking open.

The room was dark. A little light came through from Anna's side of the door, where a candle was burning; still, Ari could see Anna mostly as a silhouette, but it hardly mattered. She would recognize her anywhere, in any light.

"Anna," she whispered, sitting up, but Anna only put a finger to her lips and climbed onto the bed. She wore a silk dressing gown; it was too big for her and slid down her slender shoulders. On her knees, she reached for Ari, her lean fingers cupping Ari's face in her hands, then ducked her head to meet Ari's lips with her own.

Ari had not realized how starved for Anna's touch she had been. She gathered fistfuls of the silk dressing gown in her hands, pulling Anna closer, realizing she wore nothing under it. Her hands found the hard silk of Anna's skin, stroking her back as they kissed harder.

Ari reached for the lamp on her nightstand, but Anna caught her wrist. "No," she whispered. "No lights."

Surprised, Ari drew her hand back. She stroked Anna's short curls as Anna kissed her throat, but a sense of unease had begun to creep in, threading through the haze of her desire. There was something harsh about the way Anna was kissing her, something desperate. "Darling," she murmured, reaching to stroke Anna's cheek.

It was damp. Anna was crying.

Ari bolted upright. She scrabbled for the witchlight under her pillow and lit it, casting them both into a whitish glow; Anna, one hand holding her dressing gown closed, was sitting back on her heels. She looked at Ari defiantly, with red-rimmed eyes.

"Anna," Ari breathed. "Oh, my poor darling . . ."

Anna's eyes darkened. "I suppose you think I am weak."

"*No,*" Ari said vehemently. "Anna, you are the strongest person I know."

"I told myself not to come to you," Anna said bitterly. "You should not have to share the burden of my grief. It is mine to carry."

"It is ours," said Ari. "No one is strong and unyielding all the time, and none of us should be. We all have to let down our guard sometime. We are made up of different parts, sad and happy, strong and weak, solitary and in need of others. And there is nothing shameful about that."

Anna took Ari's hand and looked down at it, as if she were marveling at its construction. "If we are all made up of different parts, then I am quite the chessboard."

Ari turned Anna's hand over in hers, then laid it over her heart. "Never a chessboard," she said. "Nothing so plain. You are a brightly colored pachisi board. You're a backgammon set with triangles of inlaid mother-of-pearl and pieces of gold and silver. You are the queen of hearts."

"And you," Anna said softly, "are the lamp that gives light, without which the game cannot be played."

Ari felt tears burn behind her eyes, but for the first time in days, they were not unhappy tears. She held her arms out, and Anna lay down beside her, curling into her, her head on Ari's shoulder, her breathing soft as velvet against Ari's hair.

29
EXILE FROM LIGHT

At whose approach, ghosts, wandering here and there,
Troop home to churchyards: damned spirits all,
That in crossways and floods have burial,
Already to their wormy beds are gone;
For fear lest day should look their shames upon,
They willfully themselves exile from light
And must for aye consort with black-brow'd night.
—William Shakespeare, *A Midsummer Night's Dream*

A stinging fine rain had started coming down while Cordelia waited outside the gates of the cemetery. It felt like cold needles against her skin.

She had heard of the Cross Bones Graveyard, but she had never been here before tonight. It had been Lucie's decision that this was where they would enact their plan. Cordelia had seen no reason not to go along with it; Lucie knew London far better than she did.

According to Lucie, Will Herondale had often come here as a young man. It was a graveyard where the unblessed, unmourned, and unconsecrated were buried; the dead here were restless, eager to interact. Will had the Herondale gift of seeing ghosts, and the ghosts of Cross Bones would share information with him: about demons, about secret places in London, about history that only they remembered.

In the time since Will had been a boy, civilization had crept closer to Cross Bones. The city pressed in around it. Two ugly redbrick charity schools had been built and loomed over the square patch of land behind the cemetery gates. Cordelia was not sure what time it was, but no one was on the streets. The mundanes seemed less active at night, and she could not help but wonder if they were also more sensitive to places like Cross Bones in their enchanted state.

The Watchers, of course, would be a different story, and she kept an eye out for them, her hand on the hilt of Cortana. She prayed she would not have to draw it before the time was right, though she felt the joy of having it back with her, the sense of rightness that came with its presence.

She glanced back at Cross Bones. She could see Lucie only as a shadow, moving around the graveyard. She seemed to be dusting off her hands; a moment later she approached the rusted gates, her face a pale smudge against the darkness. She was dressed in gear, her hair tied back in a plait, a small rucksack over her shoulders.

"Daisy." Lucie illuminated a witchlight, keeping the light low, and began to fiddle with the mechanism on her side of the gates. "Any Watchers? Were we followed?"

Cordelia shook her head as Lucie pulled the gate open with a squeak of hinges. She ducked through the small gap and into the circle of Lucie's witchlight. "Everything's ready?" she whispered as Lucie closed the gate carefully behind her.

"Ready as it can be," Lucie said in her normal speaking voice, which sounded unnaturally loud in the stillness. "Follow me."

Cordelia did, Lucie's witchlight dancing ahead of her like a will-o'-the-wisp leading an unwary traveler to a dark fate. Still, she was grateful for the light. She could see where she was walking over rocky, uneven ground, weeds poking up through the gravelly soil. She had at least expected grave markers, but there were none. The unconsecrated dead who lay beneath their feet had had any sign of their presence erased by time and progress. It looked more like an abandoned building lot than anything else, with stacks of rotting lumber forgotten in corners, along with old pencils, notebooks, and other refuse from the charity schools.

"Grim, isn't it?" Lucie said, leading Cordelia between two conical piles of rock. Small cairns, perhaps? "They buried fallen women here, and paupers whose relatives couldn't afford a funeral. People London thought ought to be forgotten." She sighed. "Usually in a graveyard there are some souls not at rest. But here, there are *no* souls at rest. Everyone here was uncared for and unwanted. I know my father used to come here—he was friends with a ghost called Old Mol—but I don't know how he could stand it. It's so unbearably sad."

"Did you have to—you know, command them?" Cordelia asked.

"No." Lucie sounded as if she were a bit surprised herself. "They wanted to help. All right—here we are." She stopped at a spot near the cemetery's back wall. There was nothing notable about it to Cordelia, but Lucie seemed sure of herself. She raised her witchlight and said, "I suppose there's no reason to wait. Go ahead, Daisy."

"Here?" Cordelia said. "Now?"

"Yes. You're standing in exactly the right place."

Cordelia took a deep breath and drew Cortana. A ripple of power passed through her arm, followed by joy: it was clear Cortana still wanted her, still chose her. How she had missed this: the match of the sword and the wielder. It gave off a faint golden glow, a beacon in the demonic darkness. She raised her other hand and drew the blade across her palm. It was so sharp that she barely felt it as her skin opened. Fat drops of blood pattered onto the ground.

The ground shuddered. Lucie's eyes widened as a blackened glow, like a hole in the night itself, appeared, and the Mother of Demons emerged from it.

She wore a gown of silver silk, and her feet were shod in slippers of the same silver material. Her hair was coiled around her head in braids the color of hematite. The black, shining scales of the snakes in her eyes glittered as they darted back and forth, taking in the scene before her.

"Really," she said, sounding annoyed. "I had hoped that after you killed the Blackthorn woman, it would give you a taste for blood. I did not hope it would be your *own* blood." She glanced around—at the graveyard, at the sky full of rolling gray-and-black clouds. "Belial has rather outdone himself, hasn't he?" she said, with a sort of reluctant admiration. "I suppose you want me to do something about it, and that's why you're bothering me?"

"Not quite," said Cordelia. She could feel her heart pounding. She bit the inside of her cheek. She would not show Lilith fear. "I think you will find what I have to say interesting."

Lilith was looking at Lucie now, the serpents of her eyes licking the air with lazy tongues. "And I see you brought a friend. Was that wise?"

Lucie glared. "I am not afraid of you."

"You should be," Lilith said. She turned back to Cordelia. "And you. You have waited rather too long, paladin. Belial is close to the completion of his plan. I will have no use for you then, and I will not be pleased about it. Besides, I'm not going to send you out of London now. This is where Belial will come, when he is ready."

"I didn't call on you because I want to leave London," Cordelia began. "I—"

"You called me because Belial has taken your lovers from you," Lilith sneered.

Cordelia gritted her teeth. "James is my husband, and Matthew is my friend. I want them rescued. I am willing to be your paladin—I am willing to fight in your name, if you will bring them back from Edom."

Lilith's smile flickered. "I could not go to Edom even if I wanted to. They are beyond my reach. As I said, you waited too long—"

"Perhaps you cannot set foot in Edom," said Cordelia. "But you could send me there."

"Are you trying to negotiate?" Lilith sounded amused. "Oh, paladin. The knight does not 'negotiate' with her liege. The knight is the liege's will made flesh. Nothing more or less."

"Wrong." Cordelia raised Cortana in her hand. It seemed to blaze, a torch against the night. "I am more. And you are not as powerful as you think. You are bound, Mother of Demons. Bound and trapped."

Lilith laughed aloud. "Do you really think I would be so foolish as to allow myself to be bound? Look around us, child. I see no pentagram. I see no circle of salt. Only a bare ground of dirt and rock. What power would bind me?"

Cordelia looked at Lucie, who took a deep breath.

"Rise," Lucie said. "I do not command, only ask. Rise."

They shot upward from the ground, beams of silvery light that resolved themselves into translucent human figures. Dozens of them, until Cordelia felt as if she stood among a forest of lighted trees.

They were the ghosts of young women—young and shabbily dressed, with sad, empty eyes, though whether that was because of their lives or their deaths, Cordelia could not have said. There were a few transparent men scattered through the crowd as well, most of them also young. They stood with spectral hands linked, forming long lines that intersected and bisected each other to create the shape of a pentagram. In the center of the pentagram stood Cordelia—and Lilith.

"These ghosts are loyal to me," said Lucie. She had positioned herself a few steps outside the pentagram. Cordelia could see the illuminated figures of the ghosts of Cross Bones, reflected in Lucie's eyes. "They will remain in this pentagram formation as long as I ask. Even if I leave, you will be trapped here."

With a hiss, Lilith spun and struck out at the nearest ghost—but her hand passed through the spirit with only a crackle of energy. Her face twisted as fangs snapped from her mouth, her hair turning to a sleek fall of scales. Her silver slippers had dropped away; from beneath the hem of her gown a thick coil, a serpent's tail, protruded. "If you do not release me," she hissed, "I will tear Cordelia Carstairs limb from limb and shatter her bones while she screams. Do not think I cannot do it."

Lucie paled but stood her ground. Cordelia had warned her that this was what Lilith would say; she had not also said that there was every chance Lilith would do as she threatened. Lucie was safe outside the pentagram, and beyond that Cordelia did not care: this had to work. For James, for Matthew. It *had* to.

"I don't think you'll kill me," Cordelia said calmly. "I think you're cleverer than that. I am your paladin and the bearer of the blade Cortana. I am the only one who can give Belial his third wound and end him. I am the *only* one who can get your realm back for you."

"You are still negotiating." Lilith's fangs sank into her own lower lip; blood dripped down her chin. "You say you want to kill Belial—"

"I *want* to save James and Matthew," Cordelia said. "I am prepared to kill Belial. I have the will and the weapon. Send us to Edom. Myself and Lucie. Send us to Edom, and I will reclaim it for you by dispatching Belial. Before he takes London. Before he takes James. Before he is unstoppable."

"That's all you want? A chance to save your friends?" Lilith said, her voice thick with contempt.

"No. I want an agreement that when Belial is dead by my sword, you will release me from your service. I will no longer be your paladin. And I want your word that you will not harm me or my loved ones."

The snakes had vanished; Lilith's eyes were flat and black, as they had looked in the mural. "You ask a great deal."

"You will get a great deal in return," Cordelia said. "You will get a whole world."

Lilith seemed to hesitate. "Your friends are still alive in Edom," she said. "They are being held in Idumea. The great capital of Edom, where my palace stands."

Idumea. The city that had once been Alicante, in that other world, where Shadowhunters had lost the battle against demons a thousand years ago. Where Lilith had ruled, until Belial came.

"I cannot get you all the way there," Lilith said. "Belial has strengthened many parts of Edom against me. But I can get you close. After that . . ." She bared her fangs. "Once you are in Edom, you will be outside both my protection and the protection of your Angel. I cannot act there while Belial rules it. And your Nephilim Marks will fade as quickly as they are drawn. Cortana you may have, but Edom is not a welcoming place for humans. No plants grow, and any water you might find will be poisonous to you. You cannot travel at night—you will have to seek shelter once the moons rise, or die in the dark."

"Sounds lovely," Lucie muttered. "I can see why you're so desperate to get back there."

"Once we are in Edom," said Cordelia, "once we have James and Matthew—how do we return to London?"

"There is a Gard in Idumea, a dark reflection of your Gard here. It was mine, but Belial made it his stronghold during his usurpation of my realm. Within the Gard is a Portal, a Portal I myself made. You may pass through that to this world."

It was folly to trust Lilith, Cordelia knew. And yet Lilith would *want* them to succeed and to return, because Lilith wanted Belial's death more than anything else in any world.

"Then we have an agreement," said Cordelia. "But first you must swear to it. Swear that you will send us to Edom safely. Swear that if Belial dies by my blade, you will free me from my paladin's oath. Swear on Lucifer's name."

Lilith flinched. She flinched, but she swore, on the name of Lucifer, Cordelia listening very carefully to each of her words to make sure that Lilith was swearing to exactly what she had asked for. No one cared about exactitude of language more than demons; Cordelia had learned that with her paladin's oath, and she would not be tricked again.

When she was done, Lilith grinned, a ghastly snake's grin. "It is done," she said. "Remove the pentagram."

"No," Lucie said firmly. She turned to the ghosts. "When I have passed through the Portal, you may disperse and free the demon. But not before I am gone."

Lilith snarled at that but raised her hands, spreading them wide, her fingers seeming to reach out to touch Lucie and Cordelia.

Darkness poured from her hands. Cordelia could not help but think of the shadows that had swallowed James and Matthew, as the blackness curled around her and Lucie, cutting off her vision and her breath. She slammed Cortana back into its scabbard as she felt herself caught and spun upward and outward, Lilith's laughter echoing in her ears. She saw the glow of three strange moons in the sky as a searing, dry wind lifted her, twisting her body until it seemed as if her spine would snap.

She cried out for Lucie—and then she was falling, falling through a hot, choking darkness, the salt taste of blood in her mouth.

Jesse shoved his bedroom door open. He had left the candles burning; in fact, he had left the whole room a mess. And he was a mess himself, come to that: his shirt was buttoned incorrectly, and his shoes didn't match.

He had bolted out of the room the moment he'd read Lucie's note. He had no idea how long it had been since she'd left it, though he felt as if he'd barely slept—surely it couldn't have been more than half an hour before he'd rolled over and the crinkle of Lucie's note had awakened him.

He barely remembered throwing on clothes and rushing out into the street. He was halfway across the snowy courtyard when he recalled: he was a Shadowhunter. He could do better than racing into the night with no map and no plan. With Lucie's gold comb in hand, he drew a Tracking rune on the back of his hand and waited.

And felt nothing.

Cold crept into his bones. Perhaps he had drawn the rune incorrectly, though he knew in his heart that he hadn't. He did it again. Waited again.

Nothing. Only the wind blowing particles of ice and soot, and the terrible silence of a London without birdsong, traffic, or the calls of barrow boys.

Lucie was gone.

He made his way warily back to his room, and crossed most of the way to the bed before he realized it was occupied. There was a sort of nest of blankets in the center, mixed up with scattered papers, and in the middle of the nest was Grace. She was curled up, her feet bandaged, wearing a clean linen nightgown. Her pale hair was in braids. She looked years younger than she was, less like the young woman she had become and more like the little girl he had trained and protected to the best of his ability so many years ago.

"They're gone," she said. "Aren't they?"

Jesse sat down at the foot of the bed. "How did you know?"

She tugged at a braid. "I couldn't sleep. I was looking out the window and saw them go outside together. And then you rushed out, and it looked like you were trying to Track them." She frowned. "Where'd they go?"

Jesse fished Lucie's note from his trouser pocket and handed it to Grace, who unfolded it curiously. When she was done, she looked at Jesse with worried eyes.

"I knew they were planning something," she said. "I didn't know it was this. Edom, and Lilith—I don't know—"

"How did you know they were planning something?" asked Jesse, furrowing his brow.

"The way they were looking at each other," Grace said. "Like—they had a secret."

"I feel a fool," Jesse said. "I didn't notice."

"I used to have a secret with Lucie. You. I know what she looks like when she's planning something. Cordelia's harder to read, but . . ." Grace cast her eyes down. "I'm sorry I didn't guess what it was. I would have said something. Even when I saw them leave, I assumed they were just hunting Watchers, or looking for more Downworlders . . ."

"It's not your fault," Jesse said. Her eyes were huge, the color of mirrors, and fixed on him. He meant it, though—he didn't blame her; not for this, at least.

"It's strange," he said. "When I was a ghost, I could sense Lucie, you know. I could simply . . . reach out into the shadows and always find her. Appear wherever she was. But not anymore."

"Now you're alive," Grace said quietly. "You must live within human limitations. And within those, there is nothing you could have done."

"I wish Lucie had told me," Jesse said, looking down at his hands. "I could have tried to talk her out of it . . ."

Grace said, not unkindly, "I've come to know Lucie quite well, you know, these last months. She was probably as close to a friend as I have ever had. And I know—and you know, too, I don't doubt—that she is very determined. This is what she wanted, and she would have let nothing stand in her way. Not even you."

"Even if I couldn't have stopped her," Jesse said, "I could have gone with her."

"No," said Grace. "I mean—Jesse, if they've gone to Edom, it is only because Cordelia is protected by her bond with Lilith, and Lucie by her ties to Belial. It's a demon realm, and you would have been in terrible danger—it's why Lucie *didn't* tell you, or anyone. I don't know if Cordelia even told Alastair. They knew no one else could come."

"I wouldn't have minded," Jesse said, clenching and unclenching his fists. "The risk, I mean."

"Well, *I* would mind. If you risked yourself. I know you are angry with me, Jesse. I know you may never feel the same way about me again as you did once. But you are still my brother. You are part of my character, and if there is a little good in me, along with the evil, then it is there because of you."

Jesse softened. He reached out and took Grace's hand in his, and for a moment, they sat in silence.

"If it's any consolation," Grace said after a time, "I think that Lucie also went without you because she knew *we* needed you. There are only six of us here now. Six Shadowhunters to stand between London and the forever dark."

"It's a bit of consolation," Jesse said. "And—there is good in you, Gracie," he added, after a time. "The first thing you did when you escaped the Silent City was run here to warn us of Tatiana. You could simply have fled. It would have been easier, perhaps safer. Yet you took the risk."

"I didn't want her to win," Grace said. "Mama. She had taken so much from me. I wanted her defeated. I hope it was goodness; I worry it was only stubbornness. We are both stubborn, you and I."

"Is that a good thing?" Jesse said. "Maybe being stubborn will get us all killed."

"Or maybe it will make the difference between winning and losing," Grace said. "Maybe it's just what we need right now. To not give up. To never give up. To fight all the way to the end."

By the time the sun set, Matthew was shaking uncontrollably. It didn't seem to matter if he was wrapped in his own coat and James's, too; his teeth chattered together so hard that he'd gashed open his lower lip. Gasping that the taste of the blood nauseated him, he crawled some distance away and was sick, throwing up apples and water and, James worried, the last of Christopher's sedative.

How much worse might this be, he wondered grimly, if Matthew had not already started to cut down his alcohol intake. He had been suffering *before* they'd come to Edom. James could only hope that what he had already paid in pain would reduce the cost to him now.

The moon rose in the sky, an eerie gray-white—and then a second moon, and a third. The courtyard was illuminated as brightly as it had been during the day, though the shadows between the dead trees were deeper. James went to get water, and he watched the reflection of the three moons tremble on the surface of the stone bowl.

He thought of his parents, far away in Alicante, in the shadow of the true Gard. They must have learned by now what had happened to

London. To him. Someone would carry the news to them. Not Lucie—she would never agree to leave London to its fate.

When he returned to the wall, Matthew was resting his back against it, shivering. James tried to hand him the cup of water, but Matthew was shaking too hard to take it; James held the cup to his lips, encouraging him to drink until it was empty.

"I don't want to be sick again," Matthew said hoarsely, but James only shook his head.

"Better than dying of thirst," he said, setting the cup down. "Come here."

He pulled Matthew roughly toward him, Matthew's back to his chest, and wrapped his arms around his *parabatai*. He had thought Matthew might protest, but he seemed beyond that: he only sagged back, an alarmingly light weight against him.

"This is good," he said tiredly. "You're better than a coat."

James rested his chin on Matthew's shoulder. "I'm sorry," he said.

He felt Matthew tense. "Sorry for what?"

"All of it," James said. "Paris. The fight we had at the Shadow Market. When you told me that if I didn't love Cordelia, I should let someone else love her. I was too blind to see what you meant."

"You were," Matthew said, with some difficulty, "under a spell. You said yourself, it blinded you—"

"Don't," James said. "Don't excuse it. What you said, back at the Institute, about not being able to be angry with me—I'd rather you *were*. Even if you won't blame me for anything I did under the bracelet's control, what about after it was broken? I ought to have thought more about your feelings—"

"And I ought not to have run off to Paris with Cordelia," said Matthew.

"I know how I must have seemed to you," James said quietly. "Feckless, flighty, pointlessly cruel to Cordelia, and oblivious to all of it. In the name of an infatuation that made no sense to anyone but me."

"It was still selfish. I thought . . . I told myself you didn't love her. And that I loved her, loved being with her, because—"

"Because she is who she is," James said.

"But also because she never knew me, as you did, before I drank. Not really. I had feelings for Lucie once, you know, but I could see in her eyes when she looked at me that she was waiting for me to go back to my old self. The Matthew I was before I ever picked up a bottle. Cordelia only knew me after I changed." Matthew hugged his arms around his knees. "The truth is, I do not know the person I will be when I am entirely sober. I do not know if I will even like that person myself, assuming I survive to meet him."

James wished he could see the expression on Matthew's face. "Math. The drinking has not—did not—make you more witty, more charming, more worthy of love. What it did was make you forget. That is all."

Matthew sounded as if he had forgotten to breathe. "Forget what?"

"Whatever it is you are so angry at yourself about," said James. "And no, before you ask—Cordelia has told me nothing. I think you shared your secret with her; I think that is part of what has made you long for her. We so desperately want to be with those who know the truth of us. Our secrets."

"You guessed all this?" Matthew said, sounding a little amazed.

"When I am not under a spell, I am surprisingly insightful," James said dryly. "And you are the other half of my soul, my *parabatai*; how could I *not* guess?" He took a deep breath. "I cannot demand that you tell me anything; I have kept enough from you. Only . . . if you want to tell me, I swear I will listen."

There was a long silence. Then Matthew sat up a little straighter and said, "Bloody convincing Herondales." He tipped his head back, staring up at the strange triple moon. "All right. I'll tell you what happened."

"It's never been my favorite city," said Alastair, "but I have to say, I did much prefer London in its previous state."

It was midday, though one could hardly tell, and Alastair and Thomas were hunting for Watchers in Bayswater.

It had started off as more of a reconnaissance mission. Follow the Watchers without being seen, Anna had said; find out where they congregated, and if possible, how they might be harmed or killed.

It had been hours now. They had seen several Watchers and tried following them, creeping through the streets after them as they wandered, but that didn't bring them any closer to figuring out how to defeat them, since everyone in the city—mundanes, Downworlders, even animals—gave the Watchers a wide berth. There was no way of discovering what they could do in a fight, or how they could be stopped, just by watching at a distance.

They had decided: the next Watcher they saw, they would engage in battle. They were both heavily armed; Thomas carried a halberd, and Alastair a long *shamshir*, a curved Persian blade, in addition to the seraph blades and daggers in their belts. Ordinarily, Thomas would have felt fairly secure, but it was impossible to feel secure in this London.

They were walking down Westbourne Grove past the lightless, grimy windows of Whiteleys, a department store that took up half the street. It was normally thronged with stylish carriages, delivery vans, and excited shoppers. Now there were no carriages at all. One lone old gentleman sat collapsed like a beggar on the pavement outside the Gents' Hosiery window, his frock coat crumpled and his hat askew, muttering to himself about socks. Beyond him a flash of movement jolted Thomas for a moment, but it was just an abandoned and very grubby ladies' umbrella, which might have been pink once, flapping like a dying bird beside an expensive display of hats, dimly visible through the mud-splashed window. The hats also looked grubby. It was not a particularly cheering sight, and Thomas could not help but agree with Alastair.

"Do you mean, you preferred London when it was not cut off from the rest of the world, or you preferred London when the mundanes were autonomous rather than puppeteered by a demon?" Thomas said politely.

"I mean," said Alastair dryly, "I preferred when the shops were open. I miss buying hats. Come on out, Watchers!" he called in a louder voice. "Let us get a good look at you!"

"I don't think there are any in this neighborhood," said Thomas. "We've looked everywhere. But we could try Hyde Park. When I was walking Jesse and Grace to Grosvenor Square, I saw a big clump of them there."

They proceeded down Queensway, which was also deserted and equally depressing. Drifts of rubbish two feet high had blown up against the railings along the east side of the street. They both tensed as they saw a figure in a white, flapping robe—then relaxed; it was not a Watcher, but a young mundane nursemaid in a white apron, pushing a large, fancy white perambulator. "Once upon a time," she was saying brightly. "Once upon a time. Once upon a time . . ."

As they passed her, Thomas glanced under the hood of the perambulator and saw to his relief that there was no baby there, only a collection of rubbish the woman must have picked up off the street: dirty old rags, crumpled newspapers, tin cans, dead leaves. He thought he glimpsed the bright eyes of a rat staring out from the nest of litter.

How long could the mundanes go on like this? Thomas wondered. Were they feeding themselves, their children? Would they starve, or begin to wind down someday, like dying clockwork? Belial had claimed he wanted to rule over a New London—was he going to rule over a London of corpses? Would he bring in demons to populate the houses, the streets?

They had reached Bayswater Road and the park entrance. Tall black wrought-iron gates stood open on either side of a broad path lined with leafless beech trees, which stretched away into foggy gloom. There were none of the usual groups of tourists, or dog walkers or kite-flying children, or indeed anything alive at all except for a group of horses peacefully cropping the grass; a scene that should have seemed pleasantly bucolic, but they were all wearing bridles and blinkers and head-collars, and one appeared to be trailing part of the broken shaft of a hansom cab. As Thomas watched, he caught a glimpse of a redheaded figure slipping behind an oak tree—he blinked, and it was gone.

"Thomas," Alastair said. "Don't brood."

"I'm not," Thomas lied. "So what happened with Cordelia and Lucie? Did you know they were going to Edom?"

That morning Jesse had shown them all the note left by Lucie, explaining that she and Cordelia had worked out a way to get to Edom, Belial's realm, and had gone there hoping to rescue James and Matthew.

Everyone had reacted as Thomas would have expected them to. Anna was angry but resigned, Ari and Thomas had tried to be optimistic, Jesse was quiet but firm, and Grace was silent. Only Alastair's response had confused him: he had seemed as if none of this came as a surprise to him at all.

"I didn't know exactly what they had planned," Alastair said. "But Cordelia asked me for Cortana yesterday, and I gave it to her. It was clear she was brewing up some sort of scheme."

"Did you think about trying to stop her?" Thomas asked.

"I have learned," Alastair said, "that when my sister sets her mind to something, there is little point in trying to stop her. And besides, what would I be stopping her for? So she could experience more of this?" He gestured around. "If she wants to die as a Shadowhunter, in battle, defending her family, I can't deny her that."

The words were defiant, but beneath them, Thomas could sense the depth of Alastair's worry and pain. He wanted to pull Alastair close, though they had barely touched since the night of Christopher's death. Thomas had felt too raw, as if his whole body were an open wound. But the lost sound in Alastair's voice . . .

"What's that?" Alastair said, squinting. He pointed in the direction of Lancaster Gate, which led out from the park back into the city.

Thomas looked. He saw it too, after a moment. . . . A flash of white robes through the iron bars.

They hurried through the gate, keeping out of sight. Sure enough, a single white-robed, white-hooded figure was headed briskly north, its back to them. Thomas and Alastair stared at each other before dashing after the Watcher as silently as they could.

Thomas wasn't much paying attention to where they were going until Alastair tapped him on the shoulder. "Isn't that Paddington Station?" he whispered.

It was. The station didn't have a signpost or a fancy entrance: it was a rather unprepossessing, long, grimy Victorian building, accessed by a sloping pavement leading down to a covered arcade labeled GREAT WESTERN RAILWAY.

Normally there would have been paper sellers and crowds of passengers flooding through the doors. Now the place was deserted—save for their Watcher striding down the ramp.

Thomas and Alastair hurried to follow it into the arcade. It swept ahead of them, seemingly unconscious of their presence, and whisked through a doorway that led into the Second-Class Booking Office. It was dark and deserted inside; the ticket windows along the mahogany counter were shuttered and the marble floor was littered with abandoned luggage, some of which had burst open. The archway that led into the station was blocked by a large brown leather suitcase, spilling a pair of red-and-white-striped pajamas and a child's stuffed bear. Thomas and Alastair leaped over the mess and emerged into the cavernous vault of the station.

They were on platform one, which, like the booking office, was strewn with abandoned luggage and a random selection of passengers' personal items, all laid out like a stall at a giant bazaar. The big station clock, permanently stopped at a quarter to four, was wearing a red woolen scarf; an enormous, befeathered "cartwheel" hat hung at a jaunty angle from the top of a chocolate vending machine; and five cheap novels, spilled from a velvet bag, lay on the floor like collapsed dominoes.

Above them soared the huge triple arch of the great iron-and-glass roof: a gigantic cathedral, supported by rows of delicate, ornate wrought-iron columns, like the ribs of some metal giant. In normal circumstances it would have been filled with trains and clouds of steam and smog and crowds of people and *sounds*—the babble of voices and railway announcements and guards blowing whistles and slamming doors; the deafening clanking, chuffing, and whistling sounds of the trains.

Now it was empty. Belial's demon twilight filtered down from the soot-laden glass roof through a misty haze, broken sporadically by flickering lamps; there was a weird fizzing electrical hum coming from them that sounded eerie in the echoing quiet. The faint illumination from the open end of the station, where the trains came in, cast an uncanny glow across the far ends of the platforms and threw everything else into a gloom that made the deep shadows deeper. Sometimes they seemed to be moving, and small scuttling noises came from them—rats, probably. Hopefully.

Thomas and Alastair headed down platform two, hands on their weapons, their footsteps muffled by Soundless runes. The platforms were empty except for a lone train halfway down platform three, its doors standing open, waiting for the passengers who would never arrive. And—there was the Watcher, walking along beside it. As

Thomas spotted it, it turned and seemed to look directly at them. Then it stepped between two carriages of the train and disappeared.

Alastair swore and broke into a run. Thomas followed, jumping off the platform when it ended, onto the dangerous ground of the rail yard: uneven wooden railway sleepers on top of coarse, sharp chunks of gravel, crisscrossed with iron tracks.

Alastair slowed to a stop where the Watcher had disappeared, letting Thomas catch up to him. They looked around and saw nothing. The area around the train seemed deserted, the silence almost oppressive.

"We lost it," Alastair said in disgust. "By the Angel—"

"I'm not so sure," Thomas said, keeping his voice low. The silence didn't feel comforting, but wrong somehow, just like the shadows were wrong. "Draw your weapon," he whispered, reaching for his halberd.

Alastair looked at him for a moment, eyes narrowed. Then, seeming to decide that he trusted Thomas, he started to reach for his *shamshir*—just as a white-clad figure leaped from the train's roof, knocking Alastair flat.

The *shamshir* flew out of Alastair's hand as he and the Watcher rolled across the uneven ground. The Watcher pinned Alastair down; there was no way he could reach for his weapons belt. Instead he reared back and punched the Watcher in the face.

"Alastair!" Thomas shouted. He ran toward the place where Alastair was grappling with the Watcher; he was hitting it over and over, and the Watcher was bleeding, spattering red-black droplets over the gravel of the train yard. But it seemed impassive: if the blows hurt, it gave no sign. It had one long white hand wrapped around Alastair's throat, and as Thomas watched, it started to squeeze.

Something exploded behind Thomas's eyes. He did not remember closing the space between himself and the Watcher, only that he found himself standing over it, swinging his halberd. The polearm connected with the Watcher, its axe-head slamming into the thing's shoulder. It snarled but kept choking Alastair, whose lips were turning blue. Panicked, Thomas yanked the halberd free—and tore half the Watcher's cloak away with it. He caught a glimpse of its hairless skull and the back of its neck, printed with a demonic scarlet rune.

Acting on instinct, Thomas swung the halberd again, this time driving the blade straight into the rune, slashing across it, obliterating the pattern.

The Watcher sprang to its feet, releasing Alastair. The ragged remains of its white robes were soaked in red-black blood. It staggered toward Thomas, catching hold of him with hands like iron claws. It flung him, hard; he flew through the air and slammed into the side of a train car. He slid to the ground, dazed; he had lost his halberd somewhere, but his head was ringing too loudly for him to look for it.

He could taste metal in his mouth. He willed himself to get up, to move, but his body would not cooperate. He could only watch through blurred eyes as the Watcher twitched and spasmed strangely. It fell to its knees, something peculiar seeming to emerge from the bloody wound on the back of its neck. Long, spidery legs, feelers scraping at the air. They pushed the Chimera demon's body free. It crawled out of the Silent Brother's limp body, its abdomen pulsing, its green eyes glowing as they fixed on Thomas. It leaped toward him, as a merciful darkness came down like a curtain.

30
Antique Land

I met a traveller from an antique land,
Who said—"Two vast and trunkless legs of stone
Stand in the desert . . . . Near them, on the sand,
Half sunk a shattered visage lies, whose frown,
And wrinkled lip, and sneer of cold command,
Tell that its sculptor well those passions read
Which yet survive, stamped on these lifeless things,
The hand that mocked them, and the heart that fed."
—Percy Bysshe Shelley, "Ozymandias"

Cordelia had passed through many Portals in her life, but none like the one to Edom. It was an acrid whirlwind full of smoke; she spun breathless through the dark, her lungs aching, terrified that Lilith had tricked her, tricked Lucie, and they would die in the void between worlds.

Eventually the darkness faded to a fiery red-orange light. Before Cordelia's eyes could adjust, she struck a hard surface. Uneven earth; the desert floor. She rolled across gritty, dark yellow dunes, sand in her eyes and ears and lungs, clutching at the ground with her fingers until at last she came to a stop.

Coughing violently, she rolled to her knees and looked around. All around her stretched a bleak and unfriendly desert, shimmering with heat under a dark red sun. Dunes of dry sand rose and fell like waves, and between them snaked fiery lines: narrow rivers of molten fire. Black rock formations burst from the ground at intervals, jagged and ugly.

There was no indication of anything alive nearby. And no sign of Lucie.

Cordelia staggered to her feet. "Lucie!" she called, her throat burning. Her voice seemed to echo in the emptiness, and she felt the first stirrings of panic.

Steady, she told herself. She could see no footprints in the sand, only the marks where she had bounced and rolled across the ground, and the hot wind was already beginning to cover those with new sand. She narrowed her eyes against the sun's shimmer and saw a gap between two rocks at the top of a shale-and-gravel hill. The sandy ground near the gap seemed disturbed and—was that a boot print?

Cordelia scrambled up the hill, her hand on Cortana's hilt. Closer up she could see a sort of path, perhaps a place where water had once flowed, which passed between the two boulders. With some difficulty, she was able to squeeze through. Beyond the rocks, the hill fell away to more sandy wasteland, but not far away was another sizable rock formation. Leaning against it, her eyes closed and her face pale, was Lucie.

"*Lucie!*" Cordelia skated down the hill on a wave of loose sand and gravel before hurrying over to her friend. Up close, Lucie looked worse—her face was strained, and she held her hands over her chest as she struggled to breathe.

Cordelia fished her stele out. Lucie held out her wrist obediently, and Cordelia traced an *iratze* on the skin there—only to watch in horror as it rapidly faded, as if it had been drawn with water.

"Lilith said," Lucie gasped, "that runes wouldn't work here."

"I know," Cordelia muttered. "I hoped she was lying." She put down the stele and opened her flask, which she pressed into Lucie's hands. After a moment, she was relieved to see Lucie take a swallow, and then another one, a little color returning to her face. "What happened?" Cordelia said. "Are you hurt? Was it the Portal?"

Lucie took a deep breath and coughed again. "No." She looked past Cordelia at the landscape beyond: dusty with ash, studded with dozens of blackened rock formations. A burned land. A poisoned land. "It's this place."

"It's awful," Cordelia agreed. "I can't imagine why Lilith is so enamored with it. Surely there are nicer worlds she could conquer and possess."

"I think she likes . . . that it's dead," Lucie said. "I'm used to the dead, to feeling their presence and seeing them everywhere. But this . . . This is a whole dead world. Bones and rock and the skeletons of ancient things." She shook her head. "Death hangs in every part of the air. It feels like a weight pressing on me."

"We can rest here until your strength comes back," Cordelia said, unable to keep the worry out of her voice.

"No." Lucie frowned. "Every second we wait is a second James and Matthew may not have. We need to get to Idumea." She exhaled sharply, as if the name made her flinch. "I can *feel* it, Idumea. It's pulling at me. A—a dead city. So many lives lost there."

"You're sure it's Idumea?" Cordelia said. "That you're feeling?"

"I know it is," Lucie said. "I can't say how, but I know. It's like I can hear it calling out for me. Which is good, because that's where we have to go anyway."

"Luce, if it has such an effect on you, when we can't even see the city in the distance—what's going to happen when we get closer?"

Lucie looked up at Cordelia. Her eyes were the only blue thing in all the landscape; the sky shifted between orange and gray. "I feel better," she said. "I think it's because you're with me. Really," she added. "You needn't look so worried. Help me up, will you?"

Cordelia helped Lucie to her feet. As she put away her flask, she narrowed her eyes, staring at the stone Lucie had been leaning against. "Look at that," she said. "It's a statue."

Lucie turned to look. "Part of one, anyway."

Though it was eroded by years of wind and acidic air, it was clearly the head of a woman. A woman with long flowing hair, and serpents curled in her eyes. The remains, Cordelia realized, of a decapitated statue of Lilith. Where the rest of it was, she couldn't guess—buried under the sand, perhaps.

Lucie regarded the head. "When Belial won this land for himself, I suppose he destroyed all the monuments to Lilith."

"Of course he did," Cordelia said, surprising herself with the bitterness in her voice. "Like a child kicking over another child's toy. This is just a game for them. What does it matter who controls this barren world, except to Belial's and Lilith's pride? Edom is just a chessboard, and we are two of their pawns."

"But you are very good at chess," Lucie said. "James told me so." She looked out over the blood-tinted landscape of Edom, and there was strength and determination on her face, more like her usual self. "And even a pawn can topple a king."

True, Cordelia thought. *But often it must sacrifice itself in the process.* She did not say what she thought out loud, though, only smiled at Lucie and said, "Well then. The job of a pawn is to move forward, never stopping and never turning back."

"Then let's get started," Lucie said. Retrieving her rucksack by its strap, she slung it on and began to make her way across the dry land. After a moment, Cordelia followed.

By the time Ari and Anna got back to the Institute, they were exhausted. They had trekked all the way to Primrose Hill to investigate a barrow, which a few smudged maps in the Institute library had marked in a way that *perhaps* suggested an entrance to Faerie. It had been a long shot, and Ari had been pessimistic about it from the start. And indeed, if there ever had been a gate to Faerie there, it was long gone, or had been sealed by Belial without a trace.

"Back to the library, I suppose?" Ari said as Anna latched the Institute door firmly behind them. "To find the next candidate?"

"We cannot keep doing this," Anna said wearily. "If we had all the time in the world, we could try every likely hill and dale in London. But we have barely any time at all."

"Perhaps we should focus on making a longer list from our research first," Ari said. "Then at least we could check several spots in the same part of the city."

"I think we should find the five likeliest," Anna said as they started up the central staircase, "and visit them, wherever they might be."

"Only five?"

"We may not even have time for five," Anna said. "Our situation here is untenable for very much longer." She sighed. "Perhaps Grace will find a way to signal for help. Or perhaps Cordelia and Lucie will have some success in Edom. Or . . ." She trailed off, but Ari knew what she was thinking. "Or at least," Anna said in a quieter voice, "we will have made a last stand."

"Anna," Ari said, taking her by the shoulder. Anna stopped and turned to look at her. "Before we consider our last stand, may I suggest we eat something? And maybe have some tea before we go out again."

Anna smiled faintly. "Tea?"

"We will do no one any good," said Ari firmly, "if we collapse from hunger or thirst."

She was going to go on but was stopped by a muffled voice coming from the other end of the corridor. "What was that?"

"It's coming from the infirmary," Anna said, starting toward the sound. "It sounds like Alastair."

Ari hurried to follow Anna. The infirmary door was closed; Anna opened it cautiously. Inside they found Thomas, who was sitting at the end of one of the beds, and Alastair, who was standing between him and the door. Thomas was glowering. "You cannot make me stay here."

"I can," Alastair said with feeling. "I will. I shall sit on you if necessary."

Thomas folded his arms, and Ari noticed with a start that he looked as though he'd lost a fight. There was blood in his sandy hair, and bruises around one of his eyes, despite two fresh *iratzes* on his arm. He—and also Alastair, she realized—were scratched up and dusty all over.

"By the Angel," Anna said, "what happened to you two? You look as though you've been in a pub fight. And were quite outnumbered. Whereas I am fairly sure the pubs are all closed."

"We figured out how to kill the Watchers," Thomas said eagerly. "Shall I tell you the story?"

"At once," Anna said, and Thomas did, reporting their trip to Paddington Station and the battle that had ensued there. "There are runes on the backs of their necks," he said. "A bit like Belial's sigil, but modified in a few ways."

"Perhaps to signify possession," Alastair put in, "though neither of us are exactly experts on demonic runes."

"If that rune is cut or destroyed," Thomas went on, "it forces the demon out of the body. And then the demon itself can be killed with little trouble."

Anna's eyebrows went up. "Well, I don't wish to overstate our position, but that seems . . . like good news? Rather unexpectedly?"

"It is hard to think of a downside," Alastair said reluctantly. "And I have tried."

"The downside," said Ari with a frown, "is that even with this knowledge, a Watcher is a tough fight. One must find an opening to strike the back of the neck without being knocked down by strength or magic."

Thomas nodded. "And there are a lot of them," he said. "And only a few of us."

"What we need is for Jesse and Grace to make the fire-messages work," said Ari. "What we need is an army."

"Still, we are one step closer to saving London," Thomas said.

Alastair gave him a withering look. "I see the blow you have suffered to the head is worse than I had realized. We are nowhere near saving London."

"Besides, it's not quite *London* we're saving, is it?" said Anna thoughtfully. "London will remain. Only its people will be gone. Its life."

Alastair waved his hand. "Yes, yes. It has been Roman and Saxon and now it will be demon. It has survived plague and pestilence and fire—"

"Of course!" Anna shouted, causing everyone to jump. "The Great Fire!" With a wild look in her eye, she tore out of the infirmary.

The others looked at the open doorway where she had disappeared. "I don't think any of us expected that," Thomas said.

"I'll go see what's happened," Ari said hesitantly.

"Right," said Thomas. "We'll fetch Grace and Jesse from wherever they've gotten to. They must be told that the Watchers can be beaten."

He began to get up from the bed; Alastair gently pushed him back down on it. "*I* will fetch Grace and Jesse," he said. "*You* will rest."

Thomas looked over at Ari with a plaintive look.

"I'm sorry, Thomas, but he's right," Ari said. "You must allow yourself some time to recover, or you won't keep your strength up."

"But I'm *fine*—"

Leaving Thomas and Alastair to argue, Ari went and found Anna in the library, standing over one of the study tables. As Ari got closer she could see that Anna had a tattered map, deeply yellowed with age, spread out before her. When she looked up at Ari, there was—for the first time since Christopher's death—actual excitement in her eyes.

"Have you ever noticed," she said, "that the entrance to the Silent City is quite far from central London, all the way up in Highgate?"

"I have noticed," Ari said slowly. "I never thought much about it. I suppose it is a bit far from the Institute."

"Well, it wasn't always," said Anna, jabbing her finger down at the parchment. "They moved it after the Great Fire of London. This map here is from 1654, and *this* is the old entrance to the Silent City."

Ari looked. "That *is* much closer," she said. "It's just on the other side of St. Paul's from us."

"At the church of St. Peter Westcheap," Anna said. "Which burned in the Fire, in 1666." She tapped the map with her finger. "Don't you see? If we can get into the Silent City through an unguarded entrance, we can find the Path of the Dead. Retrace the route that the Watchers took from the Iron Tombs."

"You mean if we can make it to the Iron Tombs, then we will have escaped Belial's sphere of influence. We will be able to contact Alicante." Ari clasped her hands together. "Or if by some miracle the Blackthorns get fire-messages working, we could have reinforcements meet us at the Tombs—"

"And," said Anna, "we could then lead those reinforcements into the Silent City, and from there, right back to London."

Sparked by a sudden rush of hope, Ari leaned across the table and kissed Anna full on the mouth. She pulled back a little, enjoying the look of surprise on Anna's face. "You are the most devilishly clever schemer."

Anna smiled. "It's because you bring out the best in me, darling."

Later, James would guess that telling him the story was the hardest thing Matthew had ever done, his greatest act of grit and endurance.

At the time, he only listened. Matthew told the story simply and directly: Alastair's taunts about his mother, his own visit to the Shadow Market, his purchase of the faerie potion to give to an unknowing Charlotte. His mother's violent illness, her miscarriage.

"I remember," James breathed. A wind had come up; he could hear it howling over the plains beyond the courtyard walls. "When your mother lost the baby. Jem treated her—"

"Jem knew," Matthew said. "He saw it in my mind, I think, though I refused to speak about it with him. Still, I remember what he said then. 'I will not tell anybody. But you should. A secret kept too long can kill a soul by inches.' Advice," Matthew added, "that I, being a fool, did not take."

"I understand," James said. "You dreaded to tell it. To tell what happened was to live it again."

"That is true for you," Matthew observed. "I saw your face when you spoke of the bracelet, of Grace. It was as if a wound had reopened for you. But for me—I am not the one who suffered, James. My mother suffered. My family suffered. I *caused* it. I am not the victim." He sucked in a breath. "I think I might be sick again."

James ruffled Matthew's hair gently. "Try to keep the water down," he said. "Math—What I hear is a story of someone making a terrible mistake. You were young, and it was a *mistake*. It had no evil in it, no volition to harm your mother or anyone. You were rash and trusted wrongly. There was no malice."

"I've made many bad decisions. None of them have ever had consequences like this."

"Because," said James, "you ensure that the worst results of your decisions always fall upon yourself."

Matthew was silent for a moment. "I suppose that's true," he said.

"Your bad decision did have terrible, unforeseeable consequences," James went on. "But you are not the devil incarnate, or Cain condemned to wander." His voice softened. "Imagine me a few years ago. Imagine I came to you and told you this story, that *I* was the one who made the mistake. What would you say to me?"

"I would tell you to forgive yourself," said Matthew. "And to tell the truth to your family."

"You have brutalized yourself for years over this," said James. "Try now to be as kind to yourself as you would have been to me. Remember that your sin is your silence, not what you did. All this time you have pushed Charlotte and Henry away, and I know what it has cost you. What it has cost them. Matthew, you are also their child. Let them forgive you."

"That first night," Matthew said, "after it happened, I took a bottle of whiskey from my parents' cupboard and drank it. I was vilely sick afterward, but for the first few moments, when it dulled the sharpness of my thoughts and senses, the pain faded. Went away. I felt a lightness of heart, and it is that I have been seeking again and again. That surcease."

"Your heart will always want that oblivion," said James. "You will always have to fight it." He laced his fingers through Matthew's. "I will always help you."

Several dark shapes flew by overhead, shrieking. Matthew watched them go, frowning. "Belial will return tomorrow," he said. "I do not think he will leave you alone for long."

"No," James said. "Which is why I have been thinking. I have a plan."

"*Really?*" Matthew said. "Well. Thank the Angel."

"You won't like it," James said. "But I must tell it to you, regardless. I will need your help."

Time in Edom was a strange thing. It seemed to stretch out forever, like sticky taffy, yet at the same time Lucie feared it was moving too fast: that night might fall at any moment, forcing her and Cordelia to take shelter and wait. She didn't want to stay here a moment longer than she had to, and more than that, she feared what was happening to Matthew and James.

Her chest felt tight as she and Cordelia toiled up another sand dune. The sand, dust, and soot in the air made it hard to breathe, but it was more than that: it was the weight of death all around her. As she followed the sensation that drew them closer to Idumea, it pressed down on her like a stone. Her joints ached, and there was a dull pain behind her eyes. It was as though something primordial within her cried out against Edom; she was a Shadowhunter, and in her flowed the blood of angels. She had never thought what it might mean to be in a place where long ago all angels had been slain.

Heat shimmered on the horizon. At the top of the dune, they paused to orient themselves, and to drink a little water. Both of them had brought flasks, but Lucie doubted what they had would last them more than a day or two.

She squinted into the distance. Stretching out before them, at the base of the dune, was a plain of black, glittering sand, like beads of jet. Where it met the horizon, something solid rose against the sky—jagged like the peaks of hills, but far too regular to be natural.

Cordelia had tied a scarf around her hair; her eyebrows were whitened with ash. "Is that Idumea?"

"I *think* those are towers," Lucie allowed, wishing her Farsighted rune was working. She *thought* she was looking at towers and walls, but it was impossible to be entirely sure. She dusted biscuit off her hands and said, "It's in the direction of Idumea, at least. We'll have to go that way regardless."

"Hmm." Cordelia looked thoughtful but didn't object. They clambered down the dune's far side and started across the sea of black, quickly discovering that it was a mixture of sand and pitch: tarry, sulfur-smelling muck that stuck to their boots and sucked at their feet with every step.

"I haven't felt this trapped since Esme Hardcastle tried to find out how many children I intend to have with Jesse," said Lucie, yanking her foot free.

Cordelia smiled. "She did that to you, too?"

"Esme thinks she knows exactly who is going to marry who, and who is going to die when. Some people she thinks are alive are dead, and there are people who are dead who she is convinced are actually alive. This is going to be quite the family tree. It will confuse scholars for decades."

"Something to look forward to," Cordelia agreed. She hesitated a moment before she spoke again. "Luce, you can sense things about this world. Do you feel . . . anything about James and Matthew?"

"No," Lucie said. "But I think that's a good thing. I can sense the dead. If I don't sense them, then . . ."

"They're still alive." Cordelia was clearly clutching at the idea; Lucie didn't want to say she wasn't as reassured herself.

They had nearly reached the end of the black sand. Cordelia was frowning. "I don't think this is Idumea. It's just . . ."

"A wall," Lucie finished. They were in its shadow now, looking up. It rose perhaps thirty feet in the air, a construction of smooth gray stone that stretched in either direction as far as she could see. There were no other buildings or ruins to be seen: what Lucie had thought were towers were the wall's battlements high above. It was completely smooth, dashing any thought of climbing it. They would have to find a way through.

They began to pace the length of the wall, heading away from the sun, which hung halfway to the horizon now, searing across the level sand. It didn't take them long to find a gate: an elaborate carved arch that opened into the dark interior of the wall.

There was something Lucie didn't like about that darkness. It felt cave-like, and she realized they had no idea how thick the wall was. They could be walking into a tunnel, or any sort of trap. Sand blew across the entrance, dimming the interior even further.

Yet she could still feel Idumea, pulling at her even harder now, telling her she had to pass this wall and keep going. She took a hand axe from her weapons belt and glanced over at Cordelia, who had drawn Cortana. The golden sword glinted in the harsh sun. "All right," she said. "Let's see if we can get through."

They ducked through the archway and found themselves in a stone-sided corridor with a barrel roof. As they walked, the packed sand floor gave way to more stone. They were in a tunnel that bored through the wall, illuminated on the inside by a spongy, phosphorescent moss that clung to the walls. Lucie moved closer to Cordelia—the air was cold, and the smell of damp stone bitter. Lucie thought she could hear water trickling somewhere and recalled what Lilith had said about the water of Edom being poison.

Cordelia tapped her shoulder lightly. "Something's glowing," she said. "Up ahead."

For a moment, Lucie let herself hope it was the end of the

tunnel, the far side of the wall. Even the sandblasted desert of Edom seemed preferable to the tunnel. But as they drew closer and the glow intensified, the tunnel widened around them, expanding into a stone chamber filled with tallow candles: they were stuck in every crack and crevice, filling the space with flickering light.

Within a pentagram formed of dark red gems sat an oversized throne of black obsidian, on which squatted a scaly blue creature, lizard-tailed, with a downturned, froglike mouth and yellow-orange eyes. Hovering beside the throne, in midair, was a massive skull—not human or animal, but demon, with holes for far too many eyes, and threaded through those holes were a dozen black, oily tentacles. Each tentacle gripped a long silver feather, with which the skull fanned the blue demon on the throne.

"Oh my," the demon said, in a surprisingly high-pitched voice. "Nephilim. How unexpected." It shifted, and Lucie saw that in one clawed hand it held what seemed to be a bunch of grapes. "Welcome to my court. I am here to collect a toll from all who wish to pass the Wall of Kadesh."

What court? Lucie wondered. Other than the skull, and it didn't seem particularly alive, there seemed to be no courtiers here, no real place for a court, if there was one, to assemble. All she could see was a peculiar variety of sun-bleached bones, long and white, stuck into the ground at odd intervals.

"What kind of toll?" Cordelia asked. She hadn't lifted Cortana, but she was gripping the hilt tightly.

"The kind that will please me," said the demon, plucking a grape from the bunch he held and popping it into his gaping mouth. Lucie was quite sure she heard the grape scream in terror as it was eaten. "I am Carbas, Dux Operti. I am a collector of secrets. Long ago, Lilith gave me leave to set up my court here so that I may collect them from travelers passing by."

Cordelia and Lucie exchanged looks: Did Duke Carbas know that Lilith was gone, and Belial had taken her place as ruler of Edom? If he never left this spot, perhaps he didn't; either way, Lucie wasn't inclined to tell him.

"You collect secrets from passing demons?" Cordelia said.

"I didn't think demons had secrets," Lucie mused. "I thought they'd be proud of all the evil they did."

"Oh, they are," said Carbas. "Which makes it a very boring job. 'Oh, I saved a kitten from a Ravener demon, Carbas, and I'm so ashamed.' 'Oh, I failed to turn anyone toward the dark side last week, Carbas.' Whine, whine, complain. But *you*, Nephilim, with all your morals—you will have *juicy* secrets."

He popped another grape into his mouth. This one *definitely* screamed.

"What happens," said Lucie, "if we try to pass through without telling you a secret?"

Carbas leered coldly. "Then you will find yourself trapped in this tunnel, and soon enough will become a member of my court." He gestured at the bones jutting from the ground, which began to vibrate. "We'd all like that, wouldn't we?" He chuckled. "New blood, as it were."

Trapped in the tunnel. Lucie tried not to look worried: dying in battle was one thing. Being trapped in this dank, demon-haunted tunnel until they died was something else.

"So please," Carbas went on, grinning wetly, "whenever you're ready, a secret from each of you. It must be something you have told no one else, something you wish no one to know. Otherwise, it is worth nothing to me. *And* I will be able to tell if you are making something up. You must tell a secret from the heart," he added, somehow making the phrase "from the heart" sound vicious. "One that means something to tell."

"These rules seem vague," said Cordelia. "And subjective."

"That's magic for you." Carbas shrugged.

Lucie and Cordelia exchanged a look. They could try to attack Carbas, of course, but that would mean stepping into the pentagram with him, a deeply risky choice. Yet the thought of offering up her most hidden thoughts to Carbas, to snack on as he did the grapes, felt violating and cruel.

It was Cordelia who stepped forward first. "I have a secret," she said. "It isn't something nobody knows, but it is something *Lucie* doesn't know." She looked over at Lucie, her eyes pleading. Lucie bit her lip. "And that's what matters, isn't it?"

"Mmm. I'm interested," Carbas said. "Let's hear it."

"I'm in love with James Herondale," Cordelia said. "Lucie's brother."

"Well, of course you are," Lucie said, before clamping her mouth shut.

Carbas rolled his eyes. "Not off to a great start."

"No," Cordelia said, a little desperately, "you don't understand. I didn't just fall in love with him when I came to London, or when we got married. I've been in love with him for . . . for years," she went on. "Ever since he had the scalding fever."

That long ago? The thought jolted Lucie. But . . .

"I never told you about it, Lucie. Every time you mentioned him, I would lie about how I felt, or make a joke. When you suggested that I might entertain romantic thoughts about James, I would act like it was the most ridiculous idea on earth. When we got engaged, I acted as if I couldn't wait for it to be over. I didn't want to be pitied, and I didn't want to be just another of the silly girls who was in love with your brother while he only cared about Grace. So I lied to you." She took a deep breath. "It's like you said at my house that night, Lucie. I was too proud."

But you could have told me. I would never have pitied you, Lucie thought, bewildered. She didn't mind that Cordelia had been in love with James—but the lying, the hiding . . . she wished it didn't bother her, but it did. She looked away from Cordelia—and saw Carbas on his throne, smacking his lips.

"Not bad," he murmured. "Not terrible." His yellowish eyes slid over to Lucie. "Now what about you?"

Lucie stepped forward, taking Cordelia's place before the throne. She didn't look at Daisy as she did so; if she hadn't known this important thing about her best friend, had she ever really known her at all? Had Cordelia ever really trusted her?

She told herself to stop, that this was what Carbas wanted. Their pain. His amber demon's eyes were already fixed on her with anticipatory delight. "I have a secret," she said. "One *nobody* knows."

"Ooh," said Carbas.

"When Cordelia and I tried to practice our *parabatai* ceremony," she said, "I couldn't go through with it. I didn't tell her why. I pretended as if nothing had happened, but that—that wasn't true at all." She glanced over her shoulder at Cordelia, who was holding Cortana so tightly her knuckles were white. "When we began to speak the words,"

Lucie said, "the room filled with ghosts. Ghosts of Shadowhunters, though none I knew. I could see them *everywhere*, and they were staring at us. Usually I can understand the dead, but—I didn't know what they wanted. Did they disapprove of my creating a bond to someone living? Or did they *want* me to do it? I thought—what if going through with it bonded you, too, to the dead?"

Cordelia had gone a sickly color. "How could you not tell me that?" she whispered. "You were going to go ahead with the ceremony, then, without warning me? What if something had happened to you during it—what if the ghosts meant harm?"

"I *was* going to tell you," Lucie protested. "But then the thing with Lilith happened, and you told me that we couldn't become *parabatai*—"

"Yes, because *I* thought I owed you the truth before we bonded ourselves together."

Carbas moaned in pleasure. "Don't stop," he groaned. "This is wonderful! It's rare I get two people telling secrets about each other. I haven't enjoyed a revelation this much since I found out Napoleon always hid his hand inside his jacket because he kept a spare sandwich there."

He leered again.

"Oh, *ugh*," said Lucie, thoroughly revolted. "That's *enough*. We've done what you asked—by your own rules, you have to let us leave."

Carbas sighed and looked sadly at the flapping skull, as if seeking sympathy. "Well, if you return this way, do stop by and see old Carbas." As he spoke, a hidden door in the far wall swung open. Through it Lucie could see the familiar bloody orange light of Edom. "But then again," Carbas added, as Lucie and Cordelia made their way to the door, "this is Edom. Who are we trying to fool? You'll be lucky to make it to nightfall, Nephilim. You certainly won't be coming back here."

31
Bright Volumes

At the corner of Wood Street, when daylight appears,
Hangs a Thrush that sings loud, it has sung for three years:
Poor Susan has passed by the spot, and has heard
In the silence of morning the song of the Bird.

'Tis a note of enchantment; what ails her? She sees
A mountain ascending, a vision of trees;
Bright volumes of vapour through Lothbury glide,
And a river flows on through the vale of Cheapside.
—William Wordsworth,
"The Reverie of Poor Susan"

"Are you sure?" said Alastair, unable to hide the doubt in his voice.

"We're sure," Anna said. She, Ari, and Alastair stood in the entryway of the Institute. They were all in gear. They had taken just enough time for Anna to pack a small haversack in which she had placed maps, a few flasks of drinking water, and a packet of Jacob's Biscuits.

"But he's just a dog," Alastair objected.

With a deeply offended look, Oscar went to sit on Ari's feet. "Oscar is not just a dog," she said, reaching down to scratch the retriever's head. "He is a member of our team. Without him, we would have had to go through the York Gate."

"Oscar is the least of our problems," Anna said. "We have to locate the site of a church that burned down hundreds of years ago, and hope to discover a lost entrance to the Silent City. Oscar's task is simple by comparison."

Oscar barked. Alastair sighed. "I hope the hound gets a medal from the Clave after this. Though he'd probably prefer a soup bone."

"Who wouldn't?" said Ari, lifting one of Oscar's ears and letting it flop back down. "Isn't that right, best puppy pup?"

Anna raised an eyebrow. "I think Ari misses Winston," she said. "Alastair, you'll need to tell Grace and Jesse—"

"To send fire-messages instructing the Enclave to meet you at the entrance to the Iron Tombs. I know," Alastair said. "You do realize they haven't sent a successful message yet, to the Enclave or anyone else."

"I know," Anna said. "And if we reach the Iron Tombs and there's no one there, we'll know they've failed. We'll start out toward the Adamant Citadel. Once we're there, we can at least start getting messages to the Clave, and we'll bring back as many Shadowhunters as we can, as soon as we can." She did her best to sound as if it would be all right either way; the truth was that she was praying to the Angel that Christopher's pet project could be made to work.

"Are you sure you want to go now?" Alastair said. "The Silent City could be crawling with Watchers. Thomas and I would go with you—"

"Thomas needs rest," Anna said firmly. "And we have no time to waste. Every moment we are not taking action is one in which Belial could be breaking down James's resolve, or enacting some other horrible plan. Besides—you can't leave Jesse and Grace alone here. They will need you, especially traveling back and forth to Grosvenor Square—"

"I just feel that we're disappearing one by one, vanishing from London," Alastair said. He looked oddly vulnerable; Anna suspected he had been more worried about Thomas than he had let on.

"If we succeed," Anna said, "then we will return in force. And if it doesn't work, it won't be this excursion to the Silent City that makes the difference."

"If we stick together—"

"*Alastair,*" Anna said, and then, "You've surprised me, you know. I used to think you were an uncaring cad. And not in the entertaining, novelish way, but in the selfish, everyday kind of way."

"I hope this is the part where you explain you've changed your mind," Alastair muttered.

Ari hid a smile behind her hand.

"I started to think better of you when you helped Thomas, after he was arrested. And now, well—there isn't anyone I'd rather be stuck at the end of the world with." Anna put out her hand. After a moment, with a look of bemusement, Alastair shook it. "I'm glad that you'll be here, looking after London," she added. "We'll see you soon."

Alastair seemed surprised into speechlessness. Which was all right, as far as Anna was concerned; she'd said what she wanted to say. She and Ari descended the Institute steps, Oscar frolicking at their heels.

Anna was aware that Alastair was watching them go, but she didn't turn back to look at him. There had been too many goodbyes lately; she didn't need another.

"You are right," Matthew said, after a long silence. "I don't like your plan." He was still leaning against James's chest, though he'd stopped shivering. "I don't suppose you have a different, less dangerous one."

"We haven't much in the way of other choices," said James. "Belial rules here; this dead land does his bidding. He wants me to *wish* to join with him, but he is losing patience; if I simply *allow* it, even reluctantly, he will accept that as what he can get. He has planned too much, worked too hard, to give up now."

"He will think you've given up. Embraced despair."

"Good," said James. "He will assume my great weakness has finally caught up with me: that I care too much, or at all, about other people. To him, that is humiliating frailty. He will not imagine a plan behind it."

Matthew looked back at him. He had begun to shiver again and was plucking restlessly at the fabric of the coat slung over him with his fingers, like a typhus patient. "Belial has sought possession of your body all this time. Why not do this before? Why wait until now?"

"Two reasons. One, I need him to believe I am desperate. And two, I am terrified. The idea of doing this frightens me more than anything else, and yet—"

Matthew jerked in James's arms. His whole body seemed to tighten, rigid as a plank, before he went limp, gasping.

James gripped his hand tightly. When Matthew had caught his breath, he said, "Kit said—seizures."

And heart failure, James thought, feeling sick, but he did not say the words aloud. "I should get you more water."

"James, no—don't—" Matthew clawed at James's wrist before his eyes rolled up and his body began to jerk again. Swift, uncoordinated movements like a puppet being pulled too hard by its strings.

Panic bloomed in James's chest. Kit had been clear: people could die from this. That Matthew would need a fortnight to physically stop drinking, and it had been nowhere near a fortnight. Matthew could die, he thought, die right there in his arms, and they would be split apart. Divided in half. Never again would James have his *parabatai*—the infuriating, ridiculous, generous, devoted, exasperating other half of his soul.

With a shaking hand, James yanked his stele from his pocket. He caught hold of Matthew's flailing arm, held it still. Set the tip of the *stele* to his skin and drew a healing rune.

It flashed and faded, like a sputtering match. James knew, rationally: runes didn't work here. But he didn't stop. He could hear Jem's voice in his head. Soft, steady. *You must build a fortress of control around yourself. You must come to know this power, so that you may master it.*

He drew a second *iratze*. It, too, vanished. Then a third, and then a fourth, and he began to lose count as he scrawled over and over on Matthew's skin, willing his mind to concentrate on holding the *iratze* there, on keeping it from vanishing, on somehow forcing it to *work*.

Remember you are the language of angels, he thought, drawing yet another rune. *Remember there is no place in the universe you do not have some power.*

He waited for the rune to vanish. Instead it lingered. Not for more than a minute, perhaps, but as James stared, it remained, fading very slowly, on Matthew's arm.

Matthew had stopped jerking and trembling in James's grasp. As the healing rune faded slowly, James flew into action: he drew another, and then another and another, starting a new one each time the previous one dwindled.

Matthew was no longer shaking. He was taking deep, steady breaths, looking down in incredulity at his arm, where a crisscrossing map of healing runes—some new, some fading—covered his forearm. "Jamie *bach*," he said. "You can't do this all night."

"Watch me," James said grimly, and braced himself against the wall so that he could keep drawing for as long as it took.

Grace and Jesse had found a bag of miniature explosives in the laboratory and had amused themselves for nearly an hour by setting several of them off in the fireplace. They worked like fireworks, though rather than setting them alight, one tapped them with a stele and then tossed them a distance away, where they would sound a loud *crack* before exploding.

It was nice to laugh with Jesse a little bit, even if the laughter was really half exhaustion. It was astonishing what one could get used to: dodging Watchers and slinking through abandoned houses. Broken glass and turned-over carriages in the streets. On every face, a blank stare. No worse, perhaps, than living under the roof of Tatiana Blackthorn for eight years.

What Grace *couldn't* get used to was her sense of utter frustration. She had all of Christopher's notes, and her own as well. In her time in the Silent City, she had felt on the verge of a breakthrough, as if the solution to the problem with fire-messages was at the tips of her fingers. Hers and Christopher's.

But now . . . With Jesse's help, she had tried everything she could think of—swapping out ingredients, changing out the runes. Nothing worked. They had not even achieved the level of success Christopher had in managing to send half-burned, illegible messages.

It was the one thing she should have been able to contribute, she thought. She and Jesse had given up on the explosives and were instead staring at a piece of rune-covered vellum spread out on the worktable. The one good thing she could have done, the one way she could have helped after doing so much harm. But it seemed even that would be denied to her.

"How can we tell if it's working?" Jesse said, eyeing the vellum on the table. "What's it supposed to do, exactly?"

In a clear sign of rejection by the universe, the scroll of vellum let off a cough of smoke before exploding with a bang, flying backward off the table, and landing on the floor between them, where it continued to burn, not consuming the vellum.

"Not that," Grace said.

She went to fetch the fireplace tongs leaning against the far corner of the room. These she used to retrieve the vellum—still burning—and deposit it into the fireplace.

"Look on the bright side," said Jesse. "You've invented . . . ever-burning vellum. Christopher would be proud. He loved when things didn't stop burning."

"*Christopher*," Grace said, "would have finished this already. Christopher was a scientist. I *like* science. Those are two very different things." She stared down at the burning vellum. It was rather pretty, edged in white flame like lacework. "It's ironic. Belial never asked Mother to kill Christopher. Never thought about him at all. But in murdering him, she may have ensured Belial's success."

The words were not enough. She threw her pencil across the room, where it clattered unsatisfactorily against a file cabinet.

Jesse raised an eyebrow. Grace wasn't given to outbursts. "How long has it been since you've eaten anything?" he said.

Grace blinked. She couldn't recall.

"I thought so. I'll search through the pantry, all right? Hoping for biscuits, willing to make do with tinned beans." He was already headed upstairs. Grace knew he was trying to give her a moment to gather herself, but she could only scrub tiredly at her aching eyes: Jesse wasn't the problem. The problem was Christopher. She needed Christopher.

She laid her hand against the pitted, discolored wood of the worktable. How many of these blotches had Christopher made? Cutting, burning, spilling acid. Years of work, marked out here in scars, the way the lives of Shadowhunters were marked out in the pale memories of old runes on their skins.

Something flickered at the back of her mind. Something about runes. Runes and fire-messages.

Christopher would have known.

"Christopher," she said softly, running the tips of her fingers over a long knife-cut in the wooden surface of the table. "I know you're gone. And yet I feel you everywhere. In every beaker, every sample . . . every strange method of organization I run across . . . I see you everywhere, and I only wish I could have told you—that I care about you, Christopher. And I did not think that kind of feeling to be real. I thought it was a conceit of novels and plays, that one could . . . could want the happiness of another beyond even their own, beyond anything else. I wish I had understood it more when you were . . . when you were still alive."

The silence of the laboratory seemed to echo all around her. She closed her eyes.

"Maybe you *are* here, though," she said. "Maybe you're keeping an eye on this place. I know Lucie said you were gone, but—how could you keep away? How could you not be curious beyond even the pull of death to see what happens? So if you are here . . . please. I'm so close, with the fire-messages. I've gone beyond where you were, but I haven't found the solution yet. I need your help. The world needs your help. Please."

Something touched her shoulder. A light touch, as if a butterfly had landed there. She stiffened, but something told her not to open her eyes.

"Grace." A soft voice, unmistakable.

She sucked in her breath. "Oh—Christopher—"

"Don't turn around," he said. "Or look at me. I am only a very little bit here, Grace. It is taking all my strength for you to hear me. I cannot also make myself seen."

Don't turn around. She thought of Orpheus in the Greek tales, who had been forbidden from turning to look behind him at his dead wife as he escorted her from the underworld. He had failed, and lost her. Grace had always thought he was silly—surely it could not be that difficult simply not to turn around and look at someone.

But it was. She felt the ache inside her like pain, the loss of Christopher. Who had understood her, and not judged her.

"I thought," she whispered, "ghosts could only return if they had unfinished business. Are the fire-messages yours?"

"I think," he said, "that *you* are my unfinished business."

"What do you mean?"

"You don't need my help to solve this," said Christopher, and she could *see* him, behind her eyelids, looking at her with his funny quizzical smile, his eyes such a dark violet behind his spectacles. "You only need to believe that you can solve it. And you can. You are a natural scientist, Grace, and a solver of puzzles. All you have to do is silence the voice in your head that says you aren't good enough, don't know enough. I have faith in you."

"I think you are the only one who does," Grace said.

"That's not true. Jesse believes in you. In fact, all of them believe in you. They have left this task in your hands, Grace. Because they believe you can do it. It is only up to you to believe it too."

Behind her eyelids, now, she saw not Christopher, but the notes he had given her—his observations, his equations, his questions. His handwriting scrolling across the darkness, and then her own notes, intertwining with his, and Christopher believed in her. And Jesse, Jesse believed in her. And just because her mother had never thought she was worth anything didn't mean her mother had been right.

"It's not the runes," she said, almost opening her eyes with the shock of the realization. "It's not the chemicals, either. It's the steles."

"I knew you could do it." She heard the smile in his voice. "*And* you've invented ever-burning vellum. Splendid work, Grace."

Something brushed against her temple, tucking her hair behind her ear. A ghostly touch, a goodbye. A moment later, she knew he was gone.

She opened her eyes, turning to look behind her. There was nothing there, yet the wave of despair she had expected did not crash over her. Christopher was not there, but the memory of him was like a presence—and more than that, a new feeling, something blossoming under her rib cage, something that made her push aside the papers in front of her and reach for her stele, ready to get to work.

Something that she imagined felt very like the beginning of believing in herself.

The walk through London was uneventful; Anna and Ari had to duck down an alley at one point to skirt a Watcher, but otherwise the streets were mostly empty, save for the now-expected blank-faced mundanes.

As they passed a shadowy doorway, Ari glanced to the side and saw a goat-faced demon crouched in the shadows, holding four human infants. Each one was suckling at a scaled breast. Ari fought back the urge to retch.

"Don't look," said Anna. "It won't do any good."

Concentrate on the mission, Ari told herself. *On the Silent City. On the end of all this.*

St. Peter Westcheap had been utterly destroyed in the Great Fire. Ari had been worried it would have been built over with shops or houses, but they were in luck. At the corner of Cheapside and Wood Street was a small paved area, surrounded by a low iron railing—a piece of the old churchyard, most likely.

They went in through the gate. From the center of the courtyard rose a massive tree, its bare branches forming a sort of canopy over the few old graves that remained, their surfaces too worn to read. Benches had been placed at various intervals, their slatted wooden seats rubbed mostly away by years of rain and snow.

As Oscar bounded through the frozen bushes, Anna went to examine the old gravestones. Ari, however, found herself drawn to the tree in the courtyard's center. It was a black mulberry; they were not native to Britain but had been brought over by the Romans, before there had ever been Shadowhunters. The bark was not black at all, but a sort of orangey-brown, and as Ari leaned in closer, she saw a pattern slashed into it. A *familiar* pattern.

An Unseen rune. "Anna!" she called.

Oscar barked as if he'd discovered the rune himself. Anna joined Ari at the tree, looking dusty but pleased. "Oh, well done, Ari," she said, drawing her stele from her belt. "Now, Unseen runes are used to hide and conceal . . ."

With a look of fierce concentration, Anna struck a line through the rune, obliterating it. A sort of shimmer seemed to pass over the tree, and the roots began to move beneath the ground, twisting and curling aside until a black gap opened at the base of the trunk. It looked like the entrance to a cave.

Ari got down on her knees, the ground icy-cold even through the thick material of her gear. She peered into the gap, but it was utterly dark within. Even when she took out her witchlight and illuminated it, the shadows were almost too thick to pierce; leaning in as far as she could, she glimpsed the faint outline of steps leading down. Stone steps, with faint runes carved into them, half worn away by time.

She wriggled out from under the tree and threw her head back to look up at Anna. "This has to be it," she said. "The entrance to the Silent City."

Anna knelt down and reached for Oscar. He snuffled at her hands as she tucked a piece of paper into his collar. "Good boy, Oscar," she said. "Back to the Institute with you. Tell them we found it. Go on, now," she said, and went to open the courtyard gate. Oscar trotted out bravely and set off down Cheapside at a loping pace.

Anna hurried back to Ari. "It's getting darker," she said. "We ought to hurry. Do you want to go first?"

Ari found that she did. The hole at the base of the trunk was narrow and oddly shaped. She had to flip over onto her stomach and wriggle backward through the gap, sliding a little before her knees met the uneven surface of the stone steps. She scrambled down them backward, on her hands and knees, until she hit a level floor.

She stood up, her witchlight held high. Above her, Anna was making her way down the stairs, managing to make crawling backward look elegant. Ari turned around slowly, shining her light into every corner. She stood in the center of a stone room, dusty but clean, with a floor made of overlapping flagstones. When she glanced up, she saw a vaulted ceiling that soared above her, studded with semiprecious stones, each one carved with a single, shining rune.

They were inside the Silent City.

Alastair had made it most of the way to meet Grace and Jesse when the explosion went off. He was pleased to note that he barely reacted. With the events of the past few weeks, a small explosion in Grosvenor Square hardly rated more than a raised eyebrow. Besides, it was quite a small explosion—just a short burst of flame in the air a few yards ahead of him, and then the smoke that remained as it went out, and in the middle of the smoke, a piece of paper.

He lunged forward to grab it before the wind whipped it away. There were Shadowhunter runes all around its edge, most of whose meanings he couldn't remember offhand. But in the middle of the page was a note in a slightly crabbed hand:

If you are reading this, this is the first Fire-Message that has been sent with success. It has been written by Grace Blackthorn and invented by Christopher Lightwood.

He blinked at the paper for a moment, as though expecting it to disappear, or explode again, or turn out to be a hallucination.

"By the Angel," he muttered to himself, "they did it. They actually went and did it."

Still staring at the paper, he crossed Grosvenor Square toward the Consul's house, and as he approached saw Jesse—wild-haired and wild-eyed—burst from the door and run down the front steps.

"Did you get it?" he shouted. "*Did you get it?* The message? Did it arrive?"

Triumphantly, Alastair raised the fire-message over his head. "It worked," he said. "It bloody well worked."

"It was Grace who figured it out," said Jesse. "Adding a communication rune to the stele before writing the message—that was it. Can you believe it was something so simple?"

"I can believe anything at the moment," Alastair said. And madly, insanely, under the crackling black sky of possessed London, they grinned at each other as if neither of them had ever been more delighted in their lives.

32

Whatever Gods May Be

Out of the night that covers me,
Black as the Pit from pole to pole,
I thank whatever gods may be
For my unconquerable soul.
—William Ernest Henley, "Invictus"

It was near dark by the time Lucie and Cordelia reached the outskirts of Idumea.

They had struggled to the top of a hill of shale and jagged rock, the sun a low red disc hovering at the horizon. Cordelia could not help but watch Lucie worriedly out of the corner of her eye. She had thought Lucie's blood tie to Belial might help her here, but the opposite seemed true. Lucie was clearly suffering as if she were dragging a great weight behind her with every step. *A whole dead world.*

It didn't help that they'd been mostly silent since they'd left Carbas's court behind them. Cordelia wished she could go back and punch that awful blue demon in the face. He had put distance between her and Lucie at the worst possible time. Just when their friendship was recovering—

"Look," Lucie said. She had paused at the top of the hill and was gazing down. "It's Idumea."

Cordelia hurried to join her. The shale fell away sharply below them.

Beyond it, bathed in the glow of the bloody sun, was a plain studded with boulders. At the edge of the plain the city of Idumea spread out, a gargantuan dark ruin. She had expected to see the remains of streets and houses, but almost everything had collapsed into rubble. Here and there they could spot the fallen demon towers: tree trunks of *adamas*, reflecting the dull red sun. Ringing the city were the ruins of the walls that had formed its perimeter.

Like their own Alicante, the city was built around a hillside, the upper part of which was half-hidden by lowering black clouds. Still, Cordelia could make out the shape of a massive fortress at the top, circled by a stone wall, its towers silhouetted against the sky.

"Idumea," she murmured. "James and Matthew are *right there*—"

They exchanged a quick look, full of the remembrance of Lilith's warning: *You cannot travel at night—you will have to seek shelter once the moons rise, or die in the dark.*

"We could run," Lucie murmured. "If we could make it to the city, perhaps we could travel in the shelter of the rubble—"

Cordelia shook her head immediately. "No."

It hurt even to say it. She wanted as badly as Lucie did to reach the fortress *now*. But the sky was turning rapidly from red to black, and more importantly, Lucie looked drained. Even now, as she shook her head and whispered, "We can't just wait," her face was drawn tight with exhaustion, her eyelids drooping. It would be a difficult task at the best of times to dash across the sand and climb the broken walls of Idumea; for Lucie, right now, Cordelia feared, it would be suicidal.

"We *can't*." Cordelia forced the words past her dry and burning throat. "We'd have to make it to Idumea, through the city, then to the fortress—all in the pitch black, without witchlights, not knowing what's out there—and if we die, there won't be anyone to save them. You know that, just as well as I do."

And I can't risk you, Luce, Cordelia thought. *Not like that.*

After a long moment, Lucie nodded. "Fine. But we can't just stand here, either. We need to find somewhere to take shelter."

"I've an idea." Cordelia started down the slope of the hill. They reached the plain just as the sun was dipping below the horizon, creating a vast chessboard of shadow and light. Up close, it was clear that the boulders were not natural formations, but pieces of the city itself, torn from the ground and scattered across the plain by some immense and terrible force. Chunks of walls, sheets of uneven cobblestone, even an old cistern turned on its side.

Cordelia led Lucie to a spot where two slabs of broken wall leaned together, forming a sort of triangular, open-sided cave. As they neared the shelter, something flashed by overhead with an echoing shriek.

It was the call of a monstrous bird of prey. "Quick," Cordelia said, catching hold of Lucie's hand; they scrambled through the narrow entrance of the makeshift cave, ducking into the protected hollow below the broken walls just as the shadow swooped past, close enough for the massive creature's wings to stir the sand.

Lucie shuddered.

"We'd better unpack," Cordelia said, "before it's too dark to see." Lucie watched with dull exhaustion as Cordelia opened her pack, wincing—she'd cut her hand on Cortana in the mad scramble to get into the cave, and a thin cut on her palm was bleeding. At least it was her left hand, she thought, as she hurriedly took out the small blanket she'd packed and unrolled it. She unstrapped Cortana and leaned it against a wall, then retrieved a flask of water and a slab of ship's biscuit as Lucie fetched her own blanket and wrapped it around her shoulders, shivering.

It was dark, and it was going to get darker as the last light faded from the sky. They had brought nothing to make a fire, though, and one would certainly attract attention: here on this dark plain, it would be as bright and visible as a spark among ashes. Cordelia hurried to unscrew the metal flask, to pass some of the hard biscuit to Lucie, before the last of the light was gone—

"Look," Lucie said, and Cordelia realized that even though total darkness had fallen outside their small shelter, she could still see Lucie's face. Their space was enveloped in a dull golden glow—and as she turned, she saw that the source of the light was Cortana, its hilt burning dimly, like a half-doused torch.

"Why is it doing that?" Lucie whispered, breaking off a small piece of biscuit.

Cordelia shook her head. "I don't know. I'm not sure anyone

understands the blades of Wayland the Smith entirely, and what they can do."

And yet—she felt a thrum across her left palm, where she'd cut herself with the blade. As if Cortana knew of her wound, and was calling out to it. To her.

Lucie chewed thoughtfully for a moment. "Do you remember," she said, "when we were children? I was looking at the cliff and I was remembering . . . you know. When you saved my life. Do you remember?"

Of course she remembered. Lucie, tumbling from the path along the ridge. Cordelia, flat on her stomach, gripping her friend's hand as Lucie hung over the long fall below. "I was so terrified," Cordelia said. "That a bee would sting me, or I'd lose my grip, or let go of you somehow."

"I know. I was in awful danger, but the strange thing was, I felt so safe. Because you had hold of me." Lucie looked steadily at Cordelia. "I'm sorry."

"What for?"

"For not telling you about . . . well, where to start? For not telling you about Jesse. I was falling in love with him, and I knew I'd do anything at all to get him back, to make him alive again. I knew I might even do things you wouldn't approve of. Like working with Grace. I should have been truthful. I told myself Grace was never any threat to our friendship. But lying about her—that was the threat. I was scared, but—but that's no excuse. I should have told you."

"What about the *parabatai* ceremony?" said Cordelia. "Not telling me about the ghosts you saw—I don't understand it."

"I was afraid that you'd think I was a monster," Lucie said, in a small voice. "Finding out about Belial—I felt corrupted. I always thought of the *parabatai* ceremony as a perfect act of goodness. Something that would make our friendship not just special but—but holy, like what my father and Uncle Jem had. But then I felt as if perhaps I was tainted, as if I did not deserve a perfect act of goodness. I feared if you knew, you would turn away—"

"*Lucie.*" Cordelia dropped her dry biscuit somewhere in the sand. "I would never turn from you. And what a thing to imagine—do you think that because I am Lilith's paladin, I am a monster?"

Lucie shook her head. "Of course not."

"It is easy to confuse monstrousness and power," said Cordelia. "Especially when one is a woman, as one is not supposed to possess either quality. But you, Lucie—you have a great power, but it is not monstrous, because *you* are not monstrous. You have used your ability for good. To help Jesse, to get us to Edom. When you saved me from the Thames. When you comfort the dead."

"Oh, Daisy—"

"Let me finish. People fear power. That is why the Inquisitor is so afraid of your mother that he feels he must drive her from London. Belial counted on it, on the Enclave's prejudices, their fears. But Luce, I will always defend you. I will always stand up for you, and if ghosts decide to attend our *parabatai* ceremony, I will invite them around for tea afterward."

"Oh, dear," Lucie said. "I feel as if I might cry, but it's so awfully dry, I don't think I can." She rubbed at a smudge on her cheek. "I just wish I knew—why didn't you tell me how you felt about James? Earlier, I mean."

"You were right, Luce. When you said I was too proud. I was—I am. I thought I was protecting myself. I thought I didn't want to be pitied. I didn't understand, until I talked to James and realized that he had the same reasons, the same excuses, for hiding the truth about Grace and the bracelet, how much harm I was doing. James was killing himself with that secret, keeping it to himself. And I'd done the same thing. I'd been so fearful of pity I'd shut out sympathy and understanding. I'm so sorry, Lucie, so very sorry—"

"Don't," Lucie sniffled. "Oh, Daisy. I've done a dreadful thing."

"Really?" Cordelia was bewildered. "What kind of dreadful thing? It can't be that bad."

"It is," Lucie wailed, and reached for her rucksack. As she rummaged in it, she said tearfully, "I stopped writing *The Beautiful Cordelia*. I was too angry—"

"That's all right—"

"No, you don't understand." Lucie pulled a small notebook out of her pack. "I started writing a new book. *The Wicked Queen Cordelia*."

"And you brought it *with* you?" Cordelia was astonished. "To Edom?"

"Of course," said Lucie. "You can't just leave an unfinished manuscript behind. What if I had an idea?"

"Well," said Cordelia. "I mean. Clearly."

Lucie thrust the notebook toward her. "I can't hide it from you," she said, looking woebegone. "I wrote such terrible things."

"Perhaps I oughtn't read it then," Cordelia said, with some trepidation, but the look on Lucie's face made her flip the notebook open hastily. *Oh, dear,* she thought, and began to read.

The wicked Queen Cordelia tossed her long, easily managed scarlet hair. She wore a gown of gold and silver thread, and a massive diamond necklace that rested atop her large and treacherous bosoms. "Oh, foolish Princess Lucie," she said. "Did you think that your brother, Cruel Prince James, would be able to help you? I have had him executed."

"What?" Princess Lucie gasped, for even though he could be cruel, he was still her brother. "But after everything I have done for you?"

"It is true," said the wicked queen, "that I have everything that I have ever wanted. I am adored by all the people in the land, and I have countless suitors"—she indicated the long line of handsome men that stretched through the throne room, some on their knees—"my magical sword has been judged the best and most beautiful sword by the International Council of Sword Experts, and last week I wrote a thousand-page novel for which I have already received a handsome advance from a publisher in London. Indeed, you have helped me achieve all these things. But I have no further use for you."

"But you said we would always be friends!" protested Secret Princess Lucie. "That we would be princesses together!"

"I have decided that rather than being princesses together, it is preferable that I be a queen and you be a prisoner in my deepest dungeon, below the castle moat. You, Sir Jethro, take her away!"

"You will pay for this!" cried Secret Princess Lucie, but she knew in her heart that the wicked Queen Cordelia had won.

Cordelia made a muffled noise. Lucie, her eyes huge, clasped her hands together. "I am so dreadfully sorry," she said. "It was utterly wrong of me to think any of those things, much less write them down—"

Cordelia clapped her hand over her mouth, but it was too late. A giggle burst from her, and then another. Her shoulders shaking uncontrollably, she hiccuped, "Oh, Lucie—I have never—read *anything* so funny—"

"*Really?*" Lucie looked amazed.

"I do have to ask something," Cordelia said, tapping the page with her finger. "Why are my, er, the Wicked Queen's bosoms so enormous?"

"Well they *are*," Lucie explained. "Not like me. I look like a little boy. I always wanted to have a figure like yours, Daisy."

"And I," said Cordelia, "always wanted to be dainty and delicate like you, Luce." She started to giggle again. "The International Council of Sword Experts?"

"I'm sure they exist," Lucie said, starting to smile. "And if they don't, they ought to." She held her hand out. "I suppose you might as well give it back now."

Cordelia whipped the notebook away. "You can't be serious," she said. "I am simply *dying* to find out what happens to Princess Lucie in the dungeon. Should I read aloud? Will there be another mention of my bosoms?"

"Several," Lucie admitted, and for the first time in many long centuries, under the harsh glow of three moons, the sound of simple human laughter drifted across the plains of Edom.

Thomas came back to himself slowly. He was lying on a crisp, white-sheeted bed, and the familiar scent of herbs and carbolic hung in the air. The infirmary of the Institute—he knew it well, and for a disconnected, dreamlike moment, he wondered: *Is my leg broken?*

But that had been years ago. He'd been a child, still small and even a bit sickly, and had fallen out of an apple tree. He and James had played cards every night in the Institute infirmary while he'd healed. It seemed like a distant dream now, of a more innocent time, when the horrors of the present would have been unimaginable, and the loss of James and Matthew more unimaginable still.

They're not dead, he reminded himself, starting to turn over, the blankets rustling around his feet. Then he heard it. A deep, steady voice, rising and falling—Alastair Carstairs, reading aloud. He was sitting beside Thomas's bed, his eyes fixed on a leather-bound volume in his hands. Thomas closed his eyes, the better to savor the sound of Alastair reading.

> *"I have often thought of you," said Estella.*
>
> *"Have you?"*
>
> *"Of late, very often. There was a long hard time when I kept far from me the remembrance of what I had thrown away when I was quite ignorant of its worth. But, since my duty has not been incompatible with the admission of that remembrance, I have given it a place in my heart."*
>
> *"You have always held your place in my heart," I answered.*

The book snapped shut. "This is dull," Alastair said, sounding weary. "And I doubt you are appreciating it, Thomas, since you are asleep. But my sister has always insisted that there is nothing better for the ill than being read to."

I'm not ill, Thomas thought, but he kept his eyes closed.

"Perhaps I ought to tell you what's happened today since you've been laid up here," Alastair continued. "Anna and Ari found the entrance to the Silent City. I know because they sent Matthew's blasted hound back with a note to let us know. And speaking of notes, Grace and Jesse managed to get Christopher's project to work. They're in the library now, sending dozens of the things to Alicante. We can only hope they arrive—it's one thing sending them within London, and another trying to break through the barriers around the city." He sighed. "Remember the one you sent me? The one that was mostly nonsense? I spent *hours* trying to piece it together, you know. I was desperate to know what you wanted to say to me."

Thomas stayed as motionless as he could, keeping his breathing steady and regular. He knew he ought to open his eyes, tell Alastair he was awake, but he couldn't make himself do it. The raw honesty in Alastair's voice was something he had never heard before.

"You scared me today," Alastair said. "At the train station. The first *iratze* I put on you—it faded." His voice shook. "And I thought—what if I lost you? Really lost you? And I realized all the things I've been afraid of all this time—what your friends would think, what it would mean for me to stay in London—mean nothing next to what I feel for you." Thomas felt something brush his forehead gently. Alastair, pushing back a lock of his hair. "I heard what my mother said to you," Alastair added. "Before the Christmas party. And I heard what you said back—that you wish I would treat myself as I deserve to be treated. The thing is, that's exactly what I was doing. I was denying myself the thing I wanted more than anything else in the world because I didn't believe I deserved it."

Thomas could stand it no longer. He opened his eyes and saw Alastair—tired, rumple-haired, shadow-eyed—staring down at him. "Deserved what?" Thomas whispered.

"Deserved *you*," Alastair said, and shook his head. "Of course—of course you were pretending to be asleep—"

"Would you have said all those things if I was awake?" Thomas said roughly, and Alastair set down the book he'd been holding and said, "You don't have to say anything back, Thomas. I know what I hope for. I hope against hope that you could possibly feel anything like what I feel for you. It is almost impossible to imagine anyone feeling that way about me, given who I am. But I hope. Not only because I wish to have what I desire. Although I do desire you," he added in a quieter voice. "I desire you with an ardor that frightens me."

Thomas said, "Come lie down next to me."

Alastair hesitated. Then he bent down to unlace his boots. A moment later Thomas felt the bed sink, and the warm weight of Alastair's body settle next to him. "Are you all right?" Alastair said quietly, looking into his face. "Does anything hurt?"

"Only that I'm not kissing you right now," Thomas said. "Alastair, I love you—but you know that—"

Alastair kissed him. It was awkward to maneuver on the small bed, and their knees and elbows knocked together, but Thomas didn't mind. He only wanted Alastair close to him, Alastair's mouth hot and soft against his, lips parting so he could whisper, "I didn't know it—I hoped, but I wasn't sure—"

"Kheli asheghetam," Thomas whispered, and heard Alastair suck in his breath. "I love you. Let me love you," he said, and when Alastair kissed him again, a hard, hot, openmouthed kiss, Thomas lost himself in it, in the way Alastair touched him. In the way Alastair moved with careful surety, unbuttoning Thomas's shirt with deft fingers. In the way, once Thomas's shirt had been gotten rid of, Alastair stroked him with gentle fingers, his gaze sleepy and desiring and slow. He brushed touches along Thomas's wrists, up his arms, across his shoulders, opening his palms against Thomas's chest. Sliding his open palms down, until Thomas was going out of his mind, wanting more than gentle brushes of lips and fingers.

He buried his hands in Alastair's hair. "Oh, please," he said, incoherently, "now, *now*."

Alastair laughed softly. He drew off his own shirt, and then he was lowering himself over Thomas, bare skin against bare skin, and Thomas's whole being seemed to rise up in a tightening spiral, and Alastair was shaking as Thomas touched him back, shaking because it was *now*, just as Thomas had asked for, and now was a moment so immense, so profound in its pleasure and joy, that both of them forgot the shadows and peril, the grief and darkness that surrounded them. They would remember in time, and soon enough, but for the moment of *now*, there was only each other, and the brightness they wove between them on the narrow infirmary bed.

When Cordelia awoke the next morning, the dim sun of Edom was filtering into their hiding spot. She had fallen asleep with one hand on Cortana; she sat up slowly now, rubbing the sleep out of her eyes, and looked at Lucie.

Lucie was curled up in her blanket, her eyes closed, her face pale. Cordelia had woken several times in the night to find Lucie tossing and turning restlessly, sometimes crying out in distress. Even in sleep, the weight of Edom bore down on her.

It will all be over today, Cordelia told herself. *We will either succeed in finding James and Matthew, and I in slaying Belial, or we will be killed trying.*

In her sleep, Lucie plucked at her locket. There were dark shadows under her eyes. Cordelia hesitated before steeling herself to reach out and gently shake Lucie by the shoulder. There was no point in delaying; it would only make everything worse.

They parceled out what was left of the food—a few swallows of water and some hardtack each—and Lucie seemed a little revived; by the time they ducked out of their shelter and began to cross the plain to Idumea, there was color in her face again.

It was another simmering day, and a hot wind blew dust into their eyes and mouths. As they drew closer to Idumea, it grew more recognizable as what it was: a ruined Alicante. The great fortress of what had once been the Gard loomed over a tumbled mix of rubble and standing structures. All the demon towers save one had fallen, and the single glassy spire caught and held the scarlet glow of the sun, like a red-hot needle piercing the sky.

Cordelia had wondered whether they would be bothered by demons as they tried to enter the city, especially after their encounter with Carbas. But the place was almost eerily deserted: only the wind troubled them as they scrambled over the rubble of the destroyed walls.

More rubble awaited on the other side, but in between the piles of smashed and broken stone were surprising patches that had been left almost intact. As they moved closer to the city's center, Cordelia could make out what had once been Cistern Square, though a great hole had been torn through the paving stones there, as if something had burst *up* through the earth long ago. She and Lucie exchanged an uneasy look and gave the hole a wide berth.

They passed the remains of ancient canals, filled now with rotting black moss. Cordelia could see something shining in the near distance, a glint like metal or gold. A heap of rubble barred the way; she and Lucie clambered over it and found themselves in what had once been Angel Square.

She and Lucie looked around with an awful sort of fascination. Here was something so familiar, and yet not familiar at all: the great square at the heart of Alicante, with the Hall of Accords at one end, and the statue of the Angel Raziel in the center. Only there was no Hall of Accords here, only a massive pillared building made of a darkly glowing metal; this had been the glint Cordelia had seen earlier. Its sides had been engraved with words in a curling demonic script.

As for the statue of the Angel, it was gone. In its place was a statue of Belial, carved from marble. A sneer was stamped on his beautiful, inhuman face; he wore scaled armor, and wings of black onyx burst from his back.

"Look at him. Look how *pleased* he looks with himself," Lucie said, glaring viciously at the statue. "Ugh, I wish I could—" She gasped and doubled over, her hands on her stomach. "Oh—it *hurts*."

Terrified, Cordelia caught hold of Lucie's arm. "Are you all right? Lucie—"

Lucie looked up, her eyes wide, her pupils dilated and very black. "Something horrible," she whispered. "Something's wrong. I feel them—the dead—"

"It's because we're in Idumea, isn't it? You said it was a dead city—"

Lucie shook her head. "Those are old ghosts. These are new—so full of rage and hatred—like they just died, but nothing's lived here in so long, so how—?" She flinched and staggered back against the base of the statue. "Daisy—look—"

Cordelia turned to see what seemed to be a whirling cloud of dust. She thought of stories of storms in the desert, great sheets of sand moving across the sky, but this was no natural phenomenon. As it drew closer, spinning across the square, Cordelia could see that it was indeed a moving, tightly packed cloud of dust and sand, but within that cloud were shapes—faces, really, with wide eyes and gaping mouths. Like paintings of seraphim, she thought in a daze, great wings covered in eyes, wheels of fire that spoke and moved.

Lucie was moaning softly, clearly in agony as she crouched against the statue. The spinning cloud was right in front of them. Out of the dust and sand, a face began to form, and then a torso and shoulders. A mournful face, with spilling black hair and sad, dark eyes.

Filomena di Angelo. As Cordelia stared in amazement, she spoke—a strange, half-formed figure circled in whirling sand. "Cordelia Carstairs," she said, and her voice echoed like the wind that blew across the desert. "Have you at last come to save me?"

This is a demon, Cordelia thought. *Some sort of nightmare creature that preys on guilt.* Only—that did not explain Lucie's response to it. Still . . .

"You are a monster," Cordelia said. "Sent by Belial to trick me."

The dust whirled, and a new face appeared within it. An old woman, sharp-eyed, familiar. "It is no trick," said the semblance of Lilian Highsmith. "We are the souls of those Belial murdered in London. He has trapped us here for his own amusement."

The sand shifted. Basil Pounceby's grim face stared out at them. Lucie was breathing in rasping gasps; Cordelia fought back her fear, her desire to flee to protect Lucie. This creature would only follow. "We have been ordered to harry anyone who comes into Idumea and drive them away," growled the ghost of Pounceby. "Belial finds it an amusing joke to bend Shadowhunters to his will and force us to eternally witness the destruction of that which was once Alicante."

"Belial," said Cordelia. "Where in Idumea is he now?"

Another shift. It was Filomena again, her expression desperate. "In the dark Gard," she said. "That which was Lilith's palace but is now his. He flies there and back on a great dark bird. We think he has taken prisoners."

Prisoners. Cordelia's heart leaped. "You must let us through, Filomena," she said. "I failed to protect you before. Let me try now. Let us go to the Gard, for when we get there, I will kill Belial, and you will be free. His hold on you will be ended."

"How do you think you can slay Belial?" Basil Pounceby's voice, thick with scorn. "You are just a girl."

In one smooth motion, Cordelia drew her sword. Cortana glowed in her hand, a staunchly defiant gold, untouched by the bloody sun. "I am the bearer of Cortana. I have already wounded Belial twice. A third wound will end him."

Filomena's eyes widened. And then she was gone, the sand reshaping and re-forming itself, into the most familiar countenance of all. Pale hair and eyes, gray stubble, a deeply lined face. Her father.

"Cordelia," said the ghost of Elias Carstairs. "You heard my words in Paris, when I spoke to you, did you not?"

Any doubts Cordelia had entertained that these were really the spirits of the London dead vanished. "Yes," she whispered. "Oh, *Baba*—"

"Daisy," Lucie said, her voice thready. "I can't—we don't have much time—"

"I heard you in Paris," Cordelia said, staring at her father's face. "You tried to warn me."

"I reached out," Elias whispered hoarsely. "I heard your call in the darkness. But we are weak in death. . . . There is so little I could do . . ."

"Father," Cordelia said. "You were a great Shadowhunter once. The legendary Elias Carstairs. You led warriors into battle, into victory. Be a leader now. Defy Belial. Give me this chance to make it to the Gard. *Everything* depends on it. Father, please—"

She broke off as the cloud began to spin faster, and then faster still. Faces appeared and disappeared within the storm of it, eyes bulging, teeth gritted; Cordelia could no longer tell which face was which, but each wore the same look of grim determination. And then, with a great shrieking cry, the cloud burst apart into fragments, sand showering the cobblestones of Angel Square.

Cordelia's ears rang in the silence. She turned to look at Lucie, who was straightening up cautiously. She said gently, "They're gone, Daisy."

"Are *you* all right?" Cordelia lowered her sword. "Do you feel better?"

"Yes. But they'll come back, I think. They're subject to the will of Belial; they can only fight it for so long." Lucie inhaled, a long and steadying breath. "We'd better get to the Gard while they do."

Cordelia nodded, feeling solemn. She had thought she would feel more pain after seeing her father. Instead, strangely, she felt a sort of cold calm descend on her. She was the wielder of Cortana, and she was not here to mourn. She was here to avenge. She was an angel falling upon the plains of Edom, in the name of Raziel and all the Nephilim who had fought and died here long ago. She would free her father's spirit from this place. She would rescue Matthew and James; she would liberate London from Belial. This world could not be saved, but the fate of her own had not yet been decided.

Together, she and Lucie started in the direction of the dark fortress atop what had once been Gard Hill.

When the red sun rose over the courtyard the next morning, James had not slept. His eyes felt as if they were full of sand, and his mouth was bone-dry. Matthew sat next to him, his legs drawn up, his eyes fixed thoughtfully on the horizon.

At some point, James had stopped the drawing of *iratzes*. Matthew had stopped shaking and fallen asleep, breathing deeply and evenly, his head heavy against James's shoulder. Some hours later, when he had woken up, he had turned to look at James thoughtfully.

"I don't know what you did," he said. "At least, I don't know how it was possible. But—I feel better. Physically, at least."

He looked at his forearm. It was a latticework of pale white lines, the ghosts of vanished runes.

"That shouldn't have worked," he said. "But then, that's true of so many things we've done."

He was right, James thought. It shouldn't have worked. He'd put every bit of his concentration into drawing the healing runes, trying to imbue them with his own strength, his own will, hoping that if he could get each one to remain just a little while, the combined force of a hundred of them would get Matthew through the night.

As Matthew stood up now and went to get water, he was steady on his feet. There was color in his face, he wasn't shivering, and his hands didn't shake as he came back with the cup. This was not a cure, James knew. Matthew, if he survived Edom, would still crave alcohol; there was much work still to be done. But to have kept him alive so he could *do* that work—

A shadow passed overhead. Matthew reached James, held out a hand to help him up. As James brushed dust off his clothes, he said, "Do you mean that? About things we've done that shouldn't have worked?"

Matthew eyed him oddly. "Of course."

"So you'll go along with my plan," James said. "The one you hate."

Matthew glanced at James hard, and then up at the sky—where a dark, winged shape was growing closer. A pure white cloak flew on the wind like a flag.

"Belial," Matthew said flatly.

He set the cup down, and he and James moved to stand shoulder to shoulder. It was a gesture, James knew. Belial could separate them both with a snap of his fingers. Fling them to opposite sides of the courtyard. But gestures mattered. They were important.

Belial sprang off the back of Stymphalia even before the

bird-demon touched down in the pebbled black dirt. As dust flew, he marched across the courtyard to James and Matthew. He looked annoyed, James thought, which was something: he had expected gloating. This seemed a bit more complex.

"Your companions," Belial snapped. "Cordelia Carstairs, your sister, the others—you know I offered them safe passage out of London. Did they refuse it? Are they still in the city?"

James felt his heart swell. *I knew,* he thought. *I had faith.*

He spread his hands wide. "I couldn't possibly answer that," he said. "We've been here."

Belial's lip curled. "I suppose. But I imagine you have a guess."

"Why?" James said. "Are you afraid of them? A bunch of Nephilim children?" He grinned, feeling his dry lips crack. "Or just of Cordelia?"

Belial sneered. "She will not touch me with her foul blade," he said. "For I will be possessing *you*—and for her to harm me, she would have to end your life. Which she will not do. Women," he added, "are notoriously sentimental."

"Wonderful," Matthew muttered. "Advice about human women from a Prince of Hell."

"You will be quiet," Belial said. "The time for playing and posturing has come to an end. You have been an amusing adversary, grandson, but there was never a chance for you. If you do not agree to let me possess you, I will torture your *parabatai* to death in front of your eyes. After that, I will bring you with me to London. I will kill every man, woman, and child we encounter until your fragile human spirit breaks and you beg me to put an end to it."

James raised his head slowly. He met his grandfather's gaze. The urge to look away was immediate, intense. Behind those eyes something *slithered*—something primordially evil, cold, reptilian, and venomous.

He kept his gaze steady. "First, you promise not to hurt Matthew," James said. At the edge of his vision, he saw Matthew close his eyes. "And I will let you have what you want—with a few more conditions."

Belial seemed to purr. "Which are?"

"You will not hurt my friends, my family, or Cordelia."

"Having her run around freely with Cortana is inconvenient,"

Belial said. "If she attacks, I will defend myself. Surely you can see there is no agreement otherwise."

"All right," James said. He could barely breathe, but he knew better than to show it. "But as you said—she won't."

"Hmm," Belial said. There was a hunger in his expression now. A look that twisted James's insides with nausea. "We seem to have reached an agreement."

"Not yet." James shook his head. "I require something more formal. You're a Prince of Hell. You must vow on Lucifer's name."

Belial chuckled. "Ah, the Lightbringer. You had better hope, Nephilim, that you never have cause to meet *him.*" He flung out his arm, his white robe swirling around him like smoke. "I, Prince Belial, Lord of Edom, of the First Nine, do swear on the name of Lucifer, He that is everything, that I will not cause harm to befall any of those dear to my blood grandson James Herondale. May I be struck into the Pit if such comes to pass."

He looked at James; his eyes were wide and black and flickering, dark and empty as the end of all hope. "Now, come here, boy," he said. "It is time."

33
A Fortress Foiled

A fortress foiled, which reason did defend,
A siren song, a fever of the mind,
A maze wherein affection finds no end,
A raging cloud that runs before the wind,
A substance like the shadow of the sun,
A goal of grief for which the wisest run.
—Sir Walter Raleigh, "A Farewell to False Love"

To Ari's surprise, she and Anna reached the heart of the Silent City without seeing a single Watcher. They had started out keeping to the shadows, checking doors and archways before passing from one room to another, and communicating only in hand gestures. But as their map led them up from the prisons through the living quarters and on past the libraries and the Ossuarium, they exchanged puzzled glances. They had seen not a soul, nor heard so much as a mouse scrabbling behind a wall since their arrival.

"Where *are* they all?" Anna murmured. They were passing through a tunnel, which widened out into a large square. At each cardinal point of the square rose a spire of carved bone. Alternating squares of red and bronze, like a checkerboard, made up the floor. Their witchlights gave the only illumination; the torches set in brackets along the walls had long burned out.

"Perhaps out in London," Ari said. Her witchlight danced over a pattern of silver stars set into the floor. "They have no real need to occupy the Silent City, I suppose."

"I would have thought they would at least be on guard against anyone entering," said Anna. "Let me see the map again."

They bent their heads over it. "We are in the Pavilion of Truth, here," Ari said, pointing. "Usually the Mortal Sword would be on the wall—"

"But it's in Idris, thankfully," said Anna. "Here—through these rows of mausoleums—it's marked on the map. *Path of the Dead.*"

Ari nodded slowly. As she fell into step beside Anna, she thought it seemed as if she'd barely taken a real breath since they'd entered the Silent City. The scent on the air—ashes and stone—was a cold reminder of the previous time she'd been here, when she had nearly died from the poison of a Mandikhor demon. The experience had not given her any desire to return.

They continued through stone halls that led them to a vaulted room filled with mausoleums, many with Shadowhunter names or symbols carved above their stone doors. They cut down a narrow path between CROSSKILL and RAVENSCROFT and ducked through a narrow dark archway like a keyhole—

And found themselves in a long corridor. *Long* was barely enough of a descriptor: witchlight sconces on both sides of the tunnel formed an arrow of light that receded until the distance was too far for human eyes. Something about it made Ari shudder. Maybe it was only that the rest of the Silent City's tunnels had a more organic quality, often following unusual paths that Ari had assumed were accidents of geology. But this one felt alien and strange, as if a vein of peculiar magic ran beneath its floor of stone.

As they made their way down it, they passed runes carved into the walls: runes of death and mourning, but also runes of transformation and change. There were other runes too, bearing the sort of odd patterning that Ari saw when a Portal was made. They seemed to flare up as Anna and Ari neared them, before receding into the shadows. These, Ari suspected, were the runes that made the tunnel what it was: a telescoped version of real distance, a peculiar shortcut through time and space that would allow them to—at least, as they would perceive it—walk from London to Iceland in less than a day.

Every once in a while they would pass a door with a rune carved into it, or a narrow passageway that snaked off into the dark. There was no sound but their footsteps until Anna said, "You know, when I was a child, I thought I would be an Iron Sister."

"Really?" said Ari. "It seems like quite a lot of routine, for you. *And* a lot of taking orders."

"Sometimes I like taking orders," said Anna, sounding amused.

"No flirting in the Silent City," Ari said, though she felt a little shiver down her spine, as she always did when Anna teased her. "I am fairly sure that there is a Law about it."

"I thought I would like to make weapons," Anna said. "It seemed the opposite of wearing dresses and going to parties. In any case, it only lasted until I found out I would have to go live on a lava plain. I asked my mother if I would still be able to get my favorite chocolates there, and she said she doubted it very much. So that was enough for me." She paused, all lightness gone from her voice. "Do you hear that?"

Ari nodded grimly. The sound of footsteps came from up ahead—many footsteps, marching in a regular tread. She narrowed her eyes but could see only shadows—and then a flash of something white. Watchers' robes.

"Quick," Ari whispered. They were near one of the narrow passageways leading off the tunnel; she caught hold of Anna's sleeve and ducked into it, pulling Anna after her.

The passage was barely wide enough for both of them to stand facing each other. Ari could hear the sound of marching feet getting louder, an odd reminder that though the Chimera demons possessed the bodies of Silent Brothers and Iron Sisters, they were *not* them; they did not have their powers or skills.

She crouched down and peered into the corridor. There they were—a large group of Watchers, fifty or more, their death-white robes swirling around their feet as if they had been born out of smoke. They moved down the passage with blind determination, their jagged staffs in hand.

"Let me go," Anna said, and tried to push past Ari. "We know how to kill them now—"

"No!" Ari didn't think; she caught hold of Anna and yanked her back, nearly flinging her up against the wall. They had both doused their witchlights, and there was little illumination in the passage, but Ari could still see the fury in Anna's blue eyes.

"We can't just let them *go*," Anna said. "We can't just let them—"

"Anna. Please. There are far too many of them. And only two of us."

"Not *you*." Anna shook her head violently. "You need to get to the Iron Tombs. One of us does. I cannot kill them all, but think how many I could take before—"

"Before you *die?*" Ari hissed. "Is this a way to honor Christopher?"

Rage flashed across Anna's face—rage directed at herself, Ari guessed. "I couldn't protect him. I wasn't ready for an attack. But at least I can stand against these creatures *now*—"

"*No,*" Ari said. "The responsibility for Christopher's death is Belial's. They are a horror, the Watchers, because of whose bodies have been possessed. But Chimeras are *just demons*. Like any other demons. They are the instruments of Belial, and it is Belial we must defeat."

"Let me go, Ari," Anna said, her eyes burning. If Ari turned her head just a little bit, she could see the Watchers, a white flood passing by the narrow mouth of the passageway. "It will not be my hand that slays Belial, if he can even be slain. Let me do this, at least—"

"No." The determination in Ari's voice surprised even her. "It may be Cordelia's sword that kills Belial. But all of us stand behind her. Everything we have done, everything we have accomplished, has made us part of the force that drives her blade. Nor is our task done. We are still needed, Anna. *You* are still needed."

Very slowly, Anna nodded.

Carefully, Ari let go of Anna, praying she was right about the look in Anna's eyes. Praying that Anna would not bolt. And Anna didn't—only remained very still, her back flat against the wall, her eyes fixed on Ari, as the sound of the Watchers receded into the distance.

A cracked road, the remains of a once-impressive boulevard lined by shade trees, led Cordelia and Lucie to the base of the hill that loomed over Idumea. Before they started up, Cordelia glanced over at Lucie a last time. This was it—their final push, the final approach to Lilith's palace. Edom and Idumea had already taken such a toll on Lucie. Did she have the strength for this?

Cordelia decided in that moment that if she didn't, she would carry Lucie up the hill herself. They had come too far, and Lucie had pushed herself too hard, for Cordelia to abandon her now.

Lucie looked pale, strained, smudged with dirt. The encounter with the cursed ghosts seemed to have stretched her even thinner: her eyes looked huge in her face, and her expression was tight with pain. But when Cordelia glanced up the hill, a question in her eyes, Lucie only nodded and started up the uneven, zigzag path that led to the top.

The hill was steeper than it looked at first, and the terrain much rougher. It had been a long time since the path had been tended to, and petrified tree roots bulged through the dry scree that covered the hillside. Low stone cairns dotted the edges of the path. Markers of graves long forgotten? Had this been the last stand of the Nephilim in this world? Had they died protecting their fortress? Cordelia could only guess.

As they rose up the hill, the clouds thinned, and she could see what seemed like all of Edom laid out before her; she could see the plains where she and Lucie had taken shelter, and even the long line of the Wall of Kadesh in the distance. She wondered if it had once been a border with another country; she wondered what had happened to the Forest of Brocelind, with its deep wooded dells and faerie groves. She wondered, as the black clouds fell away below them, if Lilith had lied and they would find no way back to their own world from here.

She wondered where Belial was. In fact, not just Belial, but the demons who must surely serve him. She kept her hand on Cortana, but all was silent: only the sounds of the wind and Lucie's ragged breathing accompanied their ascent.

At last the slope began to level out and they could catch their breath. Before them, black in the red glow of the sun, rose the high walls that encircled the fortress. A pair of massive gates was set into them.

"There aren't even any guards," Cordelia said as they approached the gates together. "It doesn't make sense."

Lucie was silent. She was staring at the gates with an odd look on her face. They were a dark mirror of the Gard gates in Alicante, gold and iron carved with swirling runes, though these were not the runes from the Gray Book, but a demonic language, ancient and disquieting. Stone statues of angels—decapitated and acid-eaten, only their spreading wings giving a hint of what they'd once been—stood watch at either side of the gates.

The gates had no handles, nothing to grasp. Cordelia put her hand against one—the metal was icy cold—and pushed; it was like pushing against a massive boulder. Nothing happened. "No guards," she said again. "But no way to get in, either." She tipped her head back. "Maybe we can try to climb the walls—"

"Let me," Lucie said quietly. She stepped past Cordelia. "I saw this in a vision," she said, sounding very unlike herself. "I think—it was Belial that I saw. And I heard him speak."

She laid a dusty hand against the gate's surface. *"Kaal ssha ktar,"* she said.

The words sounded like stone scraping against metal. Cordelia shuddered—and stared incredulously as the gates swung open noiselessly. Beyond them she could see a moat, filled with black, oily water, and a bridge that crossed it, leading directly into the fortress.

Before them lay the heart of Lilith's palace.

After a very long minute and a half of listening to the Watchers tromp past their hiding spot, the marching had receded into the distance and silence had returned. Cautiously Ari poked her head out from the alcove and gestured to Anna.

"Where do you think they're going? The Watchers, I mean," Anna said.

Ari bit her lip. "I don't know, but I can't help but fear we're running out of time."

They walked on. And on. It was very hard to tell how much time was passing, as the corridor extended in either direction for as far as they could see now, disappearing to vanishing points ahead and behind. Ari was peering back over her shoulder, hoping they hadn't been meant to turn where they had seen the Watchers, when Anna let out a quickly muffled yelp of recognition. "Look!"

Ari hurried to join her and looked where she was pointing. There, leading off the corridor, was a pair of barred gates wrought in gold; they hung half-open, darkness visible beyond them. These, she knew, must be the gates through which Tatiana Blackthorn had let Belial and his army pass from the Iron Tombs into the Silent City.

"Who could do such a thing?" Ari whispered. She glanced over at Anna. "Do you think anyone will be there? Waiting for us?"

Anna didn't answer, only strode through the doorway. Ari followed her.

They had been passing through caverns of inhuman scale since they arrived, so another one did not have quite the same impact as the first had. Even so, the sheer scale of the Iron Tombs intimidated her. She supposed that a thousand years of Silent Brothers and Iron Sisters added up to a very large number of tombs. Whose inhabitants, she reminded herself, were now rampaging around London.

Before them was a tiled floor, easily a hundred yards in each direction, describing a huge circular chamber. Around the perimeter, dozens of stone staircases were set into the walls; these led to landings, and then more staircases, a riot of staircases stretching above them, crossing one another, forming a kind of massive, vaulted ceiling where the stairs were absent. On each of the landings, at least the ones they could see, were stone tables—no. Sarcophagi. Even from here on the ground, Ari could see that the lids had been disturbed, thrown off entirely or at least shifted from their places.

It was not as dark as it had seemed from outside. The walls were lined with witchlights, all the way up, casting everything in a gentle blue glow. The witchlights were placed regularly, but the intersecting, apparently random placement of all the staircases made them shimmer down from above like a field of stars. It was almost impossible to tell how high the staircases rose, as they disappeared into a ceiling that could have been the sky.

They crossed the crypt, the tapping of their shoes echoing through the cavernous space. The center was empty, but the floor, Ari realized, was a huge mosaic whose image she could not initially understand. She studied it as she crossed it, and realized eventually that it was of an Iron Sister and a Silent Brother, and an angel rising over them.

At the end of the mosaic was a long double staircase rising straight ahead of them to a simple door set in the wall. *The way out*, Ari thought. It had to be; it was large enough, and there were no other doors in sight except the ones they had entered through.

"Well," said Anna, and Ari realized she was nervous. "Shall we?"

"We shall," said Ari properly. She reached out and took Anna's hand in hers, as if to lead her to a dance floor. "We'll go together."

The actual opening of the door, once they reached it, was a bit of an anticlimax after all the buildup. There was a large iron key in the door, and, after another glance at Ari, Anna turned it and simply pushed the door open.

On the other side was the night sky, and a rocky volcanic plain, and silence.

Into the silence, Anna called, "Hello?"

No sound came.

They looked at one another in horror, and Ari felt a terrible fatigue. No fire-messages, it seemed. No Shadowhunter army to meet them.

Anna took a long, deep breath. "It's good to breathe clean air, at least."

"And," said Ari, "it's good we had a backup plan."

"Yes, but it's an exhausting one," Anna said, eyeing the rocky terrain rolling away from where they stood. "How long do you think it will take to get to the Adamant Citadel?"

But then Ari's eye was caught by a flash of light on the horizon. She looked, and the light became a steady glow.

"Is that a . . . Portal?" Anna said, as though saying it out loud would cause it not to be so.

As they watched, a line of figures appeared, carrying lamps that gave out their own glow. Like fireflies they danced across the lava plain, but then they grew closer, and the Shadowhunters *had* come, and Grace and Jesse *had* made fire-messages work, and perhaps there was still such a thing as hope in the world.

Anna put her arms above her head and waved. "Here! We're here!"

As they got closer, Ari could see their faces. She recognized Gideon and Sophie and Eugenia Lightwood, Piers Wentworth and Rosamund and Thoby, but most were strangers, not members of the London Enclave but Shadowhunters from elsewhere who had come to fight.

She couldn't help but feel a bit disappointed, but it was a rather silly fantasy, she thought, to have imagined that they would be met by the families she knew best.

And then she froze, as she saw her mother.

Her mother was in battle gear, her gray-brown hair swept up in a practical plait at the back of her neck, a weapons belt around her waist. Ari couldn't remember the last time Flora Bridgestock had actually put on gear.

As though she knew her daughter was looking at her, Flora's gaze came to rest directly on Ari, and they locked eyes. For a moment, Flora seemed expressionless, and Ari felt a terrible anxiety go through her.

And then, slowly, Flora smiled. There was hope in that smile, and pain and sorrow. She reached out her hand—not commandingly, but hopefully, as if to say, *Come here, please,* and Ari went to join her.

Cordelia and Lucie hurried across the bridge, the black water in the moat below surging and swirling as if *something* were alive inside it. It was nothing Cordelia wanted to look at too closely, though, and besides, she was more worried about demons pouring out of the fortress, ready to attack.

But the place was quiet. At first glance, as they ducked into the vast entryway, the fortress appeared abandoned. Dust blew across the bare stone floors. Spiderwebs—far too large and thick for Cordelia's peace of mind—coated the ceiling and hung from the corners. A double spiral staircase, beautifully constructed, soared to the second floor, but there was no motion or sound from above, any more than there was around them.

"I don't know what I expected," said Lucie, looking perplexed, "but it wasn't this. Where's the throne of skulls? The decapitated Lilith statues? The tapestries with Belial's face on them?"

"This place feels utterly dead." Cordelia felt sick to her stomach. "Lilith and Filomena both said Belial had taken it over, that he was using it, but what if Lilith was lying? Or if they were just—wrong?"

"We won't know until we search," Lucie said, with grim determination.

They headed up the curving stairs—it was two sets of spiral staircases, weaving in and out of each other, never touching—until they reached the second floor. Here there was a long stone corridor; they followed it carefully, weapons at the ready, but it was just as empty as the entryway. At the corridor's end were a pair of metal doors. Cordelia looked at Lucie, who shrugged and pushed one of them open.

Inside was another large room, semicircular in shape, with a floor of marble, badly cracked. There was a kind of bare stone platform rising against one of the walls; behind it were two huge windows. One gazed out over the bleak plains of Edom. The second was a Portal.

The surface of it swirled and danced with color, like oil on the surface of water. Through that movement, Cordelia could see what was unmistakably London. A London whose skies were gray and black, the clouds overhead riven with heat lightning. In the foreground, a bridge over a dark river; beyond it, a Gothic structure rising against the sky, a familiar clock tower—

"It's Westminster Bridge," said Lucie, in surprise. "And the Houses of Parliament."

Cordelia blinked. "Why would Belial want to go *there?*"

"I don't know, but—look at this." Cordelia glanced over and saw Lucie on her tiptoes, examining a heavy iron lever that emerged from the wall just to the left of the doors. Thick chains rose from it, disappearing into the ceiling.

"Don't—" Cordelia started, but it was already too late; Lucie had pulled the lever down. The chain began to move; they could hear it grinding in the walls and ceilings.

Abruptly, a circular piece of the floor sank out of sight, forming what looked like a well. Rushing to the edge of it, Cordelia saw stairs leading down, and at the bottom of the stairs—light.

She started down the steps. The walls on either side were polished stone, engraved with more designs and words, but this time Cordelia could read them: they were not in a demonic language, but in Aramaic. *And the woman said to the serpent, "We may eat the fruit of the trees of the garden; but of the fruit of the tree which is in the midst of the garden, God has said, 'You shall not eat it, nor shall you touch it, lest you die.'"*

"This must have been written here by the Shadowhunters," said

Lucie, following carefully after Cordelia. "I suppose because the stairs lead to—"

"A garden," Cordelia said, for she had reached the foot of the steps, where a blank stone wall stood before them—but with another iron lever emerging from the wall at one side. She looked at Lucie, who shrugged. Cordelia pulled, and again the grinding of stone upon stone, and a portion of the wall rolled away, revealing a doorway. She ducked through it and found herself outside the fortress, in a walled garden—or what had once been a garden. It was withered and blackened now, studded with the stumps of dead trees, the dry, cracked ground covered in broken bits of black rock.

Standing in the middle of the ruined garden, looking filthy and half-starved but very definitely alive, was Matthew.

While Grace and Jesse remained in the library, sending fire-messages to every Institute on a very long list, Thomas had volunteered to join Alastair on the roof to keep watch. The roof gave them the best view over the widest area: they could see if Watchers were approaching or even—and Thomas knew this was a desperate hope—if the fire-messages had reached their target, and reinforcements of Shadowhunters might be arriving in London.

It was hard to have hope that anything would change. It was the earliest hours of the morning, and under normal circumstances, the sky would have started to lighten by now. But it looked exactly as it had for the past days—the sky a boiling black cauldron, the air full of the scent of ash and burning, the water of the Thames a lightless green-black. There weren't even any Watchers to spot, for the moment.

Thomas leaned on his elbows next to Alastair, who wore an unreadable expression.

"It's so odd to see the Thames without any boats," Thomas said. "And no sounds of voices, no trains . . . it's like the city is sleeping. Behind a hedge of thorns, like in a fairy tale."

Alastair looked over at him. His eyes were dark and held a tenderness that was new. When Thomas thought of the night before, in the infirmary with Alastair, he blushed hard enough to feel it. He quickly went back to staring at London.

"I actually feel a bit hopeful," said Alastair. "Is that mad?"

"Not necessarily," said Thomas. "It could just be light-headedness, since we're running out of food."

Normally Alastair would have smiled at that, but his expression stayed serious, inward. "When I decided to stay in London," he said, "it was partly because it seemed the right thing to do, not to take Belial's offer. And partly because of Cordelia. But it was also that I didn't want . . ."

"What?" said Thomas.

"To leave you," Alastair said. Now Thomas did look at him. Alastair was leaning against the iron railing. Despite the cold, the top button of his shirt was undone. Thomas could see the wings of his collarbone, the hollow of his throat where Thomas had kissed him. Alastair's hair, usually neat, was windblown, his cheeks flushed. Thomas wanted to touch him so badly, he shoved his hands into his pockets.

"What you said to me in the library, when we were there with Christopher," Thomas said. "It sounded a bit like poetry. What did it mean?"

Alastair's eyes flicked toward the horizon. "'*Ey pesar, nik ze hadd mibebari kar-e jamal. Ba conin hosn ze to sabr konam?*' It is poetry. Or at least, a song. A Persian ghazal. *Boy, your beauty is beyond all description. How can I wait, when you are so beautiful?*" His mouth quirked up at the corner. "I always knew the words. I can't remember when it fully struck me what they meant. It is men who sing ghazals, you know; it occurred to me only then that there were others who felt as I did. Men who wrote freely about how beautiful other men were, and that they loved them."

Thomas tightened his hands in his pockets. "I don't think anyone has ever thought I was beautiful, except for you."

"That's not true," Alastair said decidedly. "You don't see how people look at you. I do. It used to make me grind my teeth—I was so jealous—I thought surely you'd choose anyone in the world who wasn't me." He reached up, cupped a hand around the back of Thomas's neck. He was biting at his lower lip, which made Thomas's skin burn. He knew what it was like to kiss Alastair now. It wasn't just a flight of imagination; it was real, and he wanted it again more than he would have thought possible. "If last night was just the once, tell me," Alastair said in a low voice. "I'd rather know."

Thomas yanked his hands out of his pockets. Taking hold of the lapels of Alastair's coat, he pulled the other boy toward him. "You," he said, brushing his lips against Alastair's, "are so *aggravating*."

"Oh?" Alastair looked up at Thomas through his lashes.

"You have to know I care about you," Thomas said, and the movement of his lips against Alastair's was making Alastair's eyes darken. He felt Alastair's hands burrowing under his coat, circling his waist. "You have to know—"

Alastair sighed. "That was the sort of thing Charles always said. 'I care for you, I have feelings for you.' Never just 'I love you—'" Alastair stiffened and jerked away, and for a moment Thomas thought it was because of him, but Alastair was staring past him, the expression on his face grim. "Look." He moved down the roof, trying to get a better angle on whatever he'd spotted. He pointed. "*There.*"

Thomas looked, and his breath caught in his throat.

They were marching as an army might march, looking neither to the right nor the left, one single column of white-robed figures making its way steadily westward, toward the heart of London.

Alastair ran an agitated hand through his hair. "They've never done this before," he said. "Usually they're just aimlessly patrolling. I've never seen more than two or three together since—"

Thomas shivered. He had been warm, cuddled up with Alastair; now he was freezing. "Since the fight with Tatiana. I know. Where can they be going?"

"They're under Belial's command," Alastair said levelly. "They can only be going where he's commanded them to go."

He and Thomas exchanged a look, before diving for the trapdoor that led back down into the Institute. They hurried to the library, where they found that Jesse had fallen asleep on the table, his cheek on a pile of blank papers, a modified stele in his hand. Beside him, Grace sat at the same table, scribbling fire-messages in the light from a single witchlight stone. She held her finger to her lips when she saw them approaching. "Jesse's just taking a nap," she said. There were dark circles under her eyes, and her pale hair hung limply. "We've been at this all night."

"The Watchers are on the move," Thomas said, keeping his voice low. "A lot of them, maybe all of them. They were making their way down the Strand, all going the same direction."

"As if they've been summoned," said Alastair, checking his weapons belt as he spoke. "Thomas and I will go see what's going on."

Grace set her stele down. "Is that wise? Just the two of you?"

Thomas exchanged a look with Alastair. Alastair said carefully, "We don't have much choice—"

"Wait," Jesse said, sitting up. He blinked and rubbed at his eyes. "I . . ." He yawned. "Sorry. I just thought—what if the fire-messages worked? If the Clave found the entrance to the Iron Tombs, and made it to London, the Watchers could be marching to battle with them." He looked at Thomas's and Alastair's dubious expressions. "We've never seen them in a large group like this, and what's changed since yesterday? Only that we've sent fire-messages out. What else could it be?"

"It could be the fire-messages," said Alastair slowly. "Or it might be that Belial . . . has gotten what he wanted."

James. Thomas felt the suggestion like a punch to the stomach. "I thought you were feeling optimistic."

"It passed," said Alastair.

"Well, whatever it is," said Jesse, standing up, "we're going with you to find out."

"No," said Alastair flatly. "You're not trained enough."

Both Grace and Jesse looked offended; in fact, their expressions of annoyance were so similar that it reminded Thomas that whether or not they were blood related, they were siblings nonetheless.

"What Alastair means," Thomas said quickly, "is it's not safe, and you've both been up all night. And we have no idea what we'll be facing out there."

"And?" said Jesse, his tone rather sharp. "What do you expect us to do? We've sent a hundred fire-messages; we can't just huddle here in the Institute, waiting to see if you ever come back."

"I see I am not the only one who has abandoned optimism," noted Alastair.

"He's just being realistic," said Grace, reaching down below the table where she'd been working and pulling out a canvas sack.

"What do you have there?" said Alastair.

"Explosives," she said. "From Christopher's lab. We *are* ready."

"The time for hiding and protecting ourselves and saving our energy is over," Jesse said. "I can feel it. Can't you?"

Thomas could not deny that it was true. Cordelia and Lucie had gone; Anna and Ariadne were trekking through the Silent City, hoping to meet the Clave at the entrance to the Iron Tombs. They were nearly out of food. And the Watchers were on the march.

"Besides," Grace said. "We're the only ones who can send fire-messages. What if we need to reach Anna and Ari, or the Clave, and tell them what the Watchers are doing? Where they've gathered? You can't say that wouldn't be helpful."

And indeed, Thomas couldn't.

"One way or another, it's going to end today," Jesse said, going to fetch the Blackthorn sword from where it leaned against the wall. "All of it. Better that we're together for whatever comes."

Thomas and Alastair exchanged a look.

"And if you don't let us come with you," added Jesse, "you'll have to lock us up in the Institute. We won't stay here otherwise."

Grace nodded in agreement.

Thomas shook his head. "You're Nephilim. We're not locking you up. If you really want to come—"

"We can die together," Alastair said. "Now, get your gear on. I don't think we have much more time."

"*Matthew,*" Cordelia breathed.

Matthew took a step back. He was staring at Cordelia as if she were an apparition, a ghost that had appeared out of nowhere. "James," he said raggedly, "James was right—you came—"

Lucie passed through the doorway into the courtyard. The red-orange sun beat down on her, and on Cordelia, who had already looked, already seen that the garden was empty of anyone but Matthew. And though Cordelia was desperately glad to see Matthew, the look on his face made her feel as if a fist were crushing her heart.

"He's gone," she said. "Isn't he? James is gone."

"He's gone?" Lucie whispered. "You don't mean—"

"He's alive." Matthew's face crumpled. "But possessed. I'm sorry—I couldn't stop it happening—"

"Math," Lucie said softly, and then she and Cordelia were running across the courtyard. They threw their arms around him, embraced him tightly, and after a moment he put his arms around them awkwardly and hugged them both back. "I am so sorry," he said, over and over. "So sorry—"

Cordelia drew back first. Lucie, she could see, had tears streaking her face, but Cordelia had none to shed; what she felt was too terrible for her to cry. "Don't apologize," she said fiercely. "You didn't *let* this happen; Belial is a Prince of Hell. He does what he wants. Just—where did he take James? Where have they gone?"

"London," Matthew said. "He's obsessed with it. A place on Earth where he rules." His voice was bitter. "Now that he has so much power over the city—he as much as swore he would murder every living person in London until James broke down and let him do what he wanted."

"Oh, poor James," Lucie said miserably. "To have such an awful choice—"

"But he would have thought of it already," Cordelia said. *Think like James,* she told herself. She had come to know him so well over the past half year, come to know the intricate, winding way he considered and schemed. The kind of plans he made; what he was willing to risk, and what he was not. "That Belial would make a threat he could not withstand. It could not have surprised him."

"It didn't," Matthew said. "Last night, James told me he had a plan. Letting Belial possess him was part of it."

"A plan?" Lucie said, urgency in her voice. "What kind of plan?"

"I'll tell you. But we must start back to London. I don't think we have much time to lose." There was dust in Matthew's bright hair, and smears of dirt on his face. But he looked more alert, more resolute and clear-eyed, than Cordelia had ever seen him.

Lucie and Cordelia exchanged a quick look. "The Portal," said Lucie. "Matthew, are you well enough—?"

"To fight?" Matthew nodded. "As long as someone has a weapon

I can use." He put his hand to his belt. "James gave me his pistol last night, to hold for him. I think he didn't want Belial to be able to make use of it in our world. But of course, it won't work for me."

"Here." Lucie drew a seraph blade from her weapons belt and handed it to him. Matthew took it with a look of grim conviction.

"All right," Cordelia said, turning back toward the archway that led into the fortress. "Matthew—tell us everything that happened."

Matthew did. As they headed up the stairs, he spoke of his and James's imprisonment, sparing nothing, not his own sickness, nor his stunned surprise when a door had opened in the blank wall of the courtyard and Lucie and Cordelia had appeared from nowhere. He told them of the threats Belial had made before that, and James's decision, and of the moment Belial had possessed James.

"I've never seen anything more horrible," he said as they emerged into the room with the Portal inside it. "Belial walked toward him, grinning this terrible grin, and James stood his ground, but Belial just passed *into* him. Like a ghost walking through a wall. He vanished into James, and James's eyes turned a kind of dead silver color. And when he looked at me again, it was James's face, but with Belial's expression. Contempt and loathing and—inhumanity." He shuddered. "I can't explain it better than that."

Cordelia thought he'd explained it quite well enough. The thought of a James who was not James anymore made her feel sick. "There has to be more," she said. "For James to let this happen the way he did . . ."

"He'd already accepted that Belial would possess him," Matthew said. "He was concerned with what would happen after. He said that we needed to get Cordelia as near to Belial as possible—"

"So I can deal him his third wound?" Cordelia demanded. "But Belial is part of James now. I cannot mortally wound him without killing James, too."

"Besides," said Lucie, "Belial knows you're a threat. He won't let you anywhere near him. And now that he's possessed James—he'll be so powerful—"

"He is powerful," said Matthew. "He is also in pain. Those two wounds Cordelia dealt him already still cause him agony. But you can heal them, with Cortana—"

"Heal Belial?" Cordelia flinched. "I would never."

"James believes the idea will tempt Belial," said Matthew. "He is not used to pain. Demons normally don't feel it. If you tell him you're willing to make a deal—"

"A deal?" Cordelia's voice rose incredulously. "What kind of deal?"

Matthew shook his head. "I'm not sure it matters. James only said you had to get close, and that you would know the right moment to act."

"The right moment to act?" Cordelia echoed faintly.

Matthew nodded. Cordelia felt a quiet panic; she'd no idea what James intended. She'd told herself to think like him, but she felt as if she were missing the integral pieces of a puzzle, the key bits that would allow it to be solved.

Yet she couldn't bear to show her doubt in front of Lucie and Matthew, both of whom were looking at her with a desperate hope. She only nodded, as if what Matthew had said made sense to her. "How did he know?" she said instead. "That you'd see us again, or be able to tell us anything?"

"He never gave up," said Matthew. "He said none of you would take Belial's offer, or leave London—"

"He was right about that," said Lucie. "Cordelia and I came here, but we never went through the York Gate to Alicante. We stayed in the Institute with the others. Thomas, Anna . . ."

"James guessed all that." Matthew was looking at the Portal, at its stormy view of London. "He said you'd come for us. Both of you. He believed in you."

"Then we must believe in him," said Lucie. "We can't delay any longer. We have to get to London."

She started toward the Portal; as she reached out for it, Cordelia saw the image within the enchanted door change from Westminster Bridge to the abbey, with its Gothic spires reaching toward the storm-struck sky.

A moment later Lucie went into the Portal and was gone. Then it was Matthew's turn, and then Cordelia's. As she stepped into the whirling darkness, letting it spin her away from Edom, she thought, *What on earth did James mean by "the right moment to act"? And what if I don't figure it out in time?*

34
Communion

Be ye not unequally yoked together with unbelievers:
for what fellowship hath righteousness
with unrighteousness?
and what communion hath light with darkness?
—2 Corinthians 6:14

It wasn't at all as James had expected. He'd thought there would be wrenching pain, a sense of violation, perhaps the feeling of being caught in a nightmare. Instead, one moment he was in the courtyard in Edom, bracing himself, and the next he was walking across Westminster Bridge, with the Palace of Westminster and its famous clock tower straight ahead.

He could feel his legs carrying him forward. He could feel the air change from the choking heat of Edom to a wet, piercing chill. He could even feel the wind in his hair—a cold dark wind, blowing off a Thames the color of dried blood—and he wondered: Had something gone wrong with Belial's plan? Was he really possessed?

The air stung his eyes; reflexively, he tried to raise his hand to shield them. And found he couldn't. He could feel the *impulse* to lift the arm in his mind, but his arm didn't respond. Without conscious planning he tried to look down at the arm, and felt a stab of horror as his gaze remained fixed on the far side of the river. Panic began to rise in him, and he realized he could feel something else—a burning ache in his chest, which flared in a stab of agony with each step.

The wounds of Cortana. Each one was a line of fire laid against his skin. How did Belial bear this constant pain?

He tried to clench his fists. Nothing. The sick panic of paralysis washed over him: his body was a cage, a prison. He was trapped. It didn't matter that he'd prepared himself for it. He was panicking, and didn't seem to be able to stop.

A familiar voice echoed through his mind.

"You're awake," his grandfather said with a terrible pleasure. James knew his mouth wasn't moving; no sound was coming from him—this was Belial speaking to him mind to mind. Belial's consciousness, locked with his own. "I'm sure you rather hoped I'd snuff your consciousness into oblivion. But what fun would that be for me?" He chuckled. "My triumph over London is at hand, as you can see. But my triumph over *you* is complete, and after anticipating it for so long, I wish to relish it as much as possible."

London. They were at the middle of the bridge; James had a fine view of the city from here, and wished he didn't. It had been transformed since he last saw it. Dark clouds hung low in the sky, casting an ashy pall over the city. London was frequently cloudy, of course, famous for its rain and its fog, but this was something else entirely. These clouds were ink black and roiling, reminding James of the sea below Malcolm's cottage in Cornwall. Every few moments, red lightning speared the horizon, spilling a bloody light.

Normally there would be dozens of mundanes on this bridge, a constant stream of traffic in front of Westminster—but all was silent. The streets were utterly empty. The buildings that lined the river were dark, and there were no boats on the Thames. A dead city, James thought. A graveyard city, where skeletons might dance under an eerie moon.

The thought sickened him—and relieved him, all at once. Because though Belial was delighted, James felt only horror. His greatest fear had been that somehow, when possessed by his grandfather, James would think as Belial did, feel as he felt. But as Belial gloated over his imminent victory, James felt only disgust and fury. *And determination*, he reminded himself. He had chosen this; it was part of his plan.

Matthew had begged him to reconsider. But James knew his time of dodging Belial was over. The only way out was through.

"Might I ask where we're going?" James said, his voice echoing oddly in his own head. "We seem to be headed for the Houses of Parliament."

"We are not," Belial said crisply. "We are going to Westminster Abbey. We are here for a coronation. Mine, that is. Twoscore generations of kings have been crowned here as rulers, and as you know, I am a stickler for tradition. I shall be crowned the king of London, as a start. After that—well, we will see how quickly the rest of the land bends its knee to me." He chuckled. "I, Belial! Who was meant to never again walk on Earth! Let the Earth stretch herself under my boots in surrender; let Heaven watch in horror." He flung back his head, staring up at the scorched sky. "You did not see the first revolt against your power coming, Great One," he hissed. "And you have not stopped this one, either. Is it possible you are as weak as the Morningstar always said?"

"Enough," James muttered, but Belial only laughed. They had reached the end of the bridge, were striding up onto the road. Parliament loomed up on their left. It was still and empty here, in the heart of the city; James could see where carriages had been abandoned, some tipped over as if they'd been dragged behind panicked horses.

"James!"

Belial whirled around as a figure slipped from behind an abandoned carriage. It was Thomas, his clear, honest face full of delight, stumbling over the debris on the ground in his haste to get to James. Behind him came Alastair, much more slowly. His expression was wary.

James felt his heart sink. *You're right, Alastair. Call out to Thomas, get him away from me—*

But Thomas was already there, sliding his seraph blade back into his weapons belt, reaching his hand out to James. "Jamie! Thank the Angel! We thought—"

Belial moved, almost lazily, taking hold of the lapel of Thomas's coat. Then, with no effort at all, he *flung* Thomas away. Thomas stumbled backward, and might have fallen had Alastair not caught him with an arm slung around his chest.

"Get away from me, you disgusting great lump," said Belial; James could feel the words scratch their way out of his throat, laced with hateful venom. "Stupid as pigs, you Nephilim. Touch me again and you die."

James felt sick at the look on Thomas's face—hurt, horrified betrayal. But the look Alastair gave James was different. Cold and furious, yes, but narrow with realization.

"That's not James, Tom," he said. "Not anymore."

Thomas paled. With every part of him, James wanted to stay, to somehow explain. But what was there to say? Alastair was right, and besides, Belial had already begun to turn away, dismissing Thomas and Alastair both.

He could try to force it, James thought. Make Belial turn back. A tiny thought, a whisper. But no. Not yet. It was too early. He pushed the thought down, forced himself to be calm, forced himself not to think about what it would mean if his plan didn't work. That not only would Belial destroy everyone James loved, he would do it with James's own hands, and James would see their fear, their pain, their pleading up close, through his own eyes.

Control yourself, James thought. *Do as Jem taught you. Control. Calm. Hold tight to who you are, inside.*

As the abbey rose in front of them, a mass of gray stone surmounted by towers, James felt another lick of horror down his spine. He watched, through eyes he could not close, as Belial approached the cathedral. There were Watchers in the streets, drifting in and out of Belial's path, falling in behind him as he went. They circled like ghosts as he made his way across the Sanctuary, past the tall column of the War Memorial, and entered the abbey through the vaulted stone archway of the Great West Door, its ancient wooden panels flung wide open to receive him.

To James's surprise, the Watchers did not follow Belial through the door. They waited outside the cathedral, clustered by the stone benches in the archway like dogs tied up outside a shop. Of course they could not come in, James thought; they were demons, and this was a holy place. But even as he thought it, he heard Belial's laughter.

"I know what you're imagining, and it's wrong," Belial said. "There are no holy places in London now, no space my influence does not touch. I could fill this ancient cathedral with all the demons in Pandemonium. They could desecrate the altar and spill their filthy blood upon the floor. But that would not serve my intentions, which are far more honorable than *that*."

James did not ask what Belial's intentions were; he knew it would mean another round of gloating. Instead, he said, "You wish to make sure you're not interrupted. You've set them outside, like guard dogs, to keep away anyone who might try to stop you."

Belial snorted. "There is no one who might try to stop me. There are your foolish little friends who stayed in London, of course, but there are too few of them to make any difference. The Watchers will see to them handily."

He sounded sure of himself in a way that made James cold inside. He took in the abbey uneasily. He had been here before, of course; it was always a strange experience to walk through the peaceful space, echoing with the quiet voices of tourists and those at prayer. To see the endless memorials and chapels dedicated to the heroes of what mundanes called Britain. No Shadowhunters were mentioned. No battles against demons were recorded. Nobody here knew what he knew: that the world had almost been destroyed as recently as 1878, that his parents had saved it before either had even turned twenty.

Now he strode through the empty nave, Belial's boots echoing against the tombstones embedded in the floor. Ghostly light from the clerestory windows illuminated the gold bosses that studded the ribs of the vaulted roof, a hundred feet above, and filtered down in dusty rays past shadowed arches upheld by massive fluted stone pillars. Behind the arches, tall stained-glass windows threw colored patterns on the myriad plaques, tombs, and memorials that lined the abbey's ancient walls.

Belial came to a sudden stop. James was not sure why—they had not reached the High Altar yet, but were in the center of the nave. Here were long rows of empty wooden pews, lit by tall wrought-iron candlesticks in which burning tapers flickered. Past the pews was an ornately carved and decorated screen and beyond that, the tiered stalls and gilded arches of the empty choir. The emptiness of the place was vast, deathly; James could not escape the feeling they were making their way through the bare rib cage of some long-dead giant.

"Kaal ssha ktar," Belial breathed. James did not know the words: the

language was guttural, sour. But he felt the anger that coursed through Belial: a bitter, sudden rage.

"James," Belial said. "I am learning some things that are making me quite upset."

Learning them how? James wondered, but there was no point speculating. Belial was a Prince of Hell. It was reasonable to assume he could hear the whisperings of the demons who served him, that he could read patterns in the universe invisible to mortals such as James.

"These friends of yours," Belial went on, his voice in James's head growing shriller, almost painful. "I mean, *really*. I offered them mercy. Do you know how rare it is for a demon to offer mercy? Much less a prince of demons? I lowered myself for their sake. For your sake! And how do they repay me? They sneak about my city, they do their best to disrupt my plans, and worst of all, my own granddaughter creeps into Edom with that girl who bears Cortana—"

"I knew it," James breathed. And he *had* known—he had been sure, somehow, that Cordelia would come after him, would find a way. And it did not surprise him at all that Lucie had not left her side.

"Oh, be quiet," snapped Belial. "If it weren't for Lilith, always interfering—" He broke off, seeming to exert control over himself with some effort. "It hardly matters," he said. "They arrived in Idumea too late to snatch you away from me. Their bones will whiten in the sun of Edom, along with those of your *parabatai*. And now . . ."

He stalked forward, passing through the choir, into the center of the abbey, between the north and south transepts. The cathedral, like most, had been built to resemble a cross: the transepts were galleries that formed the cross's arms. High above, two enormous rose windows glowed in jeweled shades of blue, red, and green; before them a set of shallow steps led up to a dais, on which was another carved screen with two doors. A table bearing a large gold cross and draped in richly embroidered cloth stood between them.

"Behold." Belial seemed to have forgotten his troubles; his voice was thick with glee. "The High Altar of my coronation."

Placed before the altar was a heavy, high-backed oak armchair with legs carved to resemble gilded lions. With a sense of nausea, James remembered seeing it on display during a visit here, long ago. The Coronation Chair of England.

"Do you know," Belial said, "that this chair has been used to crown the king of England for six hundred years?" James didn't answer. "Well, did you?" Belial demanded.

"I wouldn't think that six hundred years would impress a Prince of Hell," James said. "Isn't that but the blink of an eye for one who saw the world born?"

"You miss the point, as usual." Belial sounded disappointed. "It's not what six hundred years means to me. It's what it means to *mortals*. It is the desecration of things held holy and significant by human souls which is so very delicious. By crowning myself here, I snatch hold of the soul of London. It shall never leave my grasp, once this is done."

Belial ascended the steps—wincing, as the wounds in his side sent a stab of pain through James's body—and flung himself into the chair. Its back was too high, the seat hard and uncomfortable, but James doubted that Belial cared.

"Now, I know what you're thinking," Belial said in a singsong voice, as if he were teaching a history lesson to a small child. "The king of England can only be crowned by the archbishop of Canterbury."

"That," said James, "is *not* what I was thinking."

Belial ignored this. "You would think there would be plenty of them here," Belial said, "with all the crypts below us. But most of them are interred in Canterbury Cathedral. One has to go all the way back to the fourteenth century to find an archbishop buried here in Westminster. Right over there, in fact." He gestured behind him, toward one of the transepts. "Which provides an excellent opportunity for you to witness the power I have gained. So much, just from being here, on Earth, in your body! Out there in the heavens, or deep in Hell, my power is a pinprick of light, a star among other stars. Here—it is a bonfire."

As Belial said the word "bonfire," a wave of what felt like heat tore through James. For a moment, he thought he was truly burning, that Belial had found some way to harness the fire of Hell to burn his soul away. Then he realized it was not fire at all, but power—the power Belial had spoken of, tearing through his veins, the vast and terrifying power that had been Belial's goal, all this time.

A deafening scraping noise shattered the stillness of the cathedral. It sounded as if stone were being ripped apart like paper. It went on and on, shuddering and grinding. Belial curled James's mouth into a pensive smile, as though he were listening to beautiful music.

The sound stopped abruptly with a crash, as if something massive had fallen to the ground. A wave of cold air blasted through the abbey, air that carried with it the stench of tombs and rot.

"What," James whispered, "have you done?"

Belial chuckled, as around the nearest pillar came shuffling the corpse of a man, one bony hand wrapped around a carved ivory shepherd's crook. Some flesh still clung to his bones, and some long, yellowing hairs to his skull, but he was far more skeleton than flesh. He wore robes that were tattered and stained, but horribly similar to the ceremonial white tunic and gold-embroidered chasuble that James had last seen in a newspaper photograph of King Edward's coronation.

He reached the foot of the dais. The tomb stench hung on the air as his grinning mouth and hollow eyes turned toward Belial. He slowly inclined his skull in a gesture of obedience.

"Simon de Langham, the thirty-fifth archbishop of Canterbury," Belial announced. "After the Norman conquest, of course." James felt his own face stretch as Belial grinned down at the skeleton of de Langham. "And now, I believe, the ceremony can begin."

Anna had felt such a rush of relief at seeing the Shadowhunters outside the doors of the Iron Tombs that she had come as close as she ever had in her life to fainting. The witchlight lanterns had become a pattern of swirling stars, the ground the tilting deck of a ship beneath her feet. Ari had taken hold of her arm, steadying her as the Shadowhunters approached.

"Haven't eaten," Anna had said gruffly. "It's making me light-headed."

Ari had just nodded. Lovely Ari, who understood Anna had nearly fainted with relief, but would never press her to admit it.

Her dazed state continued even as the Shadowhunters reached them, which was probably how, while Ari walked alongside her mother,

Anna had allowed herself to be seized by Eugenia. Dressed in gear and looking thrilled by all the excitement, she chattered continuously for the entire trip back through the Silent City. Anna liked Eugenia and normally enjoyed her gossiping, but she was trying to concentrate on navigating them all back to London successfully. Anna suspected she was only hearing every other sentence, which was giving her a rather patchwork sense of Eugenia's report on the situation in Idris.

There was a great deal about how angry the Council had been when they'd realized Anna and the others had remained behind in London, which did not bother Anna, and that both Aunt Tessa and Uncle Will had cried when they realized that James and Lucie were trapped in London, which did. Apparently Sona had comforted them, and told them her children were also still in London, but it was because only they could defeat Belial; it was their hour to be warriors, and the hour for their parents to be strong for them. Oh, and Sona had had her baby, it seemed—"Right during the speech about warriors?" Anna was puzzled, but Eugenia, exasperated, said no, it had been the next day, and unrelated to the speech.

Anna missed a great deal of detail after that, because they were emerging from the Path of the Dead, along the narrow corridor between CROSSKILL and RAVENSCROFT. As they passed the Pavilion of Truth, Eugenia was telling her about how Uncle Will and Aunt Tessa had been tested by the Mortal Sword and found innocent of complicity with Belial, but that Jesse's true identity had been revealed, which had added intensity to the Inquisitor's insistence that the Herondales believed they were a law unto themselves and must be punished. Anna gathered that there had been a great deal of shouting after that among the Council in Idris, but she'd returned to focusing on finding the way out.

They were almost to the Wood Street exit when Eugenia said, ". . . and you wouldn't believe what Charles did! Right in the middle of the Council meeting! Poor Mrs. Bridgestock," Eugenia added, shaking her head. "Everyone is certain the Inquisitor won't keep his job, not after Charles's confession."

"Confession?" Anna said sharply, startling Eugenia. "What did he say?"

"It was so terribly *awkward*," said Eugenia. "No one wanted to look at the Inquisitor—"

"*Eugenia*. Please attempt to locate the point. What did Charles say?"

"He stood up at the council meeting," Eugenia said. "I think someone else was still talking but he just spoke over them. He said very loudly that the Inquisitor had engaged in *blackmail*. Of him! Of Charles! It was part of an attempt to take control of the London Institute."

Anna gave Eugenia a sidelong glance. "Did it happen to be revealed . . . what it was Charles was being blackmailed about?"

"Oh, yes," Eugenia said. "He fancies men. As if that ought to matter, but I suppose it does to some people." She sighed. "Poor Charles. Matthew always was the braver of the two of them, though no one could see it."

Anna was stunned. She glanced back over her shoulder at Ari, who had clearly overheard; she looked just as surprised as Anna felt. She supposed they had both given up on the idea that Charles might at some point do the right thing. And yet—didn't Anna believe that she herself had become a better person in the last months? Wasn't it possible to change?

Up ahead of them Anna saw a flagstone floor, a familiar set of stone stairs leading up. She began to quicken her steps, hurrying toward the exit—somehow they'd all have to crawl out of the narrow hole in the tree trunk—when a soft *plouf* sound startled her. A sheet of parchment paper had appeared in the air; it drifted down into her hands.

A fire-message.

The paper felt warm to the touch as she unfolded it with a sense of amazement—it was one thing to hear that the fire-messages had worked, and another to see it happen for herself. She didn't recognize the spiky handwriting but suspected it was Grace's. She had written only a few lines:

Anna. The moment you return to London, come immediately to Westminster Abbey. Belial is here, and the Watchers have gathered. The battle has begun.

Cordelia had braced herself for a terrible trip through the Portal between worlds: a whirlwind of darkness stealing her breath, as it had been when Lilith had sent her through to Edom.

But it was far more ordinary; she was caught and carried through a brief darkness, as if on a current of air, before being deposited onto the familiar pavement of her beloved London. Of course, she thought, straightening up and looking around for Lucie and Matthew. This was how Belial himself traveled. It was a reminder how much more power he had in Edom than Lilith, now.

She saw Lucie first, gazing around at their surroundings. They had arrived in the deserted street, looking across at St. James's Park. Shadows clustered thick under the trees, and the frozen hedgerows moved with something that was not wind. Cordelia shuddered and turned to look for Matthew: he was staring at his surroundings in horror.

"This," he said in a strangled voice, "is what Belial's done to London?"

Cordelia had nearly forgotten. Neither James nor Matthew had seen this dark version of London before. Neither had seen the abandoned carriages in the street, the dense, murky clouds that churned the air like foul water, the dead-looking sky ripped through with scarlet wounds of lightning.

"It's been like this since you left," said Cordelia. "The mundanes and Downworlders are all under some kind of enchantment. The streets have been mostly empty—except for the Watchers."

Lucie was frowning. "Listen—do you hear that?"

Cordelia listened. Her hearing felt sharper, better than it had, and she realized with relief: her runes were working again. She could hear the surge of incipient thunder overhead, the sough of the wind, and over them, the unmistakable sound of battle—of human cries and the crash of metal striking metal.

She ran toward the noise, Matthew and Lucie beside her. They raced down Great George Street and turned onto Parliament Square. Before them rose the great cathedral of Westminster. Though Cordelia had never been inside, she knew its outlines from a thousand history books, photographs, and drawings: there was no mistaking the honeycombed front window, framed by thin Gothic towers and spires connected by soaring stone arches.

In front of the cathedral's Great West Door, sprawling across the empty courtyard north of the Dean's Yard Gatehouse, a battle was taking place. White-robed Watchers with their vicious black staffs battled back and forth with at least three dozen Shadowhunters. As they raced across the empty street, Cordelia searched the roiling crowd, her heart leaping as she saw the friends she and Lucie had left behind—Anna and Ari cutting through a knot of Watchers near the abbey entrance, Thomas and Alastair flanking a single Watcher by the fence—and there were Grace and Jesse near the gatehouse. Jesse was holding off a Watcher with the Blackthorn sword; as Cordelia watched, Grace reached into a large bag and threw something that exploded at the Watcher's feet. Smoke and sparks occluded her view after that, but she heard Lucie mutter, "Oh, good *work*," and thought, with some amazement—

They were all still alive. They were all still fighting. And not just them, but others—Eugenia, Piers, Rosamund, even Flora Bridgestock and Martin Wentworth. Whatever else had happened, their friends *had* made contact with the Clave. They *had* successfully led Shadowhunters to London to fight. It was nothing short of a miracle.

It would all be for nothing, of course, if Belial could wield the power he had claimed he would have in James's body. If James could not be saved.

"But what are they doing?" Lucie wondered aloud as they drew closer to the battle. Cordelia understood her confusion. The Shadowhunters were clearly more precise fighters than the Watchers, but they were moving oddly, dancing around the Watchers rather than attacking head-on. Thomas swung a broadsword—not the blade edge, but the flat of it, knocking a Watcher to the ground. She craned her head to see what happened next, but the battle surged like a wave, blocking off her view.

"Let me see," Matthew said, and began to clamber up the side of a tall granite pillar in the courtyard's center—a war memorial. He peered out, shading his eyes with one hand, and shouted down to Lucie and Cordelia, but the wind had come up again and all Cordelia heard was the word "Chimeras."

"Cordelia!" It was Alastair, who turned to start toward them then swung around as a Watcher made a beeline for Rosamund. She plunged a seraph blade into its chest, sending it staggering back; Alastair, behind it, whipped his *shamshir* in a cutting blow across the back of its neck, slicing away its hood.

The Watcher fell to its knees. Cordelia reached for Cortana, then stopped herself; it would do no good to summon Lilith now. She had to find Belial first. She was forced to do no more than stare as the Watcher shuddered, its body twisting as something with long, arachnoid legs began to emerge from the back of its neck.

A Chimera demon. It burst free of the Silent Brother's body, hissing as it scuttled past Alastair—and was impaled immediately by Thomas's sword. As it spasmed, Rosamund hopped over its dying body, her eyes shining.

"*There* you are!" she cried, as if wondering where Lucie, Cordelia, and Matthew were had been taking up all her spare time. "I was *so* surprised when none of you came through the York Gate! Have you really been hiding out in London this whole time? How frightfully exciting!"

Matthew sprang down from the memorial, landing lightly on the balls of his feet. "We're looking for James." She looked surprised. Matthew said, more slowly, "Have you seen James?"

"Well," Rosamund said cautiously, "Piers said he's gone into Westminster Abbey and apparently he's trying to crown himself king of England. I *really* don't know what's gotten into him."

"Rosamund!" It was Thomas. He was in gear, his sandy hair disheveled, a bruise rising on his cheek. "We need you by the door. The Watchers are clustering around Eugenia." Rosamund gave a tiny shriek and, without another word, ran off. "Eugenia is fine," Thomas said the moment Rosamund was out of earshot. "She won't mind the help, I'm sure, but—you're *back*!" He gazed back and forth between the three of them as though he couldn't believe what he was seeing. "You're *all* back! And you're safe." He grasped Matthew by the arm. "I thought we'd lost you, Math. We all thought we'd lost you."

"What's going on?" Lucie said, staring after Rosamund. "How did you get everyone *here*? I mean, not everyone, it's rather an odd group, but still—"

"Grace and Jesse managed to make the fire-messages work," Thomas said, looking anxiously back over his shoulder at the fighting. "They sent them to Idris—I gather this was the group in the Council

Room at the time, so they got the messages first. They came in through the Iron Tombs, the same way the Watchers did. More are on the way. Shadowhunters, I mean, not Watchers."

"What are they doing?" Matthew said. "It's a strange manner of fighting they've chosen."

"There's only one way we've found to defeat the Watchers. There's a symbol on the backs of their necks that binds the Chimera demon to them. You can't see it with the hoods of their robes up. If you destroy it, the Chimera is forced out. So you have to try to get behind them—which isn't easy." Thomas thrust his hand out. "Here's the symbol. I wanted to be able to show people what it looked like."

Cordelia looked at the scrawl on his open palm. It resembled the sigil of Belial that she had come to know well, but with a kind of hook protruding from it.

To Cordelia's surprise, Lucie's eyes went wide. "I have to get to Jesse," she said. "There's something I must tell him." She began to back away, drawing the axe from the belt at her waist.

"Lucie—" Cordelia began.

"I *have* to," Lucie said, shaking her head almost blindly. "The rest of you, get to James—as fast as you possibly can—"

And she took off running, zigzagging through the edge of the crowded battle, heading for the gatehouse that stood at an angle to the cathedral entrance. Cordelia itched to go after her—but Lucie was right. The most pressing concern here was James. James, and Belial.

She turned back to Thomas. "Is James really inside the abbey?"

"Yes," said Thomas. He hesitated. "You know it's not James, though, right? I—encountered him." He shuddered. "It's Belial, using James's body. To what end, right now, I cannot say."

"We know it's Belial," said Matthew. "We have to get to him. All these Watchers, here—" He gestured at the battle. "They're trying to keep us away from him, from the inside of the abbey. And specifically, they're trying to keep Cordelia and Cortana away."

"We've been trying to get inside," Thomas said. "The Watchers won't let us anywhere near the door."

"There has to be another way in," said Cordelia. "The cathedral is huge."

Matthew nodded. "There are other ways. I know a few." He straightened up. "We need to gather everyone—"

Thomas seemed to know exactly what Matthew meant by "everyone." "First, we should get Cordelia away before one of the Watchers notices her," he said.

"Cordelia and I will go," said Matthew. "Tom, get the group together and meet us around the corner at Great College Street."

Thomas looked at Matthew with a slightly curious expression. Then he nodded. "And then we'll get to James?"

Cordelia put her hand on the hilt of Cortana. "And then we'll get to James."

For the third time, Ari put her foot on the Watcher's chest and, in one clean move, slid her *khanda* out of its body. She tried to catch her breath. She hadn't been able to get behind the Watcher yet, and she knew it would only get up again, but she appreciated the moment's rest while she waited for it to recover. Before it could, though, she felt a tap on her shoulder. She whirled around, ready to strike—but it was Thomas, wearing an urgent expression. "Ari, quick—come with me."

Ari didn't ask questions. If Thomas looked this desperate, he had a reason for pulling her out of the battle. As they shoved their way through the thrashing, fighting crowd, he let her know—shouting in between ducking through skirmishes—that Cordelia and Matthew and Lucie had returned, and that there was a plan for getting into the cathedral. He didn't explain further, but the relief that their friends were back—and that there was *any* sort of plan—was enough to keep Ari pushing forward.

More Shadowhunters arrived, pouring into the triangular courtyard just as Ari and Thomas were leaving, but she had no time to stop and see if there were any familiar faces. She and Thomas were already running down the street, headed around the side of the cathedral. There they found the others waiting: Alastair, Cordelia, Matthew, and Anna. Thomas immediately went up to Alastair—who was sporting quite a few bruises and cuts; there had been no time to stop for healing runes—and kissed him. Ari wanted to do the same to Anna, but decided to wait, given the ferocious light of battle in Anna's eyes.

"But why?" Cordelia was saying. She looked more grimy than Ari had ever seen her—her boots were dusty, her gear scratched, and there was dust in her dark red hair. "Why on earth would Belial be in the abbey trying to crown himself king?"

"Indeed," Anna said, "I would not have thought that would be his priority. But Piers managed to get a look inside. James—*Belial*—has the Coronation Chair up on the High Altar, and at least some of the crown jewels as well."

"He also," said Alastair, "appears to have an archbishop of Canterbury."

"He's kidnapped the archbishop of Canterbury?" Ari said, horrified. She wasn't entirely sure what an archbishop did, but it certainly seemed outside the bounds of propriety to kidnap one.

"Worse." Anna looked grim. "He's raised one from the dead. The very, *very* dead. And is attempting to have him do the honors."

"Will it make some kind of difference to his power?" Thomas asked. "Crowning himself? Does it solidify his hold over London?"

"It must," Alastair said. "But most significantly, this may be our last chance to get Cordelia near enough to him to—"

"But she can't mortally wound him," Anna interrupted before Alastair could say it. "Not without killing James."

There was an awful silence. "James told Matthew I had to get as close to him as I could," Cordelia said. "And I trust him. If that's what he wanted me to do—"

"James would be willing to sacrifice himself," Thomas said in a low voice. "We all know that. But we can't—we can't lose another—"

Anna looked away.

To Ari's surprise, it was Matthew who spoke. He stood with his back straight, and there was something very different about him. As if Edom had changed him—not just that he was thinner, and exhausted-looking, but as if the light in his eyes, always there, had changed in its quality. "He would not consider this a sacrifice," he said. "He would not want to live with Belial possessing him. If there was no other way out, he would take death as a gift."

"*Matthew,*" Cordelia said softly.

Anna's eyes flashed. "You're his *parabatai*, Math. Surely you can't be arguing for his death."

"I don't want to," Matthew said. "I know I might not survive it myself. But he asked me to be his voice when he no longer had one. And I cannot betray that promise."

"Let me ask a question," Alastair said. "Does anyone have a *different* solution? One in which Belial doesn't murder everyone in London, and perhaps everyone in the world, *and* he stops possessing James, *and* James is never in danger? Because if so, speak up now."

There was another awful silence.

"I love James like a brother," said Thomas, "but Math is right. James would never want to live with Belial controlling his every move. That would be torture."

"James said to believe in him," Cordelia said. Her chin was up, her jaw set and determined. "And I do."

Anna nodded. "Fine. That's our plan, then. We get Cordelia inside the abbey, as close to Belial as possible." She drew a seraph blade, unlit, from her belt. "Now come along. There's an entrance around the back we can use to get in."

She gestured for the others to follow her down Great College Street, a narrow cobbled lane with tall, old-fashioned houses along one side. On the other side was the abbey, protected by a high stone wall topped with spikes. Halfway down the road, they found an alcove set into the wall, containing a small wooden door with no visible latch or knob.

Anna eyed it for a moment before launching a kick at it; it flew open with a sound like a gunshot. They all piled through the doorway and found themselves in a large monastic garden. It was a manicured lawn lined with flowerbeds, and utterly deserted. The blank windows of what seemed to be a dormitory overlooked it; Ari couldn't help but wonder what had happened to the students who normally lived in the abbey. Were they wandering the streets of London, blank-faced as all the other mundanes?

Together, the Shadowhunters darted silently across the grass and through an archway into a dimly lit tunnel that led into the abbey proper. There was no movement, not a single sign of anyone living.

They passed out of the tunnel into a small walled garden, open to the sky, which was a whirlpool of colliding gray-black thunderheads. A fountain at the garden's center trickled quietly into a stone bowl. Thomas paused for a moment, blinking in the unnatural light.

"If we do succeed," he said, "if everything goes back to some sort of normal, will the mundanes remember what happened? What all of *this* was like?"

No one answered; only Alastair touched Thomas gently on the shoulder before they started moving again. Ari noticed that they had grouped themselves loosely around Cordelia, as if they were the escorts of a warrior knight. It had been completely unconscious, but they had all done it.

They cut down a passageway that led into a larger, square garden, surrounded by arcaded walls. The Great Cloister. The dry grass square was surrounded by corridors paved with ancient, pitted stone slabs and lined with arched doorways.

In the silence, the creak of metal hinges was as loud as a shriek. Ari straightened as, from the darkened hallway they'd come from, the telltale white robes of the Watchers appeared. Apparently they'd been seen; apparently they'd been followed; apparently the Watchers could enter the church unimpeded. From the far corner behind them came half a dozen more, moving fast, swarming across the cloister's lawn toward them. There was nowhere to hide, nothing to duck behind.

Anna whirled on the others. "All of you, go. We have to get Cordelia to James. I'll hold these off."

Ari thought of Anna's face in the corridor, her fierce desperation, her need to stand against the Watchers—and her apparent desire to do it alone.

Cordelia seemed paralyzed, her hand on Cortana, her face a mask of indecision. "Anna—"

"Anna's right," Alastair said. "Cordelia. Let's go."

Ari said nothing as the others raced from the cloisters, through an arched doorway that led into the abbey. But she did not follow them—only gestured, when Thomas paused to look back at her, that they should go on ahead.

"I'm staying," she said, and Anna spun to stare at her. She held a seraph blade in one hand, and her expression was furious, her blue eyes blazing.

"Ari—you idiot—get *out* of here—"

But it was too late for her to protest; they were already surrounded by Watchers. Anna swore and raised her blade: "*Kadmiel!*"

The glow of the blade seared Ari's eyes; she reached over her shoulder and drew her *khanda* free. Her mind was already passing from the place of conscious thought to the place of battle, where her hands and body seemed connected to a force outside herself. An avenging, ruthless force.

She charged at the nearest Watcher. It raised its staff, but not fast enough. Her *khanda* punched into it with a sickening thud. But it only twisted away, leaving Ari's sword bright with blood, and the Watcher's wound already beginning to close.

Ari looked past it, meeting Anna's blazing eyes with her own. With her gaze, she told Anna what she needed; she could only hope Anna understood as Ari harried the Watcher back, landing blow after blow, making it retreat, maneuvering it into just the right position—

Behind the Watcher, Kadmiel blazed. Blade in hand, Anna tore away the Watcher's hood, and sliced her weapon across the back of its neck. It crumpled to the ground, its body spasming as the smaller Chimera demon began to worm its way free of the body that could no longer hold it.

Ari didn't wait for the other Watchers to react; she immediately leaped forward, catching one that was facing away from her, ripping away its hood, destroying the mark of Belial with a single sweep of her *khanda*. As it folded in on itself, she looked over at Anna in triumph—only to see that Anna, her bloodstained seraph blade held high, was staring past her with a look of sickening dismay.

Ari turned her head and saw why: more Watchers were pouring into the cloister. Too many for the two of them to possibly handle. What had been a risk before, fighting the Watchers on their own, was now far more. Now, it was suicide.

She caught Anna's eye. They looked at each other for a long moment before, together, they turned to face the demons.

* * *

There were four of them now. Matthew, Alastair, Thomas, and Cordelia.

They had fled from the Great Cloister, leaving Anna and Ari to face the Watchers. The thought of it made Thomas feel sick to his stomach—even though he knew both were excellent warriors. Even though he knew that in reality, they'd had no choice.

They had to get Cordelia to Belial.

It was Matthew who had taken over as their navigator; he led them through a heavy oak door along the south side of the great cathedral, swung them along the lower part of the nave, and then came back up along the north wall. They stayed out of sight of the central part of the church, the High Altar blocked by the choir screen. Which was nerve-racking, Thomas thought, since they all knew that was where Belial was, doing only the Angel knew what.

Whatever Belial was doing, it was quiet. They stopped near the north transept, listening, Thomas leaning silently against the cold stone wall for a moment. There were few things that made him feel small, but he was struck by the sheer vast height of the cathedral; the great rows of impossibly high arches going up and up, like an optical illusion.

He wondered if it was that enormity that had brought Belial here. Or something about the solemnity of it, the ceremonial effigies of soldiers and poets, royalty and statesmen, that lined the walls. He realized he was facing the large statue of a Major General Sir John Malcolm, a balding gentleman leaning on a stone sword. According to the inscribed marble pillar on which he stood, *his memory is cherished by grateful millions, his fame lives in the history of nations. This statue has been erected by the friends whom he acquired by his splendid talents, eminent public services and private virtues.*

Well, thought Thomas, I've *never heard of you.*

Sir John Malcolm scowled.

Thomas jerked bolt upright. He glanced to the right, at Alastair, and then at Matthew and Cordelia. None of them seemed to have noticed anything amiss. Cordelia and Matthew seemed to be assessing Cordelia's best route to the High Altar, and Alastair was looking away, frowning.

Thomas followed his gaze and realized that Alastair was staring at another monument, a huge bas-relief of multicolored marble, featuring Britannia, the emblem of Britain, holding a massive spear. An intense scarlet light had appeared within the stone spear, as if it were being heated from below.

"Alastair," Thomas whispered—just as, with a horrendous tearing sound, Sir John Malcolm stepped down from his pillar and raised his marble sword; it, too, was burning with an intense scarlet light.

Thomas lunged out of the way just as the sword came down, slamming into the floor of the abbey and sending up a cloud of stone dust. He heard Alastair call his name, and scrambled to his feet.

In seconds, chaos had erupted in the north transept. Britannia was tearing herself free of her imprisoning stone carving, her blank gaze fixed on Cordelia. Several knights in full armor began to rise from their sleeping positions atop their tombs.

Matthew whirled, white-faced. "*Run*, Cordelia," he said.

She hesitated—just as a Roman soldier bearing a gladius lurched around the corner. He made straight for her, and without a moment's thought, Matthew stepped into its way. He raised his seraph blade, and the stone gladius slammed into it, sending him skidding back several feet. Cordelia started toward him, and so did Thomas, but it was as if the statues sensed blood—Britannia bore down on him, raising her spear—

Something lunged into Matthew, knocking him out of the way. The spear jammed into the wall just behind where he'd been standing, sending chips of stone flying as he and Alastair rolled across the abbey floor.

Alastair. Alastair had saved Matthew's life. Thomas only had a moment to take that in before he spun to hiss at Cordelia, "Run—get to James—"

The knights who had torn free of their tombs were lurching toward them, their footsteps ringing through the cathedral. Thomas thought he heard distant laughter. *Belial.*

Cordelia stood very still for a moment. Her gaze swept over Thomas, over Matthew—rising now and lifting his sword once more—and finally over Alastair, who was back on his feet. It seemed as if she were trying to memorize all of them, as if she were praying she could hold this image in her head, and never forget it.

"Go," Alastair rasped, his eyes fixed on his sister. He was bleeding from a cut at his temple. "Layla. Go."

Cordelia ran.

Even though more Shadowhunters had arrived to join the battle in front of the abbey, Lucie could tell that the Nephilim were struggling against the Watchers.

She had not thought it would take so long to get to the gatehouse. She knew now how one could kill a Watcher, but she had no time to try. She had to reach Jesse. She used her small size as an advantage, slipping through the ranks of Nephilim, ducking low to scuttle across the courtyard. When she could, she slashed with her axe at the Watchers' feet and legs, making them stumble; she upended one that was in the middle of battling with Eugenia, leaving Eugenia staring around in surprise.

Many of the Nephilim she passed were strangers, and she could not help but feel a pang at not seeing her parents. At the same time, wasn't it better that they were somewhere else, out of danger? She knew they would hurry here as soon as they could. She hoped the battle would have ended by then. That she could help it end.

But to do that, she needed to reach Jesse.

At last, she burst out from the main clutch of the fighting, and found herself at the gatehouse. At first she saw neither Grace nor Jesse, just a swath of blackened pavement and a glimpse of the green Dean's Yard through the main archway.

She felt a moment of fear—had something happened to Jesse, to Grace? Had they moved elsewhere in the battle, and now she would have to search for them, when there was so little time?

And then she heard Jesse's voice. "Lucie, *look out!*" he called, and as she whirled, she realized he was behind her, and so was a Watcher, black staff in hand. She reached for her axe, but Jesse had his sword out and was harrying the Watcher back. Something tore past the Watcher and exploded behind it, sending up licks of flame that caught the hem of its robe.

Lucie glanced up to see Grace clinging to a cornice along the gatehouse wall. She was still holding her bag, and had something clutched in her other hand—another explosive, no doubt. Her gaze was fixed on Jesse, who had taken advantage of the Watcher's distraction to slice away its hood; he spun, lashed out with the sword, and caught it across the back of the neck.

The Watcher fell forward like a tree uprooted in a storm, making no attempt to cushion its fall. As its body began to spasm, the Chimera demon wriggled free through an eye socket—Lucie shuddered—and rotated its head swiftly, seeking a hiding place.

Lucie brought her axe down, slicing it in half. It made a sound like bone crunching underfoot, and vanished.

"*Lucie.*" Jesse caught her with his free arm, swinging her hard against his body. She could feel the hammering beat of his heart. He was breathing hard; he smelled of sweat and blood and leather. Shadowhunter smells. She looked up at him—his face was cut and bruised, his green eyes stunned as he searched her face—

"Get under the *gate*," Grace hissed from above. "You can't just stand around ogling each other during a battle—"

Jesse blinked as if snapped out of a dream. "That's good advice," he noted.

Lucie could only agree. She took hold of Jesse's arm and half dragged him into the shadows of the gateway: it was deep, almost a tunnel leading through to the Dean's Yard on the other side.

"Lucie." Jesse slammed his bloody sword into its scabbard and caught hold of her. He pulled her close, his back against the stone wall. She tossed her axe aside, taking hold of his gear jacket, clinging to him tightly. "I thought you were gone forever. I thought I'd lost you."

It seemed so long ago now, the night she'd left him, placing the folded note under his pillow. "I know," she whispered, wanting to lay her head against his chest. Wanting to touch his cheek, to tell him she hadn't spent a moment since without thinking of him, of getting back to him. But there was no time. "I know, and I'm sorry. But Jesse—I need you to hold me."

"I want to." He brushed his lips against her hair. "I'm furious at you, and desperately glad to see you, and I want to hold you for hours, but it's not safe—"

"Remember when I said I'd never seen the ghost of an Iron Sister or Silent Brother?" Lucie breathed. "That wherever they were voyaging, I'd never gone that far? Well, it was true I've never seen them. But I've *heard* them. I realize that now."

"Heard them? What—?"

"Every time I was with you, every time I touched you and I saw that darkness and heard those cries—Malcolm was wrong, I think. I don't believe being with you makes me closer to Belial, more vulnerable to him. I think because of what happened to you, it brings me closer to the other side. Where souls go, the ones who don't linger here."

Outside the archway, an explosive went off, scattering dirt and sending smoke drifting into their hiding space. Lucie's stomach turned over; Grace could hold off the Watchers for only so long.

"Jesse. The sign I kept seeing—it wasn't that it was Belial's symbol; the symbol was holding them back, keeping them imprisoned—"

"Lucie," he said quietly. "I don't understand."

"I know, and there's no time to explain." She pushed herself up on her toes, wrapping her arms around his neck. "Trust me, Jesse. Hold me. Please."

He pulled her close. She gasped in relief, pressing herself against him. "Well," he whispered against her hair, "if we're going to do this—"

And then he was kissing her. She hadn't expected it consciously, but it seemed her body had: she pushed up harder on her toes, her hand stroking the back of his neck, tasting dust and salt on his lips, and something sweet and hot beneath that. Her skin prickled with yearning, and then the surge of longing became a buzzing in her head. She felt the narrowing of her perception, darkness encroaching, tunneling her vision.

She closed her eyes. She was in the great darkness, the shimmer of stars in the distance. She gritted her teeth, even though she could no longer feel them, as she reached out. Reached out to hear them, the voices, the awful cries that had become so familiar. They swelled somewhere beyond her imagining, the cries of the lost, desperate to be found. Of the unknown, desperate to be recognized.

And she recognized them now. She knew exactly who they were. And though her own body was beyond her awareness, she cried out to them with her mind. "Iron Sisters! Silent Brothers!" she called. "My name is Lucie—Lucie Herondale. I want to help you."

The howling cries continued; Lucie had no way of knowing if she'd been heard or not. No way of knowing if she could reach them, but she had to try; she could only deliver her message and hope.

"I understand now what you've been trying to tell me," she called out. "Your souls are voyaging, but still you remember your bodies, still you might return to them one day. And Belial came and violated them—he stole you from the Iron Tombs and put his demons in your bodies to use as he wishes. He can be stopped. I swear he can be stopped. But you need to *help me.* Help me, please."

She paused. She could still hear the wailing in the distance. Had it grown louder? She could not tell.

"Fight back!" she cried. "Reclaim yourselves! If you thrust the demons from your bodies, I swear we know how to destroy them! You will be freed! But you must *try*!" The cries had died away; there was a great silence now. She floated in it, in the darkness and the silence, utterly untethered. She had gone further than she had ever gone before, reached further than she had ever reached. Whether she could return or not, Lucie did not know. She raised her face to the stars, that were not really stars, and said, "We need you. The Nephilim need you. We have fought so hard."

Her vision had begun to dim, her consciousness slipping away. Lucie whispered, *"Please come back to us, please,"* and then her mind was swallowed up by darkness, and she could say no more.

35

Winged with Lightning

But see the angry Victor hath recalled
His ministers of vengeance and pursuit
Back to the gates of Heaven: The sulfurous hail
Shot after us in storm, overblown hath laid
The fiery Surge, that from the precipice
Of Heaven received us falling, and the thunder,
Winged with red lightning and impetuous rage.
—John Milton, *Paradise Lost*

Cordelia ran.

She ran from the north transept of the abbey, circling around the tomb of Edward the Confessor, and burst into the nave, where the choir turned into long rows of pews, all facing the High Altar.

Where Belial sat, sprawled in the Coronation Chair. He was still, one hand under his chin, his gaze fixed on her.

Holding Cortana crosswise, as if it were a golden shield, she began to walk toward the High Altar. She kept her back straight, her face expressionless. Let Belial watch her approach. Let him puzzle at her calm; let him wonder what she had planned.

Let him be afraid. She hoped he was afraid.

She was not afraid. Not now. She was breathless. Stunned. She had known it was true, since they had found Matthew in Edom, and he had told them what happened. But she had not been able to imagine it. Not until this moment, as she strode through the center of Westminster Abbey as if she were going to her own coronation. Not until this moment, when she looked at the High Altar, and saw James.

James. Even with everything she knew, part of her wanted to rush up the steps and throw her arms around him. He would *feel* like James; his heart would beat like James's did. His body would feel like James's body against hers, his hair like James's if she knotted her fingers into it; he would sound like James if he spoke.

Or would he? She didn't know. He had asked Matthew to be his voice; was James's voice, even the sound of it, gone forever? Would she never hear him say *Daisy, my Daisy*, ever again?

He smiled.

And it felt as if he had slapped her.

James's face—the one she could conjure up so easily with her eyes closed, the soft mouth and high cheekbones and lovely golden eyes—was set in a sneer, his expression a mixture of hatred and fear, contempt and—amusement. The sort of amusement that made her think of a schoolboy torturing an insect.

Nor were his eyes golden now. Belial's eyes, in James's face, were dark silver, the color of tarnished shillings.

He raised his hand. "Stop," he said in a voice that was nothing like James's voice, and Cordelia—stopped. She had not meant to do so, but it was as if she'd hit a wall of glass, an invisible magical barrier. She could not take one more step. "That's close enough."

Cordelia tightened her grip on Cortana. She could feel the sword tremble in her hand; it knew they had a purpose here.

"I want to talk to James," Cordelia said.

Belial smiled, a twisted expression nothing like James's smile. "Well," he said. "Don't we all want *things*." He snapped his fingers, and out of the shadows at the side of the altar lurched a horrific figure—an animated corpse, a frame of yellowed bones topped with a grinning skull. It wore an archbishop's miter and a tarnished chasuble that had once been richly embroidered with gold; the vestment was now mostly rotted through, and through the holes Cordelia could see the archbishop's ribs, hung with stringy bits of leathery flesh. In its hands it held a purple-and-golden crown, studded with gems of all colors.

She was reminded, horribly and strangely, of the play on the stage of the Hell Ruelle, the crowd applauding the peculiar coronation . . .

"I, for instance," said Belial, "wish to be crowned king of London by Simon de Langham here."

The dead archbishop wobbled.

Belial sighed. "Poor Simon; we *do* keep getting interrupted by your idiot friends. And now, of course, by you." His silver gaze slid over her like water. "I can't say it's been the coronation of my dreams."

"I don't see why you want a coronation, anyway," said Cordelia. "I thought things like royalty, and kings and queens, only mattered to mundanes."

She had not meant it to be particularly insulting, but to her surprise, rage flashed across his face. "Please," he said. "I am a *Prince* of Hell, do you think that title means nothing?"

Yes, Cordelia thought, but didn't speak.

"I am not going to accept a *demotion*," he snapped, settling back against the chair. "Besides, there is magic in ritual. This will cement my hold on London, and eventually on all of England. And after that, who knows?" He grinned brightly, his mood seemingly restored. "With this new body of mine, all is possible. There is no kingdom on Earth that would not fall before me, if I set my mind to it." He let his head fall back, James's cloudy dark hair falling charmingly over his forehead. Cordelia felt sick. "Oh, James is *miserable*." He chuckled. "I can feel it. To behold you here causes him an agony that is, I assure you, delicious. It's fascinating, the way you human beings *hurt*. Not physically, of course, that's all boringly familiar, but the *emotional* torment. The anguish of feeling. It is unique among animals."

"They say angels weep," said Cordelia. "But I suppose you've forgotten."

Belial narrowed his silver eyes.

"And speaking of physical pain," she went on. "The wounds given you by Cortana. The wounds given to you by *me*. They still hurt, do they not?"

Above her, Cordelia heard a sudden susurration of wings. She looked up sharply to see an owl flap through the arched galleries high above them.

"The wounds you have," she said, "will never close. They will burn forever." She turned Cortana, so that the engraved side of the blade faced the altar. *I am Cortana, of the same steel and temper as Joyeuse and Durendal.* "Unless I heal them."

"*Heal* them?" he echoed sharply, so sharply that the archbishop, apparently in confusion, stepped forward with the royal crown. Looking annoyed, Belial plucked the crown from the skeleton's grasp and waved him away. "How can you—ah." The shock faded from his expression. "Because it is a paladin's blade. I too have heard the stories that claim such a power. But they are just stories."

"Stories are not lies," Cordelia said. She raised her left hand. Then she brought the edge of her sword against it, the blade cool against her skin. She pressed, and it bit in, slicing open her palm. Blood welled from the cut and fell in thick drops to the marble floor.

She held up her injured hand to show Belial, who did not react, only continued watching her. Then she lay the flat of the blade upon the palm and drew it slowly across her hand. When she lowered the sword, the wound was gone, her skin showing no mark or scar, not even a white line where the cut had been. She flexed her hand a few times and then held it up again for Belial to inspect.

"Stories," Cordelia said, "are true."

"Interesting," Belial murmured, as though to himself, but his eyes stayed hooked to Cortana, even as Cordelia lowered the sword. He looked hungry, she thought. Hungry for the end of pain.

"This is the blade Cortana," Cordelia reminded him, "forged by Wayland the Smith. There is no other like it, and it can heal as well as harm. But it can only do so in the hand of its rightful bearer. You cannot simply kill me and use the sword to heal yourself."

Belial was silent for a long moment. Finally he said, "What is your proposal, then?"

"Depart from James's body," Cordelia said. She knew it was a ridiculous suggestion, but she had to keep him talking. James had said she needed to get close to him, and here she was, desperately searching Belial's face, looking for any sign of James at all.

Belial gave her a sour look. "Your gambit is sillier than I thought. I have worked far too hard and planned far too long to give up this form. It has been my primary aim all this time. However," he added, "I am not unwilling to negotiate. If you heal my wounds, I will spare your life."

Perhaps James had imagined things would be different, Cordelia thought. That he would not be trapped as he was. Or perhaps all he had wanted was for her to get close enough to kill him.

The thought made her sick. But she knew it was a possibility.

"I don't want my life spared," she whispered. "I want James."

"James is gone," said Belial dismissively. "No use being a child, crying for the toy you can't have. Think of all you have in your life, should you live." He furrowed his brow, clearly searching for anything he might consider a reason for Cordelia to keep on living. "You have a brother," Belial said thoughtfully. "And though I slew your father myself, your mother lives. And"—his eyes sparked—"what of your newborn brother? A baby who has yet to speak a word or take a step? A child who *needs* you."

He grinned loathsomely. Cordelia felt as though she had missed a step on a staircase, as if she were grasping at empty air. "The baby—?" She shook her head. "No. You're a liar. You—"

"Really, Cordelia," said Belial. He rose to his feet, the crown glittering in his hand. The light from the rose windows sparked fire from its gems as he raised it above his head. "You have made an offer you must know I will only refuse. Then you tell me I am a liar, which would suggest you are not interested in a negotiation. So, Cordelia Carstairs. Why are you *really* here? Just to watch me . . ." Belial smiled up at the crown. "Ascend?"

Cordelia raised her eyes to his. "I am here," she said, "because I believe in James."

Belial went still.

James, she thought. *If there is any piece of you there. If any part of you remains, trapped beneath Belial's will. Know that I have faith in you. Know that I love you. And nothing Belial can do can change that.*

And still, Belial was unmoving. It was not a natural sort of stillness, but looked as if he had been frozen in place by a warlock's spell. Then slowly, jerkily, his arms began to move, lowering themselves to his sides. He let go his hold on the crown, which fell heavily to the floor. Even more slowly, he raised his head and looked directly at Cordelia.

His eyes, she realized with a jolt—a jolt she felt at the very center of her soul—were gold.

"James?" she whispered.

"Cordelia," he said, and his voice, his voice was James's, the same voice that called her Daisy. "Give me Cortana."

It was the last thing she'd expected James to ask for—and the first thing Belial would have wanted. Belial was a master of lies. Surely he could change the timbre of his voice, sound like James in an effort to fool her . . . And if she chose wrong, she would doom her city and, ultimately, her world to ruin.

She hesitated. And heard Matthew's voice in her head: *He said you would know the right moment to act. And to believe in him.* She hadn't lied when she spoke before. She *was* here because she believed in James. She had to have faith, not only because James had told her to, but because she'd come this far on her own instincts and her belief in her friends. And there was no turning back.

She still could not move forward, could not walk to the High Altar. She drew her arm back and flung Cortana. She almost cried out as it hurtled away from her, spinning end over end, and James's hand shot out and caught it out of the air by the hilt.

He looked at her. His eyes were still gold, and full of sorrow.

"Daisy," he said.

And plunged the sword into his own heart.

All Shadowhunters believed that they would die in battle; indeed, they were raised from childhood to understand it as the *preferred* method of death. Ari Bridgestock was no different. She had always wondered what battle would be her last, but in the past few minutes, she had developed a strong feeling that it was going to be this one.

It was cold comfort that Anna was here with her. Anna was a great warrior, but Ari did not think that even a great warrior had a chance in this situation. There seemed an endless horde of Watchers, enough to overwhelm an army of Shadowhunters and still keep coming and coming.

They had decided without needing to discuss it aloud that there was neither time, nor room, for the subtle maneuvering necessary to destroy the possession runes. All they could do was beat back the tide, knocking down enough Watchers to give themselves some breathing space—only to see them rise to their feet again.

Anna was a long blur of movement, her ruby necklace gleaming against her chest like a drop of angelic blood. Her seraph blade moved so quickly in her hand that Ari's eye could not catch it—it seemed a silvery shimmer painted against the air. The thought appeared in Ari's mind: *I could accept dying here, right now, as long as it meant that Anna would live.*

Once she had had the thought, and knew in an instant that it was utterly true, everything became clearer. A new energy flowed into her; she redoubled her attack, using her *khanda* to harry a tall Watcher whose white robes were stained with blood. She plunged her blade into its chest.

And heard Anna scream her name. She twisted around, her blade still *in* the Watcher, and saw another of them rising up behind her, a once Iron Sister raising a barbed black staff to plunge it into Ari's back. Ari yanked her *khanda* free, leaving the first Watcher to sink to the ground, but there was no time—the second Watcher was upon her, the staff coming down—

The Watcher crumpled, hitting the ground with the force of a felled tree. The staff clattered from its hand. Ari looked immediately to Anna. Surely Anna had come from behind to injure the Watcher, to keep it from hurting Ari. And Anna *was* there, her seraph blade in hand, but she was still too far from the fallen Watcher to have touched it. Her face was a mask of shock and even fear. Ari had never seen her look afraid before.

"What on earth?" Anna whispered, and Ari realized *all* the Watchers were falling. Folding like puppets with cut strings, collapsing onto the bloodstained grass. And then, before either Anna or Ari had even lowered their weapons, came a terrible ripping sound. From the fallen bodies of the Iron Sisters and Silent Brothers the Chimera demons emerged: some crawling out of open mouths or eyes, one tearing its way free from an open wound in a shower of blood.

Ari backed up, half in revulsion, half readying herself to battle the Chimeras, as they emerged, chittering and blood-slicked, their fangs flashing. They were smaller than she'd imagined, the size of piglets, and she raised her *khanda* high—only to be startled when they turned to flee like a pack of rats, slithering and hopping across the damp grass of the cloister, scrambling up the walls to vanish onto the roof.

Silence fell. Ari stood over the bodies of the Silent Brothers and Iron Sisters, who lay as still as effigies. She could hear no sound from inside the abbey, nothing that explained what had just happened—had Cordelia reached James? Had Belial been killed? Something had happened, something huge—

"*Ari!*" Anna caught Ari by the arm, swinging her around so they faced each other. Anna had dropped her seraph blade; it sputtered in the grass like a dying candle, but she didn't seem to care. She touched Ari's face—Anna's hand was crusted with dried blood and dirt, but Ari leaned into the touch, into Anna. "I thought you were going to die," Anna whispered. "That we were both going to die." Her dark hair tumbled into her blazing blue eyes; Ari wanted nothing more in this moment than to kiss her. "And I realized—I would sacrifice myself in a moment. But not you. I could not bear to lose you."

"And I could not bear to lose you," Ari said. "So there will be no sacrificing yourself. For my sake." She let her *khanda* fall from her hand as Anna pulled her close; her hand stroked Ari's hair, which had come loose and fell about her face.

"You will not leave me," Anna said fiercely. "I want you to stay, with me, at Percy Street. I do not want you to move to some flat somewhere, with *sconces*—"

Ari was shaking her head, smiling; she could not believe they were having this conversation *now*, but when had Anna ever waited to say what she thought needed to be said?

She raised her face to Anna's; they were so close together she could feel the brush of Anna's eyelashes. "No sconces," Ari said. "No flats in Pimlico. Just us. Wherever you are is home to me."

Cordelia screamed.

The blade went into James with a sickening noise, the awful shearing of bone and muscle. Cordelia felt it through her body as if she were the one stabbed; as James sank to his knees, she threw herself at the invisible wall separating her from the High Altar, threw herself against it as if it were glass that could shatter, but it held her back, pinning her in place.

James was on his knees, his bloody hands locked around the hilt of Cortana. His head hung down; Cordelia couldn't see his face. His grip on the weapon tightened, his knuckles whitening. As Cordelia flung herself against the barrier that separated them, he wrenched savagely at the sword, and she could *feel* the blade shear against bone again as he pulled it free.

He gazed for a moment at the blade, slick with blood, before opening his hand to let it clatter to the floor. He raised his head and stared at Cordelia as the blood pulsed slowly from the wound in his chest.

His eyes were silver. As he spoke, blood bubbled to his lips; his voice was thick, but recognizable. Belial's voice.

"What," he said, his gaze flicking incredulously from the blade to his own bloody hands, "is this?"

"You're dying," said Cordelia. She found that she was no longer afraid of Belial. She was no longer afraid of anything. The worst that could happen had happened. Belial would die, and James with him.

"It's impossible," he said.

"It's not impossible," Cordelia said. "It's three wounds from Cortana."

There was a roaring sound in the distance, growing louder and louder. Cordelia could feel a trembling in the earth deep beneath her feet; off to the side, with a soft rattling sound, the dead archbishop collapsed into a dusty pile of rotted vestments and bones.

"A human soul could not overpower my will," Belial hissed. Blood ran down his chin. "My will is immutable. I am an *instrument of God*."

"No," said Cordelia. "You *were* an instrument of God."

Belial's whole face shook, his mouth trembling, and in that moment, Cordelia seemed to see through the illusion of James, to the angel that Belial had once been, before he had chosen power and war and the Fall. His silver eyes were wide and confused and full of a fear so complete it was nearly innocence. "I cannot die," he said, wiping the blood from his mouth. "I don't know how to die."

"Nor does anyone living," said Cordelia. "I suppose you will learn like the rest."

Belial slumped forward. And the roof of the abbey came off, or seemed to—it had been there, and now it was not, though there had been no sound of it ripping away, no breaking of stone. It was simply *gone*, and Cordelia stared up at a sky like a whirlpool—it had been black with opaque clouds, mazed with dark lightning, but the clouds were parting. She could see the gleam of blue, a clear cold sky, and then a shimmer—a ray of sunlight. It pierced the windows of the abbey and laid a shining golden bar across the stone floor.

Belial threw his head back. Above him, white clouds parted, illuminated by ice-bright winter sun, and with the light on his face he looked as if he were caught between agony and joy, a martyr's look. As he got to his feet, he seemed to step out of James's body, like a snake shedding its skin. James slid soundlessly to the floor of the altar, and Belial rose and stepped away, now unrecognizable. He was a burning dark light in the shape of a man, lifting his hands up, up toward the sky, toward the Heaven he had turned away from so very long ago.

"Father?" he said.

A spear of light broke through the clouds. It shot downward like lightning, like a flaming arrow, and plunged into Belial. He seemed to catch alight, his shadow burning, and he howled aloud in agony, *"Father, no!"*

But his cry was unheeded. As Cordelia stared in dazed shock, Belial was lifted into the air—he was writhing, struggling, his deep cries like thunder rolling—and carried thrashing into the sky.

The barrier that had been holding Cordelia back from the altar vanished. She raced up the crimson-slicked steps and flung herself down beside James.

He lay on his back, in a spreading pool of his own blood, his face very white. Her hand flew to his throat, her fingers pressing hard. She gasped.

He had a pulse.

Jesse slid to the ground, still holding Lucie. It had all happened suddenly: one moment he had been kissing her, her hand warm and familiar on the back of his neck.

The next, she had stiffened as if shot—and gone limp, a dead weight in his arms. He kept hold of her now, her head against his shoulder, his back pressed to the interior wall of the archway. She was alive, at least. Her breathing was shallow, and her pulse beat rapidly in her throat. Dust streaked her pale face. She felt fragile in his arms, light-boned as a bird.

"Luce," he whispered. With his free hand, he fumbled for his stele—one of the instruments Grace had adjusted so that fire-messages could be written with it—and scrawled a healing rune on Lucie's arm.

Nothing happened. The rune did not fade, but neither did Lucie's eyes open. Her blue eyes, that had haunted him as he walked the dark streets of London alone, a ghost who could not speak or be spoken to, who could not feel warmth or cold or pain. Lucie had brought feeling back into his existence: she had touched him and brought him to life. *I would give it all up*, he thought, staring desperately into her face, *just to make you all right.*

"Jesse." It was Grace, slipping into the darkness of the archway. "I'm—oh! Is she all right?"

"I don't know." Jesse looked up at his sister; it was strange to see her in gear, her white-blond hair twisted in a tight knot behind her head. "I don't . . ."

"Let me take her." Grace knelt down and held out her arms for Lucie. "I'm out of explosives. I'll watch Lucie; you'd better hold off any Watchers." There was something officious, almost doctorlike, in Grace's attitude; it reminded Jesse of Christopher, and he found himself gently easing Lucie over, so that she leaned against Grace, who took out her stele. "It's all right," she said, starting to draw another *iratze* on Lucie's arm. "I'll look after her."

Leaving Lucie was the last thing Jesse wanted to do, but Grace was right—without her explosives, the Watchers would find them here soon enough. He scrambled upright and caught up the Blackthorn sword.

The thick stone walls of the archway had muffled some of the noise of battle. It exploded into Jesse's ears the moment he stepped into the courtyard. The clang of weapons, the mixture of shouts and howls of pain and grief. Among the chaos of the fighting, he thought he glimpsed Will Herondale, and Tessa with him, battling Watchers, though he could not be sure—had they arrived in the last wave of Shadowhunters? Or was he seeing things? He could tell there were bodies on the ground: mostly Nephilim, a few Watchers. They were too hard to kill, he thought with a wave of despair.

He thought suddenly of Oscar. They had left Oscar at the Institute, safely locked in, though his howls of disappointment at being left behind had followed them to the gates. If they all died here, Jesse thought, who would take care of Oscar? Who would set him free?

Stop it, he told himself. He knew his thoughts were scattering with exhaustion and panic over Lucie. He had to focus on the battle in front of him, on the Watchers; one of them was turning toward him, an Iron Sister with a blank, unwavering stare—

Who went rigid, her eyes rolling back. As Jesse watched, sword in hand, she crumpled, her back arching even as the rest of her sprawled on the bloodstained ground. Her mouth gaped open, and a Chimera began to crawl out, pulling itself free with its feelers.

Someone shouted hoarsely. Jesse tore his gaze away from the fallen Watcher and realized—it was happening everywhere. One by one, the Watchers were toppling. One by one, the Chimera demons were emerging from their bodies, crawling and slithering and hissing, clearly furious to be so unceremoniously evicted from their hosts.

In the surge of the melee, Jesse could hear Shadowhunters shouting with joy—he saw the silver flash of seraph blades as the Nephilim attacked the Chimera demons; the stench of ichor was sour on the air. As the last Watcher fell, Jesse realized something else—a knot of the Chimera demons had gathered together and were headed straight for the gatehouse.

Lucie, he thought. He knew this was her doing: she had gone into the darkness, had called on the souls of the wandering Iron Sisters and Silent Brothers whose earthly forms had been possessed. And, it was clear, they had heard her. They had pushed back, tearing the Chimera demons out of their bodies, hurling them free to be slain by swords and seraph blades.

As the slavering Chimeras drew closer, Jesse saw the fury in their burning green eyes and thought: *They know.* That Lucie was to blame, that she had done this to them—he raised his sword, knowing that even though the Chimeras were relatively easy to defeat, he could not hope to dispatch a dozen of them at once—

"Throw me the sword, Blackthorn!"

Jesse wrenched his gaze away from the Chimeras—and stared in amazement. Halfway up the War Memorial was Bridget, wearing a flowered dress and an apron, her red curls flying, her face blazing with fury.

"I knew it!" Jesse yelled, "I *knew* you were still in London! But how? How did you escape Belial's enchantment?"

"No one tells me what to do!" Bridget shouted back. "The sword!"

So he threw the sword. It hurtled toward Bridget, who caught it out of the air and flung herself from the memorial, falling like a dropped anchor directly atop the Chimeras. As she began to hack at them viciously, Jesse snatched a seraph blade from his belt, whispered, *"Hamiel,"* and joined the battle alongside Bridget, slicing through a Chimera demon's torso with a feeling of vicious relief.

And then the sky above them tore in half.

His pulse was faint, but it was there, a rapid tap against her fingertips. James was alive.

Cordelia felt as if she'd swallowed fire. Her whole body came to life; she half lunged over James, catching up Cortana. With her free hand, she took hold of the hem of James's blood-wet shirt, and pulled it up: there, on the left side of his chest, was the slash of the wound he had dealt himself, raw and scarlet-edged.

She raised Cortana. Behind her, she heard footsteps—she glanced over her shoulder to see Matthew, Alastair, and Thomas approaching. She shook her head to say *stay back*, and they stopped a few yards away, their expressions horrified and uncertain as, with great care, Cordelia lowered her sword and laid its engraved blade along James's torso, the flat of it covering his wound, the hilt toward his hands. *Let him be the effigy atop the tomb of a knight,* she thought; let him be that warrior. He had wrought his will, and it had been more powerful than a Prince of Hell's.

There was a long moment of stillness as James lay unmoving, Cortana's golden blade gleaming against his bare, blood-slicked skin. Cordelia cupped his cold cheek in her hand, feeling the brush of his lashes against her palm.

"I am a paladin," she whispered. "This is my power. To wound, with justice. To heal, with love." She remembered long ago, holding a feverish James as he nearly tumbled into the shadow realm. She had clung to him as if, by force of will alone, she could keep him tethered to the world. "James," she said now, the same words she had said then, "you must hold on. You must. Don't go anywhere. *Stay with me.*"

James gasped. The sound went through Cordelia like lightning; Cortana flashed as his chest heaved with breath. His fingers twitched at his sides and slowly, slowly, he opened his eyes.

They were pure gold.

"Daisy," he said, his voice rough as sandpaper. He blinked up at the sky. "Am I—alive?"

"Yes," she whispered. Her mouth tasted like salt. She was laughing and weeping and touching his face: mouth, cheeks, lips, eyes. His skin was warm and flushed with color. "You're alive."

She bent to brush his mouth with hers. He winced, and Cordelia jerked back. "I'm sorry—"

"Don't be," he breathed, and glanced down. "It's just that there's a rather large sword on top of me . . ."

Cordelia caught hold of Cortana and moved it away; the wound below it had gone, though there was still a great deal of blood everywhere. She heard footsteps on the altar stairs. Turning, she saw it was Matthew, hurrying up the steps to fling himself down at James's side.

"You're all right," he murmured. A long look passed between him and James, one that told Cordelia that whatever had happened while they had been trapped in Edom had forged a new connection between them. Matthew's whole being seemed focused on James—which, Cordelia thought, was as it should be. "I felt it, you know," he said, brushing a lock of hair out of James's eyes. "My *parabatai* rune fading—" His voice caught. "And then I felt it return." He looked at Cordelia. "What you did—"

"Layla!" Alastair's voice rang out, sharp with warning.

Cordelia bolted to her feet. As she did, she felt a shadow sweep over her, and realized that the roof of the cathedral had reappeared just as swiftly as it had vanished. Above her rose its high arches, and before her, on the steps of the altar, stood Lilith.

* * *

Jesse had never seen or imagined anything like it—perhaps in old paintings of the visitations of the gods on Earth. The black clouds above seemed to collide with each other like the blades of swords, sending a reverberation through the sky louder than any thunder.

He staggered back as the ground heaved under him. A dozen jagged bolts of lightning, black as the staffs the Watchers had carried, arrowed down from the clouds: one struck the War Memorial, sending up a shower of sparks. Another struck the doors of the abbey, making them tremble. Jesse heard someone swearing loudly and was almost entirely sure it was Will.

And then another bolt, far closer, hurtled directly toward the gatehouse. Jesse staggered back as Bridget raised the Blackthorn sword, almost as if she could ward it off—

The lightning struck the sword full-on. The blade glowed for a split second, illuminated like a beacon, before it shattered apart. Bridget was hurled backward; she dropped the hilt of the broken sword and skidded across the ground as the clouds above began to peel backward.

Jesse started toward her, trying to keep his balance as the earth shook under him. Chimera demons were running wildly across the courtyard like maddened black beetles. Jesse thought he saw a dark shadow shoot upward from the abbey roof, hurtling toward the widening gap in the clouds above. He blinked, and it was gone—his eyes burned; light was streaming down, pure, golden sunlight, the kind he had nearly forgotten during all these long dark days.

He looked around. The courtyard was chaos. Chimera demons were bursting into flame as the sun touched them, running back and forth like flaming torches. Pale gold sparks were raining from the sky. One brushed Jesse's cheek—it was cool, not burning. And Bridget was sitting up, brushing the dust away from her flowered dress. She looked furious.

"Jesse!"

He whirled around. Through the falling sparks, he saw Lucie, standing in the archway, her hands clasped in front of her. Beside her was Grace, smiling at him in relief, and Jesse realized that he did not know which of them had called his name.

Perhaps it did not matter. They were two of the most important people in the world to him. The girl he loved, and his sister.

He ran toward them. Lucie was looking around in wonder, as sparks of gold dust brushed against her face. "She did it," she said. "Daisy did it. Belial is dead. I can *feel* it."

"Look," Grace said, narrowing her eyes. "Isn't that your mum and dad, Lucie?"

They all looked toward the abbey. So he hadn't imagined it, Jesse thought: there were Will and Tessa, helping Eugenia and Gideon pry the cathedral doors open. A crowd was gathering: Jesse saw Gabriel Lightwood there, and Charlotte Fairchild. They'd probably been told James and all his friends were inside the abbey, and were desperate to get inside.

"James," Lucie whispered, her eyes widening. A moment later, despite her exhaustion, she'd taken off running toward the cathedral, Jesse and Grace following in her wake.

Lilith.

She was tall and cool and pale as a marble pillar, her long black hair falling past her waist. She wore a dress made of the feathers of owls, that moved with her as she moved, in shades of cream and brown and dark orange.

"My paladin," she said, her voice deep with exultation. "You have truly worked wonders here."

Cordelia could hear footsteps, and past Lilith she could see Anna and Ari rushing into the nave, slowing as they reached the High Altar and staring at what must have been a truly bizarre tableau—Matthew kneeling with a bloody James, Thomas and Alastair at the foot of the steps staring up at Lilith and Cordelia.

This was it, Cordelia thought calmly. The end of it. She would rid herself of Lilith now, or die in the attempt.

"I am not your paladin," she said.

Lilith waved a lace-white hand dismissively. "Of course you are. And you have performed beyond my expectations. Belial is slain, and Edom liberated from his control. It is mine again. Of course," she added, "your work is not *quite* done yet. You see, surely with the death of Belial, Asmodeus will come to lay his claim to Edom next. But little does he know *I* am in possession of a slayer of Princes of Hell! You will face him as my finest warrior, and find victory again, I am sure."

Cordelia glanced back over her shoulder. At Cortana, lying shining on the floor. At Matthew holding James's shoulders, and at James, who was sitting up, his breath harsh, his eyes fixed on Lilith with cold hatred.

"You can keep them if you like," Lilith said, gesturing at Matthew and James, "either one of them or both, as long as they do not distract you from necessary tasks. I am feeling generous."

"I don't think you heard me," Cordelia said. "I am no longer your paladin, Lilith. Our deal is concluded, and I have fulfilled my end of our bargain."

The Mother of Demons chuckled lightly. "Well, not quite. In the end, *you* did not kill Belial, did you? It was James Herondale who struck the killing blow." Her lips curled into a grim smile. "What is it you Nephilim say? Something about how the Law is the Law, even if we might not wish it so?"

"*Sed lex, dura lex.* The Law is hard, but it is the Law," said Cordelia, looking down at Lilith. "Indeed, the letter of the Law, or of any vow or contract, is important. Which is why I was so careful when I asked you to make a vow to me. Do you remember what I asked you to promise?" She looked steadily at Lilith. "'Swear that if Belial dies by my blade, you will free me from my paladin's oath. Swear on Lucifer's name.'"

A dark red light had begun to burn in Lilith's eyes.

Cordelia said, "I never vowed to strike the killing blow myself. Only that it would be struck by Cortana. *Which it was.*"

Lilith bared her teeth. "Listen to me, girl—"

Cordelia laughed, a sharp bright laugh like a knife's edge. "You cannot order me to do *anything*," she said. "Not even listen to you. Your hold on me is broken; you are not my liege, and I am not your knight. You know I am telling the truth and that your vow binds you: you cannot harm me, nor anyone I love." She smiled at the look of rage on Lilith's face. "I would not remain here much longer, demon, if I were you. Belial's hold on this world is broken, and this once more shall become consecrated ground."

Lilith hissed. It was not a human sound, but rather the hiss of a snake. Black serpents burst from her eyes and lashed back and forth like whips as she started up the steps toward Cordelia. "How dare you disobey me," she snarled. "Perhaps I cannot *harm* you, but I shall return with you to Edom, immure you there, imprison you where you cannot escape; if you are not mine you shall belong to no one—"

"*Sanvi.*" A familiar voice rang out like a bell. Lilith halted where she was, her face twisting. "*Sansanvi. Semangelaf.*"

Cordelia looked behind her. James was on his feet, Matthew by his side. In James's right hand was his pistol, gleaming silver, the inscription along its side standing out starkly: LUKE 12:49. *I have come to bring a fire on the earth, and how I wish it were already kindled.*

James was swaying slightly, his clothes drenched in drying blood, but he was upright, his eyes blazing with fury.

"You recall this weapon," he said to Lilith. "You recall the pain it causes you." He grinned ferociously. "Take another step toward Cordelia, and I will riddle you with bullets. You may not die, but you will wish you had."

Lilith hissed again, her dark hair lifting, twisting, each strand a slim, venomous serpent. "Belial is dead," she said. "With him will go your power over shadow, your sister's power over the dead. I doubt you can even fire that gun—"

James cocked the hammer of the gun with a decided *click*. "Try me," he said.

Lilith hesitated. One moment, then another. James did not waver, his arm steady, the barrel of the gun pointed directly at the Mother of Demons.

And something shifted. Cordelia felt it as a change in the air, like the turning of a season. The stones on which Lilith stood began to glow a dark, molten red. Flames licked up suddenly, catching at the hem of Lilith's dress, filling the air with the scent of burnt feathers.

Now Lilith screamed, a terrible wail that rose to become an unearthly shriek. Shadows swirled up around her body; great bronze wings beat the air. As she rose into the air, in the form of an owl, James pulled the trigger of the gun.

Nothing happened. There was a dry, metallic sound, and that was all. James lowered the pistol, his eyes on the owl, whose wings beat frantically as it sailed up and up, vanishing into the air.

Lilith had been right. James could no longer use the gun.

He exhaled and let it fall to the floor with a heavy thump; when he looked up at Cordelia, he was smiling. "Good riddance," he said.

And Cordelia wanted nothing more than to go and throw her arms around him, to whisper to him that they were safe; that it was all finally, finally over. But as he smiled, great rays of illumination speared through the cathedral, turning the air to a shimmering cloud as dust motes sparkled in the sunlight—sunlight that poured through the doors of the cathedral, which had been thrown wide open.

And through the doors came Lucie, calling out Cordelia's name, and then Jesse and Grace, and Will and Tessa, racing toward James. And a little way behind them, Eugenia, Flora, Gideon and Gabriel, Sophie and Charles, and even Charlotte, who gave a cry when she saw Matthew.

And there were dozens of others as well, Shadowhunters she didn't know filling the cathedral as Cordelia sank to her knees beside James and Matthew. Matthew smiled at her and got to his feet, starting down the steps toward his mother and brother.

Beside her, James took her hand. It would only be a moment, Cordelia knew, before the others reached them, before they were caught up in a whirl of embraces and greetings and exclamations of gratitude and relief.

She looked at him—covered in blood and dirt and healing runes, with the dust of Edom still caught in his lashes. She thought of all the things she'd wanted to say, about how it was over and they were safe, and she had never thought it was possible to love someone so much as she loved him.

But he spoke first. His voice was rough, his eyes shining. "Daisy," he said. "You believed in me."

"Of course I did," she replied, and she realized as she spoke the words that that was all she really needed to say. "I always will."

Coda

Night had fallen over London. But it was not the unnatural night, heavy and black and silent, that had covered the city during the past terrible days. It was an ordinary London evening, full of life and noise: the sound of carriage wheels, the whistle of distant trains, the faraway shouts of Londoners passing under a sky full of moonlight and stars. And when Jem slipped out of the Institute and stood for a moment in the courtyard, the air was cold and clear and tasted of winter and the turn of the year.

Inside, there had been weariness and warmth, and even some laughter. Not for everyone, not yet; there was still shock, and grief and numbness. Anna Lightwood had returned to Alicante to be with her family, and Ari Bridgestock had gone with her. But as Jem had good cause to know, even after unimaginable loss, one continued: life had to be lived, and one learned to bear one's scars.

And the young were resilient. Even after all she had been through today, Cordelia had wept with happiness when she found out she had a little brother now: his name was Zachary Arash Carstairs. Sona would be arriving the next morning, bringing the baby with her, and neither Cordelia nor Alastair could wait to meet him.

All things in balance, Jem thought. Life and death; grief and happiness. They had been brave, James and his friends, incredibly brave—they had lived through the nightmare of London under Belial's control, and survived the wasteland of Edom. Outside Westminster

Abbey, James, his clothes still drenched in blood, had told Jem that it was their years of training together, of sharpening and strengthening his will, that had given him the idea that he could resist Belial, could throw off his possession even for a moment.

And that had been part of it, Jem thought. Strength of will could not be dismissed, but there was also the great weakness of demons: they did not understand either love or faith. Belial had underestimated not just Cordelia, Lucie, and James, but also their friends, and what they would all do for each other. He had not seen them as Jem had, in the drawing room tonight: Cordelia sleeping in an armchair with James holding her; Alastair and Thomas, hand in hand before the fire; Lucie and Jesse, communicating with whispers and looks. Matthew, being gentle with his parents and, for the first time in a long time, with himself. And Will and Tessa, their hands outstretched for Jem, as they always were.

Now Jem looked out over the courtyard; snow had begun to sift from the sky, whitening the black iron of the gates, dusting the steps with silver. He could hear the murmurs of his Brothers in the back of his mind: a continuous soft rumble of silent conversation. They spoke of the cruel violation Belial had visited upon those Iron Sisters and Silent Brothers whose souls had gone voyaging outside their bodies. They spoke of returning those bodies to the Iron Tombs the next morning, returning them to their more dignified state. They spoke of Bridget Daly, the mundane who had been stricken by unearthly lightning, and of what changes might be worked in her, if any. And they spoke of London: that the mundane inhabitants of the city would remember the last days as those of a terrible snowstorm that had trapped them in their houses, cutting off London from the outside world. It was already beginning: the rest of the world reporting on the extreme weather in London that had downed the telegraph lines and prevented the movement of trains.

The Clave had hired Magnus Bane to repair the destruction wrought at Westminster Abbey, but no warlock, no magic Jem knew, was responsible for this great forgetting. It seemed a direct intervention of angels. *Such has happened before,* Brother Enoch had told him, *only you, Zachariah, are too young to recall it. Belial upset the balance of things;*

sometimes Heaven rights that balance, though we can only guess at when it will do so. Angels, after all, do not answer to us.

The Downworlders who had been trapped in the city would, it seemed, remember, though Magnus had said their memories were dim and confused. From what Cordelia and Lucie had said, Jem thought, it was better that way. He did wonder about Malcolm; whether the High Warlock had been in London when it had been taken over was still an open question—

Movement caught Jem's eye, a flicker of shadow at the Institute's entrance. He heard the squeal of twisting metal. Though the gates had been locked, they creaked open, just wide enough to allow a shadow to slip through the gap.

Jem straightened, his hand on his staff, as a man strode toward him across the flagstones. A handsome man of middle years, in a well-cut suit. He had dark hair, and there was something peculiar about his face. Despite the lines on it, the marks of age and experience, he seemed oddly young. No, not young, Jem thought, tightening his grip on his weapon. *New.* As if he had just been made, shaped out of some strange clay: Jem could not quite explain it, even to himself. But he knew what he was looking at.

Demon, breathed a voice in the back of his head. *And not just any demon. There is great power here.*

Stop, Jem said, holding up a hand, and the man stopped, casually, hands in his pockets. He wore a long, leathery greatcoat, with an unpleasant-looking texture. The snow still fell, soft and white, but no flakes clung to his hair or clothes. It seemed to be falling *around* the man, as if it could not touch him. *Why have you come here, demon?*

The man grinned. An easy, lazy grin. "Now, that's rather rude," he said. "Why not give me my proper name? Belial?"

Jem drew himself up. *Belial is dead.*

"A Prince of Hell cannot die," said the demon. "Yes, the Belial *you* knew is dead—well, I might not use that word precisely, but certainly his spirit will trouble your realm no more. I have been assigned his place. I am Belial now, the eater of souls, the eldest of the nine Princes of Hell, the commander of countless armies of the damned."

I see, said Jem. *And yet I still wonder—why have you come here? What message do you hope to convey?* There was a great murmuring in the back of his mind, but he ignored it—the more ordinary human part of him was in control now. The part that loved and felt, that wished above all things to protect his family: Will, Tessa, and their children. *Your predecessor had an unhealthy obsession with a Shadowhunter family*, he said. *It caused much suffering and destruction and resulted eventually in his death. I hope you will not be continuing that fixation.*

"I will not," said the new Belial. "That was his bloodline, not mine. I do not care about the family you speak of; they are nothing to me. The previous Belial diminished his strength in his fascination with them. I wish only to build that strength back up again."

And you came by, out of the goodness of your demonic heart, to tell me this? Jem mused. *No. You fear Cortana. You know it killed your predecessor. You fear you will be the next target of its wielder.*

"Humans have such trouble understanding the ways of Heaven and Hell," said Belial, but there was a stiffness to his smile. "There would be little point in the Carstairs girl slaying me; I will only be replaced by another, one perhaps more determined to do away with her."

Quite simply, said Jem, *you are saying: if the Herondales leave you alone, you will leave them alone.*

"Eternally," said Belial. "As I said, I have no interest in them. They are only ordinary Nephilim now."

Jem was not sure he agreed with that, but he let it pass. *I will convey that information*, he said. *I am sure they will have no interest in pursuing a connection with you, either.*

Belial grinned, his teeth white and sharp. "Delightful," he said. "I will owe you a favor, then, Silent One."

No need for that, Jem protested, but Belial was already fading from view; there was only a shimmer where he had stood, and then, not even that. The only evidence of his presence was a strange bare circle of stone in the center of the courtyard where no snow had fallen.

Epilogue

Summer had come late to London this year, Cordelia thought, and at Chiswick House it seemed to have come even later, as if the place possessed its own distinct climate. Despite the blue sky overhead, the gardens of the manor seemed cast into shadow; the trees were cloaked in green, but few flowers had bloomed in the overgrown gardens. Cordelia found herself reminded of the first time she'd seen the house: at night, in demon-haunted darkness, the wind itself seeming to whisper, *Go, you are not wanted here.*

Now, things were different. The manor itself had not changed, perhaps, but Cordelia had. She was not here only with Lucie, embarking on a clandestine mission, but rather surrounded by her friends, her family, her husband, and her *parabatai*. She would not have minded had it been snowing. In this group, she could not help but be content.

The ground had been hard, rocky, and difficult to dig out; it had taken them most of the morning—even trading turns with the shovels—to hollow out a rectangle in the ground that would fit Jesse's old coffin, which was balanced precariously at the edge of the hole.

They had brought picnic baskets—though they did not intend to picnic here—and had made inroads into the ginger beer; everyone was a bit sweaty and dirty, and the boys had all stripped off their jackets and rolled up their shirtsleeves. James had done a great deal of the digging, which Cordelia had enjoyed watching. He consulted briefly with Matthew now, and, apparently having decided that the hole was big enough, he turned to the rest of the group: Lucie and Jesse, Thomas and Alastair, Anna and Ari, Matthew (and Oscar), Cordelia, and Grace.

"All right," James said, leaning on his shovel like the gravedigger in *Hamlet*. "Who wants to start?"

They all looked at each other—a bit sheepishly, like children caught breaking a rule. (Well, not Anna. Anna never looked sheepish.) But it had been Matthew's idea in the first place, so in the end all eyes fell upon Matthew, who had knelt down to ruffle Oscar's head.

Matthew looked amused. "I see," he said. "Very well. I shall show you how it's done."

Oscar barked as Matthew strode up to Jesse's empty coffin, its lid thrown back. The trees cast the shadows of leaves across it, and across Matthew's green waistcoat. His hair had grown long since the winter, almost touching his collar. He had been training hard and no longer looked too thin. There was a depth to his smile that had not been there when Cordelia had first come to London; it had not been there even when they had been in Paris together.

With a flourish, Matthew slid a bottle of brandy from inside his waistcoat. It was full, the dark amber liquid flashing gold in the sun. "Here," he said, bending to lay it in the coffin. "I don't think that anyone will be surprised by my choice."

Cordelia doubted anyone was. When winter had turned into spring, they had all felt as if they were finally coming out of a long darkness into light. It was Anna who had first remarked that in summer, they would be scattering from London, separating each of them from the group who had been their support through the long months after January. James and Cordelia would be going on their honeymoon, Matthew on his voyage; Alastair and Thomas would be off helping Sona move back into Cirenworth (her desire to move to Tehran had rather miraculously evaporated after a months-long visit from her family following Zachary's birth), and Anna and Ari would soon be in India. Life was resuming, however much they had all changed, and to mark the occasion Matthew had suggested this ceremony, in which each of them would bury a symbol of the past.

"It doesn't need to be something terrible," Matthew had said. "Just something you wish to let go of, or regard as part of your past, not your future."

He had smiled a bit ruefully at Cordelia when he had said it. There had been a distance between them since January—not a distance of hostility or anger; but that closeness she had felt with him in Paris was gone, the sense of how well they understood one another. Paradoxically, Matthew had only grown closer to James, and to Thomas, and even Alastair. "You have to let his heart heal," James had said. "That can only be managed with a bit of distance. It will resolve itself in time."

A bit of distance. Only Matthew would be going a great distance, very soon, and for how long, Cordelia did not know.

Matthew rose, brushed off his hands, and sauntered over to throw a stick for Oscar. Oscar bounded across the grass, stopped, and sniffed the air suspiciously.

Squaring her shoulders, Ari came up to take Matthew's place. She wore a simple rose-colored day dress, her hair pinned in a loose chignon. She held up a folded sheet of paper, slightly charred around the edges. "This is the letter my father wrote in his attempt to blackmail Charles," she said. "To me, it symbolizes a standard he held me to, one to which he did not hold himself. This is what my father wanted me to be—a false image. Not who I am. Not who I hope he will someday learn to be."

As she dropped it into the coffin beside the brandy bottle, her eyes were sad. Maurice Bridgestock was still in Idris, having been stripped of his role as Inquisitor. He would soon be traveling to Wrangel Island, a lonely place where he would take up the task of guarding wards. Mrs. Bridgestock had applied for a divorce, but far from seeming despondent, she appeared liberated by her new independence, and had welcomed Anna—and all of Ari's friends—into her home. It was a warm and happy place to visit, but Cordelia could not blame Ari for regretting what had happened to her father, or wishing he had been a better man. It was a feeling she herself knew all too well.

Thomas was next. A paradox, was their Thomas—he bore the marks of the loss of Christopher more visibly than any of the rest of them, in lines beside his eyes that had not been there before and were unusual in someone so young. (Cordelia thought they gave him character.) But there was also a new peace to him. He had always seemed to be trying to make himself smaller in a body he found ungainly; now he was at ease, as if he at last saw himself the way Alastair saw him: tall and graceful and strong.

Like Ari, he held up a piece of paper, though this one was not slightly charred; rather, it was extremely charred. "I shall bury one of the very earliest attempts at fire-messages," he said, "in which I may have penned some regrettable things."

Alastair smiled. "I recall that one."

Thomas let the paper fall. "It represents a time when I didn't know what I wanted." He looked at Alastair, the connection between them almost palpable. "But that is no longer the case."

Alastair took the spot after Thomas; as they passed each other, their hands touched lightly. They were always touching—Alastair straightening Thomas's tie, Thomas ruffling Alastair's hair—much to Sona's amusement. Cordelia found it quite sweet.

As Matthew had, Alastair held up a bottle, though this one was small, with a block-printed label. For a moment Cordelia wondered if it was alcohol—perhaps he was putting away thoughts of their father?—before she realized it was not that at all. It was an empty vial of hair dye. Alastair dropped it into the coffin with a wry smile. "A sign," he said, "that I have discovered that my hair looks much better in its natural state."

"Don't rubbish blonds," said Matthew, but he was smiling as Cordelia moved to take her brother's place.

Alastair nodded encouragingly at her as she went to stand beside Jesse's coffin. She looked out at her friends, feeling oddly as if she were onstage, though with a far friendlier audience than the Hell Ruelle. She sought Lucie's smile, and then James's, before taking a deep breath and reaching for the empty scabbard at her waist.

She drew it free, looking at it consideringly. It was truly a thing of loveliness. Steel like silver, inlaid with deeper gold, etched with runes and leaves, flowers and vines. The light that filtered through the branches above illuminated its beauty.

"I thought for a long time," Cordelia said, turning the scabbard over in her hands, "about what to put behind me. I had thought it should be something to do with Lilith. But in the end I chose this. It is a lovely thing. And because it was beautiful, my father wanted to give it to me, and because of that, he was late to my wedding and drunk when he did arrive." She took a deep breath, feeling Matthew's eyes on her. "He never quite understood that I did not want pretty gifts. I wanted him. My father, beside me. And—I never spoke those words to him. I kept them secret in my heart." She bent to lay the scabbard down; it lay sparkling among the odd assortment of items in the coffin. She said, "Had I told the truth to my father, it might not have changed things, but it would have changed my regrets. Had I told the truth to all of you about my plan to seek Wayland the Smith, I might have been spared a terrible mistake." She rose to her feet. "What I am putting behind me is the keeping of secrets. Not every secret"—she smiled a little—"but the kind we keep because of shame, or some imagined failing that others will judge. Our failings are always more monstrous in our own eyes than any others'; in the eyes of those who love us, we are forgiven."

Lucie clapped her hands loudly. "Now that you have a *parabatai*," she said, "you will never need to keep secrets again! At least not from me," she added. "You can keep secrets from the rest of these heathens here, if you like."

There was a chorus of cheerful boos. "Lucie, dear," said Anna. "Don't give Cordelia terrible advice. We all want to hear what she has to say, no matter how scandalous. In fact, especially if it's scandalous." She grinned lazily.

"Anna," Matthew said, in a mock-serious tone, "is it not your turn now? What will you be contributing?"

Anna sketched a wave on the air. "Nothing. I like everything I have and I approve of everything I've done."

Even Alastair laughed at that, and Ari laid her head against Anna's shoulder. Anna's waistcoat had rose stripes to match Ari's dress, Cordelia noticed—Anna had taken to matching bits of her outfits to what Ari was wearing, which for Anna was a commitment more serious than marriage runes.

"Well." They all looked around at that; Grace rarely spoke, and it was always something of a surprise to hear her voice. "As someone who has many regrets, I will take the next turn. If there are no objections."

No one said a word, and Grace walked quietly up to the coffin that had been her brother's. In the past months, she had settled into a place among them, a part of their group as Jesse's sister. It was undeniable that without her completion of Christopher's research, it was unlikely they would have achieved a victory against Belial. And Christopher's words—that if they forever blamed her for her past actions, they would be no better than Tatiana—had stayed with them all.

Even so, it had been an uneasy truce. Once James had told his parents the tale of the bracelet and the curse, they had been devastated. Cordelia had been there, had seen how acutely they felt James's pain, more acutely than they would ever, she imagined, feel pain of their own. And they had carried the guilt of parents, that they should have seen, should have guessed, should have protected their son.

James had protested, explained: the very evil of the bracelet was that it prevented knowledge, protection, help. They were not at fault. Still, it was a wound, and Grace had moved quietly out of the Institute that day, and into the Consul's house, where she was helping Henry reorganize his laboratory.

Jesse had worried—would it be awkward for her there, considering her history with Charles? But Grace had demurred: Charlotte and Henry knew everything, and she and Charles had achieved an understanding. Though Charles had been very angry indeed at first, he professed himself now grateful that Grace had disrupted his plans to marry Ari, which would have made them both miserable. He was in Idris now, working for the new Inquisitor, Kazuo Satō. (Charles sent back letters sometimes, usually to Matthew but sometimes to Ari, with news of her father. They would have made a ghastly married couple, Ari said, but as friends, they got on surprisingly well.)

Where it came to Grace, everyone's eyes had been on James, who after all was the one to whom she had dealt the greatest hurt. To everyone's surprise, his anger at her seemed to fade quickly with the death of Belial. One night, in bed with James, Cordelia had said, "I know it is not something we speak of very often, but everyone is looking to you when they try to decide how to manage with Grace. And you seem to have forgiven her." She had rolled onto her side, looking at him curiously. "Have you?"

He had rolled onto his side too, so they faced each other. His eyes were lambent gold, the color of firelight, and they left heat behind where they traced the shape of her shoulder, the curve of her neck. She did not think she would ever stop wanting him, and he had shown no sign of feeling any differently about her. "I suppose we have not spoken about it because I rarely think of it," he said. "Telling everyone was the difficult part. After that . . . Well, I do not know if it is forgiveness. But I find I cannot be angry at her when I have so much, and she has so little."

"You don't think you need to speak to her? Hear her apologize?" Cordelia had asked, and James had shaken his head.

"No. It is not something I need. As for her, she will always be marked by her childhood and the things she has done. What would punishment or apologies add to that?"

The things she has done. Cordelia thought of James's words as Grace held up two silver crescents. The shattered remains of the cursed bracelet. She looked over at James, her gray eyes level. She had a scar on her cheek now, not from the battle at Westminster, but from a beaker that had exploded in the Fairchilds' laboratory.

James nodded at her, and Cordelia realized: there needed to be no more conversation than this to resolve what had happened between Grace and James. It was long over, and James's past pain had been absorbed into who he was now: it was the memory of a needle that could no longer draw blood.

Grace dropped the broken bracelet into the coffin; the pieces rattled against something glass. She looked at them for a long moment before turning and walking away, her back straight, her fair hair lifted by the wind.

She went to Jesse's side. He laid a hand on her shoulder before making his own way up to the coffin. Out of all of them, Cordelia thought, he had changed the most since January. He had still been pale and thin then, especially for a Shadowhunter, despite his determination to work and train, to learn the skills of strength and balance that had been instilled in most Shadowhunters from early childhood. Now, with the passage of months—months in which he had trained nearly every day with Matthew and James, until he could scramble up the ropes dangling from the training room ceiling without even breathing hard—he was lean and strong, his skin a shade darker from the sun, and Marked with new runes. All the fine clothes Anna had helped him choose had needed to be let out, and let out again, to accommodate the new shape of his body. He no longer looked like a boy who had grown up in shadow: he was nearly a man, and a strong and healthy one at that.

He held up a jagged bit of metal, bright in the sun—the broken hilt of the Blackthorn sword, Cordelia realized. The etched circle of thorns was still visible against the blackened cross guard. "I," said Jesse steadily, "am letting go of the complicated history of my family. Of being a Blackthorn. There is, of course," he added, "nothing inherently evil about any family. Every family has members who are good, and those who are less so. But the terrible things my mother did, she did after taking that name. She hung the Blackthorn sword on the wall above my coffin because it was so important to her that even in near death I be reminded always that I was *her* idea of a Blackthorn. So I'm burying what my mother thought it meant to be a Blackthorn; I am putting it behind me, and I will start again as a new sort of Blackthorn. The kind I choose to be."

He laid the broken hilt among the other objects, and for a moment stood, looking at the coffin that had been his prison for so long. When he turned his back on it, it was with a determined air, and he strode over to join Lucie with his head held high.

And it was Lucie's turn next. She squeezed Jesse's hand before approaching the coffin. She had told Cordelia earlier what she was bringing—a drawing of a Pyxis, taken from the flat of the warlock Emmanuel Gast.

Cordelia knew Lucie still felt guilt over what had happened with Gast—indeed, over every time she had commanded the dead, though with Gast it had been worst. Lucie's ability to see ghosts remained, but the power to command them had vanished along with Belial's death. Lucie had confided to Cordelia that she was glad to be rid of it—she would never even be tempted to use it now.

She did not speak as she let the paper fall: Lucie, usually so full of words, seemed to have none to speak now. She watched it flutter its way down, her hands at her sides, only looking up when James came to join her beside the grave—no, Cordelia reminded herself, it was *not* a grave: this was a farewell of sorts, but not that kind.

Standing beside Lucie, James looked at Cordelia. Here, among the shadows, his eyes were the color of sunlight. Then he gazed around at the others, as slowly he drew his battered pistol from his belt. "I almost feel I should apologize to Christopher," he said. "He spent so much time—and destroyed so many objects—trying to get this to work." A rueful smile flitted across his face. "And yet, I am putting it behind me. Not because it no longer fires at my command, though that is true—but because it only ever worked for me because of Belial, and Belial is gone. The powers conferred upon me and upon Lucie due to him were never gifts—they were always burdens. They were a weight, a heavy one. A weight we both set aside with relief." He glanced sideways at Lucie, who nodded, her eyes bright. "I like to think Christopher would have understood," James said, and knelt to lay the gun flat in the coffin.

He expelled a deep breath, as someone might when, having walked a long and dusty road, they finally found a place to rest. He took the coffin lid in his hands and shut it with an audible click. As he rose to his feet, the whole group was silent; even Anna was no longer smiling, but looked thoughtful, her blue eyes grave.

"Well," James said, "that's everything."

"Constantinople," James said to Cordelia.

They were sitting on a yellow picnic blanket, flung across the green grass of Hyde Park. The Serpentine glittered silver in the distance; all around were their friends, setting down blankets and baskets; Matthew was rolling in the grass with Oscar, who was trying desperately to lick his face. At any moment, Cordelia knew, their families would arrive, but for this moment, it was just them.

Cordelia leaned back against James. She was sitting between his legs, her back to his chest. He was playing delicately with her hair; she supposed she ought to tell him that he would soon loosen all the pins and create a coiffure disaster, but she couldn't bring herself to mind. "What about it?"

"It's hard to believe that we'll be there in a fortnight." He wrapped his arms around her. "On our honeymoon."

"Really? It all seems quite ordinary to me. Ho-hum." Cordelia grinned at him over her shoulder. In truth, she could hardly believe any of it. She still woke up in the morning and pinched herself when she realized she was in the same bed as James. That they were married—now with their full sets of wedding runes, though she could not think about that without blushing.

They had turned the room that had once been James's room into a planning room, in which, James had said grandly, gesturing about with a pencil behind his ear, they would *plan adventures*. They had traveled to Constantinople and Shanghai and Timbuktu already in their minds and imaginations; now they would go there in reality. They would see the world, together, and to that end they had pinned up maps and train timetables and the addresses of Institutes all over the world.

"But what will happen when you have children, with all this gallivanting?" Will had grumbled in mock despair, but James had only laughed and said they would take them along wherever they went, perhaps in specially designed luggage.

"You're a cruel mistress, Daisy," he said now, and kissed her. Cordelia shivered all over; Rosamund had once told her kissing Thoby was boring, but Cordelia could not imagine becoming bored with kissing James. She shifted closer to him on the blanket, as he brought up one hand to gently cup her face—

"Oi!" Alastair yelled over good-naturedly. "Stop kissing my sister!"

Cordelia drew back from James and laughed. She knew Alastair didn't actually mind—he was at home now in their group of friends, at home enough to tease. Never again would he worry whether he was welcome at a meeting in the Devil Tavern, or at a party or late-night gathering at Anna's. Attitudes toward her brother had changed, but even more than that, *he* had changed. It was as if he had been locked in a room, and Thomas had opened the door: Alastair now seemed to feel free to express the love and affection for his friends and family he had always tamped down and hidden away. He had truly astonished Sona and Cordelia with the attention he paid to his new baby brother.

As long as Alastair was there, Zachary Arash never needed to fear being alone for a second: Alastair was always holding him, always tossing him into the air and catching him while he squealed. He rarely came home from a day out without a rattle or a toy to keep the baby entertained.

One night after dinner at Cornwall Gardens, Cordelia had passed the drawing room in her mother's house and seen Alastair sitting on the sofa with the baby—a swaddled mass of blankets with two pink fists visible, waving as Alastair sang, in a low voice, a Persian melody Cordelia half remembered: *You are the moon in the sky, and I am the star that circles around you.*

It was a song their father had sung to them when they were very small. How things came full circle, Cordelia could not help but think, in the last ways one would expect.

"Bakewell tarts," said Jesse. "Bridget's outdone herself."

He and Lucie were unpacking a picnic hamper the size of Buckingham Palace onto a blue-and-white-checked blanket that Lucie had laid upon the lawn under a cluster of sweet chestnut trees.

Bridget *had* outdone herself—every time Lucie thought the basket must be empty, Jesse brought out another treat: ham sandwiches, cold chicken and mayonnaise, meat pies, strawberries, Bakewell tarts and Eccles cakes, cheese and grapes, lemonade and ginger beer. Ever since Bridget had recovered from her injury at Westminster, she had been wildly active in the kitchen: in fact, she'd seemed to have more energy than ever. The gray threads had disappeared from her head; Will had remarked that it was as if she were aging backward. Even her songs had become more frequent, and more gruesome.

"I'm hiding a few. Otherwise Thomas will eat them all," Jesse said, setting aside several of the Bakewell tarts. As he moved, a thick black Mark on his right forearm flashed. *Home.* It was a rarely used Mark, symbolic rather than practical, like the runes for grief and happiness.

He had gotten it the day he returned from Idris, after his trial by Mortal Sword. Though most of the Clave's concerns about Will and Tessa's loyalties had been put to rest by their testimonies—and the death of Belial—the question of Jesse, and Lucie's actions in raising him, had remained an open one. The Clave had wanted to speak with them both, but Jesse had been insistent: he wanted to stand trial by Mortal Sword alone. He wanted it known that he was Tatiana's son, and that she had kept him half-alive until Lucie had done what she'd done—that Lucie was innocent of necromancy. He no longer wished to pretend to be Jeremy Blackthorn. He wanted to be known as who he was, and face whatever consequences came.

After all, he said, a trial would reveal how hard he had fought against Belial, how he had never cooperated with him or any demon. Lucie knew he also hoped his testimony would help not only her but also Grace, and while Lucie had respected his wishes and not accompanied him to Alicante—she had spent the two days he was gone tearing out bits of her hair and writing a novella entitled *Heroic Prince Jethro Defeats the Evil Council of Darkness*—she suspected it had.

When Jesse had returned from Idris, his name had been cleared and so had Lucie's. He was now officially Jesse Blackthorn, and there was a new resolve in him. To be part of the Enclave, to hold his head high among them—after all, many of them had seen him fight bravely at Westminster, even knew he had helped. He patrolled, attended meetings, accompanied Lucie to her *parabatai* ceremony with Cordelia. The Home Mark, which was permanent, had been given to him by Will, who had also presented him with the gift of a stele that had once belonged to Will's father (and had now been modified to create fire messages, as all current steles were). They were both gifts, Lucie thought, the rune and the stele—a sort of welcome combined, she hoped, with a promise.

"You can't tease Thomas for always being hungry when *you're* always hungry," Lucie pointed out.

"Even hours of training a day—" Jesse began indignantly, then narrowed his eyes. "Luce. What's wrong?"

"There. On the bench," she whispered.

She was aware of him turning to look: a row of park benches had been set up along the edges of a low fence, not far from a stone statue of a boy with a dolphin. On one of the benches sat Malcolm Fade, wearing a cream-colored linen suit and a straw hat pulled low over his eyes. Despite the hat, Lucie could tell he was looking at her with a focused concentration.

Her stomach did a small flip. She had not seen Malcolm since the Christmas party at the Institute, and it seemed as if a lifetime had passed since.

He crooked a finger in her direction, as if to say, *Come and speak to me.*

She hesitated. "I ought to go talk to him."

Jesse frowned. "I don't like it. Let me come with you."

Part of Lucie wished she *could* ask Jesse to accompany her. She could not really see Malcolm's face, but she felt the intensity with which he was looking at her, and she was not sure it was entirely friendly. Yet a larger part of her knew that she was the one who had bound herself to Malcolm with a promise. A promise that had now gone long unaddressed.

She glanced around; no one else in their group seemed to have noticed the warlock. Matthew was lying in the grass, face turned up to the sun, while Thomas and Alastair played fetch with Oscar; James and Cordelia had eyes only for each other, and Anna and Ari were down by the riverbank, deep in conversation.

"It'll be all right—you'll be able to see me. If I need you, I'll signal," Lucie said, dropping a kiss on Jesse's head as she rose to her feet. He was still frowning as she set off across the grass toward Malcolm.

As she drew closer to the High Warlock, she noticed how different he looked since she'd last seen him. He had always been well put together, his outfits carefully considered for fit and fashion, but he seemed a bit shabby around the edges now. There were holes in the sleeves of his white linen jacket, and what looked like bits of flowers and hay stuck to his boots.

She sat down gingerly on the park bench, not close to Malcolm, though not so far away as to insult him. She folded her hands in her lap and gazed out over the park. She could see her friends on their bright picnic blankets; Oscar a pale gold shadow darting back and forth. Jesse, watching her with serious eyes.

"It's a lovely day, isn't it," Malcolm said. His voice was remote. "When I left London, the ground was covered in ice."

"Indeed," Lucie said carefully. "Malcolm, where have you been? I thought I would have seen you after the Westminster battle." When he said nothing, she went on. "It's been six months, and—"

That seemed to surprise him. "Six months, you say? I was in the green land of Faerie. For me it has been a matter of weeks."

Lucie was astonished. She had not heard of warlocks traveling to Faerie often—if at all. But it did explain the grass and flowers on his boots. She could ask him why he'd gone, she supposed, but she sensed the question would not be welcome. Instead she said, "Malcolm, my power is gone. You must have guessed—since Belial died, I can no longer command the dead." He said nothing. "I am sorry—"

"I had hoped," he interrupted, "that perhaps your power might have started to return. Like an injury healing." He still looked out over the grass in front of them, as though searching for something there and not finding it.

"No," Lucie said. "It hasn't come back. I don't think it ever will. It was tied to my grandfather, and it died with his death."

"Have you tried? Have you tried to use it?"

"I have," Lucie said slowly. "Jessamine allowed me to attempt it. But it didn't work, and—I'm glad of it. I am sorry if I cannot help you, but I am not sorry the power is gone. It would not have been a kindness to use it on Annabel. I understand you still grieve for her, but—"

Malcolm glanced at her and then away, so quickly that Lucie was only conscious of the flaring fury in his eyes, the twist of his mouth. He looked as if he would slap her if he could. "You understand *nothing*," he hissed, "and like all Shadowhunters, when you make a promise to a Downworlder, you will inevitably break it."

Shaken, Lucie said, "Could I not help you some other way? I could try to get some kind of restitution from the Clave, an apology for what was done to Annabel—"

"*No.*" He flung himself to his feet. "I will get my own restitution. The Nephilim have reached the end of their usefulness for me." He looked past Lucie, then, at Jesse. Jesse with his black hair and green eyes, Jesse with his resemblance to the family portraits in Chiswick House. Was Malcolm thinking how much Jesse looked like Annabel, like all his ancestors? His face was without emotion—the fury had gone from it, leaving only a sort of calculating blankness. "I will not trust a Shadowhunter again," he said, and without another glance at her, walked away.

She sat for a moment on the bench, unmoving. She could not help but blame herself. She should never have made foolish promises, should not have said she would use her power, even after what had happened to Gast. She had not meant to take advantage of Malcolm—she had meant to keep her end of the bargain, however she might have regretted making it. But she knew he would never believe that.

Jesse was on his feet when she returned to the picnic blanket. He caught her hand, his expression troubled. "I was about to come over there—"

"It's all right," Lucie said. "He's upset with me. I *did* make him a promise and break it. I feel awful."

Jesse shook his head. "There's nothing you could have done. You did not know the power would be extinguished," he said. "In the end, his anger is not at you. It is at what happened a long time ago. I only hope he can let go of it. Nothing can be done for Annabel now, and dwelling on the past will poison his future."

"When did you get so wise?" she whispered, and Jesse drew her into the circle of his arms. For a moment they stayed as they were, reveling in each other's closeness. It was a wonder to be able to hold Jesse, to touch him without awful darkness surrounding her, Lucie thought. And, more practically, it was rather nice to be in Jesse's arms without her parents watching them like hawks. Though they lived together in the Institute, they were strictly forbidden from visiting each other's rooms unless the doors were left open; no amount of complaining on Lucie's part would budge Will. "I'm sure you and Mother got up to all sorts of scandalous things when you lived together in the Institute," Lucie had said.

"Exactly," Will replied darkly.

Tessa had laughed. "Maybe when you're engaged, we can loosen the rules," she said cheerfully.

It was not Jesse's fault they were not engaged, Lucie thought now; she'd told him they could marry when she sold her first novel, and he seemed to think that was a fine timeline. She was working on it now: *The Beautiful Cordelia and Secret Princess Lucie Defeat the Wicked Powers of Darkness.*

Jesse had suggested she shorten the title. Lucie had said she would think about it. She was beginning to see the value in critique.

She let herself forget her sadness over Malcolm now, as she tipped her face back and smiled up at Jesse.

"You told me once you don't believe in endings, happy or otherwise," he said, his calloused hand gently cradling the back of her head. "Is that still true?"

"Of course," she said. "We have so much yet ahead—good, bad, and everything else. I believe this is our happy middle. Don't you?"

And he kissed her, which Lucie took confidently to mean that he agreed.

"I do not see," Alastair said as Oscar deposited a stick at his feet, "why this hound here got a medal. None of the rest of us got a medal."

"Well, it isn't an *official* medal," said Thomas, dropping to his knees in the grass to rub Oscar's head and muddle his ears about. "You do know that."

"The Consul presented it," Alastair said, kneeling down as well. He caught at the little medallion attached to Oscar's collar. It was etched with the words OSCAR WILDE, HERO DOG. Charlotte had presented it to Matthew, saying that as far as she was concerned, Oscar had done as much as any human to save London.

"Because the Consul is the mother of the dog's owner," pointed out Thomas, trying—and failing—to prevent Oscar from licking his face.

"Terrible favoritism," Alastair said.

A year ago, perhaps Thomas would have thought Alastair was being serious; now he knew he was being ridiculous on purpose. He was quite a bit sillier than anyone gave him credit for. A year ago, Thomas would never have been able to picture Alastair down on his knees in the mud and grass with a dog. He would not have been able to picture Alastair *smiling*, much less smiling at *him*, and it would have been far beyond his wildest imaginings to picture what kissing Alastair would be like.

Now, he and Alastair would be helping Sona move, along with baby Zachary, to Cirenworth, and after that, Thomas would be joining Alastair to live at Cornwall Gardens. (Thomas still remembered Alastair asking him if he would like it if they lived together; Alastair had been clearly terrified that Thomas would say no, and Thomas had had to kiss him and kiss him until he was pushed up against a wall and breathless before he finally believed that Thomas's answer was yes.)

Thomas had wondered if he'd be nervous about the move, but found he was only excited at the thought of a home with Alastair. (No matter how much Cordelia teased him that Alastair snored sometimes and left his dirty socks about.) He'd been nervous to tell his parents the truth about himself and his feelings for Alastair too. He'd chosen an ordinary night in February when they were all gathered in the drawing room: Sophie had been knitting something for Charlotte, Gideon had been looking over some papers for the Clave, and Eugenia had been reading Esme Hardcastle's *History of the Shadowhunters of London* and screaming with laughter. Everything had been quite entirely ordinary until Thomas had stood up in front of the fireplace and cleared his throat loudly.

Everyone had looked at him, Sophie's knitting needles arrested in mid-motion.

"I am in love with Alastair Carstairs," Thomas had said loudly and slowly, so there could be no mistake, "and I am going to spend the rest of my life with him."

There had been a momentary silence.

"I didn't think you even *liked* Alastair," Gideon had said, looking puzzled. "Not much, at least."

Eugenia had tossed her book to the floor. Rising to her feet, she regarded her parents—the whole room, in fact, even the cat asleep by the window—with a magnificent righteousness. "If *anyone* here condemns Thomas for who he is or who he loves," she had announced, "he and I will leave this house immediately. I will reside with him and renounce the rest of you as my family."

Thomas was wondering in alarm how he would explain this business of Eugenia residing with him to Alastair, when Sophie put down her reading glasses with a click. "Eugenia," she had said, "do not be ridiculous. No one here is going to *condemn* Thomas."

Thomas had exhaled in relief. Eugenia had looked slightly deflated. "No?"

"No," Gideon had said firmly.

Sophie looked at Thomas, her eyes full of affection. "Thomas, my darling, we love you and we want you to be happy. If Alastair makes you happy, then we are delighted. Although it would be nice if you *introduced* us," she added pointedly. "Perhaps you could bring him to dinner?"

Eugenia might feel let down, but Thomas didn't. He had always known his parents loved him, but knowing that they loved the whole truth of him felt like putting down something very heavy that he'd been carrying for a long time, without realizing the weight of it.

Alastair had indeed come to dinner and charmed them all, and it had led to many other dinners—delicious Persian dinners at the Carstairs', and even dinner at the Bridgestocks', with all the families gathered. Now that Maurice was gone, Flora had found a new delight in entertaining, and Thomas was pleased to see Anna so happy—so loving with Ari, and so free with her laughter and smiles, as she had not been since she was a child. In fact, he and Alastair would be looking after Winston the parrot while Ari, Flora, and Anna went to India to visit the places Ari had lived as a child and seek out her grandmother's relatives, her aunts and uncles.

Alastair had already taught Winston some rude words in Persian and planned to continue his education in the same vein. Thomas had not bothered to try to stop him; he liked to think at this point he knew which battles were worth the trouble.

Oscar had rolled onto his back and was panting, his pink tongue lolling. Alastair scratched his stomach thoughtfully. "Do you think we should get Zachary a dog? He might like a dog."

"I think we should get him a dog in six years," said Thomas, "when he is at least able to say the word 'dog,' and perhaps feed and pet the creature. Otherwise it will not be his dog so much as your mother's, and she already has a baby to look after."

Alastair looked thoughtfully at Thomas. Thomas's heart skipped, as it always did when he felt himself the sole object of Alastair's attention. "I suppose it will fall to Zachary to carry on the family name," he said. "Most likely, anyway."

Thomas knew Anna and Ari were planning to adopt a child—there were always children needing adoption among Nephilim—but he had not thought about children for himself and Alastair, save as a hazy future question. For the moment, Zachary was enough. "Do you mind?" he asked.

"Mind?" Alastair smiled, his teeth flashing white against his summer-darkened skin. "My Thomas," he said, taking Thomas's face between his long, delicate, beautiful hands, "I am perfectly happy with everything—exactly the way that it is."

"James," Anna said imperiously, "it is beyond the bounds of ungentlemanly behavior to passionately kiss your wife in public. Do stop, and come help me set up the croquet."

James glanced up lazily. Cordelia's hair had come down as predicted, and he still had his fingers looped in the long crimson strands of it. "I haven't the faintest idea how to play croquet," he said.

"I only know what I've read in *Alice in Wonderland*," said Cordelia.

"Ah," said James. "Flamingos, then, and—hedgehogs?"

Anna put her hands on her hips. "We have croquet balls, mallets, and hoops. We will have to improvise from there. My apologies, Cordelia, but . . ."

Cordelia knew better than to try to dissuade Anna when she was set on something. She waved as James was dragged away to where Ari was trying to catch a runaway painted ball, and Grace was holding a croquet hoop with a puzzled expression.

A gleam of gold down by the river's edge caught her eye. Matthew had gone to the bank of the Serpentine and was watching the slow run of the water under the pale June sunlight. He had his hands behind his back; Cordelia could not see his expression, but she knew Matthew well enough to read his body language. She knew he was thinking of Christopher.

The thought was a pang; she rose to her feet and made her way across the cropped grass to where Matthew stood at the riverside. Ducks pecked impatiently among the rushes, and children's toy boats bobbed brightly on the water. She could sense that Matthew knew she was there, beside him, though he did not speak. She wondered if looking at the river reminded him of Christopher, as it did James; James often spoke of dreams in which he saw Christopher standing on the other side of a wide riverbank, a great band of silver water before him, waiting patiently for his friends to join him one day.

"We will miss you, you know," Cordelia said. "All of us will miss you very much."

He bent down to pick up a smooth stone and eyed it, clearly considering skipping it across the water. "Even Alastair?"

"Even Alastair. Not that he will admit it." She paused a moment, wanting very much to say something, not sure if she should. "It seems strange, for you to be leaving now, when it seems as if you have just found yourself. Please tell me that . . . your going away has nothing to do with me."

"Daisy." He turned to her in surprise. "I care about you still. I always will, in some part of my heart, and James knows that; but I am happy you are together. The last months have made me realize how very unhappy James has been, for so long, and his happiness is mine, too. You understand—you, too, have a *parabatai*."

"I think it is how James bears that you are going away," said Cordelia. "He knows you are not running *away* from something, but running *toward* some grand idea." She smiled.

"Many grand ideas," said Matthew, flipping the small rock between his fingers. It was an ordinary river stone, but bits of mica glittered inside it, like crystal. "When I was drinking, my world was so small. I could never go that far from another drink. Now my world is expansive again. I want to have adventures, to do mad, wonderful, colorful things. And now that I am free . . ."

Cordelia did not ask him what he was free of; she knew. Matthew had told his parents all the truth of what he had done years ago, and how his mother had suffered because of it—how they all had. He had brought James with him, and James had sat beside him as Matthew explained, leaving no detail spared. When he was done, he had been shaking with fear. Charlotte and Henry had looked stricken, and for a moment James had been terrified that he was going to be witness to the dissolution of their family.

Then Charlotte had taken Matthew by the hand.

"Thank the Angel you told us," she said. "We always knew something had happened, but we did not know what. Not only did we lose that child, but we lost another child—you. You grew further and further away from us, and we could not get you back."

"You forgive me, then?" Matthew had whispered.

"We know you meant no harm," Henry had said. "You did not mean to hurt your mother—you believed a terrible story, and made a terrible mistake."

"But it was a mistake," Charlotte had said firmly. "It does not change our love for you one iota. And it is truly a gift that you are telling us now"—she had exchanged a look with Henry that James had described as "treacly"—"because we have something to share with you, as well. Matthew, I am going to have another baby."

Matthew had goggled. It had, James had said at the time, been a day of many revelations.

"You're not leaving because of the baby, are you?" Cordelia said now, mischievously.

"Babies," Matthew reminded her darkly. "According to the Silent Brothers, it will be twins." He grinned. "And no, I rather fancy the idea of little sisters or brothers. By the time I return from my voyage, they will be nearly a year old and have begun to have some personality. An excellent time to teach them that their big brother Matthew is the finest and most upstanding person they will ever know."

"Ah," said Cordelia. "You intend to suborn them."

"Entirely." Matthew looked down at her; the wind off the river blew his fair hair across his eyes. "When you first came to London," he said, "all I could think was that I disliked your brother, and I expected you would be like him. But you won me over quite quickly—you were kind and brave, and so many other things I aspired to be." He took her hand, though there was nothing romantic about the gesture; he pressed the smooth river stone into her palm and closed her fingers over it. "I don't think I realized—until you sent the Merry Thieves to me at my lowest point—how much I would need someone in my life who would see the truth of me and offer me kindness, even though I had not asked for it. Even when I felt I did not deserve it. And when I travel the seas with Oscar, every time I set eyes upon a new land, I will think of you and of that kindness. I will always carry it with me, and the knowledge that it is the gifts we did not have the strength to ask for that matter the most."

Cordelia sighed. "There is a terrible selfish part of me that wants you to stay here in London, but I suppose we cannot keep you to ourselves when the rest of the world is pining away for you to brighten it up."

Matthew grinned. "Flattery. As you know, it always works on me."

And as Cordelia held the smooth little stone tightly in her hand, she realized that the distance she had felt between them seemed to have fallen away. Though he might be on the other side of the world for a year, they would not be far apart in spirit.

There was a rustle; it was James, his dark hair wildly untidy, coming toward them across the grass. He held a stack of charred paper in his hand. "I have just," he said, by way of greeting, "received a seventh fire-message from my father." He shuffled through the pages. "In this one, he says they are running late and they are ten minutes away. In this one, they are nine minutes away. In this one, they are eight minutes away. In this one . . ."

"They are seven minutes away?" Matthew guessed.

James shook his head. "No, in this one he wants to know if we have enough mustard."

"What would he have done if we didn't?" Cordelia wondered.

"The Angel only knows," James said. "He certainly won't be happy about all these ducks." He grinned at Matthew, who looked back at him in that way he had that seemed to convey everything about how he loved James: that their friendship was both very silly and terribly serious all at once. One joked during the day and risked one's life at night; that was the way of being a Shadowhunter, Cordelia thought.

James squinted into the distance. "Math, I think your family's here."

And indeed, it seemed, the others were beginning to arrive at long last. Charlotte was coming toward them along a park path, pushing Henry's Bath chair.

"Duty calls," Matthew said, and started off toward his parents. Oscar left Thomas and Alastair to join him, running along at his heels and barking a welcome.

James smiled at Cordelia—that lovely, lazy smile that always made her feel as if delightful sparks were running along her spine. She moved closer to him, dropping the stone Matthew had given her into her pocket. For a moment they stood looking at the park together in companionable silence.

"I see the croquet game is going well," Cordelia noted. In fact, Anna, Ari, and Grace seemed to have created a bizarre tower of hoops and mallets that did not resemble any croquet court she had ever seen. They were all standing back and looking at it: Anna seemed delighted, Ari and Grace puzzled. "I didn't know Grace was going to bury the bracelet," she said. "At the manor. Did she speak to you about it?"

James nodded, gold eyes thoughtful. "She asked if it was all right if she buried it, and I said yes. It is, after all, her own regret she is burying."

"And your sorrow," said Cordelia softly.

He looked down at her. There was a smudge of dirt on his cheekbone, and a grass stain on his collar. And yet when she looked at him, he seemed more beautiful to her than he ever had when she had thought of him as distant and untouchably perfect. "I have no sorrow," he said. He took her hand, locking his fingers with hers. "Life is a long chain of events, of decisions and choices," he said. "When I fell in love with you, I was changed. Belial could not alter that. Nothing could alter that. And everything that happened after, everything he tried to do through the bracelet, only strengthened what I felt for you and brought us closer to one another. It was because of him and his meddling that we married in the first place. I loved you already, but being married to you only made me fall more inescapably in love; I had never been so happy as I was every moment we were together, and it was that love that led me to shatter the bracelet, and realize that indeed I had a will that could contest Belial's." He brushed a strand of hair away from her face, his touch gentle, his eyes locked on hers. "So no, I do not feel sorrow, for all I went through brought me to where we are now. To you. We have been in the crucible, and come out as gold."

Cordelia went up on her toes and kissed him quickly on the lips. He raised an eyebrow. "Is that all?" he said. "I thought that was a very romantic speech. I expected a more passionate response, or perhaps for you to start spelling out my name in daisy chains on the riverbank—"

"It was a romantic speech," Cordelia said, "and believe me, I will have much to say about it later." She smiled at him in the particular way that always made his eyes blaze up like fire. "But our families have just arrived, so unless you wish to passionately embrace in front of your parents, we will have to save that for later, when we are home."

James turned and saw that she was indeed telling the truth: everyone had arrived at once, and were coming toward the picnic spot, waving—Will and Tessa, laughing alongside Magnus Bane, Sona pushing Zachary Arash in a pram and chatting to Flora Bridgestock, Gabriel and Cecily holding Alexander by the hand, Gideon and Sophie pausing to chat with Charlotte, Henry, and Matthew. Thomas, Lucie, and Alastair had already started across the green lawn toward their families. Jesse hung back to assist Grace with the pile of croquet implements, which had toppled over; Anna and Ari were laughing too hard to move, leaning against each other as croquet balls rolled everywhere.

"When we are home?" said James softly. "Here we are, with all those we love, and those who love us. We *are* home."

Alastair had plucked his little brother from the pram; with Zachary seated in the crook of one arm, he waved at Cordelia. Matthew, in conversation with Eugenia, smiled, and Lucie made a beckoning gesture in James and Cordelia's direction, as if to say: *What are you waiting for? Come here.*

Cordelia's heart was too full for speech. Without a word, she caught hold of her husband's hand.

Side by side with James, Cordelia ran.

Notes on the Text

As always, Shadowhunter London is a mixture of the real and the unreal. Most of the locations used in the book are real and can still be visited today. The York Watergate dates from the early seventeenth century and used to be a fancy boat dock for the house of the Duke of Buckingham; it can be reached easily by going to Charing Cross Station and walking toward the Thames. St. Peter Westcheap stood at the corner of Cheapside and Wood Street from medieval times until it was destroyed in the Great Fire of London in 1666. The tiny churchyard is still there, as is the huge old mulberry tree that Anna and Ari use to enter the Silent City.

Sir John Malcolm's statue in the north transept of Westminster Abbey is real, as is the bas-relief of Britannia nearby. Simon de Langham was archbishop of Canterbury from 1366 to 1368; he left most of his enormous estate to the abbey, which is why he is the only archbishop of Canterbury interred there. His is the oldest ecclesiastical tomb in the place.

Polperro is a real, extremely charming fishing village in south Cornwall, and the stone cottage that inspired Malcolm's house can be easily spotted on the spit of land that forms a natural barrier for the village's harbor.

The love poem quoted by Alastair to Thomas is from thirteenth-century Persian poet Šams-e Qays, who cites it as written by another poet, Natáanzi.

Aught but Death,

A BONUS STORY FEATURING

CORDELIA AND LUCIE.

April 1904

A warm, sunny day would have been nice for her *parabatai* ceremony, Cordelia thought. But this was London in early spring, and it was as damp and wet as one might expect. She made her way through the branching paths of Highgate Cemetery, thinking of the last time she'd been here, almost a year ago now. When she had followed James into shadow. When she had given Belial his first wound. Despite the peaceful quiet that hung over the graveyard this morning, she felt a shudder go through her.

When she reached the clearing where the entrance to the Silent City appeared in the form of the statue of an angel, a faint shaft of sunlight broke through the clouds, illuminating the trees. Small green buds clung to their branches, a portent of spring and growth. The stone angel's sword, with its eternal question, QUIS UT DEUS—*Who is like God?*—seemed to glow.

"No one," Cordelia said softly. "No one is like God."

The statue slid aside; the entrance to the Silent City was revealed. She started down the stone steps, her boots ringing in the hollow darkness. Drawing out her witchlight, she let the pale white glow illuminate her way.

The Silent City, like Highgate itself, had an air of peaceful quiet, as though it had never been invaded, as though an awful army of Watchers had never stalked its corridors. Later generations would read about what had happened in dusty books, she thought, but it would not seem real or immediate or terrifying. Only another chapter in a long and bloody history.

Lucie had wanted to do the ceremony somewhere else. She had many ideas, all locations she deemed to be of symbolic importance: Mount Street Gardens, Regent's Park, the middle of Tower Bridge. But Brother Zachariah had politely suggested that everyone, including Lucie and Cordelia themselves, would benefit from a return to tradition, and Brother Jeremiah had less politely pointed out that the Law was the Law, and one did not simply have *parabatai* ceremonies anywhere one pleased.

Cordelia knew exactly why Lucie was reluctant to have the ceremony in the Silent City. Lucie was haunted: haunted by fear of what might happen—that her connection to Belial, though broken, might rear its ugly head again. Cordelia had urged her a dozen times not to worry, that she would be by her side at every moment.

And perhaps she was right to be worried. Cordelia couldn't say. The ceremony was technically open to any Shadowhunter who wanted to attend, and she had worried a bit that a large crowd would put in an appearance. A lot of gawkers had come to see James and Matthew take their vows, she knew, but James had explained that most of them only wanted to see whether he, the son of a warlock, would burst into flames the moment he began to speak the ceremonial words.

James and Alastair were acting as Lucie and Cordelia's witnesses, and Cordelia suspected they had put the word out that only family were wanted at this event. Rather to her surprise, people seemed to have listened. There was no crowd around the massive doors to the ceremonial chamber when she approached, slipping her witchlight into her pocket as flaring torches took over the task of lighting the Bone City.

James and Alastair had come earlier (along with Sona, Jesse,

Will, and Tessa) so that Brother Zachariah could walk them through their witness duties. Cordelia could have come too, of course, but she had wanted to make this journey alone. It felt to her like part of the ceremony. She had woken up that morning with a sense of quiet excitement. The closest thing she could liken it to was the feeling she'd had the day she'd married James, and even then, she'd thought that despite the vows and the ceremony, the change she was making to her life was huge but temporary.

This was huge but permanent. And she had wanted to walk into it alone—not as James's wife or Alastair's sister, not as Will and Tessa's daughter-in-law or anyone's friend. She had wanted to present herself as just Cordelia, stripped down to her soul, ready to offer that soul to Lucie.

Except when she walked into the chamber—one of the biggest she'd seen, with walls of variegated marble, and blackened circles on the floor from previous ceremonies—Lucie wasn't there.

The illumination in the room was dim. The candles on the walls were hidden behind carved golden brackets, which cast patterned light across the marble floor.

On one side of the chamber was Cordelia's family. Her mother, holding Zachary Arash in her arms, smiled proudly when she came in. Next to her was her auntie Niloufar, who seemed to be lecturing Alastair sternly, wagging her finger at him. Alastair nodded along with a look on his face that Cordelia knew meant he was paying almost no attention. He caught Cordelia's eye as she came in and winked at her, which brought a fresh bout of scolding from Niloufar.

On the other side were Tessa and James, who blew her a kiss. In the center of the chamber were Jem, who raised his head to acknowledge her arrival, and Will, who was deep in conversation with Jem. Other Silent Brothers stood around the chamber—Brother Shadrach carried a censer full of smoking incense, filling the room with a sweet, spicy scent, and several other Brothers stood at the cardinal points of the room, motionless, hands folded.

Jem had his head uncovered, unusual for a Silent Brother. Knowing him, Cordelia thought it was probably for the benefit of those assembled, who had all been a bit jumpy at the sight of Silent Brother robes for the past few months. He seemed to say something to Will silently, then turned and glided toward Cordelia.

I am glad you are here, cousin, he said silently. The dim light shone on the white streak that sliced through his black hair. *Lucie—I sense that she is troubled. She has gone through that arch, around the corner. Perhaps if you were to speak with her . . .*

Cordelia felt a sudden dash of panic. What if Lucie couldn't bring herself to go through with it? She glanced around to see if everyone was staring, but they seemed occupied.

I will go over Alastair's and James's duties with them again, said Jem. *Just to make sure they're quite prepared.*

"Thank you," Cordelia breathed, and quietly hurried away, through the arch and into the shallow alcove beyond. It was a small, circular space, whose ceiling rose high above, as if she stood at the bottom of a gigantic well. Lucie was leaning against one stone wall, shaking her head; Jesse stood beside her, his head bent, murmuring softly. There was love and concern in his voice, but he turned when Cordelia came in, a look of relief crossing his face.

"Daisy's here," he said, dropping a kiss on Lucie's forehead. "Talk to her, will you? She'll understand. Even if you don't want to do it." His eyes met Cordelia's: tense, worried, but there was none of that tension in his voice. "She'll still understand, Luce."

Lucie said something inaudible. A moment later Jesse slipped out of the alcove, offering a rueful smile to Cordelia as he went.

It was just Lucie and Cordelia in the alcove now. Lucie was very pale, her back firmly against the wall as if she were cornered. But she tried to smile at Cordelia. "Look at you," she said.

"Look at *us*," said Cordelia. They were both wearing ceremonial gear, unique to the ceremony—trousers and thigh-length tunics with flared sleeves, the cuffs and hems embroidered in silver with the *parabatai* rune. "Luce—if you're frightened . . ." She took a deep breath. "We don't have to. I love you, you know that. And I want to be your *parabatai*. But even without the ceremony . . ."

"I know," Lucie said softly. She looked up at Cordelia. As always, her delicate face and wide, Herondale-blue eyes contrasted oddly with the darkness of the power she'd had: nothing about her suggested ghosts or death or restless spirits. "And I know my connection to Belial is gone. But I was so worried—what if something goes wrong—"

"I don't think it will," said Cordelia. "But if we don't try, we'll never know, will we?"

Lucie started to smile. "No—no, I suppose we won't." She shook her head. "I *was* worried," she said. "But now that I see you, I'm not. We made it through Edom together. We can surely do this."

"Whither thou goest," Cordelia said. She held out her hand, and Lucie took it.

When they returned to the chamber, the ceremony began immediately, as if the Brothers had merely been waiting for them to make their entrance. Cordelia and Alastair were guided to stand on particular tiles in the room, a few yards apart, facing Brother Zachariah. Lucie and James were directed to stand opposite them. Cordelia could see Tessa and Will clasp their hands together, both radiating happy excitement—and then two circles of white and gold fire sprang up in the dead center of the room, directly beneath the highest point of the dome, and everything outside the fire's reach vanished into shadow.

Cordelia felt Alastair squeeze her hand. She leaned into him for a moment as the Silent Brothers formed a great circle around the two flaming rings in the room's center. She knew Alastair was there only to witness, not to assist her or guide her, but his presence raised her courage nonetheless.

Cordelia Carstairs Herondale. Step forward.

It was the voices of all the Brothers, speaking as one. They rang in Cordelia's head. She knew what she was meant to do and steeled herself. Letting go of Alastair's hand, she walked into the silver ring of fire; the flames licked up around her, neither hot nor cold, but filled with a tense and vibrating energy.

Lucie Herondale. Step forward.

Through flame, Cordelia saw Lucie enter her own ring of fire, facing Cordelia; in fact, she could see nothing else. Only the flames, and Lucie, and around them, darkness. She could no longer see their families waiting on the sides of the chamber; she could not even see

James or Alastair. She sensed the Brothers were giving instruction to them as witnesses, but she could not hear it over the sound of the fire.

The flames that encircled her and Lucie rose and entwined. Suddenly a new ring of fire appeared between the two of them, connecting their previously separate circles. Cordelia moved into it and so did Lucie; when they did, the flames rose up higher, to the height of their waists, then higher still to reach their shoulders.

Outside the ring, everything was dark. Within it, Cordelia stood with Lucie, who seemed to shine brilliantly. She was looking at Cordelia, and in her eyes Cordelia could read their history: everything happy and sad and silly and angry and ridiculous that bound them together. She saw herself clinging to Lucie's wrist, keeping her from falling; she saw Lucie writing her letters every week, each letter a reminder that Cordelia was not alone; she saw herself in the arms of the drowned and dead of the Thames, as Lucie begged them to save Cordelia from the river. *Bring her out—bring her out, please!* She saw herself with Lucie on the steps of the Institute, promising her, *I won't ever leave you. I will always be right beside you.*

And weren't those the words of the oath itself, when it came down to it? With new confidence, Cordelia straightened her back and smiled at Lucie, who returned her look with a delighted sort of awe.

You will now recite the oath, the Brothers said.

Cordelia took a breath and began to speak along with Lucie.

Whither thou goest, I will go . . .

She saw herself and Lucie crossing the burning sands of Edom. Lucie, falling ever more ill but never faltering. Their voices rose together in the next line of the oath:

Where thou diest, will I die, and there will I be buried. . . .

Suddenly Lucie flinched. Cordelia turned, dread twisting in her belly, and saw the dim and flickering outlines of ghosts—ghosts surrounding them, as they had in Cross Bones Graveyard; they stood among the fire and the shadow but were not dimmed by the darkness. They shone silver-white. At first there were only a handful, but as Cordelia watched, more appeared, a dozen, two dozen. Their faces were too faint to be discerned, but they were growing more visible with each moment.

It seemed they would have a crowd present for their ceremony after all.

Lucie drew a shuddering breath. "We should stop," she whispered. "Right? We should stop the ceremony."

There was no reply from the Brothers. Cordelia still could not see past the brilliant circles of fire. She was alone with Lucie, and with the spirits of the dead. "No," Cordelia said firmly. "We are going through with the ceremony."

"But—" said Lucie.

"We have waited so long already," Cordelia said. "We are going to become *parabatai* today, for nothing can part us, and after today nothing ever will. Remember." She fixed Lucie's gaze with her own. "We are strongest together. We are *unstoppable* together."

"Daisy." Lucie's breath caught. "The ghosts . . . they're *Shadowhunters*."

Cordelia looked, and blinked in surprise: on the solidifying bodies of the ghosts were runes. Shadowhunter runes. Where the outlines of the ghosts themselves were silver, the runes glowed gold.

Their clothes suggested that some had lived recently, while others were in garb a hundred, two hundred, five hundred years out of date. And they were in *pairs*. Some were pairs of men, or women; some were mixed in gender. Some looked alike—siblings, perhaps—while others differed in appearance. Cordelia saw a dark-haired man in armor etched with angel wings, beside another man who wore ivory robes; she saw two women with drawn swords, both in medieval mail of leather and metal. And there was a tall woman, beautiful but stern-faced, in old-fashioned dress next to a man with a kind but sad face. They were among the most detailed and visible ghosts, and Lucie was staring at them.

"I think—" Lucie whispered, and shook her head. "I think that's Silas Pangborn and Eloisa Ravenscar."

"*What?*" Cordelia whispered back. She knew those names—almost all Shadowhunters did. They were a warning, a story told to children, of *parabatai* who had fallen in love and whose lives had ended in ruin. Cordelia noted that however much they had violated Shadowhunter Law in life, they were, it seemed, together in death. "How can you tell?"

"There's a portrait of Silas in the Institute," said Lucie, her voice wondering. "He was a friend of Charlotte's father."

The ghost of the man in ivory robes spoke. "Do not be afraid," he said, his voice echoing and faint. "We are here to do you honor."

"You are?" Lucie looked startled. "But—why?"

One of the women in mail spoke; she had thick blond braids. "Because of the kindness you have shown to the dead. We are the *parabatai* who have come before you, those who have fought together and died together. We are linked, all of us, a line going back to Jonathan Shadowhunter and David the Silent, and so here in this chamber we may show ourselves to you."

"Kindness," Lucie said. She looked down. "I haven't always been as kind to the dead," she said, "as I should have. I had this power—it came from a bad place—but it's gone now."

"Yes," the woman said, her voice kind. "It is good that that power has been destroyed. In your hands it did good, but it could have done great evil."

"What kindness, then?" Cordelia said.

The woman spread her hands. The *parabatai* rune shone gold on her bare forearm. "The spirits that were trapped in the land of Edom," she said. "They have been freed because of you. The spirits of Silent Brothers and Iron Sisters, though not dead but only wandering, have been restored to peace."

"Do you need our help?" Lucie said.

The woman smiled. "No," she said. "You have bested Belial, the Prince of Hell, and saved the city of London. You have brought great honor to the Nephilim, and we ask you only to receive our blessings."

Lucie and Cordelia looked at each other in amazement as two of the ghosts drifted forward. "Blessings of strength be upon you," they murmured, and faded into nothing, although the glow of their runes hung in the air after they were gone.

Then all of them were moving forward, two at a time, and each spoke a quiet word of blessing: blessings of honor, of courage, of healing, of hope. Some spoke in English, many in other languages. After each pair had spoken, they too disappeared, leaving the shimmer of runes upon the air.

It felt as though time stood still, although it must have been only a few minutes. When the last of the ghosts—the dark-haired man in armor and his *parabatai* in ivory robes—had departed, Cordelia and Lucie found themselves surrounded by a field of shining golden stars, each one a rune: runes of Angelic Power, and Insight, and Wisdom, and of course the *parabatai* rune itself, repeated over and over again in twinkling constellations.

And then these too faded, and the marble chamber returned. There was again ground beneath their feet and a stone ceiling far overhead. The white-gold flames of the circle in which they were joined blazed up again, brighter than before, and crackled with warmth and, Cordelia thought, the love of the Nephilim who had come before.

The voices of the Brothers spoke inside their heads. *It has been long and long, since the Silent City has witnessed such a wonder as that.*

"A wonder," Cordelia whispered, clasping Lucie's hand. "You were worried it would be something dreadful, Luce. But it was only good, because *you* are good."

"And you were worried about Lilith," said Lucie. "But you did good deeds with her power, because *you* are good."

Cordelia had not let go of Lucie's hand. And she decided that she would not do so now. There were only a few more words of the ceremony, after all, and she spoke them together with Lucie, both of them smiling as they did.

"Whither thou goest, I will go. Where thou diest, will I die, and there will I be buried. The Angel do so to me, and more also . . . *if aught but death part thee and me.*"

CASSANDRA CLARE is the #1 *New York Times* bestselling author of *The Last Hours*, as well as *The Mortal Instruments*, *The Infernal Devices*, *The Dark Artifices* and *The Shadowhunter's Codex*. She is the co-author of *The Bane Chronicles* with Sarah Rees Brennan and Maureen Johnson, *Tales from the Shadowhunter Academy* with Sarah Rees Brennan, Maureen Johnson and Robin Wasserman, and *Ghosts of the Shadow Market* with Sarah Rees Brennan, Maureen Johnson, Robin Wasserman and Kelly Link. She is also the co-author of the bestselling fantasy series *Magisterium* with Holly Black, and *The Red Scrolls of Magic* with Wesley Chu. Her books have more than 50 million copies in print worldwide. They have been translated into over thirty-five languages and made into a feature film and a TV show. Cassandra lives in Massachusetts, USA. Visit her online at CassandraClare.com. Learn more about the world of the Shadowhunters at UKShadowhunters.com.